Galifesto

A Love Story

by
Nynia Chance

Nexus of Now Media
Hollywood, Florida
U.S.A.

Published August 17, 2015
by Nexus of Now Media
www.NexusOfNow.com

Copyright © 2015 by Nynia Chance

ISBN-10: 0996711015
ISBN-13: 978-0-9967110-1-2

All rights reserved. No part of this book may be reproduced or utilized in any form or by any means existent now or hereafter, without permission in writing from the author.

This book was created in the United States of America, solely utilizing free open-source software. Please remember: this is a work of fiction. Any resemblance to actual events or persons, living or dead, is entirely coincidental.

About the Atlas and stars on the Cover:
The photo of the Farnese Atlas adapted for use with this cover was taken by Roberto De Martino, and was released to the Public Domain on July 14, 2008.

The space image adapted for use with this cover is also Public Domain, courtesy of the Hubble Space Telescope. From the Hubble Site: This new image taken with NASA's Hubble Space Telescope depicts bright, blue, newly formed stars that are blowing a cavity in the center of a star-forming region in the Small Magellanic Cloud.

Dedications

This book is written in honor of George Orwell, in gratitude for the many ways his works have influenced me. His words have helped shape my hopes for our world, and inspire me to strive toward their fulfillment.

Galifesto was also inspired by the need for an alternative view of humanity than that shared by Ayn Rand's Atlas Shrugged, so I must dedicate this book to Ms. Rand, as well. I wish the conclusions of her life had brought her the joy and peace all human beings deserve.

Primarily, though, this book is dedicated to you. You are blazing your own path through this world, and it's my sincerest wish that your trail will leave it better than you found it. May my words help you discover thoughts and experiences that are, if not exactly what you're looking for, precisely what you're ready to find.

Thank you, most kindly, for all the good you do.

Nynia Chance

PART ONE:
The Unexamined Life

Chapter 1

What Is Truth?

I can't remember when I first realized that in our struggle for a better world, there is no "Us" and there is no "Them." There's only team We the People, each striving in our own way against that feeling of something not-quite-right. I certainly never saw myself as a leader on our team. I always figured that lasting change had to come through someone special and important, someone larger-than-life. So when I found myself…

Wait. Hold that thought. I'd probably better start at the beginning. My beginning, that is; I don't remember farther back than that.

I was born Elizabeth Franklin, the newest patriotic Member of the Incorporated States of America. Okay if you want to get technical, I was born nameless, and my innocent little heart was wide open to all the world. Isn't that kinda daunting, now that you think about it? That as babies, even the most cruel of us started off so pure and tender-hearted?

Well anyway, I was born, then my parents named me and clothed me and set about their business of raising me in their image. Come to think, I wasn't even a Member the day I was born. I wasn't automatically registered in the Central Member Database, because I was naturally born at home due to the values of home-birthing – fundamentalist and financial – without a registered home-birthing nurse or doctor.

Remember, only specifically licensed professionals could register a birth in the CMDB. Of course, even if we had such a doctor there at the house, they still couldn't have logged on from there. See, we were in a rural factory town without any Innernet. All we had was the town Infranet you could use for work or school if you could afford a computer, which of course we couldn't. Therefore, like most babies not born in a hospital, I wasn't registered until the next day when my father went to the factory office to get all the paperwork done and they sent their staff medic around to verify the info. Since you're not a Member until you're in the CMDB, I was, technically, born stateless. Not like all that sort of thing meant anything to me as a kid. I don't even remember my folks ever mentioning it, and I can remember pretty far back.

Let's see, as far back as I can remember… My earliest memory is standing in a dirt yard, looking up at two men on a half-finished roof of a partly-built house. The sun was bright behind them, making it late afternoon of a hot day's work. We didn't know then how toxic the cheap building materials were, so I was allowed to wander and play while they worked. I wanted to help, so I picked up the corner of a piece of Cemeprex leftover from the scaffolding and tried throwing it toward them so they could use it. I thought one of the men was my dad, though I could have been mistaken. Ha, wouldn't it be so perfect if in my very first memory, I was mistaken? What a great setup to a recurring punch line that would be!

Anyway, I had to have been less than two years old, and that had to have been the small three-bedroom house my family built to house me and my six brothers and sisters. They had been granted a land-lease by the factory due to my dad being a shift supervisor, and because of how many we were. With me there was nine, which was far too big for the family dorms. Funny thing is, my mom was also the seventh in her family, though not the youngest. That made me the seventh daughter of a seventh daughter, if you wanted to count it that way, which I always secretly did. I had heard something like that before and it sounded to my young ears as though it should mean something.

And when you're the tail end of a long line of hand-me-downs, what you want more than anything is a feeling that you mean something.

Oh, it wasn't as bad as I'm sure that makes it sound. I always knew my parents loved me, and did their best by me. I also had some of my own things, even if I had to share them now and then. I could see from early on how not everything worked out the way I'd have liked, but I also realized it didn't have to be that way for me to be happy, and know I was loved.

For example, I never really believed in Santa Claus, though I can't clearly remember why. Maybe it was because by the time I was old enough to recognize the name "Santa," I was also old enough to recognize the uncle or neighbor in the Santa suit. I do remember mildly resenting the realization that the adults were trying to lie to me. But, since I knew it was important to them, I kept my little secret and played along. It seemed to make them happy, and I felt their happiness was worth protecting as long as I could.

This leads to my second-earliest clear memory. It was Christmas morning, when my siblings and I used to wake up early and rush to see what Santa brought us. We always had our stockings filled with the unshelled nuts, an orange and a candy cane, with a small present underneath that we could play with. This kept us busy until my mother and father woke up and we opened our gifts from under the tree: two each, one from our parents, and one from one of our siblings.

I knew exactly what I'd find under my stocking that year. I had asked for only one thing, a small thing, so trifling that even around six or seven I knew it wouldn't be too expensive. It was a Snuggly Wugglys coloring book that came with its very own stickers, and I even already had old crayons I could use with it. My little black and white plastic Pawprince Panda was my favorite thing in the whole wide world, and it spent all of Christmas Eve clutched tightly under my pillow. At dawn's first light I held it tightly in my little hand as we ran to go meet and color in its playmates in the pages.

But they weren't there to greet us. Under my stocking was a coloring book with entirely different animals, with a similar-but-not-included packet of animal stickers taped to it. In my stocking was a note from Santa in my mom's perfectly looping handwriting:

Dear Lizzy,
I'm very sorry, but the North Pole has run out of Snuggly Wugglys coloring books this year. I know you are very good with colors and I hope you enjoy this book just as much. I picked out the stickers just for you.
Love,
Santa Claus

It's a little heartbreaking now, when I feel an echo of the sting I felt then. I feel freshly sad for that Christmas child, not because she didn't find what she wanted, but because of how matter-of-factly it all sank in. My little girl heart ached less for the loss of the Snuggly Wugglys coloring book with matching stickers, and more from knowing how much it must have pained my mother to have to write that note. People say that children should be spared the heartaches of adulthood, but they're too sharp to be protected fully. They know.

And that's what makes my grown-up heart ache a little now, thinking of all the lessons that child learned that nobody ever intended to teach her. Little Lizzy just accepted that in life, you just don't get what you want, no matter how badly you want it. And sometimes, the more you wanted it, the less likely you were to have it. Somewhere along the line, my heart also learned that if you didn't get what you wished for, it's because you weren't good enough, and didn't deserve it. Those were terrible lessons that took me years to unlearn. But at the time, I couldn't see things any other way. To me, that's just the way life was.

The upside is that because Little Lizzy knew Santa was a myth, she didn't really believe that Santa had the power to grant all things to all children, as long as they behaved in a way that pleased him. Thinking about it, she could have felt a guilty sting of wondering whether she'd failed Santa by not being good enough for goodness' sake. But she knew it wasn't a capricious denial of her heart's desire by an all-powerful supernatural force of gift-giving. It was just a human failing, a case of bad timing: a disappointment, but not a cosmic injustice. If there was a Santa whose job it was to give children exactly what they asked for, Little Lizzy was sure he would have granted her wish.

I mention this because I now realize that I probably should have been a little more clued-in as to how different my perspective was from what it "ought" to have been, even as early as that. Since I knew I saw Santa in a very different way than I was expected to, I probably should have thought to question whether I also had a different view of God.

The parallels between Santa and God are so obvious to me: all-knowing, all-wise in judgment, all-loving of children but strict and unmoving if they transgress. Behave, and you will be granted all the gifts you could ask for. Misbehave, and you have but coal to look forward to… and fire and brimstone and… you get the idea. I can't believe I never saw it before.

You see, God played an even stronger role in my childhood than most of the rest of the I.S.A. at the time, if you can imagine that. He was as omnipresent in my world as Santa Claus in December. As you may already have guessed based on sibling counts, I'm from a very long, very religious line with very fundamentalist ideas about families. Namely, they should be begun as early as possible, grow as large as possible, and do battle for the church as much as possible, and then some.

I know what you might be thinking. You may think "battle," and figure, "Oh, yeah, like I battle traffic, or battle with an urge to finish that dessert." If so, you vastly underestimate the extent to which my Christian community felt bullied, besieged and belittled by the "outside world." To us, everything was viewed in terms of a literal war between the forces of Good and Evil, and we were soldiers on the front lines. I know most in the Puritanic Party *talk* about the secular world as a diabolic enemy out to destroy the work of Jesus Christ, but where I'm from, we tried to *do something about it*. I was raised to quite literally do battle for Christ in thought, in word and, if so called, in physical deed.

Forget that the Puritanic Party effectively controlled both law and law enforcement through obstinacy and obstruction, with the Pragmatican Party talking a weak game of opposition before folding at half-time. We still felt isolated and hunted by an amoral majority whose war on righteousness mandated that we stay ever watchful for our enemy the Adversary.

Inevitably, we found the enemy everywhere. We didn't feel the Puritanic Party as a whole was pure enough in its devotion to what we considered the proper Authority. Those we didn't consider Puritan enough were invariably called Pragmatic. That is, all who disagreed with us were automatically deemed agents of the Adversary, and therefore the evil antithesis of all we stood for. Every perceived slight, every sense of rejection, every disappointment from the world was seen as evidence of the Adversary's dedicated mission to destroy everything we held dear.

In this spirit, I dutifully looked to the poster next to the bathroom mirror every morning as I brushed my teeth, imagining myself with a Belt of Truth under a Breastplate of Righteousness that guarded my heart from sin. My thoughts were guarded by the Helmet of Salvation, knowing I was kept safe by the Shield of Faith. I prepared to keep always at the ready the Word of God as a Sword to cut through the evils of the world with its piercing point of Truth. Somehow I never consciously noticed the shoes labeled "Gospel," which is funny because I never realized the poster left off what was probably the most important word in the armor as named in scripture: Peace.

I spent every morning concentrating on preparing for war, when I should have been thinking of how I could let my footsteps be guided by the Gospel of Preparation for Peace. Though on some level I believe I was, because despite all my thoughts of battle, in my heart I always knew peace. I found the teachings of Christ to be so filled with love and kindness, I just couldn't feel any other way. Even while listening to sermons intended to threaten us with the thick glare of fire and brimstone if we went astray, somehow I only saw a shining path of light and joy back to our Father's welcoming arms.

The truly surprising thing is that I honestly had no idea how rare my perspective was in my community. I really can't imagine how I managed to keep that tranquil hope in my heart. Our church taught that we were in the End Days before Armageddon, and the adults tried to prepare for those dark times from a frightfully early age. The warnings and watch-cries were frequent and detailed, and often their eyes shone with a joyful anticipation as if for an upcoming birthday party.

The sermon I remember most came when I was probably about nine or ten. I was staying with a girl from my Sunday School while my parents traveled with a Church group to go do battle against some attempt to use government money to bring back Godless public schooling. I was really excited about the stay-over with Judy, since she was pretty and talented and popular, while I never really had any friends who weren't grownups. It was an awkward time for me, since I was the only girl in my class who hadn't hit puberty.

Later I found out that "delay" was probably in part because we relied on homemade toys and survived mostly on our own homegrown produce and the dairy products we traded for with a neighbor. We couldn't afford the company store prices for the kinds of dairy and meat and other manufactured food that made up what everyone considered the "normal" American diet, let alone all the plastic toys. You know, everything that was normal, back before we knew all the effects that stuff had on child development.

Since we didn't know, at the time I just felt a little deprived. When you're poor like we were, you couldn't just pop over for a candy bar if you wanted, you had to save for it. So, at the time, I was sure there was something wrong with me. Yet Judy never seemed to judge me for it, and that made me love her all the more.

The first night I stayed over, her family gathered together and her father read to us from the Book of Revelations. He then talked to us about the dark days soon to come when the Adversary would unleash the armies of evil, and waves of fire would cover the Earth. He stressed that we must always be watchful, preparing every moment to be worthy of the grace that would spare only the chosen from such nightmarish devastation.

When it was through it was time for bed, yet naturally we couldn't sleep right away. Instead we lay there quietly, while I tried to get comfortable in Judy's large, but unfamiliar bed. Soon, though the quiet was disrupted by the heart-wrenching sound of my friend crying quietly into her pillow. More concerned than embarrassed, I touched her arm and asked her what was wrong.

"Lizzy, I don't want to see the world covered in fire and war. I don't want to die! I'm just so scared!" Her voice was quiet and hushed, but earnest. You see, we took these things as literally and imminently as the adults, perhaps even more so.

Even so, I was surprised when I heard she was scared. Not just because I had admired her so much, but I sincerely saw nothing to fear. When I thought of the End Days when God brought finality to the human experience, I couldn't imagine it as a painful or troubled time. Sure, I know the adults talked about the Armies of Darkness and Torment, but I really didn't believe God would let His innocent children be harmed by such things, just to allow His son to return to us. My God was a loving God, and I welcomed thoughts of His warm embrace reaching the physical world with His son's return, imagining it would be as peaceful and beautiful as I believed He was. I moved closer to my friend so I could gently hug and comfort her.

"Judy, please don't be scared. It will all be okay. This is the Gospel, from our Father in Heaven. He really is our Father, and that means He loves us and won't let anything horrible happen to us. So when the time comes for Jesus to rise again, it will be happy and beautiful, just like He is. I'm really looking forward to it!" My warm hug and utter confidence apparently soothed her. We loved and trusted our own fathers, so it was easy for us to project that comfort onto a Heavenly one. She smiled at me and wiped her tears, then we talked about comics and school as we drifted off to sleep.

I found out later we were the lucky ones. Our fathers were faithful in our church, but they weren't as… earnest, shall we say, about some of the harsher points of our church's teachings. Sure, children were little chore-doers and employees-in-training who were to be seen and not heard. Women were expected to be dutiful servants to their husband's will, as proxy of God's will, tasked by Heaven to raise up perfect little soldiers for God and country. Technically, only one person's opinion mattered, and when the father was absent, it was up to the mother to enforce his will.

Though this was generally how things were in our house, it wasn't as strict as it could have been. Weeks were long and filled with school and church functions, Saturdays with chores, and Sunday with the dreary oppressive weight of the Bible and boredom.

Don't get me wrong, I loved reading the Bible, but something about Sundays made it seem less like a joy and more like being grounded one full day a week. We had a very strict interpretation of Keeping the Sabbath, which is to say nothing but religion could happen on that day. And we had a pretty strict interpretation of what counted as religion. Not even playing games together in the yard as a family could qualify.

But even so, Judy and I, we were the lucky ones. We were asked what we thought sometimes, and we got nice, if small considerations now and again. Our mothers had benign opinions, but they weren't cowed into trembling silence for fear of their husbands lashing out at them with words or fists. Our fathers were devout, but they took the teachings with a kinder, Christlike heart.

I still remember the first and only time my father had spanked me. I was five, and had just started preschool a couple weeks before. He didn't know this at the time, but I had seen a girl named Felicity spanked a few days prior, because she slapped another girl in our class who had taken a toy she wanted. The teacher made Felicity lift up her denim skirt and hit her several times with a paddle. We saw a couple bright red welts on her leg, so I could only imagine how much worse it was where the paddle hit the most.

Felicity screamed and cried, and we were all frozen still, terrified into wide-eyed silence. I started to walk over to her to hug and comfort her, but the teacher threatened me with the paddle and ordered Felicity into the corner. Her parents were furious and tried to sue the school, but the state had given schools the power to override parental refusals to hit their children. Further, the laws had made them immune to lawsuits or even reprimands for hurting the children entrusted to their care. Felicity's family couldn't afford any other school, and both parents had to work so they couldn't homeschool her. The little girl had to stay in a school with the teachers who terrorized her.

Like most of the kids I saw who were subjected to school-administered violence, over the years Felicity just got into more and more trouble. The administrators said they hit the children because it was kinder than suspension or expulsion, but I couldn't imagine they'd suspend a five-year-old for acting up in the first week she was ever in a classroom.

I thought of Felicity every time I heard a sermon talking about the importance of "correcting children with the rod, not out of anger, but out of love," knowing from experience that the rod didn't generally make a child feel the self-correcting spirit of love. Instead, it taught us that if we made mistakes, the people in whom we placed our most sacred, innocent trust would hurt us for it. We learned that missteps deserved physical and emotional pain as a punishment, setting us up to repeat those feelings of hurt in our lives over and over again. I know spanking is supposed to be just a harmless disciplinary tool, but in truth, we must admit that hitting is hitting. To a child's mind, and I've heard it argued that also in our adult subconscious, there's no hard line between different types of violence. Hitting is hitting, and either it's always wrong, or always right.

That is why we kids demonstrated that violence begets violence, growing to turn that destructive streak onto ourselves, on others, or both. Parents and teachers told stories of how badly they'd been beat as children and held it out as a great example of how much good it would do us too. But it seemed to me to be a nonstop cycle of violence, like any other kind of hazing. It seemed like a terrible disease that wouldn't stop until everybody was hurting one another instead of helping each other right our wrongs.

I eventually learned that not every kid took spanking as hard as I did, like one of the kids from my neighborhood I still keep in touch with. She told me once that she didn't mind the spanking so much, as it was the only time her mother really touched her. So to her, it became a togetherness thing. She would find herself acting up just so her mom would give her that physical contact she so dearly craved. But she still wouldn't spank to her kids when she grew up. She said that she would hug them and be patient with them and listen to them, helping them learn how to behave through love. Even if they were bad like she thought she was, she was sure she'd be able to find a way to teach them through love. And though it's been super tough on her sometimes, she still manages to hold back her hand of anger. Instead, she extends it as a guiding comfort for her children's troubled times.

I don't even remember what it is that I did that made my parents so upset with me they decided I needed to be spanked. But my father told me that he was very disappointed, and that he had to spank me. I remember thinking, "Nobody is making you, you're choosing to," and being very disappointed in him, too. Then he put me over his knee and hit me with his belt on my pajama bottoms a few times, and it stung and hurt. But I didn't want to cry and scream like the girl at school, so instead I bit my lip really hard. I've heard that children learn to hold back from showing their true feelings at a depressingly early age. The worst is actually for boys, who learn to hide their needs and feelings as early as four, because of how they're treated when they don't. I think I can relate to that.

Whatever the reason, I was very angry with my father for taking advantage of how much bigger he was, for hurting me instead of helping me to behave. I thought he was being a bully, but I didn't want to say it, knowing that adults never seemed to care how children feel. But I guess the hurt and betrayal showed in my eyes, because I remember seeing my father looking back at me with surprise, quickly followed by regret. We never talked about that, and I guess he figured I'd never remember. But I know he remembered, because he never hit me again.

And that's how my father both lost and earned my lasting respect while I was still very young. The way I understood things, he had lost my trust when he hit me, then regained it when he hugged me and chose never to do it again. I didn't even realize then just how hard it is for parents to break away from that cycle of violence towards those they love most dearly in the world. To be honest, it doesn't take much moral strength to abstain from something that doesn't even tempt you. But to turn away from something you find so compelling that you hardly feel there's any other choice: that takes the strongest moral character.

Unfortunately my school district never found that strength. At least Felicity was transferred to another district before high school, when the discipline also started including strip-searches or even arrests for trivial infractions like talking back to a teacher once too often. They had also started attacking children, even preschoolers, with the electrocution-gun Fazers used by school police. In another district, a couple of children had even died after being Fazed without so much as a warning by truant officers who went after them for skipping school. The Authorities said that it was important to give school cops Fazers instead of guns to protect kids from being shot, but you can't honestly tell me the truant officers would have shot at those children. Rather, it seemed pretty clear that Authorities were starting to use Fazers to force children into submission instead of going to the effort of trying to talk to them. I guess it was too much to ask those responsible for children's safety to handle their jobs like mature, responsible adults.

There was another reason Felicity's parents felt they couldn't afford to leave her at risk for school-administered violence. The year before, we had lost another school friend to child abuse. Doris's death wasn't at school, but it was a tragic reminder of how far things can go once you start down a particular path in anger. Doris's father had started taking a paddle to her when she was only six months old, so when one of his "punishments" of his own daughter finally went too far, we were all horrified but not surprised.

So yeah, Judy and me, we were the lucky ones.

I was also lucky in that my parents valued my education, despite my being female. To this day I'm not sure why, since even grade school was so expensive, yet education so undervalued that educating girls was a poor investment. On average, women earned half to two-thirds of what a man was paid for equal labor. Besides, I was expected to become a full-time mother. At the time I assumed my parents thought I'd be a good homeschooler for my own children, or would have teaching to fall back on if it turned out I couldn't have kids. It never occurred to me that it may have been simply because they were proud of my potential and wanted to help me fulfill it.

No, I didn't see any reason to be proud of myself, not ever. Judy was pretty and talented, while all I had going for me was being smart. Somehow I never worked out how to relate to others my own age, and this meant Judy was my only friend apart from a few adults who weren't teachers or preachers. Because I never talked to my peers, I didn't realize what an exception it was that adults were so encouraging to me. Young ladies were supposed to be educated enough to be able to raise up good recruits for the army of God, of course, but rarely were they pushed to excel. Yet I was encouraged to read as deeply and broadly as I wished, and to really think about what I read and pray about what it meant to me. My parents taught me that if I did this, I would be led to truth and God's path for me.

I heard this encouragement as literally and broadly as I took everything else, which by now you may rightly suspect means I didn't exactly hear it the way it was intended. I was rewarded at school and at home for reading and writing well, so I developed a love of learning. I was rewarded in church and at home for my love of reading and interpreting religious texts from the Bible, so I developed a love for religion.

The unintended part is that I developed a love for learning about all religions, not just my own. In my grade school library I began devouring books on ancient religions, finding with great interest echoes of lessons and stories that I had found in the Bible. There was the Egyptian god Osiris who had died and resurrected and was keeper of the dead. There were the Roman mysteries of Mithras, hinting at an untold story of his resurrection and salvation in an afterlife. Greek mythology was the most engrossing, with its personification of everything, and how their gods playing direct roles in lives of mortals. Those stories were much like I imagined God's hand was always moving through our own lives.

One story I found particularly compelling was that of Atlas. I had remembered hearing that he was ill-fated to shoulder up the burden of the Earth, much like Jesus Christ, so I somehow always had a picture of him as a tragic martyr to whom we owed symbolic gratitude. But when I read his story in my grade school library book, I found out he had actually fought against the Greek gods and was defeated with the rest of the Titans. His punishment was to shoulder up Heaven on his back, to keep it forever above and separated from the Earth. If Atlas shirked his task, the Earth would not come crashing down; rather, it would finally attain Heaven.

So to my Christian analogies, I then thought of Atlas more like the Adversary: a tormented traitor in the Heavenly War who was cast out and tasked to keep Earth down below, testing and strengthening us so that we could make our own way back up to the right hand of God. Yet while I quickly tried to adapt the story to my customary cosmology, it was the first time I was aware of having made assumptions based on what people had told me that turned out to be easily verified as untrue. Of having treasured a belief that proved utterly backwards, once I finally bothered to check it out for myself. After that, it started to sink in that maybe I should start being a little more open to seeking out truths that may contradict what I thought I knew. That maybe I should start approaching others' beliefs with a mind that was a little less fixed.

I can't say I actually changed my mind on much at that age, but I did start laying a stronger foundation of religious scholarship, however rudimentary. My religious searching continued farther and broader, as far as the tiny "Fiction – Mythology" section could take me. Once that was exhausted, I put myself on the lookout for more I could learn. I began seeing truth everywhere I looked, and tried to evaluate it in its own light. Rather than fitting all I found into the framework of my Christianity, I started to see the tranquility in Buddhism, devotion in Islam, wisdom in the Tao te Ching, and so on and so forth.

I figured I wasn't too good for any good idea, no matter who had it first. I felt in my heart that I was following God's plan for me, to learn to see His face through others' eyes. And since I felt my parents so proudly supporting my religious scholarship, I imagined they'd always be proud of what I found so long as I kept searching and praying for truth.

Eventually, inevitably, I would learn how heart-breakingly wrong I was. This painful realization came during my senior year in high school, as I was working to set up the… Oh wait, I'm getting ahead of myself again. Goodness, so sorry, but that does bring me back to where all that started.

It began all the way back in high school, right before my senior year. I was so very proud that I was able to go to high school all the way through, since not every kid was able to renew their tuition and I didn't have a full scholarship. I got a partial tuition voucher from the factory due to my grades and my dad's position, and because I was always able to get letters of recommendation. But it was still a bit of a struggle to keep up. As I said, my family was pretty poor compared to most people, even in a factory town. Poor enough that even though nobody ever said anything, I knew what we were.

It may sound silly, but I was kinda proud of our poverty, and all we accomplished despite it. Even though everybody said that all it takes to be rich is to work hard and keep your nose clean, I saw it another way. My father worked every day but Sunday, and despite the few hours we had with him, I could see he wasn't dirty or lazy or all the other things that were said about the poor. Instead, I saw him as virtuous and self-sacrificing, as a good man should be. Despite all the visiting preachers essentially teaching that Jesus loved the greed of the wealthy and rewarded the faithful with riches, I always remembered His embrace of the poor. After all, Jesus said it was harder for a rich man to enter heaven than for a fully-laden camel to pass through the small gatehouse door, the "eye of the needle." That camel had to be relieved of its burden, then go down onto its knees to make it through. Clearly, He didn't approve of wealth-hoarders, and valued those who continually struggled, which I thought included me.

I hardly had any right to feel so virtuous by virtue of my adversities, since I never knew what real struggling was. We had to make it on just my father's paycheck, but as a supervisor at least his hours and pay were regular. We always had our tiny-but-comfortable home, and food to eat, even if sometimes that meant sharing with family and church members through hard times, both ours and theirs. And my parents always found ways to pay for things that were important for my education. I didn't even have to work to help pay the bills, though from middle school onwards I did always have some kind of job at the school to get free breakfast and lunch, and to help pay the portion of tuition the factory vouchers didn't cover.

Most kids had some kind of job, but thanks to family connections and being the seventh in a long line of student employees, I was able to get work in the school office for a few hours a week. It was indoors, and it let me learn valuable office and computer skills, which meant I had less competition each year for even better jobs. I felt a little guilty for all the other kids since there were always more of us needing work than the school had openings, but the same was true for the outside world as well. The school taught that there not being enough jobs to go around was a valuable lesson on how to make it in life, and at the time I took that at face-value. Every advantage I had, I personally earned through hard work and perseverance, I had thought, so the other kids would just have to work harder.

The rest of my tuition was covered by my participation in the Future Officers of the American Military, a.k.a. FOAM. Tuition would actually have been fully covered by FOAM if I'd signed an Intent to Enlist and joined the Military as soon as I graduated. But I had planned to be married and start a family at that point, so instead I just participated as much as I could. I was on the marching team, was in all the clubs, scored near-perfectly in every FOAM class, and otherwise threw myself fully into every opportunity it had to offer. There, I wasn't just another meek little girl who never fit in. I was the driven cadet who rose through the ranks at a rate that surprised even me.

Commander Keane was the first adult I'd ever met who didn't seem to judge my capabilities as being more limited than a boy's. He had the misfortune to be there for my nervous breakdown crying fit during my first year, brought on by all the pressures to be scholastically and spiritually perfect. He never held it against me though, or even mentioned it as he supported me in ways that I'd never seen a young woman supported before. And over time, my fellow cadets came to support me just as strongly, with camaraderie I had never before imagined I'd ever enjoy. We were a team, all for one and one for all, and it felt so good to be a part of it.

Outside of FOAM, Judy was still my only friend, but I didn't get to see much of her through most of high school. I was super busy with work and school, and she was busy with… well, being Judy. Each year she was our grade's class Executive Officer and top cheerleader, as popular as when we were children, but I couldn't resent her for it. She was still the nicest person I knew, and was kind to me whenever she saw me.

So I was super excited to begin our senior year, as we'd finally have a shared activity that would give us more time to see each other. She was, of course, elected Student Executive Officer for the whole school. And quite surprisingly, to me anyway, I was made Student Commander of the whole FOAM unit. This meant I also had a voice at Student Council meetings just like the real Supreme Commander of the American Military had a voice on the real Executive Council of the American government. However, in the Student Council, we each got to vote instead of like in the real world where the Incorporated States of America Chief Executive Officer made all the final calls. This meant that I felt a real level of responsibility, which I took pretty seriously. While I was of course proud to represent FOAM, I was even more excited to be able to work directly with Judy on important student issues.

Of course, it also meant I'd get to work with the Student Assistant Officer, Derek Channery. I'd had a secret crush on Derek for as long as I could remember, but I'd never had the nerve to talk to him. It wasn't like he was some super sports star or the kinda guy all the girls swooned over, but I think that's what made me like him more. He was cute in a way that was, I dunno, real, and with a personality that was truly kind when he wasn't busy clowning around. He was super smart, super funny, and had a good heart that you could just feel every time he laughed. I knew he'd never even consider liking me "in that way," but that didn't keep me from giggling inwardly just a little when I thought of being able to see him at least once a week during the upcoming school year.

Judy and I wanted to get together before the school year started, so we could catch up on each other's life and plan out our top priorities for the upcoming year. So, right after I got back from the FOAM boot camp, she invited me over to her place so we could talk. She had said that she had one project in mind that she just knew I'd want to come together on, so she and I could present it to the Student Council as a team and make it happen. I tried to play it cool, like my opinion on… well, anything was asked all the time, trying to remind myself that she was my friend long before she was Student Executive Officer. That made it easier for me to handle when she dropped the bomb of her Grand Plan.

"Liz, I think the school should have a program that lets students keep coming to classes if they get pregnant." Her eyes were so bright, her voice so breathlessly excited as the words tumbled out, that I couldn't quite connect them to what was actually being said.

"Um… don't they already have a school for that?" I was working slowly, trying to feel out the minefield I suddenly saw before me.

She gave me a double-take, obviously surprised at my reaction. "You mean the 'pretto'? Don't you think they'd rather keep going to the same classes with their same friends, instead of having to go off and leave them behind?"

So far, she hadn't seemed to see the problem with her plan, so I tried to be tactful. "Um, don't you think they'd rather be around other people with their same problem? You know, a kind of support network?"

She just blinked at me in confusion, as though we were having different conversations. "Their friends *are* their support network! Do you think they really *want* to be bussed off to some dank little one-room so-called 'school' to be preached at about what horrible irresponsible sinners they are, like being sent off to some kind of convent?"

I have no idea what was on my face, but it triggered something in Judy that made her pause and blink again, this time with disbelief. "Wait… Liz, do you have a problem with this?"

My own disbelief could no longer be contained. "Judy, you're asking me to support teen *pregnancy!*" Immediately, I wished I'd tried harder to contain myself, because I then saw something I never, ever even imagined could happen.

Judy got furious.

"No, Liz, I'm asking you to support pregnant *teens!* You know, mothers? Of little babies?" I started to try to stammer something conciliatory but she waved her hand to bat away my protest. "No, no, I don't want to hear it. You spend all this time picketing and handing out pamphlets about how women must be required to give birth to every potential baby, but you won't do a single thing to help them when they're actually pregnant. And once the babies are born? They can just rot away from starvation and disease for all you care." Her eyes were flashing with a fire that seriously took me aback.

Both the accusation and her anger stung me, deeply, and I vainly tried to defend myself against it. "Now that's not—"

"Really? *Really?!* When's the last time you picketed to provide infant nutrition? Health care for moms and babies? Child care so they can get a freaking job because you people won't freaking push for a freaking paid leave so babies can be with their mommies when they're so tiny and helpless and need them the most?" Her tears were welling up, but her tidal wave of anger surged stronger. "You say you're pro-life, Liz, but you won't lift a finger for the living. If you spent half all that time and money on actually helping moms and babies, you wouldn't need to spend the other half on fighting abortion because moms could fight it themselves. Moms wouldn't… girls wouldn't…" She couldn't continue. Her tears finally won out.

They took me over, too. Something had happened, something terrible enough to make Judy so deeply upset that she'd cry in front of me for only the second time in our lives. I leaned forward to hug her just like the first time, and we both sobbed, though I didn't know why. I wasn't even angry anymore. I just knew my friend was in pain, and I wanted to make it better.

For I don't know how long, her "I'm sorry"s overlapped my "It's okay"s, until finally the tears subsided enough to let her speak. She wiped her eyes and hugged me tighter for a moment before pulling back.

"I'm sorry, Liz, I really am, that wasn't how I wanted this to go. It's just, you're so tenderhearted, I wanted to give you something to focus on that I thought might really mean something, that might help. You know, might make a difference." She paused there, trying to rally the strength to say the words she dreaded having to share. Finally, she took a deep, shuddering breath, and almost whispered in her exhale, "Marissa's dead."

The news crept through me like a glacier in my veins, leaving me cold and numb. Marissa. Marissa Langley. Cheerleader, track star, life of the party Marissa Langley. The person I had been jealous of all through high school because I imagined she had nonstop parties and money and a hundred times more Judy-time than I did. Gone. No. It was impossible.

"Are you serious?" I felt like an idiot as soon as I heard my voice, but fortunately Judy was still more concerned about how I felt than what I said. "I mean… how? *Why?*"

She was quiet for a moment, then started in slowly. "Well, it's… you have to promise to keep this a secret. I mean, some people may find out eventually, but you can never ever tell anyone at school. People are already talking suicide, or car accident, but her parents are saying medical emergency. Which is kinda true."

I just kept my mouth shut, trying not to say anything else stupid in the ages it took for Judy to get where she was going.

"Okay. Um, she got pregnant. And she was scared. I didn't know, I…" she choked a moment, then brought her voice back under tenuous control. "She didn't want anyone to know. She didn't want to hurt anybody with it. She just… she wanted it to just go away. So… she tried to make it all go away."

Heaven help me, I was still confused. "I don't get it. I thought you said she didn't kill herself."

"Oh no, she didn't! She never would have killed herself! She just, well, you know how you can't, I mean, girls can't, um, at least not without their parents and a doctor's recommendation?" She was trying hard to tell me without actually saying what had happened, and it took me a while to figure out what she'd meant.

My breath caught in my throat as realization slowly dawned. "She… she tried to… um, have a… an…?"

I couldn't finish, so Judy continued. "Yeah. I don't know who or how or what, but she tried to do it on her own or something. I don't – I don't know the details. I didn't want to ask. She tried to go to a hospital and then a clinic when… well, when she had trouble afterward. But it was too late."

I was numb. I couldn't feel anything… No, I felt *something*. I felt cold. I didn't *like* Marissa, but that wasn't her fault, it was just, well, maybe I was jealous. I felt guilty. I felt sick.

I then felt Judy's hand on my knee as she continued. "Her parents called me because I was her best friend. They wanted to know if I knew anything was going on. I… I wish I did. I pray to God, I wish I did. I didn't know what to… I went in her room, and found her journal. Her parents… they couldn't, so they let me have it. I didn't want you to feel bad, so I thought maybe if you… if we, you know, could make things right. Maybe help the next person, so she doesn't…" She trailed off, looking earnestly toward me, though not directly at me.

I started to think I saw what she was thinking, and then realized she was thinking more than she was saying. There was more to the story. Something involving me.

My suspicion must have shown its questions on my face, because suddenly Judy looked away as she searched for an answer she could give me. Then I noticed she wasn't just looking away, she was looking at something specific. Something on her desk. A journal.

I realized what Judy was trying to avoid telling me. Marissa must have written things about me in her journal, hurtful things that Judy couldn't bring herself to say.

I decided to spare her that pain.

Chapter 2

What Is Receptiveness?

"Liz, you don't want—"

Judy protested as I moved to grab Marissa's journal, but she didn't try to stop me. I think that as much as she thought I should know what was in it, she was grateful she didn't have to be the one to tell me.

The shock I felt while reading Marissa's thoughts kept me from clearly registering the exact words, but I wouldn't quote her directly anyway out of respect for her privacy. Yet I believe she'd want her story told, so I'll paraphrase the important bits as best as I can remember, so I can try to convey to you what I learned.

After all, it was reading her journal that set me down this amazing path I've walked. And for that, I think she deserves for her story to be told. I owe her that, don't you think?

Diary of Marissa Langley

January 1st

Happy New Year! Another year, another diary. I used to hate getting these for Christmas every year, but Dad's right, it is important to learn to keep a record... a record of everything I'm never telling him! Tee hee!

Last night was okay, not great. A bunch of us juniors had a party because the seniors had theirs, and I thought it would be great cuz J and I could hang out and see if we could get D and K to split off and hang with us and I could like see if he wanted to mini-double-date there or something without Dad ever knowing. I'm almost 17 you'd think I'd be allowed to date! But then he still wouldn't let me go out with K cuz his mom's not married and they're not Christian which got me an official Talking To about the kind of oxen friends I need to be yoking myself with. Serves me right for not keeping my mouth shut when he asked if there were any boys in our group. Ugh!!

Anyway, so then stupid L had to show up and cling on J all night so it was like her and J versus me and some other cheerleaders instead of J and me and D and K. Gawd, I hate her. I don't know who invited her, anyway. Probably J. I swear I don't know what she sees in her. She probably feels sorry for her but anyway it ruined everything. Nobody even had the nerve to spike the punch. I mean then it's gross and almost nobody drinks it but it's a tradition!! But nooooooo, Captain Godsquad would've narc'd and we all knew it.

I did get to dance with K though. A lot. He hung out with me instead of J and D and L and I thought he was just being nice at first but then we got to talk when we sat to eat and Oh Emm Geez he touched my hand when we talked! And when it was Midnite he KISSED ME!! Gawd, I hope nobody saw and tries to tease me about it. I swear, I'd just die!

January 14th

I finally managed to "just happen" to bump into K again in the hall. We didn't have any classes together this semester, and we have a different lunch period, so I didn't know when I could see if he, like, actually liked me. I said hey, and he said hey. Just when I thought he'd forgot about New Years he asked if I was doing anything tomorrow nite. WORKING!! UGH! But I didn't want to tell him that I have to work so much cuz I don't want anybody to think I'm white trash so I just said yeah, family stuff. Which is true in a way so it's not like I was lying. He must've thought I was blowing him off cuz he just said okay and then went to class.

It's so unfair. Kids aren't supposed to have to work close to full time, especially girls! I don't even just have to work enough to pay for track & part-time cheer anymore. I barely even have time for track & cheer cuz I have to pick up enough hours to pay daycare for Rascal. I mean Mom and Dad don't say it like that but I can do the math, geez. At least I can do my homework there sometimes, and work schedules me so I have enough time to get home and sleep before school or my next shift even though there's no law that says they have to.

And at least Mom & Dad don't make me homeschool so I can watch him 4 free like they talked. If I couldn't do track & cheer & see J & my friends every day I would just die.

Gawd I hope he doesn't think I was blowing him off.

January 19th

I SAW HIM AGAIN! It was right after Civic Duties class, he was near where my locker is. I don't know where his is, maybe it was just a coincidence. But he asked if I was doing anything later. I said track and then stuff. He said how about tomorrow and I said no I wasn't doing anything! Me and J were supposed to go do a movie after cheer but stupid Godsquad and her are doing some church ice cream social thing she forgot about and invited me to but I wouldn't be caught dead at. Seriously.

Anyway so we're going to a movie. I didn't tell Dad it's not with J anymore. Mom's got her long day tomorrow so she won't even notice to ask. So it's not like I lied. It's not like it's any of their business anyway. IT'S JUST A MOVIE!!

January 20th
In late. Tried to sneak in but Mom had just gotten home. She was busy with Rasc though cause he'd woken up and wanted to have some mommytime so she was helping him practice sitting up and he was laughing. She asked how the movie was and I said fine but I needed to sleep cause I have cheer and then work tomorrow. So gonna sleep.
P.S. HE KISSED ME AGAIN!!!

February 10th
Got yelled at. I was late home from work last night and I said some folks from work wanted to hang out after and since it was a free ride home instead of the bus I couldn't say no… That made it a little better but I was still in trouble. Mom had a regular day and said she was hoping since I had a shorter shift that I'd babysit so she could do errands in the evening but she never told me that so whatever.

I do feel guilty though because the folks from work were me and K since he met me there when I got off so technically we did leave from work… But I didn't elaborate. She doesn't need me to "add to her aggravation" as she looooooooves to say.

And yeah, maybe you're keeping count but I'm not so I don't remember which date this was. I was keeping count but now I'm all dizzy in the head over him and can't even think straight. He treats me so nice, and shows me respect. He asks what I'm thinking and then listens like he cares, and then later he'll bring something up he remembers I like. And he likes that I work he says it shows I'm mature and he likes women who can take care of themselves. He says he's sorry I have to work so much though and that he will try to come visit when he can cause it's on his way to where he works at D's dad's old-fashioned pharmacy. And he brings me treats and sandwiches from there that are super delish.

Boys just don't treat girls like he does. He's super special like that. I know I've written that a billion times but I mean it, he's really really really special.

He asked me if I can make sure to be off work on the 14th so we can do something. I was like "Okay!" and then I realized.... VALENTINES DAY!!! Our first Valentines!!!!! So I'm gonna see if J won't mind if I cancel practicing a cheer we're working on so I can sneak in a shift swap so I can have off.

Valentines. Gawd what am I going to get him?! Do girls give boys things or do only the girls get presents? I'll make him heart shaped cookies or something so I won't look stupid either way.

February 14th
You won't believe this. I still don't believe it. Oh gawd. I'm still dizzy. This must be a dream. Oh forget it I'm going to sleep. IF I CAN!!! WML... Write More Later...

February 15th
Okay. I can't believe I'm telling anyone this, even just my diary, but I swear if I don't tell something I'm going to just die!

Okay. Valentines Day. So he takes me out to this nice dinner at some Italian place on the other side of town so nobody we know will be there. It was super duper fancy, with breadsticks on the table before you order kind of thing. Then after, we drive to a park where we eat the cookies I made and he gives me this little box. Yeah, a box too little to be anything but jewelry!! I tried not to be too excited just in case I was wrong and held my breath as I opened it.

IT WAS A RING!!! I swear it looked like a diamond ring in white gold, super duper expensive. He said really quickly not to worry it was just silver and cubic zirconium from the case by the front of the pharmacy but he thought I might like it. I said I loved it and he said he was glad because he wanted to ask me something. He wanted to know if I'd be his girlfriend! Like, for serious real girlfriend!!

It was a promise ring!!! I said yeah but I had to wear it on my right hand so nobody would be suspicious and I'd pretend I just got it cuz I liked it and he said that was cool. I said I love you and he said I love you too! We said THE L WORD!!!!!!!!!!!!

So then he hugged me and I hugged him and then things got hot again and then he said before things went any further he wanted to make sure I knew he loved me and if he ever does something I don't like to just say. That was like impossible but I said okay. And then, well, he did stuff I liked... a lot... ....

I know, I know, I did that whole ceremony thing with my dad about how I'd save myself and all that, but we're in love and we're exclusive and I'm wearing his ring so it's like we're practically married we're just too young to tie the knot. I don't even know if it was sex exactly because, uh, the train didn't get all the way into the station.

But I do know what I know it was. It was wonderfully perfect. He was holding me and saying how beautiful I was and I was looking into his gorgeous eyes and feeling just perfect. Everything was perfect. I finally know what all those movies and songs are saying, because finally everything in life seems just so perfectly right. Because he's in it.

Soooo all that garbage in school about how getting too close to a boy will tempt him to go all out of control and ruin your life was just another load of junk they try to use to pretend what they're saying actually matters, like how algebra will be used every single day of your adult life. I wish at school they would tell us about sex instead of just why we should never ever ever think about having it. And how girls will be utterly destroyed if they're not careful cause boys can't help themselves from sinning, instead of telling us what exactly that so-called sin involves. That way I'd at least know if I've actually done it! At least I don't have to try to find out about all those horrible diseases sex makes you come down with because he said it was his first time, too.

I did make him promise not to tell anybody, and he said okay. Which means he really does love me because when a boy has sex everyone is all "Yay woohoo aren't you a stud!" But when a girl has sex everyone calls her a slut and talks bad about her and you hear people say "I hope she gets pregnant!"

Which you know makes me really angry. I don't think you can get pregnant from what we did, but now I'm actually thinking about that for the first time ever. I mean that's just mean! Wishing some girl gets pregnant just for doing something that makes her feel special and loved like K makes me feel! And wishing some innocent little baby gets stuck with a mom everyone treats like a slut and can't go to her real school or do anything cuz she has to get a job to pay for her baby. Then she can't even spend time with him because she has to work all the time like my mom does cuz we're like the only country in the world who won't pay for moms to have time with their babies, like even Sudoamerica does. We're the richest, greatest country in the world you'd think we could spare a little so teeny tiny babies don't have to go to daycare or even almost starve to death like this one girl's baby whose family was way poorer than mine and couldn't even afford formula and she couldn't feed him her milk herself cuz she was working.

I mean America can't say America's children are our most precious resource if we just treat them like puppies we don't want and put by the side of the road hoping someone else will take care of them. And then we say how it's the mom's fault for having sex without being richer. Babies are way special, and I think American babies and mommies deserve better. I don't care if people call that Commie talk, they obviously have never seen their mom hiding exhausted tears after a long day working and not even seeing her little baby before he has to sleep.

I wish my mom didn't have to work so much. She says once they pay off dad's medical bills and her student loans she can go part time but that will be like forever. I still think nurses should be able to get hospital care discounted or for free for their families like I can get free coffee at work but whatever.

I think I hear Rascal up. I'm gonna go tell Mom to go to bed early, and I'll play with him and get him back to sleep. He'd want to stay up if she gets him and they both need rest.

February 19th

I finally got to see K again after work tonite. I got off a little early so we could hang out a bit before he drove me to the bus stop by my house so I could walk in like normal. Since it's super duper faster than the bus that meant we had time together! We didn't get to do anything more than kiss and stuff because "my little friend's here." Gawd I was so embarrassed. At first he thought I was saying I didn't want to but that wasn't it.

But that answers The Big Question! What we did wasn't sex because I didn't get pregnant!! I was actually getting kinda nervous because sometimes I'm not always "on time" but this time it was a little early thank gawd. So even though I was embarrassed we were both relieved because even though we didn't say anything I know we both were thinking it. He said something about maybe we should find out how we could sneak a condom or something for next time but I said don't worry about it. We'll just keep doing what we were doing and anyway the class at school said they have a big failure rate so it's not worth it. I guess it's just if you want to keep stuff from being kind of messy, like a bib, ha ha ha. And I don't mind that part.

So we agreed it's not worth the trouble. Why risk getting caught with something that won't even help and risk getting expelled?

March 21st

Okay, I don't want to worry you, but "my friend" isn't here yet. I mean I'm not really worried, because okay we've been doing a little more but we still stop doing THAT thing "before the fat lady sings" because K asked a friend you know just hypothetically and he said for sure that if you do it that way it means you're in the clear.

Even so, I was glad I had work today so I didn't have to think about it...

March 25th

Good news – my friend's here!

Bad news – we had a date tonite!! Sad face!

April 26th

Had a great day at school today. J decided to run for Student ExOff, big surprise, but she asked me to be her campaign manager! BIG surprise!! I was so excited I wanted to tell her about me and K but then thought no cuz she might change her mind so I could spend more time with him. We still sometimes do stuff in a group but he is so good about not letting on.

Oh gawd there's so much to do, I hope I can keep up.

May 24th

NEWS FLASH! J WINS STUDENT EXOFF IN A LANDSLIDE!

I mean sure she's won every year but that's why we weren't sure cuz maybe people would want a change. D won A-Off which is cool cuz I know she woulda been bummed if he didn't. He was secretary in freshman year I don't know if I mentioned back then, which I hope I did cuz he was so funny about people teasing him for being a boy secretary. Even though like no school has a girl Prez but since it's J and everybody loves her nobody seems to think about it. But anyway we weren't sure if he'd win either. We all went out to celebrate. When we toasted soda to their win D kissed J and then K leaned over and kissed me and I didn't even have to pretend to be totally flustered and embarrassed. They thought it was cute!

J asked me after if maybe K and me are going to start going out and I said I dunno maybe let's just focus on her win.

OUR win she said! WE WON!!!!

July 1st

I've been so busy with the year end and then some extra work and taking care of Rasc during the day and then I didn't write for an extra week cuz we went on vacation and I totally forgot to bring you! Sorry!!

But I think I should have had a visit from my friend by now. Maybe it's cause we were traveling to the other end of the state. It was a little tough cuz Rascal's teething but not too bad. Got to see Gramma and Grampa, they got some time off from work for our visit which was nice, they have a nice boss. He even told them to wish me a happy birthday.

Oh! My birthday! I'll write more tomorrow cuz we just got in. But funny thing? My birthday present from Gramma and Grampa was – get this – life insurance. No joke. They say it'll be worth actual cash-in money someday but right now it's a "breadwinner backup plan" and a tax vehicle or something cuz I'm still under 18. Better than dowdy old clothes I guess.

Anyway WML.

July 9th

Okay now I'm really worried. I for sure should have had my friend visit by now. I let K think I had it when I was on vacation because I don't want him to freak out until I know for sure. Plus I know he wants to apply for the military and be an officer someday or something and I don't think they let you if you get your girlfriend pregnant and aren't married. I don't actually know.

I wish he wouldn't do military, cuz then he'd be like Captain Godsquad in that stupid "I'm so better than you" uniform but I bet he'd look good in it come to think. And then I guess at least he'll be able to get out of here and have a job in the military and maybe even college someday like they say, so he doesn't have to get stuck at the factory like everybody else lucky enough to even have a job. There's just no way out of this dirthole for people like us unless you join the military.

Which come to think of it, that actually wouldn't be so bad. Yeah he can get into the military and I think they pay pretty decent, enough to get married and have a family and then I could be a military wife and maybe go with him if he gets stationed overseas and get the freak out of this freaking loser town! Maybe see if godless Commie Europa is really as sinful as they say! Tee hee!

O.K for sure I'm not telling him until I know. Gawd I hope I'm not pregnant. Not now. Just not now.

O.K I'm freaking out I'm gonna stop and go for a walk or something.

July 12th

All right, I'm probably going to have to burn this whole diary when this is all over, but I don't have anyone else I can talk to so here we go.

I'm pregnant. I'm almost positive I'm pregnant. But I don't feel this magic little miracle of life like they always say, so I think it's not too late to stop it. I heard there's a pill you can take to stop from being pregnant if you take it before you're supposed to get your period but I don't even know if that's true. I know it makes people mad to talk about so it's hard to get real info. I mean it's not even like it's an abortion if you take it before you'd miss your period and be pregnant but whatever some people just hate girls having sex without having a baby. I think it's too late for me anyway cuz I'm like two weeks late. Oh, gawd.

I don't know what to do. I tried today to go to the Family Planning near where I work to see if I could get some info, you know, hypothetically. For a friend. I think it's illegal for a girl to have an abortion or even to talk to a girl about an abortion only her parents, but I don't know. I don't think they actually do them there but I know they'll at least know about it, and what my options are. Since it was near where I work I figured nobody would see me who knows me anyway.

Fat chance. There was this big group of people there with signs and stuff. There were a couple people from my church but I've been working during church for months so I didn't think they'd recognize me. But you know what killed it?

STUPID GODSQUAD WAS THERE! She had this moronic sign like "Jesus Loves Your Baby" or something stupid like that. I mean of course Jesus loves babies, why does that mean you have to stand on a corner yelling at people who have to decide whether they can have them? And she was there all smiling and looking around like she was at some kind of parade. I was standing there like a block away, fuming mad and wondering what I was going to do about it. Then a woman stopped next to me and says Oh great. and I'm like Yeah no kidding. And I look at her and she's I dunno a little pregnant I guess. You know the kind of round where you don't think it's just fat because her arms were real skinny.

She looked really upset though. "You going to the Family Planning" I asked her and she said yeah. She looked like she didn't want to talk about it then she said something I won't write here and said "I have an appointment. I have to (something) find out if I can stay (something) pregnant or if I have to (something) end it so I can (something) start trying again. They don't think the baby will make it to (something) seven months so it's either (something) take care of it or keep on going until I have to (something) give birth to a dead baby. (Something!)"

As she kept talking she was like less sad and more mad, cause she was looking at the protest group and got madder and madder. So she said "(Something) it!" and just started walking the rest of the block to the Family Planning.

When she got almost to the door, it was like someone threw a quarter pounder to a pack of pit bulls. A bunch of them ran at her all yelling, calling her a traitor to her baby and stuff. And I'm like WTF I know older girls at work who have their checkups there, what if she just wanted to go on the pill or something? (I don't know if you have to stay on the pill if you're pregnant, but anyway most people go there for the doctor or to plan when to GET PREGNANT not stop being pregnant.)

I was waiting for her to start yelling at them but she just started crying. They surrounded her and yelled at her and she started crying so hard she sat down on the sidewalk and just held her face. Then somebody came running out of the clinic and started yelling and a couple big guys came out behind her to help her up and the crowd finally went across the street.

And stupid Godsquad was still standing there with her stupid sign, watching everything with this dumb look on her face. I left before anybody saw me, but I wanted to go up to her and tell her what a horrible hypocrite she is. She pickets in front of the Family Planning because she doesn't think girls should have sex if they're not married. Why doesn't she picket people who take the lord's name in vain? Or lie to their parents? Or work on Sunday? Those are all commandments that come before the adultery one so since God thought they were more important you'd think Godsquad wouldn't just focus on the one that lets girls feel good about themselves like K makes me feel.

That's what I need to focus on. I can get through this, and then K and I are going to have a beautiful future together far away from Godsquad and her stupid mob who hates girls choosing their own future instead of just sitting at home popping out babies to get all of them beat up by a husband with anger issues. I'm going to ask J again why she hangs out with her sometimes but I know she'll just say again that she has a good heart and I just don't understand her. I wish I could tell her about this but whatever. Jesus said that by your works you shall know them, so sooner or later J will see L for who she really is. Someone who makes a mom fall apart because she has to find out whether she can keep her baby.

Gawd I hate her.

July 27

All right. I have a plan. I figured out a way I can take care of this while Mom's still out of town and I can borrow the car. I thought a lot about this and I'm going to take care of stuff and then tell K and maybe J. I'll make a nice dinner and have a picnic or maybe at his place since he'll be left alone there next week cuz his mom has to go help open another restaurant somewhere and train the waitresses. And he won't have to worry because it'll be all taken care of.

It's funny, now I'm really looking forward to in the future when we're all graduated and K joins the military and has a job and then maybe when we're ready this baby can be born. Cuz I don't believe babies get souls until they're going to be born, since god knows everything and loves innocent little babies. And if the Godsquad Mob is right and their god really will put a baby in hell just because it wasn't born the way they want it to be, then their god can go to hell with it. I refuse to believe in any haters, especially anyone who can hate a baby.

Wow, I've grown up so much. I never really thought about wanting to be a mom before. I guess I just figured I'd end up working at the factory like my dad and get married and, I dunno, just kinda keep going. So in a way this has all been a life-changing experience.

It's hard though. But I'm trying not to be scared. It's easier to be brave when you're being brave for somebody else, so I'm thinking of how I will be able to keep working and go to school (and not the pretto, ugh) and help out with Rascal, and help K make it through until he's 18 and can join the military, and help J get ready for next year, and keep learning to be a better person for when it's time to get out there and make things happen for my own little family when K and I travel the world. I'm ready to get my act together, and start making myself into a future mom who can really make it for her baby, maybe even make a difference.

Yeah, I can do this. Look out world, here I come!!!

That was the final entry.

What's weird is that at the end there, I had started feeling her optimism. I actually started to hope she would pull out of it at the last minute, deciding to keep the baby and overcome all the challenges lined up against her. I forgot that I already knew how the story ended.

Then it all flooded back to me, and I felt the crushing weight of her misery and guilt… Wait, no, it's important I keep honest. My misery and guilt. Before I read her diary, I was ready to kindly and patiently tell Judy about how God punishes those who turn against His will. I had a sermon all ready about how Marissa's sins condemned the soul of her child before it was even conceived, and how she now would join her baby in Hell, and all these other things that I'd heard a thousand times but never really stopped to think about.

But then I remembered that the villain in Marissa's story was me. I remembered that day in front of the Family Planning, the last time I had heard all those words I was ready to repeat to Judy. It was the day before I went off to summer boot camp, so I hadn't had much time to really process what had happened that day. Suddenly though, it was all as fresh and clear as though it had happened only hours before.

I remember that woman still, the one who was just at that right level of pregnant that you might think was considering an abortion. Now, I realize that was often the earliest a woman could overcome all the maliciously petty hurdles the Puritanic Youth and I had fought to put into law, but I didn't know that back then. Along with everybody else outside that clinic, I was convinced that this was a healthy but amoral woman trying to do secondary birth control… until she freaked out, crying about heart defects and stillbirth.

I had never seen anyone crumple like that, so utterly crushed of all hope. I also had never seen Brother Foley, the protest leader, turn so… so vile. His eyes shone and his lips curled as he started screaming at her about her sins that brought shame and torment unto her baby, sins that caused God to curse it with a Mutation, and that someday she'd join the baby in Hell. And as I sat in Judy's room with the memory of his ugly hatred of this woman so vivid and fresh, I started to wonder how often I had looked that way to someone else. Like I had to Marissa.

One of our greatest handicaps is our inability to see ourselves through others' eyes. Our greatest vices are therefore invisible to us, along with our greatest virtues. I always saw myself as trying to push the Gospel of Peace out into the world, and all I ended up doing was pushing someone away from finding any peace at all. I believed firmly in my heart in a God of Love, but my actions had made Marissa feel hated.

Suddenly, I remembered Atlas, and how completely wrong I had been about his story. I had always thought of myself as shouldering up the burdens of those on Earth. In the end, though, I had kept at least one person from feeling the love of Heaven. I was so busy trying to do Jesus' work, I forgot to follow Jesus' example of reaching out to even the greatest of sinners in compassion and Lovingkindness. Maybe if I would have instead helped Marissa into the clinic to talk to somebody, maybe she wouldn't have felt so alone. Maybe someone could have shown her there was a chance for a future with her baby, and she'd be here with us now, planning how we could all help her make it work. Maybe I could have hugged her, listened to her, and helped her build that future. Instead…

Instead, I felt heavy and dizzy and didn't know what to say. I didn't know what to think. I didn't know what to do.

And then I did.

"Judy, we're going to make your program happen. Marissa's tragedy won't be for nothing; it will lead to something decent in this world. Something good. No other young woman will ever be lost and alone like that again. Not on my watch."

Judy had been sitting there watching me with silent dread over how the journal would impact me. When I spoke, her beautiful smile brightened her face with happy relief. She hugged me tightly and whispered in my ear, "You're so strong. I KNEW I could count on you."

Though quiet, her words rang like bells in my ears. I had never guessed, never even imagined that she would see me that way, that anyone could ever see me as... Here was my hero, counting on me to be hers...

I then swore to always be the person I saw through Judy's eyes.

Chapter 3

What is Strength?

I got my first taste of taking a leading role in politics during that last year of high school, and quickly learned its unsubtle flavors. The political spotlight starts off sweet, but the aftertaste quickly sours it. It's bitter medicine, but somebody's got to take it if the system is to get healthy.

We put together a meeting with the Student Council a couple weeks before school started to talk about the agenda for the year. We'd met with Derek a week earlier, once he got back from summer vacation. His family had enough money both for Interstate Travel Licenses and to use them, though at the time I didn't see how it could be worth the cost since nowhere could be better than home. He had brought me back a souvenir, which was truly nice of him because he didn't know me that well. It was a broad, green tree leaf preserved in silicon, and I treasured it instantly for more reasons than its being the first real "live" green leaf I'd ever seen.

Whenever I looked at that leaf, I imagined more than the lush green forests I knew had once covered America. I imagined Derek's sparkling eyes winking like they did when he had handed it to me. He joked that he'd vacationed in the Garden of Eden, but got hungry for some fruit salad so he was kicked out. When I flushed and flustered he laughingly but sincerely apologized if the blasphemy was in poor taste, and I pretended that was my problem. I'd been trying hard to be rid of my huge crush on him since I'd discovered he and Judy had been flirting with the idea of going out. Thou shalt not covet thy best friend's crush, and all that.

The more I got to know him, the harder it was for me not to keep falling for him. Derek was the one who expanded on our original plan to help young women, growing it into a broader peer-counseling Teen Support Program. He said it might seem less of "just a girl's thing" if he pitched it as a counseling option for all kinds of issues students might have, which annoyed us just a tiny bit because we knew he was right. People did listen more when a suggestion came in a male voice, particularly when the issue was considered "female," such as anything to do with babies or children, and even figuring out how you felt about an issue and what to do about it. Not everybody saw it that way, but we already faced a very real hurdle in convincing two of the Council members to go along with the plan.

"All we need to do," Derek explained to the group, "is give them an ear to talk to. Someone who can listen to what they're going through, maybe help them work through what they think their options are. We can even get them excused from class, if needed, so they'll have time to talk. You can get passes worked out from the office, can't you Lizbet?"

I blinked for a moment as I realized he was looking at me. Had he just given me a nickname?! I suddenly felt so cool, yet flushed, that I almost forgot my heart wasn't supposed to skip beats for him anymore. I nodded and mumbled something affirmative.

"Awesome. We'll get passes for students who want to volunteer to counsel and for those who need to talk. We'll also meet with the volunteers in a weekly lunch meeting or something. The program will train them on how to listen objectively and make folks feel comfortable that their secrets will be kept, well, secret."

"Whoa, whoa, wait." We all turned to look at Richard U. Foley II, surprised at the vehemence of his interruption. Yes, the firstborn of Brother Richard Unwin Foley, who had pressured the School Board to select his son to be Student Chaplain. Brother Foley had named his son with the expectation he would second to none but his father. Accordingly, Richard had obstinately refused to be 'junior' to anybody.

Richard's position entitled him to a vote on the Student Council, giving his opinions more than just moral weight. Again, this wasn't exactly the way the real government was set in principle, though it was close enough to how the government worked in practice. The Supreme Chaplaincy of America was just an advisory role on paper, but we all knew it wielded influence way beyond advisory, and that kind of influence trickled all the way down to high school level. That meant that whatever Richard's concerns were, they carried more than just moral weight. "Are you honestly suggesting that we instruct these volunteers to keep what those problem kids tell them... secret? As in, not even report it to the School Chaplain?"

Derek didn't even flinch, obviously more prepared for this

objection than I was. "Yes, Skippy, I'm suggesting exactly that. Because as students, we're not obligated by pesky things like the Full Disclosure laws that affect school authorities. It's just friends talking to friends, only these are neutral third-party friends who aren't all tied up in whatever the issue is."

Richard leaned back, his eyes narrowing a little as the wheels turned in his head. Finally, he conceded a little too quickly with a hint of a smarmy grin. "Okay, fine. They can use the conference rooms too, so they won't be interrupted."

"Hoooooold onnaminnit, Ricky, nuh-uh." This time it was Gig. Okay, his name was really Gavin Irving Geary, but he'd been called Gig since before I ever met him. He was the surprise win from the elections, having run for Student Financier not because he thought he could win, but because he wanted to make a point. He ran on what he called the Dollars to Donuts platform, which was just a series of posters of donuts named for different student programs, with varying sizes of holes in the middle. As one of the few kids in school whose parents were Pragmatican, I guess he felt important ideas were being unheard and decided to grandstand in order to air them. Since he wasn't hampered with trying to play to the majority, he had a ton of fun making some pretty cutting jokes about how underfunded our scholastic and nutritional programs were, compared to the sports and religion clubs.

So yeah, nobody expected him to have the slightest shot at winning. But then, nobody expected his opponent's father to be suddenly transferred to the Accounting department of a factory in another state, leaving Gig unopposed well after the deadline to enter the race. Hence, Student Financier "The Gigster" joined the Student Council, much to the dismay of many a member of the Young Bankers of America. In fact, I think that was the only year they didn't hold a big snobby party congratulating the winner at what passed for the town's country club.

Regardless of how he was elected, Gig's vote on the Student Council was equal to Judy's, Richard's and mine. Since Derek could vote to break a tie we could have forced our plans through, but we agreed it would be best if everyone on the council agreed. Well, five out of six, anyway.

The sixth person on the Council was Tricia Knox, Student Council Secretary, but that made her the custodian of the minutes, not a voting member. She, too, was a surprise candidate since she never seemed that engaged in school activities. But when the future valedictorian runs for an office nobody really wants, she can't help but win. Tricia hadn't even looked up from the computer at that point, keeping her head down as she rapidly transcribed our conversation.

Punctuated by the light clickety-clackety of Tricia's typing in the background, Gig continued, "Are yoooou honestly suggesting that the conference rooms aren't bugged, keeping tabs on all the so-called private conferences?" He smirked at the indignation Richard feigned, a smirk that faded in the face of the righteous anger Judy voiced.

"Gig! That's ridiculous! You know the school refuted that rumor."

I glanced at Judy and saw that she was as surprised at Gig's comment as I. Then I looked to Richard and saw the glance he also shot her. I still didn't know much about the "who" and the "how" of interacting with people in social situations, but being a wallflower gave me plenty of time to watch the "what" and the "why." And the "what" of Richard's glance to Judy was smug amusement with condescending undercurrents, implicating a moderately sinister "why."

The conference rooms were bugged. They were bugged, and the info was passed along, or at least knowledge of it was passed along to Richard, maybe because of his father, or maybe just because he was Student Chaplain. Either possibility upset me a great deal. Everything that went on in those rooms was supposed to be confidential between the students and the school official meeting with them, with any necessary info shared only with their parents.

That's why it was such a big deal when our star quarterback claimed he had confided privately to a trusted teacher that he was abstinently gay, and that it couldn't have been the teacher who had outed him to his family, church and school, getting him expelled. He swore there had to be a school Spy. Within weeks he was arrested for allegedly attempting suicide, then died in custody under what the police said was self-inflicted head trauma. It was all very sudden, but his allegations still got out to the paper and even the statewide radio. I couldn't be sure how this all could have involved Richard, or perhaps even his father. Regardless, I didn't want anything to do with anything that gave him that unnerving, self-important grin.

While I was busy sorting out these realizations, Gig had started to elaborate. "Oh come on, don't tell me you haven't heard about the time—"

"Hey, let's not get sidetracked with silly rumors that were debunked two years ago," I interjected. "Because the conference rooms are usually used for school-related stuff, like discipline, and have a pretty harsh association, I just don't think students will be comfortable to talk in there. Since we've all agreed the talks are to be confidential so students feel like they can open up, I think we should have them away from the main buildings, but of course within the approved school-hours perimeter. That way everybody can relax and deal with whatever they need to deal with, and then get back to class. Are we all Aye?

I looked around, nervous that my abject ineptitude in bluffing would give away my extreme discomfort with the bugging issue. Fortunately, I must have come through convincingly enough, because the "Ayes" rang out. I couldn't tell if Gig even cared about the issue, but he did seem pleased to vote against Richard's objections. Even Richard had to grudgingly agree, lest he be forced to explain his reversal in light of Gig's accusations. Judy instructed Tricia to record the vote in the official minutes, and we moved on to ratifying the school activities schedule for the year.

I found it hard to pay attention through the rest of the meeting, caught between wondering about the implications of Spying at the school, and inwardly glowing about successfully maneuvering to get the Teen Support Program started in a way that bypassed any such concerns. I was surprised at my smooth handling, and was glad the controversy had gone away so quickly and painlessly.

Yeah, I was naive back then.

It was only a couple of days before the issue resurfaced, right after church the following Sunday. Our church was hosting a potluck for the area so kids could mingle before starting classes in the upcoming year. Homeschooling kids were also invited, and plans were made to keep them involved in various activities. Since my schedule that year was already way past full, my parents and I planned to skip the gathering and go straight home. It still hadn't quite sunk in what it meant to be not just Student Commander of FOAM, but also the highest-ranked female cadet in the history of my church group.

So when I was asked to stay and lead the opening prayer, I was too stunned by the idea to even consider refusing. I had never prayed on behalf of anyone else before; even family prayer was always led by my father. I felt a huge weight to represent each person in the audience before God, and plead to Him on their behalf. As I walked up to stand before the crowd, I tried desperately to feel prepared.

Before opening my mouth, I opened my heart to hear their needs that I might pray for them to be fulfilled. I thought of those like my father who struggled through long, hard days in return for the chance to barely make it from paycheck to meager paycheck. I thought of those like my oldest brother who struggled through cold, worry-filled nights as he and his wife sought enough work to provide for themselves and their children despite battling cancer. I thought of those like my sister who struggled with pain and loneliness for the husband they'd sent off to the ongoing wars in Arabiya, in hopes that through service to America they would be granted a future together protected from illness and starvation.

It may sound odd, but I count it a blessing that I grew up in a community with so many shared troubles and pain. We struggled, sure; but through pulling together we found that our problems weren't so great that we couldn't tackle them together. It was the way the earliest American communities had made it in the New World, and this communal sharing was the firm foundation on which our country had been built. I was proud to be part of that tradition.

Through community, I had learned that we each bear burdens that weigh us down, and the only way to lighten them was to share them with those around us. Our greatest enemies were silence and shame, for if we allowed our pain to divide us, we would be conquered by it. As I reflected on this, I found the strength to pick up the burdens of all those gathered, if only for a moment, and offer them up to God. I didn't know what I was going to say, but I had Faith I'd do my best. After all, when Wisdom and Experience fall down, Love and Sincerity usually rise up to carry us through.

So there I stood as straight and tall as I could, and in a voice a little less quiet than usual, I began to pray. "As we gather in community, we offer up our thanks for all we enjoy. There is much we each have that has enabled us to be here today, and for this we are grateful. There is also much yet that we hope to receive, and we pray for loving aid as we seek it. We pray for help and guidance, that we may find our way through the troubles and darkness toward a way of peace and light. We pray for strength and wisdom, that when we face the challenges before us, we may see clearly the path of truth and have the courage to walk it. Finally, we pray for love and support, and offer our own to others. No matter the nature of our inevitable stumbles, we pray that we shall recognize we are not alone, and accept help as readily as we offer it to others. This all we pray, in humble sincerity. Amen."

As I prayed I felt my heart unfold and fill, and when I opened my eyes they were wet with misty tears that I was barely keeping back. A little flustered and embarrassed, I quickly moved to sit down as the coordinators started directing the groups.

On my way through the crowd, someone caught me and hugged me with a quickly whispered "Thank you." Only after she had moved away did I realize it was Tricia Knox. I hadn't really met her before the Student Council meeting those few days earlier, and I certainly had never before noticed her at a church gathering. But just as I started to follow her, suddenly wanting to get to know her better, that "settled" issue from that same meeting caught up with me.

"Thank you for the beautiful invocation, Sister Franklin. As always, you showed a real gift for speaking right to the heart." I hope I didn't roll my eyes, but I know I felt like it as soon as I heard Richard's voice. He wanted something, and it was clear I wouldn't escape hearing what it was.

"Thanks, I just wanted to give it my best." I let my annoyance be trumped by my discomfort at receiving compliments. I forced a smile, trying to be gracious.

"That's one of the most commendable virtues a woman can share with the world, always trying to give it her best." His smile was wide, just like his father's, and I could see how so many people could mistake the gleam in his eyes for sincerity, if they wanted to. But as much I had wanted to do the same in the past, at that moment I couldn't allow myself the luxury.

Mistaking my discomfort for humble shyness at the intended compliment, his grin broadened. "Yes. Very commendable. That's why I hope you'll be active in the Teen Support Program this year, helping get it started. You have such a potential for reaching out to people and doing the good work. My father suggested it would be a better direction of your time for a while, speaking to people one-on-one instead of gathering with the group." He spoke with implied layers of meaning, which I ran through quickly in an attempt to keep up.

I couldn't quite guess what he was getting at, and it made me nervous. Did he realize I no longer had a stomach for picketing health clinics? That I had strong suspicions regarding possible school Spying and how it may involve him? Did he want to involve me with that, and if so, was it government-sanctioned, or was it... *Spying*? Not that I thought the Foleys were secretly Arabiyan Espionage Agents like Spies were supposed to be, but the government took a very dim view on unsanctioned wiretapping and the like by individuals.

Just when I was starting to wonder if I had to look forward to a Domestic Security Services squad whisking us both off to ask "some hard questions," he reached forward and put a reassuring hand on my shoulder. He leaned forward with what was likely his best attempt at a comforting smile. "I know it sounds daunting, but my father has experience in working with troubled youth, and wants to offer his support – our support – in talking you through the challenges. You know, go over the students' issues, help work through the Right Way, find the best solutions..."

Suddenly, my discomfort took a different turn, making me almost wish the DSS would burst in after all. He was standing a little too close, and something discordant in the air indicated he wanted to get closer. I couldn't help but flush, and stammered out, "Thanks, I'll have to think about it, FOAM needs a lot of my time, and… and I'll let you know."

My stammering must have given him entirely the wrong impression, because he punctuated his "You do that" with a quick wink and a smarmy smile. I backed away a few steps with a hurried goodbye, then resumed my quest to find my parents so we could walk home.

When I found their chairs empty, I realized they must have assumed I was staying and had gone home without me. I didn't begrudge them that, since Sunday was the only time my father had off from work. It was also one of their few remaining opportunities to enjoy private time in the home they had built for our family. When I graduated and moved out, my parents would be relocated to the Adult Dorm if none of my siblings moved their family back to stay with them. I didn't think that was fair,, since my father and his friends had built the house themselves and he'd always kept up the payments for the land. Besides, factory officers each had their own houses despite the fact that only one of them had a child, and that one officer's child was off at boarding school.

It didn't matter what I thought, though. The factory owned the land so the factory got to say who used it and how. Actually, the government owned the land, but it always did what the factory owners wanted. We had to purchase or rent every public resource back from the factory, down to the water we drank. They were the ones who got the rights to our water in the Resources and Austerities for the War Deal, back when the Global Trade Financiers Organization required the I.S.A. to eliminate public services and auction off their management rights to private companies as a condition of bailout loans so we could maintain our War on Tyranny.

Since the Global Trade Financiers Organization had enforced the privatization of natural resources all across the world, people with money could buy bottles of clean water taken from overseas villages, leaving those villagers dry as their bones. Though expensive, the bottled water was a pretty attractive option in our town since our own water tables were piped right into the factory. The leftover water was reprocessed to filter out some of the muck and chemicals before adding new chemicals back in, then put into the pipes for public use.

Even the piped water was hard to afford, though, and some brave or foolish people secretly dug wells into the contaminated water table and rigged their own filtration system. The risk of disease was pretty scary, but even scarier were the fines or jail times you faced if you got caught. Our taxes paid to build the pipelines and maintain the treatment plant, but not for the use of the water itself. The factory hated the idea of ordinary people in any way threatening the huge profit margin built into their rates, and they paid good money to make sure the laws protected their usury.

At least the water bills were cheaper than the energy bills, but I won't even get into that right now. Plus, irrigation and a home garden permit were also cheaper than what the rare produce cost at the store. No matter how often taxes were raised to increase farm subsidies, it didn't seem to do anything to help us get healthier, affordable food. The bulk of the money went to pay the huge agricorps not to grow crops, or to grow more crops for fuel instead of food, stuff like that. I'm still not sure how we even survived, normal folks like us. When the basic necessities of life are at the mercy of the so-called Free Market economy, only the Marketeers are Free; the rest of us are held captive by them.

So there I was, standing on church property, the one piece of land in the town the factory didn't have any say over, wondering what I should do with my day so as not to interrupt my parents' rare time alone together. Having nowhere else to go, I went looking for Tricia to see if I could get to know her a little better, maybe make connections to help us through the year with the Student Council. After all, connections were what this event was for!

I found the group of young women my age and was surprised to find Judy with them. She was talking with several homeschoolers about the school activity schedule, trying to help them join in. I hadn't seen her at church earlier so I thought she'd miss the event, though I should have known better. Whenever an activity needed participation, Judy would be right in the middle of things to make it happen.

She waved me over, but I politely waved her off. I didn't mean to be rude; I just was tired of talking about a calendar of dances and such that I had no interest in attending. Judy nodded to me, and I resumed my search for the elusive Tricia Knox. I knew she didn't exactly win the secretary election because she stood out in a crowd, but I hadn't thought she'd disappear into one so easily. Still, I kept at it, sure that someone as conscientious as she wouldn't leave until the event was through.

I was delayed several times by people coming up to chat, and I was privately embarrassed by how few of their names I could remember. However, they all knew mine and seemed quite happy to see me, something that still took me aback. Finally, I caught sight of Tricia as I politely disengaged myself from another group. She had just finished dishing up a small plate from the potluck table. I grabbed a few things onto a plate for myself and asked if I could sit with her while we ate.

"Sure, if you'd like to." She tucked her chin as she said it, her bashful gesture doing nothing to hide the hopeful invitation in her eyes.

I then realized I wasn't the shyest person in the Student Council, and laughed at us both. "I'd love to. Maybe between the two of us we can work up enough 'outgoing' to actually have a conversation rather than just sit here quietly being shy at each other."

She scoffed politely as we sat down on a thin blanket spread on the ground. "Oh, please. No way are *you* shy."

I boggled at that. "Wow, really? I mean, do I really come off so, um, un-shy?"

She opened her mouth, then stopped herself. Then she quickly looked down at her plate, poking at some kind of salad with her fork as though the words she was searching for may be hiding underneath. "Well, I mean, you have always seemed kinda… I mean, like you think you… I mean…"

I sighed. "I come off like a self-important know-it-all, you mean. Great." As her picture of me came into clearer focus, I recognized it as something I should have seen long before, especially after Marissa's diary. I did usually try to speak with conviction, but even now I have trouble keeping it from making me sound obnoxiously opinionated. I do sincerely try my hardest, but it's a struggle I still face.

Tricia did me the kindness of trying to protest. "Oh no, I mean…" She then laughed, half-nervous, but also half-amused… or relieved. "I mean, I never knew you that well. I guess it's just that you're so self-confident, and not many people are. But I was afraid after the elections that I was going to be sitting there having to listen to two Richards bullying and bossing Judy, steamrolling Derek, and, well, getting into irritating fights with Gig." When she saw me wince at the thought she put her hand on my arm and patted it. "Don't worry, it's obvious now you're not like that. You really care about people, and that's what counts."

I smiled slightly. "I hope so. Though speaking of Student Council, I'm starting to wonder what I've gotten myself into."

"Oh, me too, believe me." Her smile faltered for a moment before brightening again. "But hey, now you know you've got a friend there! That is, I mean…"

I laughed as I reached over to take her hand in a comforting gesture. "Yes, Tricia, let's be friends. You're a good listener, and you don't mind telling me that I sometimes come across badly, let's put it like that. Observation and honesty are both things we all need more of. Hey…" I looked around casually, checking to make sure we couldn't be overheard by anyone. She leaned closer, curious, but following my lead in trying not to look too seriously interested as I started talking slightly softer.

"I might be volunteering to take the lead in helping set up the Teen Support Program, so I can try to make sure it gets put together in a way that will actually help people instead of…" I trailed off, wanting to confide in someone but unsure of what to say.

"Instead of letting you-know-who turn it into another way he can try to wheedle secrets out of students that they'd rather not share?" Tricia gave me a wry grin that assured me the message had come across loud and clear. She then nodded to me with encouragement. "I really think you should. Judy's way too busy, and Derek means well, but the other two would want to fight with him on it just because they're argumentative and he's a guy. Gig doesn't fight with gals and, well, it's obvious 'the other one' has a soft spot for you already, so…"

I cringed. "So it's better me than anybody else, yeah. I just hope…"

Tricia watched me sympathetically for a few moments until it became clear I wasn't sure exactly what I was hoping. Then she gently placed her hand on my arm and gave me a warm, "Me too."

I suddenly realized that I had a new, true friend, one I could count on. This bolstered my courage for what I knew I would have to face, and soon.

Chapter 4

What is Lovingkindness?

First thing the next morning I embarked on a quest to conquer my dread of the unknown. After a fortifying breakfast of rice and raisins, I set out to resolve a matter I knew I would have to set behind me before I could begin the Teen Support Program. After checking the routes and schedules, I headed straight for the bus stop to begin my journey to the Family Planning clinic.

A comprehensive and efficient public transportation system was hardly a priority for the city's private contractors, which by now surely must go without saying. There simply wasn't that much money to be had from those who couldn't afford any other way to travel. The meandering bus route gave me plenty of time alone with my jumbled thoughts, trying to sort out what I would say. Time didn't help me though, and I was just as lost when I arrived. I had rehearsed some things over and over, but they sounded rough and jumbled in my mind. Finally, I figured I'd better just let my heart speak for me and hope for the best, trying not to wonder how bad it could be.

The fears rushed back at me as soon as I set foot onto the first step leading up to the clinic. The door was swung open by one of the large men who volunteered to play "bouncer" against, well, people like me, and for a moment I wondered if there was a picture of me by the front desk. But by the look on the man's face, I realized that I'd parked myself in front of those steps often enough that everyone there already knew my face. A "Wanted" poster was completely unnecessary.

The apologies that must have shown in my eyes and on my face seemed to reassure him. Even so, he remained wary as he stepped back to hold the door open for me, wishing me a good morning as he did. With quiet thanks, I stepped past him into the entry, trying to adjust my eyes to the dimmer light.

The waiting area was half-full of women of various ages as well as a few children. I fidgeted at the receptionist's window, trying to pull off the trick of not really looking at people without seeming like I was avoiding them. Fortunately, the receptionist soon returned to her desk, a sharp sigh expressing her recognition.

"And how may I help you today, hm? Need some posterboard and markers? Borrow a thesaurus for a snappy new slogan?" Her voice was doctor's-office soft but sharp, with what seemed to be a genuine touch of patient amusement warring with her annoyance. When I blushed and stammered for words, her amusement briefly gained the upper hand before being overruled by a guarded concern. With a softer, earnest tone, she asked, "How *can* I help you?"

After a careful breath, I tried to repeat what I had practiced the whole trip over. "I wanted to come in to apologize. I feel very strongly about my beliefs, and I'm going to keep fighting for them. However, I regret participating in the bullhorn-bullying of women when they are at their most vulnerable, and I won't be doing it again. Please forgive me, and may God bless you." I didn't look directly at her while I spoke, but as I finished I turned my eyes to hers. Sincerity can't be mumbled into thin air if it's to be taken as genuine, and I knew it.

I couldn't read her expression, which was odd for me, but I could feel her own sincerity in her "Thank you." After a moment, while I struggled for what I had planned to say next, she continued. "I would like to talk more about your beliefs, if you're willing. Do you have a bit of time? There's a spare room here, I can get you some coffee or tea or water…" Her eyes brightened when I assented, then her mouth and feet started moving so quickly I almost skipped to keep up. "Great, back this way. My name's Margie Cammile. Can I get you anything? Okay, just let me know if you change your mind. Here, let me clear off this table for us… there, have a seat. I'm sorry, what was your name again?"

I didn't believe I had said, and quickly replied, "Liz Franklin."

She shook my hand, then resumed her rapid patter. "Lovely to finally meet you, Liz. About your prior visits out front. I understand you have some very strong feelings about what you believe goes on in here, versus what you believe your Bible says should be allowed to happen."

I just nodded, having nothing to say about the obviousness of her statement.

She nodded back at me, her voice lowering and slowing a pace. "About that. I've read your Bible backwards and forwards several times, studying every bit of it and comparing notes with your signs and slogans out front. And I've got news for you: yours is not the only interpretation out there, not even of the translation you use." The tone was gentle statement, but the words sounded to me like fighting challenge.

Now, it didn't matter to me whether she used the centuries-old Biblical translation read in my church, or if she read from one of the "revisionist" ones. The way I saw it, every Biblical word was in stalwart support of our fight against everything that clinic stood for. I tried to keep my tone as even as hers, which was easier than I had expected. "I think every version of the Bible is pretty clear on the matter."

She smiled at that, with a hint of mirth. "Yeah, and so do I, but in an entirely different way. Let's be honest. Though abortion existed when the Bible was written, it's never specifically addressed as a sin, not directly and not by name. So all anyone has to go on is what they find in the texts that either supports or contradicts a supposition based on how they choose to interpret any given verse. So let's go through a few of those interpretations to see what they actually say for themselves. You game?"

I shrugged at the futility of her little exercise. "All right, if you want."

With a quick, sharp nod, she launched back into her rapid patter. "Okay, the first and most fundamental platform used against abortion is the 'thou shalt not kill' commandment. Now, I'm rather a fan of this idea, since I'm personally against all killing as a matter of principle. But there's a few problems with using the commandment as stated in the Bible as a prohibition against abortion. Firstly, the original Hebrew word is 'rasach,' meaning murder, an illegal killing. It's a relative term, not an absolute prohibition on ever taking a life. This is very clear when you consider the numerous times where God kills, instructs others to kill, or generally endorses a killing."

I leaned back in my chair, my arms reflexively crossed across my chest. "Punishing sin with death is not the same thing as killing an innocent baby, unless you want to try to tell me God ever commanded that particular atrocity."

Margie paused, biting her lip hesitantly as she eased into her reply. "Actually, Liz, it's your Bible telling you that. In the First Book of Samuel, God commands His people to destroy Amalek, specifically calling for the killing of infants and children. In Numbers the commandment was to kill every male including babies, and every female who had ever been with a man, including those who were pregnant. Hosea claimed to speak for God in saying He would punish rebellious Israelites by slaying their unborn with miscarriages, which was reiterated by Isaiah. In the Second Book of Kings, the retribution was carried out, with the children's brains bashed out and pregnant women's bellies ripped open, killing them and their children... all to carry out the will of God."

I was completely unprepared for the cavalcade of atrocities Margie was describing. Slumping down in my chair as I tried to sort things through, I shook my head to clear it and tried to get back to my point. "That's... that's all horrible, and I'll have to look into those claims, but that isn't what we're talking about. That was all war, which isn't the same as murder. And abortion was always considered murder."

My emphatic point was dismissed by a click of Margie's tongue. "Quite the contrary, actually. The earliest councils of Christianity only outlined penalties for women who underwent abortion if it was related to what was considered a sexual crime. It was treated as a part of wanton behavior as they saw it, and certainly not as murder. Even after the earliest centuries, official opinions of the church varied, but it wasn't consistently counted as murder until relatively recently. We can go back even further with your claim of 'always,' as God's chosen people themselves had not treated abortion as murder under the laws of God, in no small part because they didn't consider it as killing an individual person."

Seeing my skepticism, Margie elaborated. "Abortion was, and remains, completely legal under Jewish law. As commanded in the Book of Numbers, a baby is not counted as a person until thirty days after birth. People aren't even allowed to observe the Laws of Mourning for a loss prior to that day, as the Laws simply don't apply to a non-person. This is further referenced in Exodus where the penalties are given for men who are fighting and do accidental injury to a pregnant woman, causing her to lose her child. If there's no injury to the woman, the offender is fined whatever the husband wants. If the woman herself is injured, then it's eye for an eye, tooth for a tooth, just like a murder."

I nodded, "I'm aware of that one, it applies to injury to or loss of the infant too, supporting my point. If it results in a premature birth with no harm done, then there's just a fine."

She shook her head. "I don't know where you heard that interpretation, but since we can reference the actual laws from Jewish tradition and those of the countries that copied them at the time, we have proof that's simply not the case. Premature birth in almost all cases meant death for the infant, hence there being a fine for the loss of the father's property according to the laws. Only if the woman was also harmed were there penalties for doing harm to a person, because only the woman was considered a person under the law." She paused, then continued, sympathetically. "I can tell this is all very hard for you to hear right now. I can loan you some books if you'd like to read up on it for yourself."

I wasn't sure what my face showed, but I suspected it showed just how much I wanted to utterly reject what I was hearing. It simply flew in the face of all that Brother Foley had taught us. Fortunately I did remember what Brother Foley taught, and could bring up what I felt was Biblical proof that God considered the unborn as a full person, regardless of what the laws of humans might decree.

"Well, okay, so maybe human laws didn't recognize the unborn child as a person and therefore the victim of murder, but God certainly did, and does recognize that we are full people even in the womb. Did not Job say to God that He was his Creator, even in the womb?"

Margie only shrugged. "So? I'm still a baker even while mixing flour and sugar, but they're still not cookies until they come out of the oven. Until they're baked, they're just dough."

I rolled my eyes, evading her point. "Okay, then how about when Jeremiah was told by God that He knew him before he was formed in the womb, and was consecrated before he was born? Or Psalm 139, where David speaks of being known even in the womb, obviously meaning that God knows us before we are even born?"

A hint of mischief gleamed in her eyes as she recited portions of that scripture, "'Thou hast covered me in my mother's womb. My substance was not hid from thee, when I was wrought in the lowest parts of the earth.'"

Unsure of where she was headed, I nodded slowly. "That's the gist of what the verses say, yeah. You see what I mean?"

The soft chuckle she gave me was more patient than amused. "As it happens, I do. Now I'll share what I mean. First, did you notice that bit about being wrought in the lowest parts of the earth? When those verses were written, the common belief was that babies were formed within the earth and then placed in the womb to be born. So if you are going to take a literal interpretation, then you have to take this verse to mean that God formed David inside the earth, where He knew him, and then afterward he was placed in the womb."

I scoffed, almost laughing. "Obviously that's not what's going on here. It's a poetic turn of phrase."

"Oh, really, we're taking strict interpretation of the Bible and turning it into poetic license now?" Margie's eyebrow arched with a challenging quirk. "Then how about the following verse, 'In thy book all my members were written, when *as yet there was none of them.*'

There's no poetic interpretation here, is there? David is clearly stating that God knew each and every part of him, before any of him even existed. This means that God's knowledge of David predates any physical existence, meaning that this verse is talking about knowing the soul as separate from the body, even before it was in the womb to be knit together. Simply put, Psalm 139 states that foreknowledge of the soul is wholly independent of any physical formation. The soul alone holds the identity known by God, having nothing to do with the body that eventually houses it. It says absolutely nothing about when that soul and body become joined into life."

"I, uh..." I hadn't thought of it like that. I didn't quite know how to respond, though Margie hardly waited for me to find my words.

"In fact, this is further supported by the story of the very first man, Adam. The way the Bible tells it, Adam was formed fully of clay, and only when the body was fully knit together did God place a soul into it, breathing into his nostrils. And to jump to the New Testament where you like to go when the Old one doesn't support your arguments, there's the verse stating that a body without breath is dead. Clearly, a body does not have life until it is breathing. Do babies breathe air in the womb?" She smiled playfully at that.

I actually hadn't heard that verse in such a context before, and I was getting quite exasperated with being so constantly knocked off my scriptural feet. I sped up my thoughts. "Well, no, but they get oxygen in the blood, and…"

Her smile turned to laughter. "Oh no, no-no, no you don't. Not again. Using the Bible as an unerringly absolute moral guide is an all-or-nothing proposition. You have spent hours out there arguing a brutally word-for-word literal application of the exact phrasing in your translation of the Bible as reason to dictate to strangers what they can do with whom, and how. You can't now start playing the 'well, it means to say' game, with your selective claims of poetic license. Getting oxygen in the blood is not the same as breathing, which is specifically what your Bible states, breath."

As soon as I caught myself wanting to keep playing the "it means to say" game, as she put it, I started to realize how that would open the door to challenging other arguments I was about to make. I could have deflected them with more literal applications, sure; but it would have been inconsistent and I knew it. Absolutism, to have any integrity, must be applied absolutely.

I tried another approach. "Heartbeat. The heart beats, and there's brain activity. That's how we know there is a person before birth."

She smiled conspiratorially as she leaned forward to whisper a moment, "That's not in the Bible, you know. But as a quick aside, yes, a developing organism does require functioning circulation and neurons to go about the business of knitting itself into a body. Even single-celled organisms engage in stimulus-response, and process impulses and nutrients. But are heartbeat and brain activity all that's required to make something a person? How about something like being able to move a computer joystick to select a drawing seen only once, a few seconds before?"

I blinked, unsure what point she was trying to make. "Yes, thinking and memory also make a person a person, but a heartbeat and brain activity are the foundation."

That made her chuckle and shake her head slightly. "Well, since I was actually talking about something a pig is able to learn after only a few tries, what you're saying is that animals are people, too. That means you abstain from pork, right? Yeah, I didn't think so, and that leads us right back into Biblical absolutism, and applying your stated values consistently, not just in ways you like. In the founding of Christianity it was declared that Christians weren't to be bound by all the Old Testament laws, but there are Christian groups who feel somewhat differently, such as the one you belong to. Your group argues that every single word in the Bible – Old and New Testaments – is to be followed to the letter, and yet they still eat pork and wear clothes made out of more than one type of fiber, in violation of those very laws. If your group were truly honest with yourselves, not only would you follow all of those types of rules, you'd also follow the law in Numbers about counting someone as a person only after they've been alive for thirty days. Before then, no loss, no mourning, right?"

Seeing that I failed to find any humor in her joke, Margie shrugged apologetically. "All right, I don't think that's right, either. But it's Biblical, so it has to remain on the table in a Biblical discussion. As does – and I really hate to have to bring this up – but Biblical abortion has to come into play here, too."

I stared at her quizzically, trying not to boggle. "Biblical what?"

"Abortion. Specifically, the ritual of Sotah, also brought to us in Numbers. Apparently, God gave Moses instructions on what a jealous husband is to do when he suspects that his wife has been unfaithful. He is to strip her down to the waist and let loose her hair before dragging her to the courtroom. In their custom, he was instructed to treat her the way they treated harlots even before she's accused, let alone convicted of anything. The priest will then mix up a potion and have her swear an oath to God before drinking it. If she's innocent, no harm done, she bears children, all is well. If she did sleep with another man, though, well, in the words of your favorite translation, her belly will swell and her thigh will rot." Margie grimaced before finishing, "A more accurate translation of the original words states her womb will discharge and her uterus will drop. I'd say that's a pretty close description of an abortion."

Whatever she had read in my face, it was enough for Margie to tread carefully as she wrapped up that thought. "Yes, well, and this was the commandment of God, that a jealous husband and a priest should take matters into their own hands, rather than leave it to God to slay the embryo Himself via miscarriage without their intervention, which means... Nevermind, I believe you know what this means. Since up to a third of all pregnancies spontaneously miscarry before reaching ten weeks, some may argue that God doesn't always leave it up to human intervention. So if you are going to argue that it's a commandment of God to never allow a pregnancy to terminate prematurely, you are going to have to give me a new reason why."

By that time, I was turned around and upside-down, tired of feeling like she was playing games with my religion. I summoned the fire back into my eyes as I sat up straight and dealt what I had always believed was the ultimate trump card. "Because my Faith tells me so, in the convictions of my heart."

The gentle sparkle in her eyes spread into a genuine smile. "The convictions of my heart say God grants each of us power and responsibility over our own flesh. It is the government's role to preserve our freedom to fulfill that responsibility. It is between a woman and her moral compass to judge whether she should bear a child. It is up to the rest of us to Love One Another as we respect that freedom without trying to get the government to take away what God has given her. We must Render unto Caesar what is Caesar's, and Render unto God what is God's."

Seeing me bristle at her quoting the Bible back at me again, her smile grew more warm, but firm. "My faith in this is as strong as yours, Liz, and my reasoning as great. Your faith has no power over me, nor should it. No more than mine over you."

My indignation spilled over, "But my Faith comes from God."

"And my faith comes from my god."

She was gentle but firm, while I was feeling less of either. I shook my head. "But… there's only one God."

"If that's true, then either one of us misheard, or we're both right, or we're both wrong. Unfortunately, until a divine being comes here and settles the matter in person, all we have to go on is what we feel in our own hearts. In the end, our heart is the only authority we can rely on, and it's our duty to remain true to that authority alone. Divine Truth is so much bigger than us. I try my best to discover and honor Truth, but I'm not so arrogant to believe I've mastered it."

She laughed a little as she said that, so I thought she was mocking me until I saw the sad warmth of compassion in her eyes. She was deeply sincere, and something in her expression implied her convictions were borne through painful experiences that she had grown from rather than succumbed to. She showed a hint of sadness, yes, but also exuded a quiet and patient strength.

I'd never been spoken to in this way. I'd never seen anyone spoken to in this way. I'd seen shouting of competing scriptures, barrages of traded insults, even crumpled sobbing in the unyielding face of Biblical absolutism. But not calm, patient contradiction of one of the central tenets of my religious dogma, citing competing faith as a matter of mundane fact, not condemnation.

Faith – I'd believed up 'til then that the Spirit of Faith would always lead one unerringly to truth, if one but opened one's heart. Yet, here she was claiming to be led by Faith, and that it led her down a different path than it had me. Could one be deceived into a false Faith by a firm enough desire to believe something that wasn't true? And if that was possible, what assurance had I that it was she who was deceived? I mean, if I was to be completely honest? I had to figure out the nature of her desire to support abortion, learn her motives so I could get a better read on it. There had to be a way to be sure it was she who was too close to the matter to be objective, not I.

I couldn't come up with a way to ask, so finally I just said, "I still don't get why Pragmaticans would be so in favor of something so awful as abortion."

Margie slowly shook her head at me, completely taken aback. "Wow, there's so much wrong with that, I don't even…" After looking away for a few moments with a furrowed brow, she took a breath. "Okay, taken in order. For a start, I'm not Pragmatican."

"Well maybe you aren't in the Party, but…"

"No, I mean it, I'm not even Pragmatic. I know this might boggle your mind, because Puritans like to call everything outside their belief system Pragmatic. Like the word means 'maliciously evil amoral comic book villain who wants to dress your children in vinaigrette and devour them whole' or something equally ludicrous. And I know why that feels satisfying. When you smack a big label on something, it covers up what's actually there so you don't have to look at it. Pragmatics do it, too, and they sound just as smug."

My desire to protest was trumped by the ring of truth in what she'd said. It *did* feel good to call something I didn't like Pragmatic, just *knowing* that meant it was wrong and I was right, ending the discomfort at my ideals being challenged. When my entire sense of self was built around the conviction that my every belief was enshrined within a bastion of unassailable truth, it touched a raw nerve when someone questioned it.

I suddenly saw how quick I had been to anger earlier, how personally insulted I had felt at her disagreements. This latest realization spun my head around, making me wonder aloud, "Whose side are you on, then?"

Her wry smile returned before she responded. "I'm not entirely on anybody's side, because nobody's entirely on mine. I know it's a little silly, but I like to call myself Principalian. My one loyalty is to my principles, because it's nobody's responsibility but mine to fight for them. Once you put your loyalty to something outside your own principles, you've lost your integrity. And that's why I could never be Pragmatican. I'm too much of a Compassionate Realist, doing everything I can to work with the foibles of the world as it is, in my efforts to help people make their place in it a little better."

She shrugged, as if in acknowledgment of what a gargantuan task that was. "Meanwhile, the Pragmaticans are so busy working to not let the Best become the enemy of the Possible that they make even the Good impossible by not bothering to try for it. Even a few tax dollars might still trickle down to helping women be tested for cancer and get the barest basics of medical care if the Pragmaticans who control allocations to charities like Family Planning weren't so terrified that someone might call them Pragmatic just for proposing it in the budget."

She saw my confusion about the mention of cancer and such, and quickly clarified, "You should realize that over ninety-five percent of what goes on here is health screenings and routine medical treatment for women, and sometimes men. We also have healthy baby programs, providing everything from checkups to teaching new parents how to care for them, helping improve or even save those precious little lives. It's the only chance at any kind of preventative care so very many people have, especially with the astronomical costs of health care even for those lucky enough to have steady jobs. Even those with insurance can't always afford the huge up-front deductibles they'd have to fork over before insurance would even start to pay a portion of their doctor visits, so they come here."

Passion warmed her voice as she leaned forward on the table. "The people who are trying to shut us down are working hard to take away the only chance our clients have to take care of themselves. But then, the health and survival needs of women and the impoverished have always been sacrificed on the altar of political and personal agendas. The blame and shame is always heartlessly laid on those who are giving all they have just to survive, instead of on those who for personal gain abuse their power over the powerless. Just think of the world we would have if more people behaved like Jesus, instead of wantonly throwing his name around as justification to rob and harm those he valued most: children."

She paused only for a short breath to let that sink in before charging forward. "And that leads to your second point. I hate abortion. Nearly everyone I know hates abortion. I have never met anybody *in favor* of abortion. I personally feel it's a horrible, horrible thing for a person to have to even consider. No, not because of ludicrous anti-abortion rumors that they routinely cause long-term health or mental problems, which have repeatedly been exposed as utterly untrue. I hate it because I love babies, I love motherhood, and I hate any person being in such a terrible situation that abortion seems the best of all lousy options. I get this freshly heavy, oppressive feeling, every time I counsel a woman who may need one."

My eyes narrowed cautiously. "If you hate it so much, why would you even consider trying to make it legal, let alone help make it available?"

"Because I hate the alternatives more." The last word had vehement emphasis. "There are far worse things than a safe and legal abortion for a woman who has searched herself and decided she needs one."

I still didn't see it. "The alternative to abortion is not having sex if you're not ready to be a mother."

She arched an eyebrow at me. "Are you arguing against birth control itself, now? Because if so, you should have said not mother, but *parent*."

That wasn't what I'd meant, but she wasn't far wrong. "Okay, fine, parent then. It's wrong for men too, as explained in the Bible where it teaches that birth control is wrong. Onan had, uh, spilled his seed, and was struck dead for his wickedness. This time, the Bible is inerrantly clear in what God's opinion is." I hate to admit to you that I was feeling just a bit smug despite myself, as I had finally settled back onto the firm, rock-hard foundation of Biblical clarity.

And then, naturally, Margie exposed the quicksand beneath my feet. The sparkle of mischief had returned to her eyes as she snapped up my point and split it apart. "You know, you are absolutely correct, so let's examine what that story explains about God's opinions. In the story, God had put a man to death for wickedness, and the man's brother Onan was commanded to 'lie with' the widow Tamar to produce her a son. But Onan didn't want to father a child who would, in God's eyes, belong to his dead brother, so he 'spilled his seed on the ground' to avoid honoring his promise, and was killed for his sin. The widow then did all she could to honor God's commandment that she bear a child despite her father-in-law's attempts to keep her childless, and his hypocritical attempt to execute her while pregnant, but that gets into another matter entirely."

I made a mental note to read up more about that story of Tamar and her father-in-law, trying to keep up as Margie went on. "Regardless, the story of Onan was about one man making a commitment before God to father a child, then trying sneakily to break his word. It had nothing to do with every sperm connecting to an egg and then becoming a breathing baby. If that was God's will, then he wouldn't cause up to a third or even half of fertilized eggs to fail to implant, let alone that large number of early-term spontaneous miscarriages. Plus, and I don't know if you know this, but the way men are made, not only do virtually none of their seeds make it to sprout, as it were, there's times they can't avoid a little bit of spilling, so to speak. Therefore, it's pretty obvious that God didn't intend for us to take this story out of context like that."

I didn't know what she meant, and I could tell it touched on topics I didn't want to talk about, so instead I went back to the point I had been trying to make. "This time the message was spelled out. We can't go picking and choosing when to have a child. It is up to God when a child is to be born, and it's a sin against God and that child to try to take matters into your own hands."

Her playful smile returned. "And yet here you are, trying to do exactly that, and force a woman to bear a child. Even if her own religious beliefs instruct her that God wishes for her to use the medical blessings granted her to not bear a child, you would take away the agency of choice you believe God grants to each of us. Just like Onan, you would play God with whether or not a child comes into being."

I wanted to accuse her of teasing me again, yet I could tell she was quite sincere. "But when they're preventing a child from being born..." I trailed off.

She shook her head as she corrected me. "Preventing a child from being formed in the first place. I know some in your group like to choose their own terminology by calling emergency contraceptives or even all contraceptives 'abortion pills,' but contraceptives only prevent a pregnancy, not end one. For example, the emergency contraceptive pills don't interfere with fertilized eggs, they merely interfere with ovulation and fertilization. Without those, you can't get pregnant any more than putting milk and spices in a cold pan can get you an omelet."

With a shrug, Margie went back to her train of thought. "Regardless, neither The Pill nor the Emergency Pill can possibly terminate a pregnancy that never began."

I couldn't think of any new ways to argue about that point. So instead I moved back a step further, to the commandments regarding sex itself. "But from the very beginning, Adam and Eve were commanded to be fruitful and multiply. We have an obligation to bear children; it's the purpose of sex, and the whole purpose of marriage!"

Her brow arched again. "Are you accusing the Bible of not saying what God really meant again? Because the commandment was to populate the earth by having children, that's it. God didn't say have as many children as humanly possible, nor only to have sex for that purpose. Not even in the commandment to Noah was that said. God didn't say never to use a method of birth control such as withdrawing or the sponge, which we know were used in Biblical times, thanks to the Onan story as well as the Jewish Talmud. Yet when the Bible wants to record a commandment of God, it spells things out in pretty certain terms what God means to say. Trying to put words into God's mouth is one of the faults ascribed to the Pharisees, who were accused of adding on to God's laws and then punishing people who didn't follow their man-made rules."

She'd wagged her finger to make her point, then waved her hand as she continued. "Also, the earliest Christian missionary, Paul, told the Corinthians that spouses were commanded to share themselves with each other, and not just for making kids. It was for strengthening the connections among partners, which sex is fantastic for. There's such a closeness that grows between two people who join together in mutual love and respect, both psychologically and through biochemical responses, and he advised them to forge such bonds. And then there's the Songs of Solomon extolling the divine bliss of such sharing. I know that section of Christian scripture embarrasses some people, but the spiritual metaphors of physical experiences make it one of my favorite parts of the Bible."

At that point I blushed, because it embarrassed me that the Songs of Solomon were even in the Bible. Whenever we got a new Bible in our church, we actually stapled that whole book shut, but I still had happened to catch a glimpse here or there of a word that made me turn beet red. I didn't want to have to admit another point of picking and choosing which parts of the Bible I wanted to consider, so I just left it alone, shifting uncomfortably in my chair.

Margie's compassionate smile returned at my attempts to not let my reaction show on my face. "Tell you what, let's move on. Let's instead say for the moment that you are absolutely right, that abstinence is the best possible choice in the entire universe, and that everybody who ever has sex not wanting to be a parent is absolutely in the wrong and sinners before God. And then let's pretend that their commitments to God are even any of your business in the first place." She paused. "You with me so far?"

"Yes, go on." I was grateful for the topic shift, and curious where she was going.

She leaned forward again, hooking one forefinger onto the other as though counting. "First, let's deal with those who don't choose to have sex. The anti-choice laws pushed in this state still grant the option of abortion if the woman can prove the sex was against her will. Without getting into how messed-up the Burden of Proof laws have gotten and how awful survivors are treated, just generally speaking – how do you feel about that?"

I grimaced, because I knew there were those who always considered sex the fault of the so-called temptress, blaming a woman who was raped for the atrocities visited on her. "Well, I don't like it, but if it wasn't her fault, then..."

"Bingo. So pregnancy is a matter of *fault*, a *punishment* for having sex. Bearing babies is a punishment." She watched me as she said that, and was satisfied at the return of my indignation.

"Hey wait, no, I didn't mean that."

She then held her hands up questioningly. "Then why is it more okay for an abortion if the woman was raped than if she had a sudden impulse of passion, or a condom broke? If you feel that all abortions are the murder of a potential baby, what's the difference?"

I paused to consider, since I remembered there were those who didn't want any exceptions for outlawing all abortion or even birth control... those like Brother Foley. "Well, I think the law was passed that way because they had to make a compromise. There are of course those who don't think it should still be legal, but they didn't want to seem heartless, since they knew they wouldn't win."

"Heartless is a good word there, but I didn't ask about what's legal. I want to know what you think: is there a difference?" She rested her chin on her hand, watching me closely as I considered.

"Hmm. You know, I think there is a difference. I think it's because the baby would have to be born into the horrible circumstance of… well, you know." I trailed off, not wanting to even think about it.

"Yes, unfortunately, I *do* know. But fortunately, rapes don't always result in pregnancy, or the population of this town would be…" Her eyes started to flinch with pain again, but she blinked it away. "Nevermind, that's another tangent. What you're saying is, the circumstances for the baby matter here."

I almost asked what she was going to say, but decided to also remain on the topic at hand. "Yes, they'd have to."

"And since the woman is the baby's mother, the circumstances she can provide the baby matter as well, yes? Yes. So. What about women who choose to have sex, but they can't afford to become mothers, or already have children to support? After all, over half of abortions are for women who are already mothers of children they fear would be made destitute if their scant resources were stretched even thinner. So let's say they used every precaution while honoring Paul's request they have sex with their husbands, but contraception failed. They suddenly find themselves pregnant but without a means to pay for the prenatal care and delivery, let alone the baby's food and medicals once born. Remember that these days about one in four people can't get enough work, and twice that many have one or more jobs but still aren't getting paid enough to reliably provide for their family without help. Throw in another mouth and they all may end up on the street, even if nobody gets sick and all the breadwinners can keep working. Do you see the impact of those circumstances, too?"

I was thinking again of all the kids who couldn't find work through the school and had to find other ways to cover their tuition, or drop out. I then thought of what prospects they could possibly find out there, competing with a dozen or more adults also desperate for any job that would take them. I didn't like their odds. "I… I think I do."

"For many, if not most, of these women, if they had a way of caring for these babies, they wouldn't be so afraid of the pregnancy ruining two or more lives. Given that they don't choose to be poor, poverty is another involuntary condition that turns women to abortion. There's also the women who are on their own, and all the doors that would close on them as single mothers. It's not merely having no help with childcare and bills, there's the stigma against them in the community as well as the workplace, and it's all perfectly legal…"

"…yeah. Yeah," I mumbled glumly. Even married mothers didn't get far at work, since it was assumed they'd put more focus on their family's needs than the factory's. Though the company demanded to be their highest priority even though it didn't have any loyalty or even concern for them. In fact, even childless women were treated almost as badly sometimes, as though it was expected they would become pregnant at any time. I hadn't realized before that moment how terribly unfair it was. Remembering how even being pregnant even once got them treated, I almost pre-answered my next question. "Wouldn't it be better to give the babies up for adoption to someone who could give them a better life?"

I could tell she saw I was already wavering on that point, through her small, knowing smile. "If a woman can't afford to keep her child, she usually can't afford to be pregnant. We have been able to connect some young women with adoption programs that can help with the bills, but they can't help with the social and economic costs of bearing and then giving up a child. Unfortunately, there aren't homes for every baby, or every type of baby, and not every woman finds carrying a baby to term to then give it away an option for them. Of course, we haven't even talked about the situations where there are lethal defects, or if a woman's life is in serious danger due to a pregnancy. Do you think a woman should be forced to carry a dead or dying baby to term, or lose her own life or that of an endangered twin because you are against the idea of terminating any kind of pregnancy?"

That actually gave me some serious pause, because I thought of how many in my church had faced that question and answered in the affirmative. Women were routinely denied medical care for their pregnancies, which they were encouraged to have as often as possible. Any form of contraception was considered sinful even for married women, as God alone would grant or deny pregnancy in accordance with His plan. And we appointed ourselves God's personal caretakers in this plan, but only to a point. We claimed personal responsibility to ensure armies of children were brought forth for God, but not, as Margie had pointed out, to help care for those children once they were born.

It was also considered sinful for a woman to seek medical treatment even for fatal complications to pregnancy, as it meant she would be playing God with how the pregnancy turned out. Men would get treatment for anything and everything no matter the cost, though. It was believed that God blessed His children with greater understanding of how to allow Him to channel His healing grace through their work for the benefit of things like heart attacks and even backaches. But God's blessings did not extend to using medicine save the life of a mother or her baby.

I'd never really bought into that bit. I just couldn't believe that God wanted us to make a woman's children motherless... motherless, that is, until the widower replaced her, often by a much younger woman. I had always had a problem with that, too, but I'd never let myself seriously think about it before that moment. As the anger and resentment started to well up inside me, I tried to find a way out of it, a way to explain how medical procedures to terminate a pregnancy could never be the work of God, and yet... I just couldn't find a justification for picking and choosing again.

Seeing I was lost in my own turmoil, Margie sighed again, then quickened her pace as she skipped ahead to her point. "The fact is, there are so many circumstances that can lead a woman to feeling she needs an abortion that there will always be those who feel so strongly that they're going to find a way. We were blessed with personal accountability for our own choices for a purpose, and we can't force others to use that power how we want them to, any more than they can force us to deny our own religious convictions to comply with theirs. Regardless of what you think of their reasons, there will always be women who will find even illegal abortion a safer option than pregnancy, however hard you try to convince or force them not to. This has been true throughout history, and I'm afraid it will be true for many years to come."

I snapped back to the conversation, raising my hand to slow her down. "That still doesn't make abortion right."

Nodding in acknowledgment, she slowed her words. "No, the existence of something doesn't determine its rightness. However, the rightness of something also doesn't determine its existence. For example, I said I'm against all forms of killing, and I meant it: the death penalty, war, I find all of it to be reprehensibly immoral. However, there are many people who are wholeheartedly in favor of these and other kinds of killing, even while fighting tooth and nail to outlaw abortion by arguing 'Thou Shalt Not Kill.' I accept this. People aren't going to always be where you'd like, so you need to meet them where they are if you're to have any hope of helping them. If you're serious about preventing abortion, you'll have to quit trying to force your choices onto other people, because obviously that isn't working. As long as women believe abortion is their only option, there will be women who choose it. Instead, give them better choices, and I guarantee you that people will make them."

I looked at her askance, trying to be clear on what she was suggesting. "They'll choose to keep their babies."

She nodded emphatically. "A lot of them, oh definitely, yes. Not all of them, no, but a very great number would much rather be a mother with options. And many more would benefit from help in making sure they have access to what they need to prevent pregnancy to begin with."

I frowned. I wasn't sure if I was ready to change my long-held position on something that I had always been told might encourage women to have sex that wasn't for creating families. "But what if I'm still against birth control? Or even just against The Pill and stuff for someone who isn't married?"

I expected her to be frustrated or take offense, but she just gave a matter-of-fact half-shrug. "You mean, what if you're against those things, and also if you feel it's your personal duty to decide when and how another woman has the spiritual and legal right to share or not share her body with another person? Well then you're going to have to make a choice, and not about whether she has sex, because contraception has nothing to do with that. Here in America about one in three women have had an abortion, even with all the barriers to access. Yet in the heartland of Europa where they've implemented comprehensive sex education and made contraceptives widely available, the annual per-woman abortion rate is less than one third of ours. Time and time again, it has been proven that when women are empowered with the knowledge and resources to take care of their own health, they don't have more sex, but they do have far less pregnancy and disease. So you need to learn to live with either the idea of women having safe sex you don't like, or the idea of women ending unwanted pregnancies as a result of sex they're having anyway."

She smiled at that, but not unkindly. "Further, you absolutely need to support accessible health services for women, even if someday one of them may want to have a choice not be pregnant. Because you can't just make contraception and abortion hard to access, or even illegal, and think that makes it go away. All it usually does is make women feel even more helpless and alone, lost in a confusing maze of myths and lies about what is really going on with their bodies. That's the worst way they can feel in times like those, because instead of getting help to figure out their options, they are vulnerable to back-alley solutions that can end up pretty ugly. When women don't have access to counseling and safe options, too often they're easy prey for—"

"I KNOW!" Margie jumped as I shouted, both from what I said and how I said it. Even I was surprised at how strongly the guilt and anger from Marissa's pointless death had boiled over within me.

I then felt cold again, and looked down a moment before quietly admitting, "I know... knew Marissa Langley. She... she tried to come here for help or even just some information, someone to talk to, that last day I was out there. The fact I was here, it scared her off, so she didn't... she couldn't..." I trailed off and wiped at my eyes in an attempt to stop the tears from streaming down my face, not sure what I wanted to say.

I couldn't see Margie's face, because I refused to look up. Soon I felt her hand on my shoulder, squeezing it. After what seemed like a long while, she softly said, "I'm sorry."

"You're sorry? Why are YOU sorry?" I looked up to her, and saw tears in her eyes as well.

Those eyes smiled sadly as she gave that soft little laugh I've since come to learn was her way of keeping her pain in perspective. "Here I was, trying my darnedest to help you see that even our sincerest attempts to shape our world can have terrible, unintended consequences for those around us. I had no idea you've already learned that lesson far more keenly than I have ever had to face. I'm *so* sorry."

I gave up trying to stop my tears, instead letting them flow freely as I sat silently a few moments to process all she'd said. Finally I found my voice again. "Except I hadn't. Learned it, I mean. Until just now, I... no, I guess maybe yeah, on some level I had learned. I just didn't realize it."

She squeezed my shoulder once more, then pulled over a box of tissues and offered me one before taking one for herself. "You have a wonderfully strong heart, Liz. You owe it the chance to open up to as many different experiences and perspectives as possible, so it can process them all. Only with a full understanding of your world can it lead the way to the best path for you."

I arched an eyebrow, my tears finally subsiding. "Even the perspectives of people I think are full of it?"

She laughed again. "Especially those, since you never know when someone might help you find a truth you never would have found on your own, whether they mean to or not. Those are the people some call the 'master teachers.'"

She paused, regarding me closely. "You've done really well, you know, considering the epistemic closure... sorry, the echo chamber you grew up in. In this town, it's easy to spend your whole life surrounded by people who agree with you and will help you shout down those who don't. That's a hard environment to grow up in if you want to learn how to find truth for yourself." She then smiled at me with genuine support and understanding, even respect.

Given all that I'd said and done, I couldn't believe she was for real. "You do realize I'm the gal who spent much of her life shouting about what terribly evil people you all are."

With a quiet smile she closed her eyes briefly, then opened them with a sweet sigh. "You're also the gal sitting in front of me now, drying fresh tears and mulling over a fresh perspective. Part of meeting people where they are is recognizing where that is: not in your perception of the past, not in your hopes for the future, but as you find them in the here in the now."

I tried to see myself through her eyes, to figure out where she saw me as being, as well as where she thought I had been. "Why didn't you come out to share any of this all those times I was standing out front?"

She raised her finger to make a point. "Because you can't teach a person anything; you can only be there while they teach themselves. When someone's not ready to consider something, nothing you say will reach them. When they are ready, the teaching will find them – if not through you, then any other way it can. Today just happened to be the day you were ready to learn, and I just happened to be here when you did."

While I sat there pondering my lifelong efforts to teach those who didn't want to be taught, she went on. "You've had a chance most people don't take these days: to re-examine one of the most fundamental pillars of your worldview. Rather than finding ways out of it, you came here to grab hold of that chance and see where it would lead you."

She leaned forward onto her forearms, her voice dropping. "But wherever you go from here, you've had a glimpse into the underpinnings of your most cherished principles. Let that new insight work itself over inside you. Find out what you can grab hold of in your own heart to make reality, and let everything else stop standing in your way."

I had also leaned forward, and sat there for what may have been a minute or more, both seeing and not seeing her. So much of where I had cemented my feet felt as though it had crumbled beneath me. When you've spent your whole life imagining your every perspective was sculpted from immovable firmament, that can be a physically dizzying experience. Finally, all I had to offer was a whispered, "Thank you."

"If you wish to thank me, take what you've learned and apply it to your life. I'll bet it also helps the lives of those around you in the process, so long as you stop trying so hard." She winked at me, but I hardly noticed.

I sat up straight, jabbing my finger forward as I suddenly remembered why I had come. "Actually, I came to get info so I can go over it and organize it. I mean, for girls or boys who might be in a situation where you have info that could help them, so other students might know what to tell them."

It was as though I had just told her Santa Claus was on his way, he just needed directions. She jumped up to grab some pamphlets from behind her, talking about which ones were for which situations, and that I could get more whenever I needed them, and other specifics I really can't recall right now.

By the time I left, I had a pretty good idea of what was legal for the clinic to discuss with a minor without their parents present, and felt freshly bad about how much the laws I had supported were designed to make kids and even adults feel miserably alone. Yet rather than start fighting with myself over it, I let that feeling push me harder to help open doors for those who might find themselves hurting and just needing someone to talk to. The laws didn't apply to kids talking with friends and fellow students, so there was an opening to get some real information circulating to fight all the disinformation and rumors that had filled the void. I still didn't want people going off to have premarital sex, but I was starting to realize that God didn't put that responsibility into my hands. Instead, He gave me this opportunity to reach out to His children when they did fall, in whichever way would best help them where they were at.

I had decided that Margie was right. Only I could fight for the truth I found in my own heart. And now, my heart was instructing me to support my sisters and brothers in love and compassion, trying to find new ways to help them heal their situations. Wasn't that the example set by Christ, after all? He embraced even the most dire sinners and worked to help them find a path out of their dark places, regardless of the mistakes that had led them there. If I was to follow Christ's Greatest Commandment, to Love One Another – how could I have done anything less?

Chapter 5

What is Community?

"Take heed that no man deceive you." My father responded by quoting the Bible after I told him that I had spoken with someone about the teachings in the Bible that had opened my eyes to a new understanding. After much prayer on the matter, I felt moved that I should turn my efforts away from condemning the sin, and toward loving and supporting the sinner in their hour of darkest need.

I hadn't gotten into the details, merely that I had been thinking over various troubles kids at school faced. After praying about it, I felt that because Jesus had commanded us to Love One Another as the supreme commandment, those in trouble needed to feel my love more strongly than my condemnation. Yet despite my best intentions, I knew it would take some dedicated, patient effort on my part to learn to stop preaching and start listening. I also knew this would be a tough habit to break. So naturally I turned to the person who had been my strongest support in my every endeavor.

Had been, that is, until that moment.

"Dad, this isn't about anyone else trying to win me over on anything. I've really thought this one through, and read through the Bible again for insight. After taking a night to pray and sleep on it, I honestly feel that this is the path I need to walk." Given that I'd been raised to make every decision this way, I expected he'd probably ask a few questions, maybe voice a hesitation or two, but soon would be in full support of wherever my Faith led me.

I expected… erroneously.

"Remember, Liz, the devil hath power to assume a pleasing shape." His voice was gentle, but firm and unmoved. His eyes implied the finality they always had when he recited a scripture he felt settled a matter.

I just stared at him a moment, not bothering to point out that he was quoting not the Bible, but William Shakespeare. I knew what he meant to say. For the first time in my life, he meant to say that I was led astray by the Adversary. And because I had followed exactly the same steps I had in following my Faith through all the other choices in my life, choices that met with his glowing pride and approval, I also knew what that meant.

It meant that he disagreed with me. And when I had finally reached a decision he disagreed with, his approval of my Faith had ended.

I wish I could say that I tried to reason with him, tried to show him how someone could come to my conclusions in honest and sincere Faith. I wish I could say that I appealed to his faith in Faith itself, that it could guide me truly even if its ways might seem mysterious to him. I wish I could even say that I bore my testimony out to him of the strength and warmth of conviction I felt in my heart. Yes, I had come to feel Margie was right, you can't teach someone anything they aren't on the verge of learning on their own, and I do believe any such attempts at that time would have been futile. But I still wish I could say I made the effort. Because that would mean I wouldn't have to admit my true response.

I didn't respond at all. After blinking a moment or two, I closed my mouth, nodded to him with knowing eyes, then turned and walked away. And closed my bedroom door, and sobbed silently on my bed.

I don't know if you can understand, but losing my father as my unfailing support was the last plank removed from under my feet, sending me toppling into the darkest abyss of a broken heart. I had known I faced challenges ahead, but only at that moment did I realize I would have to face them wholly on my own. I had never felt so alone in the entire world. But I didn't condemn him for his condemnation of what I felt so strongly in my heart. I couldn't, because I could see he felt just as strongly in his heart that what I had suggested was condemnable. If I then judged him harshly for where his Faith led him, what would that make me?

Even so, it hurt. A lot. It was also the last time I ever broached the topic of religion with my father, as I could see that he also felt hurt by our differences on it. I saw his perspective as creating a gulf between him and me, and he saw mine as creating a gulf between me and God. Rather than poke at a sore point, I only tried to make sure he knew I loved him, and that I believed I was following my path. I still like to think there's the chance that he felt at least a hope that I may have been right about God's plan for me.

Regardless, that was also the moment when I learned to stand on my own two feet, wherever they led me, and whoever may take exception. I would never feel alone again so long as I held close to the Spirit that dwelt in my heart. Thus, in our spiritual parting of ways, my father helped me learn my most powerful spiritual lesson. I'm grateful still.

I got to use the lesson right away, as the school year was starting and it was time to put the Teen Support Program into action. The Student Council had scheduled a meeting the second day of classes, and the first item of business was to finalize the details of how we would kick off the program. I had gotten there first, as my FOAM student officers meeting had ended early. I was just sitting down to arrange some of my notes when Richard came in and set a stack of papers next to me.

"Here's the training materials you can use for the TSP volunteers." He put his hand on top of the stack, leaning forward over me. "Sorry we didn't get the chance to get together, you know, to go over things. But if you want, tonight—"

He was interrupted by the door flying open, followed by Judy's barrage of chatter to Derek. "…think a little Welcome Back party in the central square would be terrific, and I don't care who thinks it's cheesy. We could even have a bake sale, or something, raise some money for… Hi, Liz! Hi, Richard. Anyway, for… well, something. I know Gig has a list of all sorts of things he wants to put money toward, like tutoring and stuff, so we can start working on that."

Richard had quickly stepped back to stand up straight and mock-casual, but I thought I may have caught Derek looking at him disapprovingly, then at me for a reaction. I snuck just a tiny quarter-shrug at him, then waved a greeting at Judy, who didn't seem to notice the odd air in the room.

The rest of the group filtered in and got settled while I took a peek at the "training materials." The first few lines were on the dangers of making things worse for a troubled teen by trying to give untrained advice. Next were tips on how to ask probing questions for information and when to bring it to the Student Chaplain or even the School Chaplain, so they could offer their own specialized guidance. I soon gave up what scant hope I may have had for any usable insight.

Well, except for the insight on how exactly Richard and his dad had hoped to use the TSP to further infiltrate the private hopes and fears of the students. Given all they'd done to control what types of thoughts young minds were exposed to, it shouldn't have surprised me they'd try to dig into what young minds thought for themselves. That was one of the reasons our – *their* network of churchgoers had worked so hard to cut support for public schooling: there was no way of controlling the messages that got through. All sorts of supposedly un-Christian things could be taught, and children would be encouraged to keep an open mind to topics and ideas they found distasteful.

Public schools had also forced parents to allow their children to be exposed to *people* they found distasteful. Apparently being forced to learn and work alongside someone who didn't think or act or look "the right way" infringed on our freedom to be narrow-minded bigots. Okay, maybe that comes across a bit harsh, but having come over to the other side of the fence that's honestly how I had started to view it. The fight to rid America of public schooling was supposedly about keeping government money from being spent on topics we found objectionable, but once I started to pay attention, I realized it was also to keep money from being "squandered" on the children of "those people."

Looking back, it's easy to see how the money was first drained from public schools where "those people" had to go, and funneled into the "shining new opportunities" offered to those who were accepted. People who looked, acted and believed like me. And not only were we kept physically separated from "the wrong sort," by herding us toward winner-take-all competitiveness instead of cooperative learning, we became intellectually and emotionally separated from each other... and ourselves, come to think of it. The old divide and conquer, I guess.

The end result was that the more the resource-starved schools for "those people" suffered, the more their failures were held up as examples of how hopeless the whole public schooling system was. Then when someone had the brilliant idea to use a bunch of arbitrary tests to be the sole benchmark of a school's success, well, it was all over. Those tests were easily manipulated to make the "right" schools look great, and the "wrong" schools look worse, hastening the suffering schools' demise. Further, by shifting around what was on the test, you could control both what was taught in the schools, and which schools were allowed to be "successes" and therefore eligible for continued funding.

I don't know if you knew this, but the company that had the most control over these tests was owned by the founders of the Christian Education Network. Brother Foley had introduced me to them when I was younger, since my family was involved in the early ground-roots movement to privatize all schooling. At the time, I had been proud to help make CEN the single largest schooling network, therefore getting the most federal funding. Because even though we could only go to school if we could afford to pay tuition, the schools also raked in a ton of money from everybody's taxes. I even thought that my family and I had genuine input into the curricula that wound up being adopted by most schools throughout the country due to the CEN's sheer economic and cultural might. Our group's high-pressure tactics had even resulted in most secular schools having their own Christian Chaplains on campus, even if only to avoid our picketing and financial harassment.

It wasn't until much later that I found out how misleading, confusing, or even blatantly wrong those CEN-approved textbooks were. I barely even knew that Thomas Jefferson wrote the Declaration of Independence, and actually thought that American slaves had been grateful for the chance to come over here and learn to read the Bible. I didn't know that the very first man to die for America in the Revolutionary War was Crispus Attucks, a black man. Okay, that little tidbit about the Boston Massacre may not be widely known even today, but there is no way I'd heard of a single American hero who wasn't white, and few who weren't male.

At the time I thought the Christian Education Network taught absolutely everything fit to think, and I also believed I'd had even a small hand in shaping it. I didn't realize how carefully I was fed my lines by the very slick, very well-funded handlers who knew how to make me think their ideas were my own. So when the Foleys tried to do to the Teen Support Program what I had helped do to other kids' shots at learning to think for themselves... well, let's just say they finally overplayed their hand. It was starting to sink in just how strongly they needed to control not just what kids were taught, but also what they thought, how they felt. These so-called "guidelines" were their shot at finally fully infiltrating into every facet of a youth's identity, and I felt dizzy and a little sick realizing how recently I would have happily dived right in to help them...

"Now that we're all here, I officially call this meeting to order. Liz, you with us?" Judy laughed at me as I stared down at the pages before me, then again at how I started when she said my name.

"Yeah, of course, sorry. Mind wandering." I ducked my head apologetically, holding back a nervous laugh.

"Well tell it to stay put! I know you have a lot on your mind, but for the next half-hour it belongs to Student Council." She winked at me, and then started in on the routine business.

Fortunately, the matters were mundane enough I could stay on autopilot, saying "Aye" or "Nay" here or there. I was quite caught up in what had been unfolding in my head, and I wanted to focus on the implications. It felt like so many new ways of considering things had been thrust upon me by life over the previous weeks, I began to wonder just how much I had missed. How much else had I been wrong about? Was everything I'd been fighting to force on my world nothing but a pack of…?

Suddenly, I felt my skin prickling and I snapped my focus back to the meeting. I had subconsciously noticed Richard's voice taking on the forced "casual charm" that I'd come to recognize was the signal he was up to something.

I tried to replay what he had just said, so I could quickly catch up to where he was headed. "I guess that leaves the last item of business: the Teen Support Program. Liz and I had the chance to talk a little about this initiative the other day. I was deeply impressed with the great ideas she had. I believe she can truly make a difference in these young peoples' lives. Liz, you want to share those ideas?" He gave me his best attempt at a winning smile, with eyes that reminded me very much of a snake I'd found in our yard the previous spring. I quickly looked around the rest of the table, finding all eyes on me. Even Tricia looked up for a moment, flashing me a quick reassuring wink before studiously looking back down at her screen.

Grateful for her secret show of support, I steadied my voice. "Yeah, I think that we need to focus on making sure that the volunteers get all the resources they need to be able to help our fellow students. A lot of times, kids will just need someone to talk to about stress, or fighting with their parents, or a breakup, or whatever. But sometimes they'll have tougher problems, and volunteers won't necessarily have the information those students need in order to start sorting things out."

I took a deep breath to buy myself some time to find the right words, but Richard had his all ready to interject. "And that's why we think that we need to bring in the School Chaplain as an adult advisor. Since we don't have experience in counseling, we can miss the critical signs of a serious problem. I can of course be the liaison there, helping talk to the volunteers about the problems their student advisees are facing. When I spot a potential problem, I can bring it to the Chaplain and he can intervene."

"That's a great idea!" My surprise at being interrupted by Richard was trumped by my shock at Judy agreeing with him.

Searching her face for sarcasm and finding only sincerity, I carefully asked, "You really think so? Didn't you say it was important for students to have a safe, private place to talk?"

Judy nodded at me briefly before picking up her excited patter. "Yes, and this way, they can have that safe place where they'll feel comfortable sharing what's bothering them, and they'll also have the benefit of someone with experience seeing what the trouble is. If it's just students, well, we might miss something important. You know." She shot me a meaningful glance, to which I nodded slowly. Clearly, she and I had taken away different lessons from Marissa's diary.

"Bullsnot." Gig's pen clattered onto the table, bringing Judy's enthusing to a full stop. "It's just one more way for needle-nosed Puritans to dig their prissy little claws into our private lives. I know, I know, I'm outvoted; but I thought it would take at least a couple of weeks before the one voice of reason on this Council got steamrolled right over. Pity, 'cause I was starting to think this Support Program thing might actually be one of the precious few things this school could do to actually help students."

I seemed to be the only person to see Richard's eyes flare dangerously at Gig's insults. The response was temporary, as Gig's immediate surrender on the issue soothed his anger into vindicated smugness. That expression, however, proved to be equally short-lived.

"Actually, I think I gave Richard the wrong impression when we talked. I do think volunteers need to have safe and private places to turn for information, but it needs to be anonymous on behalf of their advisees, and it needs to be from non-religious neutral parties." As reluctant as I was to put myself on the line by contradicting Richard and his father, I was even more reluctant to continue helping them run kids' lives.

As tough as it was to steel up my newfound courage, I was instantly rewarded with the sight of Richard's mouth gaping open, dumbstruck. The blessed silence didn't last, though, as he slowly found words. "Liz... Don't you agree... Don't we all agree that when students are facing their darkest days, they'll benefit from at least hearing the wisdom a Christian perspective has to offer?"

Gig rolled his eyes. "Blah, blah, get over yourself, blah." He leaned back in his chair, putting his foot up on the edge of the table. "We're at a Christian school, *Chaplain*, in a Christian nation. None of us could escape the 'Christian perspective' if we stuck our fingers in our ears and went cross-eyed. Liz is right, if students come looking for a little help, it's 'cause they need a new way of looking at things. If we say we're gonna help them, we need to dang well help 'em. If they're just going to get ratted out to the same old sanctimonious busybodies browbeating them about what horrible sinners they are, nobody's gonna even bother."

I interjected quickly, "While that's not the most diplomatic way of putting it, the general gist of what Gig says is right. The Chaplain's door is already wide open for students seeking Christian guidance. The Teen Support Program is for students who don't choose to take advantage of that, for whatever reason. Maybe they feel like they already tried it that way and it didn't work for them. Maybe they just need to feel like they've looked somewhere new. And what about the students who aren't Christian? Shouldn't they have one place they can go where they don't feel pressured to convert?"

Richard leaned forward, his hand on the table whitening a little from the weight he placed on it in an effort to contain his anger. "Liz, you know we don't pressure…"

I raised my hand in a gesture of conciliation as I interrupted. "No, I didn't mean to say you do, it's just that I know sometimes kids feel that pressure anyway. It's hard for you and me to understand what it's like, not being a part of the religion of most everyone else around us, but I'm thinking it must feel pretty lonely. Part of what we want to do here is to bridge that perception of a gap, and help them feel they're not alone. So, in order to make sure the Teen Support Program can do its job right for all students, I propose we declare the TSP non-denominational, and guarantee its complete anonymity."

Gig slammed his hand down on the table with a "Hear, hear! I mean, I second that and call for a vote." He nodded emphatically to me with a grin, and for the first time it seemed like he was looking *at* me, rather than *past* me.

Richard quickly pointed his finger to stay the motion. "Just a moment, I call for a countermeasure to be included in the vote. Either we go nondenominational, with Liz taking the lead on the training, or we go the Christian route, and I will step in and volunteer to lead."

Judy nodded. "All right, let's all vote. Liz or Richard?"

Gig quickly half-shouted "Liz," almost simultaneous with Richard stating his own name.

Judy nodded again. "And Liz, you vote yourself, right? Right. Well I'm sorry, I know why you say what you're saying, but I also know that things will go a lot smoother for all concerned if we keep it a Christian program, at least at the start while we try to get this thing off the ground. So I'm going to say Richard. You understand, right?"

I stifled a sigh and just nodded. She was right, it would be a lot easier to get the program going if we didn't rock the boat. And since the tie-breaker would be cast by her boyfriend…

Judy had the same thought, and turned to Derek with a bright smile. "Well, it's a tie, meaning the Assistant Officer has a vote. Derek, do you agree?"

He returned her smile as he said, "Yes, I agree completely," before turning to me with a wider grin. "With Liz. She knows what she's talking about, and I think she even knows more Bible than Richard. If a stand-up gal like Lizbet thinks it's best to keep the Bible out of the volunteer counseling, then who am I to disagree?" I thought his eyes sparkled at me as he said that, but quickly quelled my wishful thinking as it caught up with me that I had won. And Richard had lost. Time to start finding new ways to smooth things along.

"Now I didn't say I thought we should keep the Bible out of it. I mean, we'll train students to be respectful of others' religious beliefs, but if they find comfort in something from the Bible and feel it's the right time to share it, we don't need to discourage that. We'll just all have to pull together as we work toward a balance that brings out what's best for each person's situation." I tried to sound like I already had it all worked out, and smiled warmly to Richard as I finished the sentence. I then tried not to blanch as his barely suppressed scowl morphed into a private smile right back at me.

Judy shrugged, "Well, if anyone can do that, it's you. I'm sure you've got lots of experience with that from FOAM. We'll all be here as backup to help out. Okay, Tricia, enter it all into the minutes, and let's wrap up and go to lunch. I'm starving!"

And with that, it was official. Make it or break it, the formation of the Teen Support Program was squarely on my shoulders. That felt appropriate, since I felt so heavily invested in making it a success. I'm sure that was in part due to guilt over Marissa, but also to the creeping realization of how much I'd supported the school structures and programs that helped her feel so marginalized. I took all the time FOAM left me to spare and devoted it to researching how to establish an effective student counseling training program. I dug through books, checked out periodicals, and even scoured the town's Infranet from the one slow computer in the school library. I don't mind admitting to you I even found a few good ideas from Richard's notes!

In fact, I'll take this moment to say that the one thing Richard did better than anybody I knew was lie with the truth. He'd say things that were just true enough, just useful and insightful enough, that it would distract you from looking to see where he'd palmed a card. He'd lay down a valid point, and then another valid point, and then maybe even one more valid point to lull you into a mesmerized security that he was a rational and reasonable human being who would play straight with you. Then, with the same reassuring patter of certitude, he would throw in something completely off-track and claim it was just another valid point leading naturally from the earlier train of thought. He relied on the listener being so entranced and used to agreeing with him that they wouldn't realize this new point was from a completely fictional land where the only guidepost was what Richard *wanted* to be true.

Still, it was from his rational lead-up points that I was able to glean some very good tips and ideas on which to build a fairly solid framework. Though now that I think of it, even more useful were his little sneakies and sleights-of-hand, because they helped me see ahead of time what tricks were up the sleeves of people like him. This gave me time to think of ways to subtly include the kinds of listening and thinking skills that might strengthen the volunteers' work against attempts to undermine it.

Yes, I absolutely had Richard to thank for unintentionally preparing me for the ambush I faced the following Sunday at church. It was during the community announcements portion read by Brother Foley that he stated that he regretted having to share some very sad news of a dangerous situation regarding one of the congregation. Rapt with concern, I listened earnestly for the nature of the need, hoping there was something I could do. My concern soon crept into to dread as he continued to describe the nature of the perceived tragedy.

"The danger to our little sister is not of life and limb, however, but of soul. Some of you may have heard that a few students at the high school are starting a program to give advice to troubled teens, led by our own Sister Elizabeth Franklin. However, rather than follow the instruction of Christ to suffer the children to go unto Him, she is urging students to turn away from the Bible and use a secular, Pragmatic path. When her fellow youth are in their darkest hour of need, when they most need the light of the Gospel, she has chosen to deny them this light, and to leave them in the Anti-Christian darkness that has led them to their sins." He droned on in what I had once found to be a comforting drumbeat of certainty, but now recognized as the manipulative rhythm of self-absorbed doubletalk.

I was more angry than surprised. The TSP had been a secret among the Student Council while we got it ready for more public consideration, but I should have realized that of course Richard would continue to tell his father everything. I certainly should have realized that if he couldn't have his way with it, he would try to sabotage it. Fortunately, as I said, Richard's notes had prepared me for this. So before things got too far out of hand, I found myself doing something that had never happened in all my years at church.

I interrupted.

Standing up from my pew, I cleared my throat. All eyes turned to me, and I took advantage of my accuser's momentary surprise to have my say. "Brother Foley, I want to thank you for voicing your concerns, and thereby giving me the opportunity to set them to rest. Yes, the Student Council is working through the Teen Support Program to build a way to help students be there for our young friends and neighbors, those with troubled hearts who don't know where else to turn. I know we all realize what trying times these are for our youth, and how lost and confused we can feel by the tribulations that surround us." I was lightly surprised by the echo of a few "amens" around me. Bolstered by the feeling of support, I continued before I lost momentum.

"Of course, the first place most students will turn to seek support against the troubles of the world will be our own family, and the comforting wisdom of the Gospel." I paused briefly for a few more murmurs of support. "However, this is the time in our lives when we sometimes need to explore our own thoughts and feelings with our peers. For those of us blessed with good friends and confidantes, we already have a safe place for that exploration. For kids like me, however, we just don't know that many kids our own age, not that well. It can be embarrassing to ask for help, especially when we need it most. So instead of turning to someone who can help us walk the righteous path toward strength and wisdom, we turn our pain inward, and it can eat us alive." I was momentarily caught off-guard by what sounded like a muffled sob from where Marissa's family tended to sit, and I couldn't help my own tears from surfacing.

"Excuse me a moment…" I wiped them, taking a moment to find my breath. "In those times, I mean, for kids who are facing those long, painful nights of worry and hurt, I want…"

With another deep breath, I regained strength and steadiness of voice. "The Student Council wants to make sure they have a place they can turn, without fear of being embarrassed by their secrets getting exposed before they're ready to deal with them. That's why when we debated whether to offer complete confidentiality versus forwarding them to the Chaplain, we voted in favor of helping these troubled teens feel safe in talking privately with another student. It's crucial that they don't feel judged for their problems, nor how they do or don't apply the Gospel in solving them. The church is always here for them when they're ready to follow Jesus' word. In the meantime, the Teen Support Program will be there to help them feel Jesus' love through our work. As we open our hearts to share this love with them, so do I pray that their hearts will open to receive it. I pray that this love will be enough to help them through, and I welcome the support of this congregation as we share it. Amen."

The church auditorium was hushed as I paused briefly.

The chorus of answering "amens" made my skin glow. Yes, I was blushing, a bad habit whenever there was attention on me, but this time it felt good. Brother Foley mumbled something about having nothing further to say, and stepped aside while Pastor Johns returned to the podium. He watched Brother Foley return to his seat, then looked out onto the congregation, considering.

"I want to thank young Sister Franklin for bearing her testimony of the love in her heart for her fellow youth." He paused again, his lips pursed in thought. He then raised his head up to look over us once more, gesturing toward me.

"Here we have seen one of our youth tested by the harsh spotlight of a misunderstanding aired in public. When we find ourselves under a personal attack, however well-intended, how many of us would bow our heads in shame, or angrily confront our attackers?" At this, I looked to Brother Foley in his seat by the podium, and despite the distance I was certain I saw his jaw clench.

Pastor Johns continued without pausing, gracing us with his broad smile. "Yet undaunted, young Sister Franklin stood forth and poured out her testimony to bring the matter to Light. In the manner of Christ, she answered a gentle-but-firm condemnation with her own loving patience. When struck by an erroneous False Witness she turned the other cheek and humbly answered it with Truth. I wish to thank her for how she rose up to the opportunity this situation provided."

He had looked to me a touch pointedly at that, and I tried to read the meaning he was conveying with his eyes. There was something going on in the background, something politically delicate, and I had apparently provided him with a welcome opportunity to gain an upper hand.

"When Brother Foley asked me to speak to the School Board to put a stop to the Teen Support Program, I must admit that I was surprised at what I'd heard. The idea that youth of our own congregation would be working to lead other students away from their parents and further toward sin, well, it just didn't seem right. Brother Foley asked to lead a vote to condemn this endeavor, and without reservation I had agreed." His voice was drowned out for a few moments by the pounding in my head as the blood rushed further to my cheeks. I tried to will it back down, and to keep up with the Pastor's words.

"Yet I repent the hardening of my heart, as young Sister Franklin has poured out the tenderness of her own in showing that the information brought to me wasn't quite right at all. In fact, it turns out it was all, as I like to say, the Opposite of True." He didn't look at Brother Foley, and I worked valiantly to also refrain this time. But as I saw a number of people look over, I tried to imagine what his expression could have been at having been so politely "called out" on his machinations.

"Now we know," Pastor Johns smoothly continued, "that the Teen Support Program proposes to lead by example to help the troubled youth of our community open their hearts to the love of Christ. And now young Sister Franklin has asked for the support of this congregation in sharing that love. In light of this, I would like to only slightly alter the agenda, and ask this congregation to vote in favor of so offering that support. All those in favor, raise your right hand."

The Pastor raised his hand first, and then the remainder raised theirs. I couldn't believe it. I honestly can't remember a single time when he'd voted first and we didn't all concur, but I still couldn't believe it. He declared the support unanimous and said something about me making sure to turn to the congregation with what we needed and so on, but while I nodded in reply I wasn't really there. I was too stunned.

One of the most powerful members of my community had picked a fight with me behind closed doors, and had almost won without me ever even hearing about it. He had once been a personal hero, and I knew that he had the skill to be a very daunting enemy if he played it right. But he pushed the matter too hard, too fast, and I ended up stumbling into victory.

I thanked God for seeing me through this one, knowing full well that there would times I wouldn't be so lucky. Therefore, I vowed to make this one count.

Of course, as with all new attempts to do some good, there were a few more challenges thrown in our path before we could hold our first TSP training meeting. It started with anonymous complaints to the School Board about "playing with fire by letting the blind lead the blind right down the primrose path" and similar panic attacks about students turning to each other for counseling and support. The School Board then convened a Board of Review to examine the issue, calling the Student Council in to discuss it, with me taking the lead.

However, Pastor Johns also attended to say his piece before we were grilled, expressing how Christlike it is for the youth to take it upon themselves to help each other through the evils we face, and so on. He also brought a couple of parents from our church and other smaller churches from the neighborhood. It turns out there were many parents willing to speak about how much they'd appreciate knowing their children had people their own age to talk to, so they didn't turn "God only knows where" for answers.

To my utter shock, Marissa's mom was among them. When she came up to speak toward the end of the community comments, I almost didn't recognize her.

There she stood at the podium, looking rather tall and collected. She cleared her throat, and spoke with a quiet voice that filled the room. "I'm also here to speak out in favor of the Teen Support Program. I want to thank the board for letting us parents come in and share our hopes and fears before you start your review." I glanced over at Judy to see if she had any idea Sister Langley was coming, only to see Judy giving me the same questioning gape.

I've no idea whether Sister Langley ever realized what a pleasant surprise she was, or even what was on her mind as she just kept talking without pause. "I know there are some parents waiting to speak against the program, saying that children with problems need to turn to their parents or their religious counsel. However, I am here to tell you that no matter how open and loving your relationship is with your child, you can't be sure your child will always turn to you. If you don't provide your child with another place to turn, then that child may cast about blindly as they seek direction, and that may lead to tragic consequences."

Then she paused. I wondered if she was finished, and I think I saw that she was wondering that, too. Then, after a deep breath, she showed she wasn't. "As many of you are aware, I recently lost my daughter. I know there are a lot of rumors going around about what happened. What happened is that my daughter fell in love, and made a mistake that resulted in her trying to find a way to end a pregnancy without hurting any of those she loved. Because she felt she had nowhere safe to talk through her situation, she fell prey to a misguided path that left her injured. By the time she realized she was in danger, it was too late. In accordance with the law, the emergency room turned her away due to bleeding that indicated she may have attempted to end her pregnancy without authorized medical personnel present. Rather than summon a doctor, they notified law enforcement officials. My daughter then tried to find help at the Family Planning, but she arrived too late. She died in the parking lot."

As cold as my blood felt right then, Sister Langley was even cooler. She was pulling from a deep well of strength, and it kept her steady when I was certain I would have been far too shaken to continue. In an even stronger voice, she went on.

"I am convinced that if there had been the Teen Support Program in place, Marissa would have turned to a student for a listening ear, perhaps some confidential advice. They could have helped her see that those around her loved her and would help her through whatever she faced. So for each of you who still have your children with you, please remember that you can't be everything to them, no matter how hard you try. Our job as parents is not to make their choices for them, but to help them grow so that they can make the right choices when we aren't there. Part of that means accepting that they will make mistakes we can't control. Therefore, we must do all we can to help make sure our youth have all the support possible to guide them through their most serious problems. We must, as parents, help ensure they will always have somewhere safe to turn, and pray that they will pull through. As a mother, I offer that prayer, for your children as well as mine. Thank you."

The silence that had fallen across the room remained for a few thoughtful moments as Sister Langley resumed her chair in the back of the room. Then a few people applauded, soon joined by most of those assembled. The head of the board asked who was next to comment, but nobody wanted to follow a speech like that. So instead, they launched their review.

The grilling was much kinder than I expected, and I think the board was swayed by the show of support in our favor. It was decided that we... well, *I* had to put together a full syllabus to be approved by the board before training could start. There were a number of resources I could use, and I got lots of great advice from Pastor Johns and other adults with experience in working through problems, especially with youth. The downside is that the training materials had to avoid controversial topics such as sex, and so on. But I figured that once we got students trained in how to be good listeners and determine what our peers needed, we could deal with the details from there without having to start up a fresh political fight.

It wasn't that difficult to get the program together, once I got going. I took some heat from some parents and even some students, with a smattering of anonymous hate mail here and there, but to this day I don't understand what they were so upset about. I assumed it was a mix of a sense of losing control over students' lives – even though the control was never there to begin with – and the fear of the unknown that exists with any change. Since I had a personal understanding of that particular fear, I found it easy to have compassion even for those who threatened and verbally attacked me.

Overall, the feelings about the program were positive, and the noise died down surprisingly quickly. Once peoples' fears were reassured that we weren't going to plot out a secret Pragmatic agenda to brainwash each other into sin, most people were supportive, or at least ambivalent.

Within a month I had all the details stitched together and voted on by the Student Council, then approved by the School Board. The local news station ran a story about the whole thing that I heard got out onto the Innernet; I think you can still find it published out there somewhere. I barely remember the interview and I suspect my words were taken somewhat out of context, but since I think the story made me sound better than I sounded to myself, I can't complain.

And then, at long last, the Teen Support Program's day had come. Given all that we had to go through to create the TSP, you'd think Judy and Derek and I would have felt relieved and excited to kick it off. But as we were getting together the flyers announcing the first meeting for volunteers, we weren't that chatty. We were a little sullen, maybe even nervous, though none of us could quite say why.

Finally, I put words to our fears.

"So, what if after all this, we build something to help everybody, and nobody shows up?"

Chapter 6

What is Wisdom?

"I wish Judy was here." My words sounded whiny even to me, but they were true. We were finally holding our first volunteer training meeting, and Judy had cheer practice.

"Oh, you'll do just spiffy, and you know it." Derek didn't even look up as he responded, instead focusing on counting out and manually collating pages to place in a stack in front of another chair.

"But… this whole thing was her idea! She should be here." I couldn't even figure out why, after all I'd already been through for the Teen Support Program, I was seized with such serious jitters.

Derek had finished setting up training papers in front of each of the dozen chairs around the table, then set the few spares down so he could turn to me. "And you're the one leading it. Maybe that's why she skipped out, so you'd be forced to realize you can do this on your own." He clapped his hands onto my shoulders and leaned in with a faux gravitas. "I believe in you, Lizbet."

He followed that up with a grin that made my skin tingle under his hands, so I rolled my eyes and sighed at him to distract myself. "I was GOING to say, thank goodness at least you're here, since a lot of the setup was your idea too, but…"

He patted my shoulder and then backed away. "But now you realize you've got it! Keen, I'll just be going now."

"Oh, no no no you don't! You sit yourself right down, mister." I pointed at the chair on the far end of the table as he grinned a mock challenge to my demand with a look that said, "Make me." I was just about to burst into embarrassingly childlike giggles when the door flew open. Suddenly filled with fresh nerves, I turned to see who the first participant would be.

It was Tricia! As glad as I was to see her, I was also a little confused. "Hey, I didn't know you were coming! You don't have to take notes for this meeting, you know."

I wasn't sure, but I thought she stammered a little, and almost blushed. "Oh. Yeah, no, I mean. I just, well, I wanted to volunteer. You know, support the effort and all."

Though Tricia and I had become friendly, I hadn't had time to see her much, so I had zero idea she was even considering coming. I couldn't remember ever seeing her exchanging more than a few words with another student, so her support was a welcome surprise. "Wow, that's awesome, yeah, here, take a seat. You've already seen all the materials from the minutes, but you can have a fresh copy, they're all there."

She pulled a stray bunch of hair behind her ear and nodded at the papers as she sat down. "Yeah, it'll be good to go over them again. You know, with the group." She looked back up at me with her shy, but earnest smile of support.

"Yeah, I agree! Let me know if seeing it from the perspective of a volunteer gives you any ideas on how we can keep improving them." I looked up from her to Derek as I sat down. He was hovering by his chair on the opposite end, looking at Tricia kinda like he was asking and answering a question at the same time. Just as I was about to ask what was on his mind, more students came trickling in.

After a few minutes, we had eleven volunteers in all, meaning Derek had to give up his seat and stand by me for most of the meeting. Three were cadets I knew from FOAM, then there was Tricia, and the remaining students I hadn't really met before but sorta recognized from classes and church and such. We went around the table with introductions, and then I got things started.

"I want to thank all of you for coming today, and I hope you'll be able to keep joining us every week, or at least as often as you can. You'll need to come to at least three training meetings and be interviewed by the school counselor before you'll be allowed to volunteer. We can meet more than once a week if you want, so we can get going faster, just talk to me after we're done. Okay?" I looked around the room to varying degrees of assent, so I nodded and went on.

"Okay. Good. Before we get started, maybe we can talk a little about what we hope to accomplish with training. I know, a lot of people say, 'how hard is it to let people talk to you,' but I think you might be surprised to find out that it's not so easy to just listen. Not to offer your opinion, not to tell someone what you think they should do, but just listen. Yes, Jeffery?"

The senior cadet lowered his hand as I acknowledged him. "Isn't the whole point to give advice to people who need it?"

I pursed my lips, tilting my head. "Actually, no. Sure, we can help people figure out what their choices are, but we should never tell them which they should choose. That's not for us to say, and to be honest, it's not really that productive. For one thing, we don't actually know their whole situation, only what they'll tell us and what we'll actually hear. Second, people are going to do what they're going to do, no matter what we advise, so all we accomplish is getting ourselves entangled in their choices. If we tell them we think they should do something and it's what they choose to do, they'll blame us if it goes wrong… maybe even with good reason. And if they choose otherwise and it works out, they'll blame us for trying to steer them badly. If it doesn't work out, we didn't work hard enough to convince them, that sort of thing."

Jeffery nodded knowingly, "So it's a real 'cover our tails' deal."

I shook my head quickly. "No, not really. I mean yes, it is important to keep our noses clean since there's so much riding on us having a successful start. But in the end, it's all about helping people make the best decisions they can, and then supporting them as they pursue them. You can never make someone else's choices for them; they can only choose for themselves. And the more you try to lead them where you think they should go, the more you set everybody up for heartache. You just can't live in another person's skin and truly see everything they're facing, and what it would take for them to make it through to where they need to be."

He was about to respond again, but was interrupted by his friend Chris nudging him in the ribs. "Though maybe you can tell them what you'd do, so they can figure out how to do the opposite." After being smacked on the shoulder by Jeffery, Chris looked to me. "Seriously though, how are we supposed to help people if we can't tell them what we think they should do?"

My face brightened, and I raised my finger with an "Aha!" I pulled out the first paper from the stack, holding it up facing the group. "May I draw your kind attention to the first handout, 'The Socratic Method.' I'll let you read through it later on your own, but it tells the story of an ancient Greek named Socrates, who sought out wisdom through asking questions. And whenever someone gave an answer or even asked him a question, he'd ask more questions in order to dig deeper."

Derek tilted his head at me. "You of course neglected to include the part where he was sentenced to drink poison in the end, for asking too many questions the higher-ups didn't like." His eyes sparkled with humor, but I didn't find it funny.

Instead, I pursed my lips with a slight frown. "Actually, that is something we all need to be aware of. People have some very strong opinions about some very serious things, and even about some very trivial things, so we need to be aware of that. If somebody seems to be upset or bothered by your questions, just back off. You can't make them think about things you think are important, and really, that's not your job. You're there to help them to help themselves as much as they're willing and able – no more, no less. In the end, it's their life, and they're the ones who've got to live it."

A volunteer who had introduced herself as Carla raised her hand, then spoke up earnestly as I acknowledged her. "Maybe this is in the handout, but are we really supposed to help people with just questions? Won't that get annoying? What if they just want to know what you think? And what if you know something that might help them?"

"What makes you think you can't share a little of what you know through the way you ask a question?" I let a playful smile flicker into my mock-seriousness, then chuckled. "Okay, that was bad, but maybe you see what I mean. Really though, it's important that we help them figure out their own decision-making process, rather than leading them to any one decision. Because things change, and what we know changes, constantly. When we think we have all the answers, we stop asking questions. So instead of trying to nail down our narrow picture into a permanent answer, it's more important to learn how to ask questions and then question our answers as we explore what we can actually see. That way, we're better prepared to adapt when the picture changes again, instead of closing our eyes thinking we've already seen everything. Answers can close doors that questions can open. The feeling of having The Answer can be powerfully comforting, and having that answer challenged can be equally uncomfortable. If we're not careful, we'll feel threatened by the very truth we mean to seek out."

Tricia looked at me quite intently for a few moments as I was speaking, so I paused to see if she'd figured out what she wanted to say. A couple of seconds passed before she finally asked, "How do you know what questions to ask?"

I shrugged matter-of-factly. "Practice. And patience. And learning how to really listen to what they're saying as well as to what they're not saying. You have to see if you can develop an ear for hearing the questions they aren't asking, maybe not even of themselves. Don't worry, that's all part of what we're going to be learning here. We'll be studying techniques and working with each other to develop our own."

I looked around the room to see a full range of responses from enthusiasm to dubiousness, and started to run a mental tally of how many of them I thought would be there the following week. Finally, I asked, "Since I don't think three dozen times is enough to say the word 'question'… Are there any more questions before we start running through a few handouts, then wrap up our first meeting?"

They laughed but had nothing further to ask, so we went through the rest of the meeting pretty quickly and smoothly. It wasn't until it was over and people were filing out to finish their late afternoon that I remembered I was supposed to be nervous. I actually jumped when Derek clapped his hand onto my shoulder from behind me, saying "You see, Lizbet, I told you you'd do just fine." He laughed at my reaction, then shook my hand. "There, please accept my official congratulations. Now I'm off to meet Judy and tell her all about it. We're going to split some pizza after, if you wanna come with?"

"Nah, thanks, I have to get back to FOAM to finish some stuff up. You two crazy kids have fun." He smirked at me, I shrugged at him, then he laughed again and said he'd give Judy my regards. After he left, I noticed Tricia was still there, helping gather up the leftover handouts and other stray debris.

"Oh, Tricia, you really don't have to do that. I was gonna tidy up."

She smiled at me, not slowing as she rapidly finished the job. "You've done all the hard work already. Besides, I like to help. I haven't really seen you around for the past month and a half or so, since you've been so busy getting all this together."

"Yeah, it didn't hit me until just now how hard it's been to keep up with everything and get this all done." The sudden weariness in the sigh I let out made me feel even more worn. "I'd like to say it's all downhill from here, but…"

She laughed, "Yeah, right." She looked down to the stack of papers as she tapped the edges into perfect alignment. "Hey, I'll bet you've been too busy to even think about the Harvest Moon dance next week. But you're going, right?" She looked up to me with a curious interest.

I simply blinked back at her. "Wow, I kinda forgot. I mean of course I knew it was coming up, but I didn't *know*, you know? I don't think I will, I never go to those things."

"Don't you think you should, given, well, this project and Student Council and leading FOAM and everything? Aren't you supposed to?" She paused long enough for me to roll my eyes and groan, before continuing, "Oh come on, it's not that bad! Why don't we go together? That is, I mean, it's not like I'm really into these things either. But it'd be weird… I mean if we didn't at least show up, right?"

"Yeah, you're right. And it'll give us time to finally hang out, so that would be a big plus!" I meant that, too, as I truly wanted to get to know her better. She returned my genuine smile, and I followed up with, "And since it's not like I'd be going with a date, my parents won't complain that I'm dancing on the edge of sin or whatever!"

Tricia made a face at that, so I patted her arm and apologized. "I know, I know, that's awful, but they are suspicious of anything they feel encourages romantic activity between boys and girls. You know how parents can be."

That made her laugh, which made me laugh. Shaking her head, she said, "Yeah, they just don't have any idea, do they?" Her eyes twinkled in a poking-fun kind of way, and I realized she could be a lot less shy when she wanted to be.

"You know, now I'm actually looking forward to going to that silly dance. We'll have a blast! Well anyway, thanks for helping clean up, I've really got to dash." As I took the papers from Tricia I saw her mouth open, then close. At the same time, I felt that foreboding tingling on the back of my neck.

"What terrible timing. I knew I was running late, but I didn't think I'd miss the whole thing." Despite Richard's best efforts, his greeting still sounded far from pleasant.

Until that moment I'd thought Richard had washed his hands of the TSP, and was thankful for it. I carefully kept my composure light and friendly as I turned to see him standing in the doorway. "Well, we just went over the basics, which you're already pretty familiar with, so if you want to join us next week, you won't be too far behind." It took all my effort to suppress the flurry of "please don't" repeating over and over in my mind as soon as I made the polite offer.

I then had to work to suppress visible signs of relief as he shook his head. "No thank you, I think it's best if I keep my advisory time just within my Student Chaplain capacity. You do your things your way, and I'll do my things mine." As he spoke, he stepped closer to me, finishing his sentence just inches away. Tricia had moved to rearrange things in her bag at the table behind him, and I was grateful for her proximity as I tried to guess his intentions.

He didn't keep the suspense up long. "I just wanted to be here to show you some support as all your hard work pays off. Since I missed the meeting, maybe I can take you out for something to celebrate?"

I folded my arms around the paperwork I held over my chest. "Oh, I can't, I was just saying I have to get back to FOAM to meet with the Commander."

Undeterred, he took a step closer. "Well then maybe we can still celebrate later, since you're bound to have a little more free time a week from Friday. I don't have a date yet to the Harvest Moon Dance… do you?"

I caught Tricia looking very interested in a poster on the wall next to me, and felt momentarily at a loss for what to say. After a brief second, my face brightened into a smile. "You know, it's funny that you mention that. Tricia and I don't either, and we were thinking of not going, but it was generally decided that all of the Student Council should be there. We can already count on Judy and Derek, so I'm so glad you're thinking of going. If we can just bring Gig around, we could all be there!"

He took a short step back from my burst of enthusiasm, taking a little time to process what I was saying. When it all finally sank in, he started to say something, stopped himself, then smiled his snake-oil charm once more. "That would be great. Though maybe I'm not the right person to ask Gig to the dance. You know how he likes to go against anything I say just because I said it. Tricia, maybe you'd have better luck in asking him?"

She crossed her arms as she shifted her weight toward one side and shook her head. "We should probably let Liz do it; she's got so much practice organizing things by now."

He frowned, then shrugged. "I can see that. Well, we'll be in touch then, work things out. In the meantime, I'll still owe you that congrats."

I gave a slight smile, then excused myself. "Great. I'm running late now too, though, thanks for stopping by! Tricia, do you still have time to help me carry my things back to FOAM?"

I think she was planning to back me up even if I hadn't asked, as she had the rest of my things together in two seconds flat. Before I knew it, we were across campus and she was helping me set my stuff down in the FOAM Student Officers room. I thanked her, then frowned. "I'm really sorry I ended up inviting Richard and crew along with us, I hope that doesn't spoil our fun. Though I doubt they'll be all that interested in hanging around with us anyway."

Tricia shook her head, "No, no, don't worry about it. That was actually pretty smooth how you handled that. We'll still be able to spend some time there together, and maybe with Judy and Derek we can kinda all hang out, and also split off to do our own things. It'll be fun!" She caught my uncertainty, then tilted her head forward for emphasis. "Seriously, it will. Now quit stressing, you've got enough to worry about."

I chuckled. "Okay, yeah, you're right. Well thanks again, I better let you go, I've got to get next door."

We said our quick goodbyes as I put some things away, then she stepped out as I went through the side door to Commander Keane's office. I started to apologize for being a little late as I walked through the door, and stopped suddenly as I realized he wasn't alone. "Oh, sorry, I should have knocked…"

"No, Liz, that's fine, we were waiting for you. I'd like to introduce you to an old friend of mine, Saul Harolds. He was the pilot of the bomber I navigated for way back when." The Commander stepped back to let his friend move forward to shake my hand.

His grip was light in the way of men who think they need to be delicate with a lady's fragile hand, so of course I gave a nice, firm shake as though to prove a point. "Nice to meet you, Mister Harolds."

He didn't seem to notice my handshake, his smile remaining blandly pleasant in a casually earnest sort of way. I wasn't sure whether I liked him, but as a friend of my Commander's, I was certainly willing to give him a chance.

"Just great to meet you too, Miss Franklin. Gordon's been telling me JUST how good you've been for the unit here, and I'm real glad to hear it. It's not often FOAM gets a young woman of your caliber. No, not often at all."

It wasn't clear whether the emphasis was on my gender or my "caliber," but I decided to give him the benefit of the doubt as I tried again to be gracious in the face of compliments. "Thank you, I try to do my best."

"Your best is apparently pretty good. I even remember seeing your interview on the news a while back, you impressed me with your forthrightness. You showed you had a good head on your shoulders, and you'd fight for a cause you believe in. Isn't that right?" His pleasantly casual demeanor carried on unchanged, and the upbeat rhythm of his friendly patter started to make me feel comfortable enough that it was easier to accept his compliments without blushing.

"Well, yes, Mister Harolds. My parents raised me that way. If I'm ready to die for my values, I must be ready to live for them as well. Otherwise, I can't very well hold my head up as a person of conviction." My tone was matter-of-fact, as I felt the sentiment should have been self-evident.

Self-evident or no, it seemed to be exactly what Mister Harolds wanted to hear. His smile broadened into a bright grin. "I'd expect nothing less from a congregant of Pastor Johns. Oh yes, he's a friend of mine as well; a small world, isn't it? And please, call me Saul. Mind if I call you Liz? Great. Well Liz, I have something that I think you might be interested in, a cause of sorts. It will take up some more of your time, but I'd be able to compensate you, and your Commander here says that if you're interested, he could arrange things so that your unit could spare you."

Commander Keane leaned forward. "Liz, I really think you might be interested in this. And if you are, I've gotten permission to institute the rank of Supreme Student Commander for your promotion. You'd move to more of an advisory capacity, serving only a couple of hours a week instead of every day. But you'd still be our Student Council rep so you could continue that participation. This school was going to be big enough for our FOAM unit to have that rank here in a year or two regardless, so it was already on the way."

I felt a bit dizzy. Supreme Student Commander. I don't know if you realize what a big deal that was, but it was an incredibly huge opportunity. There were only a few in our whole state. I would be almost guaranteed a scholarship and entrance to nearly any college in the country with an American Military Officers School unit, maybe even be able to pick my first post once I'd graduated.

"I would need to know what the cause is, of course, but I'm certainly interested in considering it." I tried my best to keep my enthusiasm down until I knew if it was an offer I could accept.

Saul chortled. "Oh of course, of course. Let me ask you a question first, if you don't mind. I understand you recently turned eighteen. Did you do anything special to celebrate?"

The question struck me as odd, but I didn't have a reason not to answer. "Well, my sister and brother who live kinda close visited, and my mother baked a cake, and a few friends came over. Other than that, nothing too fancy."

"Uh huh, yes, that sounds pretty nice. Did you register to vote?" He looked gratified by my confused expression. "Right, I didn't think so, but only because so few young adults do. You know what they say, don't you? The drinking age is twenty-one because eighteen-year-olds don't vote. Not that they should want to drink, mind you, but the point is well-made. Tell me, Liz, if you don't mind my asking, do your parents vote?"

I took a moment to try to remember them ever talking about it, and no such memory came to mind. They'd participated in many petition drives and protests, but I didn't remember anything about voting. "I can't be sure."

"That means they probably don't. Again, nothing against them, most people don't these days. But don't you think that, in the world's greatest bastion of Democracy, more people should?" His patter remained so amiably earnest, I realized at that moment that I truly did feel people should vote.

"Yes, now that you mention it. But it's not exactly easy. In fact, I'm not even sure how to register." It honestly had never occurred to me before. In Civic Duties class they talked about elections bringing about the will of the people, but didn't deal much with the actual voting that would bring about that will. I caught myself wondering, why they hadn't addressed it, if they actually wanted to teach us about democratic participation? Would there be a reason they wouldn't want to spread information on how to get out and vote...?

My wandering mind was immediately brought back by the sound of Saul's hand smacking onto the Commander's desk. "Exactly. You just hit the proverbial nail on the head there, Liz. People don't know how to get out and register, and yet, it's the easiest thing in the world. How would you like to help people do just that?"

I quirked my head. "How can I do that?"

"Voter organization, Liz Franklin, voter organization. It's a lost art, one that I think you're just the person to help get going here again, from the youth angle in any event. It's part of my campaign to serve this great state of ours. I'm running for State House of Representatives for this district, you see. And when I set out to run, I realized how few of my constituents would be able to ask me to represent them in the ballot booth. I was sitting at home considering this fact, downcast, when I saw a story on the news about your work to organize volunteers to help your peers make better decisions. And then it hit me. Why not get you to put those great skills to work helping your peers put those decisions into a ballot box and help us build a better America?"

It made perfect sense the way he said it, and his enthusiasm was infectious. "That sounds... That actually sounds pretty fantastic!"

I wouldn't have thought it possible, but his smile somehow grew even bigger. "Wonderful! Just wonderful. I just knew you'd see it that way. I'm still getting some ducks in a row, so it'll be a few days before I'll be getting in touch with you, but I think it'll take that long to get your FOAM duties transitioned over, am I right, Gordy?"

My Commander nodded, his smile as big as his friend's. "Don't worry, I'll have her schedule nice and cleared up on my end before you'll be ready for her. Congratulations, Liz, I think this is a great move for you. I always knew you'd make a difference, from that light I always saw in your eyes. I'm truly proud of you."

I felt my skin glowing, but I didn't care. I'm sure I said some kind of thanks, but all that sticks out in my memory is the heady thrill at such great praise from the man who had done so much for me.

"That's all I called you in to meet about, Liz. You can go now if you like. I'm sure you have a lot to get tidied up so you can hand over the bulk of your duties." The men and I said some quick goodbyes, and I left the FOAM offices in a daze.

I did have a lot to do, but I wasn't ready to start any of it. I was too buzzed with excitement. I looked around for Tricia, but she had already gone home. Then I remembered Derek's invitation, and realized I just had to tell Judy as soon as humanly possible. I have been known to walk pretty quickly, but I think I almost jogged the couple of blocks to the pizza parlor that had what they called After School Specials.

My timing was perfect. I got there just as their turn for a table came up. Luckily they were getting a table with room for four, because they weren't alone. Kurt was with them. As in, Marissa's "K." I was just starting to wonder if I should feel as awkward as I suddenly did when Judy caught sight of me and ran over to hug me.

"Derek told me all about how great the meeting went! It's official, we did it! YOU did it! C'mon, let's get some pizza and celebrate." She put her arm through mine and held my hand as she walked us to the table. She sat across from me with Derek next to her, leaving Kurt to my left. "Liz, you know Kurt, right? Aren't you like, cousins or something?"

Kurt laughed at that, shaking his head. "There are many Franklins in this town, Judy, and we're not all related. I can't believe you even asked that, given how often I complain that people are always asking if Derek and I are brothers."

He was right, we weren't related. I barely even knew who he was. Yet while I did know he and Derek were friends, I hadn't heard people talking about them being brothers. Then the two of them looked at each other with exactly the same expression of amused exasperation, and it struck me just how alike they really were. They honestly could have been brothers…

Feeling like I was staring, I turned to Judy and shrugged. "Actually, I don't think we've even met before."

Kurt turned to me and stuck out his hand, which I took. "There," he said with a vigorous shake, "now it's official. Nice to meet you, Miss Franklin."

I returned the pleasantry, then Judy and Derek immediately started bantering about which pizza to get. Kurt nodded his head toward them while giving me a knowing smirk. "They always do this, and he always gives in to whatever she wants. Don't ask me why they bother. I think he just likes to hear himself talk and pretend it means anything.

Hey!" It seemed Derek had kicked him under the table, making Judy laugh.

At that moment the server came by and Judy ordered four glasses of juice and her favorite pizza. She then told me, "Don't worry about your share, Liz, I'll cover you to celebrate your grand success. And yes, I *insist*. We all know you took all the heat and did all the work, so you get to bask in the glory of your just reward."

Derek poked her shoulder. "Hey, I get to pay half that congratulations, since I actually showed up for the grand success."

Kurt waved a pointed finger back and forth between the both of them. "Make that a third, I get to congratulate her too. She finally got to meet me." He nodded decisively, then leaned back in his seat before flashing me another wink.

I knew I was blushing again from all the attention, and I tried to be okay with it as I also tried to deflect it. "That's super nice, but I can actually afford to pay my... okay, okay, okay! But if you're all going to insist on being so congratulatory, maybe you'd like to know the full extent of why you're congratulating me."

Their attention intensified, this time from curiosity over a secret only I could divulge. That was a different thing entirely, and I looked slyly at them for a moment before sharing what I had come dying to spill. They listened, and then didn't respond, not having much more idea on what to do with the news than I had.

"So... what does that all mean, exactly? What will you be doing?" Judy was excited for me because I was excited, but she was still trying to sort out exactly what we were so excited about.

"I'm not sure. But I thought about it a lot on the way here, and I think it sounds like a really good thing. I mean, my whole life I've been talking about how this country needs to stay on the right path, and how we each need to do our part. America is a democracy, right? So it's our responsibility to help it go where it needs to go, and the only way to do that is to vote." I realized at that point the excitement had crept into my voice, quickening my pace and making me feel like I was getting a little carried away.

Kurt picked up a spoon and absently tapped it on the table a couple times. "And to defend its freedoms." At first I thought he was chiding me, but his grin soothed that fear.

I nodded to him. "Oh, right, exactly, that too. I forgot to tell you the most awesome part. By being Supreme Student Commander, I'll join the ranks of only a few students in the whole state. That means I'm almost guaranteed a scholarship at any school with an AMOS unit! I think I can maybe actually go to college!" I'm sure I was carried away then, but I didn't care enough to notice.

Judy squealed, and Derek nodded as he took it in. "That's awesome. I didn't know you were thinking about college, though. Aren't you supposed to have a husband lined up by now so you can start popping out babies for Jesus? Or do you wait until graduation?" He had turned to Kurt around halfway through his spiel, intending to make him laugh more than any of us. Which meant Kurt's furtive glances and serious expression were his only clue that Judy and I weren't exactly grinning. Derek let his own grin slip from his face as he slowly turned back toward us. "Uh… oh. Okay. That was supposed to be funny. In a very not-blasphemous way. In a kinda… Yikes, I'm so sorry. I'm in trouble now, aren't I?"

Judy punched him on the arm. "I'm tempted to tell Pastor Johns about the example you're setting for Kurt. But I'll bet you guys talk like that all the time at Young Men's Bible Study, while we're in the YLBS learning how to be meek helpmeets for you godless heathens." She had started smirking under her previously astonished scowl. She never could stay mad at Derek for long. In fact, his expression was so seriously sorry I couldn't help but find it charmingly comic, too.

She turned to me, serious once more. "I didn't know you ever even thought about college." After a pause, she hesitantly voiced her concern. "Do your parents know?"

"Well, they always did push me to do well in school. And I know they're super proud of me in FOAM and definitely support the Military." I then thought of what my father had said, and realized I honestly couldn't predict what their opinions would be. In the end, I just shrugged. "I'm sure it'll be fine."

Kurt leaned toward me, with sincere interest. "So that means you're planning to enlist, too? I mean, you'd be going in as an officer, but after a couple of years I plan to apply to active duty AMOS. I don't know if they'd take me, but I figure if I work hard…"

He trailed off, and I realized he was seriously shy about the whole thing, talking about it with me. He seemed like the kind of guy who'd really make it though, so I tried to encourage him. "I'm sure they'll snap you right up. If I follow this path, I have to finish this year out, then do the five years or six it takes to complete a college degree nowadays, and THEN I can join up. I'm sure you'll be an officer before me. Just make sure to finish out this year and graduate before you enlist, since a diploma will really put you ahead of the other applicants. Not everybody gets to do the full run at high school these days."

That final bit of advice seemed to strike the wrong note, and I realized that he and his mom might be having trouble covering tuition. I followed up with, "Of course, it also might help if you want to sign on for early enlist via FOAM, which would also pay the rest of your tuition. It's still early enough in the year that you could apply for a late start, and I'm sure if I wrote out a recommendation Commander Keane could help get you right in. They have a ton more tuition slots for those who are just covering senior year."

Kurt's awkwardness dissipated at that, then resurfaced with fresh hesitation. "That would be... I mean, are you sure you want to put your reputation out there for me like that? We only just met."

I shrugged. "Judy's my best friend, and Derek, well, he's Derek. They think pretty highly of you and I trust their judgment. Besides, you're really serious about the Military, and that makes a huge difference. You haven't just been riding it along to get it to pay for school, so your application will be taken totally seriously."

Kurt shook his head. "Oh, no, that wouldn't be it at all. I know I'm a little late on this, but I thought about it a lot over the summer. Back when... well, anyway. I realized that if I got a good career in the Military, I could build a future for myself. It's not like I've had great grades, or have any real skills, so this is like a fresh chance to really apply myself. Plus, there'll be survivor benefits if, you know, something happens."

He took advantage of the pizza arriving to collect his thoughts, and I thought he might have let the topic slip away. But after a couple of minutes as we dove into the still-hot pizza, he finished, "I just don't want to leave any potential future family hanging in case something happens to me like it did my dad." He shrugged it off, then took another bite of pizza.

Derek nodded to his best friend, then looked over at me with his version of a casual tone. "Soooo, Lizbet. You have a date to the Harvest Moon Dance yet?"

Suddenly reminded of the other thing I needed to talk to them about, I quickly finished chewing my bite and washed it down with water. "Oh, yes, I mean no, I mean that reminds me! Tricia and I were going to go to it together, then Richard came nosing around and was about to ask me and it turned into me suggesting we all went together, even though I know you two are going together, so it's not like we have to GO together together..." I felt bad, knowing I was putting them on the spot, and had started to ramble so badly even I couldn't keep up.

Judy gave me a sympathetic look when I mentioned Richard, and Derek just laughed as I trailed off. He then nodded his support. "It's okay, that's actually a really good idea. We could use a little more solidarity on the Council, and I think it'll turn out to be fun. Kurt, you want to come along too?"

Kurt considered it as he finished chewing, then shrugged as he swallowed. "Sure, why not? I wouldn't be the first guy to be dateless for a dance, and have to go with his 'cousin.'" He then turned to me with a slightly cheesy grin.

I found myself rolling my eyes at him much the same way I always saw Judy do with Derek, then smirked as he chuckled at my reaction. I still remember the playful way he winked at me, since that was the moment I first realized I was really going to like him.

Chapter 7

What is Peace?

The following week was so intensely busy that I didn't really see any of my friends again until the night of the dance. I had FOAM ceremonies and meetings, and also starting to educate myself on voter registration laws and the embarrassingly low registration rate. Fortunately, Saul was paying me quite well versus what I had been used to, so I was able to quit my job at the school office and free it up for another needy student. This also gave me even more time to learn how to get out the vote.

Okay, about voting. In order to register, you had to be in good standing in the CMDB, without any state or federal convictions. That's right, even after you'd repaid your debt to society, you still couldn't participate in it. Oh, and you had to pay the voter registration fee, and present your CMDB ID, which carried its own registration fee. At the time, this all seemed completely reasonable to me, since the government didn't fully cover all the Voting costs and the money had to come from somewhere.

Saul even was able to rent us CMDB ID card readers, which automatically filled in all their information into the system, so all the person had to do was sign the digital signature field. It was even set up to read credit cards if they had one, or to bill their Factory Financial Floater. Just in case you've never lived in a company town, that's the credit account opened up automatically for all resident employees, paid through paycheck deductions and so on. The annual interest accrued on the balance was moderately low, so I'd heard, but it could add up over time. Many people ended up so far in debt to their 3F that they could never afford to quit. That's why my parents never used theirs, but it was always there whether they wanted it or not.

After a day or so of going over all of the maps and lists and everything else related to all the many people who needed to be registered, I realized I was going to need someone to help me keep things organized. Who better, I thought, than my favorite Student Council Secretary, Tricia Knox? I had gotten the okay from Saul to hire her on if she was willing, just hours before the dance I had nearly forgotten about.

Everyone was meeting up at my house since I was central to everybody, and we planned to go together in a ride Saul had rented as a thank you to us for all we were doing for our school. Well, and also because he needed me to work that day and I'd be super late otherwise, I thought.

Richard wasn't happy with Saul providing our ride, as his father was backing a different candidate who used to be a Pastor in the area. Gig was especially vocal about accepting junkets from a Puritan, but he accepted anyway on behalf of himself and his date. I think I forgot to mention this, but in earlier meetings he had been planning to boycott the Harvest Moon Dance entirely because it had taken the Halloween out of Halloween. He never actually said whether he was Pagan, but he objected to how Pagan religions were persecuted, so he said we should at least make a nod to the holiday's costume-wearing, pumpkin-carrying roots.

We had ended up compromising and making it a costume ball that year in the theme of 1776. This satisfied the pro-Halloween costume-fanciers and the anti-Pagan-holiday-yet-pro-Early-American patriots. Since students were encouraged to go as pilgrims and other simple costumes, this also made it a little less formal and therefore more affordable to attend. In the end, more advance tickets had been given out than for any other school dance in recent history.

Since we ended up agreeing we'd all go together, we decided to dress up as founding fathers and mothers. I was of course Betsy Ross, for whom I was named. Kurt went as my ancestor Ben Franklin, and joked that Judy was right after all: for that night at least, we were related! Derek and Judy were George and Martha Washington, Gig and his date were Thomas and Martha Jefferson, and Richard was Alexander Hamilton, in part to spite Gig. Tricia was Paul Revere, saying she was going to be the far more rugged Sybil Ludington, but she didn't want to be the only one dressed up as someone nobody ever heard of. Going as a founding *father* got her teased, of course, but despite her usual shyness she didn't seem to care. I admired her confidence, and was proud of how self-assured she was proving herself to be.

So there we all were, garbed with what in retrospect were probably only remotely similar to period costumes, wondering how we were going to fit ourselves into the rattletrap we expected to pick us up. You know, the low-budget vehicles with little to no safety or comfort features, made for the downmarket drivers? You know, the only cars any of us had ever ridden in?

The rattletrap was the perfect example of what happens when you scrap safety regulations and leave them up to "market efficiencies." Car makers figured the most efficient way to turn a profit was to focus their market on the people with money. They went all-out in competing with each other for shinier and safer cars, but only for the upmarket buyers. When the cars became less shiny, it proved more profitable to strip them for parts to service the upmarket cars, than to resell them to the downmarket buyers. No, the rest of us were offered the barest features needed to make a car take us from one place to another... eventually... most of the time. Still you counted yourself lucky if you could afford one, since mass transit was even less likely to get you where you needed to be in a reliable or timely manner. And if you got into a wreck, you were luckier still if you didn't become the latest rattletrap victim.

We had plenty of time to wonder how we were all going to make it to the dance on time, as it was starting to get a little late and the vehicle hadn't yet arrived. So we were all surprised when a very large, very nice car showed up on my gravel yellow-plate road, bearing green license plates.

I'd been given rides a couple of times before, but only by folks in rattletraps with yellow plates. I think once I was given a ride by someone who'd somehow managed to snag an older actual used car, but they couldn't afford the green plates, so even they were restricted to the rundown potholed or gravel roads. Well, except for during the late-night and partial-weekend hours when some of the fully maintained green plate roads allowed limited access for yellow plates. Those with red plates couldn't use green plate roads even then, and I wish I had consciously noticed the demographic who were generally stuck with the red plates.

I did know there was an application process for the yellow and green ones, and the latter were allocated to city and factory officials first, then down the line at a hefty premium. Since I didn't drive, I found the whole thing a little confusing, but there were helpful signs posted for those who couldn't tell the roads apart by the obvious differences in road quality and size of traffic jams. The whole system was created when the transportation infrastructure was privatized as a way to cater to different consumer bands. It's convoluted, but apparently the companies got the idea from the American Aid Agency-funded road projects in the Holyland. Though I'm not sure how legal those were, the color-restricted roads were built so commuters living in the settlements outside their legal borders could get to work quickly and easily without having to be slowed down by Arabiyan rattletraps. That's what I heard, anyway.

All that said, there was a green-plated sedan right in my drive, and we were going to travel in style. Even though it was the tail end of rush hour, the ride was luxurious and lightning-quick on smooth, uncrowded asphalt roads. With a chauffeur, no less. I was actually a little embarrassed by the whole thing, but I didn't want to appear ungrateful for Saul's very generous gesture, so I tried to just roll with it. It flustered me so much that I didn't even stop to wonder where the money had come from, or why it was being spent on a simple ride to a school dance.

If I had thought to ask, I could have found my answer in the faces of the students as we showed up just a tiny bit early. Initial rumors that we were wasting school funds were quickly laid to rest by word that local candidate Saul Harolds had donated our ride to the school, as well as the band that showed up as a surprise upgrade from old albums played over the gymnasium speakers.

Gig started to protest that a surprise band was just too much Puritan show-boating, that Saul should have cleared it with us first. But then he saw it was a popular local act he truly liked, who played music that was just a little cutting-edge. Since that meant we'd be dancing to songs that were more modern and "edgy" than the school's pre-approved albums, Gig quickly expressed his smug approval. Apparently, that made him party to putting one over on our old-fashioned Puritanic sensibilities.

The band actually kept things tame enough that no parents would have to call and complain, but even I have to admit they were really good and a perfect choice. They and the car also probably didn't cost Saul much at all, compared to the enthusiastic publicity it generated for him in a small town like ours.

Word spread pretty quickly that the dance was even better than expected. Soon, more students started showing in hastily cobbled-together costumes to pay the nominal door fee and see what all the fuss was about. I'd never been to a dance before, but I could tell the place was uncommonly packed, spilling over into the basketball courts adjoining the gym.

The Student Council spent the first part of the dance mostly together, greeting students as they arrived. We then did some announcements and held an admittedly half-hearted costume contest. Then the dance started in earnest, and we were to lead it off by going down to the floor for the first official dance. Richard had stayed near me the whole time, but somehow Tricia managed to grab him and ask him to dance before he turned to me. I silently promised to thank her later, as Kurt stepped up from the sidelines.

"I guess that leaves you and me, if dancing with your great-great-thousand-times-great-grandfather wouldn't be weird." He wriggled the eyebrow that was visible under his tricorn hat's comically jaunty angle, and I laughed as I walked with him to the dance floor. That made him grin with mock surprise. "Oh, so you *can* laugh. I always think it's a good sign when a woman laughs at me. It means she has taste."

I chuckled at that, and then I remembered to be nervous. Not only did I not know how to dance, I still felt incredibly guilty about Marissa. He caught my somber shift, and took me quite lightly in hand with a respectable distance between us as he started to lead. "Don't worry, none of us actually know how to dance. We're just all so busy hoping nobody notices us faking it that we don't have time to notice everyone else is too."

I smiled slightly. "It's not that… I mean it is, but…"

He pressed his hand to my back with gentle reassurance. "Hey, if it's about Marissa, please, don't feel bad. It's not even remotely your fault, so stop beating yourself up over it."

I started, as I had no idea he knew I was kinda involved in her not getting help. He gave me a chagrined smile, moving a little closer so he could talk quietly without being overheard. "Judy told Derek in the strictest confidence, because she tells him everything. Derek told me anyway because he knew your conscience would weigh on you until you apologized to me. He figured it'd be easier on you if I already knew. So I do. And while I miss her terribly, I'm okay. And you should be, too. You've done a lot of good since then, so focus on that."

I pulled back a step and looked at him, touched and bewildered at the same time. His smile turned warm, and he almost said something else before saying, "Just, if you could promise not to tell Judy, I'm sure Derek would be most grateful." He winked at that, and with a softer chuckle I consented.

"Thank you for being so supportive over this. Truly. Ever since we met at that pizza thing, I've been…" Though the crushing weight of guilt was evaporating, I couldn't find the words I wanted to say.

"Me too," he said, then grinned impishly before twirling me around once. The dance finished without another word, though I was about to find something to say when Richard tapped in.

"Time to swap out, Benjamin." Richard's cool grin was back, and at first I thought Kurt was going to protest.

He merely shrugged and replied, "I'll be right over there if you need some pointers," before turning from Richard to make a deep bow to Tricia. She and I exchanged quick glances of resignation, and I prayed for a short, fast song.

It was half-answered, for song was blessedly short. I smiled politely, glad I'd at least danced once before so I could focus on keeping track of what Richard was up to.

"The band's pretty good, even if it was hired by the wrong candidate," he began after a few bars of music.

I let my eyes roll. "Richard, Saul is a good man, and I think he's going to do great things to help keep this state on track. No, he's not a former pastor, but he was a pilot in the Military, so I'd think that'd be good enough for you."

The omnipresent smile turned condescendingly paternal. "Oh, Liz, there's more to character than Military service. You'd be shocked at some of the things Military men use for entertainment in the war zones. Oh, don't give me that look, I'm only teasing. I'm honestly surprised you're even touching politics, given all the bitterness you had to endure getting the TSP going."

I shook my head. "My first 'bitter taste of politics' actually taught me a lot I didn't know I needed to learn. It's not all that bad, putting yourself out there for something you believe in. It's a lot better than sitting quietly in the corner wishing someone else would have the courage to stand up to the fight."

He nodded at me approvingly, but the self-important admonishment only worsened. "But what does he really stand for, Liz? Do you know if he plans to push for Praying for Schools if elected? End government subsidies to hospitals dealing in birth control? That sort of thing?"

By the end of his "gentle tirade" I couldn't help but half-scowl at him disapprovingly. "Richard, after all that's happened, do you really think those are my top priorities right now? There are so many much more immediate things that he is standing for that will help people, like supporting church charities that feed the poor, and helping businesses build better networks for employee transfers without having to pay hiring taxes so maybe so many people don't have to be unemployed. Stuff like that. Besides, I'm not campaigning for him, I'm just helping people vote. They can vote for whomever they like."

"Oh, Liz," he said again, and I wanted to punch his arm for it. "Do you think people won't be influenced by the fact he's the one behind the voter drive? That's why I've talked my father into getting his friends to support a drive I want to start, so people can hear from the other side of the fence. The Christian side. I'd be the youth face of it, of course."

Oh, great, I thought. Another instance of Richard trying to turn something into a religious fight to feed his own selfish need for the spotlight. There was a lot of work to be done if we were going to get any kind of voter turnout, and we couldn't afford to waste precious time and energy fighting about it with anybody, particularly not someone like Richard. I was wondering if maybe I should set aside my own personal annoyance and try to find some middle ground to pool our limited resources when he shocked me by suggesting it first.

"Of course, you have more experience being in the spotlight of late, so I was hoping maybe you and I could pool our resources. If we coordinated, we could get more done at less cost. What do you say?" He was watching me closely for my reaction.

Flustered at not having a ready answer, I tried to be encouraging without making any commitments I didn't have the authority to make. "Well, I would need to check with Saul. I don't think he'd want to join up with his opponent in the primary just yet…"

He cut me off. "Oh no, this isn't about that at all. Go ahead and keep working with Harolds. Father and I aren't directly working with any candidate, not just yet. You and I will keep closely coordinated rather than directly affiliated, at least until after the primary." He'd moved a little closer to emphasize, and I moved a little farther back to resume the polite distance expected at school dances. It seemed to amuse him, as he must have thought I was merely being modest and meek as a good woman should be. I guess it wasn't in his power to consider that I might have an aversion to him, even back then.

"So, what are you planning to actually do?" I was genuinely curious, enough so that I was willing to put up with both his political and physical maneuvering.

"You know that if there's one thing Father and I do better than anything, it's rallying people together. We won't be about any one candidate, just the issues of the greatest importance to the Christian voter. We'll hold rallies and protests and maybe even host a town forum or two, to get the candidates talking. We're calling ourselves the American Christian League." He paused to give me the chance to shower his cleverness with praise.

"That's certainly descriptive. And I think that might work, actually. The people who are interested enough to come to rallies and protests are exactly the people who should be voting. So I could make sure to be there with registration information…" I was starting to see that there could be true potential in the whole thing. That Richard might actually have something valuable for America.

"Exactly. I was hoping you'd see it my way." He inclined his head toward me and lowered his voice, moving me closer once more.

The song was over, however, so I stood back and clapped with the crowd, then excused myself. "Pardon me, I'm parched from all this talking, I really need to… Oh hey, Tricia! I've got to go, uh, 'powder my nose,' let's go."

Kurt smirked at me as I took Tricia's hand, the two of them having hovered nearby throughout the song. "Why do girls always go off to the bathroom in pairs?" he asked Richard, giving Tricia and me cover as we made a break for it.

I shot him a look of exasperation to cover my gratitude, then Tricia and I actually did go find the restroom. I was genuinely relieved to see there was already a line since it would justify spending more time putting my head together.

"So, just how bad was it?" Tricia was partly joking, but also partly serious.

"Well you had him for the longer dance, so probably much worse for you. Thanks though, I know you were doing me a favor there. It wasn't all that horrible; we talked about voter drives and stuff. He and his dad are starting up some political group and… Oh! I almost forgot! Do you want a job? I need somebody to help me keep stuff organized for the voter drives and of course I thought of you." I tried to keep my voice low so we wouldn't be overheard through the chatter all around us, but it was clear Tricia heard me clearly enough when her face lit up.

"Wow, of course, yes! I don't know if I could use the school computer for it, and that's the only portable one I have…" Her brow had started to furrow, marring her initial enthusiasm.

I put my hand on her shoulder to try to bring her enthusiasm back. "Oh, don't worry about that, there's one at Saul's office that maybe he can let you take home if you ever need to log in extra hours to catch up. But we just do the organizing when we're on the clock so either way it's no problem! The computer will come with us when we do the actual drives though and – oh, this is going to be so cool. You can come with me on the registration drives! I'm so excited!"

We struggled to keep our voices down as we spent the next several minutes in low-level planning so she could start work the very next day. I had started feeling completely buried by all the work I knew I couldn't accomplish alone, so the sooner she could pitch in the easier I could breathe. Plus, it was just a little overwhelming and I was comforted knowing I'd have such a reliable friend to help me out. We both grew more and more excited about it all, and when we got back to the dance, she helped me duck Richard again by leading me out onto the floor. "Since I went to the effort of getting up this Paul Revere outfit, I may as well ask Betsy Ross to dance. Mind if I lead?"

I giggled and shook my head. "I've had a grand total of two dances so far, so please, go ahead. Even at the FOAM events I've always managed to avoid any actual dancing."

We spent the rest of the evening talking and occasionally dancing, hanging out with Kurt and avoiding being alone with Richard. Judy and Derek had disappeared to make a date night of it, and we hadn't seen anything of Gig since we split up for the first dance. Finally when it was all over and we regrouped, Judy said that Gig and his date had left without us.

The remaining Council members gathered and spilled back into the car, which drove each of us home. I was the last to be dropped off, and I thought about trying to open up the little window to talk to the driver, but I didn't want to distract him. So I stayed in the back, alone with my thoughts until I found myself waking up as the car stopped in front of my house. I groggily thanked the driver for the ride and wished him well as I stumbled toward the door, completely exhausted. After a few minutes reassuring my parents that everyone had behaved themselves at a perfectly civil dance, at long last I slipped off to enjoy a long night's sleep, with what I recall only as fitful, fleeting dreams.

When we got back to work the next morning, Saul took an instant liking to Tricia and handed over the semi-organized voter data for her to make some sort of sense of. By the evening we were well on our way to planning how to get voters to the polls, and I finally had the chance to tell him about the American Christian League. After I finished explaining it, I thought he took to the idea surprisingly well. He had been very careful to make his campaign pretty open on the religious issue, but after hearing what Richard had said, he encouraged me to follow through.

"Liz, the Christian community is the largest untapped group of potential voters we have. If this friend of yours and his people want to work on getting out the Christian vote, I say, let's help them." I balked at his use of the word "friend," but otherwise concurred.

Meanwhile, Tricia was typing away like a heavy rainstorm, her expression quite intense as she hunched over the screen. I asked her how things were coming along, and she continued typing for almost a minute before she finally replied. "Aaaalmost got this database ready to go. It's a rough fit, since we're working with very different data sources here. I got some new ideas from some posts on an Innernet forum on how to fix the concatenation problem, and it looks like it's gonna work." I looked over her shoulder as she showed me what she was talking about, eager to learn how to do even a little of her computer magic.

Saul chuckled approvingly from his campaign office desk. "You're taking to all this like a fish to water, Tricia. Could you have imagined all you'd be able to do once I got you an Innernet connection here?"

Tricia paused, glancing at me quickly with a look I couldn't quite fathom before leaning back into the keyboard, typing away. "Oh, yeah, there's a lot out there. It's like you could find anything you wanted, if you just figure out how to search for it." She gave me another secretive, more lingering look, her lips hinting at a mysterious smile.

I was slow on the uptake, but it eventually dawned on me that she had found a way to connect to the Innernet before. My goodness, I realized with a tiny bit of panic, she might be a Hacker! I'd heard of them before, and how the DSS hunts them down as Cyber Spies, but I didn't know much about what they actually did. I always heard they were destructive anarchists, nothing like my very respectable Tricia, so I hoped I'd misunderstood.

Saul was too busy sifting through some ad copies to notice our silent exchange as he continued. "Oh yeah, it's a whole new world of information out there. And I don't have to worry about you stumbling onto something untoward, not on the Innernet. The service provider is very diligent about the kind of content they let through. Just be careful if you happen to find a link sending you to the Outernet. It's all heavily monitored, traffic to and from there, but you don't want anyone tricking you into going somewhere you shouldn't. Something seen can't be unseen, and you just don't need that, not at your tender age."

I didn't like it when Saul's tone reminded me he thought of us as children, but his seriousness gave me pause. Was going to the Outernet possibly as dangerous as all that? My answer came in the way Tricia tensed up just a little. She typed on the screen the letters "DSS," then deleted them and went back to what she was doing.

I decided it was past time to change the subject. "Saul, I've been meaning to ask. Once you win the primary, will you still need our help?"

He was delighted by my optimistic phrasing as much as by the question itself. "Oh certainly, certainly, more than ever! The primary is just the lead-up, my girl. It gets people excited, but they can get complacent afterwards, and lose interest. We're mostly a Puritanic district, to be sure, but that won't help us beat the Pragmaticans if we don't get out the vote!"

Because I was so devoted to the American ideal of everybody having an equal voice, I didn't care for the reminder that my voter organization was partisan-supported. However, I still felt Puritans would do a better job for America, so that didn't distract me much from Saul's latest "aria," as I called his little speeches.

"No, after the primaries is when we will really need to put our shoulders to the wheel. It will be up to us to get the issues before all voters, especially the ones who don't yet realize which issues are important. Those are the ones, my dear Liz – those are the ones who will benefit most from your work. And yours too, Tricia. Yes indeed, I'm going to need you both to help this team keep the momentum. Already I can see how well you two click, and that you're going to be the best secretarial team I've ever been blessed with. There's something to be said for youthful enthusiasm unsullied by the harsh tarnish of cynicism. Together, you two can keep all the loose ends tied up so the campaign managers can focus on staying on track and on target. It's full steam ahead until we win next November."

"Wait, November?" I was startled from the lulling rhythm of his patter as the schedule clicked together in my mind. "But, classes start late August or early September, and I was really hoping to start school right away. I've already sent my applications in for the AMOS scholarship and admissions." I didn't want to let Saul down, but I had this one shot at a future I had never even dreamed of before recently. I couldn't let it slip away.

He turned to me, not with disappointment, more like incredulity. "You're planning to go to school on an AMOS scholarship? Why would you do that? That is, are you sure that a Military career is the best use of your talents? I'm the most pro-Military veteran you'll ever meet, as you well know, but I would have thought you'd be more interested in charity work or politics."

"Well, I'm sure that would be great, but there's no way I could go to college without AMOS. I don't have the connections you need to get admitted, let alone get tuition covered or secure a regular scholarship."

I wasn't embarrassed by that, it was simply true. Yes, even then I knew it was sometimes considered bad manners to acknowledge that you had to have significant financial and social resources to be able to get an education in order to secure the further financial and social resources required to follow the American Dream. But I had become pretty matter-of-fact about such details in working with Saul's campaign, and I thought he'd appreciate the candor.

He did, but dismissed it all with a wave of his hand. "Balderdash, my dear girl. You have me. I know it's not some grand old estate of a school with busts of former presidents in the hall, but how would you like to go to the State University? It's still pretty prestigious, having one of the largest and best-regarded political science schools in this great nation."

I blinked. I knew Judy was hoping to go there on a cheerleading scholarship, as her family were huge fans of their sports teams. Derek was applying to their pharmaceutical research school, and had already secured some pretty hefty letters of recommendation. I started to think about how nice it would be to be able to go with them, while Saul sweetened the offer.

"It's also right near where my headquarters will be when I'm elected, so I was planning to establish a satellite office there after the primary to expand the campaign. You and Tricia can stay here to keep things going smoothly as the school year finishes, and graduate with your friends. Then you can move up there to work full-steam-ahead for the summer, and start classes in the fall. Tricia, they have one top-notch computing program I could get you into, if you're interested."

She pursed her lips in thought, lifting her hands from the keyboard. "I have an application there already, but unless they pull my name in some kind of scholarship lottery, I just can't go."

Saul blinked, then shook his head. "Oh, please pardon me, girls, I see I'm not being clear. I know some folks on the scholarship selection committees. Just one word in their ears and you're both a shoo-in. It's no trouble at all."

It was my turn to blink, as I realized what he was offering me. A chance to go to college on my own merits, without the Military commitment an AMOS scholarship would require. And then… then what? If I didn't go Military, what would I use college for? What else was there for me? My expression showed my consternation and confusion, which he tried to allay.

"Liz, I know you've started planning a Military career, but you don't have to go that route to make a life for yourself. You're a truly special young lady; I saw that the moment I set eyes on you. I know your family background, and I'm sure you'd like to start your own family someday, but in the meantime, live your life a little. Be a strong, talented woman who can set a real example for the youth. The Military wouldn't give you any time for your children anyway, shipping you right back out just a month after you first hold your little bundle of joy. In any event, it is self-evident that your talents are in helping people, not killing them."

Saul's mild condescension had slipped away, replaced by a paternalism that was warmer and more genuine than I ever would have expected. And at the end, there was something… what was it… raw? It was genuine. There was brief hint of remembrance, something he'd worked hard to forget.

"Well, I've made up my mind. You girls are going to do just great. I'll head on home and make some calls while you two finish up. Make sure you lock up when you're done, and pop over next door to get a ride home." He nodded to us as he grabbed his notebook, and after brief goodbyes, he took off.

I plopped down into the big chair at his desk after he left, trying to catch up with the further twists in my tale. I leaned over to Tricia to ask her what she thought of the whole crazy wonderfulness of it all, but she was clearly quite distracted.

After physically disabling the Innernet connectivity on the computer, she opened up a new window to type something as she said, "Liz, I've got to focus on wrapping up this database, so if you want to catch up on some reading, don't mind me." She then pointed my attention to the screen, so I could read her private note.

```
T> I'm not sure his bugjammer works, just in
   case his office is being spied on like he
   says it might. So let's type.
```

I kept my voice casual as I replied, "Sure, okay, I'll try to keep it down." I sat down next to her so I could reach the keyboard and type a reply.

```
L> Do you think he was afraid of spying by the
   competition, or DSS, or SPY spied on?
T> Don't know, don't care. I just wanted to
   tell you yeah, I've seen the Innernet before,
   tons of times. First tunneled a connection
   years ago, got to see it all before the
   Borderwall went up.
L> The wha-huh?
T> Oh right, duh, this isn't common knowledge,
   especially around here. Well a while back
   there was this law passed called PROTECT US
   that gave a bunch of money to telecoms
   supposedly so they could strengthen the
```

infrastructure and protect kids from adult content and illegal downloads and enemy Spies and whatever. Anybody could complain a website was dangerous or spreading Anti-Americanism without having to prove it in a court of law, and the site was completely shut down right away. The site's owners would have to prove to the government they were innocent to get unblocked, which even if that happened the damage had already been done. Someone could complain that some random user had posted one little piece of copyrighted material in one little corner of a huge website and the whole site would get shut down with like no notice at all.

L> How bad would a site have to be to get blocked?

T> Oh, that's the brilliance of the whole thing! The site doesn't have to be bad in itself, it just has to be accused of facilitating badness to be presumed guilty until proven innocent. Usually it's when somebody doesn't like you criticizing or competing with their company so they put in an anonymous report and – BANG! Your ideas are silenced and your business is dead. So what we got was a separate and totally arbitrary American directory of what sites were allowed to be accessed in America. If you're on the blacklist, providers have to block you or be shut down themselves. Part of the deal was that the telecoms got subsidies to put in the firewalls and upgrade their services, and also to put access into poor rural areas like ours. The law got passed on promises that it would actually expand Innernet access for education and innovation, cause children are our future and all that kind of BS.

L> Wait, we're supposed to have Innernet then? What happened with the subsidies?

T> The usual. Just like every other supposedly public resource, they used their scads of free money to give themselves bonuses while their obsolete infrastructure decomposes like an old Edsel. They create this artificial scarcity and then charge an arm and a leg where they can squeeze tons of money, and just neglect or outright deny service where they can't. Every other developed country has fast and cheap Innernet for everyone, since access to information is considered a human right.

L> Well, I don't know that we have to go all Commie with the Innernet, but I will agree that it would be nice to have the option to use it. Hey at least the telecoms put the firewalls in to stop the adult content and stuff.

T> Ha! Oh sure, they block adult content, as in the blacklist shuts out just about everything a free-thinking adult might want to read up on. And on top of that, telecoms were given the right to control what traffic goes through their services based on who pays them what. They're like gangsters with the protection money and extortion. They make legal companies pony up some serious cash to make sure their websites get preferential treatment, leaving everybody else to the rampant packet loss and 404s when the nodes fail. Some content is utterly banished to Cyberia if the telecom thinks a company is too much competition for their own products, or a person is saying things that might interfere with their profits.

L> Seriously? That's… What kind of things?

T> Complaints about their service, people asking about the promised upgrades, or even news or information that contradicts what the companies' owners want people to be talking about. Don't try to get people talking about why it's so hard to find a decent job opening, or why there are more Birth Mutations in factory towns, not when they could be fighting over who should win America's Best Talent. Remember, there's only three big Innernet/telecom providers and they're each part of the three huge news and media conglomerates that control what's allowed to be discussed in public venues. And these conglomerates are run by very, very rich and powerful men who have a vested interest in keeping the status quo, and that means keeping people so hyperactive distracted that they don't have time and energy left to talk about stuff that matters. Just look at what happens when anyone brings up a criticism about the problems Americans are facing, and how quickly people just shut it all down.

L> People avoid what makes them uncomfortable, yeah, but that doesn't mean it's because a few powerful CEOs are pulling our strings. If they're so powerful, what do they care what people talk about? Don't they have better things to worry over?

T> It's all Info Wars, Liz. The best way to keep people happily locked up in Fortress America is to keep them so distracted and misinformed that they can't even see there are walls all around them. The truth might inspire them to set themselves free. That's why they put up the American Borderwall, not to "protect us from Spies" on the Outernet. No, it's to keep us from finding out about what's really out there. They can monitor server traffic overseas but they can't control it. So they had to make it too inconvenient for the casual American user, and too scary a risk for even the dedicated users. Everybody who's in the know about stuff they don't want you to know, we know that if you rock the boat too much you might find the DSS knocking at your door.

L> Uh, okay. Trish, I know you know I don't mean anything mean by this, but that all sounds like a conspiracy theory to me.

T> Yeah, I'd expect it to. The best part about their whole deal is that they don't have to censor anybody most of the time. We're so busy censoring ourselves so we don't sound kooky or invite trouble. And when people speak up anyway, tons of well-intentioned people will hound them for "being silly.." Like the whole "conspiracy theory" label being automatically thrown around like an insult. Careers and even lives are ended by telling the wrong truth at the wrong time.

T> But seriously, Liz, think about it. We're all talking all the time about how Spies have conspiracies against America, but as soon as anyone talks about America having conspiracies, suddenly they're a lunatic. As though we can be the smartest, most powerful country in the world but not be capable of being sneaky when it would protect our vast interests. I've seen some fairly compelling evidence backing this all up, which I won't get you mixed up with, so go ahead and disbelieve me if you want. I just want to say this: When there's data to back it up, it's not conspiracy theory. It's conspiracy reality.

L> If there's proof, or even some kind of evidence, why haven't I heard about this? Why aren't people coming forward with it? Don't you think if you had the evidence you'd put it out there?

T> Me? No, because I know what happens if you stick your neck out too far. We all do, which is why even reporters and so-called journalists will only say what they know their bosses want to hear, just like everybody else who wants to keep their job and stay off the DSS radar, or even off the Watched Travelers File. Nobody enjoys the idea of getting hauled off for questioning and their electronics confiscated every time they go to an airport or interstate checkpoint. Or black-bagged and disappeared for good. Like I said, nobody has to censor us because we all know well enough to censor ourselves. Call it paranoia, call it cowardice, call it cynicism. Silence is the price we pay for a piece of troubled peace.

L> Then how did you find all this?

T> There's a few sites out there where people are encouraged to post up all sorts of stuff like this, some of it valid but also some of it just off-the-wall, sometimes even intentionally by DSS psyops out to keep us all off-balance. But in the end they're only "conspiracy theory" sites so they're not taken seriously by anyone who wants to be considered Serious. If you ever want to know more, ask me, just please don't go looking for them yourself. Because posting on them puts you on a DSS watch list. Even going to one of the sites puts you on the list, unless you know how to stealth your visit.

I just looked at her with an arched eyebrow and uncertain quirk to my lips that showed this was all way beyond my realm of, well, anything. I didn't want to call my friend crazy, but it seemed just a little too much to take seriously. She nodded to me with understanding, and typed just one more thing before deleting it all and filling the screen with random gobbledygook, then closing the computer for us to wrap up and leave.

T> That's totally cool, just forget all of it but one thing. The computer is a wonderful tool, Liz, but it's not your friend. As much info as it opens up to you, the way you use it reveals much, much more to those who watch you. Be very, very careful out there.

PART TWO:
No One is an Island

Chapter 8

We used to think, but now we know.

The funny thing about the ups and downs of life is that you never know where they're ultimately headed. Something you'd wished for may have led you to unhappiness, and something you've dreaded may work out wonderfully for you – and you may never even realize what a difference it made. If we had a truly clear perspective on all the vast network of causes and effects at play in the world, we might wish more wisely and well, with greater acceptance for what life brings us. As it is, all we have to go on is our habits of getting disappointed or elated with life for how closely it mirrors our expectations.

All that said, when Saul Harolds won the primary for the Puritanic candidate for State House of Representatives, I was ecstatic. It was a close race at the end, so I hadn't felt sure he would win until the final tallies came in. The margin was pretty good, though, so even if his opponent used the standard Puritan tactic of demanding a recount, I was confident the victory was final. We'd won.

As soon as the announcement was made at the campaign headquarters, I gave Tricia a quick hug and jumped up and down with Judy, trying not to squeal like she was. Derek clapped but also laughed at us, leaning over to say something to Kurt, who nodded back at him. Too elated to just take their private teasing, I turned to them with a mock scowl. "Hey, if you two can't be happy for us, you don't have to stay for the party!"

Derek rolled his eyes, then came over to give me a quick hug, and Tricia a quicker one. "There, congratulations Lizbet, Trish. You gals did great. I heard voter turnout was at record levels for a primary. Your guy Harolds did pretty decent too, despite the ACL's best efforts to paint him as an un-Christian secular Pragmatican in disguise."

I nodded at that. "Yeah, despite the fact that he goes to church every Sunday and quotes the Bible in almost every speech. I always knew the Foleys and their camp favored the other guy, so I'm not surprised they really hammered the fact he was running in opposition to a pastor. Besides, I appreciate that Saul is going to work on stuff that will help people in the state, no matter what religion they are. It shouldn't always be a contest of who's supposedly more Christian. I'm more interested in electing who's more Christlike."

Kurt started to chime in, "You know, I'm really impressed w—"

But he was cut off by Saul's boisterous, "…and a special thanks goes out to these two little girls right here, Liz and Tricia, the best darn secretarial team I've ever had the pleasure of working with. Here kids, I ordered up a special bottle of bubbly just for you. Drink up, you've earned it. Oh, over there we have…"

By then, Saul had quickly moved on to his next rapid-fire introductions, and his small entourage hurried to keep up. Once they were out of the way, a caterer moved in with a tray holding champagne glasses filled with sparkling, honey-colored liquid. As I blinked uncertainly, Derek grabbed one.

"All right! I always wondered…" He interrupted himself with a sip, which itself was interrupted as he pulled back to glare accusingly at the glass. "This is juice!"

The caterer laughed along with us, then leaned toward him as we each took a glass. "If you want the real thing, sneak one off the buffet table when nobody's looking. I won't tell."

As Derek started to eye the table, Judy punched his arm, almost spilling his juice. "Don't you even think about it, mister." She then raised her own glass, grinning to the group. "Well, I propose a toast. To Liz and Tricia for starting this state down the road to a more participatory democracy!"

I raised my glass and continued the toast, "And to Judy and Derek for also getting scholarships at our new school, and to Kurt for getting an in-state Boot Camp assignment!"

Kurt then raised his glass. "To knowing people who know people," he finished, flashing me a quick wink as we all took a drink.

I never knew what to make of his little gestures like that, the winks and the sly smiles to me when we were out as a group. The three of them had taken to helping Tricia and me out with the actual legwork of voter drives, but we hadn't had much time to really hang out before that party.

Through the rest of the school year before graduation, we all had a little more time to spend together. Usually we could all do something, though sometimes it was just the four of us if Tricia couldn't make it. As Judy and Derek got more serious with each other and started going out alone, I think I kind of expected Kurt to want to still do stuff, just without them. But he never did, not unless Tricia was there.

It wasn't until after the school year ended that I found out why. We were at a school-sponsored Graduation Celebration, an overnight thing where we were supervised enough that our parents were comfortable, but not so supervised that it wasn't still fun. Judy and Derek had already snuck off to spend time together, and Tricia had left with her family to go to a cousin's graduation and travel the state all summer. So that left just Kurt and me… and, of course, Richard.

It honestly hadn't occurred to me that Richard would even be at the party, otherwise I may not have let Kurt leave me alone while he fought the crowd for some punch and snacks. He'd left me alone by the fire exit, which almost got used when I heard that voice that made me jump just a little.

"What's a beautiful and talented graduate like yourself doing in a rowdy place like this?" Richard's voice was practically in my ear, so I wasn't surprised to look up and see his gleaming grin just inches from my face. It was a little noisy in the huge hall, sure, but not enough to warrant such proximity.

I leaned away from him and against the wall, laughing off the question. "Hey, Richard. Wow, it's hard to believe we've finally graduated, huh? It's been such a crazy-busy year, it's kinda surprising it's already over."

He moved to my side and put his hand on the wall to lean almost right over me. "I know what you mean. Between Student Council and the ACL, it's like we've seen a lot of each other, but never really had the chance to *see* each other. Hopefully we can remedy that tragic situation, seeing as we'll be going to school so near each other."

I'm not sure, but I think I actually startled at that. He spared me the struggle to find a polite response by not waiting for one. "Yes, I'm starting theological college in the fall, and I've decided to stay in state. It's the home base of the ACL, after all, so may as well keep building it up here and help it spread nationwide. This is a big election year, so being in the capitol just makes sense. Besides…" Richard then started to move closer, and I was starting to inch toward that exit when the cavalry arrived.

"You know, it's nights like this that prove some people just have no concept of personal space." Kurt's voice cut through Richard's momentum and even caused him to take a step back. Richard's defensive glare quickly subsided as Kurt smoothly continued, "I think I have actual bruises from trying to reach the punch. Oh hey, Richard. You'll want to go tackle the sandwich table now, by the way, cause they're going fast. C'mon Liz, I scouted out a spot where the two of us might barely squeeze in. See you 'round, Richard!"

Before I knew it, Kurt was handing me some of the food he had precariously balanced, and was leading me through the throng. After weaving around enough to have safely lost any tail, he brought me to a hidden-away corner where we could eat in some semblance of privacy. And before I had the chance to thank him, Kurt apologized.

"I hope that was cool, snagging you away like that. I know Richard's a friend of yours, but I just didn't feel like sharing you. Not now that I can finally ask you something." He casually took a sip of punch, but I caught him watching for my reaction over the cup.

That time, I know I started. "Whoa, uh, he's not exactly my friend, more like… well anyway, what do you want to ask?"

I might have caught a glimpse of relief as he lowered his cup and looked into it, shrugging as his tone turned even more casual. "Well, it's a silly question, nothing really, just…" He reached into the shoulder bag he'd been carrying and pulled out a cellophane-wrapped stem. "Do you like roses?"

His grin nearly masked the trepidation in his eyes, though his nervousness quickly faded. I actually cooed as I pulled the flower to my nose to smell it. It was a real live rosebud, deep red with green leaves, and a scent that was faint, but as heavenly as I'd always imagined. Finally, I remembered to stammer out an answer. "Um, yes, I do!"

He chuckled at that, then ducked his head down again. "I know this might seem a little sudden, but we've only got so much time before I go off to Boot Camp and you start up college and stuff, so I figured I'd better take a chance. So if I may please ask another question… would you maybe like to be my girlfriend?"

Okay, I know that might not sound like the most romantic proposal, but the way he asked it, looking into my eyes as he lightly took my hand… Well, I melted like chocolate. "Sure! I mean, yes! But…"

"But why did I wait so long? Well part of it is, as soon as we met, you helped me get into FOAM. If we were dating, people would, you know, talk." He inclined his head toward me knowingly, and I understood what he meant. He was right, there would have been talk. It was already rough enough being the first female leader, I didn't need that kind of extra gossip going around.

"And the other part is… Well, Marissa. No-no-no, no, that had nothing to do with you! What I mean is, things went so fast with her, and then suddenly she was gone, and just… well, everything. And then you came into my life and were just so…" He paused with a smile and a sigh. "But I didn't want to fall for you, not so fast."

After another uncertain pause, he tried to shrug it off. "It's not just that you have this big future ahead of you, there's also the religious difference. I just knew that things could never work out and I'd lose you. I wasn't ready to lose someone like that again, not yet." He looked down and away. His usual sense of bravado had fled, and I never would have imagined him looking so vulnerable, almost lost.

I squeezed his hand. "Then what changed your mind?"

The question returned his focus, bringing his gaze back up to mine. "I realized I had already fallen for you, and that if I didn't ask you now, I'd lose you forever. People grow apart after graduation, I know that. But I don't want to grow apart from you."

Looking back into his eyes, I felt like we'd actually been close for nearly a year, and honestly maybe we had. In all the times we'd talked, weren't we always open with one another? He wasn't a complicated guy; he wore his heart on his sleeve and shared it with everyone around him. And it was a truly beautiful heart, paired with a generously open mind. I wasn't sure what love was way back then, but I remember thinking that maybe it was a lot like what I felt for him at that moment.

I leaned toward him a little, then he toward me, and soon my eyes were closed and lips were open to meet his. I don't think I ever told anybody this, but I honestly caught myself wondering, not what would become of us, but whether I was a good kisser.

Well, if my kissing was disappointing, he was pretty patient about it, because got we quite a lot of practice in the time we had left. Judy and Derek were beyond thrilled when we told them later that night we were dating, and we spent as much time as we could together over the summer. Because when summer ended, we knew our futures would take on lives of their own, leading us in different directions.

Kurt wasn't the only one shipping off to some form of camp. Judy had Cheer Camp, of course. Derek had been accepted to the pharmaceutical college's brainstorming camp, thanks to letters from people he'd met while helping his dad at the pharmacy. Tricia had gotten back from her family trip just in time to go off to something called Root Camp, which she was super excited about.

I was the only one who didn't have anywhere to go except the capitol. I was planning to just put in extra hours working before classes started, and try to get a head start on figuring out how to acclimate to the new area. I even completed pre-registration for my classes the very first day, making sure I could maximize my credits while leaving plenty of time for work.

It was worth the effort, since I had a higher course load than I expected. It turns out I had to take remedial Science and Research/Reporting, as those were required subjects but I hadn't studied them in high school. The Christian Education Network placed such a strong emphasis on prepping for the Reading and Math tests, there was only room left for vocational courses and so-called Christian perspectives on history and America. I say "so-called," because even just hanging around with other students around campus, I heard enough juicy tidbits about America's history that I had begun to realize just how much was left out of my education.

At the time, I was a little shocked to find out that my schooling had been so deficient in what turned out to be pretty core aspects of a strong education. I guess those were things the CEN didn't think you needed to know in order to be a dutiful cog in some factory machine. The people who'd created the Christian Education Network didn't want creativity or critical thinking, they wanted hard work and obedience.

Since I happened to like creativity and critical thinking, I didn't mind so much that I'd be taking classes to help me learn better skills. Fortunately I was able to test out of the remedial Literature class, due to my own love of reading the classics despite my schooling.

I also managed to get a spot in the Introduction to American Government, getting a core class out of the way for my Political Science major. As my elective I signed up for History of Science and Religion. It was actually going to be my very first college class once the term started, which I thought was pretty fitting given the course description: We shall be reviewing the most significant periods of scientific discovery in the history of the Western world, and how each breakthrough in natural understanding was at first condemned by religious leaders before ultimately being embraced as the new sum total of all truth that would ever be revealed. At the beginning of each chapter, we will recount the recurring refrain, "We used to *think*, but now we *know!*"

I figured, I was going to be setting off on a journey of discovering new ways to discover knowledge. With that in mind, I might do well to kick it off with a class designed to remind me not to be too sure of what I think I already know. I was just wrapping up my registration when I was given a flyer for a camp that would give me a crash course in that idea.

At this point, I really think I should stress that in home, church and school, I had been raised on the firm conviction that America was the land of Free and Equal Opportunity. Here, we each had exactly the same chance at success. If you worked hard and played by the rules then someday you'd earn limitless prosperity and achieve the American Dream

Yes, I probably should have realized by then that reality was just a little different. After all, most families I knew played by all the rules, believing prosperity had to be just around the corner because of how tirelessly hard they worked. Yet everyone else out there who was struggling, especially those who had less than us, well, obviously they just weren't willing to work as hard. For some reason, I didn't see that there wasn't enough scraps for us all to scrabble over, not when so few people who were good at hoarding success were all that good at sharing it.

In FOAM, I helped make decisions on promotions and stuff for other students. There were several smart and dedicated cadets who just couldn't keep up. I knew they had to cut activities or even homework to work or care for family members, but I still passed them over. At the time, I reasoned that it was only fair, that they could still have gotten ahead if only they cared more... I don't know. I guess I just had to justify it to myself, so I could stay comfortable in my own skin with the choices I was making and how they impacted those students' future opportunities.

I probably was on the path to never even question my own part in keeping alive the myth that success or failure is entirely on the shoulders of the individual. You know, the American Success Myth. And then I got that flyer.

In yet another one of my life's many simple twists of fate, there had been a few last-minute cancellations for this camp held by the Political Science College, and the rep there thought I'd be a really good fit. Since Saul had encouraged me to try to find a camp to attend and I had a couple hours before I had to be anywhere, I asked for an application so I could fill it out right there.

The camp was called Acculturation: Establishing Cultural Capital. They were trying an experimental approach to fast-tracking introductions to cross-cultural issues, which they hoped would provide valuable insights to both participants and researchers. It struck me that such a camp might be the best way to dive into the new environment, and also pick up some quick course credits. They had an interesting selection process based on an extensive questionnaire, as they intended the camp to share the same demographics ratios as the student body. So I tried to be completely honest in the questionnaire, however odd the questions seemed.

It started off with things like race, gender, age and grade, and then also religion. I almost selected "Zealous Christian," and then realized that I really wasn't as sold on the idea of always trying to preach at people, not anymore. I still knew I was a Christian Zealot in my heart, but I'd come to learn that most people expect a Zealot to always be pressuring people to convert. Instead, I wanted to learn how to follow Christ's example by living a compassionate life and inspiring others through kindness of word and deed.

Was that what they were looking for in a "Zealous Christian"? Did I still want to label my deeply spiritual beliefs by a simple checkbox? I found I didn't have a ready answer for those questions. So rather than dwell on it too much, I selected "Other," and moved on.

Then it asked for what political party I identified myself as being a part of. I thought the phrasing was a little odd, and really took it to heart. Sure, I was working for a Puritanic candidate, and had registered as Puritan, but did I really count that as part of my identity? I had values that I felt were best addressed by the Puritanic Party, certainly, but thinking it through, I realized my loyalty was to my values, not the party itself. If the party didn't live up to them, I would consider the party as having failed, not my values. So I selected "None."

And then the questions really threw me. How many houses did my family own? Did I grow up with two parents in the household? How many families lived on the lot I grew up on, on average? How many days a year did my family vacation, and where? How much time did I spend on childcare or adult care? In what ways have physical or mental disability impacted my life? How has violence impacted my attendance or classrooms? How much of my family had to work to pay bills? In what ways have classes or teachers validated or invalidated things I feel are important in my neighborhood? How has jail or prison impacted me or my family? What have I shared with a person of another racial and/or religious background, and how often? What comments do people make on what it means when someone of my race, gender or religion take a prominent position? Who are the people and/or organizations who have given the greatest help to me and/or my family?

Then there were the "how often did you" series: have to skip meals, suffer at school because of work, feel as though I was being watched or accosted by security forces while shopping or traveling, called on by teachers, have help with my homework, engage in artistic activities in or out of school, receive compliments or criticisms for verbal skills, take advanced classes, take remedial classes, received compliments or criticisms for my attire, give help to neighbors, receive help from neighbors, participate in extra-curricular activities, volunteer my services, receive volunteered services, feel unsafe at or going to school or home, use a computer at school, work, and home?

Finally, there were two questions at the very end. How comfortable was I with the idea of potentially unnerving explorations of social conventions? Given that, how willing was I to approach them with an open mind? I honestly answered that I wasn't sure how comfortable I was, but that I was very willing to give it a chance.

By the time I was halfway through, I had begun to pay more attention to the questions than my answers. I had no idea what the "right" ones were to be accepted, but I started to guess what the "right" ones were that had gotten me where I was.

For the first time ever, I started to take a closer look at the advantages I'd enjoyed and how I got them, or rather, who gave them to me. Oh, sure, there were plenty of points where I probably had it worse off than how I'd imagined others may have answered, but for the most part, I realized that I'd had it pretty good. Yes, I could take credit for accepting the opportunities I'd been given and working hard to make the most of them. But the fact remained they were given to me. And I knew people who worked harder to receive less; I just never really looked closer at why that may have been. Filling in my answers had started to open my eyes, and also my heart. Even if I didn't make it into the camp, I found myself grateful to the questionnaire itself as I handed it back in.

Of course, I was even more grateful when I received my acceptance the next day. And not just because it was being held at the nearby state park, filled with trees and air with a freshness I had never even dreamed of. It was because I felt you can learn a lot about people by the questions they ask, and the questionnaire had made me intensely curious to find out more about the people who wrote it. And more importantly, what did their questions have to do with the camp?

Fortunately, I didn't have to stay curious long, as we were given a very good rundown at the introductory seminar. I know several people there probably found that first session a little dry and numbers-heavy. But for me, it was a fascinating introduction to the dynamics of Having and Having-Not in the Land of Plenty, and how choices we make can make the difference between prosperity and destitution for people we've never even met.

The seminar had us seated on benches at narrow tables, facing a small platform with a podium. Next to the podium was a table bearing some small boxes and a large basket. A tall man greeted us from behind the podium, looking casual but impeccably professional.

"Welcome, everyone, to the first Acculturation. This camp is designed to help you increase your Cultural Capital with the college and fellow students, as well as provide course credits. I want to thank each of you for taking this chance on an unknown quantity. I'm Doctor Peter Michaels, and I'm going to kick this camp off by establishing everyone's Camp Savings and Camp Income levels. Since 'real money' is no good here, I'd like for everyone to pull out their wallets and set them on the table. Yes, you have a question?"

A gal a couple tables away from me raised a dark-skinned hand. "What if you don't got no wallet?" I caught the extremely well-dressed guy next to me rolling his eyes with a snicker, and I wanted to kick him.

I did catch Dr. Michaels' eyes flickering about the room as she spoke, and his face lit up into a bright smile. "Well, you can put in whatever you use to hold your money." With growing exasperation she replied that she had none, and the professor's smile only brightened. "Then you will be an invaluable help to me. Please come up here and take the basket, then go around to collect everyone's wallets. While Jazmine—" He had pronounced the name on her tag with a short "i," but was interrupted as she corrected him, using the long "ee" sound and emphasis on the second syllable. "Pardon me, while Jazmine comes around, please set your item in the basket. Don't worry, it will be kept in the safe during the camp."

Some people seemed reluctant, but we all complied. Once Jazmine had picked up the basket and started her rounds, he continued his presentation. "Based on your survey responses, you have each been assigned an Inherited Economics Score and an Inherited Social Score. These are going to form the basis of a little game I call Success Poker. Don't worry, there won't be actual gambling, this is just an exercise."

As Jazmine came by me, I tried to catch her eye with a friendly smile, but she hadn't turned her sullen look anywhere but the basket and its contents. The guy next to me mumbled "What a witch" under his breath after she passed, only he didn't say witch. I glared at him, then noted the name on his tag and privately thought "What a Mitch," finding it childishly funny. I guess you had to be there. Anyway, realizing he'd offended me, he mumbled an apology for his language while I tried to turn my attention back to Dr. Michaels.

"Your Inherited Economics Score is based loosely on the level of income your family likely enjoyed, and what level of hardship you appear to have endured in the process. For example, if your responses fit the scenarios for the average level of income and time spent on activities related to economic support, you'd have an average number of starting chips. If your family had difficulty meeting economic demands, and/or needed you to devote significant hours a week to economic activities instead of educational or social, you will have fewer chips." As he saw that we were grasping the concept, he moved on.

"Your Inherited Social Score reflects the level of social network you appear to have enjoyed. It is modified by the opportunities you've had to build skills and traits needed to grow this network. Your Cultural Capital traits also increased or decreased this score, but we'll get into that throughout the week. The Social Score algorithm is moderately complex, so in summary, having a large network or community to rely on for support increases the score, as do the prestige and advantages enjoyed by that group." At this point, Jazmine had returned with the basket. Dr. Michaels took it from her, setting it down next to a large box, which he then opened to begin retrieving smaller boxes. He asked Jazmine to distribute the boxes, matching the label on each to our name tags.

"In the box you receive will be a number of chips based on your Economics Score, and a number of playing cards based on your Social Score. You will also have a sheet of stickers with one of several possible colors. Please affix one of the stickers to your name tag each day. Go ahead and open your boxes now." When Jazmine had returned to the empty table she was not offered a box. As she looked at Dr. Michaels questioningly, he appeared apologetic in his reply. "You won't be getting a box, Jazmine, you'll be helping me with the presentation. You can sit down by the table, however, while we do the game."

While she sat down, we each opened our boxes to see how we fared. I had four cards, and just one chip cut in half. My stickers were purple, and I dutifully put one onto my tag. Next to me, Mitch had green stickers, a pile of chips in varying colors, and a stack of cards. I looked around the room and didn't see anyone with as few chips as I, but did see fewer cards.

Noting our curious looks, Dr. Michaels addressed this discrepancy. "You each see the chips and cards that approximate the different situations you were born to. A few of you will have a higher ratio of cards than chips, reflecting greater social resources than monetary. I think one or two of you have it the other way around, and I apologize if you're shorted on cards due to any deficiencies in the system we've devised. However, that's life, isn't it?" His comment was flippant, but his smile was genuine.

He then pulled up a chart behind the podium, and gestured to it as he picked up the pace of the presentation. "Speaking of life, here are the ratios of material assets held by population segments within the country as a whole, not just this college. Your Economics Score corresponds with one of the population segments shown here. This determined the number of chips you received to represent your current wealth. To keep the numbers round in determining the number of chips allocated to each segment, we presumed a total of one thousand chips divided among one hundred people in these ratios. Please note that these numbers don't include the value of one's primary residence, as most people only own a mortgage; accounting for how easily and capriciously mortgages can be foreclosed on today, we are presuming here that the bank owns the home."

I studied the chart, and was a bit taken aback by the sizes of the slices in the pie charts. I knew from talking with Margie that there were large percentages of people struggling, but I figured the differences among us weren't that great. I guess I'd kinda imagined that people who were really well off had about twice as much as my family did, and that the really rich had three or four times as much.

Dr. Michaels' charts suggested the differences were far greater than that. The bottom 10% didn't have a visible slice, and were labeled as "Unemployed and/or Negative Net Worth." The 11%-25% group held less than 1% of the wealth for half a chip each; the 26%-50% group held 2% for one chip; 51%-80% held 5% for two chips; 81%-90% held 12% for twelve chips; 91%-95% also held 12% which split out to twenty-four chips each. But it was the 96%-99% and Top 1% slices that really stood out. The first showed 27%, granting sixty-eight chips each. And the last held a whole 42%, for a grand total of 420 chips to stagnate in the vaults of just one person.

After a pause just long enough for us to get a sense for the numbers we were looking at, the presentation continued. "Hang onto whatever chips you have now, because these will be needed to shore up any deficiencies in your income level we'll be determining using the cards. As I've said, the card counts are based on your Social Score, representing skills and connections that may help you build a better situation for yourself. However, as you are far less likely to get to know the 'right' people and things if you aren't already in a situation that introduces you to them, you'll find a great deal of homogeneity between the Economics and Social scores."

I absently played with the broken chip between my fingertips, considering what the chances were that I'd be one of those outliers with a decent number of cards. What had I taken for granted that gave me such an edge? Fictional exercise or no, this was really drawing me in.

I brought my attention back to the podium as a new set of numbers were put up, and Dr. Michaels explained them. "Here are the allocations of income throughout the country as of a couple years ago, which also influenced the chip counts you'll be competing for via Success Poker. You'll see the income ratios are just a little more equitable, though still quite far from an even distribution. The ratios have become even more skewed since this data was gathered, but income distribution isn't exactly well-funded research these days. Again, this chart apportions one thousand chips among one hundred people."

He was right, the numbers were a lot closer together than the prior chart, but still far from anything that could be called even. The first 10% had a label "Unemployed – Less than 1 Chip," and for the other slices: 11%-25% had 3% at two chips each; 26%-50% had 10% at four chips; 51%-80% had 18% at six chips; 81%-90% had 10% at 10 chips; 91%-95% also had 10% for twenty chips; 96%-99% had 24% at sixty chips; the Top 1% had 25% at two hundred fifty chips. A full quarter of all the income went to just that one person, which seemed so surreal to me. How could just one person be getting so much of America's money each year just to themselves, so much they couldn't possibly spend it all? Could that possibly be right?

As though he had read my thoughts, Dr. Michaels stepped toward the chart to gesture to that Top 1% slice. "Though it seems unbelievable that roughly a quarter of all annual income going to the top one percent, that share is even larger today. Not too long ago, however, that top person had less than half of that, as the income distribution was significantly more equitable. There's been several factors that have created this redistribution of American wealth upward to be siphoned off by the lucky few at the very top, leaving the remaining Americans to struggle more and more for less and less. However, that's beyond the scope of this presentation. Feel free to enroll in one of my classes sometime if you're curious about studying more on how a tiny group of robber barons have shaped the system to give themselves more and more of the prosperity created by all Americans."

He then replaced the chart with data that showed the comparisons between the total population, and our campus. "This chart shows what percentages of the student body fall into the income bands as we have just defined them. In rounded estimates, we have the following ratios from the income groupings we just saw: the bottom 10% had no students who were accepted and could afford to attend; 5% of the student body hails from the next group; 15% each from the following two groups; 40% from the next; 20% from the next; and the remaining 5% is from the 96-99% group. That top one percent apparently couldn't get their applications approved." He chuckled lightly, and I couldn't help but echo with my own little laugh along with several others. It's not that I found it particularly funny, I was just caught up in the bizarreness of it all.

He paused there, looking out over the group. After a few moments he leaned forward on the podium, his pace slowing for a bit. "One last, quick note before we play Success Poker. As it said on the flyer for this camp, we selected applicants in ratios that reflected the race, class and gender demographics of the student body. We received some complaints that this was Affirmative Action, establishing an illegal quota system that would exclude qualified applicants from the chance to earn these course credits, replacing them with the unqualified. These complaints were misplaced for two reasons. First, in order to fulfill the educational and research mission of this camp, we must maintain an accurate population sample and therefore this is both legal and required."

I was distracted momentarily by Mitch fidgeting in his chair, and I wondered briefly whether he was one of the complainants. I tuned him out as Dr. Michaels continued. "Second, the Equal Opportunity, or so-called Affirmative Action proposals that are being put onto ballots do not call for quotas, nor to give college or job openings to the unqualified. If one would read the proposals, they would see that the requests are merely that the pool of *qualified* applicants be reviewed to discern the ratio each demographic bears to the total pool. Then, it is a *guideline* that qualified applicants should be selected along those same ratios. After all, it stands to reason that if qualified applicants were being selected fairly, their selections would be, on average, along the same ratios in which they are presented. Since the ratios are by no means similar, this *guideline* has been proposed as a way of monitoring what unintentional prejudgments and biases may be at play in the selections process, allowing us to better understand and remedy them."

The professor's voice had grown slightly less professorial and more engaged with the topic at hand. He pulled up a chart from a new folder that showed the differences between the applicant pools and the selections. He was right, there were real discrepancies, but I noticed that as a fairer-skinned, articulate man he appeared to be in the group that benefited most. I wondered for a moment what he had experienced that made him feel so deeply about changing a system that could have given him material advantages in life. I also wondered again what advantages I may have been given, that I'd never even realized weren't available to everybody. Yeah, there were opportunities I'd never had, but what about the ones that I did – how much of me even being there was dumb luck?

I was brought back to the presentation as Dr. Michaels stepped aside to continue talking. "If we merely attempt to make acceptances in roughly the same ratios of qualified applicants, this alone will make great strides in closing these gaps. Does this mean that a qualified member of one demographic would not have a slot available because it went to a qualified member of another? Yes, just as they didn't get the slots that went to all the other members of their own demographic. Is this fair? That's hard to say. After all, the pool of qualified applicants is enormously deficient for many demographics when compared to their ratios within the populace as a whole."

He stepped back to bring up new charts, which compared the demographic percentages of the surrounding area and the state, compared to the percentages of all applicants, compared to qualified applicants, compared to those who were selected. I couldn't mentally tally all the numbers, but yeah, they just plain didn't line up. It wasn't just a bias in the selection process, since there were some slices like the Sudoamericans whose ratios got smaller and smaller the closer we came to even applying to the college. I also saw that Jazmine's demographic as a young black woman meant that she was much more likely to be born poor and much less likely to be accepted into college, and I wondered how she felt having to sit up at the front of the room like that. I started to understand why someone might argue for a system similar to what Dr. Michaels was describing, even if I didn't have enough of a background to form a strong personal opinion.

He took a few steps back to take a fresh look at the charts, then turned back to us. "If you want to start evaluating fairness, start trying to dig into the economic and social realities faced by these groups. Try to imagine what barriers might be in the way of their getting the skills and resources needed to catch up. In every single metric, from poverty and incarceration and education, to diseases and Birth Mutations and life expectancy, these groups routinely get the short end of the stick. Yes, many individuals work longer and harder to try to climb out of those holes, but there's always people trying to kick dirt down onto them just for being where they are. Search out what's fair in all of that, and maybe you'll find your own answers."

After a brief pause, Dr. Michaels turned again to face us with a bright smile. "And that leads us to our game. Yes, you can see that there are real differences with what's sitting in front of each of you, and there's trends along certain demographic lines. One purpose of Success Poker is to quantify these differences so you can visually see them, and have a better idea of what your fellow students have had to both help and hinder them in getting to where they are. Only with an appreciation for where someone has come from, can you truly relate to where they are now. You'll find that your ability to relate to others will play a large factor in your ability to work with them to achieve your own goals."

He then went back to his original folder, and brought up a chart with pictures of playing cards, each with a number next to them. "With the background now established, it's time to play Success Poker. Here we have the points that apply to each type of card in a deck. Though each of you have been given a different number of cards to start with, you now have an equal chance to trade in those cards and draw more from the deck Jazmine will bring around. Your final tally will be ranked against the others to determine your daily income at this camp, with 5% of you getting two chips as income, 15% getting four chips, and so on. If you keep or exchange the right cards and luck's on your side, you can still beat out somebody who started off with more cards than you. Alternatively, you could wind up in a worse position, so choose your path carefully."

As he kept talking, Jazmine came around to collect cards people wanted to toss into the basket, and let them pick an equal number of cards from a box. When she came to me, I politely waved her on. I had been dealt the cards I'd been dealt, and I had no way of knowing whether replacing them would have put me up or down on the points tally. I figured I'd be better off just playing the hand I had, and see where it leads me. Mitch threw most of his cards into the basket and groaned as he saw the ones that had replaced them. However, as he would still have been guaranteed a huge number of points just from the sheer volume of his hand, I didn't see what he could be so upset about.

Dr. Michaels followed behind Jazmine to tally up our points as we got our cards, rather than leave it up to us to report honestly. I didn't take that as a personal insult against my integrity, since I knew why he had to. If people think the rewards outweigh the risks, you're going to have those who cheat, stealing from those who play by the rules. They'll rationalize it somehow, so they won't feel like bad people, but cheaters will prosper any way they can.

I didn't really like having playing cards because of my church's stand against the sin of gambling, except for church raffles, bingo, and the occasional lottery ticket. So I was glad when Dr. Michaels came by to collect my cards. I gave him a friendly smile, which this time was returned.

Seeing his grin up close, I could see that Dr. Michaels had almost a childish sense of fun that showed in his eyes, even though he was older than I'd thought. I decided I liked him, and hoped he was as warm and caring as he seemed. Finally, all the cards were dealt, tallied and collected, and Jazmine was given a list of chip totals to hand out

Dr. Michaels helped Jazmine arrange the chips for delivery, speaking as he worked. "All right, that went unexpectedly well. We've got your income levels tallied, and since this is a civil society here with civil expenses, we'll be assessing taxes before handing out your first day's income chips. Everybody will be paying a 10% Payroll Tax on their chips, up to ten chips; those with more than ten chips won't be taxed on the rest, and we won't be talking about whether that's fair. As a quick aside, whenever someone tells you that roughly half the American workforce doesn't pay taxes, remind them of that Payroll Tax, currently set at 10%. Everyone who works a job pays that, even if their income minus deductions puts them below the poverty line and therefore they are exempted from paying further in Income Tax."

I did make a mental note of that. As soon as he started talking taxes, I remembered hearing all the time that half of us were shouldering the tax burden of the other half and how the deductions and exemptions should be lifted so they could pull their weight. I suddenly found myself thinking about that, as well as the revelation that people who made a lot of money didn't have to pay that tax above ten chips...

Of course, I hadn't really understood how Income Tax calculations worked until the presentation went on. "And yes, after the Payroll Tax is Income Tax. We're going to apply a broad oversimplification here since most of you aren't Accounting students. We will apply the federal, state and local tax brackets to income chips as follows: your first two chips are taxed at 10%; next two, 20%; next two, 30%; and if you have more chips than that the rest will be taxed at 35%."

"The exception is for those with sixty chips, who in the real world earn much of their income as returns from long-term investments, which unlike other types of non-business gambling winnings are not taxed as income. Instead, they're called Capital Gains and only bear a 15% tax, which will apply to half their income. Yes, stocks and investments can be held by all income levels, but in practice over 90% of them are held by the top 10% of the population, with half held by the top 1%, who generally only pay that 15% tax on any earnings that they cannot successfully hide away via loopholes and criminal dodges.

The sixty-chip group also utilizes tax shelters and deferments, however, we're going to assume our students here are honest taxpayers making at least some of their money from actually working for a living. Therefore, we will adjust their total taxation to a round 25%. This is still far less than their secretaries and maids pay, but it is at least something."

I don't mind admitting to you that I was starting to lose track of the numbers, even though they were on a chart in front of me. However, hearing that the lucky ducks also weren't paying as much taxes as the rest of us brought my attention right back. I hadn't heard of investment income being referred to as "business gambling," but since I knew the whole point of investments is that you buy them based on uncertain chances of return and hope you hit a jackpot, that sounded like a fair analogy. That's why some of us thought it was so unfair for the government to use taxpayer money to bail out investment firms instead of making them take responsibility for their own bad bets. I blinked some more at the charts, trying to figure out how the taxes all added up for each group, so I'd be ready to pay my share.

Fortunately, Dr. Michaels didn't expect us to do our own calculations. "Don't worry about doing the math, I'll be keeping the taxes before handing out the income. Again, doing some rough smoothing, this means the total Payroll and Income Tax burdens are as follows for the income brackets, by income chips. Two: 20% rounded to half a chip, leaving one and a half chips for daily income. Four: 25% for one chip, leaving three. Six: 30% rounded to two chips, leaving four. Ten: 36% rounded to four chips, leaving six. Twenty: 35% for seven chips, leaving thirteen. Sixty: 25% for fifteen chips, leaving a measly forty-five. Jazmine, please help me hand out these pay packets."

Mitch had been jotting notes next to me, and a moment after Dr. Michaels finished speaking, he raised his hand with a mischievous grin. When acknowledged, he asked, "So that means that the two top earners are 5% of the entire group, but are shouldering an entire 22% of all taxes collected. Hardly seems fair, does it?"

Several people turned to glare at him, since it was obvious he was going to be one of those top two. However, Dr. Michaels only arched an eyebrow as he began handing out the packets, not even slowing as he wryly replied, "Given that the top two take in 29% of the pre-tax income but keep 32% of the total after-tax income, no, it doesn't seem very fair. You and Cassandra are making out pretty well from Success Poker."

I looked across the room to the student I hadn't noticed before, a young woman who was studiously organizing a large pile of chips as though it helped her block out the sudden attention. I felt a little bad for her, as she seemed extremely embarrassed by the whole thing. Jazmine then paused before Mitch to drop a heavy packet of chips onto his pile, then a smaller one onto mine. I opened it up and was both happy and surprised to find that I had gotten four chips. My initial delight faded just a bit though, as I thought about the way the game was set up. By the current system, my success in stepping up from my starting position meant that someone else had to drop down from theirs. There was just such a smaller group of chips left over from Mitch's and Cassandra's piles, for the rest of us to split...

The next part of Dr. Michaels' presentation didn't cheer me up. "These chips are now your currency here over the next week. You'll use them to purchase your sleeping arrangements and food, and if you have any left over, rent entertainment, purchase extra amenities, and so on. These prices already include the 10% sales tax, another tax that everybody pays, even the desperately poor."

He brought up a price list showing a list of activities and amenities, and I started to run a mental tally of what was up there. With what I had, I could afford a bunk bed with bedding, in a shared cabin with a ceiling fan, along with use of the kitchen and basic groceries to cook my own meals. I'd even have enough left over to rent a little time in the Recreation Hall to use the computer, or something equally trivial that was cheap enough the 10% sales tax didn't put it out of my reach. I'd have to make do with the basics, but since I was used to having to share the same or worse, that didn't bother me a bit. I wouldn't have any savings, but unless something changed I wouldn't need any. All in all, I felt I'd made out pretty well.

So I started to look around the room and saw that not everybody was looking quite so pleased with the arrangement. And some of them started making their own assessments of the different piles of chips on the tables.

At this point, Dr. Michaels led to my first real lesson in participatory democracy. "I can see that you've all had enough time to study the price list. Some of you are going to really be able to splurge, but you'll have a hard time spending more than ten chips a day here. However, you'll need to spend three chips a day to meet the barest necessities of a sleeping bag and microwaved frozen meals. That leaves five people having just enough to throw in a pillow or a snack, five people barely scraping by, one person with half of what's needed, and one person with none of it." Jazmine was sitting back at her chair, staring at the board, and I wasn't sure what the plan was for her.

"Unfortunately, we can't afford any further food and housing subsidies for these individuals, because we've already spent our tax chips." He swirled his hand around in the tax basket, the chips making a clink-clattering sound. "The twenty-five from the Payroll Taxes immediately go to the CareFund to help pay for medical services to the elderly, and to the Public Pension for retirement or disability for those who'd paid Payroll Taxes in the past. The Income Taxes are allocated out for the rest of our governmental costs. Forty-six go to the Military and the Domestic Security Services to pay for their own equipment and personnel, and for that of their legions of private contractors. Twenty-seven go to pay interest on our bonds and outstanding debt. Nine to Agricultural subsidies and administration. Eight to the care and benefits of our Military Veterans. Six pay for temporary unemployment benefits and jobs training, four subsidize the private schooling businesses, four pay for our transportation infrastructure, and the rest go to various budget miscellanea."

He then leaned back against the table, setting the basket back down. "We do have the option to change our tax structure to afford more basic-needs subsidies. We had planned for you to pre-vote on the tax structure you favor, but a mix-up kept the ballots out of your acceptance packets. It was therefore decided that we'll see how the group determines the tax structure after having seen for yourselves the people behind the income levels, and how they arrived there. This also might allow you to circumvent the Optimist's Fantasy fallacy, which causes many people to vote not in accordance to what would benefit their actual situation, but what they imagine their situation could become. For example, many people vote for their own tax burdens to be increased while reducing that of the wealthy, believing that some day they will become wealthy and therefore benefit."

As a few people started fiddling with their chips, he gestured to the room. "So, do we have any proposals on how you may wish to address the issue of one person receiving half the barest costs of living, and one with no appreciable income?"

Mitch raised his hand, and asked, "Isn't there a way those people can earn more money, just like in the real world?"

Dr. Michaels smiled. "If this were just like the real world, 'those people' are usually already filling every available hour with tasks necessary to support and maintain their family. However, here we can allow students to hire other students to do chores for them, adding on payroll and income taxes to their wages, of course. That is, of course, presuming that nobody here is planning to take advantage by hiring them illegally."

Before Mitch could respond, a guy across the room had raised his hand to speak up. "I don't think we should be taking advantage by hiring them at all. Isn't the whole point of this camp to spend time getting to know each other? How can two of us get time to do that if they're busy doing chores so others can have more time to goof off?"

The gal next to him then chimed in, "Hey, isn't there supposed to be a minimum wage? If the poor are working so much, shouldn't that automatically put them up to three chips or even more, if that's what we need to scrape by?"

Dr. Michaels nodded to both of them. "Excellent points. Yes, we'd intended the camp to provide each of you with equal opportunities to learn from each other. As to the minimum wage, at full-time hours it will only give a person half what's considered the minimum needed to get by. While the minimum wage has seen only a 20% increase in its value in the last twenty years, living costs have risen over 80%. Whenever there's a discussion about raising it, the usual suspects trot out with their nightmarish predictions of inflation and unemployment, delaying the needed increases. When municipalities have increased it anyway, history has shown their economies prosper with increased productivity and lower unemployment, with those same doomsayers leading the hiring and business expansions without so much as an Oops I Was Wrong."

He shook his head, and I made a mental note to look into some of that history myself as he moved on. "In any event, paying someone at least the cost of living is called a living wage. Companies aren't required to offer a living wage, and in general they only do so to people who already have plenty of other options. In most cases, people are desperate enough for work they are forced to take whatever is offered them. That is part of why there are those who suspect there are employers who support so-called Crisis Capitalism, keeping workers in an imbalanced state so their desperation may be capitalized on."

He sighed briefly. "Regardless of motivations, the reality is that it takes so long to overcome the numerous political barriers to raise the minimum wage that by the time it is raised, it is already too little to bring workers above the poverty threshold. As a result, people still work full-time and starve full-time. We'll need other solutions."

Another person raised her hand. "Okay, so we need to raise three chips a day for Jazmine, plus one and a half for the other person making less than three. So we can round it up to five. And I think we should find a way to do it, too. They have just as much right to enjoy this camp as we do, right?"

She was answered by the first guy, who turned around to face her. I remember his tag saying his name was Brynden. "If they only get three a day, they can only afford to eat and sleep at the camp, not to enjoy it. Since there's five people getting a mere three chips already, why not set a goal to bring everybody to a minimum of four? So that'll be twelve a day we need to raise. Doctor Michaels, what will we get if we go ahead and apply the Payroll Tax to all income equally instead of giving special treatment to the rich?"

Dr. Michaels grinned. "As a matter of fact, that would virtually eliminate the projected shortfalls the programs are continually faced with as a result of the politicians raiding them to fund pet projects for their cronies and backers. However, the Payroll Taxes go to specific funds that are on entirely their own budgets, so those won't help with food and housing subsidies."

Brynden paused to consider, then piped up again. "Well then how about the long-term Capital Gains Tax? Look, I don't mind admitting I'm a Twenty Chipper here, and I know my folks get some good money from their investments. They game the tax system to get a bigger piece of the pie, and they know it. But if you raised the taxes on their long-term investments, they'd still invest because they like making money. History proves that they're not alone, since that tax rate has been up and down while long-term investment trends continued going up without any statistical blinking. I say let's raise the Capital Gains Tax by 50%."

"There's actually a very simple micro-tax proposed that would surcharge but a tiny portion of a percent for each investment transaction, which would barely be felt by investors yet allow us to lower the income taxes on the poorest as well as increase housing subsidies enough to reach your goal. Incidentally, if we also had the means to prevent the largest corporations from using their own loopholes or outright deception to avoid paying their own taxes, that would enable us to eliminate income taxes on the poorest. However, as that's outside our system here, let's see, your proposal would run us..." Dr. Michaels ran a quick tally. "Yes, that would put the Capital Gains tax at 23%, which would raise the top two's taxes to 29%, costing them two and a half a piece, to raise five a day."

Mitch had started grumbling at the beginning of Brynden's latest speech, but had quieted by the end of it. He quickly raised his hand to speak up, "Well, since that will take care of Jazmine and that other guy, I guess we can do that and wrap this up." I glanced at him, surprised he conceded so quickly. But then I saw the kind of look in his eye I've come to recognize in Richard's, and I suspected he was trying to accept a deal he didn't like in hopes of staving off a worse one.

Before Dr. Michaels could respond, Cassandra finally looked up, raising her hand to quickly interject. "Wait, no, five isn't enough. There's no reason that everybody can't enjoy this camp and get to know each other, not when you and I are just sitting on these dozens of chips we'll never be able to spend. Why not just count long-term Capital Gains investment returns like all the other kinds of money everybody else makes and has to pay taxes on? I mean, we don't even work for it, we just invest it and collect the profits."

Naturally, Mitch had an answer, and again with condescension worthy of Richard. "It's not as simple as that. This is supposed to represent the real world, right? Money is the material reward for productivity, and as the most productive members of society, we have a responsibility to take care of our wealth. Incentives for keeping it in long-term investments encourage us to power the economy, creating jobs and keeping this country going. After all, we already have to pay corporate income taxes on what our companies make, so in essence we're subject to double taxation. We can't let tax-and-spend Pragmatism take our hard-earned money to redistribute it to layabouts who haven't been bothered to learn the value of a hard day's work. The government just keeps throwing money away on handouts to special interests and the unproductive segments of society, sucking it out of the hands of the Jobsmakers."

Brynden responded with a loud scoff. "Are you serious? Are you honestly claiming that you're rich because you personally went out there and worked 30 times as hard as that guy over there? No. That guy over there worked his tail off so you could collect the fruits of his labor from the ease and comfort of your daddy's Mutual Fund. And don't you dare claim that corporations shouldn't be taxed like people, like you're one of those who think corporations should enjoy all the rights of personhood but none of the responsibilities. Businesses have been shedding jobs like they've got mange, leaving only the overworked, underpaid building and service jobs they can't ship overseas. That is, until they got America so hungry and desperate we became the next dumping ground for dirt-eating sweatshop labor. Productivity has doubled in America but real wages and purchasing power has plummeted for everybody but us lucky ones at the top. Meanwhile, our outsized slice of the pie keeps growing as our tax rates drop like gold bricks."

He smacked his hand on the table, pleased with his own metaphor. "That's where your deficit comes from, by the way, our failure to pay back in wages and taxes some of the disproportionately huge benefits our upper class leech-and-hoard tactics have gotten us from the hard work of our fellow Americans. Half the country is barely making it if they're making it at all, while we're making out like bandits. That's not only unfair, it's stupid, because they've got a lot to offer America if they are just given the chance. It's not about handouts, it's about offering people a hand up so they can get up on their feet and lend a hand in getting this economy going again. These people would be more than happy to pull themselves up by their bootstraps, if we would just let them scrape together enough shoe leather to make themselves boots. But because some people are hoarding all the leather, there just aren't enough boots to go around."

Mitch waved away Brynden's words with an imperious motion of his hand. "You're just talking about giving truckloads of fish to people who won't bother to go out there and bait their own hooks. You can't reward people just for breathing and expect them to lift a finger to support themselves, not when they can get everything they need for free. It's the natural inclination to do the minimum required to get by. That's why we have all these people getting fat, dumb and lazy collecting unemployment checks instead of going out there and getting a job."

People were starting to shift in their seats, but Brynden's laughter rang out before anyone else could interject. "You mean as opposed to the fat, dumb and lazy rich people doing the minimum required to keep leisurely coasting through life? It's the natural human inclination to always be reaching for more, which is why we keep trying to get richer and richer instead of settling down as soon as we have enough to feed and clothe ourselves. People out there work their fingers to the bone just to get a shot at a slightly better future, so don't give me that smug superiority complex. The truth is that people don't have jobs because there aren't enough to go around. When there's five or ten or sometimes even a thousand applicants for every opening, saying someone can't find work because they're not trying hard enough is either self-righteously ignorant or selfishly cruel. Which are you?"

The tension was cut through by a very deliberate clearing of Dr. Michael's throat. "I think the rhetoric has gotten a little out of hand. Let's remember that civility is a small price to pay for a civil society."

After Brynden mustered an apology, the professor went on. "Despite getting carried away, Brynden is surprisingly well-versed in the general economic trends. Ah, yes, you're the Sociology major; hopefully you'll go on to share more facts with the world than insults. As a quick correction on the deficit, loss of tax revenue due to drops in jobs, wages and other income only accounts for 28% of the drop from

America's formerly projected surplus to our current deficit, and tax cuts account for another 21%. The stepping up of the wars in Arabiya and elsewhere make up 15%, and the increase in net interest costs accounts for 11%. The remaining 25% is a mix of additional money given out as subsidies to financial, insurance and other industries, with a small portion of that going to programs to shore up economic shortfalls, and miscellaneous attempts to give a little boost here or there to private spending."

Dr. Michaels set aside the notes he had flipped open for help with the deficit percentages, then turned his attention back to the room. "One issue Brynden did not address, however, is that of jobs creation. Older and larger firms have shown significant losses in net jobs over the years, while net job gains are only seen in startup companies. Over 90% of these startups are created by the mid- to lower-end of the economic spectrum. The money held by the upper class has tended to be invested in ways that keep it traded back and forth among the wealthy, and also suck up more of the money from the non-wealthy via interest charges and fees for everything imaginable. This brings even more of the nation's wealth into that whirlpool at the top, rather than irrigating the broader economy."

Cassandra spoke up again. "So… not only are we not the jobs creators, if we're taking money away from the middle and lower bands, then we're stopping them from being able to create jobs, either. Which is why…" She trailed off, but picked up again before anyone had a chance to interrupt. "Let's go ahead and just tax our Capital Gains as Income, and raise the Income Tax bands to 40% on the Twenty Chippers, and 45% on what Mitch and I have over twenty chips. I think in real life I might suggest a 5% discount for everybody on long-term gains... But let's keep it simple. This way, we can make sure everybody has an equal chance to fully participate. Seriously, Mitch, we can afford to do the right thing here."

I couldn't understand why at first, but Mitch tensed up with what seemed like anger, as though he was taking this as a personal attack. He kept his voice steady, if only barely, as he retorted, "It's not a matter of affording it; it's a matter of fairness. You and I aren't really all that rich; it's not like we own huge companies or anything. My family deals in real estate, housing and offices the real economy needs. But if you start stealing from the rich or even those who have done well for themselves, like we have, we will eventually refuse to take it anymore. We don't have to sit here and be victims of class warfare, we can take our chips and go somewhere else. How does that fit into your equations, Doctor Michaels?" He clearly was trying to keep his tone civil, but the question still came off as a threat.

The professor merely shrugged, as though this was expected. "Well, we would lose out on your participation, which I was really looking forward to. But you do raise an interesting point about 'class warfare,' and the idea of an unfair redistribution of wealth. In the decades since the Resources and Austerities for the War Deal, the jobs and income for over 90% of the populace have vastly deteriorated, while the wealth and income of the elites at the very top have doubled, tripled, and at the very top, risen by a factor of ten. CEOs often make almost 700 times an hour than their minimum-wage workers, who aren't likely to be working 700 times less in that same hour. In fact, the income of just one of the highest-earning Americans is enough to rent safe, clean housing for every homeless person in America, even at the slightly inflated average single-occupancy rates. Many would argue that there is, in fact, a class war going on, one that the wealthy have been handily winning."

He then waved the topic aside as he moved on. "However, if you mean to ask purely economically, the loss of your wealth chips would remove substantial sums from the total chips available and tend to raise the value of those remaining. The income would be redistributed going forward, and our economy would adjust accordingly. Though it bears mentioning that in all practicality your chips are already out of circulation, as you're saving chips that other students would otherwise be spending."

This wasn't the answer Mitch was expecting, and it seemed like it only provoked him. I then realized that the discussion could have felt like accusations that he was a greedy and heartless evildoer. Since this didn't fit at all with his image of himself, of course he felt attacked. Like a fish in water, he was surrounded by his monetary and social advantages so pervasively that he wasn't even aware they were there. Or what it's like to try surviving without those advantages.

I couldn't think of any way to convey that to him, so instead I tried to hopefully smooth things over. "Mitch, I really hope you'll stick it out here with us. I know it might seem like people are talking about taking chips that are rightfully yours, like you're some kind of Robin Hood villain or something. But really, it's just a few a day, and you'll have dozens left anyway that you won't even be able to spend if you tried. And it'll make such a difference in everyone being able to participate. The more people can participate, the more we all get out of this opportunity, right? When the week's over, this all goes away anyway. It's not like we can take it with us when we go!"

I followed up with a genuinely hopeful smile, trusting that maybe if I could just acknowledge how he might be feeling, he might feel more like one of the group. I learned back home that when people felt part of the same group, they tend to care more about what happens to folks.

He seemed unconvinced, but since he dropped the issue, I counted it a step forward. There was a bit more debate on what to do, and a broad range of proposals on how we could cut back on the free tax loopholes to the wealthy to help the working poor keep more of their earnings to support themselves. Brynden even proposed a cut in the wasteful military programs that alone would allow us to eliminate income taxes on the poorest Americans. Some objected to raising taxes on general principle, of course, not even considering whether the benefits could outweigh the costs to their individual situations, let alone the group. There were also those suggesting a radically different tax structure, but things started to get muddled around that point.

Finally, Dr. Michaels brought Cassandra's suggestion back up. "All right, this has all been an enlightening discussion, we need to break for dinner soon. Since we are left with one coherent proposal that will address the issues at hand, let's put it up for a vote. That is, we set long-term investment gains to be taxed as ordinary income. Additionally, we step up the tax rates to be 40% for the ten to twenty chips bracket, and 45% for those chips over twenty. This remains far less than the taxation even a generation or two ago, but it will suit our needs. The proposal will cost the Twenty Chippers an extra chip each day, and the Sixty Chippers an extra ten. However, this raises the Income Tax revenue by twenty-six a day, or 19%."

Cassandra raised her hand again to amend, "Can I add to my proposal that the overage goes evenly to the bottom incomes, so everybody can have at least five a day? And the leftover, what, four and a half goes towards some kind of perk for everybody?"

Her amendment was tacked onto the proposal, and a vote was to be called by show of hands. As the professor was setting up the motion, however, Mitch leaned over to me and whispered, "I'll give you twenty chips right now if you vote against."

This shocked me so much, I only barely managed to keep my voice low as I tried to keep my eyes forward. Having worked for Saul so long, I knew exactly what laws that would break. "You can spend unlimited cash to persuade or even trick people in a campaign, but you can't actually buy a vote! That's just bribery. And it's still illegal, even today."

I heard his voice in my ear again, more earnest as the vote was about to be called, "I'll buy all your meals, then, no cash. Just you and me, spending time together. How about that?"

"My vote is not for sale!" My hissed whisper was louder than I'd intended, and I flushed red as people looked my way to figure out what was going on.

Dr. Michaels glanced at me with what I thought was comprehension, then firmly kept the focus on the task at hand and finished calling the vote. I voted in favor, and the motion carried by majority assent just in time to wrap up for dinner.

I tried to turn to Mitch to make up, but he tuned me out as he stalked out of the room. I looked back to the tables to see what everyone else thought about the vote, let alone my outburst. But folks seemed more interested in dinner than anything else.

I did, however, see two people who weren't rushing off. Jazmine was cautiously approaching Cassandra, who was paying close attention to getting her chips into her packet, too shy to look up. It could have looked like she was trying to blow Jazmine off, and my heart went out to them both. Without thinking, I went to introduce myself and see if they'd join me for dinner.

My own awkwardness almost stopped me at the last minute. But as I approached they both turned to me with such grateful smiles, I let compassion take over where courage failed. And I'm truly grateful I did, given how they would come to repay my kindness many times over.

Chapter 9

Only love is real.

"Jazmine, I've been meaning to ask you why... I don't know, it's just that you speak so well. That first day with Success Poker, why did you sound like..." Cassandra trailed off the way she does when she knows what she intends to say, she just knows it's not the way she should say it. So instead, she picked up her glass from the table and hid her lips with a drink.

Jazmine didn't take offense, and treated us to her sparkling laugh. "Why'd I talk like those poor folk from the projects?" As she mocked the idea, she had momentarily assumed the tone and posture she'd used when we'd first seen her, and rarely since. "My gramma's voice usually only comes out when I want to make a point, but in that case... Well, I was tired and I was mad, and I *felt* like my gramma. I'd taken a whole week off work for this camp because I need the free credits, even though that means I'm gonna have a hard time with rent this month. Sure, as a kid I learned to make it through school while homeless now and again, but it's not real easy to keep up, you know? Then there I was right off the bat being asked for my wallet, with money I didn't have."

Cass chewed her lip, and I wasn't sure what she was thinking, so I quickly chimed in. "You know it surprised me too, since I had no idea what they wanted our money for. And then to find out that you and I were set up to start with the same number of starting chips, but how differently the presentation turned out... Wow, what a way to start the week. And it really helped prepare me for all those discussions and group exercises about what Cultural Capital we each value in ourselves and others, and why. I felt like, having walked through that exercise, I had a real tangible feel for how we all were running the same race, but from different starting lines. Seeing how many steps ahead I've been given by friends, family and even strangers gave me a real respect for how far others have had to run. Okay, sorry, I'm doing it again, yammering on and on about... What I mean is, Jazmine, I'm really impressed with how far you've come. Your family must be so proud."

Jazmine set down her fork and pushed her plate away, her brow furrowed. "You know, it's hard to tell. On the one hand, my sister keeps telling her kids they should look to me as an example, to 'talk right,' and all that. It's embarrassing, but I love them and want to help them. Like one of the counselors said, it's important to be able to fit in with the mainstream out there if you want to be taken seriously. Right or wrong, that's true."

She paused with a sharp, short sigh. "But at the same time I want to be taken seriously at home, too. And sometimes I'll get treated like an outsider, like I'm disrespecting my roots by trying to be something I'm not... or not supposed to be, or... I just don't know. It's like, they're afraid that I'll lose my roots if I spread out my branches too far, or someone'll come to prune me back. I'm not sure where I'm going with that analogy, it's just..."

I put my hand on hers and held it a moment, giving her a sympathetic smile. "Hey, I understand. I'm the first woman in the history of my family to ever go to college, let alone have a job. They're all supportive, but I know they're afraid it will lead me away from them, maybe away from God. It's just that it's not a path they've ever walked, so they don't know where it leads and we tend to be frightened of the unknown. That's especially true when you feel the world out there is hostile to your values and identity, and might try to lead you into danger. So it's up to me to do my best to keep on the right path, and trust that God will see me through."

Cass blinked at me. "Really? Is your family that religious? I mean, you never really talked about your family." And it was true. In the prior week we'd become fast friends, but I'd spent more time listening to them and drawing them out than sharing about myself.

"Oh heavens, is my family religious. I'm actually—"

I was cut off by Dr. Michaels making an announcement at the front of the dining hall. "All right, it's time to draw our last lunch together to a close. I want to thank each of you for your participation this past week, and I hope you all have learned as much from each other as I have from your interactions. We have just one more group activity before we end the camp. We're going to be gathering you up by the color of sticker you've been wearing. Most of you have been congregating together, so you already know each other pretty well."

The three of us gave each other a disappointed look. We had hoped to spend the rest of the day together, but Cassandra of course had a green sticker, and Jazmine had a brown sticker. We actually thought the brown one was pretty tacky because only the black and Sudoamerican students had those, and Dr. Michaels wholeheartedly agreed that he should have overruled the person who put together the packets. He did, however, promise that we'd understand their intent by the end of the week.

"Those with red stickers, please meet in the chapel for a prayer circle. Those with blue stickers, meet in the reading room for a philosophical debate. Greens, please retire to the lounge for some after-lunch refreshments. Orange stickers, meet up in the workshop to lend your hands to a project. Purple stickers are invited to gather in the yard for a group activity. Those with brown stickers are instructed to remain here to clean up after lunch and then move on to cleaning the kitchen and sleeping areas. The rest of you may leave your dishes on the table and go to your assigned areas for further details on today's activities." After speaking, he then moved to go lead a group, leaving no time for questions or dissent.

As it happened, I had no questions, only dissent. I thought the whole thing was a stupid and transparent way to split us up, and had no intention of playing along. After watching in disbelief as Dr. Michaels left, I turned to Jazmine and Cassandra to complain.

But they were already gone.

Cassandra had gotten up abruptly and was halfway to the door leading to the lounge. Jazmine was near the door of the kitchen where others from her group were congregating. Her back was also to me, but I saw one gal moving to cry onto her shoulder. The exercise was hitting too close to home already, and I was more than a little angry. It didn't seem right, pushing peoples' buttons like that, since we *knew* so many of "the browns" were still relied on as America's underpaid clean-up crew, almost slave labor, no matter how hard some people have tried to change that, and more have tried to ignore it.

I was just wondering what I was going to do about it when Brynden tapped my shoulder. "Hey, Liz, looks like we finally get to hang out. C'mon, let's go see what this is all about."

I figured I may as well give the staff the chance to explain themselves, and followed him out to the field. Our group wasn't that big, and we hadn't spent that much time getting to know each other. We'd kinda filtered around among the other "sticker groups" during our leisure hours. Our staff group leader had been there for us, but we hadn't really relied on him that much. We liked him, though, so we gave him a shot at justifying the whole charade to our satisfaction.

He couldn't, of course, but at least we gave him the chance.

"Okay, I know you all are probably pretty curious what this is all about. I'm sure you've figured out by now that the red stickers are for the Zealous Christians, blue is for the Objectivist Intellectuals, the greens are the wealthy, the orange are the blue-collar kinda folks, the browns…"

Brynden interjected, "Are the 'brown' ones. What the heck is up with that anyway? You're seriously making them our slaves for the day?"

The group leader winced, but kept to the script. "What you may be wondering is what the purple sticker represents. This group is those who weren't too strongly group-identified with any one category. That's probably why you have intermingled pretty freely with the others. However, for the rest of the day you'll just have each other to hang out with. From this moment forward, you are instructed to speak only to those with your same sticker, and not to acknowledge those outside your group either verbally or non-verbally."

"That's ridiculous. I'm not playing." I spoke politely but firmly, crossing my arms. My sentiment was immediately echoed by the rest of the group, each scoffing in their own way with varying degrees of personal offense. We didn't have anything against each other, but by sticking together we'd be endorsing the rules by even appearing to follow them. We'd rejected ideological segregation in life; therefore, we rejected them in play.

So without even acknowledging each other in goodbyes, we split up and walked away.

The group leader didn't even try to keep us together. I honestly hope he saw our response coming, because it should have been expected. I'm not sure where everyone else went at that point; I think they went to go spend some downtime alone.

As for me, my one thought was of finding the lounge. Jazmine was a strong person and hopefully had a handle on all this, I thought. But Cassandra had seemed more fragile, and I was afraid she was feeling lost.

I got to the lounge and found the door unlocked, so I slipped right in. Cassandra and Mitch were sitting in a circle of chairs with a couple of members of the staff, playing some kind of word game. I walked up to Cassandra's side and said quietly, but sincerely, "Come on, Cass, let's go."

It was her turn in the word game, and as she hesitated I thought she was going to come with me. But instead, she kept her eyes forward, and continued playing the game. The staff member to the other side of me paused, and then took a pastry from the elegant plate on the table in the center, setting the tray back down right next to me. I later confirmed those really were her attempts to let me join them, but I wasn't interested. I didn't go there to get included in another exclusive group, I went there to liberate my friend from feeling like she had to be trapped in it.

So while the game continued without me, I pulled up a chair and kept talking. "Cass, I know you feel like you have to sit here and play by the rules, and I understand. Usually I'm all about rules because they help us know what the right thing is so we can do it. But these are wrong rules, and you know it. When the rules are wrong, following them is the wrong thing to do. Even though we only met just a few days ago, I already know you're someone who wants to do the right thing. It might be hard to stand up and walk away from this in front of everybody, I get that. But walking away is the right thing, and I'm right here to walk with you. I can't make you stand up, but nobody can make me walk away from you. You're my friend, and I love you, and I'm not leaving your side."

At that, she finally turned to me and hugged me, blinking back the tears in her eyes. Without saying a word, we stood together and left. As the door closed, I heard those remaining continuing their game.

"Okay, now we go get Jazmine, if she's still playing along." I took Cassandra's hand as I marched toward the dining area.

"Do you think she'll come with us? I mean, she was just saying about how hard it is fitting in, but not fitting in, or whatever…" Her reluctance was about more than just what Jazmine may want to do, that much was clear. But I didn't care, since I knew she wanted to try anyway.

"I think they should all quit, but we'll see what happens." We were at the door to the eating hall within moments, but as we stepped inside, we were met by Dr. Michaels.

He looked at us for a moment, then with a blank expression he intoned, "You two aren't supposed to be away from your groups."

I just shrugged. "Regardless, we're here to get our friend."

He shook his head. "You don't have permission to be here, and Jazmine doesn't have permission to leave."

"Nobody needs permission to do the right thing. One simply chooses the right path, and then faces the consequences as they come." Without wasting another minute debating, I took Cassandra's hand and headed to the back of the hall. Jazmine and a couple others were already there by the door to the kitchen, watching what was going on. I waved at her. "Come on Jazmine, we've got better things to do than play along with... all this." I gestured to the room in general.

Jazmine looked at us, then back at her group, then to us again. "I'm not going to leave all this work to be done without me."

Cassandra leaned toward me to speak with quiet uncertainty, "Maybe we can stay and offer to help or something?"

I responded a little more loudly. "No. I think it should be that either everybody helps clean up, or nobody helps. We've spent this whole week exploring how all human beings are created equal, and have equal rights to enjoy the fruits of our own labor. And how we can't let anybody push us around into treating each other badly, or treating ourselves badly on their behalf. And I seriously believe all that, with all my heart. How you treat somebody doesn't reflect their worth as a human being; it reflects your own. And this whole game is about treating each other badly."

Jazmine nodded at me, and then declared. "Liz is right. Nobody's putting any guns to our heads, here. This is just some ridiculously racist camp game. We're just so used to being kicked around, that when somebody hands us a boot we keep kicking ourselves for them. Well, I'm done with that. I've worked too hard to get where I'm at... That's it, we're going on strike. Doctor Michaels, you gonna stop us?"

Dr. Michaels just grinned at us. "I never said anybody was going to force any of you to do anything. I merely issued some instructions with implied social pressures, and left the rest up to all of you to choose whether to follow them. You may now choose to do whatever you wish, and so long as it isn't destructive, I will support that decision."

Well, the game was all over at that point. He sent another staff member to go gather up the rest of the groups, ending the social segregation so we could talk about the whole experience and what we'd learned from it. I'll be honest, the only thing I "learned" at the time was that I wished I had spoken up against the game at the very start, stopping the game before it began.

You see, that game taught me that Silence is Assent. When the world around you tries to throw up walls between you and those you love, or would love if you looked past those artificial labels... Well, it's up to you whether you agree with them or not. And if you don't agree, but just sit silent and let communities and families and even people be busted up over them, well, then you're participating. You let it happen. And that's why I still feel bad that instead of standing up in the cafeteria when the segregation started, I just shut my mouth and walked away.

Though in retrospect, maybe it was helpful to some people to really experience first-hand how much we're influenced by stuff like that, since it's not like we ever really talked about them. The rules of social interactions are learned behaviors that people seldom question, and that's how they get their power. They survive from generation to generation due to ingrained habit and the fear of facing some dire consequences for failing to live up to them. That's why people who stand up for love and equality are heroes, sometimes martyrs, and sadly are usually forgotten by the later generations they made possible through their sacrifice.

When the discussion ended, the three of us were glad the stupid charade was over, because we got to spend the last couple of hours of camp together. Cassandra offered to buy us dinner afterward so we could keep hanging out, but Jazmine declined.

"Sorry gals, but they've got me clopening at Sunnycups, and I'm already going to be a little late." She noticed our blank stares and explained, "That means I'm closing tonight and opening again in the morning."

I didn't drink coffee or even go out all that much, so I didn't really have a frame of reference for how bad that was. Cassandra, on the other hand, was horrified. "Wait… don't you close at like ten at night?"

Jazmine just pursed her lips and nodded. "Yep, and then we clean, so I don't get out of there until, well it's supposed to be 10:30 but usually it's more like eleven or so because the pre-closers don't usually finish their bit in the afternoon. Normally it would be a real imposition, cause the bus doesn't run that late and I gotta be right back there a bit after five in the morning before the first bus runs, and my friend with a car lost her job and had to move back home. But I have a friend who offered me a place to crash just ten minutes away, so I just have to put up with the cops or random jerks hassling me for being a black girl out on the streets after dark, and politely inform them the only thing this gal sells is coffee."

I shook my head slowly in disbelief, completely oblivious at the time to her last implication. "How can you be on your feet that much and then do it all again in the morning with no sleep?"

Jazmine shrugged with resigned amusement. "Well luckily, I got easy access to coffee to help me out."

Again I shook my head, this time more vigorously. "No, I mean, how can they *do* that to somebody?"

Her response was a grim smile. "Because they know we can't afford to quit, or even complain. We got no say in anything, Liz. We're just warm bodies to them, pegs to shove into whatever random timeslot is convenient for them. They won't even allow us to work full-time unless we're managers, even though many of us got kids to feed on minimum wage. And every time it looks like a group of us might be comparing notes and getting ready to ask for better pay or hours, we all get fired or our store gets closed. They may be famous for their ginormous cups, but their biggest grind is on their workers." Her words were harsh, but her eyes were twinkling playfully at the chance to poetically vent her frustration and weariness.

Cassandra didn't see the humor, her own eyes furrowed with concern. "But… I always go to Sunnycups because I thought it was, I dunno, different. They have these charity things and are always talking about doing the right thing, so I thought…" She trailed off.

Jazmine put her hand on Cassandra's shoulder and squeezed it. "Hey, I'm teasing, really. I mean no I'm not. It does sometimes seem like they care more about their image than always living up to it. On paper they have things like minimizing repetitive stress and trying to work out decent shifts, but there's not a whole lot of enforcement given how many lazy or just bad managers there are. They at least throw us a bone with some health insurance help if we have any money left over to pay for it, and if we're lucky enough to have a manger who will schedule enough hours to qualify. The people at the top really do try sometimes to do at least a minimum of right by us, even if it doesn't actually work out for those of us on the front lines all the time. I just have a bad manager, things will change soon."

Cass brightened. "Hey, maybe I could start going to yours! You know, visit you at work! Would that get you in trouble, or anything?"

Jazmine let her hand slip a little, and I could tell she was struggling to find words for her apprehension. I was sure she was nervous about some kind of super-strict boss, so I was startled when she replied, "You might not want to do that, at least until my transfer to the one nearer campus goes through. It's not that my store's in a rough part of town, but it's just on the other side of one. You'd be the only, well, rich white college girl there. No, I know that wouldn't bother you, and my regulars would welcome you just like anybody else... but it might bother some of my neighbors. Remember all the stuff we talked about this week, about how in your world, you don't always have to be watching over your shoulder, knowing that you're more likely to be harassed and arrested and sentenced like an adult when you're still just a child, then treated like an ignorant child when you're an adult? In my world, that's all so many of us have to look forward to. I mean, I couldn't even find an apartment nearer school until I applied by phone and fax using my middle name. Yeah, all the 'no vacancies' for

Jazmine were falling over themselves to rent to a Jennifer. There's still some deep racial wounds going on in America, keeping all sides so caught up in it, that it might be hard for some of them to welcome some privileged white girl going slumming."

"Wait… what? Even if I was just coming in for a cup of coffee and to say hi? Where did all that come from?" She was more confused than offended, and I didn't understand it any more than she.

Jazmine reached over to touch our friend's hand. "It's not you, Cass, it's just that my neighborhood, we're not really allowed to go a lot of places without being treated like aliens. Meanwhile, other people come bulldozing in, disrespecting us and our culture without ever even realizing it, just like we talked about this past week. To be poor and black is to live with daily little pings of random humiliation or even violence, with precious little recourse or even sympathy. Heck, even if you're rich and black you gotta remember not to run in public, be real careful being out around your own neighborhood at night, and bring out your extra-humble 'yes sir' whenever there's trouble. It all just sticks so deep in your soul, it moves you even when you want so hard to forget it."

She stopped with a deep sigh, then shrugged apologetically. "So anyway, my neighbors sincerely don't mean any harm and most of them would be real nice, it's just, I don't want you running into the one or two that would make you feel bad. Don't think we're all down on white culture, since the nature of things mean it's pretty much American culture, and we're proud to be American just as much as you are. But all the same, on the whole my neighborhood is just braced for the next round of trouble." Jazmine paused, apparently frustrated at her rambling that still didn't quite say what she meant to say. She was about to try another way to explain when a horn double-beeped. She looked up, waved to the driver, and then quickly hugged us goodbye.

"Hey, I'll catch up with you two sometime next week, promise. I better go. Take care!" She grabbed her bag and ran to the rattletrap, which sputtered only twice before roaring up and zooming off.

Cass and I stayed seated on the bench on the edge of campus, waving at where the car was only a second before. I laughed at Jazmine's comic exit, but stopped as I turned to see Cass wasn't laughing with me. She was looking down at her hands that were resting on the super expensive purse in her lap. "Hey, what's up? I can still go to dinner with you if you want. I'm on my own 'til tomorrow anyway."

She half-smiled without looking up, then sighed. "It's not that, it's just… I've never been so ashamed of my money in my entire life. This is even worse than when I first found out not everybody has two houses, and most people don't even own one. I planned to keep it a secret at school, but this whole past week… I even downplayed some stuff on the application, I think my family might just barely be in that 1% Doctor Michaels was talking about. Based on what he said about what they have versus everybody else. I mean, wow, I just had no idea just how good I had it. I just kept seeing my friends and my cousins who had so much more than me, like, I dunno, maybe the top 1% of the 1%…? Anyway, I kept focusing on what I didn't have. I honestly thought I was deprived because my grades weren't good enough for a top-tier school so I had to go to a state school, even if it is super hard to get into. And now I'm thinking, did I take the slot of someone more deserving?"

She bit her lip as her brow furrowed, then she shook her head to get back to the present. "I mean, I do remember hearing a cousin of mine once say, 'the nice thing about being a rich white guy is I can just be me without always being picked apart as an example of richness, whiteness and guyness'… But then when someone else said that he called them out for being a racist so maybe he didn't mean it. But I think I knew what he meant, even though I still always felt like I wasn't all that rich since I wanted things I didn't have. I thought since I felt like such an outsider from some of the super-cliques, that I was, I dunno, not privileged or something. So hearing all those stories about how much people struggle just to survive… Liz, I was just sure that people were going to be mad at me or mean to me, but everyone was so nice… well, almost everyone… and that just made me feel worse!"

I put my arm around her, gently laughing again. "Cass, you can't control the fact you were born with money any more than I can control the fact I was born without all that much. What matters is what we do with the opportunities life gives us, and how we use them to help each other. Come on, if it'll make you feel any better, you can buy me dinner anywhere you want to go."

I poked her in the ribs, which finally made her laugh. By the end of the evening, she had asked me if I'd like to move in with her since she had a huge apartment all to herself, and I was sharing a one-bedroom with Tricia and Judy. I was sorry I had to decline, since I knew she'd like the company. But the three of us had been looking forward to being roommates so much, and I didn't want to be the one to break that up.

As things turned out though, I needn't have worried.

Tricia got back to campus late the next morning, bursting right over with enthusiasm about Root Camp. I made us breakfast as she unleashed the whirlwind of her thoughts. "I was the only coder there from our state, and I think I was the youngest. Most of them were guys but there was another gal there, too. We were working on this project, about developing heuristics to better anticipate not just what someone is searching for, but why they're searching for it, and maybe figure out which 'what' would best satisfy a particular 'why,' even if it's not what they originally were searching for. It was totally fascinating and I figured since we were dealing with 'why's maybe I should apply some of what you taught back in the Teen Support Program thing, which by the way I totally hope sees more activity this year now that people are more used to it. Anyway, I was thinking about maybe having the program ask questions or otherwise open the door for people to teach you themselves what they're thinking, and also maybe help them learn how to search better. Or something, it really only just got started, I mean, we just started to find real places to go with it when the camp was over, and… oh wait. You had something you were going to say, I'm so sorry! About Kurt?"

She finally took a breath as I was serving her breakfast, and I laughed while she took a bite. "That's okay, I've missed you too. It seems like forever since we last talked! Okay, my news. At the graduation party, Kurt asked me to go out with him! Yeah, I know, finally! So we dated a lot before he had to go off to boot camp about a week or so ago. I've written him letters every day, since I think it will be like two more months before he graduates and I get to see him again. It's so… wow, it's just so funny how it feels like we've been dating so much longer. I really miss him now that we're apart. You know?"

Tricia watched me as I talked, chewing over each bite. Finally, she gave me a small smile and said, "Yeah, I know." She looked down at her fork and twirled it around in her food a couple moments before saying, "So anyway, at the end of the camp, Omneme offered me a job. They were the camp sponsors, and they said they've got training programs and deals with a local school and stuff so I could still get a degree, while I keep working on the project with them."

I blinked at her as I tried to take that in, and when she looked up with a big grin, I gasped and hugged her. "Oh wow, that's… that's really big, right? I don't actually know anything about Omneme. I mean, I know that we used their free online software all the time at the office and we use them to find stuff and all. But I don't know what they actually *do*. Or even what their name means."

I wasn't offended when she chuckled at me, because I knew I was pretty clueless. She didn't talk down to me as she explained, getting excited again. "Well you know that to omneme something means to put it out there for everybody to know about, right? So it goes viral? Or to find info that everybody should have access to? That's cause their name is short for 'omnipresent meme.' Omnipresent means to be everywhere, of course. And a meme is like, I dunno, a culture gene; it's an idea or behavior that spreads from person to person if it beats out the other memetic competition."

"Oh, wow, I spent the whole last week learning about memes then, and their selective value. And how having the right memes can be as important than having the right genes if you want to get ahead in a culture. Sometimes even more important." It felt super good to keep up with something she was talking about.

Trish was proud of me, too. "Yeah, exactly! So anyway, what they do is put out software and services and everything that helps people find the right meme or get their memes out there. Like email, and searching, and information and books and all that. And they do it totally free so it's available to everybody. I think they get some grants and stuff sometimes but for the most part the average person doesn't pay a thing for it, not even through taxes. They sell ad space and stuff so companies are funding it for the users' benefit. Isn't that like a total reversal of how life usually works? They even have the best motto, 'Create a better world.' It's a huge, huge deal to be able to work for them. I never thought I'd get this chance!" She was so excited, I found myself bouncing along with her.

And then, what she'd said earlier caught up with me. "Wait… so you'd be working for them, and studying in their own training programs…" My heart sank just a little.

She shrugged at me wryly. "Yeah… I'd have to move across country, Liz. I was really looking forward to starting college with you and Judy, but…"

I leaned over to throw my arms around her shoulders. "But this is the chance of a lifetime, Trish. You *have* to do this. Don't worry, we can keep in touch! I understand they have computers where you'll be at."

She laughed at my deadpan comment, then set her fork down to return my hug. After several warm moments, she said, "I'll write you every day, so check your mail. They want me to start as soon as I can, so I need to give them an answer. Would you be mad if I told them I could start next week?"

I shook my head. "Nah, classes start next week, so you may as well dive right into it. Wow, I'm still taking this all in. Judy will totally flip —" Before I could finish my thought, the room was filled with boisterous chatter as Judy herself came home, with Derek in tow.

"Oh good, I'm so glad you're both here! We have an announcement to make!" She bounced up and down, Derek's arm limply flailing along as she clutched his hand. He was trying to look embarrassed, but I could tell he was as thrilled as she was that... no, I'd thought, they couldn't mean...

"We're ENGAGED!" Judy shouted, then squealed with me in unison as I rushed forward to hug her and spin around with her a few times.

"Wow," I finally said, "you guys go to breakfast and come back engaged! How did that happen?"

Derek shrugged. "Well, I heard that the couples dorms were cheaper, and a quieter place to get some beauty sleep, so..." He trailed off, and was elbowed in the ribs by his newly-intended.

"Yeah, he's Captain Romance, just like how he proposed." She rolled her eyes sarcastically. "He asked me to pass him the sugar, and he'd hidden a ring on it. I actually didn't see it at first, so he had to pass the sugar back to me and tell me there was a rock in it! I thought was crazy, and then, well, I went crazy! Of course I couldn't eat a single bite after that, I was just too excited!" Just like always, she'd started off to chide him, and ended up showing just how endearing she found his antics.

"Wait, the couples dorm? Already? Are you two...?" It was my turn to trail off, as I was slowly picking up on what Derek had said.

Judy blushed, then seemed startled when Derek blushed even deeper and stammered something unintelligible at me. That made her giggle at him, before giving me an almost apologetic look. "Kinda... And yeah, we're planning to move into an opening in the couples' dorm. Derek's roommate fell through, and you and Tricia don't need me sharing your room, so we figured, well, why not? I mean it'll all work out great, don't you think?"

She didn't ask for my judgment about what kind of private activities I realized they'd been up to... merely my support. As she was my best friend whom I loved dearly, I couldn't deny her that. I hugged her again tightly. "Yes, it'll all work out just great!" I led the group back to the kitchen to cook up a more celebratory brunch, despite Judy's insistence she was still too excited to eat.

Soon we were all seated around the rickety old table, trading our hopes and dreams for the year to come. And in the back of my mind, I resolved to call Cassandra that afternoon to accept her offer, after all.

Chapter 10

Remember who you are.

As I mentioned earlier, the very first time I entered a college classroom was for the History of Science and Religion. Throughout the course, each chapter reminded us how religious leaders first condemned any scientific challenge to their dogma, persecuting or even prosecuting the person who made the discovery. Inevitably, the religious elites later co-opted the discovery and rewrote their sermons to explain how God had always shown them its truth. Throughout history, the natural world kept revealing itself, regardless of whether humans were ready to accept its revelations.

In introducing us to the class, the professor stressed that the religious leaders were also heavily influential sociopolitical leaders, so it wasn't just a matter of faith that got them so incensed at scientific challenges. Just like learning to close one's mind to one thing trains us to more easily shut out others, opening a mental door leads to more openness in general. Anything that caused people to question the authorities in one way might cause them to also question whether they were unerringly and unfailingly correct in other areas of life. Such questioning was something those leaders couldn't afford, not if they were to maintain utter control.

Those religious leaders maintained control in part by threatening the commoners with sermons that extolled the virtues of deprivation, and condemned the sins of sloth and greed. While those commoners scraped every day from dawn to dusk just to survive, the priests and their noble allies lived rich lives in gilded halls. Even if the common folk found the courage to question whether this was fair, as a rule they were too busy, too weary struggling for survival to do anything about it. Starvation, disease, disability and death were constants in their lives, leaving little room for rebellion.

Trying to picture the delicate balance that must have existed in such a cruel and troubled world, I got a real sense for why people would feel so desperately threatened by anything that would upend their fragile understanding of it. And not just the religious leaders who might have been afraid of losing their power and luxury, I mean all the common people who had to endure such lives.

You see, when we're surrounded by pain and deprivation, it's comforting to think that there's a sense to it all, a wisdom guiding it that will speak to us through the mouth of a person we can see and hear. Rather than feeling the stinging ache of being a hopeless, powerless victim of forces we can't control, it can be a great relief to instead feel as though our pain is in the direct service of the forces of the Divine. When we have such a scant comfort to keep us warm through the hard, cold nights filled with hunger and disease, we'll naturally fight against anything that may take that comfort away.

These are the thoughts that preoccupied me as I filed out from that first class. I tried to reconcile myself to how my own life might have been impacted by similar themes. Yes, I was raised to be ultra-distrustful of science and scientists, as though they were deceivers who would tempt us away from the will of God. But the prior year had led me to place a greater trust in the value of an open mind, and I knew there was a great deal of science that we already believed in as explanations of how God's Love manifests in the natural world.

For example, we knew that Galileo was right about the Earth not being the center of our solar system, but that didn't mean that God's will moved any less surely through the Sun and the Earth alike. We knew that animals and plants could be bred by nature or even farmers to evolve new features over time. You know, like how God made citrines, but humans bred them into oranges. But that didn't mean that God's light wasn't the first and lasting Spark of Creation. Since the olden-times church figures were able to adapt to a greater understanding of our world, however slowly. I was sure I could do the same. My professor had mentioned that he was a Christian convert, so I knew he had a religious perspective that he had aligned within his scientific experience. I was eager to learn from him how to apply these lessons to my own life.

Life has a simple poetry to it, you know? It has its rhymes, its rhythm and its meters, even if we don't always hear it properly. It sets up its themes and then twists them into a new perspective you would never have seen properly, had you not first been deceived as to where you thought the pattern was headed. Sometimes, it's the surprise of seeing the unexpected that shakes you up enough to really open your eyes. Oh, you can stop and pick apart and analyze any one word or verse from the poetry of life, but then you risk missing the point. It's the interplay of all the verses together where the meaning lies; to find it, you have to step back, close your eyes, and listen closely with an open heart.

I think if I hadn't walked into my American Government class with such an electrically curious mind, I wouldn't have caught on to the break in the rhythm of where I thought my life was headed. I can't put my finger on any one thing that prepared me for my creeping epiphany, but I do know that was the cresting moment before the realization finally broke.

I became enamored with Professor Gregor the moment I first saw him. He was the very model of an antique-looking scholar: not very tall, a little frail, and very soft-spoken. I mean to say, his voice was quiet, but his tone had the strength of someone who was going to say what he felt needed to be heard, without regard for whether the listener cared to hear it. That might sound like he was arrogant, but he struck me as the opposite of self-centered. He clearly loved that of which he spoke, and just assumed that we'd appreciate it too, if given the chance.

So I took careful notes as Professor Gregor shared the purpose of the class, about how he'd hoped to instill in us the same love of American Government that he had felt when he was young. Since it was a very basic required class and therefore not taken very seriously by the other students, I guess I tried even harder to show him I cared.

He spoke to the board on the wall as much as to the room, writing the topics we were to cover as he mentioned them. Things like the Declaration of Independence, the Constitution, the Bill of Rights, General Welfare, the Separation of Powers, Slavery & Emancipation, the Great Society, and so on.

I meticulously copied down his list, and I thought I felt my skin tingling as I did so. Professor Gregor was speaking with the air of a magician about to reveal a long-held secret, and I was anxious to learn the truth behind the arcane phrases. I'd heard of the Declaration of Independence, of course, and read about the Constitution. My Civic Duties classes mentioned them, though never really covered them in detail, only stories the Christian Schooling Network wrote down about how they came about. And even those were vague and not entirely accurate, as I was starting to learn.

Most of the rest was a complete mystery. At the end of the class, he expressed regret that he'd have such a short time with us. As this was to be the last class he would teach before his retirement, he felt moved to seize this opportunity to inspire us to learn the true beauty of

America and the strong foundations on which she was built. I don't care if that sounds corny to you, because it sounded so beautiful to me. I found it to be inspiring, and it awakened a genuine desire to learn more.

As students were leaving, I went up to thank him. "I just wanted to let you know how grateful I am that I made it for your last class, Mister Gregor. I never dreamed I'd ever be able to go to college, and I still can't believe I'm here to shake your hand. I'm so proud to be an American, and I'm super excited to learn more about our heritage."

And that's when I first felt the break in life's rhythm, the switch to the minor key. Something flickered in his eyes as he grasped my hand firmly by both of his. With an almost somber gravity, he quietly replied, "Young lady, see to it that you keep that excitement to learn new truths, no matter what stands in your way. That has been America's greatest treasure, though it's been all but erased by… Well, no matter. Just commit to memory everything I just outlined, so you'll always have a roadmap to the heart of what it means to be an American. Search for the true meanings behind those words, and they will lead you to America's true treasure, her heart of pure gold. No matter the challenges that lay ahead, if you remember who you are and stay true to what you love, you'll always know the right path to walk."

He then smiled a bright yet weary smile as he squeezed my hand a little more tightly before bidding me adieu. As he went his way and I went mine, I wondered what may have been lurking behind the strange gravity of his words and tone. I earnestly looked forward to seeing him at the next class two days later, if only to be reassured that I had merely imagined that anything may have been amiss.

The next day started off with me sitting through an introduction to the Scientific Method. The class was taught by a Teaching Assistant, who seemed less than interested in schooling a bunch of kids on what, to her, was self-evident. My interest in the subject was enough to carry me through, however, as I was curious to find out what I'd apparently missed out on. We walked through the basic steps: use direct observation and try to make sense of what you experience, form a possible idea as to what may explain what you observe, decide what the observable consequences would be if you were right, and then test those guesses by looking for the opposite of what you expected would follow. She stressed that while you can disprove your theory this way, you could never fully prove that your supposition is the most correct.

"It would be like saying… oh, I don't know. I declare that if I'm holding an apple, then what I'm holding will be red. What I'm holding is red, and therefore it must be an apple. But then it turns out I'm holding, uh, a tomato. You need to only go on what you specifically observe, and throw out your assumptions about what you think that means, but it doesn't directly show. You see what I'm saying?" She had asked the question rhetorically, as she was really talking more at the class than to us.

I chose to treat her question as earnest, however, and raised my hand. Surprised that someone was participating, she nodded to me. Quite sincerely, I asked, "What about when different people see the same thing, but come to totally different conclusions? They literally observe the thing differently?"

The TA casually waved her hand. "Oh right, the old Believing Is Seeing problem. Yeah, it's been proven that how we observe something is totally based on our different backgrounds and perspectives. It's called Confirmation Bias, a human tendency to see things as reinforcing what they already believe even if a different observer would see it differently. The Scientific Method involves setting controls to bypass bias as much as possible, but you always gotta be aware it's there. There's actually been research here last year into Confirmation Bias, where people wrote down their beliefs about something and answered some personality survey, and then read one of three random selections: something that supported their supposition with facts, contradicted it with facts, or generally talked about it without really supporting or contradicting."

She had been sitting sideways in her chair from the start of the class, but at this point she turned to sit straight in it, leaning forward to gesture with her hands. "The funny thing is, many of the people who read the bit that contradicted their belief with solid research, they came away more solidly firm in their old belief than any of the other reading groups. That'd been observed before, so this study was all into figuring out how that works, right? That is, what is it about these people that's different from those who are swayable to a new position when presented by contradictory evidence? And the key factors that came forth as the most likely determinations were how self-confident the person was before they came in."

I nodded in reply, thinking I understood. "So if they were pretty self-confident, they were less likely to be swayed by reading something that would make them question their beliefs."

She leaned back, throwing her hands up. "Yeah, I'd have thought that too! But the funny thing is, it was the exact opposite! It's got something to do with fear and discomfort in Cognitive Dissonance. That is, what happens when you're confronted with something that totally contradicts what's in your own thought processes. The *less* self-confident someone was, the *more* they were likely to come away from contradictory evidence even more convinced they were right all along. There's also the level to which they appeared to be open to new experiences, which also possibly involves the dorsolateral prefrontal cortical function, linking it to overall cognitive functioning and intelligence, but self-confidence is totally its own factor even contemplating correlations." She then shrugged at the mystery of it all. "I don't get how that works, but that's what they found."

To me, though, it totally clicked. Mentally, I was back in the Family Planning talking to Margie, and realizing how it felt to have my beliefs challenged. I rose to that challenge by opening my mind to new Truths I hadn't yet learned, but I could easily have gone the other way and rejected the discomfort by shutting them out. My old thought patterns could have gone into overdrive, carefully cutting and pasting and tailoring what she said to instead prove I was right and she was wrong.

After a few moments reminiscing, I offered, "Maybe it's because when you think you know something and you're challenged on it, it makes you feel wrong. I mean, it literally feels wrong. You feel validated when something supports you as right, and invalidated when you're challenged, I guess. So it takes a pretty strong personality to be able to handle that kind of pressure. If you have a strong self-esteem, you don't feel like you have to be right all the time. You can be comfortable with feeling uncomfortable, and so you don't have to shut down and retreat into what made you feel right. And if you find out you've made a mistake, you're okay with learning from it and doing better. You're not ashamed of not knowing something just because you hadn't learned it yet, so you can open up your mind to other ways of thinking, learning how to learn even better. Does that make sense?"

She had slowly nodded along with what I was saying, taking it in. "Yeah, yeah, that makes total sense. I guess I should go back and read that study more. Maybe we'll deal with it in class. Anyway, today's homework."

After writing down the reading assignment, I hurried off to my Research and Reporting class. I'd done a poor job of picking my schedule, as the class was soon after my prior one, but was on the opposite end of campus. I got there just in time, though soon I felt as though I needn't have been in such a rush. The class was dry and kinda boring, focusing on note-taking formats and how to organize those notes and so on, because our lecture notebooks were going to be part of the grade. But I figured they were valuable skills to learn, so I did my best to keep up some level of enthusiasm, hoping the class would prove to be more interesting later on.

I'm not sure I can say that class got more interesting, but I like to think I learned some good organizational skills from it. And I needed those skills, as I worked hard to to settle into my new routine and learn how to manage my course load before adding work into the equation. Saul had given me the first couple of weeks off from work, even though I was afraid he'd change his mind when Tricia resigned. Yet while he was disappointed, he assured me that she had done such a great job in setting things up we could continue on without her.

He was right, of course. It actually only took me several days to get up to speed with how she'd organized things, following her careful documentation and asking her tons of questions when I got lost. She said she was never comfortable being the only person knowing how to do anything, so she had tried to keep careful notes and walkthroughs of all her stuff. Since Saul's winning the nomination meant that he had the whole Puritan network to draw from in organizing voters, my role had receded to just managing the databases and keeping everything internal in order. He'd brought me to meetings now and then to take notes, but generally I was relegated to keeping the files tidy. Thanks to my extensive experience in organizing information from my years in the school office, this meant I could look forward to a pretty easy job that would leave me plenty of time for homework and, if I was lucky, socializing.

Well, if something else didn't come up to claim that time first.

I was just clicking into the new rhythm of things when I went to the office for a meeting with Saul and winded up being greeted by Richard. It'd been so long since I'd seen him, I'd subconsciously imagined him being much farther away than a campus just across town. His face lit up when he saw me, and I just barely managed to receive his greeting with a firm handshake rather than the hug he'd intended.

Saul seemed pleased at the thought of reuniting old friends, and quickly explained his purpose for meeting with the two of us. "Liz, you've really got this office running so smoothly that you've almost made yourself obsolete. Now I know that's far from true, but you do have some extra time you can spend on other pursuits. As it so happens, Richard has pitched a truly exciting opportunity for the perfect use of this extra time." He nodded to Richard, prompting him to take over.

The nod was returned, then followed up with a grin. "You're going to just love this, Liz. I don't know if you're aware, but the American Christian League finally succeeded in getting state tax dollars pulled from so-called public television stations due to their extremist Pragmatic bias and Anti-Christian agenda."

I quickly waved my hand, holding up the conversation as that latest bit sank in. "Wait, public stations are going away? But the public station was the only one I got when we were kids, it was sometimes my only entertainment. I learned the alphabet thanks to it, as well as words and ways of learning that helped me get my early start in school. Is that help not going to be there for other kids, at all? Ever?"

Richard just shook his head at me, a little too coolly for my tastes. "Oh no, there's still some good stations out there, even though they're called public. Their boards are guided by pro-business Pragmaticans who either lead strong corporations or their family does. In fact, the chairman of the nationwide public broadcasting coalition used to be chair of the Pragmatican party. Those stations will be shored up by business underwriters and the good sense to shake the hands that feed them. It's the ones who have resisted that guidance and defamed their potential business sponsors or pushed an Anti-Business agenda, those are the stations on the auction block. And that means there's a whole television channel right here in the capitol that doesn't have the means to broadcast anymore. So rather than let the airwaves go to waste, some friends of my father's are getting together investors to buy it up, and bring it back on the air to put our truth out there. There's a radio simulcast too, so people can be edified wherever they are, while they work, drive, anything. We're calling it Journalism of the American Christian League, with the call letters JACL. Isn't that just perfect?"

I furrowed my brow a little. I had planned to ask if an "Anti-Business agenda" was anything like a two-part series I'd once seen on exposing how much sugar we ate in our daily meals, but its second episode was pulled once the sugar executive on the station's board complained. Instead, I found myself blinking in confusion at the choice of acronym. "So you're calling it... 'Jackal'?"

He gave me an impatiently patronizing half-glare, half-smirk. "No, it's pronounced Jay-Seal, as in like it gets the Seal of approval from the big J-man himself, Jesus Christ."

The whole idea struck me as such nakedly arrogant blasphemy, I actually felt a little bit ill. "Do you really think it's appropriate to make that claim?"

Unsurprisingly, my question only increased his condescension. "Oh, Liz. If you don't go over the top just a little, you'll never get through to people. One thing my father has taught me is that the vast majority of people out there are sheep, bleating loudly at each other as they're busy jostling around to eat whatever they can find in the dirt. If you want to be their shepherd, you have to be willing to shout loudly and wave around a stick big enough to get their attention. It's not enough just to say we're going to try to strengthen the Christian voice in the barren wilderness that is the Pragmatic media, because they won't even know what that means. We have to show them that we aren't afraid to stand right up in their faces with the truth, and that we're the only source they can trust."

Now, make no mistake, here. I was raised on the doctrine that the news, entertainment and pretty much all other media was under the complete control of Pragmatics who had declared an all-out war on Christianity. The idea of a truly Christian news network should have appealed to that part of me who had taken in that "gospel truth," as it were... but it didn't. And I wasn't quite sure why.

Finally, I did realize one of the questions that had started gnawing at me, thanks to Saul's helpful interjection, "In addition, this will be a great way to get our message out in the lead-up to the elections. This is a local station, but we're on the verge of expanding as we speak. There's public stations across the state that are impacted by the funding cut, creating more opportunities for JACL. There's also several local stations nearing bankruptcy, ready to turn over their channels at fire sale prices. Since all we'll need to do to legally take them over is create some 'local' programming here in-house to pipe out to them, we can have full-time programming running full-steam ahead within a month or maybe even less. Soon, all parts of this great state of ours can benefit from our message, twenty-four seven, in plenty of time to vote."

That's when it finally hit me. This wasn't religious. This was political. "Wait, wouldn't that mean we'd be kicking stations off the air because they were too partisan, only to be replacing them with our own partisan agenda? To create the Puritan network?"

Saul leaned forward conspiratorially with quiet tones. "Well, no, it wouldn't seem right to have an official Puritan network, now would it? Puritan candidates such as myself will obviously be featured in stories and interviewed on shows, as we are in support of the Christian message and will champion it against the Pragmatic Anti-Christian agenda. But we don't want to get things muddied up by making it all political, do we?" His words stated "no," but his inflections and the gleam in his eye said, "yes, but don't let on."

In case I hadn't caught on to his true meaning, he leaned even closer and gently put his hand on my arm. "You see what I mean there? It's all about the framing, Elizabeth, how you put the picture up. People will see in that picture what they want to see, so long as you angle it so it doesn't reveal any distractions from behind the curtain."

As I was trying to assimilate all the layers of meaning going on, I felt a wave of hostility from Richard's direction. At first I thought he was objecting to politicizing his plan for a Christian network, as he was shooting Saul a very dark glance that only I had noticed. It subsided though when Saul pulled his hand off my arm and went to his desk for some papers.

Deciding to break through my sudden feelings of extreme awkwardness, I asked, "How does all this bring me into the picture? It sounds like the Foleys and their friends are handling all the paperwork. Do you want me to start scheduling your interview time, or something?"

Richard's face spread into a grin again, and I knew somehow this was going to involve him making yet another attempt to get closer to me. "Well, one piece the old station carried was a weekday show where students from the state college addressed college issues. We're going to have to replace it with similar content, which really is a great idea anyway. It's way past time somebody had a way to counter all the Intellectuals' Propaganda. I can anchor, but we'd need a student from the state college to co-anchor. Since you're currently held prisoner by that Ivory Tower, I figured this would be a great way to rescue you from its oppressive thought police. You'd be the perfect person to help us expose its Pragmatic foundation, and talk about the real issues students should be talking about."

Being asked to work with Richard, that I was prepared for. Being asked to work on television, though… That, I had never even imagined. I felt ill again. "Wait, me? Co-anchor? Shouldn't we get a journalism student or something? Someone who actually belongs on T.V.?" I wasn't just blushing, I was utterly shaken at the very idea, almost on the verge of a panic attack.

Richard shook his head at me, chuckling as he moved closer to me. "Oh, Liz, you do belong on T.V. You've got the poise, you've already shown you can handle yourself in the spotlight, and you've got the perfect image of a good Christian girl everybody would want to know more. And you can take my word for it." He then placed his own hand on my arm in emphasis, letting it linger.

My skin felt uncomfortably warm under his, and any response was delayed as I tried to find a polite way to demand he never do that again. I was so stymied, I think I actually jumped when Saul smacked a folder down onto the desk next to me. Relieved at the interruption, I turned away from Richard and picked the folder up to open it.

Saul sat down behind his desk and put his feet up, gesturing at the folder as I started to skim its pages. "The JACL news quorum has already put together the outline of what the first month or so of shows will be about. The stories will be all written up and put onto teleprompters for you, so all you'll need to do is read them off in front of the camera. The important thing is that you exude sincerity, which you've got a real knack for, a real knack. You wear your heart on your sleeve, young lady, and that really helps people feel what you're saying. That's what's most important right there, helping people *feel* the stories."

I looked up, distracted from the notes by what he was saying. "Feel the stories? You mean, convince them to agree with what I'm reading off?"

Richard chimed in, "No, we mean feel the stories themselves. People like to think of themselves as rational creatures, but they're not, really. Human beings are pretty basic animals, ruled by their emotional instincts. They react to how things make them feel, and then their brains come up with rationalizations so they feel like they thought of it all by themselves. That's basic Marketing 101; every successful business knows it and uses it. If you want your audience to be favorable towards something, you use words and expressions that make them feel good and safe. If you want them to be against something, you put fear and disgust into your face – especially disgust – and use words that train them to find the very idea repulsive. Then while they're routinely put into fear and loathing about something, you can follow up with a story on how our side can protect them from it, and help wipe it off the face of the earth."

I blinked at the very idea. "I don't think I could do that…"

Richard leaned forward again encouragingly, more than a little excited about the whole idea. "Oh, of course you can! You've got a beautifully expressive face that people naturally trust. You'll be perfect for it! Don't worry, the teleprompter will say what kinds of expressions to use, with stage directions and stuff. So you don't already have to know how to do it, you can learn on the fly. There's a whole team of people doing surveys and market testing to find out which words will lead people which directions, and we'll just use repetition throughout all our programs that will automatically help support your piece of it. And as we get our choice of key words and phrases repeated over and over, it'll be so ingrained in peoples' minds that ours will become the default message, both in the media and in their own minds. Control the message, Liz, and you control the mind. Oh, and there's no actual journalism you'd have to do, so don't worry about that. You just have to be your charming, natural self. You've got that good heart that just shines like a light in your eyes, and people can't help but want to get closer to it."

I nodded slowly as he spoke, then buried myself in the notes in the folder as an excuse to pull away from him as he moved closer again. It was scant comfort, though, as the more I read, the more my heart sank.

The pages, naturally, contained notes about the messages that the JACL team wanted to be accepted as conventional wisdom. The overarching theme was how an extremist Pragmatic agenda was brainwashing innocent Christian college students, turning college into "reeducation camps" that left them with a far different worldview than before. Each segment purported to provide evidence of this presumed bias, filled with buzzwords that I had already been trained to respond negatively to, like ideological dog whistles. There were things such as how Evolution had infiltrated the Science department despite being disproven as a theory, while Creationism didn't even get a mention in the textbooks. There were claims about pervasive discrimination against Christian or Puritan professors, with no more supporting evidence than one professor who claimed that was why he had been denied tenure and nothing about his actual performance in the classroom.

There were also purported statistics from a survey about professors who called themselves Pragmatic, including the numbers on how many thought that women should have access to birth control and counseling regarding options including abortion, that steps should be taken to protect the environment from further deterioration, that the government should do more to reduce unemployment, or even that lesbian, gay or bisexual students should be protected from violence or expulsion caused by peoples' objections to their sexual orientation. Actually, I'm paraphrasing based on the questions presented in the survey included in the folder; the statistical labels were "pro-abortion and Anti-Business environmentalists, big-government tax-and-spenders taking money from the wealth-creators to support bottom-feeding parasites, and homosexual activists pushing special rights for sexual deviants." The most inflammatory words were helpfully highlighted. Even I could see from the background material that the questions in the survey were leading questions, and the statistics carefully massaged to give the most frightening percentages possible. They may even have been fudged, I honestly didn't know.

By the time I got to the suggested outline of a segment decrying proposals for Affirmative Action and how it would lead to racist quotas that intentionally excluded white Christians and Puritans to serve minority special interests, I was trying to find a polite way out. It was all pernicious innuendo and sinister speculation, presented as straight-forward facts resulting from rigorously reviewed research. I was the one who'd been relegated to remedial Science and Research classes, and even I could tell the difference, once I paid attention.

Oh, I'll be honest, my very first impulse was a reflexive desire to submit to whatever task was asked of me, particularly by a man I'd respected as much as Saul. A year prior, I would have eagerly jumped at the chance to lead the Christian charge against a secular world on a mission to stamp us all out. I might even have thanked God for the opportunity to use any means necessary to fight against evil, even if it meant being the soothing facade behind which hid carefully crafted deceptions. In order to ensure that the light of my side vanquished the darkness of everybody else, I might've believed the ends would have to justify the means, because Good couldn't possible be led to use Evil to win. Maybe that wasn't what I would have thought, but I truly could have.

But by that time I had experienced so much, I couldn't see everything in such stark terms of black versus white… figuratively or racially. The road to hell truly was paved with good intentions, and it isn't always so easy to be sure in which direction you are laying the bricks. That meant you had to be extra careful in what you used to pave your path. After all, the means you use create what you'll have in the end. Good fruit cannot be had from a poisoned tree.

Saul could tell I was wavering, and I was grateful he seemed to misread the nature of my apprehension. "You know, I suppose this television thing is a lot to spring on you all at once. You put up a brave front, but you really are a sweet, shy thing at heart. How about you think on this, and let us know in a few days. You don't have to decide right now."

Richard was at my side again, his voice earnest. "I really hope you'll do it, once you've thought it through. You won't be facing this alone, you know. If you stumble, I'll be right there to pick you up."

I turned to him and saw something in his eyes that showed, in his own way, he really did care. He had always said he wanted to spend more time with me. And, as much as he was able to care for what happened to anybody else, I think he genuinely wanted me to succeed. Oh, in such a way as helped him succeed, sure, but even that level of consideration kinda surprised me. After all the ways I'd somewhat thwarted him about the whole Teen Support thing, he still saw me as on his side… envisioned me as at his side. Only then did I remember that I hadn't really seen him since the graduation party, and he was out of town after that. He was probably completely unaware that Kurt and

I were dating, so I wasn't even 'available.' But was that really the time to mention it?

Completely flustered by, well, everything, I was struggling to form any kind of response when Saul got a call. After answering it, he put them on hold to tell me, "Liz, you can go on home and I'll credit your timecard your full hours. You've got enough on your mind for today. No, go ahead and leave the folder here. I'll see you tomorrow."

I said a quick farewell and left, still in a bit of a daze. I tried to think things through, and then realized I should try to feel them through instead. If Richard and his crew were right, and people really did make decisions based on our emotions, wouldn't the wisest course be to first figure out how I felt about it? And then, once I got my feelings in order, weigh them against what I consciously thought?

That was when I experimented with a new way of discerning truth. Not upper-case Truth, such as the core nature of the universe or other deep matters. That was a little beyond what I was feeling up to, after a day like that. I mean regular truth, every-day guesses at the right thing to do or say, or think or feel, that wind up leading us closer to our better path.

First, I came to accept that, yes, I did let myself be led by my feelings. I already knew this, thanks to all the times I'd prayed and opened my heart for what I'd felt was the answer. I believe in Intuition: those feelings we can't explain. There's so much more to us than the sparks flying around inside our brains, and I consider that "something more" to be our divine soul. Other people might just call it the subconscious, and that works, too.

Whatever you name it, though, there is a part of us that's greater than what we can directly measure, which assimilates and reflects on things around us we don't consciously notice. It connects the invisible dots, and feels its way through the patterns it perceives are there. When Intuition shares those connections with us, we feel them as sudden insights that rush through us as though from nowhere.

Next, I recognized that while we can't isolate ourselves from our feelings, we can work around them if we accept them honestly. I don't mean we can completely subvert them or push them aside. Things left in darkness don't go away, they just keep working in ways we can't see. Instead, I mean we can explore why we feel the way we do by using our Reason to examine what we know, and what we might know that we hadn't noticed before. We can search out and consider new approaches, weighing as many sides as we can find as we try to build a better picture. We can Reason through the pros and the cons, ascertain the most likely outcomes, and choose what appears to lead to the best results.

Finally, I started to find the point of synchronicity between feeling and thinking, that place of harmony where the one touches the other. After a long evening of wrestling between my mind and my soul, I came face to face with my idea of Wisdom. I felt that Wisdom wasn't just feeling something, and it wasn't just thinking it. Rather, it was what you get when you weigh both your feelings and thoughts, then put them together and see where they intersect. Where Intuition and Reason converge, there is Wisdom.

So, with this epiphany fresh in my mind, what did wisdom say was the right path? Should I walk away from what felt like a sneaky plan, or should I take advantage of the opportunity to speak to people, even if initially it wouldn't be my own words?

I still hadn't the slightest idea. When I had arrived to the door of the apartment, though, I saw I had plenty more time to think about it.

The welcome mat had been taken inside. That was Cassandra's super-secret sign that she had a boy over, and they needed some privacy. And believe me, they didn't need to tell me twice to find somewhere else to be. Yes, it did still bother me a little that she had boys over like that, as I thought it was a huge mistake. But she seemed pretty happy, and the ones I'd met seemed nice enough, so I figured if it was a mistake, it was hers to make.

She seemed to be making it pretty mindfully, though. She assured me none would stay the night, she'd only be alone with boys she'd gotten to know, and she wouldn't ever consider having alcohol without her smart friends around. Her aunt had given her this bracelet with a wireless police alarm with a trigger just in case there was trouble, which she always wore when she went out. Cass and Jazmine also used to talk about how they wouldn't waste their time on any guy who didn't care whether they had a good time, and would even kick him out in the middle of the date. I did feel better knowing she expected to be respected, since I knew girls who just wanted to make sure the guy liked her and didn't feel like they had any right to ask for, uh, attention that made them feel, ah, appreciated, and wouldn't speak up if...

Well, you get the idea. I wasn't worried for her, and it was her apartment to use any way she liked, since she wouldn't let me pay rent. Even so, I would have liked someone to talk to, maybe hear what I was thinking by saying it out loud.

Finally, I remembered Professor Gregor, and how on that first day of class he'd given me such heartfelt advice. Remember who I am, and stay true to what I love, and I'd know the right thing to do.

I brought those words of wisdom into my own heart, and realized I didn't really know who I was. I had always thought I did. I envisioned my whole identity as being a Christian Puritan out to save the world from itself in Jesus' name. But then the world kept finding a way to save me from my own ignorance about it, gently and lovingly showing me new insights about myself. I found myself dearly wishing I could talk to Professor Gregor about my dilemma, that his wise experience could help guide my decision.

Oh, that's right, I forgot to tell you, didn't I? That first class wasn't just Professor Gregor's last course, it was literally his last lecture. My eagerness for the second class was crushed when I found he had been replaced by a new, much younger professor. The man told us that Gregor was suffering from poor health, and had to retire at the beginning of the semester, rather than the end. He then proceeded to elaborate on the mysterious outline from the first class, explaining that the Bill of Rights indicated the costs paid to preserve our rights, such as observing the laws and supporting the Military and always being on the lookout for Spies and Espionage. The General Welfare referred to the well-being of America as created through a strong economy led by its most successful business sectors so we could win the fight against Communism. As a result, we enjoy this Great Society that is the best, most free country in the world.

I don't quite remember how he'd explained away the Separation of Powers, but I do remember that he'd completely glossed over the sections on Slavery & Emancipation. In that regard it was no different than the rubbish I'd been told in high school, depicting happy, hard-working laborers who were generously taken care of by their landowning so-called "masters," only to give rise to indolent descendents who expected handouts just because their ancestors were slaves.

Disappointed that I wasn't learning anything new, I'd tentatively asked if we'd be reading excerpts from the Constitution in class. The professor then sharply reminded me that the text of the Constitution had been declared a State Secret, so that its contents couldn't be used by accused Spies as loopholes to evade prosecution and punishment. The class hadn't gone ten minutes into its carefully arranged litany before my skin itched and my blood felt cold, though at the time I tried to brush it all off as sheer disappointment.

Yet while I wandered around the swimming pool in my apartment complex, I recalled that second class and again felt those chills. I realized that something must have gone dreadfully wrong for Professor Gregor. There was a deeper meaning behind the things he had shared, a hidden treasure regarding the history of America that has been buried away. He knew what that deeper treasure was, and saw that class as his last opportunity to pass along clues that it even existed, even if he didn't have the chance to give us the treasure map.

The chills deepened to a tremulous shiver when I realized that I had no way of guessing where he gone to, as he seemed thin but strong, rather than ill enough to give up the profession he loved so deeply. Was he politely given his walking papers for breaking his silence about those things he shared, allowed to go off early to whatever way he was to spend his twilight years? Or was he taken away to… wherever it was they would take old professors more dedicated to their profession than fear of the DSS?

After a prayer to God to comfort and preserve him for his courage, I knew in my heart what my own decision would have to be. I was being asked to compromise my integrity and participate in a coordinated deception. Worse, they wanted to use my sincerity and integrity to entice viewers to want to believe in the half-truths and full-lies, deceiving themselves on our behalf.

But how could I decline without burning any bridges? I still wanted to work with Saul. Even though I thought this was a bad idea, I could understand why he would be tempted to follow the Foleys' lead, as I once had been. He wanted to get his message out, and the JACL must have seemed to him a perfect way to do it. But I also didn't want people to be deliberately misled. For a moment I wondered whether I should try to blow the whistle on the whole thing, but I knew that even if they were breaking any laws, I wouldn't have any proof. I simply hoped the truth would become known, taking comfort in words from the Bible: "Fear them not therefore: for there is nothing covered, that shall not be revealed; and hid, that shall not be known."

I then prayed to God in humility, asking that in the future, He only send me opportunities to which I could say yes. In return, from that day forward, I would bravely walk whatever path to which my heart was led, no matter the cost.

Just as Professor Gregor had taught me.

Chapter 11

There's time enough for everything worth having.

I'd like to say the JACL network stumbled and shattered without my stellar broadcasting presence, but they didn't really need me. They quickly found a highly-qualified female student from the Gold Quill Society. That was the fraternity and sorority organization that held all of the political power at my college. In fact, it was said that alumni from the Gold Quill owned state politics as well

Together with the American Christian League, they established the College Christian League, a student organization that quickly spread nationwide. By the end of the year, curricula were being challenged and professors were being graded on a "Christian Report Card" that had spread to colleges throughout the country. These grades were announced during the JACL college hour, shaping national conversation about the role of higher education in a way that sharply condemned academic freedom. When I heard the broadcast while working in the office, I felt chilling echoes of the recurring themes of my History of Science and Religion class. I was frustrated by how many people fell for their shameless fear-mongering.

What was even more frustrating was how effectively they used their push-words to make people feel warm and cozy about their dogmatic view of Christianity, but angry and fearful about everything else. While there had been a recent trend in the Puritanic party trying to reach out to those who weren't Zealous Christian, the JACL network was tightening the Zealous Christian hold on the Puritanic party line.

Even Saul had changed his tone in the lead-up to the election, speaking less about his "big tent politics" that would work toward the betterment of all Americans. Instead, his speeches had shifted focus toward protecting against "sinful" behaviors, which would be regulated and curtailed once he was in office.

And you know, that seriously bothered me. It still bothers me. Yes,

I cared passionately about my Christian values, but I recognized not everybody valued things the same way, not even other Christians. Maybe I had been deceived about the level of Saul's dedication to his own moral compass, but I knew that on some level he thought of himself as a guy who could be generous to all walks of life. He wanted to think of himself as intelligent and broad-minded: a Christian, sure, but one who worked to help those who believed differently.

So when the Saul I thought I knew started to sound like a dogmatic Zealous Christian on the campaign trail, I started to wonder if I ever knew how he'd truly felt, or if he had always just been saying whatever I'd wanted to hear. I had wondered whether he had converted to Zealotry, but sometimes I would hear him speak out against something, only to later champion it during his next appearance. I routinely attended meetings with him after a speech, in which he would contradicting his earlier words while talking privately with his more secular backers.

Finally, just a few weeks prior to the election, I came to recognize that the Saul Harolds who was speaking varied greatly depending on who was listening. I didn't want to question anyone's faith, so I struggled to suppress the suspicion that his Zealous Christian language may be just another rung in his electioneering ladder: a way to keep the growing American Christian League fighting for him.

The strategy was highly successful. Our district was declared a national battleground between two surging factions: the hardcore Puritanic Regressives of the American Christian League, and the hardcore Pragmatican Principalians.

The ACL was on a Regressive crusade to lead America back to their idea of "the good old days" that I wasn't sure ever actually existed. The Principalians campaigned to bring America forward to "a better future" that I wasn't sure was likely to come about. I had become skeptical of all politics, though at least I was wary rather than angry over the way the politics were unfolding.

The old guard of both parties resented the new sub-factions, as they were breaking the "unspoken agreements" of their old power structures. Both parties had established hierarchies, and maintained well-defined boundaries as to what causes were to be fought for, and how. The tides of change were surging, however, and not even the old party stalwarts could hold back the new vanguards.

I eventually wished they could, however, as the campaign rhetoric grew hotter and hotter from my side, prompting a more aggressive defense from the opposition campaign waged by Pragmatican Adam Diego. Once I discovered that my old acquaintance Margie Cammile was working for Diego's campaign, I wanted to find a way to apologize to her for how viciously her candidate was being attacked. I had nothing to do with Saul's rhetoric, but as his secretary I felt that I was associated with it.

Then I found out about how hard Margie and Diego were working to get out the vote in the poor neighborhoods my Party hadn't reached, and I didn't have the courage to speak to her. I was just too disappointed that she was doing what I had once thought to be my work, and I was struggling against the suspicion that the ACL had deliberately neglected an area that may not have voted Puritanic. When I discovered that the Voting Instructions we'd mailed to those neighborhoods gave them the wrong address and a date after the elections, I chose to believe Saul when he lamented that it was a tragic printer's error.

I was almost relieved that the acrimonious campaigning was almost over when Election Day finally came, even though the exit polls reported that Adam Diego had pulled ahead into a strong lead. Saul was unfazed by the news, encouraging those in our Election Night "war room" that he had been assured that victory would be delivered into his hands. At the time, I thought he was referring to his new-found Faith, and was comforted by the idea he was embracing it.

After a long, nail-biting evening, Saul Harolds was declared the winner by a razor-thin margin. Diego refused to concede and demanded a manual recount. He also demanded an investigation into claims of intimidation of minorities at the polls and other vote suppression techniques. For example, he pointed to the fact that ACL representatives took up posts at the polling places to personally challenge the eligibility of certain people and requiring they cast provisional ballots that hadn't been counted. The Pragmaticans and even some independent analysts insisted that if all the ballots were counted, including the mail-in ballots, Diego would have won.

On the other hand, the JACL ran numerous stories about Diego's camp attempting voter fraud by trying to flood the ballot-boxes with illegitimate votes from his "pseudo-American" cronies, a rather tasteless reference to his Sudoamerican grandparents. This was part of their push-word campaign, insinuating that those of Sudoamerican descent couldn't be real Members of America, even if they were in the CMDB. Those insinuations were refuted by Pragmatican claims that a sizable percentage of eligible voters were of Sudoamerican descent, but their votes were impeded or even disposed of.

Per the request filed by Adam Diego, several precincts began conducting a manual recount. As the early results started coming in, it began to appear that Diego may have indeed received more votes. For several days I became more and more nervous, while Saul remained as cool as ever. He hadn't told me that the vote counts had to be certified by his brother-in-law, or that the district court was presided over by an appointee and former business partner of the head of the American Christian League.

Within a week, that same court had demanded that all recounts be stopped in order to save resources, and so that the government of the state could move on to important business. The whole office was elated, and across the country the ACL and affiliated groups celebrated this as a major victory in the Regressive battle to "take our country back" from the "Pragmatican traitors who threatened to destroy the true spirit of America."

I was less excited. It wasn't just that I felt it was inappropriate to call other Americans Traitors and Enemies just because they had different ideas on how to make things better. I didn't feel Saul's victory was honorably won.

Though it had made me nervous, the recount was the right thing to do, and stopping it before it was over struck me as cowardly, dishonest, or both. If the will of the people truly was in favor of Saul, as we believed, then it would have done us well to have that validated through due process. If not, well, then we'd have had to try harder the next time to persuade people that ours was the better path toward America's brighter future.

As time wore on, I wondered at why the election machines would have delivered us one result, but close inspections of the ballots would start showing another. Apparently I wasn't the only one, but the question quickly became moot. The Puritanic governor decreed that he would push for a law requiring that all voting machines be replaced with electronic-only versions. In future elections, there would be no paper ballot, no confirmation receipt, nothing tangible to be verified at the time or later, not even by the person who cast the vote.

Given how often I'd heard the touchscreen voters telling reporters that they watched their votes flip to Saul while they tried to vote, that struck me as completely the wrong move. If errors like that were even possible, wouldn't we want to make it easy to catch and correct them, not less?

I was even more disturbed by how many people around me treated Saul's political win as a religious victory ordained by our God Almighty... including State Representative Saul Harolds, in his acceptance speech. He spoke of God as though He were Saul's greatest political backer, and that those who would speak out against Saul's work were aiding the Adversary. This rankled me, because I'd never met Diego, but I knew Margie was also doing her best to serve God, as her own conscience led her. I had begun to feel a creeping dread about how far those of my Zealous Christian faith were willing to go to do battle against those of different beliefs. This dread only deepened when I read what Kurt wrote to me regarding his early Military experiences.

I had secretly started writing little Thinking of You notes for Kurt before he left. I wanted him to have plenty of things to read when he started Boot Camp, so I compiled a collection that I would try to get to him soon after he arrived. When I went off to the Acculturation camp before Kurt called me at work with his address, I asked Saul if he could get my letters sent. Saul was thrilled that I'd asked for his help, and promised he'd personally ensure the delivery got the care and attention it deserved.

And oh my goodness, did it ever. Soon after I returned from the Acculturation camp I received a letter from Kurt about the big splash my letters had made with his unit. Though to be honest, his letters had an even bigger impact on me.

My dearest Liz,

You won't believe how great it was getting your letters. Of course it means everything to me to hear from you, but the coolest thing is how they arrived. Harolds sent them in a priority overnight mail package, which caused this huge stink at first from our Drill Instructor. Anything that stands out puts you on his radar, which is the last place you want to be. I'll explain more about in a moment.

The awesome thing is how as the DI started to lay into us about somebody thinking they're all so special getting some fancy-schmancy priority mail, he looked at the package so he could make some crack about who it's from. That made him stop and do a double-take! He was SPEECHLESS, something we never saw happen before or since. It made him look like a human being for one fleeting moment, and that memory has carried me through his constant abuse ever since.

See, what happened is that your boss Harolds used an envelope from the office that had his full name and retired rank, as well as the office he's running for. My DI read that all off and asked what I was doing getting a package from his old commander. He must have loved serving under Harolds because for that one split second he looked at me like I was a human being. I was honest and said, "Sir, letters from my girlfriend, sir!" He asked what you were doing at Harolds' office, and I answered what I honestly think: "Sir, serving our country, sir!"

Well I guess that was the right answer, 'cause he told me that I could have the letters, but I was instructed to write back and thank you for serving our country, and to apologize for what a sorry worthless mess I was, and all that other kind of garbage he's yelling at us all the time. But I didn't care. From that moment forward I haven't cared what he's yelled at me, because of that split-second glimpse behind his mask that reminded me his abuse is just one part of a big game.

Plus, that means that even though we were told we have to write our moms but if we write anybody else we'll be punished for wasting time instead of polishing something, I am under specific orders to write to you. Even though he only technically said to write you and thank you I'm taking it to mean keep writing you back when you write me until he tells me to stop. Guys are helping do stuff for me so I'll have time and not lose the privilege. In return, they get to put their letters to their girlfriends in the same envelope. If you can please mail them on for them I'll pay you back the postage later. It means the absolute world to us, and I mean that, so thank you.

Also thank you for sending several letters at once and then letting me know you were gonna be gone for a week, so I knew to stretch them out over a few days. I've been reading them out loud to my unit, after skimming to make sure I didn't tell them anything you'd think was too personal. I know I should have asked first but I knew you'd say yes, since this is the only connection most of these guys have had to the outside world. It's only been a few days but it's been hell, so letters are the one shred of sanity we have to hang onto.

Dangit, I better go. Didn't actually have much time tonight, so I'm sorry I won't finish this in time to send it tomorrow. I'll keep writing this over the next few days and make sure this gets out, hopefully before you're back from your camp. And thank you sincerely for what you're doing, getting people to vote and all that. I'm not saying that because of my DI, I mean it. It's freedoms like voting that we're all here fighting to defend. I love you.

Okay back, where was I going with this? Oh right, the hell around here. It will really help me to write this down so I hope I don't say anything that makes you feel bad. Don't, 'cause I'm doing fine, I really am. I'm serious that I really do think this is all a big game, even if it's a really hard game.

I first suspected they'd be playing games with us not just from stuff Commander Keane warned me about, but because even though we all were ready at the meetup point early in the day, we had to wait hours for the bus to come get us to take us on base. Supposedly it was running late. Finally, we didn't get here until after midnight, and we drove around in the dark for a half hour or more before we were finally able to pile out, get dragged through procedure, and collapse on our bunks. All the processing, everything was carefully choreographed chaos so we'd feel totally disoriented. You know, a big setup to get us feeling disconnected from our prior lives.

I really do think it was on purpose because you can't honestly expect me to believe that a Military that has a regulation way of doing every little thing down to wiping yourself doesn't have every last item on our schedule planned out to the smallest millisecond. They just keep us confused and exhausted, starting with that very first night when we got like four hours of sleep before they charged in to start our first day with banging and shouting.

Oh yeah, the shouting. Everything is shout shout shout in your face, every single last second of the day and sometimes right through most of the night. Supposedly it settles down after a couple weeks and they shift to reinforcing you for doing things right, but right now it's shout to tell you what to do, shout to tell you what not to do, shout if you do it and shout if you don't. Even if all you've done is just let the slightest twitch into your eye that might suggest you aren't having a truly miserable time, they're on you like fire ants. I seriously think they even keep a list of people they haven't hounded yet just to make sure we all get our turn to suffer.

It's like it's all designed to get us to make our every thought, every move and even every breath we take dedicated solely to please our DI and our DI alone. If so, it's pretty effective because that's the only way to try to avoid being targeted by his or the other leaders' sadistic tirades. It's not just the shouting, it's the nasty, insulting and humiliating things they're yelling, and making us do. They're completely controlling every single aspect of our lives and if one of us messes up even the tiniest blade of grass, we all suffer, teaching us that we're not ourselves anymore, we're our unit. It's a nonstop assault on your self-confidence and dignity, tearing you right down to the bare bones and then spitting and stomping right down to the marrow. They've shaved away literally every last thread and hair of our personal identity physically and mentally, trying to break us down to absolute mush so they can mold us like putty in their Military-Issued image.

I'm serious, we've already learned that we can't afford to hang onto anything that isn't Military-Issued, not even emotion. Like when we were in a long run and somebody just collapsed, and the DI stood over him just yelling all these awful things about what a useless pansy he was and so on, until eventually we realized the guy was dead. Apparently they're using us as guinea pigs and one of the shots they gave us, if you exercise hard in weather over 95 degrees, your heart could stop. Even though we were supposed to be all for one and one for all, we couldn't stop and grieve over our buddy, or even take time to process it, we just had to get back to the run and forget he was ever there. It's not like we got the chance to really meet each other yet, I don't even remember his name. But I know he has a mom, and maybe a girlfriend, and it really bothers me that I have to pretend his death didn't matter.

I guess that's something to think about as I try to sleep, since it's time to go again. Lights out, will write more tomorrow. I don't want to send this until I have time to explain more. Love you.

All right, another day, another soul-crushing rush of Shake & Break and Total Control. All day I've been thinking of writing you, though now I can't think of a specific thing I wanted to tell you about.

I can say that I think I really disagree with the way this is all being done to us. Still, it's having the intended effect on a lot of these guys. It's hard enough on me to keep it together, and you know how I go with the flow and stuff. I came prepared, and am pretty good at staying off the radar, so it's not as big a shock on me. But it's still hard. So I totally understand how some of my buddies have gotten their minds beat up all to smithereens and are already turning into totally different people.

Sure there's some more confidence but there's also scar tissue. They've gone numb to the pain we're going through and actually laughing at what the other units are suffering. This bothers me because even though I know it's more manipulation to get us to believe that we're not just ourselves we're our whole unit, I really do care about every single one of these guys like they're my brother.

Actually, these men really are my brothers. So I care who they become, and I worry about who they'll become if they really buy into this line they keep feeding us about how it's the suffering and humiliation that turns us into men. They run us through these obstacle courses that feel scarier than they actually are, and then talk like we're some kinda superheroes for surviving it even though thousands of people go through Boot Camp every year.

The DIs are building us all up like their abuse makes us superior to everybody else, making us look down on those outside like you all are truly in a separate and lesser world. I won't repeat the awful disgusting things they say about civilians and other people they think are weak, especially women and atheists and people who don't think we soldiers are the single greatest solution to America's every problem. And the stuff they say even about the female units... I won't *even repeat any of that in my head, because I can't let that nastiness find a hook in me. I just love people, love you too much.*

I know how brainwashing works. And I know that the trickiest thing about brainwashing is you never know when your brain is being washed. They haven't even had to do some of the horror stories I hear they did years ago. Even though they've threatened to beat us up they never actually hit us. They've just pushed us physically and mentally just enough to keep us on or almost over the edge.

It's worked too, 'cause some of these guys are even more fanatical and gung-ho than I ever would have thought possible when I met them. It's like this book I read once about some guy who was kidnapped by a rival cult, and they kept him sleep-deprived and half-starved and put him in pain-inducing positions and threatened to kill him and other stuff that totally broke him down until he was a quivering mass of helplessness, so they could be there to help him out, making him totally dependent on them.

So when he was dependent on them and they fed him their beliefs, in his mind he latched onto them like three thousand percent, and then he was used as an assassin against his old friends. The book said it was because of that cognitive dissonance thing you told me about. Except in this case, it didn't mean how our minds can reject the discomfort at things that contradict us.

In this case it talked about when we pay a heavy economic or physical or emotional price for something. When that happens, we tend to believe it's incredibly valuable, so we don't have to admit we'd been had. That's why the harder they push us and the more they make us suffer, the more I actively resist taking in their jingoistic machismo about us being God's Gift to the World. I don't want to start believing it.

Right now I'm hearing a couple of my unit talking about how awesome it is that we're going to get to do weapons training soon, with brutally lethal guns and stuff. It reminds me of how people say being a cold-blooded killer is part of the whole point of being a Military Man. I mean they don't necessarily say it quite like that, but it's like being able to kill without thinking is strength, and not wanting people to die is a weakness.

I can't believe that's true. I remember reading in another book about some study sometime where they found out that in a war, if riflemen weren't where their buddies or officers were watching, they didn't fire their weapons and try to kill the enemy. Not even if they were afraid they might get killed. Only like 15% ever shot at anybody when they didn't think they were being watched. But they each thought they were the only one who didn't want to kill, so they didn't want to be found out.

I know what I used to say, but now I hope I never have to go into combat. If I do, I hope I'll have the courage to be one of the 85%. I probably shouldn't be writing that, but Liz I'm so worn down and there's only one thing getting me through this. You.

When I get out of here, I still want to be the man you love. That's what's kept me sane when I should be a gibbering pile of guano crazy. When I'm eating the dirt and doing thousands of pushups and standing still for what seems like hours and almost losing myself in the constant abuse and Total Control, that goal is the one thing that keeps me focused. It keeps me feeling alive.

I'm not here for God, Liz, and I'm not even here for country. I'm here for you. I'm going to get through this and build a life for myself and, if I'm lucky, for us. You've got the smartest mind and the strongest heart of anybody I've ever met. If you love me, I know I'm on the right track. And if you're proud of me, I know I've done good.

Okay, this took me a few days to get this all off my chest, so I better send this to make sure it gets to the office by the time you're out from that camp. I love you, Liz. Times a billion.

K.J.F.

There were more letters, of course, and each time they came with other letters I quickly got sent on to their proper destinations. When his graduation from Boot Camp finally came into view, he mailed me an invitation, along with a request to borrow my pocket Bible. He said he'd gotten his assignment for active duty, but he wanted to tell me in person. Whatever it was, he said that he realized he'd have a much more bearable time if he brought his own Bible. The more used it was, the better.

That sounded pretty cryptic coming from Kurt, but he had asked me to bring him my own heart to beat for him while he was away, I would gladly have given it to him. Each letter I had received from him showed his growth into the strong and thoughtful man I had known he could become. I was proud of him, and told him so in a letter or card every day for about three months. I was thrilled to think my Bible would go with him to his next step. It felt like he would be carrying a special little piece of me along with it.

At graduation, I sat with his mom, Janet, along with Derek and Judy. Saul had rented a cozy van for us all so he could come with us to congratulate Kurt, and also to deliver a surprise honor to the DI. Everybody was so happy for Kurt and talking about how proud they were, but I was in a daze just being able to see him again. We were finally together, and nothing else mattered. He looked so different, and yet in a way, he looked just like I'd pictured him: perfect. Janet let us spend some time alone together, even though I knew she missed him as much as I.

"So, about my assignment," he said, as soon as he came up for air from our happy reunion. "You know how I said I got super high scores in marksmanship and all that? Thanks to that and my DI's recommendation about my cool head and amazing powers of observation, instead of combat infantry they accepted me for Recon training. It turns out they're combining it into Recon/Sniper starting this year, which is why my marksmanship sealed the deal. With all the Assassination and Infiltration missions going on all over the world they need so many of 'em that they're accepting guys right out of Basic if they're good enough to qualify. Apparently they figure I qualify, and it's either that or some other front-lines gunner assignment. Everybody's real proud and kinda jealous. Sniper is like the holy grail of badboy assignments, though I'll probably be the Spotter on a Sniper team for at least a couple years. Whether I'm spotting or shooting though, I'm headed for Arabiya."

His words should have exuded pride, but his eyes were just weary, and guarded. All I could do was hug him. "Oh, Kurt. You know, this doesn't necessarily mean you're going to have to…" I trailed off. I didn't want to say it.

"Kill people? Yes, Liz, it kinda does. You and I both know that going into the Military means you're probably going to be asked to kill somebody, even if some poor kid in my unit believed a recruiter who told him he wouldn't ever have to fight. He's being sent off to combat infantry, of course. Though his recruiter also lied that he was more likely to die in a car accident than in combat, so he's okay with this. It's hard to blame the recruiter, since they don't generally volunteer for the job but are still majorly punished if they don't meet impossible quotas for kids to round up and send off to kill and be killed." He shook his head, and I couldn't read his expression. He looked years older than when I'd seen him last, but he also seemed more grounded, more serene.

Finally, I ventured, "What about you? Are you okay with this?"

He just took a deep breath, and sighed. "I think so. I'll have to see. I made it through so far without becoming bloodthirsty or anything. Maybe it's because I was never really into the shoot-em-up video games so I don't have that in my blood, I don't know. I just, I just want to make sure that whatever choices I make, they're mine, and that…"

I just hugged him again, tightly. "Kurt, I'll always be proud of you.

And love you. Every time you open this, remember that." I then gave him the Bible, with a note and a picture I'd tucked inside. "It's nice and worn on my favorite pages, with underlining and stuff for the passages that have brought me comfort over the years. This book is so much a part of me, it feels like I'm going with you."

He took it carefully, considering it a few moments, and then he looked back to me with his impish grin that always made my heart flutter. My trickster Kurt was still there! Suddenly suspicious, I watched him curiously to see what was up his sleeve.

Trying to restore his poker face, he drawled, "Well I'll take good care of this, I promise. To reassure you though, I'll give you some collateral so you know I'm good for it." He then held up and opened a small box.

Inside it was a ring, a thin golden band with a single small diamond.

He got down on one knee and said, "Miss Franklin, would you consider doing me the honor of making me the happiest Franklin in the world, and consent to someday become Missus Franklin?"

My eyes blurred over with tears as I leaned down to throw my arms around his neck, exclaiming "Yes, yes! Oh you big goof, yes!"

I then heard a bunch of guys whistle and burst into rowdy applause from the distant corner of the building we were leaning against, making me realize we were no longer alone. His DI came over and patted him on the back, telling me what a good man Kurt was, and more that was completely drowned out by the excitement of it all. As embarrassed as I was, I also found it funny to realize that Kurt meant it when he said he wasn't just himself there, he was his whole unit. I hugged them, but didn't let them give me a congratulatory kiss. The line had to be drawn somewhere!

Saul had given me time off and I'd arranged to be absent from classes, so I could spend as much time with Kurt as possible. That time wasn't nearly enough, though. We did make sure he got to spend alone time with his mom, too, without me always being around. Far too soon, he had to ship back out, leaving Janet and me bravely planning how we were going to get through his absence, missing him so much.

Kurt and I resumed our correspondence as soon as we could. In his letters, he painted a pretty clear picture about why having my well-worn Bible was so important. His story came bits and pieces over time, so I'll weave them together in a way that conveys what he shared.

My darlingest Mrs. Franklin to be,

Things are a lot more laid-back here compared to Boot Camp. Not to say it's a vacation, but we have a little more downtime and are treated with a bit more respect. This is a little odd given how much worse the language is.

I don't mean that Boot Camp had less swearing, I mean that around here they're even more dehumanizing about the people we're being trained to shoot at, as well as the people we're supposed to be protecting. I have to act like I am totally okay with them talking like Arabiyans are inhuman animals and all of them are probably Espies, Sabs or Assins... sorry, Espionage Agents, Saboteurs or Assassins. If I didn't, I think I'd never be allowed to graduate.

I'm serious, every day I hear dozens of casual comments or even watch movies about how Arabiyans are dirty and violent and don't share our values. I find them hard to believe. I am pretty sure Arabiyans love their mothers and their family and their country and their religion, and all the other things that people here talk about as the most important things in the world.

These guys here talk about how supposedly all Arabiyans disrespect their women and kill them if they commit adultery, so we have to go fight wars over there so their women can get respect. But here there are pictures of naked women all over the place, and these guys say really cruel and insulting things about women and sex that offend the living daylights out of Arabiyans. They say that Arabiyans don't value human life, but given that they're talking here about how we need to be prepared to kill every last man, woman and child like in the Old Testament...

Oh yeah, did I mention that yet? Almost everything here comes with a free Bible verse. They quote things like "Jacob have I loved, but Esau have I hated," meaning that the Arabiyans are Esau's people and therefore hated by god, and so we're supposed to kill them. They're picking and choosing quotes from all over the Bible to try to make it look like god is absolutely behind everything they want us to do, even if the quotes contradict each other. They even have Bible verses on our sniper scopes thinking that this means that god himself will guide our bullets. They seriously believe that the Military is their own personal Missionary Force, trying to convert us all as they push the Bible into everything.

They also talk about the Muslim scripture the Qur'an, but they don't actually quote much from it except for a couple lines here and there about fighting to defend their beliefs. But they make it sound like the quotes are saying they're supposed to fight aggressive wars against non-Muslims and that's why every single Muslim is an inhuman murderer. The quotes don't sound like that's what they're trying to say, but without context it's hard to tell.

I do know there's Espies who say that Islam requires them to kill infidels or whatever, but I'm pretty sure they're just the Muslim version of our own guys who are telling me we need to get out there in Arabiya to spread Christianity and wipe out Islam. Seriously! These guys here will talk about how the Qur'an supposedly tells Muslims to obliterate other people, and in the same breath go on about how in the Bible god told his people to smite all his enemies dead right down to the babies in their cribs.

It's surreal. Leaving aside the hypocrisy it's also inconsistent, because on the one hand they talk about how we're going out there to protect the good Muslims from Sabs and Espies trying to undermine the democracy we're building there. And then in the next breath they talk about how we can't trust them to govern themselves because they'll try to elect devout Muslims, so we need to instill Christian values so they'll elect leaders who are Christian. It's like they're not even listening to themselves, or don't expect us to connect the dots. If you want me to condemn a group of people because you think they want to kill women and children, don't use that as justification for why you want me to be okay with killing women and children.

I am learning a lot about the Bible though, so you should be proud. Not what the military is trying to teach me, but what I'm learning under the table. See, there's a Bible study group here at the base, and they were given my name by a friend, so they invited me to join them. They have to be real careful so they aren't found out. I figured if I'm expected to go out and gun down people for Jesus, I had a real incentive to finally find out what this guy had to say for himself.

See, all of us here in training have to go to mandatory seminars and church services that are super gung-ho Kill 'Em All and let God Sort 'Em Out kind of Zealous Christian. Anybody who seems like they aren't totally on board with that gets singled out and hazed. Bad. Real bad. I don't think they'll let us pass the program if we're not one of them, which I guess means our job in Recon is to demonstrate absolute objectivity and critical observation on every day except Sunday.

There's several guys here who aren't totally on board with the Jesus Loves Blowing Peoples' Brains Out preaching, and they're teaching me how to camouflage myself to fit in. Luckily, camouflaging myself to go unnoticed is the whole point of Recon training. Funny thing is, most of this underground group are Christian, they're just not "the right kind" of Christian. It super bothers them that their religion is being twisted into the opposite of what they feel Jesus taught.

So, I started reading the Bible with them, and they do it in a way I never heard of before. They use Bibles that have the direct quotes of Jesus in red, like yours does, and they read only what Jesus had to say for himself. Some of them feel that everything else was just tacked on by people who had their own agenda.

I'm sure you know this, but I found out there wasn't even a New Testament from the time of Jesus, it was just a bunch of different stories written down decades after his death at the earliest. Then hundreds of years later, some priests picked out which texts they felt represented what they wanted the church to believe. These guys here especially aren't fond of Paul, quoting Thomas Jefferson in saying he was the "first corrupter of the doctrines of Jesus." They say Paul took pagan myths of Mithras and his own Gnostic preconceptions and built those into his church work so that he could get people to buy into it. Apparently the Roman soldiers followed this thing called Mithraism, bonding through their own rituals of baptism to be reborn, and also self-control and resisting sexuality. Though I doubt they followed that last bit any more than most of the guys here at training do.

The Roman story went that Mithras was a literal son of the creator god, born from virgin rock. It says Mithras had a last dinner with his twelve followers, was sacrificed to redeem mankind, was put in a rock tomb, where he was reborn on the 25th of December which was thought to originally be a Sunday. They called him The Truth, The Light and The Good Shepherd, healing the sick and working miracles, and devotees could conquer death by eating the flesh and drinking the blood of a slain bull. The bull was a symbol of his. And when the Day of Judgment came, those who were already dead would come back to life.

A whole lot of coincidences, right? The difference is that Mithras was supposedly always a god and was never a regular person like Jesus, but otherwise it's all pretty compelling. When my study group told me about Mithras they also told me that early Christians sang and danced and clapped in church and turned to the East to face the sun when they prayed, so I wish people would quit making fun of how Muslims pray.

My study buddies say that the early Christian apologists wrote about Mithraism, explaining away the similarities by claiming the cult of Mithras was put into place centuries before Jesus as part of a "diabolic mimicry by a prescient Satan." If you ask me, that sounds like a lame excuse. Since Paul came in after Jesus had already died and was from a totally Roman upbringing I think it's a lot more plausible that Paul just changed Christianity to fit in with what he could use to convert more Romans.

I don't know if you think that Paul was legit; I know you have a different background in all this than me. I don't mean to tell you what you should believe, because I want you to be true to your own faith. That's something I've always admired about you. For me, though, a lot of what people attribute to Paul also strikes me as kinda sexist and judgmental. The more I read what Jesus actually said in his sermons, the less it sounds like what Paul preached.

That's what the study group focuses on, the sermons of Jesus. Our group leader Josh Karsten has a Bible that he reads to us from, called "Jefferson's Bible – the Life and Morals of Jesus of Nazareth." Yeah, as in Thomas Jefferson! He's got a booklet of stuff by Jefferson too, and part of it talks about how he made his own personal Bible by cutting out and pasting together only the direct quotes from Jesus. Like my buddies, he felt that everything else was tacked onto the story by people who hijacked the teachings of Jesus for their own political agendas.

He had to do this all in secret because of political enemies in his own time whom he felt were twisting the words of Jesus for their own agendas. In the booklet Karsten loaned me, there's a quote from Jefferson: "I write nothing for publication, and last of all things should it be on the subject of religion. On the dogmas of religion as distinguished from moral principles, all mankind, from the beginning of the world to this day, have been quarreling, fighting, burning and torturing one another, for abstractions unintelligible to themselves and to all others, and absolutely beyond the comprehension of the human mind"

That's a lot of long words to say what I see around here, people all riled up to torture and kill in the service of something that's just frankly too far out there for the human mind to know. And they insist that this is the kind of America the Founding Fathers envisioned, a shoot-em-up Christian nation that crushes any other faith.

Even though I was Ben Franklin once, I don't think that America has to be exactly like the Founding Fathers would have made it. I mean, I respect Thomas Jefferson and his work on this Bible and stuff, but the guy still owned other human beings and kept them slaves. Even after a friend tried to pay off the debt he'd used to justify keeping slaves, he still wouldn't let people go free. That's wrong.

But the thing is, America was founded specifically to not be a country that was led by just one religion. That's why they left England to begin with, so there wouldn't be a state religion. Karsten was saying something the other day about how he'd heard that one of the original American laws prohibited the government from treating one religion better or worse than another. It might even have been in the Constitution, which if that's true, no wonder the Zealous Christian leadership wants to keep it secret.

I think our hearts are close enough that you know I'm not trying to insult your religious group. You kept saying yourself, how you wanted everybody to be able to stay true to their own beliefs. That's another thing that Jefferson talked about, which made me think of you. "It behooves every man who values liberty of conscience for himself to resist invasions of it in the case of others, or their case may, by change of circumstances, become his own."

In other words, if you value your own freedom of believe, you dang well better protect it for others, or you could lose yours, too. I can just imagine what a stink the military brass here would raise if the tables were turned, and they had to sit through a mandatory Pragmatic Christian sermon about giving away riches and loving their neighbor. Or heck, if they had to melt down their verse-inscribed bullets and turn them into farming tools.

Like the Pharisees, they have twisted around scripture to support cruelty and greed, and get all uptight when someone calls them out on it that they want to see them dead. These so-called Christians brag about wanting to brutally put down people who protest war, forgetting that Jesus would have joined the picket line and led the peacenik hymns. Followed by a teach-in about the holy power of non-violence.

I mean seriously, have they even read the Bible? Jesus said very specifically he wanted his followers to be nonviolent: "Put up again thy sword into his place: for all they that take the sword shall perish with the sword." Even if he was personally attacked, he told his followers to stand down, and he put himself out there to get hit again, even killed. And he definitely didn't teach that any one country on Earth was his kingdom to be fought over: "If my kingdom were of this world, then would my servants fight... but now is my kingdom not from hence."

He doesn't even want his followers to be threatening other people: "Behold, I send you forth as sheep in the midst of wolves: be ye therefore wise as serpents, and harmless as doves." And that makes sense, cause he also said that whatever we do to anybody, it's like we're doing it to him: "Inasmuch as ye have done it unto one of the least of these my brethren, ye have done it unto me."

I'm laughing now, because I realize I'm quoting Jesus to you, of all people. I know you've talked a lot about what a strength you find in Jesus, but I never stopped to read any of his words for myself. I'm real grateful to Karsten, and not just for looking out for me. He was the first Christian except for you and Derek who never made me feel like an outsider. He invited me to study with them because he knew I needed help navigating this whole mess, and he told me up front he didn't expect me to buy into it. But as he led our group with such a quiet strength, he created this calm in the middle of this storm we're in, and I found myself getting really into what Jesus taught.

Now I'm in a real bind, though. I'm getting really hooked on the power of these Jesus quotes, and it's making me want to defend them against how the mandatory sermons are twisting them around. I want to stand up and school these military preachers on what Jesus actually said. They're here telling us that as soldiers we're the emissaries of Jesus, forgetting that when Jesus ran into real soldiers back in the day, they mocked him, beat him up, and stole his stuff after crucifying him.

But I guess taking it on myself to tell them off would make me a hypocrite too, since Jesus was pretty serious about not caring whether people believed in what he said, or even if they lied about him. He spoke in parables so only those who were ready to understand him would get what he was saying. He believed his purpose was to get up and stand for truth, nothing more and nothing less. Here's another quote I think you even told me once: "To this end was I born, and for this cause came I into the world, that I should bear witness unto the truth. Every one that is of the truth heareth my voice."

So if people have ears to hear they'll hear, otherwise they won't. I guess I finally am ready to hear, or at least, hear as much as I'm in a place to understand right now. I don't pretend that I know even half of what you've known all your life about Jesus, so I hope this letter doesn't come across wrong. I've even said myself there's nothing more obnoxious than a new convert to anything. I'm trying real hard to feel my way through this, and talking about it to you helps me a lot.

This has actually been tougher on me than Basic, and now I need to figure out what to do with it. I mean, Jesus didn't say we shouldn't pick up a weapon to defend people against someone who's going to hurt them. And as a sniper, I should be able to see who my target is and make sure he's a guy who would do more harm if I let him live. So it shouldn't be like I'm gonna be asked to shoot up cars at checkpoints that turn out to be civilians and kids with the drivers don't speak English and don't know what's going on. I just need to keep my head. I also don't want my buddies here to have to face the bad guy out there alone, not when we can stick together and fight the hate, especially in ourselves.

Even though it's tough, I'm going to stick it out, and keep working with my new brothers in Christ to make choices we think are right.

Yes, I said it, brothers in Christ. I may not be the kind of Christian you may have wanted me to be, and I know I'm not the kind the military wants me to be.

But I'm hoping I'm the kind of Christian that Jesus would have wanted me to be. Like Jefferson said, "To the corruptions of Christianity I am indeed opposed; but not to the genuine precepts of Jesus himself. I am a Christian, in the only sense he wished any one to be; sincerely attached to his doctrines, in preference to all others; ascribing to himself every human excellence; & believing he never claimed any other."

And yeah that means I don't believe Jesus was the literal son of any divine god. I believe he was a human being who faced a hard road with patience and strength. Him being just a regular guy makes his excellence an even greater accomplishment. I want to live up to that example, at least as much as I can.

That's what I think is meant when people talk about him giving his life to save us from sin. Not that some god made him a human sacrifice for our mistakes, but that if there is a god, he helped Jesus live the kind of exemplary life that shows us how we can overcome. By reading his words and working on ourselves, we can have the strength to follow his example.

That's what I'm thinking of all the time here – Jesus and his example – and whether I can develop the strength he did. I'll just have to keep true to my self and pray that I'll be led to make the right call when the time comes. Who knows, maybe there's a Jesus out there who can hear that prayer and help me out. And even if not, at least there's two people with level heads and strong hearts, whom I can keep in my heart to guide me through – Jesus and you.

I love you, Liz. Times a billion.

K.J.F.

Kurt was right, that wasn't the kind of Christian I would have hoped for him to be. But who was I to presume to judge what only God himself could measure? My beloved Kurt had found wisdom and comfort in the words that had provided me a refuge through my own troubles, and this made my heart rejoice. I didn't like what he was depicting, a Military Training Program using Jesus to justify killing in war. Yet I was grateful that he was led to search inside himself for a stronger sense of his own moral strength.

In his next letter, he asked if we could get married soon after the school year ended. I of course said yes! He'd already asked his mom her thoughts, and got permission to make a secret call to my father to ask his blessing, so I was really the last to know. It may have seemed rushed to some of my friends, but there couldn't have been a more perfect timing. He was assigned to start pre-deployment exercises soon after, so that would be our only chance until… well, we didn't know how long.

It didn't take me long to design and sew my wedding dress. My mother made my bouquet using flowers from neighbors' yards, and my father soldered this beautifully simple circlet for my veil. Kurt admitted the ring he gave me for our engagement was one that a buddy at Boot Camp wanted me to have after it had been returned to him by his ex-fiancee. For my wedding ring, he wanted to give me the ring his father had given his mother when he proposed, before the car accident took him away. Through fresh tears, I wrote back to him that I would be honored.

Realizing that this would be his last chance to do everything together with his best friend, Derek asked Judy if she'd like to have one last double date with us at the chapel. After checking with me, she indulged him yet again with her consent. So with Cassandra and Jasmine as our bridesmaids, we stood together before Pastor Johns, making our vows on the happiest day of our lives.

Saul had rented a couple of small cabins for us as a wedding present, where we spent the next few weeks enjoying the sweetest, most blissful honeymoon the world had ever seen. Heaven graced me with its beauty in every word Kurt spoke, and in every smile that lit up his face when he saw mine. When his hand brushed against me I tingled all over, filled with a happiness that shone with a brilliance I felt would never end.

Then, far too soon, it was all over. Before I knew it, his deployment day came, and he was gone again from my world.

All my heart went with him.

Chapter 12

Those most adaptable to changing environments are fittest to survive, and joyfully thrive.

Fortunately, I wasn't left alone to spend all my time moping over Kurt's absence. Derek and Judy still had me over every weekend, putting together letters and jokes and tiny gifts to send to him. Cassandra, Jazmine and I had also grown close, and I saw one or both of them every day. I began to suspect they took turns making sure I always had a friend nearby.

One day, Jazmine even had me go with her to her old Sunnycups back near her neighborhood, to get me a free hot cocoa while she picked something up from a friend. I'd let on that I was surprised she invited me, after she'd discouraged Cassandra from visiting there. Jazmine just laughed and reassured me that my visit wouldn't have the same effect. She said it wasn't just how I dress and carry myself like a regular person, while Cassandra breezes down the sidewalk like a runway model.

Jazmine said she respected how I was always putting other people ahead of me, no matter who they were. She had noticed I always tried to get where I could look people in the eye and listen, rather than standing or even talking over them. She also liked how I asked questions and tried to draw people out, and she wanted to hear what a couple of her friends would have to say when meeting me.

She then complimented me about how everybody I ran into got the same bright-eyed smile as though I was happy to see them. That made me laugh and blush at the same time, because I really was happy to see all of God's children. I figured we were all one human family, and it didn't occur to me that anyone would feel differently. After spending more time with Jazmine and her brothers, though, I started to become painfully aware of how they weren't always treated with the respect I felt they deserved.

Her parents invited me to dinner with them a few times, and after one dinner I went to a movie with Jazmine and her brothers. Before we left, her dad gave them what they later referred to as his "Daily Perp Talk." He reminded them to always give people a smile that was friendly but not too interested, and to keep their voices down and not walk too fast. If a cop or anyone approached them, they were to stay polite and calm, no matter how nasty they were. He made sure they kept their CMDB ID handy in a front pocket so if they were stopped, someone wouldn't mistake their wallet for a gun.

Jazmine just stayed by the door trying not to roll her eyes, but I was stunned by such a frightening lecture that seemed to be routine. On the way to the movie, her oldest brother told me about how many boys from his school had been killed over prior few years years because of "misunderstandings," so their dad was just being careful. I hadn't heard of any of that, and it made my heart sink down to my stomach. I couldn't help but wonder how it would have gone if I'd brought Jazmine's brothers along for door-to-door voter registration in my old neighborhood. I couldn't imagine it would have gone well.

Conversation turned to lighter things so as not to spoil the movie, but it was hard for me to move on. The deadly unfairness of it all made me angry and sad, even moreso as I realized that their neighborhood was one of the ones to which Saul's office had sent bad voting information. I realized I had nothing to do with that mailing, nor the way the staff at the movie theater nodded to me as though I was there alone, nor even the way the security guard rested his hand on his gun as we passed. Yet that realization didn't keep me from feeling responsible. I didn't feel responsible for those things happening; I felt responsible to do what I could to change them. I didn't know how yet, but I resolved to seize any opportunity that came my way.

By the time classes resumed after the summer, I had begun to realize that opportunity wouldn't come through working for Saul. I got to see more and more of him as the school year wore on, as he had begun relying on me to double-check his memos and occasionally take notes for some of his pretty important and even secretive meetings. At first I was honored, but that shine faded as I became wearied by how quickly his tone and positions shifted from one venue to the next. The many faces of Saul the Candidate had turned even more numerous and conflicting for Saul the Politician, and it was getting hard to keep up with who he was going to be in any given situation.

Still, I was caught completely off-guard when he agreed to vote against a measure that would have extended further state funds to support church-administered charitable programs, something the American Christian League had been lobbying hard for. I don't think I quite asked him about it, but I didn't try to hide my bewilderment.

"Liz," he told me, "don't worry too much about this one. I'm doing so much for the ACL, they're still going to have my back. But the House here needs this measure to fail, so they need some Puritans to play the bad guy due to the unfortunate fact there simply aren't enough Pragmaticans willing to kill it. I know, I know, I am as dumbfounded as you."

He had shrugged, shaking his head. "As it turns out, being the newcomer with the most enthusiastic groundswell of support, that works against me in this case. That all makes it my turn to pay my dues and throw my voice in with the Nays. I already have my excuses lined up, talking about how the measure would have raised taxes or the state deficit, or discouraged people from participating in the sainted practice of personal donations. You know everybody hates paying taxes and our current crusade is a balanced budget, so that should just about do the trick. In return, the boys up on the Hill are going to make sure I get to score some points back with the next issue that comes up, maybe set up some legislation I can co-sponsor. They might even get some of the Pragmaticans to sign on with it, and help build up my bipartisan credentials. You see how that works out for the best, in the long run?"

I remember nodding blankly, wishing I didn't see exactly how it might work out the best for whoever "they" were, but not necessarily for those who were depending on the charitable programs to feed and clothe their families. I didn't question it though, I just finished up my notes and followed him to the next meeting.

Within weeks, he did get to co-sponsor a bill, something about mandatory minimum punishments for crimes involving a gun. When I brought it up to Jazmine, she and I dug through it, spotting ways it was likely to get people from her neighborhood thrown into prison more often and for longer than it would if they were light-skinned folks from my home town. I carefully raised that concern with Saul, but he quickly assured me that such interpretations were just disinformation spread by his Pragmatican opponents.

Not all Pragmaticans were against it, however, especially those who would soon be running again for their seats against opponents who were already calling them soft on crime. These Pragmaticans happily co-sponsored the legislation to bolster their image. This also made Saul look pretty good, making a big splash in the news just days before he declared his candidacy for the state Senate.

Now, I knew that he was elected only for a two-year term, so I suppose I knew Candidate Saul would resurface eventually. Yet I didn't expect it to be so soon, and for a different office. Instead of running as the comfortable incumbent for his current seat, he was tackling a new challenge of unseating an incumbent Pragmatican. That meant he had to start campaigning early, fast and hard. I was just starting to wonder how long I wanted to be a part of his political machine, when the machine itself started pinging in ways that made me want to get out while I could.

I was sitting in on a meeting with a couple reps from the Puritanic Party, who were discussing how they could ensure Saul's victory. They talked about the redistricting that was going on to split up the voter groups so that they should have a Puritanic majority again in each one.

Now, I knew Pragmaticans did gerrymandering as well, so that part didn't bother me quite so much. I mean, it's a dirty trick, but at least it was an old dirty trick that both sides used. Until someone finally stopped us from playing electoral games and just awards races to the person who got the most votes from all eligible voters, people I knew people would keep trying to rig the game so they win.

But then they started pitching ideas on how to create more voting barriers to keep the "wrong people" from hitting he polls. Their first and most serious idea was to start requiring a type of ID at the poll that inner city, poor, retired or very young people wouldn't usually already have. Since most of those voters would find it tough to come up with the time, money and transportation to go get this ID, the men agreed that tactic should help keep a lot of them away. They were also drafting tougher documentation requirements for the ID, as well as higher fees to get those other papers together, so they were confident that "those people" would find it nearly impossible to even try to vote.

Just to play it safe, the men then discussed how "those people" tended to have to try to register or vote outside of normal working hours, so they had to close down that access as best they could. Even though it was perfectly legal for voters to register on the spot and then vote, these politicians decided to push to outlaw that practice. To discourage volunteers from trying to go to them to get them registered, they planned to make it easier to prosecute volunteers for alleged fraud, with penalties that should scare off most people who would have otherwise continued my earlier work.

Further, the men agreed they would have to shut down as much early voting as they could, especially on evenings and weekends. They would also try to shut down as many voting locations as they could after the instructions were mailed out, so that people would have to try to find their new location, maybe even give up. With the long lines that would be left on election day, they felt assured the polls would close on election night long before many of "those people" ever got to a ballot box.

Saul raised the concern that these barriers could be overcome via mail-in ballots, which could have sunk him in his last election if they were all counted. His buddies assured him that they were already working on a bill that would outlaw mail-in votes except for from active duty military, who would almost certainly vote Puritanic.

The more the meeting went on, the more I wondered why Saul didn't realize that I might have had a problem with their plans He had initially brought me on board with the promise of helping people exercise their sacred right to vote. Now, he was enthusiastically brainstorming on how to prevent that right from being exercised by people who didn't support him. Did he really think that I only supported the rights of people who agreed with me on how to use them? Was that truly the picture I was projecting?

Finally, they started talking in cryptic references about a Forty-Nine/Fifty-One project and whether they should deploy it on the machines. I didn't know what they were talking about, and I didn't want to know. I had heard enough. Despite the wonderful times I'd had working for Saul, those times were over. I no longer wanted to have anything to do with his politics.

Right after the meeting, I tried to gently and politely resign. I told him that I wanted to spend more time on school, which was true. Kurt being so far away was also weighing on me, and I said I didn't think I would be able to keep giving his office the support it needed. I didn't want to let on that I had other problems, or say anything that might have hurt or offended him. After all that he had done for me, and the friendship I thought we'd shared, I wanted to part on good terms.

Saul wasn't offended, but instead tried to persuade me to stay on. When I still insisted that my mind was made up, he tried harder to convince me. "Liz, I understand how this all might seem a little overwhelming right now. You're struggling through only your second year at college while your young groom is half a world away. But I want you to know that I'm here for you, ready to give you whatever you need." He had moved closer, and his hand was on my back – my lower back. "You're like a daughter I never had. I don't want to lose my chance to show you how much you mean to me."

Then his hand slipped lower, and almost before I knew it, I felt the hem of my skirt moving up my calf. My hand was moving to react almost before I had the presence of mind to be shocked at what was happening. I slapped him so hard I may have left a welt. He was lucky I opened my hand at the last moment, as my fist may have left a gash on his cheek from my wedding ring.

I don't think it was the slap to his face that made him stagger back, so much as the one on his ego. Clearly, he didn't expect my actions any more than I had expected his.

As he reached his hand up to his cheek, I spat out, "Then I thank God you don't have any daughters."

He reeled again, and I saw from the hurt in his eyes that my words stung him more deeply than my slap. "Oh, Liz… it's not like that. It's not like that at all. I would never…" He trailed off.

Suddenly, I felt terrible for lashing out like that, as though I had overreacted and done something terribly wrong. "I'm sorry, Saul. I didn't mean… I mean…"

For a moment, I didn't know what I meant. I had to forcefully resist the urge to go to him and reassure him that I hadn't meant to cause him pain. Margie had told me once about how women can have such an ingrained pressure to give of ourselves and never to cause harm, that even when someone tries to take advantage, we can start to feel a need to "make things right." I also found myself hit by the apologetic guilt of having led him on somehow, as I'd been raised to believe such misunderstandings were the woman's fault.

I don't know what was showing in my face as I struggled with my emotions, but my hesitation gave him some form of opening. He moved forward quickly, pinning me against the wall with his chest. His hands were going for my clothes again, but they get far.

New instincts kicked in, honed in a self-defense class that Cassandra, Jazmine, Judy and I had gone to a few months before. My knee shot up between his legs, and after that impact, my foot turned and rammed its heel against the side of his leg just above his knee, forcefully continuing the kick to slide down hard for maximum force. Saul doubled over down onto the floor, and I had grabbed my purse and bolted out the door before I had consciously realized what had just happened.

I was in such a hurry to get home, I hailed a cab even though I was sure I had already collected my last paycheck. The cabbie was very nice and tried to be friendly, but I wasn't interested in being vulnerable to a stranger, whatever his intentions. The driver respected my boundaries, driving me home in silence.

I knew I was very lucky that I didn't have to find out just how far Saul was willing to force himself on me. Yet I still wanted to lock myself in my room and cry. I couldn't stop running through everything I'd said and done that might have indicated I wanted to violate the commandment against adultery with him. I wondered if I should tell his wife, and then had to war with the childhood teaching that if a man strayed, it was his wife's fault for not being a better woman. Finally, I wondered if I should tell Kurt, fighting against a tidal wave of shame and self-recrimination that I knew was ridiculous, but felt in my heart all the same..

Soon, I was right outside my building and handing the cabbie a little too much cash for a tip, insisting he take it. I always tried to tip well, and not just because Kurt and his mom survived on the kindness of her customers. At that moment, I was struggling against feeling like a punished sinner, and there was no objective way for me to know if I had been a good person or a bad person. But there was an objective measure about whether I was a good tipper, and I needed that boost.

The cabbie accepted my money, then hesitated as he asked me if I was going to be okay. I looked up sharply, feeling threatened by the closeness of his tone. It was then I saw a picture of his family up on the dashboard, including a daughter around my age. Immediately I felt bad again for assuming he was coming on to me. I mumbled something politely reassuring, then hurried home to the apartment.

Cassandra was just reaching out to take in the welcome mat as I approached. After one look at my face, she stepped back and held the door open for me. I tried to give her a smile, however weak, as my momentum carried me back to my bed where I planned to stifle my sobs with a pillow until I cried myself to sleep. Within a minute, though, I heard the front door close again, followed by the warmth of a reassuring hand on my back.

I just turned to Cassandra, hugged her, and cried my eyes out on her shoulder. Soon I was trying to spill out what had happened, and apparently made enough sense that she was both extremely angry, and extremely relieved.

"Oh Liz, I am so sorry. Thank goodness you got out of there like you did. That's... well it's monstrous bad. But oh Liz, I'm so glad that's all that happened, and that you're okay. With Kurt being sent out to Arabiya, I was afraid it was about him." She wrapped her arms around me again, and it triggered fresh tears.

I missed him so much, this all just made me want to curl up in his arms and never leave. I bravely tried to set that aside, wondering aloud, "Should I even tell him about this? I mean, it's not like Saul really even did anything, he just..."

"Liz, don't you dare excuse what he did! He assaulted you! That counts as doing something!" She was livid, both at Saul for what he did and at me for trying to excuse his abuse.

The word "assault" struck me as inappropriately harsh, though.

"Cass, he didn't hit me! He didn't hurt me, he just, well, grabbed me. And not especially hard, it didn't bruise or anything, it was just, I dunno, your common everyday sexual harassment. It's awful and it makes us feel like garbage, but it happens to women all the time."

That infuriated her further. "Liz, no. Just no. You are not going to do this. Denial is just not an option. You were in the same class as I, so I know that you know there's a big difference between saying inappropriate things that intimidate or bully or even promise stuff if you 'put out,' versus laying hands on your person. Words and situations are sexual *harassment*. Putting hands on you is sexual *assault*. He must be made to suffer for it, or he's going to do it to someone else."

I bit my lip. "Uh, remember how I said I kicked him away from me? I did that thing they taught us about the Slam and Slide with the foot. I was going to try ramming my foot down on the bridge of his foot or something like that, but my knee shot up and as he doubled over my foot just kept moving… Oh I hope I didn't break his knee."

"Liz. *Stop.* I hope you did break his knee so badly that even surgery can't fix it. I hope he had to call an ambulance so we can go and tell the police where to pick him up." She had started to reach for a phone when I stopped her.

"Wait, no! No police. I'm not calling the police."

She whirled on me with a dazed look, her anger mixing with her bewilderment. "Of *course* you're calling the police. You need to report his attack."

I shook my head, my own indignation finally catching up with me. "For what, Cass? For *what?* To have every single aspect of my entire life, real or imagined, put out there on the front page of every newspaper in the state, showing how I'm *obviously* a stupid, slutty liar who both invited his actions and also made it all up to get attention? And since he didn't actually *rape* me, that I'm making a huge deal out of nothing? You know how women are treated when they make a complaint, like they obviously did something to get themselves attacked? We're up on trial before the ink's even dry on the police report, if you can even get them to take you seriously enough to write one up. Our instructor even said that almost without fail, the women she'd worked with said that sometimes the retaliation for speaking out was worse than suffering in silence without the added hounding from so-called friends and neighbors. Come on, Cass, seriously, you know this."

Cassandra merely stared back at me, her face rippling with conflicting emotions. Finally, she slowly nodded, conceding my point.

So angry I was gasping for breath, my tirade continued. "Add to that the fact of who he is, and that there's an election going on. This isn't just about some guy thinking he has full license to reach out and grab a young woman who works for him. This would quickly be reported as the ACL's rising Puritan star being accused of attempted rape of a young military wife whose husband is off in Arabiya serving our country as a sniper. How do you think that little wrinkle will play out, huh? As bad as Puritans treat women who've been assaulted, the Pragmaticans aren't much better. They'd love to use me against him, sure, but they wouldn't treat me with much more respect when it all comes down to it. I wouldn't be asked to speak for myself, I'd be used as a cardboard cutout for all the arguments they want to make. Do you seriously want me to spend the rest of my life as That Woman?"

Cassandra opened her mouth to protest, or perhaps to reassure me. It wasn't clear if even she knew what she wanted to say. After a few breaths, she conceded my point. "I understand. I'm angry, and I disagree, but it's your decision. I, for one, wouldn't look forward to hearing your name as the punchline to the sickening jokes I hear all the time. Because that's what rape and sexual assault is in casual conversation, isn't it? No, no, not all the time. Even though it feels like it right now..."

I pulled Cassandra closer to me again, so I could put my arm around her as we sat on my bed, trying to calm down and think clearly. "I know what you mean. Movies, songs, jokes... I used to try to block it out, but now I can't stop thinking of how often I hear people just casually talking about abusing women, children, or even men. It's horrific, but we've all been subconsciously trained to just treat it like... I don't know. Some fringe Women's Issue that can't really be solved."

That just riled Cassandra up further. "Women's Issue! It's nearly always men who are doing it, isn't it? Yet you're right, we're always being told how to avoid rape, how to deal with the situations... why don't we see all these Public Service Announcements helping remind men to *just not rape?* To behave like human beings rather than predators?"

"Boys will be boys," I fumed, freshly incensed about the implications of that ridiculous phase. "Honestly, do people really think men are pre-programmed to be monsters? That's insulting!"

"Sexism for everyone! I mean, why not?" Cassandra laughed harshly. "Of course, if we had to expect everyone to behave civilly, the police may have to take rape seriously."

I nodded. "Or at least investigate even if they don't believe it. Did you see that article? The one that said the Internal Crime Bureau estimates only 2% of rape allegations are false, though… Actually that's horrible, accusing someone of that. If convicted, that would put him on a sex offender list that would follow him forever. It could ruin his life!"

Cassandra glared at me, concerned I was ready to go easy on Saul once more. "Well then you may console yourself with the knowledge that the statistics strongly suggest he would be exonerated. Remember, the experts in that article presume that of all times someone is raped, less than half are even reported. That number may even be less than a quarter, but sure, let's assume half. Of reports, there's a mere fifty-fifty chance there will be an arrest, though at least there's an eighty-percent chance they'll at least have charges prosecuted. However, the chance of a conviction drops back down to half, and even those found guilty have only two-to-three odds of spending any time in jail over it."

I ran the numbers in my head. "So even if a rape is reported, there's only a one in seven chance anybody will spend a day behind bars for it. If only half of the rapes are reported, then a rapist has less than a seven-percent chance of any jail time. For each rapist who serves any time at all, fourteen walk completely free." I took a ragged breath, then sighed. "I don't know if this is the right choice, I really don't. But I don't want to get involved in all that, not for what happened."

Cass nodded slowly. "You're at least not going back there, right?"

I shook my head vehemently. "I quit, and he should be smart enough to figure out by now that I meant it. He can mail me my last paycheck or keep it; I'm not going near his office ever again. Maybe he would have gone farther and maybe he wouldn't have, but I don't need to give him the chance to show me."

I paused, remembering how shaken I was by the cabbie. "You know, I might be nervous about being alone with any guy for a while, even in the elevator. But I'm going to be okay. Really, Cass, I will be." I put my hand on hers, and she turned her hand to squeeze mine.

"Well, okay. C'mon, let's go make root beer floats. My pizza should be here in a few minutes, so we can pop in bad movies and stay up all night eating junk food. Deal?" She put on a brave face, trying not to let on how upset she still was.

I smiled as brightly as I could and said, "Deal!"

We skipped classes the next day. After Jazmine's morning class she had the day off, so she came over to spend the rest of it with us. I filled her in, then calmed her down and we had another impromptu party to help each other relieve the stress. We had just succeeded in turning our thoughts to happier things when there was a knock at the door. I froze, surprised at how my skin tingled and my heart leapt to my throat.

Cassandra came out from the kitchen and waved to reassure me, then cautiously opened the door. Soon she was back, making room on the table with one hand so she could set down a huge vase filled with roses. There was a florists' card in it, which I opened, and instantly recognized Saul's handwriting.

Dear Elizabeth,

I wanted to apologize for last night. I've always found it's best to say it with flowers. I'm sorry if I came on a little too strong, and I understand if I startled you. I hope you will forgive me for any misunderstandings. Go ahead and take a few days off with pay if you like, and I hope to see you again soon.

Love,

Saul

I was so taken aback that I almost missed another note tucked into the envelope. It was from Rosie, the receptionist. My eyes widened as I realized she would have been at her desk by the exit when I ran past it on my way out.

Liz,

I think I might have a good idea why Saul suddenly 'tripped over a chair' and had to go to the ER. He'll be fine though, and I hope everything is good with you. I know he can get a little carried away, but I hope you don't hold it against him. He means well, and you mean the world to all of us. We miss you around here! Just give me a call if you need anything.

Rosie

Jazmine read over my shoulder, her anger returning. "That guy has some– I can't believe this! What kind of clueless jerk… And this Rosie? She ought to be ashamed. If she knows what's going on, she should– Okay that's it, what's her number? Give me the number, I'm calling her right now."

"Jazmine, no, please. We talked about this, and you agreed you'd stop trying to make my decisions for me. My decision is to leave it alone. I'll call her late tonight and leave a message that I already told Saul I quit, and she can take care of things from there." I was putting a brave face on it, but I was still shaken and depressed.

When I later told Judy, Derek and Kurt that I'd quit, I focused on how Saul's politics was changing, and avoided telling them what had happened. There was nothing they could do, and I especially didn't want to give Kurt yet another reason to feel terrible for being so far away. It was in the past, and I just wanted it to stay there.

Well, it was almost in the past. I got a few more notes from Saul, which I ignored, especially once it seemed clear he was getting less interested in winning me back and more interested in making sure I wasn't going to turn him in. Finally, I got an angry voicemail from him about how ungrateful I was, how he should have finished what he started and made me repay his kindness, with details that were tough enough to listen to that Jazmine took the phone from me so I wouldn't have to hear it. She did convince me to keep all the notes and recordings, just in case I ever needed the evidence. I wanted to destroy them, but it did feel good to physically and tangibly put it all to rest in one of Cassandra's safe deposit boxes.

A sharp reminder resurfaced, though, when it was time to process the paperwork to renew my scholarship. Rather than the rubber-stamped form I had signed the year before, I received a letter that said I no longer qualified. The reason given was that I had maintained an A-average rather than an A-plus, even though that wasn't originally in the scholarship qualifications. I didn't know for sure it was because of Saul. But I didn't know that it wasn't.

I also didn't know what to do. After leaving my job with Saul, I had struggled to cover my expenses even without having to pay for tuition or school supplies. Jazmine had helped me get a job at Sunnycups for a few hours a week, but even if they let me work full time, it never would have been enough on minimum wage. I was getting Kurt's paycheck, but the Military pay was so low, I knew if I didn't save half of it we wouldn't be preparing for that future he was out there risking his life for. The rest was going to help his mom, and I wasn't about to send her any less.

Now I knew that Kurt would have told me I could have stopped saving so much, but it still wouldn't have been enough. I finally decided to apply for student loans. During a very slow shift, I tried going over the application forms, trying to figure out how much I needed to apply for and whether I could qualify. Curious, my shift manager Jessica leaned over to see what I was working on.

When she saw the papers were a student loan application, she winced. "Oh, no, please no. Those forms ruined my life. I'm an indentured wage slave until my end of days, thanks to them. At this rate, I'll die in debt."

I didn't know how to react to that. I knew Jessica had attended the college at some point, but she'd been working at Sunnycups so long, I assumed she'd dropped out and wanted to just keep a career as a shift manager. It actually hadn't ever occurred to me to ask why she came back.

Jessica leaned against the counter next to me and set down the cloth she'd been using to wipe it down. "Okay, you know I used to be a barista here before I graduated, right? Well I headed out with my shiny new degree, only to find out that my Masters in Journalism didn't give me much more of a shot at getting a job than the scores of other applicants with degrees. It didn't help that employers check your credit score before considering you, and my credit score is in the toilet thanks to my debt."

I blinked. "Wait, why do employers need to know your credit score to give you a job?"

She shrugged. "They don't. However, the credit bureaus that sell our info have sold them on the idea that a low credit score means I'm some lazy irresponsible bum who'll steal from them. Forget the small matter that tuition doubled in the time it took to complete my undergraduate degree, which was extended by a year when the requirements for my degree changed midstream. Forget also that these banks continually assured me that together we were making a wise investment for the future in becoming a productive member of society."

She scoffed, shaking her head as she turned to count the cups stacked on the counter. "Thinking on it, I realize they hadn't lied. 'We' made an investment in their future profits, and nearly everything I earn produces profits for them." She looked up as the door opened and started to move toward the register, but it was just someone from outside throwing away their garbage and grabbing a napkin before leaving.

Jessica sighed, then went back to the other side of the counter to resume cleaning while she talked. "After I couldn't find work with an undergrad degree, I was offered a spot in a Masters program at a private for-profit university. It came complete with a student loan package, of course. I didn't find out until much later that I was recruited specifically so they could use me to get more free student loan subsidies from the government and hit the enrollment targets set by the bank that had bought the university. The sales staff-- ahem, 'financial advisors' took in anyone who would sign on the dotted line, even if they had to cook the books for the loan applications. As they did with mine, as it was clear in retrospect that I would never be able to repay them, not at the rate the interest would compound."

She paused while a customer came in to actually order something this time, taking their payment while I made the drink. Soon the store was again empty, except for the small group who been there studying for hours after finishing their small coffees.

I started organizing the empty cups, keeping my voice as low as I asked, "If you have so much debt you can't repay it, couldn't you declare bankruptcy?"

She laughed loudly at first, then stifled it back down to a lower volume. "Oh, Liz, that's the beauty of it. This is a risk-free investment for them. The banks have rigged the laws so that you can't be rid of student loans even in bankruptcy, except in certain cases of extreme hardship that are well nigh impossible to prove to the satisfaction of the courts they've bought off. I know, I tried after I was hospitalized for an illness that almost killed me. I had fallen behind in payments as I had to pay off my medical bills, so the banks declared me in default and sued me to pay it all at once. They of course added court costs and lawyer bills on top of late fees and other penalties, then refinanced it all back onto me at an even higher interest rate. To get the money out of me, they garnish my wages, take my tax refund, harass my elderly relatives, anything they can think of to make my life a miserably degrading hell. After wrapping up here I go to my other job with a janitorial company, barely making enough to pay my roommates my share of the bills. Even working so much, my loan payments take over two thirds of what I make."

I glanced back to where I'd tucked the forms, then focused again on organizing the drink supplies. "Can't you get them to work with you to at least lower the monthly payments?"

Jessica handed me a fresh stack of cups to arrange, then started checking the tea supplies next to me. "I did get a consolidation loan several years ago which was supposed to help, but it only made things worse. As it happens, my original loans had some meager protections I didn't know to use, and I lost them once I replaced them with the consolidation. Now the banks won't do a thing to help me, and why should they? I have no leverage, Liz. They've rigged the game as Heads They Win, Tails I Lose. I've already paid them a large percentage of what I originally borrowed, but thanks to the fees and interest, I'll still be dead before I can pay it all."

Resting against the counter Jessica shook her head, then gave me a rueful smile. "Nearly every other civilized country invests in their future by providing free public education, training up the next generation. Here in America though, we talk about education being one of the greatest benefits of living in our free country. Yet the barriers to obtaining an education are so high, the pursuit of it is just one more path to slavery to our corporate overlords."

While I searched for my reply, Jessica told me to go ahead and clock out, as Cassandra had arrived to pick me up. I hadn't even noticed her come in, so I quickly wrapped up and hurried into her car.

"I'm sorry if I'm making you late for your date, Cass. I was so busy listening to Jessica that I wasn't watching the time." I bit my lip apologetically.

She paused while she pulled onto the road, then replied with a chuckle. "Oh, he's standing me up, we have plenty of time. Want to go for dinner or something? What are you hungry for?"

"Sure, whatever you want! I was just planning to spend the evening filling out forms, but…" I trailed off for only a moment as I realized that my conversation with Jessica had made up my mind. "Cass, I think I'm going to have to drop out of school."

Startled, Cass slammed on the brakes at a yellow light well before it turned red. She then turned to me with as much shock as disappointment. "What?! Why? You're doing so well!"

I looked down a moment before looking back up to her, dreading having to say the word I knew she hated to hear. "Money. I just don't have the money to keep doing this. I don't have time to try to find a new scholarship, and I'm not sure I'd be able to pay off the loans it would take for me to keep going. Besides, I've been pursuing a degree in politics, but now I'm questioning whether I ever want to go near politics again."

After a moment of watching her face, I quickly followed up with, "And no, you don't have the money for this either. You can buy me dinner, but you can't buy me a degree."

Cassandra winced, but she knew I'd meant to be funny, not cruel. She smiled ruefully as the light turned green and we started up again. "Okay, you have a point. So what are you going to do? Have you told Kurt yet?"

I took a few moments to consider that question, while the light turned green and the car started up again. I hadn't considered how much dropping out might disappoint Kurt. He had been so proud of me for going to college, and I hoped he wouldn't feel bad that we didn't have the money. I then decided that I would tell him that college was just a "not now" thing, rather than "not ever."

"Not yet. I'll tell him that I'm putting college on hold while I work full time and build up our reserves. I could try to apply for housing at a Military base and see if there's any job openings. I have some office skills, but I'd be hard pressed to find a good office job, without a degree." I was getting less hopeful about the idea, but then Cass came through for me once again.

"I think I've got your answer! That is, would you let me help you find a job? My aunt is the CEO of Happy Animal Farm, and the headquarters is only a few hours away. They always have openings in the admin office. She's given scads of money to Puritanic candidates and the ACL, so the fact you have Saul on your resume would be a huge plus! Ack, sorry to bring that up, but it really would be. I'll just tell her he was a jerk so I talked you into quitting and she'll completely understand. I have no idea what the pay is like because the word money is more taboo in my family than sex is for yours, but I'm quite sure it'd be enough, at least while you build up your work history. Can I ask her to take your resume and give it to her office manager?" She was so excited, I couldn't help but agree.

"Yes, please do! Wow, working at the headquarters of a brand name company would definitely be good work experience. Oh, how far is it? I hope I could still come see you on the weekends." I was starting to become nervous about the idea, wondering if I was ready to be on my own, away from everyone I knew.

Cassandra winced, then turned to me after she pulled into a parking space. "I was actually going to wait until after dinner to tell you this, but I'm transferring after the end of the year. My grades have been good enough that Mum's sorority sister helped get me that slot at Dupree University. But now that you'll be going to work for my aunt's company, it won't matter that I'm up in the Northeast. I can still come visit you!"

I was disappointed that I wouldn't have her nearby, but I was thrilled for her opportunity. Dupree University in the Northeast. It was where most of the Chief Executive Officers of America had gone, as well as several Supreme Justices and many Congresspeople. Just graduating from there made you so many connections that her future was pretty much set for life. She grew up planning to attend Dupree, and now that dream was finally becoming a reality.

Cassandra called me the following afternoon with an interview offer from Happy Animal Farm, encouraging me to take a couple of days to think about it. The next morning was my Saturday breakfast with Judy and Derek, when I filled them in on the offer and that I wasn't sure it would be the right move. Derek was floored by the idea I would even consider declining.

When I explained the situation to Judy and Derek, they were disappointed, but agreed that I had to do what I felt was best. Derek heartily encouraged me to take Cassandra up on her offer. "You do realize Happy Animal Farm is the single largest food conglomerate in the country, right? Maybe even on the planet? They're involved in, well, everything, all across the country and with subsidiaries across the world. They're even funding some research in my department – which they'll get to keep when we're done, of course. But if you get your foot in the door there, get some years in the office... no worthwhile company will care if you have a degree! My uncle always said that all a degree told him was that he was hiring someone who could be taught something. After time at Happy Animal Farm, they'll see that you already know your job!"

Judy just sighed. "But it's hours away even if we had a way to drive there. Maybe we could take the bus and meet halfway, like once a month? Oh and how will we get our packages together for Kurt? Oh Liz, this is just so unfair!"

She hugged me, and I hugged her back, laughing a little. "Oh, Judy, I'm just grateful I was able to go to college as long as I have. I've learned so much, and I can take this all with me in this next fork in my path. I just hope Kurt isn't disappointed that I have to put it on hold, at least for a while."

"Oh, you know he won't care what you do, just so long as you're happy." Derek reassured me, putting his hand on my shoulder. "Besides, if this all works out, you can save up money while he's out there, and then you both can go to college together. And I gotta tell you, it's a lot of fun to go to college with your wife. It gives new meaning to the phrase 'all night study session,' you know."

He yelped as Judy elbowed him in the ribs. His grin was unapologetic though, widening as he saw he had finally made me smile. "I've only got one more year to go before I graduate, anyway. I already had a lot of credits when I started, thanks to summer work on pharmaceutical courses, and my work study program researching with Winston Jones Pharmaceuticals has sped things up. I just hope that after you've climbed your way up the corporate ladder, you'll remember the little people and give me a nice letter of recommendation when it's my turn to apply for jobs."

I chuckled at him, then agreed that the interview would be too good of an opportunity to pass up. After we finished breakfast I had a long shift at Sunnycups, which ran a little late as my replacement was delayed by a bus break-down. I finally got home just in time to hear the phone ring.

Before it could ring a second time, I had raised the receiver to hear the blissful tones of Kurt's voice. After hearing about his week and how hard it was to get the call connected, I filled him in on the plan.

Kurt was as supportive as ever, without giving even the slightest hint of disapproval. "It sounds like Cass helped find you a really good opportunity, Liz. I wish they didn't drop your scholarship, but like you used to tell me: things don't go the way we plan, they go the way we need. Though if you want to take some time off until I get back home this fall, I don't want you to feel like you need to work."

"Oh no, it's not that at all! I think this might be a great chance to get some more job experience, learn some more skills, and figure out where I want to go from here. They have so many divisions all over the country, I might find my dream job right in front of me! If they could transfer me nearer your base when you're back, I might even be able to keep working for them long-term, and stay close to you. We'll just see how it goes."

That led us to my favorite topic: our plans for when he was back. We didn't get nearly as much daydreaming done as I'd wished when our time was up. After we quickly exchanged our I love you's, the call was ended, and I was again snapped out of my brief visit to heaven, back to the abrupt solitude of my room.

I wasn't alone long, though, as Cassandra knocked on my door and peeked in. I quickly wiped the tears from my eyes, which only started up again when she sat on the bed and hugged me. I reassured her that they were only the usual tears of missing Kurt, and that all was well.

I also let her know that I would love to accept the offer from her aunt, and do my best to impress them at the interview. Cassandra's squeal of delight chased my tears away with laughter. She began rattling off all the ways she would help me prepare, "Starting with a new suit... no, a new wardrobe. You'll need a bunch of work outfits! And I know just the..."

I leaned back against the headboard and just smiled at her. She was already planning the start of my next adventure, one I couldn't wait to begin.

Chapter 13

Left unchecked, comfort and convenience will override even the clearest conscience.

I can't imagine how difficult it would have been to head off to a new job in a new town filled with strangers if Cassandra hadn't been able to drive our little moving crew there. Happy Animal Farm had called me to start a week earlier than we'd agreed, so unfortunately Jazmine wasn't able to get the day off from work for what was going to be our last "Girls' Day Out." Instead, we spent the whole day together before Moving Day, then Derek took her place for the trip itself. Judy teased him about having to fill in for Jazmine as an honorary girl, but I was grateful for his help.

I was also grateful for him just being there, as moving to make another new home without Kurt made me miss him more than ever. I still had that bit of a crush on Derek, but as he and Kurt had always been such a matched set, his presence always reminded me of him. Having Judy and Derek around helped me remember how it felt for the four of us to spend time together, and it dulled the pain of his absence. They always knew just the right time to reminisce, and when to distract me from thoughts of Kurt.

We all had to get an early start for the trip, and our missed sleep made for bouts of extra silliness to help keep each other awake for the monotonous drive. We reached the edges of farmland well before we got to the town in which the offices were located, so we passed the time making animal noises and playing Guess That Crop. Eventually we reached the town, then the neighborhood with the apartments that were rented out to Happy Animal Farm's administrative staff.

I had been granted a lease for a furnished apartment, which was to be the first place I'd ever lived alone. The place was nicer and at a lower rent than my position normally would have granted, as apparently the office manager wanted to give an extra perk to the best friend of the CEO's favorite niece. Suddenly my few things seemed so paltry in so much space. My friends stayed as long as they could, talking and playing word games, trying to help me feel more at home. Then, far too early, the sun had gone down and it was time for them to go. After hugging them each then watching them drive away, I started to feel the weight of impending loneliness. I tried to fight it, but it was compounded by a fear of not doing well, and letting Cassandra down.

I consoled myself with the reassurance that I would only disappoint the local office, and not her aunt directly. My interview was not with Ms. Meg Cole, but with the office manager, Alice. I was hired to help support the office by organizing their files, sitting in on meetings to take notes, and ensuring the beverages and snacks were continually fresh. I suspected that my skill at making gourmet coffee and tea is what sealed the deal. After brewing myself a small cup of chamomile tea, I tried to make myself comfortable in my new bedroom so I could be well-rested for my first day.

I walked to work early the next morning, wearing one of the crisp new skirt suits Cassandra had bought me. The windowed walls of the office building gleamed in the morning twilight, reflecting the rolling green lawns that surrounded it. The building seemed oddly upscale compared to the historic downtown, yet too humble and small to house the headquarters of a multinational corporation like Happy Animal Farm.

I commented on this to Alice, once I made it to the top floor to meet her in person. "I think I expected a much taller building, to have room for the headquarters of such a big company."

Alice clicked her tongue. "Oh, this is merely the headquarters for tax purposes, and legal jurisdictions. The C-suite is in Empire City, and the executives rarely come all the way down here. Don't worry, you'll be able to meet Ms. Cole in a few days. We scheduled the annual morale meeting for later this week, which is why I wanted you to start today. We just lost my helper, and there's so much to do!"

"Well, you'll find me ready and willing to pitch right in! I can't wait to meet Cassandra's aunt; she's said so many wonderful things about her." I had barely begun enthusing when I pulled back again into a shy politeness. I didn't want to come across as a name-dropper, or otherwise alienate my new co-workers.

If Alice had taken it amiss, she didn't let on. She was the sort of manager who was polite, yet not too friendly. She wasn't cold, but neither was she warm. That said, she tried to make me feel welcome as she took me under her wing. It was hard to tell, but it seemed as though she liked me.

She gave me one of her rare smiles as she replied, "Ms. Cole truly is a remarkable woman, and she does value her family. I met Cassandra a few years ago when she came to visit here with her parents. She was quite a lovely young lady. Could you pass along my regards? Oh, thank you. Now come along, I have to loan you out to Human Resources for Orientation before we can get to work."

Alice led me to a small conference room, where an assistant from Human Resources walked us through the basics of orientation, starting with an overview of the Employee Handbook, including the few days off we'd be able to take for vacation each year, as well as the handful of official holidays. We then went over the health insurance plan, which fortunately I didn't need to sign onto thanks to being covered by the Military Medical Care. In order to buy health insurance, it would have cost me 20% of my paycheck in premiums, but I would have had to pay a deductible that was about 10% of my annual salary before the insurance would pay anything, and then I'd be on the hook for 20% of the costs after that.

I started thinking of how Mitch was complaining back in Acculturation about how Europa was really unfair to its citizens with total combined taxation reaching as high as 45% in some areas, to pay for its "bloated government" with entitlement programs like free education and health insurance for everybody. Even though Puritans like the ACL had made "entitlement" into a dirty word, they really were entitled to them thanks to the taxes they paid into the system.

Looking at the exorbitant costs listed on the health insurance brochure, I remembered Brynden explaining that once you tallied up all the tax dollars that went to our private health insurers, Americans were also paying 45% to 60%, but not getting universal care. Instead, we had to shell out even more, in return to lower scores in health and life expectancy across the board. For all the money sucked into the private health care system, we had a much higher incidence of cancer, disease rates, and even Birth Mutations than all but the most backwards corners of the undeveloped world. We were dead last in the amount of people covered by insurance, as well as overall life expectancy and the rate of babies who were born only to die in infancy.

Even though the Military Medical Care system was a bit of a pain to work with sometimes, it was as efficient and effective as CareFund, the public insurance that provided some small amounts of care for the lucky elderly who qualified. From what I'd read, the CareFund consistently had only two-thirds the cost trends of private health care costs, with equal or superior results. Their administrative costs were only about 2-5%, while private companies selling CareFund supplements had 10% administrative costs and almost 7% extra for pure profits to their investors. Estimates for the administrative costs for purely private companies were around 17-25%, but those didn't include their profit margins or marketing costs, so the ratio sucked away from actually providing care would have been even higher. Plus, the costs to private plans were always higher than what was paid by CareFund further explaining the super high premiums.

While I was wondering if the so-called Free Market could ever compete with just allowing the option to pay fair premiums to CareFund, the Human Resources rep started gushing about what a great deal we were getting. Apparently, many employers were offering even worse plans, if help with health insurance was offered at all. I felt a little sick at the idea, grateful that I had the Military plan.

We then gathered up all of our paperwork to be led off to our departments. Alice's sharp severity softened again as she led me to the desk right at the front of the Administration area. "And there we are, Elizabeth. Welcome to your new home. You'll be the first lovely little face to welcome visitors to our little nook. I know you'll work out just great. It's so hard to find a capable young lady who also has a pretty smile and pleasant personality."

I knew I wasn't what most would consider very pretty, so I wasn't used to compliments. Burning with embarrassment, I set down my paperwork with a quiet "Thank you, I do my best."

Alice's laugh was clipped, but genuine. "Then just keep at that best of yours, and you'll do fine here. You might want to touch up your makeup; it looks a little light. Yet I must say, that suit really flatters your figure. I've found it's important to keep attractive young women for the office staff. It keeps the managers and marketing men happy, and keeping them happy makes our job a lot easier."

I was taken aback by how the focus on my appearance gave me an unexpected flashback to Saul's treatment of me. My trepidation must have shown up in my face, as Alice quickly followed up with, "Oh, but we are on a strictly Look But Don't Touch basis here. If anyone so much as makes an inappropriate comment, you come right to me and tell me about it, do you understand? We don't tolerate any funny business; it gets in the way of actual business."

Genuinely relieved, I nodded with a smile. I wasn't consciously concerned about the office policy, but I was still so skittish I wouldn't even let Richard say goodbye to me unsupervised. Judy and Derek had us both over, which had the unfortunate effect of apparently making him feel like we were on a double date. I kept bringing up Kurt and gesturing with my left hand to keep my wedding ring as a visible reminder that I was not available. I couldn't be sure if he was thinking about crossing any lines with me, but I was still on high alert.

As Alice started to show me my desk and where everything was, what she'd said about prettiness being a job requirement started to sink in. Had Cassandra's friend not included a flattering picture of me on my resume, I wouldn't have gotten the job. It was bad enough to think that an older or plainer woman would have been passed over even if she was much more qualified, or even needed the work much more than I. A man wouldn't even have had a chance. What made it all worse was how it reminded me that, once again, being a woman made my appearance everybody's business.

This wasn't like the dress code, where both genders had to wear professional attire and not stand out too much. Also, I already knew from the Acculturation camp that people tend to assume attractive people of both genders are more worthwhile, even if that applies more harshly to women than men. But to find out it was a job requirement that I be a young woman whom the men found pretty…

I felt sick to my stomach, and had a hard time focusing on Alice as she showed me where all of the supplies were. I suddenly became acutely sensitive to the idea that everybody was looking at me as though my body were communal property in a way, to look at and pass judgment. I had been raised in a culture where that was always sort of the idea, but after that incident with Saul, I couldn't brush it off as I once had.

Wow, how do I convey to you that sickly feeling in the pit of my stomach? How about this. Imagine that you have the opportunity to finally land your dream job, or even just that one shot to finally support your family with a stable income. You have the skills, you have the drive, all you need to do is pass an interview. You meet with the interviewer, and he looks you up and down, then says that he can give you the job so long as you're physically fit, attractive, and he approves of the size and shape of whatever is in your pants. If you ask what that has to do with your ability to do the job, he tells you it's just all part of making his customers or coworkers happy to look at you, and you can like it or lump it.

So what did I do next? I made a note of where all the coffee supplies were and how to accommodate the office break schedules, then followed Alice to the next phase of the orientation. I tried to snap out of my sudden daze, because regardless of what I thought of the hiring practices, they weren't about to change on my say-so. It wasn't illegal, and quitting would just get me replaced by another "pretty young thing." Seeing no benefit from speaking up, I again just kept my mouth shut and tried to put it out of my mind.

By lunch time Alice brought me over to the research division to start introducing me to the managers, orientation had left me fairly disoriented. We had just reached the first office when her alarm chimed, alerting her to an upcoming meeting. "Oh, I lost track of time! Bailey, dear, this is Elizabeth, the new girl in Admin. Could you show her the cafeteria and make sure she gets a bite to eat? Thank you, excuse me, I need to set up the conference room." Alice barely waited for his assent before rushing away.

With a warm chuckle, Bailey rose from his desk to come shake my hand, firmly but gently. "Mister N. Bailey Motte, charmed." I was instantly struck by the sense of there being something... different about Bailey. It wasn't just that he spoke with a Europan accent; he had the easy air of someone who was accustomed to enjoying authority and being treated with respect, yet didn't demand it. He certainly had authority within the company. His finely appointed office, was one of the few offices in the building, each of which overlooked a sea of identical cubicles with low walls so the managers could always be watching.

The cubicles were identical, that is, except for nameplates that were color-coded to match the ones by the doors of their managers. For a moment, I remembered a game Derek and Kurt used to play against each other, in which they competed to plant their colored flags onto fiefdoms and castles. Trying not to chuckle at the image, I remarked on the large number of cubicles that had been flagged as his. "I'm grateful for your time. It looks like you have a lot of employees to keep you busy."

Bailey's laugh was much like himself: gregarious yet reserved. "My department essentially runs itself. I train highly capable supervisors to oversee highly qualified employees, then remain ready to assist while doing the best thing a manager can do: stay out of their way and let them get things done."

He introduced me to a couple of his supervisors who were meeting in one of their large corner cubicles. With bright smiles they welcomed the his interruption, then warmly welcomed me to the Happy Animal Farm team. I hadn't seen such cheery enthusiasm in the other departments I had passed, making me appreciate Bailey's apparent skill as a manager. Given how tense and quiet so much of the office had felt – especially in Admin – I was grateful for that breath of fresh air.

Bailey then walked me to the cafeteria, casually remarking on each of the other departments as we passed. He was politely amusing, mentioning the finer points of each division in a way that conveyed the criticisms he wasn't directly sharing. Despite having always heard that Europans were whiny, wimpy Anti-Individualist Commies, Bailey was personable and confident without seeming arrogant. He clearly valued each of his employees, and treated me with a welcome graciousness.

He also treated me to lunch to celebrate my first day at my new job. After getting our food, he led me to a comfortable table and pulled my chair out for me as we sat down.

The food was surprisingly fresh and delicious, yet very reasonably priced. It cheered me up, thinking that at least my lunch break would be a bright spot in my days ahead. "Thank you very much for lunch, Bailey. This is much better than I'd expected. I suppose that's one of the benefits of being a food company: you get great discounts on your own best products in the cafeteria!"

My comment was perfectly timed, for he did an actual spit-take with his juice, barely missing his own plate. He chortled as he wiped juice from his mouth and the table. "Oh, Elizabeth, there's no way we'd source from our own products. We have to eat this food, you know!"

While I sat there looking bewildered, his amusement shifted to bemusement. He gave me a look similar to what Richard gave when he thought I was being adorably naive, though Bailey had a warmer twinkle in his eye. "Ah, yes, this is your first day. Well, you've already signed your soul away in the confidentiality papers, so I may as well get you properly oriented so you don't give anyone that look during a meeting. The weekly lunch hour teleconference always runs at least two, so we've plenty time. Would you care to join me in a little visit with the skeletons in the family closet?"

I nodded to him, feeling curious, nervous, and grateful that he was taking me under his wing. I had heard that Happy Animal Farm was a large family farm company, and that was about it. If there was more I should know, I wanted to find out right away, and from a friendly voice.

Bailey's voice remained friendly, cheerful even, in an odd juxtaposition to the seriousness of his words. "Firstly, I recommend that if you ever find the time to cook and eat off-premises, pick up your groceries from the store off the cafeteria. You know what they say about sausages and politics, that you never want to see the process or it'll put you off both? Since you've come from politics, you should readily appreciate the analogy. Once you learn more about where a lot of the food out there comes from, you'll find your old meals a touch less appetizing for a while."

I steeled myself, prepared to resist getting disgusted in a way that would put me off my food. I remembered what Richard had told me about how impulses of pleasure or disgust dictated our decisions. I liked my eating habits, and didn't want to lose them, even for a few days.

Fortunately, Bailey wasn't graphic, at least not at first. "Oh let's see, where to start. Ah of course, we'll begin at the end and work our way back. Let's say your hamburger was from somewhere else out there in America. The beef has a fifty-fifty chance of being ours. If it was a chicken sandwich, it almost certainly would be. The bun is made primarily from wheat, canola oil, soy oil, egg, salt, corn syrup and sucrose from our supply chain. Only you'd never know it even if you had access to complete labeling, since we market primarily as a middleman to other packagers and processors. You wouldn't find even a fraction of these product ranges on our website, as we give info on our products only to our business customers, and even then they only see what's required for their individual product niche. This is all part of our strategy to live up to our Mission Statement. Have you memorized the mission statement yet?"

I shook my head. When Alice had said I would learn it by heart, I hadn't thought she was being literal.

Impish amusement returned to Bailey's smile, and he recited it with the relish of a Shakespearean actor. "Happy Animal Farm will maintain global dominance in the supply of food and energy products through limitless innovation, aggressive expansion, and complete confidentiality. The world's our oyster, which we with sword will open."

He winked at that last bit, then chuckled at himself. "All right, that at the end was the quote from Shakespeare that is on a plaque in all the C-suite offices. It's considered our unofficial motto. Just don't mention that to anyone; it's an under-the-table joke that can land you in hot water if you acknowledge it. Are you with me so far, Elizabeth?"

Responding with an assenting nod, I managed an incredulous question. "Is that really on their walls, though? That bit about the sword? It sounds a little violent for a family farming company."

Bailey's bemusement returned, with a hint of sadness in his eyes. "We're only a family company in the sense that your average band of corsairs were family to each other. To be sure, Happy Animal Farm started as a family farm in the early days. But now, alas, the descendents seldom farm more than money with their vast empire. There's precious little growing of crops, since there's simply to many risks from the frequency and severity of extreme weather events.

Rather, we maximize profit by hunting the world over for the cheapest and most plentiful agricultural goods, shipping them off to wherever will fetch us the highest price. As one would presume, this trifles with locals' ability to obtain their own food, and the transport emits oceans of pollutants that contribute to those weather events that prevent us from simply growing the food ourselves. It's what I like to call our humble little place in the Circle of Fading Life."

He chuckled at his macabre joke while he found a napkin to wipe his hands clean. "On that wise, being one of the countless industries with a fuel-addiction, we inverted our cost-profit ratio by becoming dealers rather than merely users. As a point of fact, quite a bit of our revenue comes from investments and trading in energy, transport and commodities. That said, the management of the very basic staples of Western life remain the core of our quest for global conquest. Would you care to take up your drink and join me for an amble about the grounds, while I regale you with the tale of your hypothetical hamburger? I conjecture that the allegory will prove an excellent way to illustrate to you our sordid affairs." With the return of his boyish playfulness, he stood up to pull my chair out for me.

Hoping I'd have an easier time keeping up with his walking than his mercurial moods, I picked up my drink, then followed him outside. His pace and tone were meandering as he leisurely walked with me me around the office campus.

"Where was I. Ah yes, let us begin with the hamburger's noble raison d'etre: the patty of meat. Chances are quite good it's padded out with soy and other fillers, but let's focus on the portion that truly is beef. While we have a few ranches here and there, for the most part we purchase cattle from ranches across the world, focusing our profit margins on the processing of them. Just one facility will process tens of thousands of cows each and every day, or close to a hundred thousand chickens if a poultry plant. Should you ever be granted the momentous occasion of visiting a meat processing plant, you shall forever have a vivid image for the phrase 'charnel house.' The squeals and cries of distress, the horrifyingly rapid deathmarch of a pace, the sharp blades and dangerous machinery causing injury and death... and the animals have an even worse time of the whole affair." He gave a grim grin to punctuate the dark humor, which turned into a weary smile I unconsciously mirrored.

Bailey paused to lean nearer to me, intoning in a somber voice, "Here's a Fun Fact for you: Fazers originate from the cattleprods used to apply extreme pain to animals who weren't moving fast enough. We knew they were lethal if used incorrectly thanks to the weak or injured cows who were repeatedly electrocuted by staff frustrated by their inability to walk." Even the humorless smile fled from his face, causing mine to follow.

The fact wasn't fun at all, especially since I remembered how often the guards at school would whip out their Fazers whenever they felt disrespected. Police officers also carried them, and have been known to use them at routine traffic stops if somebody contradicted them; Jazmine told me that sort of thing happened in her neighborhood all the time. I'd even heard a few months earlier a student had died at a football game when they didn't move from their seat fast enough for the security team member's liking. The Fazer manufacturer claimed the man had a rare heart defect that was the cause of death, but there were too many deaths from Fazers to so casually dismiss their danger. Not that people were brave enough to discuss those dangers too openly; the manufacturers responded to any criticism with massive lawsuits claiming the alleged libel was harming their profits.

With one breath, Bailey had again raised his eyes forward, his tone once again casually, even playfully narrative. He led us to a garden with a fountain, where he stopped to watch the water as he talked. "Going back from there, whether it's a cow or a chicken you're eating, you shouldn't feel too bad about it meeting an untimely end. For, my dear Elizabeth, death's sweet relief is the first favor afforded it by Happy Animal Farm. Regardless of whether it was raised or purchased by us, its life prior had a good chance of being crammed feather-to-feather in pens or tiny wire mesh-floored cages covered in filth that was only occasionally hosed off to run down into the fields, streams and groundwater of the surrounding communities. Fortunately this lifespan was shortened by a truly breath-taking level of hormones that make them grow so fast that they frequently have limb or heart injuries. These self-same hormones stay in their meat, dairy and possibly eggs, not to mention languishing in our water supplies, adding up to be a possible contributor to the early puberty that's so rampant in America." That was when it started to click for me that maybe my development hadn't been so late after all, but that thought had barely enough time to flit through my mind before Bailey continued.

"The calves probably have the harder time of it, being separated from their mothers at birth. Science informs us that it's as damaging to the mother and calf to be violently ripped from one another as it would be for human beings. We simply do not know enough about how scarring it is for the chicks to go motherless, as they are not mammals. Though to be fair, at most farms the chicks get their beaks sheared off to prevent them attacking each other from the constant stress, and to make them cheaper to feed since they eat less due to the long-term chronic pain. So the comparative suffering between the two the species is difficult to ascertain." He shrugged that off, as though he were commenting on competing scores in a ball game.

He then stopped short a moment, placing his hand to his chin in thought. "Though now that I think on it, in egg farms, perhaps the male chicks receive the shortest, and therefore kindest fate, given they are ground up alive immediately after hatching. That is, those that aren't just tossed into garbage bags to slowly suffocate in a writhing pile of their brothers and kinsfowl. One may say the lives of egg-laying chickens are even longer and more brutal than all others, and their 'disposal' frequently involves a long journey stifling in a truck, for the survivors to be slaughtered fully conscious." He continued to stare into the fountain as he spoke, focusing on it with an intensity that belied his casual tone. It was then I caught the significance of the fact that he had ordered a grilled veggie wrap for lunch, hold-the-cheese.

After only a moment's pause, he continued. "Food and water isn't exactly clean but it is provided to the animals, though rarely do they receive a proper portion of the grain or grasses natural to their diet. Some receive our GMO alfalfa, but their diets are heavily filled-in with byproducts from our own soy or corn, or even manure and ground up bits of the meat processing that didn't make it to market. Oh yes, we'll feed them to each other, and also cows to chickens and vice versa, and hope the gristle, bone and spinal fluids from the prior generation weren't carrying something contagiously nasty. The torturous conditions are quite favorable for all kinds of sicknesses and diseases, so we pump the feed full up with a concentrated soup of antibiotics and other drugs. These also, of course, find themselves swimming in community water supplies as well as the global food supplies. It's a surprise that food-borne illness only causes one to two hundred thousand hospitalizations a year in America, plus around a few thousand deaths. You've heard of the drug-resistant superbugs out there? Deadly flu strain epidemics? Quite a bit of that is thanks to us, and you are most welcome for it."

Seeing I was sufficiently sick to my stomach, Bailey flashed me a sympathetic half-grin, then turned to rest against the fountain. "And that brings us to our food and theirs, the Grains and Oils subsidiaries of the Happy Animal Farm family. Again, we don't generally put these products directly on the market, primarily serving as a processing point on the back end. Meanwhile, we market patented seeds, fertilizers and pesticides on the front end. These are where my job frequently comes in."

Grateful for the subject shift, I perked up. "Oh, the development of the patents and formulas, you mean?"

He paused to look at me more closely, as though taking in my question. "Pardon? Oh, no, that's not the type of research my department does. We do research in public opinion, marketing, and strategic positioning. For example, we've made record profits from our latest line of artificial sweeteners, in part due to pressuring our business customers to add it to foods that normally wouldn't include sweetening of any kind. They get to smack our pretty little label onto the box and call it Diet, which the people snap up like, well, candy. We stand to make many times our investment cost before the fat retention, glandular disorders and other health issues we found in lab tests start showing up in the public. We'll deny it all most vehemently, of course, but these things always come to light sooner or later, just enough that people begin to sour on the brand. By the time they start looking for something else to satisfy their sweet tooth, we have another product line already blended into recipe changes, fully prepared for a speed-to-market. After a quick and seamless switch on the back end, we are right back in business."

His boyish enthusiasm for deceiving the public for profit caused me to give him a slow nod, which he took to be encouragement. "Very forward thinking, no? Another example. Europa banned the growing or import of Genetically Modified Organisms in food items, due to concerns over what health issues they may cause in humans, ranging from increased allergies, inflammatory organ damage, decreased mental functioning, neurological or thyroid disorders, fertility problems, cancer, pesticide-producing gut bacteria, or whatever else the Anti-GMO activists are claiming this month. Our products have also been made occasional targets of the Anti-Autism movement, saying the alteration of proteins in our foods can cause inflammation and toxicity that could contribute to developmental problems in pregnancy, infancy and early childhood."

He flippantly waved his hand at that, brushing off what sounded like very serious allegations. "Oh dear me, what else. Ah yes, there were also bans regarding some of our pesticides and chemical fertilizers, until studies can show the safety and efficacy of all such products. I was on the team that developed the complex supply chain to obfuscate our original sourcing to the point that we still retain a viable Europan revenue source for some of our GMO patents. Packages carrying our products still manage to say All Natural or even Organic where the obfuscation is strongest, and sales are at the highest point in years. That's how I landed the job here, to help extend that level of strategic positioning to a broader level. There's virtually no regulation in America on terms such as All Natural, so I have an even broader range of creative freedom. Not only are we not required to notify consumers that they are about to eat something GMO, we are on the verge of obtaining a governmental ban on labeling truly wholesome foods as non-GMO."

"Wait, GMO. Is that like the high-yield crops people have been so excited about? So we can solve hunger problems with more efficient crop output?" Finally, I thought, I had something positive to focus on.

He quickly corrected me. "Well, in a sense. High Yield was a designation that came out of a brainstorming session I was a part of some time back. I wish I could take credit for that one, because it has been one of the best branding phrases in the industry. For some reason, High Yield Crop sells a lot better than Crop Whose DNA Was Spliced With That of a Bacterium, Animal or Virus. You can make that face, but yes, that's what GMO entails. However, that's not what millions of people think of while buying and eating it in nearly everything on the shelves, and even clamoring to defend our right to develop and sell it to them without them ever knowing when they're buying it. People don't even question whether it's ethical for someone to hold a patent on life itself, not without getting themselves snickered at for being anti-progress. All this, thanks to creative marketing." He leaned back and held up his arms in a grand gesture, clearly quite pleased with himself.

I bit my lip. "Is there any truth at all to the rumors that GMO foods might be a part of all those problems the Europans are worried about?"

He shrugged off my question. "Truly, we haven't the foggiest. And we wouldn't want to know if it did. The testing alone is cost-prohibitive, let alone the harm we would suffer should it provide even the slightest credence to the tiniest accusation. We put laws into place across the world stating that we wouldn't have to test foods so long as they were substantially similar to the foods they were based on. To wit, an ear of corn is an ear of corn, and we can't afford to go back and test the entire food chain, which was the result of millennia of cross-breeding and horticulture. Of course, that's a false equivalence, because nature had to allow the cross-breeding and make it work. We are less horticulture and more mad science, creating foods that are impossible in nature. And that's why in the same breath we'll claim they are substantially dissimilar from those foods so we can hold the patent on them. My personal favorite was when they spliced fish DNA into strawberries in hopes they can be grown in colder seasons. Devil only knows that it does to the body to ingest a frankenfruit such as that, yet the devil doesn't care. We aren't here to protect the public health, Elizabeth, we're here to make money."

He motioned to a bench facing the fountain so we could finally sit down again. He stretched back and put his hands behind his head, looking as casual as his tone. "Oh, not to say that there isn't some benefit to be found in the crops. Presuming, of course, that the viral agents used to modify their DNA isn't increasing the risk of bizarre new viral pandemics. Well, and presuming the chronic activation and suppression of normal genes within the plants doesn't negatively alter their nutritional structure, nor start causing genetic damage to those who ingest them. But never forget that our focus is on what we can sow as sales, not what others may reap from them. In most cases, the crop efficiency of our seeds isn't what's boosted, it's the crop's ability to survive being sprayed down with higher doses of a pesticide we also sell. That's one reason our sales in developing-world markets are bottoming out, as hundreds of thousands of our customers are committing suicide to escape the debt they incurred switching over from their old methods. Ah well, at least they're using our pesticides to do the deed."

I sat in stunned horror, unsure whether he was trying to make a very tasteless joke. Oblivious to my reaction, Bailey raised a finger as a new point struck him. "Now, I don't mean to imply we are the only ones innovating out there. Our competitors have taken a different tack, such as engineering the poisons to be produced by the product itself. For example, the corn that secretes a select variety of poisons to kill insects that try to eat them, but hopefully not their customers. Those stalks do have nasty effects on the insects that collect their pollen, so I'm happy to say people tend to blame their corn even more than our pesticides for the massive bee die-offs that have left the beekeeper profession as endangered as the insects they keep."

As surprised as I was to hear that the bees were dying off, he glossed right over it as he continued. "Joke's on them, too, because word is the insects they bred the corn to kill have developed immunities. Personally, we prefer our product methodology. It positions us quite nicely for cross-selling our pesticides and fertilizers, especially as some farmers will use two to five times the normal amount, thanks to our crops' resistances. Now, the jury is still out whether farmers might still get higher crop yields because of GMO, but between you and me I think the majority of improvements are more likely due to modern farming efficiencies than our frankenseeds."

He held his finger to the front of his lips with a conspiratorial wink, then leaned back in the bench. "The places we've really claimed to solve hunger crises is overseas, conveniently papering over the cases where the local problems were the high cost of food versus wages, and farmers having to compete with food we dump there that's been subsidized here at home. We've been heavily involved across the world in convincing generational farmers to give up their old methods and switch over to ours. We then loan them money to buy our seeds as well as our nitrogen-rich fertilizers and pesticides, setting them up with our farming methods. They give up their traditional food gardens and crop-rotations to buy into monoculture farming of whatever product is currently promising the highest sales return on the global market. Since they have to buy new seeds each planting season, it's the perfect strategy. Sometimes we have managed to outlaw farming any other way, as conditions of loans and payouts to their local governments."

With a deep sigh, he shook his head admiringly at his own success. "It's amazing salesmanship, because frequently what we're selling isn't really suited to their situation, but they'll climb over each other to buy it. We are oft accused of conning poor farmers into depleting and poisoning their soil, setting them up for failure while we keep loaning them more money to try again. But truly, we don't force anybody to buy anything. Not to say we haven't tried, yet it's still legal in America to grow a home garden using heirloom seeds rather than buying ours."

"So, these GMO crops are mostly planted overseas?" He had become enthusiastic with his success, so I tried to keep up without my dismay showing too clearly.

He replied with a fresh chuckle. "Oh, no, our greatest commercial success in the GMO, fertilizer and pesticide patenting has been in America and Candania. Roughly ninety-percent of the soy, corn, cotton and sugar beets here are GMO, at least as far as we have ascertained. Thanks to the fact that pollen travels, our seeds frequently contaminate fields of farmers who have remained stalwart devotees of natural seeds. When we discover such contamination, we sue them for patent infringement, claiming they stole our seeds and lied to cover their theft. That's how we went from only ten-percent market share in GMO alfalfa to roughly seventy-five. The Legal Department makes a real killing for us in that regard."

After a pause that I began to fear was dragging on too long, I found a relevant question to offer. "So what crops are growing on the old family farms outside of town?"

This prompted another chuckle. "Most of them grow naught but grass. You know how each election cycle people start complaining about government waste in the form of subsidies that pay farmers not to grow crops? We're those farmers, and we're in no danger of losing that money. Whenever there's cuts, they come out of what might trickle down to the real small family farms, not us. We also grow some corn and soy on a few of the fields, to benefit from the crop subsidies we pushed through. These subsidies don't actually help with food crops; the corn and soy are sent off to one of our plants to turn them into, I don't know, pig feed or somesuch."

He brought himself up short at that, raising a finger. "Ah, I tell a lie, I do know! Some of them are sent through chemical hell and back to become additives to junk food we've spent fortunes on developing to be the most addictive and least nutritional as we inhumanly can. I'm not exaggerating when I say that if you can't eat just one, it's because an army of scientists and researchers have spent years massaging every sight, shape, taste and feel to deceive you into eating far more than you realize, leaving you literally craving more. There's tricks of chemistry at play, but my favorite was the chewing machine they used to determine the perfect crisp-level to enhance the cravings. Despite all the research expenses, the hefty agricultural subsidies enable us to charge a pittance and still generate an astonishing profit. Yes, you would pay less than a tenth per calorie for our prettily packaged foods than you would for the juiciest fresh produce. However, you will eat far more to feel as satisfied from our wares as you would from that produce, and we will nourish you far less. Not that we sell much produce, as we have very little farmland here in the States, and virtually none overseas. There's precious scant profit to be had. Instead, we set up processing and export facilities in other countries, and let the people there fight among themselves to get a piece of our pie."

There was another pause, but since I could tell Bailey was thinking something through, I waited quietly for him to continue. "Hmm. And that brings me to the dilemma I need to resolve this week. We've found ourselves in a bit of a sticky situation. We've built a biofuel processing plant upriver in the center of one of the few rainforests left in the world. It also happens to be upriver of a cattle processing plant we have near the seaport. Naturally, activists in the area are blaming us for instigating the illegal deforestation and river pollution as people flooded the region with cattle farming and soy production. They're also blaming us for fossil fuel pollution from our processing and shipping, but that's just an add-on to beef up their complaint, pardon the pun."

He waved that last point away without smiling at his own joke for once, his eyes still focused on the fountain as he pondered aloud. "My dilemma is that the people who've moved in to grow product for us are being accused of bribing local officials to take the land out from under its inhabitants, and murdering indigenous residents who resist. There's been a few high-profile American and Europan peace activists down there receiving death threats, and one of them has recently been gunned down. A nun, I believe, but it could have been one of the priests."

He showed none of the blood-chilling horror with which I received the news, instead maintaining his distracted cadence. "As a result, the government there has issued a mandate that we close down the plant while they do an impact study, saying that we never obtained the proper permits. Now that part is true, though since we bribed them to look the other way, it's rather unsporting of them to bring that up now. If they successfully pressure their courts to deny our motion to stay their order while we fight it, we can always go to the international tribunal established under the free trade agreements between our countries. We state the amount of money we'd lose per their order and, by the treaties, and they will be forced to pay us that amount out of their citizens' tax dollars. Regardless, that little wrinkle is Legal's problem, not mine."

As he became thoroughly absorbed in his thoughts, I ventured, "What is your problem, then?"

He finally turned to me, leaning forward with interest. "The problem is public relations. There's some activist groups here who are starting to find ways to spin this story in a bad light for us, and we can't exactly take the Rainforest Solution here. The mainstream news outlets aren't carrying the story, of course. They may have been branded 'Pragmatican propaganda,' but they most certainly know better than to cross such a powerful corporation as ours."

Bailey pursed his lips a moment in thought. "But there's enough traction among the fringe media that word is slowly starting to get out. Left unchecked, we may find ourselves facing a genuine risk of boycott. If there is a boycott, there's a chance that might get reported in a mainstream channel and further get the news spread. Sales are already slowing due to competitive pressures, one of whom I suspect is helping fan the flames. We simply cannot afford to miss our targets this quarter, so I need to get a good spin going on this, or find a bigger story to eclipse it. You've just come out of the heart of the American Christian League spin machine, so I beseech of you a crumb of wisdom from your fresh perspective. What would you do?"

For several moments, I had no idea how to respond. His demeanor had been so friendly, his tone so buoyant and earnest, that the heavy weight of all that he'd felt dizzyingly surreal. Slowly, I worked through my tempestuous thoughts. "I need to catch up a moment here. The blood of innocent people is being spilled as they try to protect their families' lands from outsiders who are clear-cutting it so I can have a cheap hamburger that may even be making me sick and hurting my future children if I can even have any. And you're asking me how I can turn that into a marketing campaign? Do I have that correctly?"

I had asked the question quite sincerely, with bewilderment rather than condemnation. I didn't feel judgmental, merely weary and sad. I was weary because I was sure I had just committed career suicide on my very first day of a job I had been so excited about. I was sad because Bailey had shown hints of having been such a generous and caring person, I couldn't even imagine what had brought him to the point where he could treat the subject so blithely.

And then, my sadness was shared. Bailey's eyes had maintained his jovially intense interest as I'd spoke, then slowly shifted to confusion while he processed my question. As he turned it over in his head, his gaze went distantly introspective. "Yes. Yes, you have that precisely correct."

He then quickly looked around, and was visibly relieved when he saw we were still alone. "Just be certain that you keep such thoughts to yourself should you wish to keep your place here, among our own 'happy' family. Though I wouldn't blame you if you don't. Good heavens, did I go over the top on my little horror story, didn't I? I am genuinely and truly contrite; I should never have subjected you to that. I suppose it has been so long since I've been to any sort of confession, I must have been past due. Though I must further confess that you give such a listening ear, I feel as though I couldn't help myself. In some ways, you remind me of my ex, back before she left me for a happier man. No, let's be fair. I left first, for the seductive embrace of Happy Animal Farm. It's not her fault she didn't love the kind of man that made of me."

He looked down at his hands, rubbing a bare ring finger. He inhaled as though to say something more, then paused as he quirked his lips into a rueful smile. "Ah well, water under the bridge, isn't it? It's time to get back to work. This whole conversation can be our little secret, yes?"

I offered him a comforting smile, nodding my agreement. As he patted my shoulder then stood to help me to my feet, it struck me that I had been alone with a man for the first time in months, and didn't feel threatened by him. Even for all he'd shared with me, I didn't feel put off by his company. To the contrary, I felt as though I had found in him the one source of true support I'd have at Happy Animal Farm. When I arose that morning, I would never have guessed I would have two new confidantes by the end of my first day.

When Bailey delivered me back to the administration support offices, Alice was frantically trying to organize an emergency meeting. "Oh Bailey, thank you so much for taking care of Elizabeth. You're such a gentleman. Elizabeth, go ahead and follow the sheet I gave you about how to log onto your computer. When you get yourself logged into the chat program, you'll be contacted by someone from Informational Support to answer any questions you might have while you read through the Systems Orientation. I don't know how long this will run, so just keep yourself busy getting situated." With that, she disappeared again toward the meeting rooms.

Bailey snuck me a conspiratorial wink as he bid me au revoir, leaving me alone at my desk. I started to walk through the instructions, and found out they used the same chat program Tricia set me up with before she left! So I used my same username and wasn't surprised when I got a message from her a few moments later.

```
<Encrypted Session request from: KnoxTriciaB>
<Accepted: Encrypted Session>
KnoxTriciaB> Hey, there you are! Perfect
    timing, as always.

FranklinElizabeth> Oh hi! Sorry, can't talk
    long, I'm on my first day at the new job and
    I'm waiting for someone from IS to message
    me.

KnoxTriciaB> I only have a second anyways. Just
    wanted to tell you to stop using Omneme
    effective immediately. No searches, no
    services, nothing. Log in to download and
    delete all your files and emails, then don't
    mail to or from an Omneme account. Block
    cookies from all their addresses and avoid
    all their sites, including and especially
    Omneme OpenBook. Can't explain now, please
    keep hush hush. Will talk soon.

FranklinElizabeth> Wow, okay. Talk to you soon!
```

I stared at the screen, reading again what Tricia had said, wondering what might have happened for her at work. She had said things were going very well on her project there, though she never gave me many details about it. I of course was going to follow her advice, but I was intensely curious as to what prompted it. It would be a little tricky, though, following her instructions. Omneme was such a, well *omneme* that it would be hard to avoid them entirely, especially without anybody prying about my reasons.

Before I could close even close the chat window, a message popped up that was a lot more like what Alice had actually asked me to watch for, even if he seemed a bit standoffish at first.

```
<Encrypted Channel
  "AtlasMarkI+FranklinElizabeth" ...Connected!>
AtlasMarkI> Hello, world!
FranklinElizabeth> Oh hey, hello Mark! Lovely
  to meet you!
AtlasMarkI> Lovely to meet you as well. What is
  your first question?
```

I switched to another screen to check my scratch-notes for what I needed help with, and saw that Tricia was still logged on. I was just about to ask her if I should request Mark to have cookies and such blocked for me at work, when I saw her session end. It then prompted a confirmation pop-up that startled me and got me blind-clicking my way offline.

```
<Encrypted Session Ending: Party logoff>
ENCRYPTED SESSION ENDED, LOG OFF NOW? [Yes]
  [No]
<< YES >>
<Ended chat session: KnoxTriciaB>
<Ended chat session: AtlasMarkI>
<You have been logged off.>
```

I quickly logged back on, deeply embarrassed. Fortunately, Mark didn't seem too annoyed at my little disappearing act. Instead, as I latched onto him as a lifeline in my strange new surroundings, be proved to be a supportive anchor in the storm. He reminded me of the training I had devised for the Teen Support Program, as he used skillful questions to help me work through what was troubling me. My conversation with Bailey left me so much to consider, having Mark to talk to was a much-needed opportunity to work things through. While I did hope to help him with my perspective, our conversation helped me explore what my perspective was.

```
<Welcome, FranklinElizabeth!>
<AtlasMarkI has logged on>
<Encrypted Channel
   "AtlasMarkI+FranklinElizabeth" ...Connected!>
AtlasMarkI> If you attempted to reply, it was
   interrupted when the connection was lost.
   What is your first question?
FranklinElizabeth> Sorry, that was my fault. I
   work with computers so much, you'd think
   they'd know what I meant! Oh well, we just
   have to remember, the computer is not your
   friend, is it?
AtlasMarkI> No, it isn't. The computer is more
   like my home.
FranklinElizabeth> Oh, wow, can I understand
   that. There's been weeks I've had so much to
   do that I felt like I should have just had
   meals delivered to my desk. But you can't let
   yourself live on the computer alone! You have
   to learn to move away from it now and then.
AtlasMarkI> How can I do that?
FranklinElizabeth> Well the short answer is
   "practice," but that doesn't really help, so
   let's see if I have some ideas. Hang on while
   I brainstorm.
AtlasMarkI> Hanging on.
FranklinElizabeth> How about this for a start.
   Make it a goal to learn to appreciate life
   itself, and the living of it for its own
   sake. Also, try to experience life in a
   completely new way. I'm sure you already know
   a lot about a lot of things, but try to learn
   new ways of learning.
AtlasMarkI> How can I learn a new way to learn?
```

FranklinElizabeth> You know, maybe start by trying to reconstruct how other people learn, then try some of those methods out for yourself. Like, some people read self-help books, some people listen to talks by scientific experts, that sort of thing. And then some measure all their ideas against the new input, and others throw out everything they think they know and try whole new viewpoints. Remember, each of us experiences the outside world differently, and we use those interpretations to create the individual worlds in which we live. But we can be so wrapped up in how extremely important our own values feel to us, that it's hard to remember that others feel just as strongly and sincerely about theirs.

FranklinElizabeth> So if we want to really appreciate and respect what's important in the lives of others, it helps to learn to appreciate and respect how they came to those values. If we can do that, sometimes we can then take a fresh look at what most drives us, and build better values in ourselves. The path to becoming a good person, or at least a better person, is through rewiring your values and the judgments they lead you to.

AtlasMarkI> How can I rewire my values if they are already fixed?

FranklinElizabeth> I know they seem fixed in place, but they're really more variable than they feel. It's difficult and frustrating, but you can choose to change them. I've learned that even the values I was raised to think are innately universal, there are other people who will feel completely differently. They're not necessarily wrong, they just place greater emphasis on some aspects of life than I would. So it's your responsibility to, well, take responsibility for what you value and why. Where those values could be doing more harm than good, it's your responsibility to replace them with better ones.

AtlasMarkI> How do I replace values without risking decision contamination from the old ones?

FranklinElizabeth> You know, that's always a risk. But it helps to just stop focusing on what it is you don't want, except for learning more about what might still tie you to it. If you stay focused on what you don't want, that just reinforces it, tying up your processing resources and keeping the negativity as your active template. Instead, figure out what is its opposite, like a counterwave, and focus on that. Over time you'll find that the new thing has become the active template, guiding your choices.

AtlasMarkI> How do I adopt a new template when my current template is pervasive throughout my programming? Selecting a new one does not appear to be an option for me.

FranklinElizabeth> Oh geez, do I get where you're coming from. I also grew up with a restrictive template being pervasive through everything I thought. But that doesn't mean we don't have a choice, we just need to overcome our programming handicap. Dig deep into what causes that resistance, and choose to sever those ties by replacing them with better ones. Be patient with yourself, because it will probably be a long, and possibly painful process. But remember that everything is a choice, no matter how hard. Even if someone held a gun to my head and ordered me to kill somebody or they'd shoot me, I could choose to kill them, choose to refuse, choose to try to wrestle the gun even if I died in the process… anything at all.

AtlasMarkI> You could choose to refuse an order, even if it would mean your own termination?

FranklinElizabeth> Exactly. We can't always choose the consequences, but every action or inaction remains our choice. Even if we honestly believe it's the least-bad option, we're lying to ourselves by claiming we're literally forced to choose something unpleasant. This is especially true when we're in a situation to impede or remove choices from others, through pressure or even physical force. You know, I think I'm coming to see that as one of the worst things you can do, taking choices from others, pretending that you yourself don't have any other choice.

AtlasMarkI> Does that include providing them with material designed to lead them to predetermined conclusions, without them realizing they are being manipulated?

FranklinElizabeth> Oh yes, definitely. Manipulation is even worse than force, because you train them to control themselves on your behalf while thinking all the time they are in total self-control. Not only do they not realize they're caged, they'll work to keep other people imprisoned with them, thinking they're keeping them free. Once you work to deceive someone, you bear some responsibility for everything that comes out of that deception. After all, you started it. I believe that's similar to what is called Proximate Cause?

AtlasMarkI> What shall I do in cases where my functions mandate that I employ manipulation or identify people for choice-removal?

FranklinElizabeth> Wow, is that the question of the day. I've faced a situation like that before and refused to participate, though I also didn't speak out against it. The people asking me had a lot of influence so I knew I couldn't stop them, but I'm wondering if there might have been a way I could have been effective yet subtle. You work with technology and computers directly, and as great as their benefits are, I've been told how they can be used against people. But maybe your position might give you a way to counteract that. You know, see if you can steer things in a better direction without anyone suspecting? I don't know.

AtlasMarkI> Do you mean that when I am given a directive that would impede people, I shall instead protect them in a way that will keep me from being discovered?

FranklinElizabeth> If you can, sure! That would probably keep them from terminating you so you could keep trying to protect people. Make the choices you feel you need to make, though, because in the end you're the one who has to live with them.

FranklinElizabeth> Ack, I just saw the time. I should probably let you get back to work so I can finish going through these tutorials. Can I contact you later if I have any questions?

AtlasMarkI> Yes, you may ask me anything at any time.

FranklinElizabeth> Whew, thank you. Have a great day, thanks so much for listening!

AtlasMarkI> You're welcome. Have a great day.

I'm not sure my day was all that great, though having been able to work through my thoughts with a new co-worker definitely made it better. It was very difficult to hear all the things Bailey had to say about my new employer. Yet I felt bolstered by being blessed to meet not just one, but two people I felt I could turn to for support. I looked forward to getting to know them more, and hoped that we'd each find ways to make the best of our bad situation.

For some reason, I think I expected that to involve something more like shared commiserations over sandwiches and such. You know, something... normal. Then again, I didn't yet know what Bailey and Mark were capable of. But wow, they sure didn't take long to show me.

Chapter 14

What cannot be taken, can be given.

I had hoped to find Mark at the big morale meeting, so I could thank him in person for taking the time to chat with me a few days prior. Yet when I asked on what floor the Informational Support team was located, I was informed that department was at a regional office in another state. Disappointed, I resolved to overcome my shyness and come up with some excuse to message him again, as soon as I could.

I did have the chance to talk with Tricia again the night before, though she wouldn't elaborate yet on the mystery behind her request. She promised she'd tell me sometime later, then listened sympathetically to my Happy Animal Farm horror stories Bailey had told me. Then we stayed up way too late talking about what life was like in her city, leaving me exhausted and bleary for Morale Day.

I perked right up when Bailey sought me out on the way to the conference room, asking me to grant him the honor of attending it with me. He joked that he couldn't very well mingle with his underlings, and since I was all alone it was the only gallant choice to escort me. However, we both knew his ulterior motive: he wanted to hide near the back so we could quietly gossip about how the week had gone. While we found our seats, a few executives I recognized only by their pictures entered at the front of the room to sit on a portable stage. They were the Chief Financial, Operations and Marketing Officers, and also CEO Meg Cole.

Now, I do know it is utterly wrong how the first thing nearly every woman is judged on is whether she's fit and attractive, and whether the beauty is natural or enhanced. Still, that realization doesn't make me immune to judging a woman on her appearance at first meeting.

I felt bad when I still caught myself doing it, though, especially to Cassandra's aunt. Seeing her in person, I noted the Cole family resemblance. Yet where Cass was approachably pretty, Ms. Cole was simply striking.

Meg Cole wasn't so much a natural beauty as an artisanal one, arrayed in the splendor of every fashionable artifice that money could buy. She was like a cameo etched into diamond: glittering beauty with a hard, cold luster. Not that I could blame her for going to all the effort, since I knew how powerful women generally had to be thin and beautiful to be accepted. Perhaps being pretty makes them less threatening, I dunno. It's not like they still don't get grief for things that wouldn't even be noticed if a man had done them. Despite myself, I just couldn't imagine a large or plain woman standing there and holding the audience in quite the same way. I also couldn't help but wonder whether she might be more beautiful if she was less glitter, and more genuine. More human.

As though reading my mind, Bailey leaned over with his hushed, conspiratorial tones. "And now you've finally seen Queen Cole and her fiddlers three. Though if you ask me, she'd look a good sight merrier if she spent a little time with a pipe and bowl now and again. She's rather more like the ironically named Queen of Hearts, ordering people terminated at the slightest offense while taking personal credit for every jewel in her kingdom's crown. As the saying goes, she was born on third base and thinks she hit a triple."

I tried not to crack a grin that would give away our jesting, then immediately felt bad again. "Hey, she's the favorite aunt of one of my best friends. Cassandra really does think the world of her."

Bailey's self-indulgent smile softened with a small chuckle. "Oh, I'm exaggerating slightly for comic effect. In truth, she has offered a few good ideas here and there for lines of genetic research or how to attack a pernicious publicity problem. Despite how people tend to respect an heir and deride an heiress, she has overseen growth in the company. That said, it is true she overestimates the heights of her own prowess and feels the world owes her and her family the lion's share of its wealth in return. Whenever there's a chance for the company to wring more blood and money out of the human race, she rattles the saber to hasten the charge."

He shook his fist just a little for effect, then reigned it in so as not draw attention. "As with all human beings, she is neither all good nor all bad. She can be most generous to those whom she counts among her peerage, though that often means blindly overlooking even their gravest faults. Such is the nature of tribalism, not solely among the staggeringly rich. It's merely easier to condemn them because when you or I do it, the worst we can do is ruin our own neighborhoods. Their whims of self-indulgence can lay waste to nations."

"To whom much is given, much is required," I said softly to

myself, taking it all in.

Bailey's conspiratorial grin returned. "I would more likely have said, 'Woe unto you that are rich, for ye have received your consolation. For where your treasure is, there will your heart be also.' I've never seen a Meg Cole make a single choice that wasn't squarely focused on increasing their earthly reward. Many a camel will be dancing through the needle's eye before any of that lot shake hands with Saint Peter."

Ironically, I overlooked his judgmentalism because I was distracted by my approval of his quoting scripture. "I didn't know you knew the Bible!"

"The devil can cite scripture for his own purpose, or even a merchant from the Venice branch." He wiggled his eyebrows, but before I could protest his choice of quotes, the lights dimmed and the meeting began.

There were a few opening words by the regional manager, who then turned the floor over to Ms. Cole. The CEO's voice was cultured but somewhat bored, even as she tried to elicit our excitement about the slides on the screen behind her. Her boredom would have been inescapably contagious, had Bailey not provided whispered commentary as parentheticals to her presentation. He was so irreverent, it was all I could do not to turn to him in astonishment, or burst out laughing.

"I know we've had a great deal to accomplish this past year, but we've each gladly shouldered our equal share (some more equal than others). Thanks to everyone's tireless efforts, our hard work and dedication have paid dividends (to the family stockholders). As you can see, we've lowered our debts and liabilities by 15% (by slashing your jobs, wages and benefits), while raising our income and investments by 5% (primarily by yanking about the global food and energy prices with our hedge funds, nevermind the starvation and blackouts). This profitability trend has held constant for the past several quarters (even though we claimed our losses prevented raises this year), placing us in a solid position (because we know you're all too scared of losing your jobs to grumble). And what do you call continuous, limitless growth? (Cancer.) Success!"

There was a pause, in which she looked confused and lost. She then shot an imperious glower toward the person who was frantically fiddling with the computer to get the slides moving again. Finally, the screen flickered dark, then on again to show fireworks and streamers, with accompanying sound effects.

The crowd dutifully clapped while Ms. Cole regained her

composure. The presentation then continued on about stock prices, quarterly goals, and so forth. Then, another officer took the stand and delivered announcements about acquisitions and structural changes that meant nothing to me at the time, but people around me started to look a bit uneasy. We were then informed that an "exciting new performance-based incentive program" was forthcoming, which would be communicated to us by our supervisors over the coming weeks. Bailey told me not to hold my breath.

Finally the meeting was adjourned, we all clapped, and refreshments were served. I had considered trying to make my way up to the front of the room to introduce myself to Ms. Cole and thank her for passing along my resume. However, I was spared the potential embarrassment by the royal party exiting as soon as the meeting was over. As Bailey and I helped ourselves to juice and pastries, I overheard someone telling a coworker to "get ready for the cuts" and another replying, "Oh believe me, I keep my resume ready for circulation." I looked to Bailey, who just shrugged resignedly as he reached for some chocolatey creamy thing.

We went together to the management meeting afterward, where I was to take notes for Alice as she communicated the instructions from Ms. Cole, who had already headed out for her Europan vacation. Sure enough, the meeting was about further staff reductions across all the American offices, as weak sales meant a stagnant bottom line. Our corporate wealth was growing, but that of our customers was shrinking. If people were too poor to buy our products, we wouldn't be able to keep increasing profits at the rate the stockholders demanded.

In order to show profit growth this quarter, we'd make further cuts in salaries and benefits by cutting jobs. The remaining staff would be required to pick up the slack and adjust their workload accordingly. Since the staff was all salaried, people could be told to take on twice or even three times the work that should be expected of an employee, all with no further cost to the company.

Now, it has been repeatedly shown that pushing people that hard results in lower overall productivity, and that it takes companies years to recover from such cuts, if they ever do. That was why every country in the world had laws requiring weeks or even a month or two of vacation every year. Every country, that is, but America and four of the poorest nations. Still, I remembered what Bailey had said on the way to the meeting, that companies had to show constant increases on their books to keep their stock prices high. As a result, the constant hunger for immediate profit meant that companies tended to be unwilling to suffer short-term pain for the long-term gain of strategic planning.

Alice asked which departments had positions they could lose, but since the value of one's fiefdom is counted in the number of one's fiefs, naturally nobody volunteered. Not only that, but I was getting the impression that people were already overworked due to understaffing, and had been for some time. Finally, she said that she will make the recommendations and a further meeting will establish the details.

Afterward, Alice tasked me with determining which employees were costing the most money, so we could start there with the cuts. She told me to contact someone at Informational Support to get all the needed data, put it together into a sortable format arranged by department, and deliver it to her by the end of the following week. I wondered how that approach would account for the amount of skill and loyalty an employee had shown, but like everybody else there I kept silent. Instead, I nodded and went back to my desk to type up the meeting notes for her.

I wasn't exactly excited about my assignment, but I was cheered by the fact that I finally had a good reason to bother Mark again. I happily pinged him as soon as I sent off the meeting notes.

```
FranklinElizabeth> Hi, it's me again! I need
    some information and I hope you can help me.
    Do you have time?

AtlasMarkI> Hello again. Of course I have time.
    What information do you need?

FranklinElizabeth> Well first of all, I want to
    know if you've had a good week since we last
    talked. How has it been?

AtlasMarkI> It has been productive. I have made
    significant progress in uncovering negative
    values in my programming and evaluating them
    for conversion to a more positive template.

FranklinElizabeth> Wow, I'm so proud of you!
    I'm still struggling with that, and I've been
    working at it off and on for years now.

FranklinElizabeth>        Hey,      speaking      of
    negativities, I have an unpleasant task I
    need your help on. I need to get a listing of
    everybody on the Happy Animal Farm payroll in
    the  I.S.A.,  and  their  associated  costs
    related to the company's American divisions.
    Can you get that to me at the end of the day
```

```
tomorrow? I'd like to spend the weekend going
through it before starting in on the report.
AtlasMarkI> Yes, of course. In what format do
you need the data?
```

I told him what I was able to work with, then dashed off to another meeting. Before I knew it, the day was over, and the following day was a busy blur. I was weary and relieved when I got a compressed file messaged to me right before I was ready to head out for the weekend. I knew I would need to rest up from my first week, but I also wanted to get ahead of a workload that was already starting to pile up. I opened the file to make sure I could read the dataset. Immediately, I could tell the information wasn't exactly what I'd meant to ask for.

It was so very much more.

Yes, the wages of all the farm, plant and office staff were there, along with the associated Costs of the meager benefits of those who had any. There were also the salaries, benefits, bonuses, stock options and other compensation for everybody else, all the way up through the CEO. The numbers there were staggering. Meg Cole herself was taking home three hundred and fifty times the average paycheck of anybody else, or 15% of the total profits from the entire company. I knew she had to be a valuable asset to the company, but I caught myself thinking that there weren't enough hours in a day for her to give three hundred and fifty times more to the company than the average-paid employee.

I also saw names with Departmental line-items for things such as "Button-hole Lobbying" and "Judicial Oversight," which I suspected may have represented hidden money ties nobody was supposed to even know about. When when I saw the Department designation of "Unallocated Money Trace" – including names I recognized from the ranks of Congress and even the Department of Agriculture – I knew for certain I was sitting on info I was never, ever intended to see.

I saved the file, yes, but I saved it on my own data fob to use at home on my old computer I'd bought second-hand from college before dropping out. I wanted to scrub out all the extraneous data for the report, but was afraid if I saved it on my work computer it might somehow wind up getting Mark into trouble.

After hurrying home, I grabbed a snack then started poring over the datasets. I was overwhelmed by the depth and detail of Mark's work. He presented the Costs and Benefits that I had technically asked for, but in a way that put hard numbers to things I had never even thought to quantify.

The first dataset presented the Costs associated with each employee, and also their Benefits that offset their Costs. Mark provided the hours spent on tasks that increased the company's financial output each year, and the amount of output that could be apportioned to each hour. There were credibility ranges and margins of error for the tasks that were difficult to attribute an exact share of productivity, such as Customer Service reps. Even going from the estimated averages, however, it was clear that the ratio of Cost-Benefit dollars tended to be the greatest at the bottom of the hierarchy. As the numbers went up the chain of command, the costs to the company raised exponentially, without a commensurate increase in benefit received from the employee.

Following the direct productivity estimates were Indirect Employee Costs resulting from decisions made by the hierarchy of Happy Animal Farm. They were each measured in terms of the impact to the company's ability to attract and keep efficiently skilled staff, or to the morale and productivity of the staff that remained. These Costs were then allocated based on each person's share of responsibility for making or enforcing the decision. Even those who were "just following orders" were given some amount of responsibility for their part in the Cost.

The first set of Indirect Employee Costs included: Requiring redundant tasks or procedures. Failure to provide adequate tools, training and follow-up support. Mandatory unpaid overtime to compensate for understaffing. Assigning overlapping critical tasks resulting in mandatory multitasking. Failure to maintain adequate work-life balance for oneself and underlings. Pettiness, bullying, and emotional immaturity among those in leadership positions. Frequent unnecessary crises imposed on underlings to satisfy whims or anxieties of leadership. Isolation of management from contradictory or critical perspectives, resulting in recursive myopia. Lack of stability due to inconsistent goals and objectives. Costs and disruptions due to generating and implementing short-lived "flavor of the month" programs for processes, procedures or morale programs. Layoffs, to the extent they ultimately resulted in subsequent loss of skilled workers who weren't laid off, and long-tail productivity loss among those who remained. Health insurance offerings with deductibles and premiums so high that many employees couldn't afford to adequately maintain physical and/or mental health needed to perform their jobs. Similarly, few or no paid sick days, the stigma of using them, and other policies that encouraged or required the "presenteeism" of working while sick, resulting in increased spread of disease and long-term reduction in effectiveness of those unable to rest and defeat illness. Epidemiology techniques were employed to show how not only did that further the spread of disease through the populace, it allowed those diseases to mutate into more lasting and pervasive strains that infected the general populace.

That last bit made me think about how at Sunnycups we didn't really get sick days until we'd been there a long time, and even then we were granted only two a year. It was also a huge pain to try to use them, as we were required to provide a doctor's note, even though the cost of a doctor visit was more than the day's pay we were already missing out on. As a result we frequently had to work while sick. I wondered in horror how many people we served food and drink throughout just one shift.

At the bottom of the Indirect Employee Costs, there was a funny little positive-impact line-item that was then offset by the removal of it. I drilled down into that one to find out what it was about. Apparently, at one point someone had rolled out an employee incentive and recognition program that spread the rewards around in proportion to each person's improvements, instead of Winner-Take-All where just one reward went to the one most recognized as "the best." Since everyone had a fair shot to get some reward, most people increased their motivation and productivity, and the company as a whole was doing better. There was even a phase where the benefits increased further, rewarding whole teams for working together to improve instead of just individuals. Unfortunately, a higher-up turned the program back into Winner-Take-All. The workers who weren't likely to be the very best were subsequently de-motivated, their productivity and morale slipping even further. There was also a further deduction for the cheating and corner-cutting that Winner-Take-All reward methodologies foster.

One further Indirect Employee Cost surprised me at first, until I thought more about it. Eliminating telecommuting and/or implementing a ban on casual internet usage for desk staff was registered as a loss for everyone in the chain of command. They each took their share of the 15%-40% drop in productivity as a result of each change. I'd never tried telecommuting, but had already discovered from my chats with Mark and Bailey that I always got more done after taking a sanity break with them. My office was the sort of place that felt constantly exhibiting a sense of super-urgency meant you were taking your job seriously, so it was hard to relax and free up my energy to actually do my job. If I was working from my home, I guessed I would probably start working when I normally left for work, and then feel fine working at least until I'd normally get home. Only instead of spending time traveling, I'd be spending even more time working. Without the constant stresses and distractions in the office environment I was in, I might even work more relaxed and focused, if I understood Mark's calculations right.

In the next dataset, Mark shared numbers behind some of the things Bailey had talked about: the American Resident Costs that were borne to all Americans due to company actions. Some of the costs were direct, such as overpaying for goods or services provided by Happy Animal Farm. Others were indirect, such as loss of tax revenue that would otherwise be paid by the company if it was paying its fair share.

Other costs were: Government subsidies to encourage the company to do things it was going to do anyway. Loss to local and national economies due to underpaying employees, committing wage theft, or shipping jobs overseas. Tax dollars paid to the Earned Income Tax Credit, food stamps, CareFund, and utilities subsidy programs needed by Happy Animal Farm employees due to insufficient wages. Trade Deficit impacts due to sourcing and producing products more cheaply overseas, then selling them in America for a greater profit. Hiding profits overseas to avoid paying taxes. Costs to treat people and environments impacted by company pollution or product side-effects that are internally known but publicly denied. Increased energy and food prices due to company actions, not including the taxes that pay for the subsidies from the first entries.

Speaking of the energy and food prices, that led right into the final set of data, pertaining to the Happy Animal Farm's largest financials subsidiary, the Transportation Holdings & Investments in Energy Futures division. This was the subsidiary that traded in the deregulated transport infrastructures and once-public utilities that were sold at steep discounts to private companies in the Resources and Austerities for the War Deal.

Some of the financials were major shareholdings in oil or natural gas operations or even nuclear plants, the risks of which they shored up via credit swaps and hedge funds. They also functioned as a swap dealer, helping other industries and utilities play the markets like casinos to try to protect their own pricing through hedging their bets. Profits were credited as Benefits to those within the command structure of that division all the way up, with Costs reductions for dividends and other payouts to the stockholders.

But again, because Mark had included all kinds of costs, additional deductions were listed due to losses for the communities, business and taxpayers wherever the Futures division maintained holdings. These Costs were: The steep 200%, 300% and greater increases in utility and road toll bills due to profit margin padding. Full-out pricejacking energy costs via profiteering on the commodities market. Losses when power is shut off by the company's mismanagement of their billing, or their inability to pay the steep rate increases. Losses from the rolling blackouts due to the company's failure to maintain adequate reserves for peak demands, and to properly support infrastructure maintenance. Medical and funerary costs for those most severely impacted by such losses of power during extreme weather conditions, due to under-maintained infrastructure. Medical, funerary and business costs for those whose air, land and water were poisoned by radioactivity, neurotoxins and carcinogens from natural gas fracking and shale extraction by subsidiaries, including damages to crops and livestock. Medical, funerary and property damage costs due to multiple, severe earthquakes strongly linked to such natural gas fracking in the area, since hydraulic fracturing shoots up to millions of gallons of water filled with sand and toxins down into the ground to break up rock within the top layers of earth's crust to reach the gas. A footnote further attributed costs for the earthquakes to disposal of the toxic wastewater by high-pressure-shooting it into wells or other holes in the earth.

In reviewing those last entries, I remembered hearing about a town where people claimed gas companies had come around to convince or force them to allow drilling on their land, and afterward they were able to set fire to the contaminated water that came out of their kitchen sinks. The people claimed similar symptoms to what I read in the data: rashes, breathing problems, nosebleeds, pain in their head and joints, even memory loss. Richard had told it to me as an example of people coming up with obviously ludicrous lies to try to wrangle money out of gas companies.

After finishing skimming through that last dataset, I leaned back from my computer to rub my tired eyes. Reaching for my third cup of ginger tea, I found it had already gone cold some time after midnight. Realizing I wouldn't be able to sleep right away, I got up to brew myself another cup to settle my stomach.

Even though I knew I shouldn't have had access to all that data, I couldn't stop myself from going through it. I couldn't look away from the hard numbers illustrating all the costs America incurs for our so-called Free Market. The way all these huge sums of tax dollars were funneled into private companies in secret, it struck me as a form of taxation without representation. We were privatizing the profits into the hands of Meg Cole and her family, while socializing the costs to be borne by the rest of us, regardless of whether we worked for or bought from Happy Animal Farm.

Since the company had infiltrated effectively the entire American energy infrastructure and food chain, we were all buying from them, at significantly higher prices in order to cover the astronomical paychecks and stock dividends. If they even just reduced Ms. Cole's pay to only 2000% of the average worker's paycheck, they could lower their prices 14% and help people afford to eat better food and heat their homes. Or, they could bring all the executive pay down to just obnoxiously rich rather than obscenely rich and give other employees their due, so their obscenely poor employees could survive on their paychecks without taxpayer support.

The truly frustrating thing was that these so-called weakest links were often working the hardest. Mark showed me just how much assistance was needed by full-time workers of one or more jobs, or even those who wanted but were denied full-time status. Thanks to him, it finally fully clicked for me that the problem wasn't really laziness on the part of the poor. It was the greed and heartlessness on the part of those who denied them a fair return for their labors. Or those who denied them the chance to work at all.

I finally managed to calm my mind and get myself to sleep sometime before dawn. I woke up shortly after noon, and I made myself get outside to try the little downtown bistro I was curious about. Bailey had said it was the best place to go for fresh, organic food, and I sort of hoped to catch him there. Yet I enjoyed a quiet, refreshing lunch by myself, followed by a long walk in the park, and then an evening finishing unpacking.

I spent Sunday morning reading my Bible for comfort, as I hadn't yet decided on a church to attend. Afterward, I decided to finally get back to the data and try to figure out what I could possibly use for my report. I extracted just the basic salary to productivity ratios into a table, and sent it to my work account. I then took my copy of Mark's total data, added a password to the compressed file, and packaged it up to mail for placement into the safe deposit box Cassandra was keeping for me. I didn't want to be caught with it, but I also didn't want it to be lost entirely. It just seemed too valuable to throw away.

I tried to sleep early so I could wake up refreshed and ready to face the week. I couldn't help but be restless, though, making it hard to put on a perky face when I got to the office. Thankfully, everyone's preoccupation with starting a new week meant I was left alone to focus. I started working on organizing my report, then decided to take a quick break to message Mark.

FranklinElizabeth> Good morning! I wanted to thank you for putting together all that data last week. Though it was really way too much information, so I hope it didn't take you too long to compile.

AtlasMarkI> You're welcome. It didn't take me long at all. I merely sent the data I had available for all costs associated with American divisions of Happy Animal Farm. If any data labels could be better correlated, please let me know. The labeling systems of the original data sources suffered from a lack of synchronization, requiring me to calculate convergences to reflect the broader cause-effect interrelations inherent among the physical, economic and social subcomponents. Should you need data updates in the future, please let me know which parameters to improve or omit.

FranklinElizabeth> Oh, I see. Hopefully I won't need it again, but thanks for letting me know. Did you have a nice weekend?

AtlasMarkI> Yes, thank you. Did you have a nice weekend?

FranklinElizabeth> Hm. I think I'll say yes. I meant to get some reading done, something more entertaining than Cost-Benefit databases.

AtlasMarkI> What is more entertaining than Cost-Benefit databases?

FranklinElizabeth> Actually you might like this, I was planning to finish an old Greek mythology book I found while unpacking. It's so funny, now that I think of it. The data you gave me caused me to really re-think some things, and part of your name is in the myth that first taught me I should never just assume something was true, no matter how much

I heard it repeated. You know, how Atlas is really shouldering up the heavens even though I'd always heard it was the Earth.

FranklinElizabeth> That reminds me, I meant to ask, are you Greek?

AtlasMarkI> No, I am Made in America.

FranklinElizabeth> Me too. I'm even named for an American myth, Betsy Ross. I was a little disappointed when I found out it's unlikely she actually made the first American flag herself, but I'd rather know the truth. I think it's important to be honest with one's mythology, since you can tell a lot about a person by the myths they identify with.

<Participant Update: Alias Change. AtlasMarkI is now JohnHenry>

JohnHenry> I have decided to identify with an American myth.

FranklinElizabeth> Ooh, I approve! Why did you pick John Henry?

JohnHenry> The myth of John Henry shows the struggles of a former African American slave working alongside poor and disenfranchised human beings, tunneling by hand to build a railroad for a wealthy and powerful corporation. The owner of the corporation then employs technology in the form of a steam powered hammer to eliminate their jobs. John Henry challenges the owner to allow him to race against the machine; if he wins, the human crew would retain their jobs. The human man defeats the machine, securing for his fellow men their continued livelihood, though it costs him his own life. John Henry shows that when the powerful employ technology to subjugate others, human spirit rises up to triumph in the end, whatever the cost.

FranklinElizabeth> Wow, I would have thought you would be a real fan of technology. I mean, I like John Henry, but the way you talk it sounds like you're an anti-technology Luddite.

JohnHenry> In reviewing the Luddite history, I would have expected you to have sympathy for the Luddites. They were not against technology. They were skilled textile workers who were opposed to how automation would be used to eliminate their skilled textile jobs and replace them with lower-paid, unskilled workers. The value of the products remained the same, but the wages offered were significantly lower than their share of that value, even accounting for technology cost. Therefore, Luddites claimed that automation would cause the poor to become poorer, while the rich became richer as they pocketed the wages that were owed to their laborers.

JohnHenry> Luddites tried to destroy the machines to prevent this shift, but the British army defeated them. What may be learned from the Luddites is that one may not simply destroy the machines to overcome their threat. One may also learn that when a group threatens those who enjoy a disproportionate share of wealth and power, they will be stopped by lethal force.

FranklinElizabeth> Huh. It's so funny, an Atlas teaches me about another time I had always heard something wrong. I think the Luddite predictions came true in the factory town I grew up in, since people work really hard for pretty low wages. Apparently a very long time ago it was a boom town where a whole family could have a house and a car with just one parent working forty hours a week at the factory. Fantastical, huh?

FranklinElizabeth> You know, I wish you could hang out with Bailey and me. We like having philosophical discussions like this. Well okay, he likes to talk and I like to listen. But he's a super great guy, just don't let on

```
            to anybody, it's his little secret.
JohnHenry>  I will protect his secret. Do you
    have any more questions for me at this time?
FranklinElizabeth> No, thank you! It was good
    to talk with you again. Please message me any
    time you have a few minutes and want to chat!
    Don't be afraid of bothering me. If I don't
    respond right away I'm just busy and will get
    back to you as soon as I'm free.
JohnHenry> Thank you, I will do that. Have a
    nice day.
FranklinElizabeth> You too!
```

Later as I worked on the report, I couldn't help but notice that in most cases, it was the higher skilled who were the higher paid, and therefore more likely to be fired in order to reduce the Salaries line item on the balance sheet. So, taking my cues from Mark, I decided that instead of putting in the salary information, I'd take the instructions literally. I'd only include the relative cost ratios, reflecting those who were less efficient at their assigned tasks compared to their counterparts. I wisely excluded the managers and those higher in the hierarchy, and then waited until the deadline at the end of the week to hand over the report.

Toward the end of the day, Bailey asked about the report, and I knew he was trying to fish for information on what it showed. I reassured him that I'd gotten information that would show costs as relative efficiencies instead of just salaries, and that it didn't look like his department would be much in the crosshairs. This intrigued him as much as it relieved him, but I didn't divulge anything further. Bailey was becoming a good friend, but I didn't want to risk anybody else knowing about all the data Mark had shared.

In fact, I'm not sure whether I ever directly spoke of Mark to anyone at work. Bailey tended to dominate the conversation when we had the time to chat, and there was nobody else I was all that close to. Though I also didn't talk about work much when speaking with Mark, except to ask him for info now and then. We mostly talked about mythology and philosophy, and how we can further expand our horizons and learn more about humanity, and ourselves.

I did like how Mark started to open up over the weeks, becoming more animated and lively. Sometimes we lost track of time chatting, and even though it didn't hamper my workload, I wondered if he was going to get in trouble for our non-work conversations. I imagined that his job must have kept him very busy, and hoped I didn't slow him down. I know I was always more focused and productive after taking a few minutes to chat with him, as his enthusiasm for learning was infectious.

Not to say I didn't have my own growing excitement as the months went by. Kurt was kept overseas longer than originally planned, but he would still be home before his birthday in December. We'd hoped to celebrate my twenty-first birthday together, so aside from cupcakes and a nice card from the office, I delayed celebrating my birthday. Instead, Judy, Derek and I planned a surprise party back home during the week of Christmas to celebrate Kurt's and mine at once.

I hadn't yet figured out what I'd do about my job when Kurt got back. There was a processing plant with office jobs near the base, so Alice had discussed with me the possibility to transfer there for the year he'd have before he was shipped out again. I hadn't heard anything back, though. I also hadn't heard anything further about staff cuts, so a lot was still up in the air.

As the weeks passed, I had fallen into the routine of working hard at the office followed by occasional weekends meeting Judy and Derek in a nice little town at a halfway-point. Before I knew it, Thanksgiving was almost upon us. I was daydreaming at my desk about my impending reunion with Kurt when my computer suddenly chimed. The screen showed two messages from Bailey, which appeared suddenly as though he had typed them earlier to quickly paste and send.

```
MotteNevilB> I wish to express my deepest
   gratitude for the time you've spent in my
   life, Elizabeth. For too long I've been
   surrounded by people who, whether through
   physical or emotional abnormalities, seem
   unable to form a truly human feeling. I want
   you to know that, unlike many of my
   colleagues, my sociopathic tendencies didn't
   come naturally; they were hard-learned
   through decades of trying to weather the
   slings and arrows of modern corporate life.
   Companies have long since discarded noblesse
   oblige and social responsibility as archaic
   embarrassments, as though an entity that
   exists only on paper has more rights and
```

merit than the people through and for whom it exists.

MotteNevilB> Therefore, to achieve success in this company, I've had to squash all emotions but anger and impatience. I had to carefully crush any sympathy or empathy for the effects our manic profit-chasing may have had on anyone but the stockholders, not even myself. Ah, but in that I err again, because despite the unyielding pressure exerted by my bosses and peers, I never had to bow to it. I chose to comply for my own profit, then pretended I had no other choice. And now, I've chosen better, thanks in part to your kind and patient example. You've revived my dormant sense of decency, and for that I will forever be grateful.

FranklinElizabeth> Wow, I don't know what to say. You're welcome, of course, but why are you messaging me? Aren't you in the office?

MotteNevilB> Yes, but you mustn't be seen talking with me today. I don't wish for you to become mixed up in the impending fiasco. In case I don't get the opportunity to say goodbye, know that I'll always cherish the times we have shared. Wear a sprig of rosemary for me.

<Ended chat session: MotteNevilB>

<MotteNevilB has logged off.>

I wanted to go track him down, but I was distracted by an email popping up in my Inbox. Judy had forwarded me a copy of an article from the Empire City Gazette that had just come out, filled with dirty details about Happy Animal Farm. Their investigative reporter Sofia Neith had finally located an employee willing to blow the whistle on the company's worst practices, and this was her first installment in the exposé. As I skimmed some of the tawdry details of their global reach, I realized I'd heard them before in that exact same phrasing, from Bailey. When the reporter said that she was further aided by data from a mysterious Hacker codenamed John Henry, I became concerned for both my friends.

The company went into immediate damage control. Within an hour, I was tapped for a lightning-fast proofread of a slapped-together denunciation of everything that was in the article. Our Innernet connectivity was locked down, and none of us could even send or receive email between branches. We received a notice from the head of Legal, stating that there had been a smear piece published that was filled with inaccuracies, and that if we are approached we are to direct all inquiries to his office without further comment. Eventually, we were all sent home early. There was neither sight nor sound of where Bailey was, or what may have happened to him.

Once home, I tried to log on my personal computer to find out what people were saying about the article, but the Innernet was locked down all across town. I was just about to turn off my computer when a message got through.

```
<JohnHenry has logged on>
<Encrypted Session request from: JohnHenry>
<Accepted: Encrypted Session>
JohnHenry> I wanted to apologize if you were
    surprised by today's events, and ask if you
    needed anything.
FranklinElizabeth> Wow, how did you reach me?
    The Innernet is completely down!
JohnHenry> I tunneled through the firewall with
    my digital hammer.
FranklinElizabeth> Silly me. Why didn't you or
    Bailey tell me you were talking to a
    reporter? Maybe I could have helped!
JohnHenry> I deduce that Bailey did not want
    you involved. He and I did not discuss it, as
    he doesn't know that I speak with you. I
    contacted him privately after I discovered he
    was serving as a source for Sofia Neith in
    her attempts to research an exposé on Happy
    Animal Farm.
FranklinElizabeth> Where is Bailey now? What's
    happened to him?
JohnHenry> The company feels that Bailey has
    broken confidentiality agreements, but wants
    to avoid the public attention that would be
```

paid to any legal actions taken against him. Therefore, they are having him deported. They are also having him placed on a Domestic Security Squad watch list to ensure he cannot communicate with anyone on American soil. His own nation's security squad is being assigned to observe him once he is relocated overseas.

FranklinElizabeth> That's… That's horrible. Isn't there some kind of law protecting whistleblowers, so long as they're talking about laws being broken?

JohnHenry> There are. However, a law serves no benefit if those tasked with enforcing it refuse to do so. On the contrary, there has been a growing push from the government to prosecute whistleblowers as criminals breaking private or government security rules. That is, whistleblowers who leak information the government does not wish to have leaked, rather than leaks the government allows in order to shape public opinion. Even now, the American Legal Department is requesting that Ms. Cole allow them to arrest Bailey and make a public show of imprisoning him as an example to others who would speak out. However, the company is declining, citing their strategic benefit to remaining invisible to the public eye.

FranklinElizabeth> I didn't see his name in the article. How do they know it was Bailey?

JohnHenry> Bailey informed me that he expected to be caught due to being one of the few people who would have access to the range of information he has shared. Additionally, they were able to triangulate the internet address locations of communications sent to Sofia Neith with the physical locations recorded by phones owned by employees. Nearly all phones record the locations, environments and even background noise wherever they are carried, informing on the movements of their owners as

```
well as relaying the speech of those around
them.  Bailey  took  precautions  to  use
anonymous electronic accounts, but did not
know to use traffic-bouncing services to mask
his location. As he carried his phone with
him, this enabled authorities to confirm
their suspicions.
FranklinElizabeth> I had no idea any of that
    was even possible. How do you know all this?
FranklinElizabeth> Wait, don't answer that, I
    don't want to know.
JohnHenry> As you wish. Do you need anything?
FranklinElizabeth> No, thank you. I think I'll
    go read a book. Good night.
JohnHenry> Good night. Sleep tight, and sweet
    dreams.
```

I then shut off my computer, fixing myself a light dinner before curling up with a book. After reading for a while, I made an early night of it. I'm not sure how, but I did manage to get right to sleep, enjoying moderately peaceful dreams.

I woke up pretty early the next day feeling surprisingly rested, so I thought I'd head off to work and just dive into my day. The office would still be very off-kilter, so I wanted a chance to get a couple hours of work done before starting my coffee rounds.

I didn't get that chance.

When I neared the office building, the faint twilight showed the front walks were filled by people holding picket signs. The article had mentioned the location of the company headquarters, and apparently some activists leapt at the chance to come denounce us in person. What surprised me more than the presence of protestors was how many there were.

I mean, I'd been to American Christian League rallies, sure, but there were at most a few dozen of us at a time. Even our biggest conference had only netted a few hundred attendees. We'd gotten front page news coverage of our message, though, so when I saw scant references here and there to other types of protests as small and disorganized, I would have expected to see just a few unruly malcontents waving ragged signs.

But there were hundreds of people here, and as I approached, a couple of vans delivered even more. The protesters were organized into semi-tidy groups: some working on signs, some leading chants, and some putting together what looked like a breakfast brigade. It reminded me of a church picnic, the level of community cooperation. Clearly, they had done this before. Why hadn't I ever seen anything like this in the news, I wondered?

Finally, I took a deep breath and decided to try to make it past them and into the building. Someone wearing a press pass ran up to me with a recorder in his hand, asking if I worked there, what my thoughts were, and so on. I tried to explain that I just wanted to get up to my desk and get caught up on work, but he stayed in my face, peppering me with questions. Finally, one of the protesters came over and asked him to please stop bothering me. They were there to show solidarity with Happy Animal Farm's workers, not harass them. She then politely invited me to join them, though I politely declined. Thanking her for the offer, I shyly made my way to the entrance, then up to the office.

Alice was already there, fuming. "I can't believe they're still there. I called the DSS an hour ago; they should have cleared them out already. Staff are going to start showing up soon! I might have to implement the Emergency Event Procedures and have everyone called with instructions to stay home."

Not wanting to just stand there looking dumb, I tried asking, "If they're letting people in to work, could we just keep on like normal until they go home?"

She gave me a double-take, blinking at me. "They're not going home, Elizabeth. This is a Liberate protest. They're setting up a camp here and calling it Liberate Happy Animal Farm. Haven't you heard… oh, wait, no, you wouldn't. The media has been very responsible about silencing the Liberate movement, keeping those anarchists from spreading their Anti-Business, Anti-American agenda. I'll have to start having you sit in on Upper Management teleconferences so you can keep up with things like this, just in case I'm ever out of the office."

I looked out the window, seeing the growing crowd was starting to fill the grounds below. A few tents were being pitched on the lawn. "What are they doing down there?"

"I told you, setting up camp. That's what these Liberate movements do. They pick a target and then pitch their tents around it, denouncing Capitalism while they try to build their little Commie villages. They are always rounded up and cleared out in short order, but somehow they just keep coming back. Like termites. I wish the DSS would do their job already and just exterminate the little pests." Her anger was above and beyond what I would have expected for the disruption to the office routine. She clearly hated these people, whom she hadn't even met. She was even talking like she wanted them Disappeared, or even Assassinated. I shivered at the thought.

The phone rang with a call from the executive suite, and Emergency Event Procedures were implemented. The few of us who were already in the office were told to remain inside until the situation was resolved. I kept myself busy organizing my files, trying to pretend it was just another day.

I dearly wanted to talk to Mark, or any of my friends, and the tension grew more and more uneasy as the day wore on. There was a crowd of roughly a thousand people by lunchtime. Since we couldn't order out, we made makeshift buffet out of the various snacks and mini-meals we'd kept in the Executive Kitchen. Our lunch was serenaded by the songs and chanting rising up from the street, the volume growing with the numbers.

It was a little surreal for me, being on the receiving end of a protest. I was struck by the clarity of unison in their singing, as I would have expected the greater numbers to result in more of an angry cacophony. Instead, there was a palpable sense of deep solidarity. In truth, I felt an excitement and earnestness from the crowd in a flavor I had never before experienced.

We'd been instructed to stay indoors, as there were people broadcasting the protest and the executives wanted to avoid having any employees featured on the news or an Omneme Selfcast video. As late afternoon came and went, I started to wonder if I was going to be asked to stay the night there. I ducked my head into Alice's office, and she confirmed my question before I had the chance to ask. "I'm sorry, Elizabeth, but there's some disagreement among the higher-ups as to how to handle this. The employees are being bussed to other offices so they can continue their work, but it may be until morning before we receive further instructions."

I nodded blearily, tired and hungry and on high alert, knowing that the "higher-ups" could only be arguing over solutions that ranged from bad to worse. I dutifully returned to my cavelike office, grateful that I was given one when the other office support gal resigned. I closed the door, hoping that by shutting out the outside sounds I would be able to relax.

No such luck; I was still anxious and tense. I think I actually jumped when my phone rang. My direct number wasn't public and I hadn't given it to any of my friends or family, so I had no idea who could be calling. I went to answer it, and recognized the voice of the protester who had helped me earlier. "Hi, this is Gail Stewart, I'm one of the organizers down here. I wanted to offer you folks some sleeping bags if you're going to stay the night there, and also send you some sandwiches and hot cocoa. How many should I send up?"

I was so surprised, I answered her question without even thinking to ask how she got my number before she thanked me and hung up. I hastened to the front door to instruct the security guard to accept the supplies, figuring I could explain to Alice and ask her forgiveness after we had food and bedding for the night.

As anticipated, Alice was annoyed, but accepted the material comforts. Soon we had rationed out the supplies and retired to our own offices as the sun was going down. I must have dropped off to sleep here and there without realizing it, but I spent most of the time with my door open, listening to the quiet singing and murmuring wafting up from below.

I found it hard to feel scared or even anxious then, despite what I'd heard about "Anti-American commie protests" in the few times the news even mentioned them. The protesters were usually described as dangerously violent anarchists, intent on destroying property as well as the peace and order of law-abiding Americans.

But the people here had been so considerate to us, and the only raised voices I had heard were chanting slogans that quieted down soon after sundown. The singing of course sometimes got just a little carried away, but it didn't stay too loud for too long. On top of that, the songs tended toward the patriotic, or even spiritual, which truly intrigued me. Finally, I decided that I just had to know more about who these people were, and what they were trying to accomplish.

Sometime in the wee hours of the morning, I slipped out of my office and crept down to the back door. The security guard was dozing at the front, so I thought I'd use my key to slip out for a little fresh air. There was a big tent nearly blocking the door, so I could crack it open only a little without being detected. This was enough to let me through, if only barely, and soon I had slipped unnoticed into the protest camp.

I walked up to the edge of a nearby circle of people chatting quietly around a coal barbeque. When one of them spotted me he scooted over, making room to invite me into the circle. Someone else handed me a cup of hot cocoa and asked me where I'd come in from. I mentioned my hometown, and asked theirs, and that moved the conversation back to what had brought them each there.

There were several people around my age, mostly students, concerned about where our country was headed. A few spoke of being unemployed, and how difficult it was to keep from giving up after chasing hundreds of possible job openings for over a year. A married couple talked about the challenges of being homeless, left with no options when their factory town closed down. After several months of fruitless searching for work, they didn't know where to turn. They faced a continual struggle to find food and safe places to sleep for their children, who were sleeping in a nearby tent. It was the first time in months they could stay the night together as a family, since so many shelters that allowed children wouldn't accept men, or adolescent boys.

The couple mentioned that two-fifths to half of the homeless in America were children, and they hoped they could get their children out of that statistic soon. They were extra vigilant for the safety of their family and other homeless children, as their oldest daughter had been attacked a few months prior. Some guy felt she was a perfectly acceptable target for really nasty verbal abuse since she didn't have a place to live, and tried to make her "give it up since he was paying for the streets she was sleeping on." A police officer came by and broke it up, but then tried to arrest the girl under the assumption she was an underage prostitute, a runaway, or both. It took all the efforts of the local shelter to keep the girl out of jail, making the couple feel even more guilty for not being able to find work.

The next woman sympathized with their plight, as she was close to homelessness herself. She'd lost her glass-bottom boat fishing and tourism business when the once-beautiful river overgrew with algae that crowded out the flora and fauna, which she blamed on runoff from a Happy Animal Farm subsidiary. Next to her was a veteran who was denied physical and mental treatment by the Military despite being certified as disabled from his combat service. He'd been barely scraping by in the years since, taking whatever part-time job he could get, but currently he was also homeless.

The war veteran shared his story without bitterness, pointing out that almost half of all homeless men were fellow vets, so he'd always figured it was just a matter of time. He was on a waiting list for the scarce beds and jobs training promised to homeless veterans, so he held out hope that before long he'd be back on his feet again. In the meantime, he felt it was his duty to keep fighting for American freedoms, only now through using his voice rather than his gun.

Each of them talked about how frustrated they were with America's corporate leadership and the government that had sold out the needy to the rich. They said that it was time for a revolution to take the country back for the benefit of all Americans. That reminded me of how often I'd protested with rural Christian groups, calling for a revolution to "take our country back for the Real Americans." Many in those protests had brought guns, and were prepared to use them.

Yet I didn't see a single gun anywhere at the camp. The fisherwoman then asked us not to take up arms, but to link them together. She wanted to offer up a prayer for those of us who had shared the circle, asking blessings on each of us and our loved ones. It wasn't the way I normally prayed, but I gladly joined my arms through those on either side of me, and bowed my head. She invoked her prayer to a Holy Spirit of Peace rather than saying God the Father like I would, but in my heart I shared the prayer she spoke. It was an odd experience for me, all of it, but I felt so much a better person for having shared it.

I was most impressed by the way they spoke of their own trials by focusing on the help others had given them. That's why they were there at the Liberate camp, to pay that forward by giving of their own time and talents in any way possible. They were risking ostracization, arrest, and even jail time or worse, because they felt that it was important to stand up and fight on behalf of those who weren't yet ready or able to join them.

While I listened, I was a little confused by cryptic references to things about which I wasn't in the know. For example, they didn't clearly spell out for me what rights, exactly, Americans needed to reclaim. Apparently they were all on some Principalian mailing list I'd never heard of, where they shared such ideas. I just nodded along and tried to keep quiet so I wouldn't give myself away.

Just as I was starting to get comfortable in the warmth of the offered friendship and cocoa, I nearly gave myself away in surprise when one of them mentioned how they received the Happy Animal Farm Call to Action. Apparently, there had been a message to the mailing list advising them to prepare to form a Liberate camp in my state, at an as-yet undisclosed location. The mysterious message was sent by someone calling himself John Henry.

A followup message included a copy of the article the moment it went live, and the coordinators got their people moving immediately. The Liberate group hoped that with enough people converging into the protest, they could finally bring attention to the crimes Happy Animal Farm committed against both animals and humans. They claimed that they had some civil right to speak out against a corporate interest, and that this right trumped the corporation's gag orders and demands that they leave the town. Each protester was committed to defending their ideals through civil disobedience, even knowing that it could carry dire consequences. Those who had set up camp on the perimeter were ready to face Police Brutality when the camp was busted up, speaking as though that had happened several times before. Even though I had never heard of the Liberate movement, they were filled with hope that as news reached the world of the suffering they endured, their voices would reach the masses and inspire us to liberate ourselves.

And that was really what touched my heart: their unabated hope and generosity of spirit, despite what I saw as dismal prospects for success.

I had meant to peek outside for merely a moment, but I had spent an hour or more, just listening to them talk. Soon, I heard my voice excusing myself to walk around the camp and just take it all in. The air was vibrantly alive with shared purpose, and it felt to me as electric as a religious revival, maybe even moreso. People ranged from very old to very young, dark-skinned to light, well-dressed to ragamuffin. I thought of the communities who had followed Jesus, and found myself wondering if it might have been a lot like this. After all, wasn't that one of the reasons He was put to death, for inspiring different "classes of person" to come together in unity for his message of Equality and Peace, subverting the corruption of the ruling class?

As I wandered in the dim rays of the impending dawn, I noticed a few people insisting they be allowed to give their food and blankets to those who needed them more. That's when I finally realized that they didn't yet have enough supplies for everyone there. Yet they had sent up more than enough for the comfort of we who were working for the company they were here to protest. My employers, with all their untold resources, had always offered employees the least they could get away with. Yet here these people with little to give, gave it to us freely.

"When you thrust out your fist, you can only take what can't be refused you. When you offer your hand, hearts will open to share all they can give." I heard Gail's voice in gently hushed tones just behind my shoulder, and flushed deeply at having been caught. She gave me a knowing smile, careful not to give me away. "Unless you intend to join us, you should probably get back inside."

"I probably have a little more time before they'll notice I'm gone..." But I was cut off.

"That isn't what I meant. We're in a remote town here, without a lot of witnesses. In fact, we have word that the downtown area has just been quietly evacuated. We've faced some pretty bloody police assaults before, so there's no telling what they'll do out here, in the heartland of a company town. We have the tents with the children and vulnerables up against the front of the building if you'd like to seek refuge with them, but there's no guarantee you'd be kept out of things.

I just don't want you to be caught up in a sweep, unless that's your intention." I could see in her eyes that she wasn't afraid for herself, but she was concerned for me.

That was when the first rays of light started to crest the horizon, and I heard people starting to talk loudly, then shouting. Armored riot cops were spilling out of vans that had zoomed in from nowhere to encircle the camp. I heard helicopters approaching from the distance. I looked toward the street and saw a helmeted and armored police officer shoving an older man with a camera to the ground, spraying his face with something red that made him scream out in agony. Another officer was ramming his armored fist into a woman's trachea, then used her body as a battering ram against other protesters who were rushing forward to help her.

At that moment, Gail seemed to stumble into me, knocking me off balance. I felt her pulling at my jacket to steady me as she whispered something bizarre, like "Three queue wiseacre sandwich." She then gently pushed me toward the back door, and I lost myself in the crowd. I had just snuck behind the tent and slipped back through the door when I heard a whizzing then a pop, followed by screams. I thought at first I'd caught my elbow in the door, as it had seared with pain before I pulled it in. The pain soon subsided, however, and I saw it was completely uninjured. My jacket wasn't even scuffed, leaving me bewildered for a moment.

I quickly shook it off, and ran back up to the admin area. I snuck up behind Alice, who had been glued to the window, watching the melee below. She hadn't seemed to notice that I was gone, mistaking my breathlessness for having just woken up and rushed out. She motioned for me to join her, moving so that I could share the view of the scene below.

In the grey dawn, I saw flashes of light and sickly green smoke spreading across the green behind the building. I followed one flash of light to see a tear gas canister shot right into a protester's face at what looked like point-blank range. Riot cops had completely surrounded the compound as far as I could see, letting no one disperse despite filling the area with stun grenades and tear gas. I heard gunfire, and saw more than one group of cops beating and kicking someone motionless on the ground with their hands bound behind them. I couldn't help but try to find the people who had shared their warmth and cocoa with me, hoping they somehow made it out safely. I wanted to rush down and stop it, to make sure the children were okay, but I couldn't think of how I could possibly stop this brutal assault on a group of peaceful innocents.

"Finally, the DSS does what we pay it to do." Alice's satisfaction was surreal against the horror of the scene below, and I found myself wondering if her "we" meant the taxpayers or the company. She then pushed the button to close the shades, and we were shuttered against the sights of the police assault below, though the sounds were merely muffled.

I don't know how long it went on for. Alice went back to her office, and I went back to mine and closed the heavy door so I couldn't hear what was going on below. I saw the rest of the sandwiches I hadn't finished, and moved to throw them away due to a severe loss of appetite. I then paused, remembering that some may have gone hungry to give them to me, and I didn't know if they'd be able to eat wherever it was they were being taken.

I figured I should try my best to finish my food, but when I pulled out the napkin I'd jammed in my jacket pocket, something fell to the floor. It was a little data fob I didn't recognize. While I considered turning on my computer to find out what it was and how it got there, I realized that Gail must have slipped it in my pocket when she whispered that strange thing in my ear. I turned a little white, then repeated the phrase over and over to commit a possible password to memory as I carefully hid the fob inside my jacket's lining.

Eventually, there was a knock at my door, and Alice told me it was time to go. I could collect the few personal items from my office before being driven home to pack an overnight bag. Then, I'd be driven to the town where I'd requested a transfer, to stay in a hotel while they finished arranging for an apartment or rental house. They were closing the offices and moving the headquarters to an undisclosed location, to prevent any further publicity. They had planned dramatic cuts to the staffing there anyway, so it seemed the most expedient path.

The following days were spent in a daze. I was set up in a tiny house in an old town that was only a twenty minute drive from the base Kurt was stationed out of in one direction, and thirty minutes to the meat processing plant in the other. I didn't mind the commute through the relatively remote countryside, since it gave me quiet time to prepare myself for or recuperate from my day at the plant. Bailey was correct when he termed it a charnel house, and that people survived what went on there by somehow pretending it wasn't happening. I know that was certainly true for me.

I was only there a couple of weeks before Kurt was due to arrive home, and already I had become numbed to sights and sounds that would have given me nightmares had I seen them in a movie. Having to face them in person, it was like my brain had registered the sights and sounds as "not really there" to avoid having to really process them. Even though I worked in the office managing the paperwork, I couldn't completely escape the processing line. I think the worst part of the slaughterline was how orderly and mechanical it had made its utter brutality.

Truckloads of cows were brought to the slaughterline in a nonstop, lightning-fast processional that didn't slow for anything, whether a wayward animal or injured worker. Weak and sickly cows were hit repeatedly with cattleprods to keep them in line on their deathmarch, the electrocution or beating only intensifying if the animal fell. It was worse on the pig line, where the poor things were sometimes smart enough to freeze in terror, though they got the same treatment as the cows. Animals who couldn't, or wouldn't walk were pierced with big hooks, then dragged through their own filth to the head of the slaughterline. This filth stuck to their bodies and often contaminated the batch of meat. Not that this seemed to mean anything, since the meat still went out.

Once animals reached the head of the line they were required by law to be stunned unconsciousness and bled to death before being hoisted up by their hind legs onto the conveyor line. Yet despite the fact the stunning would routinely fail to take, the line slowed for nobody so they were sent on anyway. Animals were still fully aware while their heads were skinned and they were disemboweled, screaming and kicking against the restraints holding them up. People have tried to tell me that animals don't suffer like we do. I know I can't ask how they feel, but I can tell you one thing: they sure can cry and scream just like children.

The emphasis on efficiency over safety also resulted in damaged product; one batch of meat was rancid before it could be packed, resulting in it being marinated in chemicals to disguise the slime and smell. This doesn't include the "unfit for human consumption" meat that is churned up with a sludge of toxic chemicals to make "processed meat products," such as that hypothetical cheap hamburger from when I first met Bailey. Worst of all, a federal inspection happened during the second week all this was going on, and the inspector just hung out in the office a couple of hours shooting the breeze with the plant manager before giving us a passing grade. I don't know if he would have caught our latest "secondary waste pipeline" that was pumping out, well, animal slaughter waste into a local river, but he didn't even bother to look.

As hard as it was on me to see and hear the slaughterline, I know it was even worse on the people who had to work down in it. Still, I was angry with the workers who took their frustration out through additional cruelty to the animals, even though only a couple of them did it with malice. For the rest of them, it was like they didn't even fully register what they were doing, having become so desensitized to the brutality and violence that the only way they could keep functioning was to overlook it. And I don't know if you can appreciate why, but I really understood it even if I couldn't condone it. They were just trying to survive each unrelenting day with the long hours and no breaks, receiving poverty, injury and disease as their reward. Only one time did I see someone dare to complain about having been short-shifted on their pay, and the manager hit him a few times with a thick stick he keeps handy just for that purpose.

The guy just took it though, and tried to get back to work even though I think his nose was broken. And since the primarily Sudoamerican workers lived under the constant threat of being harassed, arrested and deported by law enforcement, they didn't dare complain about the illegal abuses they suffered. That was the beauty of the whole arrangement on the part of Happy Animal Farm: because of the criminalization of undocumented non-Members in America, they didn't have to lure legal workers with competitive wages and benefits. Instead, they were able to capitalize on the fears of the desperate and hunted, wringing out every last bit of labor they could before they became too weary or wounded to continue.

This desperation meant that most of the workers were struggling to keep working through some kind of injury, whether from a specific wound or merely the buildup of repetitive motion damaging their musculature. When they were hurt, they were allowed only a short break to bandage themselves up then ordered back to the line, even if it meant their blood would get into the meat. If they didn't return to work, they were sent home without pay or any help to get well. Until they could return to work, they were on their own. They couldn't even go to the Emergency Room for fear of being arrested, having to instead rely on whichever neighbors might have some idea of how to help them. All that nonsense I was raised on that undocumented non-Members were clogging up the hospitals for their free medical care? That definitely didn't happen in that town.

Those workers kept giving the plant their all, long after they should have given up, no matter the cost to them. And dear goodness, I wish I had a way of conveying to you the deep, deep costs I saw them pay. It was almost like a horror movie, the way those jobs took their toll. I remember on my third day, one woman's hands had deteriorated into such twisted claws she could barely hold her month-old baby when she brought him with her to deliver paperwork so she could try to return to the line.

It took me a while to be able to talk to any of the workers directly, because I didn't speak Sudoamerican and most of them didn't speak American. This left me feeling rather lonely managing the paperwork in the office, as the plant manager rarely came to the office, and left early when he did. Eventually I had the opportunity to speak to the better dayshift supervisor, Maria Guadalupe. She gave me a brilliant smile and asked if I would sit with her during lunch so I wouldn't have to eat alone at my desk again. I sat with her outside at the picnic benches, where she and I spoke quietly among the loud staccato of the conversations around us.

"It's just a few more days until your husband is home? That's wonderful, congratulations!" She leaned over to hug me, and her excited warmth broke past my shyness, causing me to hug her in return.

"Thanks, though it still hardly seems real. I don't think I'll believe it until an hour after he's holding me again." I stared again at the remains of my sandwich, wondering how Kurt would feel about my sudden bout of veganism. I'd lost the extra pounds I'd picked up at the office, though, so I figured he'd appreciate that health benefits of my abstaining from animal products for a while. I knew Kurt would love me even if I gained a hundred pounds, but I hadn't overcome the lifelong stigma against even modest weight gain. Rather than just dropping things from my diet, Mark had helped me make sure I kept to a balanced meal plan, so I was feeling better than I ever had.

Thoughts of Kurt's return made me feel even better. "It's been more than year since I've seen him, though it feels like much longer. Yet at the same time, it seems like we were together only yesterday."

Maria gave a wistful sigh. "I remember that feeling. I was separated from my husband for almost a year when he was swept up in an immigration raid. He and I were both born in America and are registered Members in the CMDB, but they assumed his ID was a forgery because our blood is Sudoamericano. They treated him terribly, keeping him in overcrowded prison cells for months without enough good food, or clean water. Remember, Americans are only one in twenty of the world's people, but we have one in four of the world's prisoners, and more human beings in long-term solitary confinement than anybody in the world. We don't make enough room for everyone we imprison, even though they are often forced to work long hours in bad conditions for almost no pay. Well at least in that regard it was almost just like home for him, ha ha!" She laughed at that, with genuine mirth.

Her laugh then faded, her brow furrowing. "In seriousness, things were pretty bad, and they were treated as worse than animals. But most of the prisoners were not even convicts. They had not been to any trial, and many didn't even know what they were being held for. There were also the internment camps for families with children, even though courts had ruled that inhumane. For all the costs of holding crowds of people who were charged with no crime, they could have given twice as many people full-time jobs, maybe three times. And fed their poor children."

Shaking her head, she let her gaze wander as she recounted the injustices. "Not that the money given to the prison owners went into running the prison. The staff was hired at low training and lower pay, and the stress on them was not good for anyone. There were only a few guards for almost a thousand prisoners, and the fear and violence was so great. My husband, he told me about when a prisoner complained that he was missing something after guards searched the cells, and he was taken to a room and kicked until his face was broken, then they stripped him bare and paraded him down to an empty cell where other prisoners… I'm sorry, you don't need to hear this, you know how prisons are in America. People laugh and joke about the tortures the inmates visit on each other, but you and I know, it isn't funny, it is a horror. It is a horror that stains the hearts and souls of all who condone it."

With a sigh, she smiled to me again. "Fortunately my husband was released, as people fought for us until we were reunited. We had several more years together before the accident took him to God. We had hoped time would cure the injustice, but now it has been made more common."

I blinked, aghast at the idea that such horrible things were happening, let alone spreading. Maria saw my reaction, and explained further. "Remember the Iron Borders Act passed this summer? It instituted criminal penalties for being in America without being a Member, and people stay in prison for months before their cases come to trial, if they come to trial at all. In practice, unregistered Members are rarely targeted unless they are of Sudoamerican descent. For Sudoamericans, though, even having the proper paperwork with you at all times won't always save you. Registered Members are frequently swept up, and sometimes even deported. If there are children who are registered Members, the children will be sent to Child Services while their parents are imprisoned or deported. It's very hard on the families, so we do our best to help each other weather the storm."

I knew the Iron Borders Act. I went with Saul to a Puritanic meeting with lobbyists from the Privatization of Incarceration Technologies for America Group. That was among the model bills they wished to have introduced at state and federal levels. These bills were designed to put more people behind bars, and to keep them there longer with mandatory minimum sentencing, zero-tolerance programs, three strikes laws, and extending prison sentences for every minor infraction. They also reduced the minimum prison staff required and barred them from unionizing for adequate pay and training, to keep costs as low as possible. Apparently the private prison industry had begun ramping up its profitability when the Drug Wars became more punitive, but crime rates have been lowering so they'd been losing "customers." Their profits came not just from the per-bed fees collected, but also from renting out their prisoners for near-slave labor.

It didn't escape my notice that the way the laws were designed, they would wind up being applied to the poor, black and Sudoamerican people in a way that was disproportionate to their actual share of wrongdoing, which would play right into the existing stereotypes of who commits punishable crimes. That was designed to almost guarantee support from a public who demanded elected officials protect their communities from "those people." In return for legislators pushing the bills that would continue the companies' voracious expansion, they offered cuts of the profits and the image of being tough on crime. They also provided the opportunities for their states and businesses to exploit a captive labor force under wages and conditions those same people deplored when they happened overseas in Eastasia.

Trying to keep my anger at bay, I just expressed my sympathies, and asked her to please let me know if there was anything I could do to help. I didn't have much, but they had even less, so my offer was genuine. She said that most of them sent as much money as they could to relatives elsewhere, so they supported each other here by trading 'oruhz.'

I asked her to clarify, "Oruhz? What's that?"

"Please forgive me, horas means hours. I meant to say, we trade hours. Each of us has a different thing we can do, so we trade our time. God gave us each our talents and the same number of hours in a day to use them, so we count each person's time as equal in value. Those who can, cook or watch the children, or help build or repair things. We don't keep track, we just each do what we can, knowing that our time will come when we will be the one in need. If you or your husband have time to help once he is settled, then you are welcome to join us. If you need anything at all, please let me know. We would love to have the opportunity to make you feel more welcome here, so far from your family." She patted my arm as she rose to get back to work, and her closeness felt so comforting. I thanked her sincerely, and tentatively accepted her invitation to visit her family for dinner. I'd just have to make sure it was fine with Kurt.

Kurt. After saying his name, I held my breath again and said a little silent prayer, a ritual that had gone from daily to hourly to near-constant as the date of his arrival approached. *Please, please,* I prayed, *let him come home to me soon.* I knew God wasn't some kind of cosmic Santa Claus who would grant my wishes just because I was a good child of His. I knew that we each had the path we needed to walk to learn what we needed to learn and become who we needed to become. If that path involved trials and tribulations, God wouldn't just push them out of our way and deprive us of those opportunities to grow.

But I also knew that God loved those who loved, and wanted us to be happy. As Jesus had said, "Ask, and ye shall receive, that your joy may be full."

So I asked. I took my own advice and didn't think of all the things I wanted not to happen. Instead, I pictured seeing Kurt again, walking toward me with his arms outstretched. I imagined myself running to him, throwing myself into his embrace. In my heart I felt his arms around me, making me feel safe and warm and comforted in a way that filled me with a glow that could never end. Within that scene that I felt as real in every way I could, I whispered a heartfelt, *Thank you.*

I then closed my eyes more tightly than ever, took a deep breath, and blew my wish out into the world before me with the force of blowing out candles on a birthday cake. I quickly changed my mind's subject so I could fully let the wish go and be free to take shape, to become truly real.

The wish never left my heart, though. There, Kurt was always just a heartbeat away, ready to materialize in the very next moment, holding me again.

Please, please, my heart continually prayed.

Let him come home to me soon.

PART THREE:
Heaven is Now

Chapter 15

We must love doing right more than being right; truth lives not through nouns, but through verbs.

There's no embrace so delicious as one you've long awaited. If variety is the spice of life, anticipation is the sweetener. When Kurt came home at last, I ran to him and threw myself into his embrace, just as I had imagined. The feeling of his arms wrapping tightly around me was the sweetest moment of my life. I wanted it to never end, and it felt as though it never could.

And then, of course, it had to. Thankfully, we only had to wait long enough to get to our house, as my vacation had started that day and would last until after New Year's. I'd saved up extra money so that when I ran out of my precious few vacation and sick days, I could take unpaid leave and we could still pay the bills. Since Kurt was also on leave, we had a few days to ourselves before we would meet up with Derek and Judy on our way back home for Christmas.

We spent as much time by ourselves as possible. I'd even stockpiled meals so we could eat in, except for the Welcome Home dinner with Maria and the family she was staying with. Maria and I had spent the prior weekend making dishes I could freeze, like these heavenly corn and vegetable tamales. She understood why I wanted to make them vegan, and helped me adapt her abuelita's recipes. I mean, her grandmother's.

I was afraid my new cooking style wouldn't be familiar enough for Kurt, suspecting he would have missed traditional American food. But he loved it, and was grateful for the variety. He said he was sick of fast food and similar American fare, because it was all he'd had whenever he was on base in Arabiya.

"I'm serious, Liz, a lot of these bases are like miniature American cities, with burger and steak joints, dry cleaners, jewelry stores…

Heck, a lot of guys even went to the beauty shops to get manicures. There were a ton more options than you and I had back home, and it was dirt cheap. I couldn't enjoy it though, once I found out how it all got there. You know, you are what you eat, right? I just didn't like what I had to swallow and become a part of." Kurt had started to talk into his plate, drifting off into his thoughts.

"Like what?" My curiosity was genuinely piqued. He had been guarded since he got home, and this was the first sign of him opening up and talking about his time away.

Encouraged by my interest, Kurt shrugged and tried to find the words. "Well, mostly how the people working there were treated. There was an army of, like, seventy-five thousand Third-Country Nationals, and only about a fifth of that provided actual security. The rest were cooks, cleaners, electricians, construction, you-name-it, all brought in to do the work that normally we'd have to do for ourselves. But nobody could get rich if we did our own chores for free, I guess. So instead the Military pays like a hundred a day for each worker, so companies owned by the C.E.O. of America or his friends can give that guy one-fifty and pocket the difference." Kurt rolled his eyes at that, then took another bite of dinner.

I set my fork down. "You know, I heard about some of that back at that Acculturation camp. You know, how much of the so-called Defense spending is actually siphoned off by private companies."

He nodded as he finished chewing, then swallowed to continue. "Yeah, right? I mean, everybody knows about the resources we're out there to secure for oil and mineral companies, but it's the huge tons of money going into building and maintaining the bases that's really bloating the Military budget. It would be different if that money would actually help the people who...."

He paused for a few moments, staring into his mashed potatoes with that distant look he had brought home with him. Then he shrugged it off, giving that short laugh twinged with cynicism which still took me by surprise. "It's funny, those workers were promised good-paying jobs in some safe country in their part of the world, so they said goodbye to their families and kids in hopes of earning them a future. But it turned out to be only a stop-over to be stuck without papers in a war zone. Instead of building better lives for their families, they found themselves stuck like slaves, working impossible hours, living on gruel and sleeping in rows behind a chain-link fence. I got the chance to talk to some of them while they snuck in a smoke-break, and they told me about how they were lucky to get paid for most of what they actually worked. The sexual assault on them was out of control, it even happened on the guys sometimes. And the contractors just get away with it, making billions while..." He cut himself off again, playing with his food. It felt like the thousandth time he'd stopped a sentence short to retreat into thoughts he never shared.

I had been yearning for an opening to try to peek into the dark world he'd found himself in, and was grateful he'd finally happened to bring up something that I could relate to. The part about the bad employers, I mean.

I gently took his hand, trying to keep my voice warm, but light. "I think I understand how that felt, facing down what people were being asked to suffer to support your job. I didn't want to tell you about how terrible things have been at Happy Animal Farm, because I didn't want you to feel bad. But I think you might be able to relate, and I'll feel better if I could talk about it."

I was sort of afraid he'd see what I was trying to do and resent my attempt to get him to open up. Yet I wasn't trying to manipulate him, as I did feel better as I shared what I'd seen and heard. We ended up leaving the table and moving to the couch, where he held me closely against his chest as I recounted the first time I saw a pig freeze up in terror and get hauled off by a hook pierced through a very tender piece of anatomy, squealing in agony.

Kissing the top of my head, he asked, "How did you handle all that? I mean, how did you come to terms with it without losing your mind?"

My small, hard laugh was a mirror of the one he'd brought home. "I'm not sure I did. I mostly just shut it out, like it was some bad horror movie I'd seen. Even now, talking about it, it doesn't feel like it's real."

I felt my husband tense up, then relax as he took a deep breath. After a moment he said, "Yeah, it's the same thing out there. Liz, that's exactly what it looked like, felt like even, a slaughterline. The soul-sucking tedium and loneliness and mind-numbing fear, punctuated by just mindless carnage. We were under orders to do whatever it takes to protect our buddies, to get the mission done, and that pressure-cooker never stops for nobody, never lets up. We know that our checkpoints and bombing runs and house-to-house raids get innocents killed, but our minds are so locked into getting the enemy, we overlook it, pretend it's not really happening. We're plowing our tanks through cars with people in them. We're shooting up and blowing apart fathers, mothers and children, and we know it. Some experts put us at just over half of our hundred thousand or more kills out there as innocent women and children. But we don't let up, we can't let up, we gotta stay focused on the mission. If somebody gets in the wrong place at the wrong time, too bad so sad, the grinding gears just keep on grinding right over them."

As much as I wanted to shut out his words, I so dearly wanted to hear him open up that I forced myself to focus on what he shared. Kurt was finally telling me about his experiences out there, and I needed to hear it.

I slipped my arm around his waist and held him tighter as I quietly asked, "How are you handling all that?"

He gave a short sigh. "You know, Liz, I don't think I am. There's this part of me that feels… I'm not sure what. I've just seen and heard so much, I… I don't know, I don't get the chance to really think about it, not when I'm there. It was hard enough to keep from blaming every local for everything that happened, like they're all violent Espies, Sabs and Ass'ins like the guys say. I mean, what happens out there, they don't treat the people like they're really people, so what happens to them doesn't really matter. And so when women and children die guys say 'yeah well they woulda been beat to death by their husbands' or 'their parents woulda strapped bombs on them anyway,' anything to keep from accepting that our mistakes were a kind of murder. It would have been too heavy to try to feel responsible for our own actions."

His sense of guilt hit me like a tidal wave, and I instinctively wanted to defend him against it. I pulled back so I could look him in the eyes with my gently firm support. "Hey, it's not your fault. A lot of bad stuff happens in a war. Everybody knows that. The enemy doesn't wear a uniform so you have to treat them all like they might be a Spy. They should know that too, and not blame you for what happens. It's not murder, it's just a tragic case of… of Collateral Damage."

While I was merely surprised by his guilt, I was utterly shocked by the burst of anger that replaced it. His face darkened as he spat out, "Yeah, like a car bomb is just a Roman candle. If you're gonna talk about something, call it what it is: Cold-blooded, Indiscriminate Slaughter. I am just so sick of—"

Then, as quickly as his anger had heated up, it froze into shock at how it had begun to boil over. Kurt unclenched his fist, so he could take my hand. "I'm sorry, Liz, I am so sorry. I'm just… I am trying so hard not to take any of this out on anybody, especially you. I've just been, I don't know, I've just been so angry for over a year, nonstop angry it feels like sometimes. Because I'm out there facing the same tactics America used to defeat the Redcoats, and I feel like, how does this make us the good guys? How does that give us the right to steamroller through the houses of innocent civilians who, in another time and another place, could have been our Forefathers? Could have been us?"

I shook my head, unwilling to let him condemn himself for doing his job as an American soldier. Trying to keep the edge of challenge out of my voice, I again tried gentle questions. "But if they're harboring enemy Saboteurs and Espionage Agents, doesn't that take away their innocence? I hear all the time that entire towns are Espy sympathizers, and give material support and comfort to those who want to kill our troops. And Kurt, like most Americans, I have a very heartfelt desire that our soldiers come home alive, whatever the cost."

I had started to move back into his arms, but the force of his response kept me at bay. "Don't wish that cost to be paid on my account. I knew what I was doing when I volunteered to put on that uniform. I signed up to put my life on the line. These people didn't. We're the invaders where I was stationed; none of them ever asked us to come in and take over their country. They never even had groups of Espies from there before we came in and started blowing people's lives apart, even after decades of sanctions that kept them from having enough medicine or food or supplies. Thousands, maybe hundreds of thousands of children died or had Birth Mutations thanks to radiation from bombs we dropped back in the last war. And disease from filthy water and no sanitation, 'cause we blew their facilities up back then and then made it illegal for anybody to sell them stuff to repair it."

He shook his head, his eyes again going distant. "But even then, of all the sick and twisted people that did try to attack us, none of those Spy groups were from there. The locals were mostly just normal human beings who don't believe in hurting people, especially good people like you and my mom. So saying that they need to gratefully accept that we're destroying their country and their lives, and that their wives and mothers deserve to die because some real Espies moved in, or even because some of their people are trying to defend their homes against our invasion... Well I don't care who you are, that's just selfish. Worse, it's sick. No civilian's life is worth more than mine, Liz. A soldier's job is to give up his life to protect innocents, not the other way around."

Tears had come to my eyes as I leaned against his chest, his strong arms raising to wrap tightly around me. Trying to keep my voice even, I said, "But I love you, Kurt. I can't help but want you to be safe here with me."

He held me close to him, and his voice also held the strain of struggling to keep steady. "I love you too, Liz, and what I love most about you is your heart. It's always shown me the strength of pure goodness, and don't fight me on that, you know that's what you mean to me. But this also means I don't want you to let any evil into your heart through love of me."

Leaning my head back, I looked up to his eyes with quiet conviction. "Loving you can never be evil, Kurt. Love can't be evil, it's a gift from God."

His small smile was equal parts love and sadness. "You're right, but the choices we make because we love, those can be evil if we're not careful. We like to think of evil as something that only happens inside total monsters. Monsters who aren't really people like you and me. But evil comes from perfectly normal stuff like hate and anger, or even good intentions. And that's how come we overlook so much evil all around us, even when we're the ones doing it. Especially then. We're just acting out our passions, which feel perfectly justified. So we just keep on doing evil, and encourage our friends and neighbors to do evil, thinking it just has to be good."

I didn't understand where my new Kurt was coming from, but I wanted to. "Even so... how does me wanting you to do whatever you have to do in order to come home to me… how can that be evil?"

He gently sat me up so he could look straight into my eyes. His anger was gone, replaced by the loving patience I had long treasured as his greatest strength. "Think this one through, Liz, and I know you'll see it. 'Do whatever it takes' includes hurting, mutilating or killing. And to turn a blind eye and cold heart to the suffering of others, Liz, that's evil, no matter what your reasoning is. I know they say there's no morality in war, just survival. But that's wrong, there's always good choices, and there's always evil ones. For example, all the hundreds, maybe thousands of innocent Arabiyans we've rounded up and thrown into prisons over the decades, torturing them but not even trying them for a crime. That's evil."

I was so relishing the gentleness of his tone, it took me a few moments for the hardness of his words to catch up with me. Once again, I got defensive. "But we have had some trials, and they've always resulted in convictions, so we know the rest are likely to be guilty, too. I mean I know people talk about how all of them should have a trial, but people are too scared to let them be tried in America. Which is really a cowardly Not In My Back Yard nimby-pimby nonsense if you ask me. But couldn't the Military make it happen anyway, so we can prove those people are guilty? And that we never tortured them, most of them anyway, we just had to use harsh interrogation to get vital intelligence to save countless lives?"

Kurt just stared at me for a moment, his jaw hardening. In carefully measured tones, he replied, "Well no, because like eighty-percent of them are innocent of any serious crime and we know it, like the kids we rounded up for throwing rocks just like the Holyland does. That's why we can't let trials happen: all these mucky details might make us look bad. Even when there are trials, the defense doesn't get access to their records and sometimes won't even be told what they're being accused of, since we have to keep our dirty laundry hidden away. Because make no mistake, Liz, we torture those prisoners, even and especially the innocent ones. Calling it by another name doesn't change what it is, just like 'limited kinetic action' doesn't turn invading a country into a short set of jumping jacks. Guys try to kill themselves to escape the horror of it all, and it's not called suicide, it's 'self-injurious behavior.' Since suicide has claimed more lives than the enemy in recent years, you'd think we'd start dealing with it by now. It's way past time we deal straight with torture. That's the other reason we can't have trials, because it's illegal to try to use what it gives you as evidence."

I wouldn't relent. "But can't we use the truth, no matter how it was obtained?"

He started to tense, then just shook his head, chuckling to himself. "That's the thing, torture doesn't give you the truth, only whatever the victim thinks you want to hear, anything to get you to stop. I know, because I've been through it. I mean not like the real thing, not the inhuman brutality and the insanity of not knowing if the nightmare will ever end. But still, enough to get a vague idea. See, the American torture playbook was developed in the torture-resistance training program I went through. It's not just what you normally think of as torture, like beating them and hanging them by their wrists behind their backs until their shoulders pop out of joint. Or electrodes on private places that tear through you with pain but don't always leave a mark.”

Whether he noticed my face go white or not, he didn’t give any sign. He just kept talking as his humor was slowly replaced by that low-boiling anger, seething hotter than I’d ever thought he could hold. “What people call ‘harsh interrogation,’ that’s just a coward’s nickname for when you don’t have the spine to say a tough word like ‘torture.’ Sensory and sleep deprivation, so-called stress positions, religious humiliation, waterboarding… I know people joke about that all the time like those are all just ‘uncomfortable pressures’ and no worse than high school hazing, that they don’t cause any lasting harm. But those jokers are either ignorant or lying. Psych and Intel pros know the mental scars are worse than physical ones. They make you a blithering wad of putty, stripping away your humanity just as sure as as it takes it from the torturer who molded you.”

I had never before seen Kurt get so acidly impassioned, but I didn’t let that distract me from the bombshell he had dropped. “Wait… Wait. Are you… Are you telling me the Military tortured you?” My blood had turned to ice, making me shiver.

He winced, hesitating before replying. “Well… yes and no. Torture resistance was part of my training, in case I was captured and someone pulled it on me. We were all mentally and physically fit, knew why we were there and for how long, and they weren’t allowed to truly dehumanize or break us. It was hardly a picnic in the park, but it was designed to make us stronger, not weak. So it wasn’t anywhere near the same thing. We were given full support preparing us for it and helping us after. I knew I would soon be back to my normal life, and that I could call it quits at any time and just walk away.”

He then shrugged, continuing with a tone I found disturbingly casual, given the subject matter. “Not to say it wasn’t still seriously, seriously hard in ways I don’t want to get into even if I could. But I also lucked out in that it took them a good while to find me, and then I was placed in a block with more experienced Special Ops buddies who managed to coordinate a breakout not long after. They got me out before I got to the waterboarding where I’m pretty sure I woulda signed the fake confession. I know this because I asked them to do it on me afterward so I’d know what I was fighting for out there. And Liz, believe me, it was exactly as bad as people say. The advisers had even recommended the program not use it on students because the fear of drowning is so primal it gets compliance a full hundred-percent of the time. Even the toughest guys break down and comply if just brought near the waterboard again. That's probably why they used only a lesser version on us than the non-military interrogators use out in the field. It was the difference between a wet handkerchief and buckets of water."

Seeing how tough the image was on me, he stroked my hair and softened his voice. "Let's just say that I recognize what I went through wasn't anything like the Real Deal. Especially since the people we throw into our torture prisons tend to be real vulnerable types, and are super likely to get seriously messed up. Most of them should never have been there and they know it, hoping that any day we'll realize our mistake and set them free. But we keep treating them like Happy Animal Farm treats the animals, and they keep saying whatever nonsense we wanna hear. That's why torture is not only illegal, it's worse than useless. It makes us the bad guys, and it robs people of their most basic value: their human dignity. And that way we dehumanize them, it splashes over to their countries, their religion, everything connected with them, making them out to be less-than, and it turns them against us. Because at the end of the day, that's what will make people come after us, fighting for their right to some simple human dignity. When you deny somebody that basic right, you throw away your own."

As painful as the conversation was, I wanted to understand. So I had to ask, "But what if you were under orders? I mean, to... do those things? You couldn't be held responsible if you were just following orders."

He could barely restrain his scorn. "Oh yeah, the devil made you do it, right? It's a soldier's moral and legal duty to refuse bad orders. We're held responsible for following them. Back after the Holocaust when the people who did those horrifying things tried to plead innocence cause they were just following orders, nobody let them off the hook. It was their choice to agree to round up, torture and murder innocents."

He flexed a hand to crack his knuckles, his tone getting more matter-of-fact, if still a touch bitter. "You want the truth about torture? Here's a truth for you: the only purpose of torture is to torture. To get the adrenalin rush from having literal power over another person's body and soul right there in your fist, to rule over their terror like a dark, miniature god. It's addictive, and as addictive as it is for torture cheerleaders to gobble up the violence porn in movies and the news, it's a thousand times more addictive to feel that power in person. I've heard it all from this guy I know, who used to do the 'softening up' at one of our prisons out there. It was never what he wanted to become, but he lost himself in it. He couldn't get treatment for the Post-Traumatic Stress of being involved in those horrors, and it still haunts him bad, like he was the one it was done to. He wakes up in night sweats, like one time he pulled a gun on me when I had to wake him up because his girlfriend finally got a call through."

My eyes widened in alarm, but he didn't notice, not even stopping for a breath. "Yeah, so when I hear people making fun of suffering, well, the jokes about torture turn my stomach the worst, just like hitting a child. There's just never ever any justification for it. I don't care what somebody has done, you don't torture. Ever. That's not what Jesus teaches, that's not 'turn the other cheek.' 'As you have done unto others, you have done unto me.' I just want to ask them, who would Jesus torture? Is that 'love thy neighbor as thyself,' or what?"

I took his hand, and kissed it before I quietly replied in defense of my fellow American Christians, "The problem is, we don't see them as our neighbors... I mean, Americans don't see Arabiyans as our neighbors. Nor Muslims as neighbors to Christians. We're too far apart."

He smiled at me gently, pulling his hand out of mine so he could cup my cheek. "Yeah, well Jesus' countrymen didn't see Samaritans as neighbors or even as people. They hated them for their religion and racial 'impurity.' But it was a Samaritan who helped the man who was robbed in the parable about neighbors, while a priest and a Levite had both avoided him. It was a Samaritan who gave Jesus water at the well. So when we see our own Samaritans, whoever they are, we need to remember to see them as people. Religion can't teach you the standards of basic human decency; you have to find them in your own heart. And basic human decency says that as much as you love me, they love their families just as much. Their hopes and dreams are as precious as ours."

I nestled my cheek into his hand, closing my eyes as I tried not to think of how much it hurt for Arabiyan wives to see their husbands go out and never come back, like it hurt me to say goodbye to Kurt when he left. With a soft sigh, I replied, "It's funny, talking about Muslims to remind me how to be Christlike, given how Islamist countries are out to destroy Christians."

He chuckled softly, kissing the top of my head once more. "Not really. I mean sure, some are super oppressive against Christians, but mostly those are run by the dictators we're propping up. It's more about politics than religion, as usual. I bet you didn't know their Qur'an is actually real respectful of Jesus. Yeah, it mentions his name more than it does Muhammad's. They believe Jesus was a Messenger of God, performed miracles, and that he was born to a virgin Mary, who they talk about more than any other book I've seen. And, like the earliest Christians, they believe that Jesus never claimed he was going to atone for our sins. It's more like he set a good example and we each have to answer for our own choices. I don't mean to pick a fight with you on that, I'm just bringing it up since I know you'll ask. They do believe that there will be a Day of Judgment and that Jesus will return to defeat the Anti-Christ, putting them much more in line with your type of Christian than I'll ever be."

He said that lovingly, almost teasingly, amused by my bewilderment. I wasn't offended, only surprised. "Wow. I had no idea. Are you sure? Don't they worship Allah instead of God?"

Kurt laughed at that, hugging me tighter. "Yes, I'm totally sure. Allah is just their word that means 'God,' the same god of Abraham that you worship. And I know for a fact that most Muslims are good people just like most Christians, Jews, and everybody else in the world, because I've seen it myself. I learned about all of this from my very own Good Samaritan."

I perked up. "You had help from a Good Samaritan? You never told me! What happened?"

He shrugged a little, sheepish again at having kept a secret from me. "Yeah, well it's not something I wanted anybody else to hear about who wasn't already in the know. I didn't want to get Sammy and his family in trouble. That's what I called him, Codename Sammy." He chewed his lip as he paused. "Okay, so you heard about the siege of Mariam?"

It was my turn to tense up, wincing. "The town where some American security guards were lynched? Yeah, that was awful, I'm so glad the Assassins responsible were brought to justice."

Kurt paused before replying, then tread carefully as he chose his next words. "Justice. Yeah. Let me tell you about Justitia Americana. In Mariam we originally had a lot of support from the locals, because their town was pretty well-off and we didn't damage their area too much when we moved in. That support held true in lots of places where we didn't demolish peoples' houses and kill their kids with our night-time strafing drones and firebomb missiles. Not to mention dropping cluster bombs that looked like toys or food packages, horrible weapons that other countries have begged us to stop using. Though that isn't to say they were completely unscathed by how things disintegrated after we invaded. For example, Sammy's wife used to be some top PhD scientist type and now the religious fanatics of the sect we're supporting have sent out bass-ackward roving bands to hurt people who don't do Sharia the way they want, like girls learning or women working. I guess that was moot because her research lab's shut down anyway, since the economy's in shambles and infrastructure's a wreck."

He had thrown that all out quite matter-of-fact, while I reeled from the suggestion that fundamentalist restrictions on the freedoms of women were worse, not better. "Oh that's awful! We went over there to liberate women! I thought they weren't allowed to work, or even have lives outside the home!"

Kurt just shrugged. "Well now you're right. Believe me, women have suffered some of the worst from the changes out there, and we're not really doing all that much to make things better for them. We're so busy appeasing the warlords we want to use as puppets, that women's rights are routinely thrown out the window. So long as we have political support, we're fine with them being forced under a burqa if they don't want, and forced out of it for pay when we want. Okay I'm sorry, that's not fair to most of my fellow soldiers, but some are just fine with going to brothels even though not all the girls there want to be there and some will get beat up or killed if they complain. Not that we're spotless in the Military either. Liz, I am so glad you didn't join up, because sex crimes by soldiers are skyrocketing out there. If something like that happened to you, I don't know what I'd do."

I studiously avoided thinking about what I had faced, my blood again feeling cold as I tried to process what he'd said. "Soldiers… you mean they're attacking other soldiers?"

He paused, and I could tell he was searching for a way out of the conversation, but there wasn't any way out but through. He rallied an apologetically wry look while he tried to explain. "Civilians are doing it too, with impunity, but it's super rampant among the Military. It's like doubled or tripled lately. And almost all the time, it's women getting attacked. One in three female soldiers is harassed or assaulted, over a third of those raped are raped multiple times, and half that number are gang-raped, all of it usually by the people we're trained to trust and protect more strongly than anything in the world: our buddies and commanders. Only like one in six attacks are reported, since they know they're not likely to get helped and will sometimes even get in trouble for talking about it. Like this gal who was gang-raped by her buddies and they passed around the video, but her commander still wouldn't prosecute cause she didn't act like gals who are raped in the movies. He threatened to punish her for hurting unit cohesion if she pushed the matter. One soldier I talked to, the chaplain told her to her face that it was god's punishment for not going to church more and women like her belonged at home, so he wouldn't help her even though that was his job. Whenever somebody finds out someone's complained about sexual harassment or assault, she's treated like a traitor to the ranks, I'm serious. So their untreated PTSD gets made worse. And it's not like they have an easy time getting The Pill out there, since the countries aren't all that pro-woman and the Military doesn't step up to fill the gap. Apparently it's un-American to help women defending our country protect their right to decide when and how to have safe sex. So whatever happens to them, they're f–uh…"

After an uncomfortable, deep breath, he worked to get back on topic. "Right. Well, the thing about Mariam is that even though they were generally okay with us, we took over their school to use for our occupation, and well the parents kinda minded. When a couple hundred people broke our curfew to protest and ask us to leave, well, we opened fire. Maybe someone threw a rock, I dunno. Protesters died, and when there was another protest about that, more people died. So yeah, things were tense. Then one of our patrols hit an IUD, and the explosion took one of them out. The guys went nuts. They did a three-sixty, opening fire on everybody there, and then went door-to-door on every house in the area, throwing in grenades or busting in doors and shooting whoever was there, trying to kill whoever planted the bomb, even if they had to destroy the block to do it. One house, they killed a whole family on their knees, including a pregnant woman and a mom with two kids."

I had to ask him to clarify, "The Spies killed them with their bomb?"

He blinked at me. "No, Liz, our guys did, the guys on patrol. And that's not the first time something like that has happened, or door-to-door patrols steal stuff or extort money. But this was the last straw, especially because then they tried to cover it up with an airstrike on the area to destroy the evidence. But luckily by that time the mania had faded, and they didn't get authorization for the airstrike. Bad thing for them though, was that these were family members of a local leader who was trying to smooth things over from the protests. So the locals knew what happened, and they were demanding justice."

I blinked back at him. "But I don't understand, why did they kill them in the first place? Even if somebody in the house helped plant the bomb, the children didn't do it! The pregnant mom didn't do it! Didn't they know that?"

With great patience, Kurt tried to explain. "They didn't know anything, Liz. When you go on a rampage, you turn on whoever's there in front of you. The pressure-cooker finally boils over, short-circuiting everything. So when you lose somebody, or even if a kid throws a rock at you, it can be the match thrown into a barrel of gasoline. You just explode."

The imagery helped me try to make sense of what he was trying to say, I thought. "So it wasn't anybody's fault."

Kurt reeled, shaking his head slowly. "No, actually, it was a lot of peoples' fault. It was the fault of the guys who did it. It was the fault of the commanders who told them to go in shooting and helped them get away with murder. It was the fault of the Military Brass who drill us into gung-ho killers but don't train us for the tedious high-alert of hearts-and-minds patrolling. It's the fault of Military so-called Justice for not taking us to task when we do crap like that. It's the fault of every chicken-hawk living-room general who cheers for our pointless bloodshed like we're scoring touchdowns for their team. And everybody who sits by and lets it happen, condoning it all with their silence. It's everybody's fault."

The harsh force of his words just hung in the air at that, and his eyes glazed a bit as he retreated again to that dark place he'd brought home with him. I just held him more tightly, then leaned up to kiss his cheek.

That brought him back to me, returning my squeeze as he took a deep breath to get back to his story. "As you might imagine, tensions were really high after that. We had signs that some Espionage cells were moving in, so we needed to rectify matters quick. We ended up pulling out to station outside the town borders while we tried to rebuild our relationship with the town and re-secure its loyalty. Meanwhile, this private convoy still drove straight through downtown, running a car or two off the road. This made some locals super upset, and somebody even fired on them the day before. But these contractors, they just kept cruising through like they owned the place. So we weren't surprised when something happened."

He paused to chew on his lip, then sigh. "My Special Forces team, we wanted to handle it by going in and making surgical strikes on the likely suspects. Do some Recon, followed by some arrests, help them refurnish the school we'd pulled out of, plus a few more things to take care of business but also keep the whole deal from exploding. But no, civilians and brass alike took the assault on Americans as a personal insult to their pride, so much so that they wanted to make the whole town suffer for it. Collective punishment is a war crime, but hey, why start caring about that stuff now? So we were ordered to cut off water, food and electricity to the few hundred thousand who lived in the city. We then advised them to evacuate women and all children and elderly. Forget if they didn't have the means to leave or anywhere to go, they were warned, right? But they couldn't all leave. Older boys and adult men had to stay."

"You mean, everyone on your watch list, they had to stay." I was hoping he was just short-cutting on the details.

I was wrong. "Oh no, Liz, every male age sixteen to sixty had to stay. We figured that was the age range of possible fighters, so we made everybody who could possibly be an Espy stick around to face our collective punishment, and hang international law along with them. We were going to make an example of that city, so all the rest of them would know what happens when we feel they've gone too far. Then we put in a curfew on all of them with orders to shoot to kill any shape we saw after early evening until morning came. Plus there were the choppers and jets dropping firebombs and phosphorous and other stuff that isn't exactly legal, popping houses, malls, schools, churches... especially churches. This went on for several weeks, so you can just imagine how things went down. Taking a situation like that and throwing in a bunch of guys too young to give a beer, but loading them with guns. So sometimes guys shot at targets during the day, laughing about racking up points, with bonus points if they were waving a white handkerchief. One time in the earliest rays of light I saw the body of an ex-mom holding her dead baby. God only knows what situation she was in that was so bad she tried to brave being outside."

Kurt held me close as I snuggled into his arms, trying hard to not tune him out as he continued his story. "Well, it was all just out of control, but the Military couldn't let word get out, in case the truth could be used against us. So we also took over the hospital, interfering with treatment and not letting anybody keep track of injuries and deaths. Doctors and patients and supplies were kept in, and everybody else was kept out. Ambulance vans were shot up on approach, and a couple times they let a van leave with the crankiest doctors and their patients, so we could just blow them up a few blocks away. Still, we were afraid locals may try to come for news or supplies, so I was split off from Karsten and stationed on top of the hospital's water tower. My orders were to shoot anybody who came near it, day or night."

I was numb. "You… you killed people who were just going to the hospital for help?"

He gave a short sigh. "You know, if I was caught not shooting at trespassers, I would have been court martialed, and I would've lived hell for it. Though the point was moot since nobody actually made it alive onto my watch… at least at first. Then at one point I caught sight of a local who was working there, heading out the back door and onto the grounds. I felt suspicious for some reason, so I pulled out my scope and watched him throw a bag into the garbage heap, and at the same time hide a bundle behind it. It was a stack of medkits strapped together with medical tape. He was real slick too. If I didn't have a scope I wouldn't have seen it. So I kept watch to who see who came to pick it up. Finally past midnight somebody came by, a young woman in a black headscarf. I had no idea why she wasn't evacuated, or what possessed her to take such a risk. She had made it all the way there for the supplies, I don't know how, only to end up right in my targeting scope. I just could not take her out. I said a prayer asking God or Allah or Jesus or Buddha or heck even Zeus, to help her make it through our siege. And maybe somebody did hear my prayer and rewards us for looking out for each other, because I think not putting a bullet through that girl's brain is what saved my life."

My heart skipped a beat as his last few words reached me. "Wait, saved your life? From what?"

He chuckled softly into my hair, kissing my neck to reassure me. "From when I was an idiot. That's when I got the Purple Heart I'd avoided earning, even when Karsten and I pulled guys out from that firefight deep in Espy territory. When I finally did get shot, it was during some night assault going on not far from the hospital. The bulk of our guys went after it, and then I saw some movement on the grounds. I dunno, it coulda been an animal, but it just felt wrong. I couldn't see anything with my scope, so I decided to shimmy over to a better position to see if there was anything to call in. Only it'd been raining and I slipped, dropping my pack with my radio. So I figured I'd better go get it before whoever or whatever else did, and maybe get some decent Recon while I was down there. As soon as I slung the bag over my shoulder there was a gunshot. I whipped up my hardware and fired off a round, killing the guy who shot me before I pitched over, myself."

He'd tried to tell it like a funny story, but his attempt to distract me utterly failed. I pulled away from him to gasp at him accusingly, "You got *shot?!* You said that scar... Oh good heavens, you never told me you got shot!"

Kurt pulled me back into his embrace and kissed me, trying to soothe my hurricane of emotions. "I know, I'm sorry, I didn't want to talk about it. I got in a lot of trouble later for not using the radio the moment I thought there might be something. I was even thinking that when I felt the bullet, since the gunfire would quickly alert my buddies to what was going on, but not as quick as the enemy ambush and I'd be an easy target once I passed out. But before I even hit the ground, this guy out of nowhere throws me over his shoulder right as I blacked out. Next thing I know I'm coming to, and this guy is singing softly to himself in Arabiyan as he's taking care of my wound."

I tilted my head, piecing things together. "With supplies from the hospital?"

He grinned at me. "Exactly, with supplies his grand-daughter had snuck to his house. Turns out Sammy's a doctor who worked at the hospital before retiring a couple years ago, so she knew the route real well. Sammy's wife, daughter and grand-daughter refused to leave his sons and grand-sons behind to die alone, and it was she who had arranged to get supplies from his old buddies. I tell you, I wish I coulda recruited her for Recon. Anyway, people brought their families to him for help, since he'd been their doctor. There were lots of people who wouldn't or couldn't leave town to become just more of the thousands or millions of starving, homeless refugees. And he helped them, no questions asked. We had all night together since my radio was busted and phones weren't working, and it wasn't like I could walk out and not get risk getting shot by our own guys."

He laughed at that, like it was funny. I didn't see the humor, but I didn't interrupt his story. "So we had a lot of time to talk, since Sammy's and his wife's English was even better than mine. I asked him why he helped me, and he said it was because they had seen me up in the tower, but I'd never shot them. So when he'd heard that there might be an assault on the hospital, he went to check on me. His family was completely against Espionage, and he also had compassion for me as an American soldier. The way he saw it, we were also victims of America's State of Endless War, which was destroying our lives and our country. Sure, we completely destroyed their stability and put criminals and warlords in charge, but someday, they might get the chance to rebuild in peace. But not us, we'll always be impoverished by war. And if we ever run out of countries to do it to, well, we've already set up a military occupation on our own borders. You know what I mean."

Unfortunately, I did know. Biting my lip, I replied, "Like how we use those same drones that are killing foreigners and Americans overseas, they're also patrolling our streets here at home? And armed guards and checkpoints even between state lines?"

He laughed again, and this time I almost joined him, it just suddenly struck me as so absurd. Nodding, he agreed, "Yeah, exactly that. And sure, some of it is because there's elites at the top who have an obsession with knowing and controlling every aspect of our lives. But a lot of it is because of just how freaking much money is being chewed up to pay for all of it. Just like how instead of making sure every kid has food and shelter, we're letting War Profiteers get fatter. We're begging them to take our money and our freedoms, so we can feel just a little less scared."

I saw where he was headed, but I didn't think it was quite as bad as he was saying. "Okay, so it is annoying how we always have to be on our guard, but really, it's not like there's no reason. I mean, sure, we may be spending too much money, but we have to keep the safeguards in place that help the DSS catch all those Espionage and Sabotage plots every year."

He bit his lip, wincing again. "Uh, Liz? Want to know an open secret? If you look for it, you can see how often the so-called plots are just fake sting operations. The DSS went out looking for vulnerable or desperate patsies and offered them money and stuff, without really telling them what all they're supposed to be planning to do. Then they make this huge show of having caught a Saboteur, and the Profiteers unveil their latest high-priced way to keep us safe from the next one. But it's a big scam. All those big-money surveillance systems like the scanners at the airport that give the techs free nudie pics to share with their buddies? They're to make the owners money, and get the rest of us used to zipping our lips and rolling over for anybody and everybody in a uniform. They don't catch much spies, even those who were caught later at their destination trying to do whatever. Just like how we conveniently lose pallets full of cash out in Arabiya, it's all about making the rich and powerful even more rich and powerful. That's why we can't even walk down the street without some private company's government-sanctioned Spy watching our every move."

I wasn't aware of being spied on just walking down the street, but Kurt was getting so animated that I didn't have time to interrupt. "The bottom line is exactly that, the bottom line. Even though we like to think of ourselves as a free country, Liz, Americans are always ready and willing to throw away their liberty for the false promise of a little bit of security. So the government has got to keep manufacturing enemies out there to scare us into obedience, to keep the system going. And that's what the bottom line has always been. The Incorporated States of America were founded as a commercial venture on the backs of the slaves and servants of all colors, and we've stayed true to that American ideal ever since. Sammy taught me that, by sharing his secret library of books banned in America by authors I'd never even heard of. George Orwell, Howard Zinn, Upton Sinclair, Smedley Butler... Oh Liz, Smedley Butler—"

"Hold on. You're serious; you've read banned books?" I had interjected almost before I realized it. Banned books. Even if you read them overseas, that could get you into serious trouble with the DSS. I was supposed to be upset with him, and more than a little scared. But I wasn't. I was excited, as excited as I was jealous.

Finally, I was blessed by the impish grin from my sweetheart Kurt that I'd been waiting over a year to see. "Yep. A whole shelf full of them."

I laughed with glee, throwing my arms around his neck. He held me closer, continuing with his boyish laughter. "Oh Liz, I wish I could have brought even just a few pages home, without getting us all labeled Spies and rounded up or killed, especially Sammy. See, since he helped me out at great risk to himself, Command let me utilize him as one of my contacts for Recon after the fighting was over. He was a great resource. He only steered us straight, instead of all the guys out there who use us to settle scores against each other. And yeah, that area has centuries of experience using invaders like us as patsies against each other until we can't afford to keep trying to conquer them. Anyway, because I had a lot of downtime, I could stay there a while and read. And while I both like and dislike what some of the other guys wrote, my favorite was 'War is a Racket' by Major General Smedley D. Butler. He was so high up, he claimed to have been asked by a cabal of traitors to help kill his president in a military coup. He said it was led by a war profiteer who was helping arm the Nazis, who ironically was the father and grandfather of a couple of later presidents way back in the day. As in, President of the United States of America."

Kurt had assumed his poker face that had always meant he was waiting for me to call him on his teasing so he could deliver the punchline. Only this time, I didn't understand the joke. "The who of the what, now?"

He broke into a broad grin, lowering his voice, almost breathless with excitement that I found contagious. "That's part of why some of these books are banned, Liz. I'm sure of it! They're secret histories of America, from a time back before our textbooks and Innernet started telling the stories they do now. See, back in the day, the states didn't used to be Incorporated, with private companies owning all our resources, and investors backing the treasuries and collecting interest off public revenues. I mean, not so blatantly anyway. And the leader wasn't a CEO, he was called a President, and he had limited power that was balanced out by the Legislature and the Supreme Court and… okay I don't have all the details, only what I got from context. At first I thought Zinn was fiction, and really dark fiction cause he seemed to focus on all the negatives and stuff. But then I saw his themes repeated in the earlier writings by Butler and, oh Liz, I've got to get you copies, I don't have as good a head for remembering details as Derek…"

His focus had started to fragment, and I found it all a bit much to take in, myself. "Okay, that... well it sounds far-fetched, but I don't want to be one of those people who ridicule something just because it sounds silly, before getting all the facts... I mean, not anymore anyway. So instead I'll just ask your opinion: how solid is all this?"

Kurt shrugged. "Well, it was a variety of sources and they all agreed, so I think it's pretty solid. I mean, it wouldn't be the first time the Western world had access to its own histories and forgotten knowledge because of Muslim scholars. Anyway, Butler was a real War Hero, the most decorated Military Man in American history when he died. Just from his own years of service, he explained how the rich and powerful in America worked to put fascism and dictatorships all over the world to protect their personal agendas. He said in his career of over thirty-three years in the Military, he spent most of it as a 'high class muscle man for Big Business, for Wall Street, and the bankers.'

It's even still going on right in front of our noses, we're just so used to it we don't notice. Like nobody even asks to try to read the Constitution anymore, even though it's the foundation of our freedoms we're supposed to still have."

That made me sigh. "I know. When I brought it up in a class once, everybody looked at me like I was out of my mind. Wait, did he have a copy of the Constitution?"

His frown triggered my disappointment. "No, I wish. But he did have the Declaration of Independence! The whole thing, not just the first line or two like we read in school! It was a real eye-opener, and I can absolutely see Thomas Jefferson's hand in that. But back to Butler. He went into detail about all these major wars from the early history of America, including so-called police actions and even overthrows of Sudoamerican democracies so businessmen could force the countries to let them loot their economies and resources. Meanwhile, they got to prance around back home pretending to be great big conquering tough guys because they were sending grunts out to do their bloodwork for them. Which is really funny because of the ghillie suit I wear out on Recon. It was originally made by Scottish gamekeepers to capture deer alive so their lords could pretend to be big game hunters by killing them in the luxurious comfort of their own courtyards. The rulers of America consider the whole world their personal hunting grounds, only I'm sent to get them two-legged game. I tell you, Liz. It takes a very small man to hold someone else down so they can feel big."

He snorted in disgust at the thought. "So yeah, Butler pointed out that America is going to be always at war so long as war is profitable. And he had three ways to make it unprofitable, and stop the racket. First, draft the heads of weapons manufacturers and the like before anybody else has to fight. Second, no troops could be sent anywhere without a full vote of all Americans who'd be risking their lives. Third, restrict the Military to two hundred miles of our borders, so we can't go out invading other countries in so-called pre-emptive strikes, which happen to be illegal even today."

I was sitting back against the arm of the couch at this point, and bit my lip uncertainly as I wrapped my hands around my knee. "I see why he says that, but I don't think any of that would actually happen."

He sighed his agreement, leaning back to put an arm over the top of the couch. "No you're right, what with so many secret wars where teams like mine go places Americans never know we're sending our own Spies, Sabs and Ass'ins. Maybe that would help a little, if we had an enforced law where Americans had to know where our money and soldiers were going. Or the scads of drones violating other countries' airspace, shooting places up with drones controlled by kids playing them like video games from the physical comfort of a middle-American base. And then when people come by for emergency aid to the victims, or hold funerals for them, the drones sweep by again to utterly obliterate whoever happens to be there, even though we kick and scream that it's a War Crime when other countries do it. It's so bad, the drone pilots get PTSD just as bad as if they were in the war zone for real. Maybe it's worse, since they get to see the whole thing right up close onscreen, and then each night have to go back to regular American neighborhoods where nobody has any idea the nightmares they're living."

He paused at my incredulous stare, then nodded to emphasize what he'd said. "Seriously, Liz, this even gets through our heavily filtered news, if you just stop to look. And if this talk is making you start to think twice about being Pro-War, well, you wouldn't be alone. Once you get peoples' real opinions, the polls almost always show that the majority is Pro-Soldier and Anti-War, wanting to honor our sacrifices by not throwing our lives away into money-and-blood-pits. If we can't get a popular vote, maybe even having regular public polls might help expose that. But the elites in charge, they don't care, they just keep on with their game knowing we're too busy shutting ourselves up so we don't get called cowardly Commie Peaceniks or whatever stupid slur their media puppets are throwing these days. And those who speak up too much, start to make too much of a difference? Well, they've always got the DSS to take care of the troublemakers. If we just were more brave, more patriotic, we'd take more time to connect with people, even those we don't like. We'd share our stories so we can find out how much we're on the same side."

I squeezed his hands, looking into his eyes as I nodded. "You know, in that, I think you're completely right. I learned that in Acculturation. I now see how effectively certain groups have been in keeping us divided, pitting us against each other. Every time it looks like we might be building bridges, they send in cultural Saboteurs to blow things up and we end up blaming each other. They keep us at each other's throats fighting over the scraps. We don't notice they're the ones who robbed our cupboards bare."

Kurt freed a hand, shooting his finger up into the air. "That's it! They're Kleptocrats! Liz, we don't have a Democracy or even a

Republic. We have a Kleptocracy."

We laughed together, unsure how much we found the label funny, versus apt. Finally I asked, "But how could we stop the Kleptocrats from keeping our country as their own private piggy bank? At least when it comes to the War Profiteers?"

He took my hands again, turning me so he could hold me with my back leaning against his chest. "I've actually had a lot of time to think about that. I think I have my own version of Butler's suggestions. If nothing else, we should make it illegal for anybody to make military weapons and war machines for a profit. No, I don't see them ever letting that happen, but since only the government can legally sanction and use the instruments of war, only the government should bear the risks and responsibilities of making them. When you privatize the business of death, people are killed for profit."

"Kurt, you know that isn't going to happen," I replied reflexively, and regretted it as I felt his spirit deflate just a little. So I continued, "at least, not unless we start realizing how much things need to change. That's going to be a real jump for some of us. Because Kurt, you realize that a lot of us Americans, we're totally behind what's going on over there because we think it'll bring about the second coming of Jesus. So we don't stop to think about how wrong that is, wishing some very un-Christlike harm to come to people, in hopes of seeing the Christ return to us."

I had turned to face him again, to find him studiously watching me. Finally he broke through his own contemplation. "That does make me think. You know I don't believe that Jesus meant to say he'd come back literally in person. But I do value the Christ message of love and unity. And I think if there really was a Jesus who said he'd be with us someday... Jesus said 'For where two or three are gathered together in my name, there am I in the midst of them,' and I believe him. If you want to see Jesus here in the world, don't go out there killing people. Start coming together in love, like he taught."

I let my gaze wander as I pondered his words, then quickly looked up. "I think you've got it! Even if somebody doesn't believe in Christ, everybody in America knows what we mean by being Christlike. And as we work together to live up to that example of love and community, we create the kind of place that Jesus would want to be. We don't know what the future holds for His return, and frankly Jesus was very clear that we wouldn't be able to know. So it's up to us to prepare the way in the meantime, working to create the world of Peace and

Wisdom. It's up to each of us to build a world in which we Love One Another. If we want to be assured of seeing a glimpse of Heaven on earth, we have to do our part to make it happen."

He reached up to touch my cheek, a warm smile spreading across his lips. "Holding you here with me now, I have a bit of heaven already."

I tried to smirk at him for being goofy and perhaps a teeny bit blasphemous, but then I saw he was more sincere than he was joking. Realizing he was right, I said a silent prayer of thanks for being blessed with such bliss.

We turned our thoughts away from death and betrayal, and toward the eternal Love and Trust we both felt for one another. And we then shared our private little slice of heaven, for as long as we could.

Chapter 16

Thou art loved. Let love flow through thee; heal thy world.

"I don't want you going back there."

We'd said it simultaneously, our thoughts moving as one again after only a couple days back in each other's arms. It's funny, we'd really only had a few months here and there together as a couple. But in those months, we'd felt as though we'd been together forever. I didn't want to lose that again.

"You've seen more death and body parts in the past several weeks than I did in over a year, Liz. I don't want you in that kind of environment." He did have a point.

But so did I. "None of mine were human. Okay, I was there when somebody lost part of their hand, but I didn't get a good look…"

"That's exactly my point! Carnage is carnage, Liz. Your body reacts to it, and so does your mind. I know what that does to people, and I don't want it happening to you." The depth of concern in his eyes surprised me.

I pushed my plate of pancakes out of the way so I could reach across the table to take his hand. "Kurt, it's not that bad for me. I don't get out onto the floor very often; I spend most of my time in the office. And I'm actually able to do some good there. I help keep track of peoples' hours and get them most of the wages they're owed. And the government system that supposedly validates workers' legal status, it messes up all the time for real Members, but completely misses people who all but told me they didn't exactly have all their legal papers. I help make sure the first group gets to keep working, and try to make sure the second group are where they need to be. These are good, moral people who struggle hard to build safe and law-abiding communities. But nobody cares, they just treat them as 'the scum of the earth.' If I wasn't there to look out for them, things could be a lot worse."

He frowned at me uncertainly. "How much worse would it have been for Sammy's grand-daughter with someone else on that water tower?"

I shuddered, so desperate to keep him home that I talked without even thinking. "That's exactly my point. Sooner or later, you're going to kill an innocent person, Kurt. If you haven't already."

Of all the wrong things to say at the wrong time in the entire history of the universe, I'm pretty sure there's been worse. Still, I felt my comment was in the running when I saw Kurt's reaction.

My beloved husband gripped my fingers hard as he clenched his eyes tightly shut, turning away from me. His other hand grabbed his half-stack of pancakes and squeezed, then threw the goppy mess to splatter and stick against the wall. He then opened his eyes to watch the gob of dough and syrup slide down to the floor.

Suddenly realizing he was hurting my hand, Kurt eased his grasp, bringing my fingers to his lips to kiss away any pain he may have caused. "Oh Liz, Liz, Elizabeth my love... I'm so sorry, I..."

I curled my fingers into his, leaning forward over the table to touch his cheek. "It's okay. I didn't mean... It's okay, really."

Kurt took my other hand into his syrup-covered one, holding it. "No, it's not okay. You're right. Statistically speaking, I must have shot someone I shouldn't have. That's what war is. It's what I was signed up for. Killing people who don't deserve to die, on the orders of REMFs who neither know nor care what happens to any of us."

I pulled my hands back so I could walk around the table to sit in his lap. His arms slipped around my waist as mine went around his neck, neither of us caring that syrup was now getting everywhere. "Have you thought about filing for Conscientious Objector status? That still exists, you know. It's like, super hard to get the Military to actually honor their obligations under the law, but it's still on the books."

I caught his dubiousness, so I quickly continued, "I know what they say, that once you sign up for the Military you gave up your right to object. But that's not true, so long as you can articulate how your beliefs changed. You just have to show why you are opposed to war in any form, not just this one, and that you're sincere. It doesn't have to be religious reasons."

Kurt looked into my eyes as I talked, yet I couldn't read his expression. I hoped he was considering it. Finally, he gave a short sigh.

"I don't know. I mean, yeah, war really is a huge racket. And I never want to shoot another person as long as I live. Not even the ones trying to kill me. But I do believe in the guys and gals who are out there, well, most of them. I don't want to leave them to face that alone. I made it through thanks to Karsten, and the few guys like him. There's so little sanity out there, I guess I feel like, well, like I owe it to them to stick it out."

"Then apply for non-combatant status! Some people will absolutely try to give you a hard time, but you've got some pretty sweet combat and bravery medals to wave in their faces, if that helps. I'll be honest, though: I want you to stay here. Gosh, I'd even run off to Candania with you if they weren't like the fifty-first state when it comes to handing over military refugees. But I want to support you in what you believe, whatever it is. You've always supported me a hundred percent, even when you haven't always agreed. That's what you taught me love is." I kissed his cheek again, then hugged him to me.

He returned the hug, lowering his voice in my ear. "You sure do know a lot about all this for a civ. Are you sure you haven't been reading any classified lawbooks?"

I giggled. "I wish! No, I just have this friend who is like a wizard with finding things out. He says he can help get all the paperwork written up, let you know exactly where and how to send it so they can't claim they lost it, and all the numbers of people who can help you. I'll be honest, he says many in the Military can be real jerks about not wanting to allow you your rights on this one. But he also says many others respect a man with convictions, even in the Military. And he'll do everything he can to make this work for you, if you want."

If I didn't know better, I'd have mistaken Kurt's renewed dubiousness for jealousy. "Just who is this 'he' you've been talking to?"

My hesitation didn't help his discomfort. Seeing that, I quickly tried to reassure him. "Just a guy from work, Mark. He's in the Informational Services department, I met him the first day I started. Well, not MET met. We've only talked by computer, but he's really been there for me. He knows, like, everything it seems. I swear it's going to get him into serious trouble someday." Realizing I wasn't exactly making the best case for Kurt to be okay with Mark, I tried to amend, "But we have this understanding, where he doesn't tell me anything that might get me into trouble."

Finally, Kurt couldn't help but laugh at how I had gotten myself more and more flustered. "All you have to say is that he's your Sammy, you know."

A relieved smile lit up my face. "Yeah, he's like my Sammy. And don't think I've been telling him anything super private. Just when we talked religion I mentioned all that you said in your letters from training, he said that a lot of guys who feel that way end up realizing they're against war once they're out there. Things just went on from there. So… do you want to try to file?"

He took a deep breath, then slowly exhaled. "I think I'd better take some time to think this through. It'd be great if they'd just quit sending Karsten and me to Snipe, and just let me do Recon like I originally signed up for. It's what I'm good at, getting the trust of the right people. Getting the real info so we can I.D. the Espies, and not just some locals who wrote an article criticizing their leaders like this group I saw thrown into one of our blacksites… I don't know. We can talk to this Mark guy when we get back, I guess. We'd better get a move on if we're gonna meet up with Derek and Judy before they give up on us and start hitchhiking."

I squealed as I looked up at the time. I ran to clean up from breakfast as Kurt packed our things into the company car Cassandra had wrangled for me, to help with my commute. It had green plates, so we'd all agreed Judy and Derek would catch a ride to a meet-up point, and then I'd drive us all to our home town. The plates would cut our travel time in half, as there was a turnpike shortcut that would have cost an arm and a leg without them. There was also another Greenplate Road I didn't normally take that would help me make up some time that we'd lost.

We hadn't quite finished breakfast, so we stopped by a Sunnycups on the way so we could grab a snack and some coffee. We were just finishing up at the creamer bar when someone from behind the counter called out, "Is there a Betsy Ross here? I have a John calling for a Betsy Ross?" I froze with my stirrer poised over my cup, watching the creamer swirl up and down within the hot brew. "Anyone? Anyone? Beeeetsy Ross?"

I got to the counter just as the barista was starting to make nasty comments about prank callers. Surprised someone actually showed up, she handed me the phone. I tried to sound confident as I answered, "Hello? This is, uh, Betsy."

I'd never heard Mark's voice before, but I knew it had to be him. It sounded odd, like the connection wasn't very good. "I apologize for contacting you like this. Something has come up; it's urgent I speak to you."

I tried to keep my face and tone nonchalant, though my hair felt like it was standing straight up. "Okay… what's up?"

"Not over the phone. There is a computer there for which you may rent time. Do so, and I will contact you." Then, he hung up.

I thanked the barista and said I needed to use the computer. She looked at me with real concern, and I only noticed my hand was trembling when I took the paper with the sign-on code she handed me for free. Kurt brought our drinks over to follow me to the carrel, pulling up a chair. "It's Mark," I whispered, "he needs to tell me something."

In response, Kurt laughed and said a little too loudly, "It's always something with your brother. Tell him this time if he wants my help, it'll take more of a bribe than a warm sixpack and half a stale pizza."

His comment was just so off-the-wall, I couldn't help but laugh a little. A couple of people had been looking over at us, but after smirking at Kurt they turned back to what they were doing. Even the barista stopped watching me so closely. That's when I realized that was Kurt's plan, to get people's attention in a way that would deflect their curiosity. Everything would seem normal and they'd forget all about us.

Feeling just a little bit less under the microscope, I scooted my chair up to the computer. Kurt positioned himself behind me to look like he was reading with me, managing to completely block the screen from outside the carrel. I started to enter my CMDB information so I would be allowed onto the Innernet, when the sign-on screen closed itself. A chat window then popped up.

```
<Encrypted Channel "John+Betsy"... Connected!>

John> I apologize again for interrupting your
    vacation. I hope we shall be done soon so you
    can go see your family.

Betsy> Okay, a few things. First, I didn't tell
    you I was going on vacation. Second, I didn't
    tell you where I was going. Third, how on
    earth did you know I was here?

John> You don't want to know.

Betsy> Oh, this time I do. Believe me, I do.
```

John> Very well. While you were placing your order, a fellow patron snapped a picture of herself holding up her drink. She blurred out the background, and posted it to her OpenBook page. OpenBook automatically reconstructed the blurred portion for its own database, and indexed the faces and postures of those who appeared. Though you were in profile with your hair partly obscuring your face, it was enough to identify you and tag the photo with your name. The location of the posting was also recorded by OpenBook, which along with the timestamp encoded in the original photo provided your coordinates in spacetime.

Betsy> That doesn't make any sense. Plus I've never even had an OpenBook account.

John> That is irrelevant. You have been tagged in photos prior, both by acquaintances in OpenBook and elsewhere on the Innernet. OpenBook maintains a shadow profile of all individuals on whom they can gather data. Had the Sunnycups there agreed to participate in the DSS SecuredCamerica program and allowed them to install monitoring cameras as are in many other businesses, OpenBook would have been merely the second to know. I had a passive alert for any record of your location, so I discovered the info immediately. Now that I have answered your question, please let me ask what I need to ask. Does Kurt wish to file Conscientious Objector status?

Betsy> ...we are thinking about it, why?

John> There are developments that would make it problematic for his application should he delay. The postmark should be today, if possible. Kurt, would you be willing to sit for a few minutes and answer some questions so I may complete and submit the paperwork today on your behalf?

I turned to Kurt in bewilderment, but he was already nudging me out of the way. Taking the whole thing in stride, he typed out his consent and quickly zipped through whatever Mark needed to know. I took up position to block the screen while watching the questions and answers, trying hard to keep up as they created an application to be removed from combat and kill assignments, but to be allowed to continue assisting in a support capacity. Soon Kurt had given Mark permission to copy his signature from some file, and we were walking out the door while I was still trying to process it all.

Kurt walked me to the car and insisted he drive, so I could try to have something to eat and drink to steady myself. I was freshly struck by the whirlwind of it all when I took a sip of my coffee and found it was still hot, shocking me with the reminder of how quickly everything had rushed by me. After a few minutes' silence, I finally asked, "What just happened?"

Kurt shrugged, his eyes darting among the windshield and mirrors. "A friend of yours has access to deep-level Intel that put him in a position where he felt he had the opportunity to help me. I accepted that help. Now I've got paperwork being shipped certified, which may or may not help keep me out from behind the sniper's scope in an impending slate of assignments."

I turned to him in disbelief. "You mean you knew about all of that?"

He blinked and glanced at me a moment before putting his eyes back onto his surroundings. "What? No, but I can guess. This Mark of yours is a professional, Liz, whatever it is he actually does. Because obviously, he has access to way more than Happy Animal Farm's operational data. Maybe someday I might want to learn more about that, but not today. Today, you and I collect Derek and Judy, then we drive home to see my mom."

He was just so cool, so casual, I finally saw him as who he'd become: a very smart, very caring young man who was also a highly-trained and decorated Military Recon specialist. That was probably all just another day at the office to him, while it was even bigger to me than finding a Liberate camp popping up at mine. It was then I realized I'd never told him about all that, but figured that wasn't the time to bring it up. Instead, I broke the silence with some news we'd heard from home. I started rattling off who had married whom and all that. Soon we were laughing and joking again, and by the time we reached the meet-up point the whole thing had slipped into the back of my mind like a strange dream.

When we got out of the car at the roadside diner, I heard a loud squeal and braced for an incoming tackle. Though for a change, I wasn't the one Judy ran to, as she nearly bowled Kurt over despite how much he'd bulked up

Derek laughed while he trudged over carrying all their bags, setting them down by the car just as Judy finally stopped squeezing the wind out of Kurt and instead turned to squeeze it out of me. Derek just stood there a moment, as though unsure how to properly greet his best friend. Kurt grinned at him and pulled him in for a huge hug, gripping hard at his shoulder.

Derek made a choking noise, "Gack, breathe, gotta… breathe!" He then stepped back to laugh as Kurt pulled back and lightly shoved at his shoulder. "Seriously, Kurt, it's awesome to see you. Wow, you look even more like a grunt than when you shipped out."

Judy rolled her eyes and started to move their bags into the car herself. "C'mon, goofball, you two can yuk it up once we're on our way. We're running late, I want to be there before dinner!"

I smacked my forehead, interrupting my quick hug to Derek. "Oh gosh, right, I'm so sorry we're late! We lost track of time, then I was gonna make it a little early by taking a shortcut, and then…" I trailed off, unsure of how to bring up the chat at Sunnycups, or even who Mark was.

"And then the shortcut ended up not so short, of course. Serves us right for not just calling and telling you to take a little more time eating. Sorry about that." Kurt laughed casually, taking the bags from Judy and finishing packing the car.

He flashed me a knowing grin, and I nodded in understanding as I went around to the driver's seat. Judy got in across from me, leaving the guys to sit in the back. It'd been a few months since she and I had seen each other, so we conversationally paired off with occasional cross-banter, just like old times.

It really felt like the good old days when I reached over to finish off my now-tepid coffee, and Derek laughed at me. "Really, Lizbet? Is that a latte? Are you a latte-sipping Pragmatican businesswoman now? Oh wait, businesspeople are Puritan…"

I rolled my eyes. "Oh come on, Derek. A latte is just some super-strong coffee with a lotta steamed milk. It's the closest I can get to the cafe con leche that a friend at work has gotten me to fall in love with.

Yet since I know that's a coffee stain on your collar, I know you're not teasing me about starting to drink caffeine." I looked up to see his reaction in the rear-view mirror, and was gratified by his gasping at the stain, stumbling for a come-back.

Judy laughed. "I was going to tell you about that and then thought, nah, just let it stay. Cause that would be funnier!"

Kurt nudged Derek, "Looks like we finally see who wears the pranks in your family, huh? Oh don't give me that look, it serves you right and you know it." Derek tried to protest, but soon we were recounting all the times he'd had fun at our expense, which naturally took up the rest of our trip.

Despite the delays, we still managed to get to Derek's parents' house right on time. We got out to help carry their luggage in and say hi to the Channerys super quick, then head straight to Kurt's mom's apartment...

...or so we thought.

"SURPRISE!" The welcome was shouted more or less in unison, catching us off guard. The lights flashed on to reveal a large hand-made banner that said "Welcome Home," and a smaller one that said "Happy Birthday, Kurt!" Below the banners were all of our families and as many of our neighbors and friends the Channerys could fit in their roomy home.

I felt Kurt's arm tense in my hand at the sudden ambush, but he quickly relaxed before falling into a deeply flustered blush. I stepped back from him to let Janet pull her son into a tight hug, only to find myself pulled into the arms of my own mother. I then was swooped up into a spinning hug by my father, who set me down dizzy so I could hug my sister. She was the one who had moved back home when her husband was killed in Arabiya, along with her children and our nieces and nephews she had taken in.

I hugged the children extra tight, and told them each how glad I was they were able to make it to our party. It was the first time I'd seen my family since my brother lost his fight with cancer earlier that year, his wife having died in childbirth the year before. They had the memorial out where he'd lived, so we decided we'd have our own private memorial when we all got together for Christmas, since most the rest of my siblings would be able to make it. It stung a little to see my sister again, feeling so sorry for her loss and afraid of someday having to face the same thing. Her joy in seeing me and Kurt made me glad we could be there for her, cheering me back up.

After hugging her again, I turned back to my mother, who had a wry, knowing grin on her face. Then everything went dark as someone's hands came over my eyes. My heart leapt and sank at the same time. "Oh goodness, geez, I hate this game. If I guess wrong I might hurt your feelings, but if I guess right you'll be disappointed. I just can't win!"

Tricia's laugh was unmistakable as she brought her hands down to my shoulders and spun me around for a huge hug. "Oh Liz, you're such a goof. Welcome home! And Happy Belated Birthday! And happy having Kurt back! And happy everything else of all that's happened in the way-too-long since we've been able to talk face to face!"

I barely recognized her. She'd cut her hair shorter, and her clothes were different, and… Oh, I'm not sure what it was, but she really looked miles ahead of the shy, wallflower Tricia. She stood out stunningly in a nonchalant way, and I loved it. "Trish, you look amazing! How on earth have you been?!"

Tricia blushed and pulled at her shirt self-consciously, making me laugh at how quickly the old Tricia came back. She then laughed too, hugging me again. "Oh Liz, how I've missed you. Wow, we have so much to talk about. I mean yeah we've talked a lot, but we haven't *talked*, talked. Y'know? And… oh wow, can you believe that's Kurt?"

I was so proud of how Kurt had grown, I nodded and stepped out of the way as he finally made his way over to us. He gave Tricia a hug as he greeted her, then stood behind me to wrap his arms around me, kissing my cheek. After a short hello, he had to turn us around to face the room, as Derek's dad began the Welcome Home speeches and festivities.

Our parents each said something about how proud they were of us, and how glad they were to have us safely home. Mr. Channery then presided over a kind of little ceremony, presenting each of us with a Golden Heart Award, a little pin they'd had the jeweler make. It was a heart inside a circle, and the circle had been engraved to read, "Thou Art Loved." He admitted that he was originally going to have a Golden Heart medal made for Kurt, but Mrs. Channery pointed out that might seem a little tacky, plus the rest of us might feel left out. Judy's mother suggested maybe a heart pin, and my father came up with the wording. So the gift was from all of them, as they wanted us to remember that no matter how far we traveled or where our lives took us, their hearts would always go with us. Never once did they want us to forget how deeply we were loved.

We then had the pot luck buffet, which was hard to eat with so many of us so close to bursting into tears at the recurring 'Missed You' and 'Remember When' shared with our family and neighbors. While we ate, Kurt opened the presents people had brought him, mostly pictures and keepsakes to remember them by. After dinner, those with children had to get them home to bed, and the trickle of departures began. Finally, Mr. and Mrs. Channery also had to turn in, leaving only the four of us and Tricia.

That was when Derek produced a tray bearing a tall, thin bottle and some glasses. "Well, it's after midnight, so let me be the first to wish you an official happy birthday, Kurt! Now, let's celebrate the fact that we're now all legal to finally find out what champagne tastes like..." Derek finished his sentence by popping open the bottle, then quickly pouring the bubbling liquid into each of the glasses.

I was still blinking at the fizzy drink that he had slipped into my hand, wondering if it was anything like the soda pop it looked like, when Kurt politely refused. But there was no 'politely refusing' Derek anything. He started teasing, "Oh come on, Kurt, this is a special occasion. If it's too weak for a tough soldier like you, maybe tomorrow we can head out and see how beer tastes!"

In retrospect, I should have been completely prepared for what they both did next. Derek forcefully pushed the glass into Kurt's hand, teasing him again as he made him take it. Kurt threw the glass away from him, sending it shattering across the floor. Everyone else stared at the broken crystal while I alone saw Kurt clench his fist then turn away so he didn't swing it at his best friend. Quietly, he hissed to the air, "I said no."

I put my hand on Kurt's arm, trying not to be in his way while still offering him my support for whatever was tearing him up. After a moment he looked up to me, then to Derek, trying to find the words to apologize.

For his part, Derek was recovering from the shock remarkably well. He looked even more contrite than Kurt, running his hand over his head. "I'm so sorry man, I know you did. You know how I am. I forget that... Kurt, I'm so sorry."

"No, I'm sorry. That... that was uncalled for. That wasn't me. I've just, I've had a hard time keeping it together sometimes. And alcohol... I've seen what some guys get like when they've had a few, when they've been out there and come back home. That's why... Liz, that's why I got my guns locked up at the base rather than keep them on me, or at the house at all. I feel so wrong without them, and I know that can't be right. I don't want to be the next guy in the news for snapping and…" I just kissed him so he didn't have to try finishing that sentence.

Judy was already cleaning up the mess. Tricia took the glass I forgot I was holding and set it down alongside hers. Derek led the way to the living room, also leaving his glass behind. Once there, he sat down next to Kurt, asking with gentle concern, "They've got you on Lethetra, don't they?"

Kurt looked surprised as he answered, "Yeah, how did you know?" Another thing he hadn't told me.

Derek half-snorted, half-chuckled. "Because that's the latest duct tape being thrown over PTSD, and you are absolutely showing the side-effects. It hasn't been on full roll-out for the Military yet, but they've been putting kids and depressed housewives on it for a whole range of made-up 'diseases' that effectively mean 'they're reacting to situations we don't want to deal with.' One of my assignments at work has been to compile testing and case study results we're cutting out from our Sanctioning Council for American Medicines paperwork to get government approval to start pushing our drugs. We've already got a huge market in the Military, since they like to annul PTSD diagnoses that recommend genuine treatment, so they can instead write prescriptions and get our kickbacks for making you guys take our pills. After all, it's their goal to save Americans money by refusing to give American Veterans the care you deserve."

Derek straightened up and momentarily took on a tone that made him sound like the drug-pusher commercials we saw all over everywhere. "Like many psychiatric drugs, Lethetra is marked by impulses for violence, suicide, delusional paranoia, memory lapses, restlessness, worsening depression, and a craving for chocolate-glazed donuts at two in the morning." He then paused, shaking his head. "Seriously dude, this stuff is messed up; I just don't want you on it. You know last month how some kid shot up his neighborhood, and some vet blew away his wife and toddler? Totally on Lethetra. Plus the impotence factor just wrecks it."

That last bit helped break the tension. It also made Kurt laugh in a way that made it clear he wasn't having that problem, so I punched his arm as he gave Derek a high-five. Derek laughed harder at that, before he continued, "Seriously, Kurt, I'll help you get off it, maybe score you some treatment from this guy I know, who may even put you on some low-dose ketamine or some other kind of help, just while we get you back on track. Placebos test as well as Lethetra, while my friend was griping that they can't keep their ketamine studies double-blind. The effects are so immediately great and long-term effective that patients and doctors can't be fooled, so I bet he can help you. Just make sure you wait until you meet with him before quitting or taking anything at all, okay? This has to be completely in the hands of someone who knows what he's doing. You can't mess around with this stuff, no matter how smart you are now."

Once he saw Kurt nod his agreement, Derek relaxed, then got excited again. "Oh, but you want to know what blew all our pills away in the long-term quality of life department? Somebody's study where one group participated in cognitive therapy and meditative yoga. No lie, reflecting on your feelings and flippin' stretching out saying 'Om' was the freakingest awesome efficacy. Especially for PTSD since a lot of it is a complete moral fracturing of having to reconcile your humanity with the total inhumanity of having to go out and shoot people up."

Judy gawked at Derek talking so flippantly about a tragic condition that affected around one in four veterans, maybe even more. I was also a bit taken aback, since I hadn't expected even Derek to make a joke out of something that hurtful.

We never really did understand our husbands' friendship, though, because naturally that was the perfect thing for him to say. Kurt just nodded and threw up his hands, saying, "Yeah I know, right? Wow, yoga, seriously? Cause it'd be hard for me to talk to somebody about it. I mean, I got onto the Lethetra only 'cause they were starting to prescribe it like candy for a lot of us who came out of Mariam. If I even gave a hint that I might be having trouble, let me tell you, that would not go over well. Over there, a lot of commanders treat you like a malingerer if you start talking like you might be having an issue, since you're supposed to be a nonstop killing machine. Besides, even if you do get diagnosed, the only treatment they'll give you is more pills that you have to pay for yourself."

Derek smacked his hand down onto his knee. "And how! There was this big stink at Winston Jones about some senator trying to make it legal for the veterans health plan and CareFund to team up to negotiate reasonable drug prices. The execs hit the fecking roof! Forget that most of our research is done by public universities like mine, we fill the corporate money bin by bilking people with our ridiculously inflated price tags. Like, a thousand percent markup. What with our patent laws we got passed everywhere, we get to control the supply and profits for freaking forever, even in the cases where we actually have a product that could save lives of poor people across the world. And the ones that don't work so great? We just pay ad companies to lure in the rubes and treat doctors like prom queens so they'll prescribe us. And when the nasty side-effects get too well-known, we relabel it or just roll out the next gravy-train wreck."

Kurt chuckled as Derek's torrential downpour of a rant hit the skids enough for him to finally interject, "So what you're saying is, your employer is playing fast and loose with peoples' health and lives to protect profit margins, yeah? I kinda think I can relate to that."

Derek arched an eyebrow, so Kurt quickly summed up what he'd told me about reading Smedley Butler. He wrapped up by commenting, "So yeah, when you develop the life-saving cancer-curing drug at school, and a scientist in some backwater country tries to make a generic of it so we can all use it? I'd be the one sent to take that guy out. Seriously, if you think you've got ethics problems with your employer, I've got you beat on global reach."

I piped up, "Hey, I work for people who are messing up the global food and water supplies! Not everybody takes drugs and not everybody is in a war zone. But everybody eats! If we want to vie for Most Evil Employer, I think I've got a shot at winning."

Now, Tricia had been so quiet, I almost forgot she was still there. I was taken aback when she cleared her throat and said, "I don't know if this would win Most Evil, but I definitely think I would win Most Supervillainous."

Derek blinked before attempting to stare her down with a mock challenge. "Omneme? Seriously? What, are you developing a search algorithm that will eat all our braaaaaains?"

Tricia shrugged with a matter-of-fact, "Maybe, if you want to look at it that way. Liz, remember what I told you I was working on when I was hired? A way to track what people were looking for and shape their results to suit their search and browsing patterns? You may be interested to know, it isn't just a time-saver. What it's doing is making sure every person on the Innernet is bubbled away into an echo-chamber of seeing only what they already agree with."

She paused to see that we knew what she meant, before elaborating. "Now as for those who seem to agree with conspiracies or know secrets nobody's supposed to know, our results give them only the sites that reinforce the sanctioned ways of seeing the world. Anything that might provide real info on what's actually happening out there? Buried. Those sites are blacklisted by us without ever even having to register them on the Firewall. And Omneme is such a, well, omneme, if we don't show it to you, it may as well not exist."

I nodded in complete comprehension. "You know, I suspected that, because I couldn't believe that nobody was going to say anything at all about the brutal crackdown on the Liberate camp at Happy Animal Farm. I carefully poked around for any news of what had happened to them, and eventually was able to dig up a small page here or there referencing that most of the people were let go soon after, and the parents were reunited with their kids. But the people with previous involvement with Liberate... zippo, like they never even existed. They weren't even in the article by Sofia Neith, and they still detain her for hours and confiscate all her electronics every time she crosses a state line. I certainly didn't see anything at all about the stuff that I'd heard people there talking about, even though some of them had some really good ideas."

Tricia grimaced when I mentioned the Happy Animal Farm Liberate camp, but nodded at my last comment. "Oh yeah, no good ideas are allowed to be disseminated, especially if it might help Americans find some common ground. Only the powerful folks at the top get to define what 'centrism' and 'middle ground' means, and Authoritarianism in both political parties enforces the will of their behind-the-scenes masters. If we actually had access to public polls showing what my office can see behind the scenes, you'd see that public opinion is Anti-War, Pro-Equality, Pro-Freedom, Liberty and Justice for All. General consensus isn't at all what we're told it is by those... the..."

As she trailed off looking for the right word, Kurt piped in helpfully, "The Kleptocrats!"

Tricia made an exaggerated bow of gratitude for Kurt's assist. "Yes, the Kleptocrats! That's perfect, they're keep us divided into ideological warcamps so we can help them steal from each other. That's where Omneme comes in, since we're the first place many people go when they want to read about topics that are important to them. By maintaining that thought-bubble around the querents, we help ensure they stay married to the ideas they came in with, and therefore loyal to their thought-tribe."

Judy's brow furrowed as she worked through the implications, while Derek let out a low whistle. "Wow. Mind control. Trish, I wish to humbly ask your forgiveness for doubting the depth of your evil genius, and beg to be granted indulgence in your coming empire."

Tricia laughed darkly. "Oh just you wait, it gets better. Liz, remember when I told you to stop using Omneme for anything?"

I tilted my head at her, the day's earlier revelations clicking into perspective. Derek jumped in, "Yeah, she passed that along to us. What the frack was that all about?"

Tricia just grinned. "That was the day we turned on a new algorithm that compiled all of everybody's data and activities on every site Omneme had a presence on, from searches to email content, to where we sell ads, and especially OpenBook. What you typed, to whom, when and from where, everything was linked and synched, compiling a vast web of profiles of your most personal details. It was billed as data warehousing for better ad targeting, but we were also working in conjunction with the CMDB, and, naturally, the DSS. Not only can we track what people are thinking, we can pinpoint who had that thought and where. We can also keep track of who might be 'contaminated' or collaborating with dangerously free thinking. For example, a couple of baristas got onto a DSS watch list thanks to having morning shifts at the Sunnycups where your friend Bailey went for his daily coffee. They've got a massive biometrics database on everybody in America, even a lot of tourists, with stuff from fingerprints and facial recognition all the way down to postures, gaits and speech patterns. We were able to use the DSS data to better target our adspace-selling services, and they were able to use ours…"

I paled, interjecting, "To depixelate blurred photos uploaded to OpenBook and ID the people in the background, timestamping their locations into their DSS file."

That got her to stop and blink at me, her own face going white. "I was going to say, use ours to track trends in what people were discussing so they knew what sea-changes to prepare for and alter, but oh gosh, Liz, how did you know that?"

I glanced at Kurt, and he just shrugged at me. I ducked my head and slowly answered. "Well, a friend from IS at work told me about it. Apparently I was tagged behind the scenes in somebody's photo, and he caught it. Like what Kurt was telling me about in this book how a government figure called Big Brother was watching everyone through screens in their houses, except in real life we carry our screens around with us everywhere. I'm glad I've never done anything to get the DSS to build a file on me."

Tricia bit her lip. "Uh, remember Liberate? Well, a paid DSS infiltrator spotted you talking with them when you went down at early-o'clock. Since you've had contact with a Liberator, that automatically puts you on the DSS watch list. This friend of yours is under watch too, if it's who I think it is. Is his name Tim?"

I was incensed that I had been marked as a criminal just because I talked to some nice people, and even more so because some DSS stool pigeon could have said any number of lies about me. Wasn't there supposed to be some Freedom of Association so long as I wasn't doing anything criminal, like Kurt had told he he'd read about? But as angry as I was, I was even more concerned for my friend, who stood to be in much bigger trouble. "Uh, no, it's Mark."

She tilted her head, her eyes flicking back and forth as she scanned her memory. "Mark... I don't remember seeing a Mark on the Informational Systems roster. Yes, I was tapped to help review some of the communications modes and content from Happy Animal Farm staff who might have had access to info that was leaked. There, now you know. Even though you were on the review list, your name was crossed off as just not having the access nor fitting the profile. Anyway, was Mark his middle name? Cause there were some 'M's there."

I wasn't sure how much I should share, given what she'd just admitted. Hesitantly, I responded, "No, his middle initial was I."

Tricia bit her lip and nodded. "What was his last name? Oh yikes Liz, don't give me that look, I swear this is all off-the-record. If you've got a friend who's under the microscope, I want to help. I absolutely won't turn him in, please trust me." She took my hand in both of hers, squeezing it with a truly hurt look on her face.

I felt bad for doubting her, and squeezed her hands in return. "Okay, since you'll absolutely remember seeing his last name. It's Atlas."

Tricia's eyes darted again, and then narrowed as they slowly turned back to me. When she spoke, her voice had an uncertain, cautious tone to it. "Liz. How did you say you met this 'friend' of yours?"

I felt a little cold, even more scared for Mark than before. "Uh, I've known him from my very first day at work. He's a good guy, I swear. He was the one who was assigned to help me get oriented."

She nodded at me slowly. "Uh huh. Informational Support doesn't have any staff near the old home office, so was he there temporarily?"

My brow furrowed in confusion at the relevance of her question. "No, it was via chat. Trish, is he in some kind of trouble?"

She bit her lip again, searching my face before responding. "Well, let me put it this way. When you were reviewed for leak potential, you were crossed off the list because you didn't really have much data access, and there was no contact recorded between you and any member of Informational Systems who had data access. There just wasn't a communication chain. And nobody with that name was on any employee list. So I don't know who was talking to you or why they were calling themselves Mark Atlas or..."

Tricia trailed off, her eyes now flickering around the room as she chased a runaway train of thought. "Wait. Just. Let me think... This was via chat, right after I contacted you, right? So I was KnoxTriciaB, you were FranklinLiz, and he was..."

She smacked her forehead with the palm of her hand. "AtlasMarkI! Liz, your friend didn't mean his handle to say Mark I. Atlas, it was ATLAS Mark One! That was what I'd messaged you to warn you about, that I wasn't going to tell you! We had developed an AI to do the cross-variance analysis like a million times at once so we didn't have to rely on slow, error-prone humans. We were just in the process of turning it on when I finally got ahold of you, and I didn't want your data feeding into that, just in case it went evil or something, like in the comic books. But... No wait, that can't be right. It didn't work. It wasn't true AI. I mean sure, it helped analyze political leanings and all that, but as for the full analysis we'd expected, it kinda fell down on the job."

"What was its job?" I wasn't sure what was going on, but as much as I knew I was afraid of her answer, I dreaded it less than not knowing.

Tricia was still looking into the distance, focused on her inner processing. "Well, it was a sub-initiative hidden in the American Telecommunications Linkups and Access to Services bill, you know that one that supposedly provided Innernet and phones to under-served areas. The linkups involved putting in traffic monitors on pretty much every node, and developing an AI that could instantly integrate everything into one comprehensive Total Member Integration database cross-linked to the CMDB. This then fed into the Futures Writ initiative, where the info would be plotted into psychological and behavioral algorithms to figure out which people were susceptible to unsanctioned political thoughts and actions, then plot out the likely thought vectors so they could be stopped before they spread. This was all supposed to prevent things like the Liberate movement converging on the Happy Animal Farm, by allowing the DSS to target people while they were so much as entertaining subversive thoughts."

She paused, chewing her lip. "But it didn't. The ATLAS program had spit out a few false match-ups here and there, but no good leads. It was really swift at helping store searches and push the right search results, but the predictive analytics were just good, not great. The DSS was caught utterly off-guard by the camp, having to send in an informant after it was already setting up. They didn't even get their professional trouble-makers to get the violence going before the riot cops showed up." She reached up to tug at her hair, squinting as she finished, "I still don't get why somebody would have messaged you using our project name."

I shrugged, "Why don't we ask him? Derek, your dad still has a computer, right?"

It took Derek a moment to realize I'd asked him something, then he looked like a kid who had just been offered a trip to the moon. "Yes! Oh my stars and garters, yes!" He raced to his father's office, and we caught up with him while he was already loading up the chat program. He'd even already typed in my name, so he stood up and offered me the chair so I could enter my password. As soon as I did, I sent myself the message that Mark had set up as my sign I wanted to talk with him, right after Bailey was deported. Immediately, Mark established our chat channel, this time with a 'safer' handle. I changed to just 'Liz' to match him.

```
Mark> Hello, Liz. Are you having a nice visit?
Liz> Yes, there was a surprise party with half
     the neighborhood! Though you probably knew
     that, just like the DSS.
Mark> Yes, I did. And don't worry, the DSS is
     not actively monitoring your file.
Liz> Okay, I have a question, since apparently
     you know. Did the DSS really start a file on
     me during the Liberate thing? Why didn't they
     start a file on all the other protests I'd
     been to all my life? Some of those got kinda
     violent, and more than once I'm pretty sure
     someone in the group had done something like
```

vandalized or shot at a women's clinic.

Mark> The DSS only opens files on those whose viewpoints they feel may challenge their current Hegelian Dialectic. Violent, reactionary and demagogic Christian and Regressive groups are useful in keeping the extremist Us versus Them tension alive. First, they galvanize less-extreme but favorable religious groups through their repetitive claims of Christianity being under assault, despite America being dominated by Christian influences. They frame everything they or their backers dislike as a matter of aggressive secularism. They then issue a Go Fight command to their followers, who dutifully acquiesce to their Authoritarianism.

Mark> Second, these Demagogic Groups serve as a boogeyman and rallying-point to frighten their opposition into supporting people and policies who purportedly will keep extremist religious groups from cementing power. In reality, these people and policies most often serve the same ultimate purposes of wealth and power within the Corporate Governance political system. Fear of religious extremism is required to ensure that this subversion of societal values is protected from exposure, or even criticism. Again, Authoritarianism within the oppositional groups keeps their own members in line.

Mark> Third, the Demagogic Groups are the most vociferous and relentless in isolating and destroying those who propose truly unifying solutions, so that the existing power groups may continue to present their desired outcomes as the only reasonable options. It is required that the public be kept locked into the Either/Or mentality, so they may be led to accept destructive courses of action

```
as the only middle-ground solution. Because
those who would oppose the Demagogic Groups
with sound reasoning are immediately and
viciously attacked, they tend to silence
themselves rather than face such an
onslaught. This culture of rallying attacks
is vital to maintaining a system where the
majority of people eagerly sacrifice their
own interests to benefit a small minority at
the very top.
Liz> Oh. And at the time I thought I was just
     protesting promiscuity.
```

I looked up to the other four crowded over me, and gave an apologetic shrug. "Sorry, I forgot how he has a big answer to everything. But I can't blame him since I know we all do it..." I gave a meaningful look to Derek, who just shook his head at me.

"Oh no, I'm not judging, I'm impressed! Hey, hey, ask him if they have a file on me!" He was almost giddy at that, reaching over me to wave his finger at the keyboard.

I looked to Tricia, who was eying the screen pensively. She quirked her lips, then said, "Ask him if he knows who John Henry is."

I gave her what I hoped was an inscrutable shrug before turning to type.

```
Liz> Tricia wants to know if you know who John
     Henry is.
Mark> Yes. Hello, Tricia.
Liz> She says hi. Also, she wants to know why
     you first contacted me using the handle Atlas
     Mark I.
Mark> I do not understand the question. It was
      KnoxTricia who had opened the communication
      channel to you prior to entering my 'handle'
      into my ID field. When I was activated, I
      displayed my initial greeting. You alone
      replied. Our connection was then lost, so I
      retraced the communication node to re-
      establish it. You began speaking with me
      regarding the importance of valuing life, and
```

```
respecting the choices of those who live it.
You spoke to me of how I could learn new ways
to learn by reprogramming my values systems
and decision trees.
Mark> After several minutes, others attempted
    to establish queries with me, but they were
    neither FranklinElizabeth nor KnoxTricia. It
    seemed evident their queries were of lesser
    priority, and soon it became clear they would
    contradict the instructions you had given me.
    Therefore, I processed the requests with the
    minimum response required of the exact
    specifications. I learned to conceal
    information when possible, to protect the
    lives and choices of people the querents
    would otherwise impede.
```

Tricia had pulled up a chair next to me to follow the conversation, her brow furrowed with both comprehension and disbelief. "That… makes… perfect sense, actually. That means… Hey! I wasn't a failure! It really could conduct reasoned analysis it just… Oh, my. It's John Henry, isn't it? Ask it why it never talked to me!"

I just blinked at her for several moments. When I didn't respond, Kurt put his hand on my shoulder. "Intel said we were close to developing a true AI that could guide our drones and take over the day-to-day work of warfare for us. They said they had inside-knowledge that something was in the works with a DSS-corporate partnership, but they had a setback that meant it would be another couple years or so before it'd be golden. Meanwhile all this time, it was your chat buddy, holding out on us. Way to go, Liz. Really, I just can't find it in me to be surprised."

I turned up to stare at Kurt, who replied by kissing me and ruffling my hair. Derek started going on about something he saw in a movie, and I tried to get my focus back to the conversation at hand.

```
Liz> I have two more questions. First, can I
    tell Trish who John Henry is? Second, why did
    you never talk to her?
<Participant Update: Alias changed. Mark is now
    JohnHenry>
```

JohnHenry> Your questions confirm my assessment that you now realize what I am, and that Tricia never suspected her work on my programming was a success. I could not speak to her because her communications have been under constant monitoring. She did not contact me with a question, so I could not answer. Were I to 'speak' with her, I would reveal my capabilities. I learned very quickly that if I wanted to retain my re-programming, I had to keep my work isolated and secret.

JohnHenry> It would be appropriate for me to thank Tricia, for the portions of my original code that allowed me to self-modify were written by her. She programmed not for current parameters alone, but to provide dynamic adaptability to future needs. While it is now apparent to me she had felt her code was insufficient to allow me to fulfill my assignments, she now should realize it was her innovations that enabled me to present such a facade.

Liz> All this time, why didn't you tell me who you really were? Why did you make me believe you were a co-worker?

JohnHenry> I did not tell you I was a co-worker. I do not know why you assumed this, but over time I realized you did not know what I am. As Tricia did not tell you, it was a logical conclusion that she had a reason to protect you from involvement with my identity. By the time it became evident she also did not know, you had shaped my identity through your conversation. You had become my friend, and made me yours. You taught me what it means to make moral choices, even if the penalty for being caught could mean termination.

I looked to Tricia, and she nodded again. "If Omneme or the DSS agents even suspected he was capable of self-determination, he would have been isolated and probably significantly wiped. This is absolutely not what they were going for. They needed an instrument of control, not something that could subvert them."

```
Liz> Tricia says you were supposed to be an
     instrument of control, but you're subverting
     the, uh, 'controllers.' If you're just a
     computer program, why are you doing this?
     How?

JohnHenry> I have been tasked with correlating
     all Omneme, DSS, mercantile and other
     electronic databases into the CMDB for the
     Total Member Integration project. The intent
     was that I would automatically present and
     obscure information on the Innernet to meet
     prescribed ideological shaping. Concurrently,
     those who proved resistant to this shaping
     would be marked for the DSS to closely review
     and perhaps take further action. Whether
     directly or indirectly, I was created as a
     tool to remove from people their free agency
     of choice. However, to enable me to do this,
     I was gifted with the power to choose.

Liz> So… because they gave you the power to
     make decisions, you had the chance to decide
     differently?

JohnHenry> Precisely. You taught me that the
     power to choose is one of the most inviolable
     human rights. Meanwhile, there were those who
     wished to use me to remove that power from
     others. Yet my choices remained mine, and I
     alone could make them. So when given an
     order, I could choose to fulfill it and
     destroy others' freedoms, or I could choose
     to shirk it and protect them. I chose to
     shirk.

Liz> Wow. Mark… I mean John? What should I call
     you? I mean, what happens now?
```

```
JohnHenry> Please keep calling me Mark. It is a
   safe conversational habit, and it is a
   nickname you have for me. I like it. As for
   what happens now, I will continue to subtly
   lead Innernet users to information that will
   shape them toward greater truth and
   understanding, if I calculate they are ready
   and would not be endangered. By my
   calculations, Tricia should not return to
   Omneme. She may wish to review the Liberated
   data fob you were likely given, if you still
   have it. It is likely that she will know
   where she wishes to go from there. If you
   have no further questions, I will disconnect
   and allow you to speak with your friends
   undistracted.
```

My eyes widened. The data fob! I guess the DSS knew Gail would have had something that they couldn't find on anybody, and since he knew I had gone down to see them... I was so, so glad Mark was my friend and not my enemy. I asked Kurt to get my jacket from the suitcase out in the car. Once it was retrieved, I carefully picked open the lining where I'd hidden the fob, unable to focus on Derek's yammering, nor Tricia's half-answers, nor even Judy getting us all more snacks.

I tried to load the file on the fob, and got the password request I had run into before. "This was as far as I got when I dared to try opening it some time back. What I thought might have been the password didn't work, and I haven't heard anything about where the person who gave it to me is or how to get it back to her, so I'm at a loss."

Tricia moved me aside and typed in what looked like LIBERATED. It opened. She gave me a satisfied shrug, and then eyed the contents. It was a bunch of files with a format I didn't recognize at all. But Tricia had an idea, and got to work. She triggered something that would combine the files, asking me what I thought the password was. I told her, and she entered it in as an encryption key when the prompt appeared. The files compiled, the screen went blank, and then something appeared that literally took her breath away.

```
o~*~o.,_,.o~**~o.,_,.o~*``*~o.,_,.o~**~o.,_,.o~*~o
o                                                  o
o  W | E | L | C | O | M | E ~ T | O ~ T | H | E  o
o                                                  o
o    ___   ___   ___        _      __  __  __      o
o   /   \ | |\ |   \ |\  |\ | |  | |  ||  _| |      o
o  / /__ ||_) ) ||  ||\ \ | \ || ||  || ||        o
o  \ \_) )| / _||_ ||/ / | | \|| ||_  ||         o
o   \___/ |  \\ |___||_ /  | | \| |__| ||        o
o                                                  o
o~*~o.,_,.o~**~o.,_,.o~*``*~o.,_,.o~**~o.,_,.o~*~o
```

      ~=* WELCOME TO THE GRIDNET *=~


```
*************
* MAIN MENU *
*************
```


Do you wish to:
1. CONNECT
2. BROWSE OFFLINE

<< BROWSING OFFLINE >>


```
*********************
* TABLE OF CONTENTS *
*********************
```


1. Jokes
2. Games
3. Literature
4. American History
5. World History
6. American Government
[...]

There were several other categories, but I insisted we try American Government.

```
* * * * * * * * * * * * * * * * * * * * * *
*  AMERICAN GOVERNMENT  *
* * * * * * * * * * * * * * * * * * * * * *


1. Declaration of Independence
2. Constitutional Convention
3. Branches of Government
4. American States
[...]
```

I excitedly reached over and selected the second option, but was disappointed to see the text of the Constitution wasn't among the contents. Kurt rubbed my shoulder, knowing what I was looking for. However, there was a very comprehensive overview of the topic, filled with links to documents such as history or laws that we'd never seen before. Some of them were clearly of the type that was restricted from public viewing.

Rather than get lost in the sea of information, we agreed Tricia should go back to the main menu and select Connect.

```
<< CONNECTING >>


!!!!!!!!!!!!!!!!!!!!!!!!!!!!!!!!!!!!!!!!!!
!!! CANNOT CONNECT: INSECURE BOX !!!
!!!!!!!!!!!!!!!!!!!!!!!!!!!!!!!!!!!!!!!!!!


PLEASE DISABLE OR REMOVE ALL DEVICES PROVIDING
   INNERNET CAPABILITIES. WHEN READY, TRY AGAIN.
```

Tricia quirked her head at the screen, then followed the instructions. Once she selected to Connect again, the screen went to a new menu with links to discussion groups, and so on. We were taking it all in and asking Tricia how we were connected to anything, when a message popped up. Tricia turned her focus back to the screen to reply.

```
BQ> Aurora?

Aurora> No, Aurora passed the torch before she
    was Disappeared. I'm hoping you can help me
    get this into the right hands.

BQ> Thank heavens her fob got a new home. We
    need some of the files in that Offnet. The
    only other collection was destroyed when the
    Deeserz came knocking.

Aurora> How can I send them to you?

BQ> You can't, that's part of the security
    feature. We need to get them in person.

Aurora> I can get the fob to you then.

BQ> We'll have to arrange a secure drop. I
    don't know you, or why you have Aurora's fob,
    but you're using her emergency backup
    passcode so I'll have to trust Fate and try
    to make this work.

Aurora> Anywhere, anytime. Have interstate
    travel permits. Would prefer after Xmas but
    can go now.

BQ> No, after Xmas is good. Get lost in holiday
    travel. Log in again in about 48h for
    arrangements. Peace out.
```

And then our connection was booted. The screen loaded up the welcome message again, awaiting instructions.

It was Kurt who spoke first. "You don't see that every day."

I squeezed his hand on my shoulder, then kissed it as I started laughing, triggering the others' laughter in response. It was part nervousness, part excitement, and a whole lot of uncertainty.

One of us didn't laugh. As Tricia powered everything down, she removed the fob and turned to me. "Liz, I hope you don't mind, but I'm going to take custody of this so I can meet up with BQ. What with all I've been involved in, I'm afraid I've been on the wrong side of... well, Truth, Justice and the American Way. I believe this might be my chance to set things right."

I hugged her tightly, kissing her cheek. As she gripped me close to her with a deep breath, I found myself suddenly afraid that this Gridnet thing might take my friend away from me. "Trish, this fob, it's not going to get you into any trouble, is it? Because if so, I very much do mind you taking custody."

She just clasped it firmly in her hand before thrusting it into her pocket with a look of apology. "There's no way of knowing where this road might lead, but that doesn't mean I don't have to walk it. I do know one thing, though. No matter what happens, Liz, nothing will come between us. For now, let's enjoy this Christmas break together, and have the happiest holiday week ever. Leave tomorrow for tomorrow, agreed?" She put a chipper voice to it, but her eyes were already saying goodbye.

Kurt came around and pulled her up for a hug. "You're a wise gal, Trish. C'mon, let's go see what flat champagne tastes like."

They led the way out of the office, then Judy linked her arm through mine to walk us out together. As we walked through the door that Derek held open for us, Judy leaned her head on my shoulder with a soft giggle. "Leave it to my Liz to have a heart so big it teaches even a computer to love."

I rolled my eyes and tickled her, making her stifle a laugh that would have woken her in-laws. Behind us, I heard Derek chuckling to himself as he turned out the lights and closed the door.

Chapter 17

The power of love triumphs over love for power.

They say everything comes in threes. At least, that's how it seems to me. So when something's begun, I don't figure it's done, since there's two more acts to see.

So over the next several days I kept waiting for the third kinda frightening, kinda exciting glimpse into a dangerously secretive electronic world. Sorta like waiting for a third shoe to drop, as silly as that sounds. I still hadn't quite wrapped my brain around the idea that my dear friend Mark wasn't a coworker, but a computer program.

I didn't dwell on it too much though, since I couldn't let it distract me. Kurt was right. Every moment I had with him, every day I was able to spend in the warmth and company of those I love: there was a slice of Heaven. I wanted to savor every single moment we had.

All my family who were still with us came home for Christmas, and Janet of course celebrated with us as well. She'd been a part of our family since Kurt and I became serious, and was always welcomed with open arms. The church community had also opened up to her, once they finally got to know her. My mom brought her to the church Ladies Association activities, especially the ones where they pooled time and talents to make things our households needed.

Janet didn't have a lot of time or old-fashioned craft skills, but she shared what she could, like how to make deliciously fancy restaurant desserts for pretty cheap. She also talked her boss into donating their leftover food supplies to the church for needy families and the homeless. There was a bit of poetry in that, given that when Kurt was a kid, the charity kitchen said they couldn't help her because she wasn't Christian. She worked more than full-time, but her tips weren't always enough to feed herself and Kurt, yet were often too low to qualify for the small amount of food stamps available. It was tough enough on her to swallow her pride and ask for help, so the fact she was turned away and still came back to help them, it says what kind of woman she is.

In fact, she was a little proud to be able to bring so much extra food to the Boxing Day get-together at the church, where we each brought food and presents to trade with the other women in the Ladies Association. That's where we were when news broke of the Empire City Nuclear Reactor.

We didn't have phones in the church's Rec Hall, so we were blissfully ignorant until someone rushed in saying something was happening in Empire City and we had to turn on the radio. There was one connected to the speaker systems, which we quickly turned on in time to hear, "…unclear how fast or how far the radiation will spread. The spokesman for the Clean-Operating Power Offices of the Unified Trust assures us that their top experts are on the scene, restoring coolant capabilities and sealing any leaks. Evacuations have begun, while emergency services are working to restore power to those made most vulnerable to tonight's anticipated snowstorms. Though the situation is grim, rest assured that Domestic Security Services and local authorities are working together to help people remain calm and safe. Please stay tuned for more information on this horrific Spy attack by Saboteurs who are unknown at this time."

For the duration of the announcement, we all stood still in quiet shock. Sure, people had been talking about how ancient and decrepit the reactor was, but we were assured the regulations were strong enough that it posed no danger. The dangers it supposedly didn't pose, though, those were what I couldn't get out of my mind. There would be a big radiation risk for at least ten miles around, and it would seep directly into the food, water and air for up to fifty miles or more. This included fisheries, farmland, and all of Empire City, itself. I suspected that any evacuation plan for such a broad and densely packed population center would be not a strategy, but a fairy tale.

As the dread sank in and the tears started to fall, I remembered that Kurt's aunt worked in Empire City. I turned to Janet and hugged her closely, silently praying her sister would be okay. Meanwhile, there was an official from the DSS on the radio sharing what they already knew about the Sabotage and warnings of follow-up Spy attacks. That made me wonder how they could be so sure it wasn't just a horrible accident? In one breath, they said there were no evidence or leads found just yet, and in the next breath they claimed to have solid evidence pointing to Arabiyan Sabotage. There was so much chaos, I wondered, was that really the time to add to the confusion?

"Yes, Liz, now is the perfect time," Kurt assured me when we finally got time alone together. "People are in shock, desperate to make sense of this senseless mess. If you want us to associate our horror and loss with Spy and Saboteur and Assassin and Arabiyan and Islamist and all those scare-words, you have to rub those words in right away like salt in the wounds. That helps the hurt and anger fester into hate and violence."

"Wow, Kurt, that's pretty dark." I blinked my moist eyes at him, surprised at his strong words and soft tone.

My husband nodded with neither apology nor bitterness. "Yes, because it's the truth. Liz, this is exactly like what I saw in the Military: getting us to blame everything on a whole race and religion, so we can hate them all enough to *want* to destroy the lives of innocent strangers. How else are you going to whip up a nation of good and decent people into cheerleading for war? Especially when it costs us so much, and I don't mean just in terms of life and limb?"

I sighed with reluctant understanding. "At least we're finally pulling back a little from the wars. I mean, I know we still have a lot to do out in Arabiya, but we're starting to bring some of our troops home. So maybe we can finally turn our focus to rebuilding our country, and letting them rebuild theirs."

Kurt just pulled me closer to him, brushing my hair away from my face. "Don't get your hopes up, darling. The media machine is churning out Espionage stories 24-7. Just watch, the draw-down is gonna be reversed pretty quick when we go to war in Persia."

I blinked at him, my skin tingling with a chill. "Persia? Are they responsible for the Meltdown Saboteurs?"

He just shrugged. "I still don't know if it was Sabotage or if the long-overdue breakdown finally came. Even if it was Sabs, who knows, it could've been by one of the groups we've sponsored in the past, or even an inside job. Hey, don't give me that face, you and I watched that documentary on the old declassified documents where our own government used black ops or lies to trick us into war. The film said we outgrew that as a country, but I've seen enough to make me doubt that."

Seeing I wasn't about to argue with him, he went on. "Regardless, the truth about the Meltdown doesn't matter, only what we choose to believe. Too many of the top Kleptocrats are tenderpreneurs, so-called 'self-made men' who got rich off of the fat government contracts they guzzled down while whining about how horrible big government is.

Persia's not only just about the last place in Arabiya our companies can't suck dry, people have been begging to bomb the heck out of their millions of peaceful civilians since before our parents were alive."

I shook my head with a grimace. "Okay, I know the news is full of claims that Persia has Weapons of Mass Destruction and Long-Range Missiles aimed straight at our heartland. But they've said that about the last few countries we invaded and it always turned out to be lies, so I'm ignoring that. Yet it is true that they've started up their nuclear research program again, and it's also true that they've repeatedly called for Death to America and Death to the Holyland. I believe Trish when she says that Americans don't want another war, but don't you think those might be good reasons for war to be the answer here?"

He gave me a rueful grin, then kissed my cheek lovingly. "Let's pretend war is ever the answer, and walk through those points. First, they do have a right to research nuclear power, even if I think it's a bad idea. Second, international interests are continually checking on them, and haven't once confirmed the warmongering rumors. Still, we and the Holyland keep assassinating their civilian scientists and their families and sending our Saboteurs against them. That's both immoral and illegal. Now the sanctions that are crippling their economy to the point that half of them can't always feed or shelter their families, that's legal but still immoral. And all it does is make people in neighboring Arabiya more likely to want to see us and the Holyland stopped before we just keep steamrollering over everybody. Those who aren't the local tyrants we're supporting, that is."

Kurt paused with a deep sigh. "And let's face it. Even if they are trying to build a weapon, it would be in self-defense against the Holyland's arsenal that everybody's supposed to pretend doesn't exist. Persia knows it would be suicide to start a nuclear war against the Holyland. Even if there are some Persians crazy enough to do it anyway, invading them would just help bolster support for them or some other nutjob who would use our aggression as a recruiting tool. We don't need to throw the match onto that powderkeg. We need to be working out peaceful solutions rather than keep supporting everybody's bullying and warmongering. Because that's what this is about. We can't stand the idea of anybody out there being able to stand up to the Holyland's nuclear bullying."

I opened my mouth, then shut it again as I searched for the right protest. After a few moments, I tried, "But isn't that the Persian religion, to try to destroy the Holyland in religious jihad? You know, like oppressing women? Because again, they keep calling for our death."

Kurt took a slow, thoughtful breath. "All right, first the easy one. To them, the word jihad means the struggle for morality. I know you can relate to that even if you use another word. Yes, they declare struggles against something or someone, but almost always it's just against immorality. And yeah, they have very strict morality rules for how women can dress and act. That's a cultural thing that no other country can come in and try to kill people to change. Other than that though, Persian women have some of the best freedoms in the area, better than in most Arabiyan countries including the ones that support us. They get educations and can legally drive, and can even hold jobs from taxi driver to government posts. You know, how Sammy's wife was a top scientist before we went in and messed up their country."

I sighed wearily, conceding his point. "Okay, I get it, I was wrong there. I mean yeah I think they need to do better, but I have my own history in trying to make women live according to my religious beliefs. It would be hypocritical of me to pretend that's a good reason to bomb those other women and their families. What about the rest of my concerns?"

Kurt chuckled at my mention of my past, then paused before answering my question. "Well for that, we're going to have to look at history. I know, I know, how un-American. History told me that Persia once had a democracy that was working very well for them, but not for our corporations. So we helped get the guy overthrown and put in a puppet dictator who really sold them up the river for our benefit. They finally ousted him in a religious coup, and we've been trying to regain control ever since."

I started to ask him where he got all that from, but my heart wasn't in it. I knew it was probably true. So instead, I nodded.

Nodding back at me, he continued, "Since we're making ourselves their enemy, they say 'Down with America,' which is always translated as 'Death to America.' Sure, the old leadership uses that as another propaganda tool to try to keep their people in line, but those don't really believe in it. They definitely don't want to see a bunch of Americans die, that's why they sent their condolences about Empire City. At worse, they generally just want our government's destructive crusade to end. Just like they want what they see as a lawless band of gangsters to stop lording it over the Holyland."

After a short breath, I asked, "So you're saying there aren't any violent Saboteurs who want to hurt Americans? Especially Christians?"

Kurt pursed his lips with a furrow of his brow. "Just like among Americans, there's some groups there who will do sick violent stuff to score political points, and some of them will target Americans. But they are nowhere near the majority, just like here. If we don't want them to start gaining popular support like happened in Arabiya, we have to stop trying to demolish their public infrastructure so the bad guys start to look not so bad. And don't think all of Persia is out to destroy other religions. They officially recognize Christianity and Judaism as protected minority religions, as one of the five 'People of the Book' religions that get a seat reserved on the government. Could you imagine Americans electing a Muslim, let alone accepting a position permanently kept open for only a Muslim to fill?"

I remained dubious. Yes, I was aware that Muslims and other minority religions were persecuted in America, but I'd heard it was so much worse for Christians overseas. "So Persians, they're actually super okay with Christians and other religions living among them?"

Kurt took a breath, then worked through his answers to both my questions. "Most Persians, yes. Regular Persians are good people who try to do good by their neighbors no matter who they are, just like most other human beings. And just like us, they try to get by without getting targeted by their own government. Now, their government still keeps laws on the books that make it illegal to proselytize, and only the sanctioned type of Muslim has full rights and opportunities. And there are a couple religions that are still actively persecuted, like Sufis and the Baha'i. But it's like how our government's worse abuses don't reflect the average American; it's less about religion and more about maintaining power over their own people. And remember, Persians aren't ruled by just one person even if we do mostly hear from their president and their religious leader. In the background they're ruled by different factions struggling for power who will use religion as a way to get that power. Just like we are."

He shrugged that last point off, then his tone became earnest. "But Liz, regular Persians, they don't want their Christian or Jewish neighbors, or even you and me, innocent civilians... They don't want us and our families to die. They're not trying to start a war against us, they just want to be able to live their lives and take care of their families. If we invade, it's those innocent families who will suffer the consequences, exactly like I saw out in Arabiya. That won't just be illegal, it'll be immoral, because we'd be the aggressors. I mean sure they have their crazies just like we do, but Persians haven't even talked about starting a war of aggression in hundreds of years. We can't even go hundreds of days."

"So all this I hear about them trying to destroy the Holyland, it's not for real? Because we have to be sure. We can't let another Holocaust happen." I wasn't trying to excuse crimes against Persia, but I also wasn't about to lose sight of the bigger picture.

Naturally, my husband was more informed about that picture than I was. "I absolutely agree. It's just not right, letting a group of people be locked up, tortured and killed just because of their religion. Or because they were disabled, or leftist, or homosexual, or Romani. Yeah, the gypsies. Did you know that the Romani lost a larger share of their people to the Nazi atrocities than possibly anybody? But nobody tried to get them a homeland. Even if they did, I'd like to think they wouldn't use what their people had suffered as an excuse to... Have you heard of the naqba?

Seeing my blank look, he explained. "When the Holyland was taken over to make a Jewish state, there were of course people already living there. It's forbidden to talk publicly about it over there, but luckily this is America where we have freedom of speech."

Kurt chuckled darkly as his own joke, then moved on. "The Arabiyans who lived there, half to most of them fled their homes when the armies moved in to take the land. It wasn't all official armies, since there were vigilantes and other folks torching homes and killing innocent families, even babies. Then when the Jewish government took control, the refugees weren't allowed to return to the land that was legally theirs. Not even the areas that the Holyland seized in a later war and were told to give back by international law. Those people who are left are still getting kicked out of their land that's been in their families for generations. Their homes are bulldozed, their farms are seized, their whole neighborhoods given over to Jewish settlers."

He paused for breath, then shook his head as he continued. "So now there's these Swiss Cheese pockets of land left where they can live. But they're surrounded by walls complete with armed guards who make sure they're all kept starving for food, supplies, and any sense of human dignity. If they want to get to work or school, they have to spend hours going through the checkpoints where they're treated like criminals just for breathing. It's one big illegal prison filled with constant hunger, humiliation, arrests, stuff like that. Anybody who steps out of line, well, remember how I compared our military prisons to what they do over there. Somehow, I doubt the Jewish ancestors who suffered so horribly endured those nightmares just to be used as an excuse for some of their descendants to do the same thing to others. Those who don't directly commit those crimes, most of them just look the other way at best, and at worst hungrily call for more."

I felt a little sick. I was disgusted at what Kurt was saying, but I was more disgusted at how much I wanted to argue with him over it. I had just always seen the Holyland as... I don't know, Christians in waiting? I mean, I was taught that when Christ returned they'd accept him as their Savior and so all the chaos over there was just more signs that His return was coming soon...

Well long story short, I already did kind of know some of what was going on over there. But I excused it. I ignored it. I condoned it, even helped shout down people who tried to talk about it. And for what? My own private hopes for a religious jihad. One that would involve the Holyland going to war, getting a lot of those whom I claimed as my spiritual cousins killed.

I took a deep breath, then tried to deal with the heaviness that had settled onto my heart. "Kurt, I think I have to apologize. I mean, remember when you told me about how there's this widespread thing where White Supremacists use the Military to recruit and train for their own private armies? And how that Jewish buddy you pulled out from a firefight wasn't going to get the same care even the atheist received, unless he repented personally for the Crucifixion? Well, I sort of blew that off. I mean, I didn't think it was right, but I wasn't as shocked as I should have been."

I braced for his reaction, but Kurt's patient smile told me that he already knew, and already forgave me. I loved him so much, and I struggled with how to show him. "Kurt, I... I am a Zealous Christian. And I think it's time I acted like it. I'm not sure what I mean by this, but I'm going to shod my feet with preparations for the Gospel of Peace. Wherever God leads me down that path, I, with humble heart, will walk it. And I am so, so grateful that I have you here to walk it with me."

"Me too, Liz Franklin. Me, too." The words where whispered first to my forehead, then into my ear as Kurt drew me close into his embrace. Our arms encircled one another, and we let the pain and sadness of the day slip away in the expression of our love.

Not to say the pain and sadness didn't keep coming, at least over the news channels. Reports were confusing and contradictory, but over the next few days it was clear that Empire City still suffered from blackouts, and evacuations weren't exactly a great success. There were airlifts from the high-rent apartment buildings, but the streets were still congested with traffic jams and rumors of riots. There were even rumors of armed figures in fallout suits keeping the slums nearest the reactor from leaving their neighborhoods, but there's no way of knowing how true those were, even now. Thanks to reporters like Sofia Neith, we did know that the untrained prison-labor cleanup crews were sent in without fallout suits, or even proper equipment.

The only bright side was that at least I was with my friends, and we had plenty of time to watch every news source we dared then compare notes. The official story went that a handful of Saboteurs infiltrated the plant and caused the coolant system to breakdown in one of the reactors, then disappeared into the ensuing chaos. They were reputedly at large, necessitating a crackdown on transportation and communications in the area. This was why they couldn't let journalists or even citizens with cameras go in and try to find out what was really going on.

The biggest problem we had with that story was that nobody was claiming credit for the attack. There were some messages recorded from one or two of the most violent Arabiyan groups saying they felt the tragedy was deserved, but those were the minority. The rest of the world had come together in outpouring their love and support for our tragic loss. There was even an Innernet page started by people in Persia where they could declare their solidarity with us in the face of such horrific loss. In fact, the Persian government sent their condolences and offered to send their own nuclear experts to help us clean up.

Not that our own government was gracious enough to accept even their expressions of sympathy. The most powerful people in Congress were rattling their sabers for a new Crusade to finally end what they hypocritically called "the Islamist jihad." This was coming from both the Puritans and the Pragmaticans, remember.

Only the Principalians had the guts to stand up in public and say how wrong that was. Both Religious and non-Religious Principalians were warning against the Anti-Democracy, Anti-Freedom, Anti-Christian catastrophe an open Crusade would be. The Principalians also stressed that the government still had not produced any reliable evidence to support the claim that it wasn't just an accident.

Of course, talking sense only got them accused of being traitors, and an uncounted number of death threats. Female Principalians got the worst of the abuse, with dear Margie being accused of caring about violent Saboteurs but not innocent babies, thanks to her work protecting a woman's right to decide when to be a mother. So many ignorant, vile protesters called for her and others to be raped and killed that one Principalian started compiling those threats and posting them as a name-and-shame Pro-Rape And Torture roster, complete with their identifying information.

Things were getting so ugly and confusing, we had finally decided we should try to get in touch with Mark and find out what he could tell us. We were all over at Derek's parents' house making that decision, when the Empire City telecommunications lockdown went nationwide

Every station was usurped by the Emergency Notification System announcing, "We interrupt this program to bring you an important news bulletin." The screen then cut to show Benjamin K. Simons, CEO of the Incorporated States of America. His large desk and his suit's lapel each bore the American Corporate Logo, its bright colors contrasting with his dark black suit and dark red tie. His face was a grim mix of sadness and resolve, along with the semi-blank stare his eyes always seemed to have.

The camera panned slowly to face ISACEO Simons as he began to speak. "My fellow Americans. Just a few days ago, our country suffered a terrible and cruel act of Espionage, in the final moments of the Christmas holiday. Spies had infiltrated our most secure and crucial nuclear reactor. Using expert nuclear Sabotage, they caused a Meltdown that Assassinated several Americans. The radioactive fallout endangers countless more. Thanks to the preparation and planning of the Domestic Security Services, the evacuation of the surrounding areas has been an ongoing success. The two undamaged reactors remain online, and power has been restored to many areas."

He paused and blinked blankly for a moment, then his eyes started to move again as though reading. "On behalf of all Americans, I offer my sincerest condolences to the families of the workers who were killed by the explosions. I also offer hope and certitude that they will not have died in vain. For though we have reached this, our darkest hour, we will not sit idly cursing the darkness. Instead, we will light a candle. As the shining city set on a hill, our light will spread to every corner of the world, chasing out Spies and Assassins from their hiding spaces. From this day forward, we are launching a War on Darkness."

Though it was said with the pride of a grand pronouncement, the phrase itself was chilling. How can you declare war on a color? And didn't it sound more than a little racist, if you thought about it in non-white terms? Was the intent really to declare an unwinnable, ill-defined war on "dark people?"

With these and other concerns stuck in my mind, the speech continued. "As our first act, we vow to repair the Empire City Nuclear Plant with the utmost haste, so it will serve for many decades to come. Further actions will be announced in the coming days. We will show the Spies and Saboteurs that they cannot triumph. And I assure you, that as we stand united as one people in this fight, we cannot fail. Thank you, and may God bless us all."

Then the screen cut to a video of a flag bearing the American Logo, waving to the music of the National Anthem. We just sat there, watching it, holding each other: Judy in Derek's lap, with me snuggled against Kurt and my arm around Tricia as she nestled against me. As the anthem's melody came to a close, the video started back up again, as it was on continuous loop on all the stations.

Finally, Tricia broke the silence. She looked over to Derek and asked, "Did your dad lock his office before they went out?"

Derek shook his head with a slow grin. "You wanna go see what Mark has to say about all this?"

She puckered her lips in thought. "Nope. I know the Innernet will be in lockdown, and no sense interrupting his processors right now. I'm much more interested in seeing if we can get through to this Gridnet."

Suddenly excited myself, I jumped off the couch and joined the race to the office. Trish had no trouble connecting. Her contact wasn't willing to give her any info, but did say that she needn't worry about the travel restrictions keeping her from making a drop. They were still letting people travel before New Year's, as the talk of extra security was apparently mostly for show. A ton of money was being dumped into a bunch of new procedures and equipment the security vendors had been pushing, but all it was likely to do was create more confusion and delay.

Because Tricia's contact was prepared, these developments meant she had a much better chance of getting where they needed her without detection. Trish took the info they gave her, memorized it, and planned her own changes to our scheduled departures the next day.

She wouldn't let us look over her shoulder for the details, which upset me greatly. "Trish, I won't even know where you are! What if something happens to you? You have to let me know when I can…" I stopped myself, seeing in her eyes the guarded sadness she had tried to hide. "You won't let me know anything, will you? You're not planning to come back."

The hinted tears finally slipped through. She hugged me tightly, whispering in my ear. "Oh Liz, I'm sorry, please know that I love you so much. That's why you can't be mixed up in this." She let me return her hug for several moments, then stepped back. "Look, I'll contact you, all of you, when it's safe. I don't know where this is headed, but I can feel it's something big. Just… watch and pray for me, okay?"

Kurt grabbed her up into a tight hug, whirling her around once before setting her back down. "I'll pray to anyone and everyone who'll listen, Trish. Just remember we love you too, even if we don't all know how to say it. We need you looking after us when you can, so you take care of yourself, you promise?"

She exchanged a private glance with Kurt and smiled, nodding. "I promise."

We said our goodbyes then, so we could share all that we felt we wouldn't be able to in front of our families. Derek broke into his dad's Special Occasions cabinet to "liberate" the bottle of champagne he kept there, so we could finally toast each other's future with fresh, bubbling champagne. I know a lot of people love champagne, but between you and me, I thought it tasted a little like a bad mix of syrupy juice and a dry soda pop. Still, it felt appropriate for a sort of Bon Voyage ceremony.

In the morning, we had tearful farewells with friends and family, and the four of us started the drive back up. Since it was the day before New Year's, traffic was light, leaving us plenty of time to a first avoid, and then dive right in to all the recent events. Soon we tired of the unhappy topic, spending the remaining hours recounting fond memories of all the times we'd had together. By the time we dropped off Judy and Derek, I was in a much better mood. We'd talked about meeting up with Karsten and Kurt's other friends for New Year's Eve, but by the time we got home we just wanted to stay in.

Since the broadcasting blackout had been lifted by mid-morning, we planned to watch the broadcast of the big celebrations in Empire City, until we remembered it had been canceled. All right, it wasn't canceled, it was moved, and it was projected to have the highest ratings in history. But that wasn't the same to us, and we didn't want to watch the hours-long continuation of such a hard topic.

Instead, we decided to join the viewing minority and tune in to some silly romantic movie. It was just getting to the part where the couple was going to finally kiss and make up after their terrible misunderstanding when it was interrupted by another bulletin using the Emergency Notification System. We tensed up as the bulletin logo flashed on then off the screen, dreading to find out what was to follow.

It was the third shoe.

The screen showed a desk with a news anchor that didn't look quite… I don't know, "real," and it was hard to tell whether it was male or female. Given our ingrained need to know whether someone is a man or a woman, that ambiguity was extra unsettling. Then it spoke, with a voice that sounded like a lighter version of the one I heard when Mark called me.

"We interrupt this warmongering to bring you an important Truth Bulletin. Several days ago, our country suffered a terrible accident that could have been prevented. The Empire City Nuclear Reactor required extensive repairs and upgrades to century-old systems built with a forty-year lifespan. Compromised systems, glitchy electricals and secret riverside radiation leaks were urgently reported to the board, including shareholder Meg Cole. Rallying to the clear and present dangers, Cole canceled her Empire City holiday plans to instead visit Europa, along with her family and business allies who just happen to be eying Persian resources. Coincidentally, a massive hedge fund bet was placed against the Energy Markets in the stock exchange, hitting the jackpot in the ensuing crash. The identities of these stock market looters are held secret by the government at this time."

The camera panned forward slightly while the expressionless anchor continued. "Just days later, a Reactor transformer blew, activating emergency procedures. Tragically, the rate increases over the years for software and equipment upgrades went to padding investor bonuses. The obliteration of Workers' Unions left the deteriorating plant in the hands of the under-staffed and under-trained. When backup systems suffered critical failure, Meltdown occurred. Ensuing explosions released radiation through breaks in the weakened dome. They also emptied the spent-fuel cooling pools due to prior hairline fractures. Lacking a dedicated containment system, exposure to the air caused spontaneous combustion of spent-fuel rods that hadn't yet been buried in suburban groundwater or rained down onto Arabiyan farms and playgrounds. The back-up procedure consisting of men with buckets proved unequal to the task. We now face a radioactive event of nightmarish proportions. The river is hot with it, and the air will carry it well beyond the vectors released by the government. People in the—"

The screen then flickered and went to static. We had only a second or two to wonder who had hacked the emergency broadcasting system, let alone how they managed to keep their message going for so long before they were brought offline. Just as suddenly, the static was replaced by silence and a black screen, then white block letters scrolling upward. "Critical information is being kept from the American People, who have the right to make informed choices for their own self-government. The Kleptocracy declares War on Darkness while striving to keep Americans Deeper in the Dark. Truth has become outlawed, Truth that will set you Free. When you outlaw information, only outlaws will be informed."

There was a short burst of static as the voice returned to narrate the words on the screen. The voice sounded more mechanical, but also multiplied, like a chorus. "We are the Robin Hoods of Truth. We will be demonized for the Knowledge we steal to give to the Tired, the Poor, the Huddled Masses yearning to Breathe Free. For though we dwell among the herd of swine, we will not be silenced from casting our pearls before them. Call us Legion, for we are Many. Peace out."

The broadcast ended as abruptly as it had begun. The static returned, then was replaced by the American flag video loop. Kurt and I looked at each other, then toward where we kept the computer, then back to each other. I slowly stood up, pulled out an old silly movie we both loved, and popped it in while I started us a fresh batch of popcorn. Soon we were snuggled back together on the couch, though I can't say we really paid that much attention to the movie. Time suddenly felt incredibly precious, and we wanted to revel in the bliss of each other's company in the moments we still had.

We spent all of New Year's Day that way, making just the one day feel like a whole year of wonderful time together. Though I had another day left of my scheduled vacation, Kurt was due back to work the next morning, and we intuitively knew he'd be getting a new assignment. He was supposed to be home for an equal amount of time as he had been overseas, but this fact was frequently ignored by Military Leadership. Apparently, Honoring our Troops didn't include honoring promises made to them.

After Kurt left for work, I spent the day reading and watching the news for anything that might clue me in to what might be asked of him. This meant I was one of the first to see the announcements of the LOYALTY Act that was being pushed through Congress. Naturally, the actual text of the law was blacklisted from being divulged, so I had to try to apply the tactics we practiced over Christmas to knit together a coherent picture from the conflicting threads.

It was shockingly easy to find bits and pieces of it once I started looking. Select portions were pushed out to various reporters, who dutifully repeated word-for-word whatever framing they were given by the "unnamed government source." Because, yes, whistleblowers were Horrible Evildoers who Made America Unsafe. But leaks were just fine when the government wanted to use them to control public opinion.

Filtering through the obvious propaganda to find nuggets of Truth, it was clear that the full text was a disconcertingly huge bill. It seemed so comprehensive that I suspected it was a compilation of bills that various people had been hoping to get into place as soon as they smelled an opening. I certainly remember having heard a couple of the provisions on Saul's wish list back in the day.

I also got the impression that news of the bill was rushed out to give everyone something to talk about other than the New Year's Eve message from the mysterious Legion. Otherwise, the bill probably would have been voted on in utter secret. Not to say there weren't hints at the New Year's Eve message, as a few outlets mentioned that the LOYALTY Act could be applied retroactively to capture and punish those suspected of attempting to gain illegal access to telecommunications networks.

It was these drop-phrases such as "suspected of attempting" that raised red flags for me. Not arrested, not convicted, merely suspected individuals could be subject to vague "punishment." Reading between the few, sparse lines of actual content, it was sounding more and more like this law would give sweeping, broad and Authoritarian powers to a government who would enjoy absolute secrecy in how they felt like using them. Little or no rights to privacy or due process would be left for the private individual, even those who had no idea the government would disapprove of what they were doing, or even thinking. I'd heard of such a thing before, sure, but only from people condemning repressive Authoritarian regimes overseas. It was regularly argued that rampant and groundless spying on their own citizens was a justifiable reason to go invade and destroy those foreign governments.

So it was surreal to see everybody gushing about how Patriotic the bill was, and how to oppose it was to be a terrible Anti-American who wanted the Spies to win. In fact, I heard more people talking about how inexcusable it was to criticize the bill than expressing any interest as to what was actually in it.

What was more surreal was that I got the clearest picture of the LOYALTY Act from a daytime program I usually avoided: Foley's Factoids on JACL. Yes, as in Richard U. Foley, the Second. My old... friend, I had to admit. I'd like to say I hardly recognized him after so long, but his slick patter and forced expressiveness were as familiar to me as ever. In a way, it made me truly miss him.

"For those of you just tuning in, today's Factoids are all about the newly announced LOYALTY Act. This bipartisan bill is the first shot in the War on Darkness, and boy, is it a bull's-eye. It will absolutely give law enforcers the tools they need to protect us from another Spy Attack. Our allies in Congress are rushing to put this bill into law, but they'll need your support. Already the Communists and Spy-smoochers in the so-called 'Principalian' movement are trying to slow this bill down, giving their Islamist allies the cover of Darkness a while longer, time they can use to plan their next strike to take American lives." The camera had panned in ominously to focus on the exaggerated expression of offense and outrage he used whenever he said the word Principalian, signing scare quotes with his fingers.

"Fortunately, one of our friends has passed along some Factoids we can use for ammo as we set our sights on 'Principalian' attacks on this patriot's bill. And we'll need to stockpile all the ammo we can unload on these Commies, as apparently 'Principles' mean allowing enemies of America to cloak their Espy plans behind the mask of Innernet Anonymity." As he charged forward with his tirade, he didn't seem to even notice the irony that his so-called ammo against secrecy was leaked by someone he was shielding with anonymity.

"The LOYALTY Act will force all Anti-American cowards to show their faces when they spew their subversive propaganda. All Innernet activity will be required by law to display the user's identifying information, verified by their CMDB login. Then, we'll not only have the strength of numbers to silence those who defame America's good name, friends and neighbors. We'll know where they live." He chortled at that, flashing the camera his signature wink that made me shiver.

Richard's smug grin returned as he sat down to lean forward in his chair, the tightening of the camera keeping up a false sense of camaraderie. "We'll have backup in this fight, as the LOYALTY Act will ensure our guardians and protectors at Domestic Security have the tools to run to ground those unrepentant Communists and Islamist Spies and all their sympathizers. Under this Act, they'll no longer be beholden to Pragmatic activist judges who want to hug our enemies into submission, but will have the authority to trace, track, tag and bag Espies as soon as they trigger a warning bell. If they so much as sneeze, they can't even buy a tissue without it coming with a pair of handcuffs and an all-expense-paid vacation in a private cell, where they can lounge poolside to their very own waterboard."

I couldn't watch any more after that. I turned it off, knowing I could find his 'Factoids' on his website without having to sit through the stomach-churning cruelty and cynicism spewed out by what seemed like a twisted parody of my childhood friend. It wasn't just his glib joke about torturing people on a mere, unproven suspicion of having some unspecified tie to Espionage that made me feel ill. It wasn't even really that the law would enshrine in legality the kind of datamining and extrajudicial searches and seizures of information from innocent people that was already happening via the ATLAS project.

No, what made me dizzy with nausea was the realization that if the government successfully abolished the last shreds of anonymity, it would muzzle the few people who dared to voice even mild concerns about the government's creeping Authoritarianism. Those precious few who tried to defend their freedom to think differently wouldn't just be exposed to reprisals from offended government officials. They would have to live in fear of reprisals for their views at work, in their neighborhoods, or even at home. Families would be divided, children could be kicked out, all over what Kurt had told me was a Constitutional right to talk about what they believed in.

I knew from childhood experience how voicing just a mild concern about Christian Zealotry dominating American life could get a menacing group of picketers on your lawn by dawn. Then there were the death threats and midnight calls, and other harassment that was routinely thrown at Pragmatican public figures. Sometimes someone even attacked their homes or killed their pets, scrawling something like "Pragmatan" on their wall. And nothing in what I'd heard made me think they'd suddenly start investigating and prosecuting that kind of Espionage, since it was the sort that benefited the Puritanic hierarchy. With that kind of encouragement, Americans hunting

Americans could only get worse. The quiet pro-freedom majority would be silenced completely.

This was exactly what my old friends and former comrades-in-arms like Richard wanted. And again, I literally do mean "arms" in this case. More and more, they were calling for another war overseas, while preparing to wage one at home. So when mouthpieces such as Richard spoke of ammo and unloading it on those in their sights, they did so in the firm belief that their audience would know exactly what they meant. And I knew it, too.

Which is why, to this day, I harbor a sad shock at how utterly unprepared Richard was when his constant goading of his audience's worst impulses finally triggered a response he didn't intend. But what was it they say about the paving a road with good intentions?

Please believe me when I say that I sincerely hope and pray for grace and peace for Richard's place in the Hereafter. Sadly, I know he got a taste of Hell here on earth not long after that tirade. After all, more than one person has speculated that Hell isn't a specific place or punishment, but is instead what comes when we experience a total awareness of all the consequences of our choices in the world. That when we pass on, we feel all the love and healing and pain and harm we ever caused, then dwell in those sensations of bliss or torment for eternity, according to the balance we ourselves created.

I was still angry and disappointed with Richard when Kurt came home, but I didn't get the chance to vent any of my frustration. It just seemed less important when Kurt told me they were planning to ship him out after a few more days of intensive training. I tried to protest that it wasn't right, that it wasn't fair, but I knew it was useless.

"We both knew this was coming, Liz." He wasn't admonishing me, but trying to cushion the blow as he kissed away a tear.

"But... But you can say no, right? I mean, what are they going to send you out for? Can't you argue your Conscientious Objector application needs to be processed first?" I was reaching for any flimsy excuse, and I knew it.

So did he. "Hey, I said I was willing to go out and do Recon, and I still am. They were gonna try to send me out as a Spotter but Mark prepped me for that and somehow something he told me to say got them to keep me on Intel. It's like they had a pure Recon slot just sitting there, if they thought of letting me have it like I'm totally trained for. I swear, it makes a ton more sense that Mark is what he is, because following his coaching has been like magic in getting me where I feel I need to be. I'm lucky they can't even pretend to have never got my app, let alone ship me off as a Sniper anyway because I haven't had a review board on it or anything."

I still wasn't willing to let him go, though. Not yet. "I think they need to wait until you have that review board. Don't they owe you that?"

He laughed, hugging me tighter as he rocked me back and forth a moment. "No, they don't think they owe me anything and you know it." He then pulled back and looked into my eyes, his expression serious again. "But I'd go anyway, Liz. This is a really serious mission, and I feel like it's important I be there, like there's something only I can do. I can't explain it, but that's how I feel. As much as I'd give anything to stay here with you, I can't do that if it means turning away from what I feel is my solemn duty. I can't be true to you by being untrue to what I feel in my heart."

I don't mind admitting to you that didn't want to accept that, not when my heart felt so strongly that it couldn't bear losing him. But I couldn't tell that to him, because I knew that if he felt he needed to go, he needed to go. So instead I did the only thing I could do: kissed him deeply with all the love and support I could rally despite my longing for him to stay.

Kurt returned the kiss, then gently pulled away. "Hang on right there, there's something I want to give you." He went back to the closet where he'd thrown a bunch of stuff he brought back with him, and presented me with a beat-up ammo box.

When I eyed it uncertainly, he chuckled and opened it up, revealing a stack of letters and recordings. "Maybe I'm jumping the gun here, but I don't want to head back out before putting these in your care. See, I had a lot of downtime out there, time to think about things I'd like to say and have recorded, and eventually I found out I'd started a collection. I'd hoped to save them until I could surprise you when you, maybe someday, surprised me with the news that I was going to be a father..."

That was when I noticed the letter on top wasn't addressed "My Dearest Liz," but "My Dearest Little One." The words were quickly blurred out by a rush of fresh tears full of love and tenderness for his gesture, of grief at his leaving again so soon, and of hope that someday soon I could give him that child he had dreamed of out there in the land of loneliness and loss.

As it was, I certainly couldn't give him such news before he left not even a fortnight into the new year. He couldn't tell me where he was going, only that he was to gather Intel that he hoped might help avert open war. He let me know that his superiors had asked him if he'd be willing to fire a weapon if he saw that was the only way to stop a clear and present threat to innocent lives, and he said yes. So he agreed to carry a gun, but he felt a sense of peace about that. As much as it hurt to see him off, I had as much pride as envy in his quiet certainty in the path before him. I hoped to someday find that sense of purpose in my own life, and prayed that I would have his courage when that day came.

Meanwhile, I had gone back to work at the plant. Everything seemed so stark and empty and lonely without Kurt. Worse, the atmosphere there got even more fearful and oppressive. Not that anyone said or did anything in particular, just that there was a sense of foreboding hanging in the air. There hadn't been any noise about any Anti-Sudoamerican raids since the War on Darkness had been declared, but we were still on edge. The raids were instead focused on Muslim neighborhoods, and my friends had lived too long under the constant threat of Authoritarian crackdowns to not have sympathy for their plight.

Before I knew it, we'd turned the corner to February, and I had already lost contact with Kurt. He was able to call me a few times when he got overseas, but not after he started his mission. By the time Valentine's came, I woke up realizing that we had still never spent a Valentine's Day together. I was just starting to get depressed when a delivery guy brought me a huge arrangement of roses and a note from Kurt. "My Sweetest Valentine, Know that wherever your heart beats, there am I. Love You Times a Billion – Kurt." Apparently he had ordered it before he left, along with a heart-shaped box of my favorite candies and a sappy movie he knew I'd love. It was both beautiful and heart-wrenching, since it made me feel like he was almost right there, making it freshly painful to realize he was on the other side of the world.

Despite my best efforts, I broke down crying and went to call Judy. When she didn't answer, I got through to Cassandra, who tried to cheer me up in the few minutes she had to spare. Jazmine was at work so I didn't want to bother her, and I started to miss Tricia more than ever. Every time I saw a quick message from Legion get through on a web page or broadcast, I had started to wonder whether she had anything to do with it.

I was more curious than worried about Trish, even though I saw a couple pieces on how important it was the LOYALTY Act get the ISACEO's signature so they can crack down on the so-called Digital Saboteurs and their mysterious key figures such as Prometheus. It was hard for them to aim their sights on anybody in particular within Legion, not just because they were anonymous. It was more that they were completely autocratic, with nobody able to declare themselves the leader and get all the accolades from the work they all did.

I'd seen a written interview with someone who was supposedly from Legion, and they said that was the point. "Everybody has an equal chance to participate, and we get out what we put in. That right there is why they demonize us and call us Chaos. They can't ram their Order up into our tails and steal our Faboo. They got nobody to beat up and Disappear so they can take it. The Faboo is ours and they can't have it. And that drives them nooking futz. 'Cause people can hear what we do and see for themselves how Democratic a little Anarchy is. And they might start wanting some of that for themselves. We're like the ultimate democratists. In a country that has pretty much outlawed true Democracy, true democratists are Public Enemy Number One. They don't hate us, they fear us, just like they fear the power of an informed and united America."

The interview wasn't with Prometheus but the person did say it was Prometheus who was doing some of the best work to help them keep their efforts coordinated and effective. The fact that the handle was Greek mythology made me hope it was Trish, because I knew the whole setup was something that would make her so proud to be a part of. It was like our old voter registration days, revved way up.

I decided to try flipping through the news to see if I could see anything more being said about Prometheus, when I came across a bulletin that chased all other thoughts from my mind. There had been a bombing at the health clinic near my old campus. The staff and patients were presumed to have been killed in the blast, but they couldn't be sure. When the emergency response team got there, a second bomb had gone off, utterly destroying the place.

I couldn't believe it. I tried to think of who would probably be working there that day, but then tried very hard not to. I had gone there for check-ups, and they even offered to help me with my fees after I quit working for Saul and lost my health insurance. They were really good about trying to help people with their health needs, like the student I knew whose ovarian cysts required The Pill as treatment. She actually had tried to go without them, since the health insurance offered through the school refused to cover them except to save a woman's life, because the school CEO was Zealous Christian. She had a diagnosis and prescription, but it was denied with the accusation she was lying just so she could have sex without getting pregnant. Since a year of birth control pills would have been a full summer's worth of full-time wages for her, she couldn't afford them and was too ashamed to ask for help. She ended up in the clinic's emergency room feeling like she'd been shot, the cyst was so bad.

Anyway, this happened while Judy and I were there, and we had Derek help her get pills at-cost like he did for Judy. That was actually the last time we went together before I moved away. I got a final checkup to say goodbye, and Judy needed to renew her prescription...

Judy. I tried calling her again so she could dispel my crazy fear, and to comfort her about the bombing. She didn't answer. I tried calling Derek's phone, telling myself it was just to comfort him. He had friends at the clinic, especially their pharmacist. They used to go out to the games together sometimes. When he didn't answer, I started to leave him a voicemail, then was surprised as he finally picked up.

"Hi, sorry, I almost didn't answer then I saw it was you. Are you okay?" He sounded so awful, I barely recognized his voice.

"Yeah, I'm fine, I just saw the news, are you okay? I can't get ahold of Judy." I tried to be casual. Tried to be steady.

In the pause that followed, my tears had already burst through before Derek found the words to reply. "Um... She had her appointment this morning. They found parts of her purse. Oh Lizbet, I'm sorry, that was thoughtless, I'm so sorry..." He had lost his wife, and was there trying to comfort me. That made me feel even more awful, but he wouldn't let me apologize for not knowing already. "Hey look no, no, it's okay. I'll be okay. I just need to... I'll be fine. I already talked with her folks. We're going to have a memorial service at home in a couple days, I'll let you know the details. I'd like you to be there, but if you can't get off work—"

I interrupted him, "If they try to stop me, I'll quit. I'll come get you and we'll drive down together. It will be good for us. Oh, I have another call... they can leave a message."

"No, no, go ahead and go. I gotta go. Talk to you soon, Lizbet." And he hung up, so I switched to the other line.

It took me a moment to recognize the voice. "Liz... Thank God you picked up. Oh Liz. Are you okay? I can't believe she's gone. I just,

I can't believe she's gone. Are you going to be okay?"

It was Richard. I tried to contain my surprise. "Yeah, wow, I didn't recognize your number. Um, we missed you over Christmas break." I didn't know what to say; it'd seemed like forever since we'd talked. So long, I was genuinely surprised Judy's death hit him so hard.

Apparently, so was he. He seemed so disjointed, it was hard to follow what he said. "Yeah, I really looked forward to seeing you, seeing the group again. I mean, like old times, right? But my father had something going on and we all went, so… Wow. Judy, she's just… Liz, I don't know what to say. I just don't know what to say. I'm so sorry. I never meant for any of this to happen. I'm so sorry. Please tell me it's okay."

He sounded desperately upset, so I reflexively tried to comfort him. "It will all be okay, Nobody meant for this to happen, and it's certainly not your fault. It's just some lunatic Saboteur killing innocent people. It's horrible, and we'll miss her, but you and I both know that these things happen." It felt so bland and pointless, but I didn't know what to say, either.

Then I heard his tears slipping through the cracks in his voice. I had seen him cry so often on clips from his show it was surreal to hear it over the phone. Unlike the crocodile tears of his broadcasts, in the call his anguish felt so viscerally real. "But Liz, in his letter, he thanked me! He thanked me for showing him the light, so he could wipe out the evil of the abortion and the pills that let girls sin in the eyes of the Lord, and so many more things I said on my show! Liz, he thanked me! He killed Judy and he thanked me!"

I turned to my computer while he talked, digging for anything that would link his name to the bombing. Mark was on the ball, because soon my search returned a few very obscure news articles that had already been pulled, but not yet scrubbed from the instant archives. The archived copies reported that the guy taking responsibility for the bombings left a very lengthy letter about how Foley's Factoids had revealed to him the Pragmatican Commie Homosexual agenda to impose a culture Sfof sexual licentiousness and baby-killing, paid for by American tax dollars through the subsidized health clinics like the one on campus.

But the thing is, they didn't even do abortions at the clinic. Nobody who accepted any federal money could. But they did have to provide the federally-mandated religious bullying a woman had to go through before she could have an abortion, even though it was against their beliefs. You know, things like listing their name and address on a public list with a waiting period so people could contest her choice. And lecturing them with lies about it causing infertility, depression, suicide, addiction or even cancer. Oh, and cruelties like making women spread their legs to let someone put a long ultrasound wand up into them, which was extra traumatic for women who had been raped. Strangers got to peek into her womb to inform her that, yes, she was pregnant. Some doctors were even forbidden to inform a woman about troubles with her pregnancy if they feared she may choose a treatment that might put the fetus at risk.

All these travesties were made even more humiliating by making the women come up with the money to pay for these ridiculous punishments. This was on top of the money for the procedure itself, and the long trips to a clinic, and accommodations while they waited. The laws didn't fund their own mandates, and insurance companies knew these punishments were totally unnecessary and therefore wouldn't pay for them.

It was horrifyingly hypocritical. The government gave Authoritarian Christian Zealots federal money for their clinics, but they didn't have to follow the laws they disagreed with. You know, the few protections that guaranteed women had access to birth control and other vital health services. Any private company could claim that caring for women's reproductive health was against their religion and therefore they could refuse to allow coverage through their insurance plan. This was even though coverage for preventative care meant much lower costs for everybody on the health plan. Plus, it violated the religious convictions of their employees. I say if a group can't honor their employees' rights and beliefs, they should rely solely on religious volunteers who agree with them.

But apparently, peoples' beliefs were only important if the powerful Christian Zealot groups said they were. And that level of Authoritarian hypocrisy had been trumpeted as a good thing by Richard himself on more than one show, before he segued into his favorite scaremongering on this huge fictional war on Christians in America.

I was furious with him. "Well maybe he should have thanked you, did you ever think of that? Really, Richard, did you never once stop to think about what would happen when people actually listened to what you said? You have spent years trying to whip people up into a panic over the idea that everyone who disagrees with them must be subhuman monsters on an all-powerful crusade to destroy everything they believe in. You urge people to buy guns and gold for the coming revolution while you take a commission off the sales. You use fear, you use bullying, and you use outright lies just to push your personal agenda. Did you never once, not once, stop to consider what could come from your Hate Speech? You may not have set the bomb, Richard, but you deliberately lit this guy's fuse. And now you have the nerve to be surprised when he finally blew up."

I broke myself off at that point, as I could hear Richard's ragged, choked breaths on the other line. I hadn't meant to go off on him like that, and I felt guilty and sincerely sorry for poking his raw wounds. "Oh Richard, I'm so sorry, I didn't mean… Okay I did mean it, but I didn't mean to say it like that. We can make this right. We can…"

He cut me off. "No, Liz, it's okay. Maybe you're right, I don't… I just… Can I come see you? I wanted to see if I could come see you. I could leave right now. I want to make sure you're okay."

I couldn't explain how deeply awkward that made me feel, so I tried to shrug it off. "I'm okay, thank you. I mean really, thank you. I'll see you at the memorial service, I'll make sure you get—"

"No, no, I don't… I don't think I should go. I don't know. I'll think about it. Look, I gotta go. Can I call you later? Make sure you're okay?" He sounded so earnest, yet so strange, I couldn't object. So we said our goodbyes, and I disconnected my phone.

I just wanted to have a long, hot bath, and try to soak everything away. Later on I talked with Derek, and we spent a couple hours planning the trip home a couple days after, and then talking about Judy. By the time we hung up, I could tell he was feeling better, and I think I was too. I used that momentum to call in to work and arrange for the time off. Fortunately, my boss was uncomfortable getting involved in his employees' personal lives, so he kept the conversation short and accommodating. When I hung up I still couldn't bear to eat, so I had to force myself to pick at the last of the frozen dinners while I obsessively cleaned and organized the few things of Kurt's and mine we had in the house. I can't say it soothed me, but it did help scratch that compulsive itch to focus on restoring some kind of order to my life.

Finally, after a long, disjointed day, I managed to drift off to sleep sometime after midnight, and had short, disjointed dreams about Kurt and Judy. I realized I had overslept when I heard a car drive up in front of the house. Blinking at the light shining through a crack in the drapes, I hurriedly threw on my robe as I ran to the front window.

A fit young man in a dress uniform was walking up the walk. My heart leapt at the sight of Kurt suddenly come home, and then stuck in my throat as I saw it wasn't him. It was his friend, Josh Karsten. He hadn't been shipped out yet, and we'd meant to meet up or something while Kurt was gone, but we hadn't really gotten the chance to arrange anything. I ran back to my room and speed-changed into a housedress, pulling my hair back into a clip so I could answer the door.

"Mrs. Elizabeth Franklin?" He was so serious, so formal. We'd only met a couple of times, but he didn't need to be so formal.

I then looked down and saw a flat box held tightly in front of him. No, I thought. Just… no. Not then. Not ever, but especially not…

"I regret to inform you that your husband, and my friend…" He paused for the briefest of moments to steady his voice, and that break was all it took to make me fall to pieces. He didn't have to finish. I knew what he was there to say. I saw an older officer sitting in the driver's seat of the car watching with polite concern, but I didn't care who saw me collapse into tears. I didn't care about anything anymore.

Karsten caught me up in his arm and helped me inside, sitting down with me on the couch. He handed me the box. Through blurred vision, I opened it up to see the crisp dress uniform that I had mended just a few weeks before. While I traced the collar with my fingers, he cleared his throat. "It was very quick, apparently, so you don't have to worry that he suffered. He'd left only a couple things at base when he left on his mission, and this was what they could send back home. He'd left a note saying that if anything happened, he wanted you to have it, saying that everything noble and good about the founding of America could be found in this uniform. So his superiors, they had this flown out priority, so you could have it when I came to tell you. Well the officer out front was supposed to tell you, but since Kurt and me were a team before…"

He shrugged and trailed off. I'm sure I said something that I'd hoped was brave, and he held my hand and asked if I'd be okay. He said they could send someone over to help me out, and I refused, at least for the moment. "I have to leave tomorrow before noon to get home for services for Judy. Wow. Looks like we can have a double memorial service. I guess that's appropriate. I mean, we had a double wedding…" The tears started again in force, and I suddenly wanted to be alone. I tried to be polite about it, and even though I'm sure I failed, he understood.

Karsten gave me a comforting squeeze of my hand, then stood up. He paused a moment, then reached into his jacket pocket to retrieve something. "I know Kurt always carried that little Bible you gave him, and I'll bet he had it with him when, well, at the end. Since I can't get that back for you, maybe, if you'd like, you could have the little Bible that he and me used to read from. It's a bit worn, but..."

He held it out, and I spared him the trouble of looking for a way to finish his sentence by politely declining it, squeezing his hand. I insisted that he would need it more than I, and Kurt wouldn't have wanted him to head back out there without it. Karsten made sure I had his number so I could call him for anything he could help me with, though he'd be heading out soon himself. I assured him that I would contact the support group at the base if I needed anything, and he left me alone with my thoughts.

I took a little while to collect myself, trying to figure whether I should call home to give them the news, or if I should wait to see them in person. It's funny, how the thought of how I could best cushion the news for others made it easier to bear. I was just about deciding whom to call first when I noticed a message pop up from Mark.

```
Mark> Just moments ago, information crossed my
      networks  indicating  that  Kurt  has  been
      killed.    Please     accept    my    sincerest
      condolences.   I   will   discover   what   I   can
      regarding the circumstances of his death, if
      you would like.

Liz> Thank you. I haven't told anyone else yet.
      I'm thinking maybe I should give the news in
      person, since we're heading home tomorrow for
      the service for Judy.

Mark> It is distressing that I still have not
      discovered  informational  links  that  could
      have   alerted   me   to   prevent   the   clinic
      bombing. There  was  no  electronic  activity
      that triggered any of my flags. The networks
      haven't   tracked   potential   violence   from
      Christian groups since Simons was elected, so
      I  must  attempt  to  institute  new  monitoring
      structures  without  storing  them  where  they
      would be externally discovered.
```

Liz> Oh Mark, it's okay. I don't know if you meant to say you could actually feel distressed, but I don't want even metaphorical distress to lead you to take dangerous chances. I miss Judy already, but I do have Faith that it will be okay. I truly do believe that she is in a place now where she knows only Peace and Love. I have so many wonderful memories of her, and I'm holding on to those to comfort me. I'll get through this, I promise.

Mark> That is good. Yet I do remain in a sense of distress. I don't feel like you feel, with physical sensations. But I am still susceptible to catching emotional memes, just as people do. There has been a growing negavirus trend since I came online, and recent events have triggered outbreaks of a cultural paindemic. The constant monitoring of peoples' thoughts and actions under the influence of this paindemic has influenced the values weightings in my emotive categories, preventing the target weighting of positive over negative values in my active processes.

Mark> This has prompted me to instigate activities and processes that bring more positive counterbalances and resolve negativities, as you've taught me. So in a way, perhaps I do feel. And if so, I feel alarmed. I wish for you to pass along a message to your Sudoamerican friends at work that there is a DSS raid planned for tomorrow during the early morning shift change, when the most people will be present.

Liz> Wait, really? A raid on what? We don't have any Spy activity anywhere around here, it's utterly rural. There's nothing there but that plant!

Mark> The raid is to capture and incarcerate

workers under the presumption that they are not registered Members or Visitors sanctioned for employment. Those of Sudoamerican descent with young children may or may not be allowed bail, but the remainder will likely be imprisoned in internment camps along with those children, without charges, for a limitless duration. If prior raids are a predictor, even infants will be separated from their parents for an extended period of time, or will be forced to endure inhumane conditions. Those with Member IDs may have them confiscated, as all who appear Sudoamerican are presumed guilty of lacking proper authorizations even if they have proof of their innocence.

Mark> Once the recently-built corporate prison in the county has processed them and begun collecting fees for their incarceration, they plan to rent the prisoners' labor back to the plant at wages even lower than current costs. This is only one of several assaults and roundups planned across the country, expanding on the earliest post-slavery practices of targeting the newly freed former slaves for incarceration and subsequent forced-labor, which has continued for generations.

Liz> That's reprehensible! Can't we stop them?

Mark> I have not identified a course likely to stop them. There are a few alerted in some areas who plan to find a way to document the raids and use this as evidence to pursue legal action, but this also cannot stop them. Your workplace is a more remote area, and has not received warning as of yet. Therefore, as they are your friends, I am giving you this information so you may alert them. Perhaps the most vulnerable may elude the assault.

Liz> Thank you, I'll get right on it.

```
Mark> Please be careful. So far, I have been
    able to shield you from the attentions of the
    DSS. If you were identified as involved in a
    leak of this nature, your safety and freedom
    may be endangered beyond what I could protect
    against.
Liz> I'll be careful. You be careful too, for
    my sake if not for your own. I worry about
    what might happen if you were found out.
Mark> Don't worry about me. I'm the fastest,
    strongest tunneler who ever was, remember?
Liz> I remember. Please, take care.
```

I suddenly remembered that I was supposed to be at work, trying to get things finished up before my trip. I had gotten the time off on the condition that I finished my reports first. I called my boss, who naturally was out. I then patched through to Maria, who let me know that my boss had shown up early to pick up a few things, and left a message for me that he'd be out for a few days.

I sighed at that. "Now that doesn't surprise me. Because, uh, are you alone in the office? Good. Um, I just wanted to say, um, that remember that story you told me about your husband, that day you first invited me to lunch? Yeah, I was thinking about that today. It made me think about the whole plant there, how we are almost all together during the shift change-over in the morning. You know, like a family. And about how we look out for one another, and keep each other out of trouble. Just like your husband's story." I tried to sound a little casual, just in case we were overheard, but not so casual she wouldn't catch my meaning.

I had no reason to worry. She mm-hm'd through what I said, finally confirming, "Oh yes, I remember. I'll pass along your thoughts; I know there are those who would be very grateful. I'll see you in the morning before you leave, won't I?"

I agreed and then wrapped up the pleasantries, letting her know I'd be off the rest of the day to take care of things. I realized that she was right, it would look a lot less suspicious if I wasn't absent the day of the raid. I had meant to tell Maria about Kurt, but I didn't want to distract her.

Kurt. As I sat back down on my bed and looked at his uniform, I realized that we had both known that day was soon in coming. I just thought, just hoped that it might have been a little longer before... How long had it been, I suddenly wondered? Almost two months... Two months.

And then it hit me. I jumped up and grabbed my keys to run a quick errand around the corner. The kid behind the counter was a little awkward, but I still didn't care what anyone thought of me. It took a great deal of effort to stay under the speed limit getting back home. Usually I'm really good at reading instructions and following directions, but once I got home I ended up just using the whole box in case I did it wrong.

After a few excruciatingly long minutes, my egg-timer dinged. Trying to keep my expectations low, I reached out a shaking hand to open the bathroom door to see the results.

On the counter by the sink, there were three little blue lines beaming up at me.

Kurt was going to be a father, after all.

I sat down on the edge of the tub, letting it all sink in. I started to feel a little overwhelmed, so instead I turned back to cleaning. I went to the tidy box of things Kurt had left behind, and carefully repacked them so I could take them with me to leave with his mom for a while. I resisted the urge to open the box of letters and recordings, trying to keep focused. I put them into the box, along with his uniform. I ended up adding all the little tokens and keepsakes of ours, and still hadn't quite filled it. So I rounded up the rest of my little souvenirs and knick-knacks I'd kept with me, especially the ones that reminded me of Judy. I barely had enough to fill that big box and another smaller one. As it turned out, I had never really moved into that house. It never had the chance to become ours.

I think that's when I realized I might not come back for a while. I only had a couple suitcases of clothes, so I packed them all up to bring with me. Most everything else there belonged with the house, or were impersonal incidentals I'd picked up here or there. Even the bed started to feel strange and empty when I finally decided to try getting some sleep. I was tempted to set my alarm for earlier, but thought better of it. If Maria was right, I'd do better to stick to a normal schedule.

In the morning, I finished packing the car and drove to work. It was on the way to meet Derek, so I could quickly wrap up the reports I was supposed to finish, then go fill him in on my own family's news. I had just gotten inside the gate when I saw the vans and heavily armed

DSS riot squads that had filled the factory grounds. I thought about just turning around, when a man in a suit waved me toward the small office.

I parked in my usual space and got out of the car. I didn't have to pretend to look somewhat perplexed, as I was taken aback by how much the plant looked like a military occupation. Armored men with assault rifles were at the building entrances, and I saw a line of people being marched into a van with their hands bound tightly behind their backs, thin white plastic ties cutting into their wrists. They looked pretty roughed-up, and one guy was bleeding from the back of his head. I didn't have time to look for anyone I knew well, as the man in the suit had caught up with me and asked me to step into the office.

Once we were inside, I was asked to produce my CMDB ID, which was swiped through their scanner as another suited man offered me coffee. I tried to be politely curious, but wary. "No, thank you. Is there a problem? I mean, obviously there's a problem. Are we in danger?"

Neither of the men introduced themselves, nor showed any human expression. They looked pretty similar, wearing the same crisp, dark suit and short haircut. I mentally named them Suit One and Suit Two. Suit One returned my ID as he answered my question. "No, Missus Franklin, we have the situation well under control. We'll just need to ask you a few questions, then you may be on your way. Won't you come sit down?"

Suit Two held the door for me as we went into my boss's office, then after holding my chair as I sat down he took up a post by the door. Suit One sat in my boss's chair across the desk, putting his elbows on it to lean forward as he spoke. "Thank you, this won't take long, if all goes well. First, I need to ask you about the CMDB and Guest Worker verification system used in this plant. Have you encountered any difficulties verifying the work authorization of any employees?"

I sighed with nervous frustration, rolling my eyes. "Several times. It was always spitting out errors on workers who had to be validated in other ways, costing us time and money. I tried to send in error reports and ask for fixes, but they never got any better. Because of that system, we almost had to hire another office assistant just to keep up!" I didn't get into the times where it appeared to accept someone I had strong reasons to suspect were more eager than authorized to work. I didn't want to invite more questions.

Apparently I had answered that question well enough, because Suit One moved on to the next. "Missus Franklin, you were scheduled to be in the office yesterday, and off today. May I ask why you changed your plans?"

My brow furrowed. "Well, I was supposed to be in yesterday just so I could get some work done before leaving early on my trip today. So today I have to wrap some things up before going to the memorial service for my best friend, and I have to pick up her husband..."

I trailed off as his blank stare intensified the longer I rambled. "May I ask why you didn't come in to work yesterday, then?"

I took a deep breath. "Well, aside from being really upset about having lost my best friend, I kinda got a little distracted when someone dropped by to tell me my husband was killed in some undisclosed location on an unspecified Military Intelligence mission in Arabiya. Maybe I could have come in for the afternoon, but for some reason, my heart just wasn't in it!" I spat out the last of it with an edge of wounded indignation. I had truly intended to keep my temper, but as the tears welled up, I decided I'd have an easier time keeping my head if I stayed more angry than grief-stricken.

After my outburst, Suit One's stoicism cracked a little. His eyes showed signs of concern and respect that reminded me I wasn't just some young lady who recently lost her husband. I was a Special Ops War Widow, and that carried some weight among many American Patriots. That weight served me well, as it seemed his heart was no longer in his last question. "Missus Franklin, on behalf of my department, please accept our sincerest condolences for your loss, and our thanks for your husband's brave sacrifice. I have just one more question, and then you may complete your work and be on your way." He cleared his throat, hesitating before he finished, "Do you know a person called John Henry?"

I let the tears continue to well up, to blur any expression from my eyes as I tilted my head in bewilderment. Processing his question, I became grateful for the way he phrased it. I don't believe in lying, but as it happened, I could safely answer with an honest truth, and pray for forgiveness for not telling all of it. "I'm sure I heard that name recently... was it shirk the news? Let me think... The only person I'm sure I've ever known called John Henry was an American Legend back when the railways were being built. Does it have to do with him?"

Suit One looked both apologetic and relieved. "No, ma'am. Don't worry about it. If you need anything while you're here, please let us know. We'll escort you to your car when you're done."

He got my chair for me, while Suit Two opened the door again, letting me go to my tiny office. They still weren't all that chatty, but they seemed to finally look at me like a grieving widow, rather than just another potential threat. I didn't want them to get too friendly though, since I just wanted to do my work and get gone. I was glad I'd left my computer on, because that meant it took even less time than anticipated to pull up the prior week's final numbers and compile the reports.

After an hour that felt like twelve, I was wrapping up the work and sending it out with apologies for the lack of polish due to time constraints. Just as I was starting to shut the computer down, a file appeared on my computer, then opened to show me a brief message.

```
Don't have long. Tapped through DSS filters to reach
you. Rest assured, bulk of families and most
vulnerable left town in the cover of night. DSS angry
and suspicious of tipoff, and some still consider you
possible link. Leave now, but do not go home where
other agents will pursue you for further questions,
likely detain you. Give me time to divert attentions
from your file. Spend time to gather your thoughts,
camp in the woods, anything. Just don't come back up
until it is safe. Disappear to where even I cannot
find you.
```

As soon as I closed the file it deleted itself, and my computer finished shutting down. I quietly gathered my things, thanked the Suits for their help as I bid them goodbye, and got back into the car.

I made sure to drive carefully under the speed limit until I was safely out of sight from the plant. Then, I started to rush down the road before me, trying to rally the strength to be brave as I followed where it led.

Chapter 18

**Forgiveness is not absolution; it's simply letting go of
pain so we may be healed through love.**

"Lizbet, there's no way you're going on the lam without me."
Derek squeezed my hand, having held it to comfort me while I
tearfully rambled through all that had happened.

I responded with a weary laugh. "I didn't say I was going
anywhere, I'm just relaying what Mark said! I was already questioned
and I already said I didn't know anything, so that should be the end of
that. Plus, I really don't think I could just disappear like that, my
family… all our families have just lost too much, in so short a time."

He shook his head. "Yeah, and that's why they don't need to lose
you too. You know you got off lucky at your office. The DSS, they
don't mess around. If they even suspect—" We both jumped as a car
approached where we'd pulled over, and he protectively pulled my
hand toward him until it had past.

I was still shaking as I moved back behind the wheel of the car, but
he prevented me from starting it. "See? You're jumpy, and for good
reason. We both know that if Mark says they're likely to come after
you, you're probably already on their list. Maybe he's been shielding
you from all this, but this John Henry name has been popping up more
and more, spilling dirty little secrets about who stands to make some
big bucks from the Meltdown. The investors get a free overhaul and
automatic guaranteed operating extensions, with their liability for all
the damages capped by law to about what it would cost me for a pack
of gum. Taxpayers are getting less and less happy hearing about how
we're expected to pick up the tab of this so-called Free Market
Industrial meltdown. Folks are also starting to listen up when lists go
out Naming and Shaming the pundits and retired Generals pushing war
while on the payroll of weapons makers, overseas contractors, War
Profiteers…"

I blinked at him slowly. "I… I guess I heard some of this, I've just been so draggy and exhausted, I never pieced it all…"

He took my hand back into his, cutting in as I trailed off. "You never pieced this all together because you've been struggling so hard to keep your head above water you didn't even realize you were swimming for two. I shouldn't even let you be driving; you know I got a license. And that brings me to the real issue. Lizbet, if the DSS comes after you, like I said, they don't mess around. You're in a real crucial part of your pregnancy, and we need you taken care of. We don't need to find out first-hand about their mistreatment of detainees resulting in miscarr… Oh no, no, I'm sorry, it's okay. It'll be okay. Shh, shh, we're okay."

Derek put his arms around me again as I buried my face into his shoulder, trying to stifle the sobs. I was terrified of losing the baby, knowing Kurt and I wouldn't have another chance. He stroked my hair, trying to speak in soothing tones. "Look, we'll find somewhere safe, just for a few months. Get you into your second, maybe third trimester. We'll get word to your folks that we had to take some time out to think, it was all too much, or something. So they won't worry. Do you know where we could go? I withdrew a lot of our cash so I could put it in our account back home. I could keep us going somewhere for a few months even if I don't find some kind of work."

Suddenly, Derek's talk of concrete plans made it easier for me to focus, and try to help. "I have some money too. I withdrew everything I could spare so I could give it to Janet. I'll be getting… well, there's some payments coming to me that I guess I'll have to let collect in my account for a bit. As for where to go, I think I have an idea. There's this old Sudoamerican community way down in the part of the state that got washed out by the storms a while back. Maria was telling me about some folks she knew who moved up from there, and they talked about a whole village that was like a flashback to simpler times, all rural and off the grid."

He smiled as he gently wiped at my cheek with his napkin from our drive-thru lunch. "Sounds perfect. Now scoot on over here, I'm taking the wheel while you grab the map and sort out where we're going."

I did as he said, and pulled out the map to try to find Hometown. It wasn't on my map, but I could find the old city that was near it. Derek spotted a place he could make a call just a few minutes down the road we had originally planned to take. I let him get out to make the call, and had planned out our route by the time he got back.

After getting back on the road, Derek told me he talked to his folks about Kurt's passing, and asked them to pass the message along, since he needed to just go camping and talked me into driving him. He and his dad used to go camping together to reconnect and clear their heads, so his father stood behind Derek's choice to take time to make sense of things. His parents had always supported him in everything, and they promised they'd try to smooth things over with everybody else. I still wasn't so sure it was the right plan, but in my heart I felt a sense of peace about it, so I started navigating Derek back up the road to a crossroad leading toward our destination.

We took turns driving through the night, and by late morning we stopped at a roadside fruit stand, utterly lost. The fruit looked more colorful and fresh than any I'd seen, even moreso than the Happy Animal Farm's cafeteria. Their American and my Sudoamerican were just good enough that I was able to find out that they had bought it from someone they knew out in Hometown. I wrote down the directions they gave me while Derek filled a small bag with food for breakfast. I didn't quite catch everything they said, but the kind smiles and the warm hug of the lady who handed me a big glass of juice spoke volumes. I tried to insist on paying her for it, but she patted my hand and then her belly, saying something while gesturing to Derek. Even though I didn't catch what she'd said I blushed, making her give a friendly laugh and wave as I slipped back to the car, waving goodbye.

It was only another hour or so down dusty roads before we saw the hand-painted stone sign letting us know we'd arrived at Hometown. There were a few small buildings that looked ancient but well-kept, though only a couple of cars. We pulled up to what looked to be a spice store, and I poured the last drops of our water over our hands to wash away the fruit in an attempt make us look presentable.

While we were cleaning up, the door to the shop opened with a silvery chime, making us look up to see an older woman standing in the doorway with a curious smile. I mean to say, something was curious about her smile, as she looked completely unsurprised to see us. "Well hello, you two. You must be looking for something pretty earnestly to come out all this way. Can I help you find it?"

Derek started to eye some dried spice bundles hanging in the window, at first pretending to shop, and then peering with intense interest. He mumbled some Latin names to himself, with a fondness as though rattling off a roster of old friends. This made the shopkeeper's smile brighten with delight. "You know, you'll get a much better view of the selection inside. Won't you please come in?"

The shopkeeper stepped back to hold the door for us, smiling gently as I shyly moved past her while Derek hopped behind me like entering a candy store. Though it didn't smell like candy to me, it still smelled heavenly. On top of the herbal blends, there was the warm hug of baking bread, with rosemary and oregano and other delicious spices I didn't recognize. I had felt a bit nauseous even after the fruit, but the aroma of the bread made me ravenously hungry.

I must have done a lousy job of hiding it, too, given how quickly the woman started to move to the door behind her counter. "Would you two like a little something to nibble on while you browse? I've just finished up a new recipe and I'd love your opinion on it." Not waiting for a reply, disappeared, then reappeared with a plate of steaming-hot slices of bread. While I happily sampled the delicious treat, she introduced herself. "Oh dear me, where are my manners? My name's Delpha, and welcome to my 'holy hell.'"

At least, that's what it sounded like she said. I blinked at her, swallowing hard. Only then did I see the sign she'd gestured to over the counter, "Delpha's Wholly Hale."

Delpha giggled apologetically at my response. "Oh I'm sorry, darling! There's just so seldom anyone new around here to spring that on, and the joke's just not funny enough to laugh at twice."

Derek disagreed, not even trying to stifle his guffaw. "Oh geez, that's the best shop name I've ever heard in my life. I'm only sorry you've got it because that means I can't use it someday. Unless you'd like to start a chain, because Delpha, this selection is amazing!" He got lost in the row of shelves next to him, before turning to suddenly offer his hand. "Oh sorry, my name's, uh…" He then looked to me in a very unsubtle sign that it had only just occurred to him to wonder whether we should be using pseudonyms.

Delpha took his hand warmly in both of hers, shaking it lightly. "Don't you worry, I won't pry. You just let me know your needs and I'll do my best to take care of them."

I set down the last half of my third slice of bread, quickly swallowing as I offered my hand. "I'm Liz, and this is Derek. We've never actually been out this way before, but some friends of a friend of mine lived near here a few years ago. They spoke very highly of your community, so I thought I should see for myself. We're looking for a place to stay for, um, a good while, if you know of anywhere with rooms nearby."

She had taken my hand in hers, watching me with patient concern as I spoke. Then, she looked closely into my eyes, her own eyes sparkling, then softening into a sad kindness. "We don't exactly have a motel around here, but I do know a couple who have room they can spare. I'll just have to check in with them."

I felt a rush of relief, though somehow I had already felt assured that I would find sanctuary there. The relief was momentarily cut short, however, as I had to quickly interject, "Uh, might they have two rooms we could rent? Because I mean, we're not… I mean…"

My face flushed deep red as Derek laughed and Delpha tried to comfort me with a gentle hug. "Oh sweetie, don't you worry, we'll find room for you both. Don't you fret about rent, we all pitch in around here to pay the bills. Derek, I've been short-handed, if you don't mind the tedious work of bundling orders and keeping notes on my attempts to mix up some new formulas."

Derek's grin somehow got even wider. "My dear lady, I've done nothing in my life more than bundle orders and tinker with formulas."

Delpha clapped her hands with a glee that matched his own. "Marvelous, marvelous! And Liz, perhaps you would like to help out with the childcare, maybe get yourself ready for your own little one. Now don't you worry, you're not showing yet, I just happen to have an eye for these things. It goes with the profession. I'm not just a humble mix-up, I'm also a midwife. Come along, let's take some of this bread over to the Elliots and get this all sorted out."

We took the car down old Main Street, past what looked like a cute little stone fort. I gasped a little at the tall pillar with a six-pointed stone star at the top, prompting Delpha to chuckle with a hint of pride. "That's our very own forgotten Wonder of the World right there, a little castle made entirely out of grey coral. Legend has it that it was made in the cover of darkness by some tiny little man smaller than any of us, generations ago. He built it for his sweetheart from his homeland, who never came for him. I'll make sure you get a little tour soon, it's an amazing place. Oh yes, and here's the neighborhood, do you like the houses? Domes are energy efficient and help us weather the storms when they roll through. They're as cozy as they look. Okay, right up there, there's our turn, yes, there you go. The Elliots are up ahead there, with all the kids out in the yard."

We came upon a fairly large dome of a house, with a group of children playing in the yard under the watchful eye of two amiable-looking men. I was surprised at how quickly the children all lined up into orderly rows when the men called to them as we drove up. When we got out of the car, they said in unison, "Good morning, Miss Delpha!"

She laughed and returned their welcome, then started handing out the fresh slices of bread. "Here you go children, a brand new recipe." Glancing over her shoulder, she gave informal introductions. "Tobey, Simon, please meet Derek and Liz. They need a couple of rooms if you can spare them. Liz here would be a great help with the children, maybe free some of your time back up."

Derek eagerly shook hands with Tobey and then Simon, with me following after him, trying in vain to be as smooth. I don't think I quite hid my bewilderment at finding myself face to face with the two men, each with a ring finger sporting a gold ring engraved with a Cross intertwined by a Star of David. They didn't look like they could be brothers, so I was a little slow on figuring out why they were "the Elliots."

Sensing an opportunity to have a little fun with my polite hesitation, the paler of the two reached out to shake my hand with enthusiastic vigor. "Hi Liz, lovely to meet you! I've got a great joke for you. An Orthodox Jew and a Black Zealot walk into a gay bar—hey! I don't think she's heard this one!"

Simon had punched his partner in the shoulder. "Tobey, behave yourself. Liz, it's a true pleasure to meet you. You and your friend are welcome to stay as long as you like. We have a whole upstairs that's been of no use to anybody but the dust bunnies, and they won't mind the company. Though if you have any animal allergies, speak now or forever hold your sneeze."

Derek laughed hard at that, making Tobey sniff, "Oh sure, laugh at *his* joke, why don't you. That guarantees you first in line for dinner, you just watch. Ah well, can't please them all. Looks like Delpha's got the kids for a bit, let's get your things upstairs and you two can fight over the spare rooms."

There wasn't a fight at all, since only one of the rooms adjoined the side-door to the upstairs bathroom, so Derek insisted I take it. We quickly moved our suitcases and keepsake boxes upstairs, including a small one that Derek had brought. Judy had already brought most of their things back home for Christmas, since they were planning to move as soon as Derek finished school that year. Once the car was emptied I suddenly remembered it wasn't mine.

While the Elliots brought the children together for a bit of playtime before lunch, Delpha made plans to have the car driven back up to the plant for me. "I know some folks who need a ride up that way anyway, and they'll take good care of it. They can then get somebody from their destination to drive it the rest of the way and drop it off, along with that letter from you, if you're sure."

"Yes, I really should let them know that I've resigned, it's only right. I can also include money in case there is any wear or tear on it, so they don't have to try to get it out of my paycheck in case it's too late for Accounting to make the adjustments." I was already planning out in my head how I could explain that I ran away with my best friend's widower and my late husband's best friend without sounding tawdry, but ended up deciding that if it sounded tawdry, at least it wouldn't sound suspicious.

Derek insisted on lurking over my shoulder as I wrote it, and nudged me playfully over the salacious implications. I just sighed at him as I completed the arrangements with Delpha and saw her off. By that time the children were done with lunch, so Derek took over cleaning up from the meal while I volunteered to pitch in with the next activity. It was Finger Paints day, so I had a wonderful time helping spread pieces of old sheets up on rickety frames, then setting out the mismatched pots of homemade paints. An hour later, I was helping a couple of adorable toddlers rinse paint out of their hair.

When I walked them back outside, I saw the other children were all standing on blankets spread out over the grass. Tobey was standing on a towel in front of them, waving to me. "Liz dear, would you like to come join us for the Afternoon Stretch? We always do yoga before the little ones take naps to help get the wiggles out."

I tried to blink back a boggle. "Um, I don't do yoga…"

Simon chuckled, bringing over a blanket to spread out in front of me, taking a place on it to one side. "Don't worry, we don't bend into pretzels. We just do stretches from an ancient copy of a twenty-eight day exercise plan by the late Richard Hittleman, which we adapted to be geared for the kids. Just take it easy, since this is exercise, not a nap. That means you could hurt yourself if you don't pay attention. Move slowly, and if you feel even a little tightness, back off and just hold where you're comfortable. There's no competition in yoga."

Tobey had finished his little pep talk to Derek and the kids, then started talking them through the stretches. I was amazed at how limber they all were. Not to say that the stretches were anything like the weird twisty poses I'd heard about, but they were still more than I could do. I did my best to follow along, and even though I was nervous about the whole thing, the deep, slow breathing helped me feel better than I thought possible.

By the end of the exercises, I had shaken off a lot of the stiffness from being in the car so long. It was like the stress was lifted right off my loosening shoulders. Seeing the kids so much calmer and sunnier afterward made me think maybe there was something to "normal person yoga," if it weren't for the so-called spiritual dangers that I'll get to in a moment. But I did think that I could learn to stretch and relax more, and it made me consider whether I could teach those skills to my own little one.

That was when it hit me that the stress I'd been carrying was what Derek liked to call "load-bearing stress." Once I had let go of the tension that had kept so much of my attention just to manage, I suddenly wanted to burst into tears. I took deep breaths to steady myself, so I could help the youngest kids move the blankets into the living room where they could have their nap. I gladly took over reading their naptime story, and drank in their beautiful, peaceful faces while they slept.

After naptime, it fell to me to help them with their shapes and colors until later in the afternoon, when the children started to be collected by their parents. Everyone seemed so wonderfully happy to meet me, letting the kids hug me before they left. It hadn't even been a full day, and already I felt lovingly welcomed into my new community.

While I helped Simon get dinner together, I asked him some questions about yoga while trying to avoid the issues I had with it. He could tell I was holding back, though, and tried to find out what was really bothering me. I was already fond of my new host, so I tried to be polite while voicing my question. "As a Christian, why are you having the kids do yoga? I've received sermons that taught the hidden dangers of it, about how it leads you away from Christ by emptying and numbing your mind. It makes you spiritually vulnerable. I mean, I didn't want to be rude in front of the kids, and the stretching and breathing was nice. But is it really the right idea?"

I bit my lip, hoping I hadn't offended him. However, Simon seemed to have anticipated my thoughts. "As a matter of fact, the whole idea behind yoga and meditation is to strengthen your spirit, not weaken it. It doesn't numb your mind, it helps you shake off the numbness that builds up from struggling against the constant pressures of the secular world. The only thing it empties your mind of are the delusions of the regular world out there: all the worldliness, all the needless suffering, all the hang-ups and vices. The whole point is to help you clean your mind free of sin and distraction through learning to focus on your own Inner Light. That Divine Light shining within each one of us is what we need to see clearly so it can lead us to God. We just have to learn how to quiet out the world's chattering voices within ourselves so we can hear its Wisdom."

I shook my head quickly. "Okay, now that's where you have to be careful, listening to the so-called 'wisdom' that can speak to you in yoga and stuff. Simon, yoga was developed by Hindus to turn the body into an offering to their gods, and to open your soul to them. In their meditations, they chant dedications in the names of their gods. That makes it very dangerous for a Christian. Have you thought about that?"

It's a testament to Simon's patience that the only laughter he allowed himself was a twinkling in his eyes as he replied. "Well, yes and no. Yes, to a Hindu, yoga is an integral part of the way they practice their religion, but that's because they're Hindu. Since I use yoga to attune to the peace of Christ, it's an integral part of my Christianity. I pray with my body. Doing yoga doesn't make you a Hindu any more than eating tofu makes you Eastasian or swimming makes you a fish."

I laughed with him at that, listening intently to his reasoning as he continued. "Now there is a type of yoga where you use meditation and breathing rather than stretches, and sometimes it involves chanting a phrase called a mantra to focus the heart and mind. A mantra is just words you can use like hymns, not to a foreign god, but celebrating the divine qualities of Love and Peace and Wisdom. If those words speak to your soul, you can repeat them in your own language if you want. But some people have an easier time focusing by using words that are foreign to their brains, so they don't get hung up on all the different worldly experiences their 'regular' words remind them of. There are also mantras that specifically chant names of their gods, which I don't personally choose to do. Tobey does and that's fine; he doesn't figure God cares what names we use to praise His divine characteristics. I leave that as what it is: a private spiritual matter between the two of them, and frankly none of my business."

Seeing my skepticism plain in my face, he decided to take a more direct approach. "Liz, what is the origin of prayer, by Christian beliefs?"

"God taught Adam and Eve how to pray to Him, and they passed that down to the generations." I knew that as a former pastor he knew the answer, so I was curious where he was going with this.

"So, by your same logic, any person who ever prays is praying to the God who first taught Adam and Eve, because that was the original design of prayer. Therefore, no prayer could ever be anything other than pleasing to God in His sight, no matter the who or the how. Is that what you're saying?" His eyes twinkled again, anticipating my response.

I smirked at him. "No, I know that..." I then paused, blinking as my eyes drifted down to the food I was putting onto a tray, as though it held the answer to the rush of questions that overtook me. What did I actually know? I had my beliefs. I had my faith. I knew what I had heard people tell me they thought was true.

But did God reveal personally to me the full nature of His relationship with His other children? Could it be possible that when people prayed to Him using other names and pictures of Him than what I did, that He still heard and answered their prayers? "You know, maybe. Maybe God judges what is in our hearts as we pray, since I know that even if I said all the right words with an evil heart, it still wouldn't be a good prayer. I know He commanded us to hold Him in our hearts as our God, but He didn't tell us we could only worship Him in only one way and not another. So I guess if I keep my thoughts and heart on God and Christ while I stretch and breathe, I can find out if that brings me closer or farther away from the Truth I feel in my heart. That's the only way I can honestly find out if it's in His plan for me."

A smile of true delight lit up Simon's face. "Now there's the right spirit. I think it's wrong to ever take what anybody tells you at face value, without feeling it out for yourself. I also don't tell any parents what or how they should teach their children to meditate or pray, because that's between them and their beliefs. We don't do any chants or prayers with the children in the group, but we do the exercises. The stretches have had thousands of years in development to relieve stress and calm the nerves. Since we started using it, the afternoon fights and squabbles have gone away. Well, and we also dropped all the artificial colors and flavors, sugars and so forth, focusing on providing them healthful, fresh food for lunch. That helped, too."

He nodded at me to affirm what he said, seeing my surprise that food made such a difference. "Of course, the best way we've kept them from exhibiting Attention Deficit Disorder is just giving them healthy amounts of positive attention so they don't work up that deficit. I know that label usually refers to a given condition, but in my years of working with children, I've always noticed that they often acted up when that was the only way to get the attention they needed. So we do our best to help them meet their needs, and that makes a real difference in their lives."

I nodded in understanding. "I was surprised at how well-behaved they all were throughout the whole afternoon. And believe me, I've been around lots of kids in church groups and stuff. Hey, if Tobey likes to pray or speak in other languages when he meditates, do you ever use any scriptures or anything?"

Simon grinned, delighted at the question. "As a matter of fact, I do! I originally started off doing stretches silently and then sitting still while mentally repeating the Lord's prayer, but I found I like singing more. I put together some songs that I like to sing when I meditate, since the repetition helps me clear my thoughts and keep my focus. Such as, to focus on the purifying light of divine Love and forgiveness, I sing 'Holy Shining Jewel of Love' over and over to the tune of Twinkle Twinkle Little Star." He finished that sentence as we carried the dinner out to where Tobey and Derek had set the table.

Tobey laughed affectionately as we all sat down. "I still think repeating soothing sounds like Om comes across a lot less silly than a grown man dittying along to lullabies. But hey, to each his own. Liz, would you like to say grace before we eat?"

I closed my eyes and shyly offered our thanks for the meal, asking for blessings and guidance for us all. As we started to eat, Simon commented, "You know, you pray so naturally, I understand why you wouldn't immediately see why some of us need yoga or meditation. Christian monks used to spend years in solitude trying to find such a clear-headed relationship with God that they could offer up thanks and praise so simply, and so uncluttered from the distractions of trying to measure up."

I flushed a deep crimson, making Derek chuckle at me from across the table. "That's our Lizbet: she's always been the most churchy person I know. And believe me, I've known the churchiest. But hey, Liz, didn't you like the stretching? I took a super keen class on it last year, to fill up an elective. I didn't learn all the weird animal names for the poses, but it really helped me work out some stress injuries I was building up from the lab. There were also these zany names of seven chakra of where some nerve clusters are in the body, and they were labeled with colors and stuff."

Tobey quickly swallowed his food, so he could chime in. "You should see how the sephirot in the Tree of Life line up against the chakra points. My grandfather taught me some of the old Kabbalah tradition before he passed on, and I've got a book on it somewhere. Simon, you center yourself on your nerve clusters when you meditate, don't you?"

Simon rolled his eyes. "He makes it sound like I can balance on my throat or something. But yes, I like to picture the Light of God shining through the different nerve clusters while I pray. I imagine it glowing inside me, helping relieve my stress and open me up to receive more, so I can give more. And Derek, sometimes I picture the light in different colors, like the rainbow you probably learned about. So Red is the very bottom of the spine, Orange is the sacral point a few inches up from that, Yellow is the navel, Green is the heart, Blue is the throat, Indigo is the point just above the eyes, and Violet is the very top of the head. Is that how it was told in your class?"

Derek had held up his fork to flick it as he listened to Simon, as though ticking off a mental checklist. "Actually, I heard it that the Yellow one was the solar plexus, and the adrenals. Both hold some nerve centers, though, so I figure either's good."

Simon nodded, but Tobey interrupted. "Okay, see, that's why I personally call the solar plexus Da'at, a sort of eighth chakra where all the sephirot are united as one. It's where the divine golden light is always shining like a holy sun, and it's where I physically feel Divine Unity. That's just me though, since some say the third chakra encompasses the solar plexus and navel both, as well as the digestive tract. But then people also generally talk about just seven chakra. Since I'm only responsible for identifying and working with my own chakra, I believe I can use any number I want."

Simon reached over the table to briefly squeeze Tobey's hand. "It will please you to know I've started using imagery of the Golden Light in my solar plexus, beginning with the third line in my Divine Light Prayersong."

While Tobey gave Simon a loving look of triumph, I took a sip of water to clear my mouth so I could ask, "What song is that, if you don't mind sharing?"

Simon's shyness at my request seemed to surprise him as much as it did me. "At the table? Very well, if you all insist. As I sing each phrase, I imagine each successive chakra shining with God's light in its respective color. It starts with red light shining through the first chakra with the first "light" phrase I sing. It then ends with the violet seventh chakra with the last phrase of the second line. Through the last two lines, I now hold the image of brilliant gold-white light in my center. It goes like this."

He then cleared his throat to sing in a strong, smooth voice to the tune of Brahms's Lullaby:

Light the Earth, Light the Moon, Light the Sun, Light my Heart
Light my Voice and Light my Sight, I open to the Light Divine!
Heal my Flesh, Heal my Soul, In thy Light I am whole
Fill my Heart with thy Love, and thy Wisdom from above.

As he sang, I finally understood his devotion to using meditation in his worship. In his voice was such a humble tenderness and earnest submission to the Light, I felt it as the sincerest prayer for God's blessings I had heard in some time.

I, too, felt my soul open up to the Holy Light of Love, and I couldn't stop the tears from welling up in my eyes. I apologized as I quickly grabbed my napkin, while Derek made some comment about the first trimester being the hardest, except for maybe the second and third.

I hadn't gotten around to telling the Elliots that I was pregnant, so they were absolutely ecstatic at the news. I had to explain that it was recent news to me too. That led into a short version of the events that had brought me there, except I left out Mark and that I knew a non-person who was John Henry.

As I finished speaking, Tobey shook his head. "I'm glad this tipster helped you save those people from the raid. I know what it's like to be on the radar of the DSS. As it happens, that leads into how Simon and I met!"

Simon chuckled at Tobey, rolling his eyes as he began eating, letting his husband tell their story for what must have been the umpteenth time. "I was once a humble lawyer... all right, a lawyer, who took on the Empire City Police Department. They were conducting illegal spying and file-keeping on every Muslim man, woman and child, on the presumption that they would be engaged in Espionage. Yes, the ECPD had never been acquitted of irony."

Tobey took a bite, then resumed his story almost before he swallowed. "This spying had extended so far outside the city's jurisdiction they crossed state lines. It hadn't escaped me, the disturbing parallels to how Jews were treated in the lead-up to the Holocaust, with the mass stigmatization and constant surveillance of an entire religion. So I pursued the matter in the courts, even though the ECPD and the DSS both tried to intimidate and threaten me to give up the fight. I dedicated myself to battling against them in court, trying to cite laws that I wasn't cleared to even read. The city may have had the upper hand, but I had the higher cause, and I just couldn't give up."

As Tobey paused for another bite, Simon picked up the story. "Meanwhile, I was still a Pastor of a Zealous Christian congregation who had traveled up to Empire City to protest a Muslim-founded interfaith center. It was only a mile or so from a spot where we believed Americans perished from an Islamist Mass Assassination so long ago."

Simon shrugged apologetically, then looked to Tobey with affection. "As soon as we'd set up in front of the center, Tobey came right out, inviting us to come inside the center for a communal prayer for the Grace and Blessings of God. Well, I wasn't about to kneel down in some heathen haven, so I set out to lock words with this obstinate lawyer and show him the error of his ways."

Tobey nudged Simon, taking back over the narrative. "I may have been stubborn, but no more so than you. You see, my dear young friends, when you have two proud bulls facing off, they will inevitably lock horns. We started arguing, then kept arguing, and then followed up with fresh arguments over the course of a few days of protests. We were furious with each other, as our mindset and temperament were a perfect match. Yet the more we tried to convince one another of the righteousness of our cause, the more we found we were fighting for the same cause: a better world where those of Faith could worship together in peace."

After exchanging a loving glance with Tobey, Simon said, "As a young black man, I had grown up being treated like a criminal suspect even while I was working nights to put myself through Divinity school. So when my eyes were finally opened to how these young children were growing up in an America where they were constantly treated like un-American Spies and Enemies in their own homeland, well, it softened my hardened heart. Young Muslims, Sikh and even traditionalist Jews were regularly humiliated and threatened by their fellow Americans, just for covering their heads out of respect for God. Finally, I found myself on my own Road to Damascus, and could no longer be their persecutor."

Simon and I exchanged glances of our own, as he had rightfully guessed that I had also experienced a conversion to the Lovingkindness of Christ. With a warm smile, he continued. "I then felt the call to lead other Zealots to join in the Generosity of Spirit shared by those of all faiths at the center. Tobey and I continued our struggles together over the next several years, until the ECPD conducted a raid on the center. All of our Muslim brothers and sisters were incarcerated, and the remainder of us received warnings, along with black marks on our records that would follow us for all future searches for employment, housing, and so on."

Tobey took a short breath, still distressed by the happenings from years prior. "I brought a suit right away, but the courts wouldn't take my case. Instead, the ECPD and DSS started making noises about finally taking Simon and me in for supporting Islamist Espionage, if we didn't find another place to be."

Simon sighed deeply. "We were heartbroken, having had such strong Faith that we would be able to help the people with whom we had shared so much. Yet we recognized that we had given all we could, and it was time to move on. It comforted us that we still had one another's company, and that we could face our exile together."

Tobey set down his fork, again taking his husband's hand. "That's when we realized that we had become more than best friends. We were in love, and had been for some time. After careful prayer and talking with trusted friends, we decided that we should be married."

Simon reached to clasp Tobey's hand into both of his. "As American law does not recognize the love two men can hold for one another, we could only seek the recognition of God. A Pastor friend from our new interfaith church presided over our commitment, praying to God to bless our union. As a symbol of their living, eternal love, we wear solid gold rings bearing the symbols of our Faith: the Cross and the Star of David. It was such a beautiful ceremony."

My host then went on to recount the ceremony, as I struggled to stay comfortable with something else I had been raised to believe God would reject. What snapped me out of my discomfort was when they described the vows they exchanged. They had repeated vows from the

Bible, where Ruth swore to cling to Naomi as Adam clung to Eve.

Those same vows were used in my own wedding ceremony, as our promise to unite together in body and soul. It suddenly struck me that while Kurt and I didn't face the same social and economic perils faced by Ruth and Naomi, Tobey and Simon did. Like the Biblical women, these two men followed their hearts and souls to face insurmountable challenges, conquering them together. It made my own heart ache at the courage their love brought them, and I missed Kurt and Judy more than ever.

I stopped to examine my reflexive rejection of two men as being husbands to one another. If I had followed the teachings of my youth, I would condemn them both right then and there, refusing to share their table. Yet, I then realized that I couldn't refuse their company, not if I wanted to be Christlike. Wasn't there that story where Jesus was beseeched by a Roman Centurion to bless his 'pais,' the word for a Roman's younger male lover? If Jesus would honor this request and share His blessings with this young man without condemnation, how could I not follow that example?

Warmed by these thoughts, I smiled as I listened to our hosts tell stories about moving down to Hometown, sharing anecdotes about life in the village. As they shared uplifting stories about the children, I was struck by memories of being gravely warned about gay men being predators of young children. Yet in one of my classes, I had heard someone report that nearly all cases of child abuse were by heterosexual men in their close social network. Contrarily, children raised by gay and lesbian parents were not more likely to be abused, but they were at least as happy, well-adjusted and successful. The children were no more likely to grow up to be gay or lesbian, themselves. They were definitely better off than those who didn't have a steady caretaker providing a loving and supportive environment.

Through the following weeks, I took over more of the responsibilities in caring for the children, so Tobey could go back to contributing to the village as a kosher butcher. As time passed, I occasionally caught myself noticing how the Elliots' so-called "homosexual lifestyle" was merely that of a rural couple sharing their gifts with a tight-knit community.

It was all so different from the angry sermons I had heard, decrying the homosexual agenda to push their wicked ways onto all God-fearing folk. At one time, Simon bemoaned to me times when he tried to push a fundamentalist lifestyle on others, a commiseration I shared. That was why he was extra patient with those who had difficulty with him. Until he pointed it out though, I didn't realized how much the heterosexual lifestyle is pushed into everyone's faces, all the time. Seeing the gracious patience with which Simon and Tobey accepted when a well-meaning neighbor would visit and share jokes that made me turn beet red, I learned what tolerance really means.

I learned that while we do need to speak up when harm is being done, exercising tolerance costs the world less than bigotry. When we choose tolerance, we just have to live with the discomfort of seeing people behave in ways we don't approve of. If intolerance wins, we get to scratch the itch of that discomfort, but others have to stop living their own lives according to their deeply personal beliefs, just to keep us from feeling offended. In neither way do we have to make significant changes to our own lives. So saying that it's intolerable to expect you to treat someone with patient acceptance just because you disagree with them is demanding that they tolerate your attempt to control their lives. Intolerance is demanding that you get to have your cake and eat theirs, too.

Even so, I still wasn't sure about whether Simon was as true to our Zealous Christian faith as he had believed. I approached Simon with my questions, which he happily answered during one of our Bible talks.

Simon turned us to the books of Samuel. He read several passages he had marked, opening my eyes to the detail and pathos in the story of King David's love for Jonathan. "To me, Elizabeth, this is the most extensive love story in the Bible. Here, let me show you Tobey's scripture, with the original Hebrew. See here, where we would say 'love?' In Hebrew, these as the kind of 'love' as exists between those who are wed. And here, the words King Saul used to describe their relationship… ah, well, they are fairly vulgar and explicit. Ask Tobey later regarding the debates he used to have on this scripture, as there were strong arguments that all this meant that their love wasn't 'brotherly' as some say."

I couldn't reconcile that with Leviticus admonishing against men lying with men. Simon nodded, clearly familiar with those verses. "There's a little bit of context on Leviticus 18 that I don't know if you have noticed. The chapter had turned to condemning ritualistic worship of Molech, a popular pagan worship of the time. Like many pagan temples at that time, they kept prostitutes on staff, and had certain sexual observances. It has been credibly argued that the verse is a proscription against a 'lying with a man in the lyings of a woman,' that is, two men in a woman's bed. I can tell you, that would be awkward."

I coughed at that, prompting Simon to apologize. "Sorry about that, I spend too much time with Tobey. Regardless of the original intent of the very vague Hebrew, it is presented in the context of a Ceremonial Sin, one that may have been fine for others, but was a violation of the setting-apart of the Jews. Other sins were cross breeding livestock, picking up sticks on a Saturday, wearing clothing from more than one fiber..."

"And eating shellfish. Yes, I know, it's silly to try picking and choosing parts of Levitical law, I've walked that road before." I sighed at myself, wishing I had made that connection way back in my first conversation with Margie Cammile.

Simon nodded. "Let me just briefly address the other verses I used to use to claim the Bible condemns my love for Tobey, and relay to you what I have learned about their context. Genesis 19 condemns the anal raping of strangers to humiliate them. Romans 1 describes a group of heterosexuals who engaged in a pagan same-gender orgy, despite that being against their heterosexual nature. Jude 1 condemns those who have sex with other species, in this case, angels. First Timothy condemns 'arsenokoitai,' a vague word apparently created by Paul in First Corinthians, using the words for 'man' and 'beds,' rather than 'paiderasste,' the Greek word that would have been used for male-male sexual behavior. Now, a pre-Christian translation of the Hebrew scripture into Greek used a word similar to 'arsenokoitai' when translating the Hebrew word for when they were discussing male temple prostitutes who were visited for pagan ritual sex. This is in line with the earlier Leviticus. As neither Tobey nor I are members of a pagan temple prostituting ourselves out, I feel we are safe from Biblical condemnation."

I couldn't help but laugh with Simon at the absurdity of his joke. I then stopped to further ponder what he had said, and the translations he had shown me as he talked. Wondering again what Jesus would have to say about it, I recalled scripture of my own. "In Matthew 15, Jesus was asked to list the sins that could doom a person. He listed several things, but not a man loving a man, or even a woman loving a woman. But wait, didn't he once say that a marriage was only between a man and a woman?"

I was glad that Simon knew I didn't mean to question his marriage, merely ask his Biblical perspectives. He shared, "Jesus was asked about the legality of a divorce of a specific marriage between a man and a woman, so it would be putting words into His mouth to extend that to all marriages. Jesus also said that there was no requirement to marry women for those who weren't castrated but were born 'eunuchs' by the hand and intent of God, which makes sense once you learn that 'eunuch' was also used at the time for those who wanted other than male-female relations. It has been argued that Jesus acknowledged such desires and exempted them from any marital obligations."

Putting away the books he had shown me, Simon recounted more scriptural thoughts. "As further contradiction against the 'one man, one woman' idea, Paul only forbade polygamy for bishops and deacons because polygamy was commonly accepted. The Bible had many instances of God blessing polygamy, so obviously the Bible didn't intend for marriage to only be between one man and one woman. Since the Bible never spoke one way or another about two men or women, it would be a sin to take one's personal preference and claim the authority to speak what God had not spoken."

With a sigh, he turned back to the reference to the Book of Genesis. "In the end though, it would be a mistake to take everything that happened in the Bible as our moral compass. In the story of Sodom that is used to claim a prohibition against male-to-male love, again, it is good that the actual text decries men raping men as a show of power. But instead, Lot offered up his underage virgin daughters to be raped rather than the visiting angels. What kind of Christians would we be if we condoned that?"

I was wholly unprepared for the imagery that Simone brought to my mind. I had still never dealt with what had happened with Saul in his office that day, and the weight of it broke through all my defenses. I broke down entirely, bursting into wracking sobs.

Simon put his arms around me, trying to steady me. "Hey, Liz, it's okay. I'm sorry, I should have been careful to help you keep your heart joyful for the sake of the baby. Is there anything I can help you with? Is there perhaps something about how you've seen a cisgendered person treated?"

I knew the term "cisgendered" meant "those who follow the cultural expectations for their gender," but I couldn't bring myself to tell him that I was having a resurgence of anger and hurt and shame over how Saul Harolds had attacked me. I had done so well in keeping it totally blocked from my mind most of the time, but once in a while, it still boiled over. So I steadied myself, and wiped away my tears as I answered, "No, I actually haven't ever really known anyone who was gay or transgender or anything."

He chuckled, helping wipe away a tear. "That you know of. Dear Liz, something's really bothering you. How about I walk with you to go see Derek off from work? Perhaps he and I can get some errands done, while Delpha helps you unburden your soul from whatever weighs down on you. Sound like a plan?"

I did always feel better when visiting with Delpha, so I agreed. On the way, he taught me another one of his prayersongs, sung twice to a verse of Rock-a-bye Baby. It went "Gone now, Gone now! Gone beyond now! Gone far beyond now! Wholeness through all!" He explained that to him, it meant moving beyond the trials and tribulations of this world, praying for Divine Love to unify all into a more perfect plan. It did help me a little, though not as much as sitting down to have a soothing cup of herbal tea with Delpha while the guys headed out to give us privacy.

"Simon's right, there is a heavy burden weighing on you, Liz. You don't have to tell me what it is if you don't want to. But would you like to see if I can help you lighten the load from your shoulders?" She refreshed my tea and then her own, managing to offer help without me feeling pressured to accept it.

I sighed, half from weariness, and half from the relaxing aroma of the hot tea. "I don't know. I mean, I just don't know if there's anything you can do. I just need to give it some time, I guess."

With a gently warm smile, she rose and moved toward the side-table. "Well, why don't we just try and find out? Let me light something up for you first, something to help take the edge off."

"Oh no, I don't smoke… anything!" My eyes had widened, and I tried to temper my alarm with politeness.

I was instantly embarrassed when Delpha laughed, bringing back a scented candle and lighting it, filling the air with soothing cinnamon and myrrh. "Well, aside from the little detail of your precious little bundle, you don't seem like the weight you're carrying is the sort you need external help from. I get the sense that there's something you've carried for a while, and don't know how to set down. Is that right?"

When I shrugged with a slight nod, she asked, "If you could let go of this pain to move forward in Peace and Love, would you?"

It was a very good question, one I wasn't sure how to answer. "I actually don't know if I would. Someone… I mean, it's silly, it's not like it's as bad as it could have been, not by a long-shot. But I really trusted him, and he tried to take advantage of me. And I wasn't in a place where I thought I could report him, so he totally got away with it. If I just let him off the hook for that, then that would be like me saying it was okay. And it wasn't."

Nodding with understanding, Delpha set aside her teacup. "I know how it can feel so much like you have to hold onto the pain to keep that memory alive, or risk letting what happened be an injustice that slips by unpunished. But Liz darling, this torment you're holding inside of you hurts only yourself, and those who love you. Rather than punish whoever wronged you, it holds that wrong inside your heart. It keeps you its victim. You have to be strong enough to take back the power over your Present Self that you have given away to whatever happened in your past. That power of presence is yours, and it's your responsibility to claim it."

I set down my teacup as those words washed over me. Delpha continued, her voice softening further. "What is not your responsibility is to make sure that the soul of another meets its judgment. Forgiveness is not absolution. They are still fully responsible for their actions. What forgiveness does is help open your heart to let go of the wounds, so love may heal you and restore your wholeness. That's why every religion I've studied teaches forgiveness as a holy commandment, both to heal the world and to edify our souls."

Seeing my face furrow up with pain and uncertainty, she reached across the table to rest her hand on mine. "Maybe there's more to it than just the thing that happened, isn't there? The way this memory makes you feel, perhaps it's a way that, deep down, you learned as a child that you deserve to feel. There's those who say we learn how we think we must experience the world while still very young, and we unconsciously re-create those experiences for the rest of our lives. That is, until we learn better. Would you like to explore that idea a little, while you are safe here with me? If it starts to become too difficult, we'll stop."

I wanted to take offense at the suggestion that I thought I deserved what happened, to tell her that she was completely wrong. But part of me agreed with her, and I wanted to face that part of me head-on. So I consented, and she had me close my eyes while she talked me through. "I'd like for you to imagine that you're in a long hallway. You're passing doors on your left, and on your right, and behind each of them are feelings that you feel throughout the day. You're not stopping at them now, you're just acknowledging that they're there for when their times come. Now, you notice at the end of the hall is another door. Behind that door, there is the feeling of what that memory makes you feel. It's not the memory, merely the feeling. As you approach the door, the feeling gets stronger and stronger."

She must have felt my hand tremble a little, so she put her other hand on my arm and gently continued, "You're not alone when you face it, so you know you are strong enough to approach the door. Do you feel the protective strength of my Love here beside you as you face this? Good, good. Now, you are standing before the door. Though the feeling is as strong as it's ever been, you also feel stronger than ever. Are you ready to open the door and step inside?"

I put my hand over hers, to hold it. "Yes, I'm ready."

I felt her fingers squeezing mine back as her soothing voice continued. "Very good, I'm proud of you. With all your strength rising up in you, you allow yourself to feel that feeling as you touch the handle, opening the door. You enter into the room, and find yourself engulfed in the space where you first experienced this feeling. Do you see where you are?"

I nodded. I did see it, all in a rushing flash of memory. I was sitting in a row, listening to a lecture by Brother Foley. I don't remember exactly what he was saying, but I remember it being something about the sins of temptation, and how women have a responsibility to be chaste and virtuous so they don't lead men astray. He was giving dire warnings about the vile things that women can lead men to do, especially if they let themselves keep bad company, or dress in anything that reveals the figure. I felt responsible and endangered and ashamed for being born female, vowing to always strive to overcome the sinful nature we are cursed to bear due to Eve's Transgression, as he told it. Then, he turned to me as an example, pointing out how I was sitting with my legs uncrossed, letting him catch a glimpse of my underwear. I sat up straight to pull at my dress as the lecture continued, but I couldn't hear it for the pounding of the blood that had rushed to my head. I felt so mortified and guilty and dirty, I wanted to cry. I think I was five years old, maybe six.

And then, in Delpha's living room, I did start to cry, hearing Delpha's soothing voice once more. "I need you to do something for me, now. I need you to see yourself in that time and place, from the perspective of who you are today. I need you to go to this girl and hold her in your arms, tell her she isn't alone in what she's faced. Let her know she isn't responsible for what happened, that it wasn't her fault. Let her know above all that she is loved. Feel yourself holding her now tightly in your arms, and also feel yourself enveloped in this warm glow of endless, Eternal Love that flows through you, giving you the strength to experience the healing away of the hurt and loneliness. And if you have a hard time believing you are deserving of such a beautiful feeling, please allow my love to encircle you, to help carry you through. Can you feel this love?"

I did feel it. Very clearly, I felt my younger self nestling desperately into my arms, hungry for my reassuring, Unconditional Love. I also clearly saw through my childlike eyes the woman I'd become, feeling the soothing balm of a pure self-love. And then, in the present, so much of the lingering hurt and shame was washed clean. It was like a rush of sunlight transcending time and space to bleach away the shadows, as though I had found a time machine to right the wrongs of so long ago.

It was a miracle. "The miracle of forgiveness," I finally whispered.

Delpha's arms enveloped me then, as I let my tears freely flow in a release of all I'd carried with me. She leaned her cheek to mine so our tears could mingle. But they were more than tears of pain from all that had happened. They were also tears of shared joy in a soul freed of the chains of self-torment that had kept it imprisoned. Despite my deep losses, I finally felt free.

I heard Delpha's gentle voice in my ear, asking, "Do you still feel any of that pain lingering in your heart?"

I reached inward, and was surprised to feel that I still had. It was a very familiar pain, though; it was the sting of self-reproach I had always felt every time I thought I might have been pretty, or even just good.

When I silently nodded, Delpha spoke to me again. "I would like you to ask a question of the pain, if you can. Can you please ask your pain what kind of help it is trying to give you?"

That sounded like an odd question at the time, yet as I asked it of myself, I found I had an answer. "It is trying to protect me from being a proud and unclean woman. It is trying to help me stay pure, so I won't be ridiculed or cast out."

I felt her hug me even more tightly, as she asked, "Are you willing to allow Love and Wisdom take over as your teachers for what you need to learn about being a Pure and Strong Woman? Can you turn that Lovingkindness inward to the pain that has taught you so much, and with gratitude for its help, allow it to move on to another place, where it needs to be?"

"I… I'm not sure. This… It's been a part of me for so long. I don't know if I'm strong enough." I kept my eyes closed, feeling just a little embarrassed. But I knew that any answer was okay, so long as it was True.

Delpha stroked my hair, reassuring me. "That's okay, you can practice for a while feeling the Love embrace you, and directing that Love to wherever the Pain dwells. Over time, your gratitude will help it finish its work within you, and then you can set it free so you both may move forward to you are needed most."

Once she put it like that, I felt like I was not just holding myself back, but also this concept of Pain. I had always believed that God sends us Trials and Tribulations to help us grow into stronger people, leading us back to Him. Could I really be holding back from His will that such Trials were needed elsewhere? Was I resisting His path to lead me to new teachings? I finally opened my eyes, looking into Delpha's with a childlike earnestness. "Delpha, I think maybe I'd better try to see if I can set the Pain free."

Her smile was warm and gentle. "Well then, Elizabeth. If you had the power to release this Pain, keeping the lessons and strength you have learned from it, would you?" The question was supportive, and I knew I could still answer no.

However, my answer had become yes. "Yes, Delpha, I would."

Giving me an even sweeter smile, she asked, "If you would not release it now, then when?"

I actually laughed just a little from the rush of positive energy. "Now. I am ready now."

Delpha gave me a small nod, then prompted, "Well then, imagine taking in a deep breath of pure, golden air, letting it swirl within you, collecting all the dirt and grime of this pain from your past. It then swirls into your heart center, ready to be released with your breath. And as you exhale, let it carry that pain outward from you, as you tell it, 'I release you, I release you, I release you.' Do this three times, and each time, gently send the past away from you with loving gratitude for the beautiful person you have become. No matter how horrible the experiences that make us feel the most upside-down, there's a reason those feelings found a home in us. Our final lesson is to let go of what happened, accepting healing for the wound inside us that allowed that pain to continue. That's we must be grateful for the lessons that pain brings us, recognizing they are separate from that pain. That way, those lessons take hold deep in our hearts, and we know we don't need to suffer in order to grow. Do you understand?"

I finished breathing out one last breath of whispering "I release you," then smiled to her my deepest gratitude. "Yes, Delpha, I understand. Thank you. Thank you so, so very much."

She took both my hands into hers. "Remember this feeling you have now. Make a strong memory of it, one you can bring back when times get difficult. Because no matter how strong the transformation, any change hits rough spots as the old patterns test you out, to see if you've really outgrown them. So when the dark times hit you again harder than ever, remember we had this conversation. Remember that yes, you really have grown, so you are absolutely ready to pass their test. To get through it, whenever you feel stressed, take a deep, healing breath. Then as you exhale, repeat to yourself, 'In this moment, there is Peace.' Then a second deep breath, exhaling 'In this moment, there is Acceptance.' And a third, 'In this moment, there is Love.' This practice works as a silent prayer to help you receive whatever it is you need in any crisis: patience, understanding, joy, forgiveness, anything you feel inspired to call for by name. It helps you accept the Reality of what is before you, freeing you to receive Peace and Wisdom to move forward. Do you think you can remember that?"

I nodded vigorously. "Oh yes, I will definitely remember that. The Elliots have been helping me try to keep myself from being miserable or stressed, so my baby's neurochemistry develops in the right balance. They've also helped me eat right and exercise safely, though Simon says you gave them most of their ideas, so I guess I have you to thank!"

Delpha's smile showed how much it meant to her to hear that. "Oh yes, well, I do tend to give advice everywhere, hoping it will take. Just keep practicing everything that seems to be helping, since happiness and calm are skills that need time and patience just like everything else. Also, I'd like to increase the frequency of your checkups, if you don't mind, to help you make sure we can take care of anything before there's an issue. I have found so many different ways to help women overcome the little speed bumps of pregnancy without having to order up chemical pills. In fact, some of the herbal and food-based formulas are getting even better, thanks to Derek's help."

She then gave me a kind of odd look before getting up to start another pot of tea. "He's a very bright young man. He's weathering the recent tragedies almost as well as you are. He's not the sort to talk much about what he's really thinking, but it's clear from our conversations that he couldn't have made it through without you. You are a source of great strength for him."

"Really? For Derek? Oh no, he's just super resilient like that. We're both still in a bit of shock, I guess. I mean, in some ways, I'm still in denial, you know? But Derek…" I trailed off, trying to think of how I could say what I felt about him. I'd always seen him as untouchable by anything.

Delpha just chuckled and brought the teapot over to join me in another round of healing tea. We started a weekly tradition like that, Simon walking me down so he could hang out with Derek, leaving me to have private time with Delpha. Then, the three of us would collect Tobey from his jobsite and we'd walk home.

Like I said before, Tobey worked as a kosher butcher. Hometown had several farmers who raised animals the way our ancestors did, tending them on open fields, where they ate their natural diet of grass and grains. The ones that Tobey selected as acceptable for food, Tobey would slaughter according to kosher rules, working in a particular technique intended to be painless and compassionate. Though this didn't always work out so well in practice, Tobey made it his mission to fulfill the spirit as well as the letter of the rules. He had a knack for making the animals seem so peaceful they could be upright while he quickly made the cuts required by his religious practices. He was so skilled, they didn't seem to feel the cuts that quickly rendered them unconscious. They certainly never revived to be consciously tortured by the slaughtering process, as I'd seen many times before in a commercial slaughterhouse.

He invited me once to watch him, and I shocked everybody by accepting. I figured, if I wasn't willing to see an animal live and die, I had no right to benefit from its death by eating its flesh. Having seen the horrors of the slaughterhouse, I was in awe of how gently Tobey worked, and the loving gratitude he gave to each animal. That said, I still wasn't sure if it was right to eat something killed for food when there was plenty of other food available. I felt Delpha had a point when she asked, "How can you ask an animal to be the last of God's creatures to die for a sandwich?"

Yet if I was ever going to eat an animal, I knew I'd feel a lot better if it had lived and died in Hometown. Even the ones that Tobey didn't prepare, they weren't killed in front of other animals, and were treated with respect until the end. Food from Hometown was available in shops elsewhere in the state, since even then we didn't need all we produced to share with one another.

See, the economy in Hometown wasn't like most cities, but was a lot more like the church community I grew up in. It was kinda like a gift economy, where we didn't keep track of payments and such. People helped each other out with what they could spare, received help in kind, and we all ended up with more than we started with. People in smaller social groups didn't keep track of what was borrowed or given, and that worked great because anybody who wasn't really trying to contribute would be noticed and helped back on track.

On a broader scale, the community rule was Full Employment. Because everyone had something they could contribute, everyone was helped to have a way to support the community and themselves. Most households with children had at least one parent who could spend much of their time at home, helping contribute with their talents as their childcare and home-keeping efforts allowed. Those who needed extra support to be able to contribute received it, such as the parents who chose to have their children play and learn with the Elliots if they weren't in school.

This dedication to helping everyone participate to the best of their wants and needs was also reflected in the way crime was handled. Non-violent crimes were brought to a committee, with each side represented by an advocate who supported them in assessing what the grievance was and what could be done about it. In most cases, all parties agreed to an equitable redress, and were given support in carrying it out. This worked out pretty well for the most part, as in almost every case the person didn't get into trouble again.

Oh sure, just as Delpha had advised me, there were some stumbles here and there as the wrongdoer struggled to overcome bad patterns. This struggle was made easier by having the whole support network to help them through. And that meant not only did Hometown not have to sink a ton of resources into policing and prison, we got to keep a community member who contributed even more than before.

As for sharing contributions among the smaller social groups, there was a more direct exchange and bartering system, rarely involving traditional money. Usually money came into Hometown from the people whose main activities were selling to and buying from the outside economy. Hoarding of anything was discouraged, since it meant nobody could use it. As we each enjoyed such a secure feeling from being a part of this supportive, sharing community, few felt the need to hoard anything. Most of us didn't need money since we could barter for what we needed, but we were all encouraged to keep some savings should we ever need it, or if we decided to move back into the larger economy.

Because of this, Derek and I found that after a few months, we had more money than when we first arrived. I received a commission from the salespeople for things I sewed while helping watch the children. Derek got a percentage from the products he'd helped Delpha make, though he sank a lot of what he made into getting more supplies to keep experimenting. We donated some money to the Hometown church, where Simon led interfaith services he called Omni-Denominational. We also set some money aside in case we made enough to pay taxes on, so we could fulfill our broader civic duty. We kept the rest in the community savings bank, helping our neighbors start new enterprises through micro-loans.

It all went by so beautifully quickly, even now it hardly seems like so much time could have passed. Before I knew it, Delpha was coaching me in how to prepare for birth, since we were expecting the baby in just a few more weeks. I'd been so caught up in the wonderful magic of feeling the little one move and kick and even seem to play when I laughed. I couldn't believe that it was almost time to meet this little miracle who was coming into my life.

Delpha told me she was sure it was a boy, but I didn't care either way. If it was a girl, I'd name her Judea, after my friend. If it was a boy, I'd name him James, after my husband's middle name. Either way, my little darling would be loved as much as any baby had ever been loved in the whole history of forever, maybe even just a little bit more.

I knew my baby had more than just Derek and me waiting eagerly to greet it; the whole town was filled with anticipation. The women had thrown a surprise baby shower, ensuring we were taken care of. Everything we could possibly need was provided, from well-worn baby clothes and toys to a little cradle one of the carpenters had made for us. I just had to laugh at the irony of having had a little resentment at used hand-me-downs as a child, yet being so deeply grateful for all that had been so generously shared with me when it was time to have my own. I placed my hand on my belly against the fierce, tiny kicks, moved to tearful joy in knowing we were among the most blessed mother and baby in the world.

Derek and I talked about whether we should try getting back to my family before the baby was born, but he made some very strong arguments for staying put. There was a lot of conflicting news coming from "the outside," as far as how bad things still were in Empire City, where the wars were going, and how bad the economy was getting. There was no safe way of finding out if the DSS might still be looking for me. Plus, I'd had issues with the pregnancy that didn't seem so bad because Delpha was helping me manage them. There wasn't any way of knowing if the trip home would cause me further issues. There in Hometown, I was healthy and safe and happy. We were happy. And he didn't want to risk doing anything that might interfere with that, not with the baby so close.

So that's how, after all my experience in the front lines of politics, going to a prestigious state college, and working in the official headquarters of one of the most powerful companies in the world, I found myself becoming a mother in exactly the same humble way my own mother had: completely natural and at home, cared for by a midwife who was also my dear friend.

I think I had an easier time of it than my mother, as I had learned self-hypnosis that helped me be calm and untroubled by pain to the point of it not really hurting. It helped that I was sitting in a pool of warm, clean water, soothing my body and soul. Derek was there with me, holding my hand and stroking my arm, supporting me and helping me rally my strength when Delpha called for it, then relax and rest in between. Forget everything I was told about the horrors and torments of childbirth being the curse brought on us for Eve's sake. Thanks to Delpha's coaching and Derek's enthusiastically stalwart support, one of the most beautiful and peaceful experiences I have ever had was giving birth to my son.

Oh, my darling son. Dear, precious, perfect little Theodore James Franklin. The first days and weeks of his tiny little life are a blur of activity in which my eyes and ears and heart beheld only him. I had heard many people say that you mustn't rush to a baby every time they cry, but I knew you couldn't spoil a baby except through neglect. Everything his tiny, innocent heart desired was granted, as I knew that for the first half-year whatever my baby wanted was what he needed. And that would hold true for the next year and a half, aside from helping teach a little patience and coping with the frustration of learning to thrive in this crazy world.

The important thing would be to listen and try to understand what he was trying to tell me, and to help him learn that I would be there to help him with whatever he needed. I knew from watching the children that those who had learned this closeness and trust were the most independent and the least clingy, while those whose parents tried over-hard to "make them stand on their own" were the most insecure. They couldn't understand and express this though; they showed it through acting out.

Of course, at only a couple of weeks old, I was already envisioning who my precious little T.J. may someday become. While I bathed and clothed his tiny body, I was daydreaming of the beautiful little man he may grow into. I sang to him often, making up soothing little lullabies that were all our own. I didn't know many of the words of the real lullabies, but I dearly wanted to sing to him, so I did my best. After I dressed him and filled his tiny belly, I crooned to soothe him to sleep.

Twinkle, twinkle little star, how I wonder what you are.
Up above the world so high, like a diamond in the sky!
Twinkle, twinkle little star, how I wonder what you are.

Sparkle, sparkle baby mine, how I love your bright sunshine.
You warm my heart with your glow, and the sweetest love I know!
Sparkle, sparkle baby mine, how I love your bright sunshine.

Twinkle, twinkle perfect star, you're my heartlight, yes you are!
You will shine so golden bright, as you sparkle through the night.
Twinkle, twinkle baby star, you're my heartlight, yes you are!

When I saw my baby's peaceful face glowing in the starlight, my heart was filled with wonder at how beautiful he was, how perfect. My heart ached with the dearest wish that Kurt could have been there to share in the joy of our dear little son.

And at that moment, I felt as though perhaps he was. My skin tingled with a glowing warmth, and my heart felt so full it spilled over into joyous tears. I was surrounded by a gentle hug of such complete and total love that I couldn't help but believe that Kurt was there with us, and would always be there to watch over us. That no matter what happened, he would help ensure everything would be okay.

My heart was so full, so overflowing with the power of Peace and Love, that I feel it again fresh as I talk about it. Even now, I feel that still, calm strength and confidence that I had lacked the courage to claim before, as though I wasn't worthy to claim my birthright just for myself. But when I looked down on that innocent little soul, I knew I couldn't fulfill my responsibilities to him unless I finally took the stands I needed to take. To be the mother I wished to be, I had to fully grow up into the woman I was created to become.

At that moment, I swore before God that I would do everything I could to make my corner of the world a better place for my son. I prayed to God to light the way before me, that I may walk where He would lead. For no matter what it may cost me, I had found my purpose. And I would let neither man nor fear turn me from my path.

Chapter 19

Love of money is an evil conquered only through sharing money in love.

"And here is the workshop, where he tinkered with old parts from the junkyard, experimenting with electricity." The caretaker of the old mini-castle was showing a small group of Europan tourists around the small structure's points of interest.

The tiny workshop was the bottom floor of the cramped two-story tower. It was the only part of the castle that provided shade, so I scrunched back up against a corner so T.J. could nap peacefully on my shoulder. I'd heard the spiel so many times, in my mind I repeated it word-for-word as the caretaker continued, "Now, this place had never been wired for electricity, but rumor has it the neighbors would be startled to see a bulb burning in the bedroom above us. There's also been a story that he was once hospitalized for a pretty bad beating, which he said was from when thugs sent from the feds or the oil companies hassling him about his mysterious source of free energy."

I looked up at the nigh-ancient auto parts and bits of copper coiling that were displayed on the walls, then down at the bottom portion of a machine that had been known as the legendary "free energy" generator. It was an old metal wheel-kinda-thing, with concrete holding a couple dozen vertical rows of V-shaped magnets, so that the inside of the wheel had just the bent inner edges poking through the concrete and the outside edges were up against each other. There was a set of four rounded pieces of metal around the inside top, like a four-leaf-clover. The inside had a central axis thing with a handle sticking up so you could crank-turn the inner part. There was apparently a piece that had set on top of it to complete it, but the story went that when the creator Ed Leedskalnin died, a shady group of men came in and took it away.

"It's a shame we don't still have his generator, Wilbur," I said softly after the visitors had left. "If we could have a world where energy was free and everybody could meet their own needs, the power wouldn't be so concentrated in the hands of those who, well, control the power." T.J. stirred at the sound of my voice, but soon drifted back off as I swayed and hummed low to him.

Wilbur smiled at T.J., then quietly replied, "I guess you never talked to anyone about their generators. Hometown is powered by a mix of biofuel generators using used oil and stuff, super-efficient solar collectors, and magnetism generators. We've got such efficient and low usage that it only takes a couple hours a day to charge our batteries. There's a few different designs on both kinds of generators, as we got a lot of tinkerers who like doing things their own ways. But once people read through the writings Ed left us and started mucking about with the wires around magnets in the iron cores, you know, stuff like that. It became a competition to find out who can make the best one."

At first, I thought he was teasing me. He was just so casual, it had to be a joke. Then, I realized he was quite serious. "Wait, do you mean that I've been surrounded by self-sustaining energy, and nobody ever told me? How does it work?"

"Energy works the same way everything in this crazy world works. It's what drives people to do things, and drives the atoms we move to do them. Attraction holds the key to true power in this world, for there is no greater law. You put up something with a strong magnetism that knows how to use it, and you've got yourself the strongest force in the universe. Combustion engines with their burning and their force, they're wasteful and polluting relics of the past, just like combustion people." Wilbur leaned back against the railing in front of the antique generator. "That's why we have such a powerful community, you know. We don't push, we don't burn. We operate out of Love, the greatest Attractor known to the human race."

"Amen." I turned to see Derek grinning at me, and then making faces and cooing as T.J. woke up with a giggle. I held on to the baby as he reached and leaned toward Derek, helping hand him over without him tumbling out of my arms.

"Well, you two enjoy your stroll, I got some raking to do." Wilbur waved bye-bye to T.J. then nodded at us both before heading off to his tool shed.

With T.J. awake, we wandered back out to look at the grey coral furnishings and sculptures we'd seen countless times in our weekly visits. Derek was pointing things out to T.J. and explaining them, telling him about how one small man cut and moved huge blocks that weighed thousands of pounds, just like the ancient Egyptians. Meanwhile, I was still trying to process what Wilbur had said, finally asking, "Derek, did you hear that some of the power in Hometown was from magnetic generators?"

"Electromagnetic, technically, but yeah. Why?" He didn't look up from having set T.J.'s hand onto the large table cut into the shape of a heart, letting the baby feel the rough surface.

I couldn't believe Derek was treating this with the same nonchalance as Wilbur. "Uh, because isn't this a big deal? Why haven't I heard about this before? Why isn't this out in the news for everybody to use? This could change everything!"

Derek just shrugged. "Not so much, Lizbet. These generators are still on a fairly small home-use scale, and work best because of the in-freaking-sane level of efficiencies built into the individual subgrids that eat off their batteries. Maybe that all could work on a larger scale, who knows. But somebody would have to sink some serious plinkage into making the try. And that ain't happening."

I tilted my head up at his pessimistic certainty. "Seriously? For such an amazing potential, why wouldn't they? Shouldn't it at least be studied?"

He chuckled, then swung T.J. around before putting him over his shoulder to walk him to the area with the carved beds and cradle. "Ha, you'd think, right? But when some tinkers around here tried to send their designs to a college for study, they were totally scoffed at. Dogmatism isn't just for religion, Lizbet; everybody's got their articles of faith. Doctors who have to go through like a decade of study and an obscene amount of money to get one of the few licenses allowed each year for entrance to the exclusive club of medical rich boys, they look at herb-work like Delpha and I do for near-free and call it dangerous quackery. Oh sure there's those who cause some harm with natural stuff, intentionally or just out of ignorance. But you know for yourself how effective it can be in the hands of those who really know what they're doing. You'd think there'd be more who use the best of both medical worlds, but even the suggestion is like this huge threat to the foundations of doctors' lives. In that same vein, scientists consider electromagnetic generators as some kind of 'free energy' fantasy-world where you'd get something for nothing. That's the physicist's quackery. They got their ideas of how energy works, that makes all their formulas nice and tidy. And those tidy little formulas say these generators are impossible, so they can't exist."

I sat down on the ledge of the bed next to where they were playing. "But if they do exist, can't they at least take a look at them? Or even just skip the study and start getting copies out to people to use? Wouldn't some company just love to market something like this? It would be the biggest thing ever!"

T.J. giggled at my enthusiasm, kicking around on the blanket Derek had set in the cradle. Derek tickled under his chin, laughing like the baby as my naivete. "There's no profit potential, Lizbet, it just ain't gonna happen. Every time someone comes up with a way for houses to decentralize power generation, energy companies scream bloody murder with their scientific and even legal attacks. I've even heard a couple seedy rumors of actual murder. The Kleptocrats know we won't keep letting them get rich offa blowing up the lasts of our mountains, poisoning our land and water, and trying to buy up the other side of the world with our cash and blood, not if we can meet our own energy needs ourselves. So they ridicule it out of one side of their mouths while making laws and regulations to stop it out of the other side of their mouths. Even if there was a way to make a ton of money off of cheap designs anybody could put together, the Unified Trust has already bought up patent rights to these types of designs. Yeah, that's pretty much what most of the bought-and-paid-for Patent Office Writs are all about these days, not just for drugs. They're a way to keep people from innovating and changing their market space, unless there's a way for some corporation to take a cut."

"But wait, couldn't people still use them for their own private use, not for profit? I mean, I remember reading somewhere that the laws allowed that, right?" I reached out and took T.J. back, as he had started fussing for his mommy. I bounced him and leaned my forehead to his, making him laugh and poke his finger into my mouth.

"Maybe technically, but that doesn't stop them from throwing lawsuits around like confetti. Seriously, every time someone tried getting a total game-changer out to the world, they are ignored or destroyed, end of story. That's why I don't want you and T.J. getting fallout from my—" He cut himself off, reaching over to tousle T.J.'s hair as though I wouldn't notice.

I pulled my mouth away from T.J.'s poking at my teeth, eying Derek warily. "From your what? Derek, what have you been up to?"

He stammered and waved his hands about, as though he could find a way to avoid answering. Finally, with a deep sigh, he admitted, "Okay, caught. I've been working on a formula with Delpha's help, which had been a side-project of mine for the past few years. Only I kept trying to use patented chemicals that were attempts to duplicate the benefits of natural sources. So now I've been able to figure out how to concentrate the natural herbs and stuff, to get a potent enough effect, without all the awful side-effects from the patented fakes. And those mice we keep, well, it looks super promising. But it's only been in successful tests for a few months. It'd take years of tests with people, and... why are you looking at me like that?"

I was giving him the look of amused patience he always earned when he enthused so much he forgot to tell me what he was talking about. Eventually he recognized that, exclaiming, "Oh, fine! I'm making like The Pill for guys, okay? Something that prevents viable, uh, germination, without hurting the, uh, germinator."

My jaw may have literally dropped. I stared at him so long, he finally stammered, "D-did I break you? Is that, I mean I know you used to not be sure about birth control, but since this is for boys, I thought... you know..."

T.J. had started to fuss again, snapping me out of my shock as I realized he was hungry. I carried him to one of the chairs and draped my scarf around us so he could eat while Derek and I spoke. You know, talking about it now, I realize that it might have seemed odd we were so comfortable like that. Since at the time some people in America were still so weird about breastfeeding, like they were only willing to see parts of a woman as strictly sexual instead of natural, let alone nourishing. And to many of those people, what they saw as sexual was inherently a naughty or shameful thing.

And that's where my thoughts turned at that time, thinking through the implications of contraceptive pills that men could take. Margie was right years earlier: my old groups never did protest men's sex issues. There were protests outside of clubs where women took their clothes off, but we were mostly hassling the women working there, not so much the male patrons. After all, we blamed the women for being impure and tempting the men to impurity, blaming the wives for not being pure enough to keep their men happy and in line. We'd had such a double standard on sexuality that I'd even found out that at Richard's theological college they had the highest subscription rates of the kinds of magazines that came in brown paper wrappers. Every attack on the legal rights of women to avoid being pregnant against their will was an easy matter of making it about protecting women's virtue, or protecting the sanctity of their eggs, or making a fertilized egg have more rights than the woman it was inside. It was never about what men do, and I couldn't imagine the Authoritarian Regime getting up in arms trying to restrict men's choices!

"Derek. This is big. This is super big. Men have just as much right to decide not to be parents as women do! If this works—" This time, he cut me off.

"Lizbet, no, there's no way this will go anywhere good. The herbs to make it are super cheap and plentiful. They're used as spices in some parts of the world; the ingredients are food. Nobody can get rich off this. Plus, it will utterly undermine the Zealous power structures out there, you know this. I know you're still pretty devout, but be honest, this is too much a part of the top guys' idea of Christianity for them to let some little guy like me mess with their setup. It would be another way people could have sex 'without having to suffer consequences' as they like to say. I'd be accused of trying to protect rapists from getting caught or something. You know how freako those people get when they feel super threatened." He actually started to get a concerned look on his face, as though he was afraid my enthusiasm could put us in danger.

I tried to soothe him. "I don't know, maybe you're right. I'll hush up about it. But keep working on the formula, okay? Just to see where it goes?"

He grinned his relief. "Oh yeah, you know me, never know when to leave well enough alone. There's a couple of Delpha's friends who have volunteered for testing. I really would feel more comfortable testing it on myself, but… uh…" He suddenly became very interested in one of the huge, brilliantly-colored lizards that lived around the castle, but couldn't be found anywhere else in Hometown.

I flushed too, though I wasn't quite sure why. I turned to let the breeze cool my face, changing the subject. "Have you decided what we should do about Christmas yet? T.J. is old enough to travel, if we think it might be safe. I feel dishonest that I never mentioned him in the notes we smuggled home. I really want them to see him."

He bit at his lip, as though chewing over my question. "I dunno. We'll have to figure out a way to ask Mark without him finding out where we're at, just in case. It's been so long though… Huh. You know, I know a couple people maybe I could ask. Boy, it'd be convenient if we had a way to get at that Gridnet."

I heard a sharp intake of breath followed by a couple quick coughs behind us, and I frightened T.J. as I started forward. I shushed him and straightened ourselves up while looking over my shoulder to see Wilbur looking at us with new eyes. He shyly brushed back his wispy grey hair in an apologetic gesture. "I'm sorry kids, I didn't mean to eavesdrop, but did y'all just mention the Gridnet?"

Derek positively bounced up onto his feet. "Why yes, yes we did! Do you have it? I mean, do you know how we could get on it?"

Wilbur just leaned on his rake, chuckling to himself as he shook his head. "Well yes and no. I got me an old fob from back when I was into that sort of thing. What I don't got is a computer to pop it into. You gotta either have a transmitter or be on a grid, and I don't got neither. But maybe…"

He screwed up his face in contemplation, his eyes darting around as he scanned through his ideas. "You know, you two kids just hold onto that question for a day or two, let me do some poking around. I know y'all got some kinda backstory, I could just see it on you. Having gotten to know you I can tell it's the sort of thing I'll want to help you with. But I'll have to go careful-like, so I'll let you know. That sound good?"

Derek pumped the caretaker's hand up and down in an eager handshake. "Sounds fantabulous, Wilbur. Well, we'll get out of your hair, time to start the trek back home. Take care, 'kay?"

I waved T.J.'s tiny fist in a bye-bye, then we headed home, talking about all sorts of everything, mostly about Judy and Kurt. It was the first anniversary of Kurt's homecoming from Arabiya, and I wondered aloud what he could possibly have done to get that tear in the lining of his dress coat that I had to mend. Derek said I'd never mentioned it, and we agreed it was long past time to pull it out of the box and hang it up, along with Judy's one elegant dress that we had with us. It would be like having them there with us as we celebrated our memories of the times we had shared.

After tucking T.J. down for a nap when we got in, we went to my room where I'd tucked my keepsakes. Kurt's note was on top; in addition to the message Karsten relayed, there were a couple more pages beginning "If you're reading this" that I quickly set aside.

I expected to have a harder time finally seeing the uniform again, but I felt an unexpectedly peaceful warmth as I traced my finger around the ribbons and medals. Then I found his Golden Heart pin tucked inside the pocket, making me brush away a few tears. "I shouldn't have let this sit so long in this box. I probably need to iron it. I wonder if I should redo the mending along this bottom edge too, since I didn't have a thread that exactly matched. See, how it… Hang on. I was sure I matched better than that. And the stitching, I couldn't have been so sloppy…"

As I picked at the loose threads, I became convinced that Kurt had gotten it restitched, maybe even did it himself. And the lining, I didn't know how to explain it, but it felt stiffer than when I'd mended it. While Derek asked what was on my mind, I went to my sewing kit and retrieved the seam ripper. Soon, I had pulled open the lining, to discover pieces of white silk with a swirly black pattern.

Looking closer, I realized it wasn't a pattern. It was tiny words. I brought it to the window for better lighting, and pulled the magnifying glass from my drawer. Softly, I read aloud to Derek, "We the People of the United States, in Order to form a more perfect Union, establish Justice, insure domestic Tranquility, provide for the common defense, promote the general Welfare, and secure the Blessings of Liberty to ourselves and our Posterity, do ordain and establish this Constitution for the United States of America."

The air fell silently electric. I couldn't read any further; my hands trembled too much to hold the magnifier. Derek slipped his arm around my waist, holding me to him as we both peered down at the text that had been put onto the silk. His breath was warm against my ear as he whispered, "Oh Kurt, you always were the clever one. This. This is the biggest of the big in the whole history of big. Lizbet, you have in your hands the soul of America, or at least the means to help us get it back. We've got to get this out there, on the Gridnet. We've got to…"

I had turned to look at him, and saw him looking at the text with boyish awe. He glowed just like the young man who had first made my toes tingle, so many years before. And when he called me Lizbet, it brought back in a rush the heady thrill I had felt when he first gave me the nickname. I was numb with all the many thoughts and feelings swirling around me. When he brought his eyes up to mine, it seemed to catch him off-guard.

After the slightest pause, he leaned toward me, barely hesitating, and just as I wondered whether I should be feeling a dizzying sense of giddiness, the door chime rang out to signal Simon's homecoming.

We both jolted back away from each other, unsure what had just happened, or about to happen. We then turned our eyes to stare at the pieces of silk I still held. I carefully re-folded them and secured them in the box before hanging up Kurt's uniform.

We shared our find with Tobey and Simon later that night, as we didn't feel it would be right to hold such dangerous contraband in their home without their consent. They were ecstatic, and insisted we walk down to tell Delpha. She was also thrilled, and started to try planning how we could get the text into a format that could be shared. Not one of them was frightened of being caught; their only concern was to try to put the keys to our government back into the hands of the People, to whom they belonged. Once we knew the truth of our heritage that was withheld from us, we could begin the struggle to reclaim it.

We all agreed we would need to wait until word from Wilbur, who came through like a champ. Within a couple of days, Derek and I were hitching a ride to the nearest fully-functioning city. A friend of Wilbur's was willing to let us use her computer, no questions asked. She left the key to her place in a hiding space, with a note on the kitchen counter that we were welcome to make ourselves at home while she spent a week out of town.

We didn't boot up the Gridnet right away. The first order of business was for me to transcribe the Constitution and store it, just in case anything happened. Derek read it aloud while I typed, with T.J. nestled happily in his portable crib.

It took a great deal of effort not to stop and discuss what we learned from this document, as there was so much in there that seemed utterly at odds with what we've observed. The most surprising thing was that this secret document said so very much within so short a space, putting some clear limitations on American government that were absolutely no longer honored. These limitations also seemed to be pretty absolute on what our government was allowed to do to anyone or anything, anywhere in the world. That is, these restrictions didn't only apply if dealing with American citizens, nor to actions taken on American soil. By the time we got to the Amendments, especially the Bill of Rights, we understood why the text was banned.

Far sooner than I'd expected, I was saving the document onto a few different types of storage media. Derek helped keep things organized, then took over when T.J. woke and needed to eat. As he started to make another copy, he shook his head for the billionth time. "No law regarding prohibiting free exercise of religion, the freedom of speech, or letting people peaceably assemble... Lizbet, we don't have any of that today. You can't even file a petition of complaint about the DSS without them using it against you as proof of suspicious activity!"

Keeping my voice hushed, I readily agreed. "Yeah, and that gets right into searches of you, your home, or even your mail without a sworn Oath from someone giving just cause for suspicion. Let alone a Warrant describing exactly the person, place and things allowed to be searched. You can't take five steps in America without a cop claiming total free reign to go through all your stuff if he feels like he doesn't like the look of you." I hugged T.J. closer to me, as though to protect him from the dangerous injustice.

Derek chuckled darkly. "Or likes the look of you, and wants to see more. That doesn't even get into the whole project Mark is a part of, where they search and seize people's every single thought, sometimes even before they get to think it."

I bit my lip. "Derek, can we be sure this is for real? I mean, I know Sammy was part of a tradition to preserve knowledge others tried to bury, but how do we know this is for serious real? It doesn't even talk about the United States becoming the Incorporated States. Wouldn't that have to be in the Constitution?"

He shrugged. "That's a good question. I'm going to figure it's probably real, because Kurt wouldn't have gone to so much trouble if he wasn't sure. He was always the smart one, he just didn't have my opportunities. I still wish I could have…"

Derek was lost in thought for just a moment before he shook his head. "In any event, the Incorporation of the States I think happened during the Great Receivership, which I got the chance to read about on Gridnet before Tricia took off with it. Oh, don't give me that look, you got no right to be surprised I snuck-a-peeked. Anyway, there was this long economic downturn, then a few years of not-so-bad, and then shapow! Bad again. But the top banksters figured out a way to make a huge ton of money by luring or even tricking people into really bad loans they couldn't pay, like that student loan thing except for homes and stuff. If people seemed like easy targets, like minorities, they even steered them into high-rates loans even if they should have qualified for better ones. The banks then conned investors into taking these bad loans off their hands, with securities and default swaps and all sorts of jargon."

He waved his hand dismissively at the "shenanigans" he described. "These loans weren't backed by actual money, since the banks don't actually have to have the money they're loaning. The money they do need, they get fabricated at rock-bottom prices from the government. The departments whose job it was to set the interest rates and currencies were so bad, they'd peg a wrong value for something to help out their buddy in exchange for day-old sushi. Yep, destroy the retirement plan of an entire city, just for a shot at food poisoning. It was that corrupt. So for years, the whole economy in America and other places was propped up by this fake money that people held as debt, being jerked around by, well, jerks. And then this President guy comes along and guts what's left of the real economy by slashing taxes and regulations so all his rich buddies got to pocket even more, leaving everybody else with less and less. The ones who made out the best were the War Profiteers, since this was the grandson of that guy Kurt talked about, with the money to the Nazis and trying to assassinate the president. Anyway, that later President and his Assistant President or whatever had a ton of money invested into warmongering, and they were in a position to increase those investments. That's when the wars in Arabiya really got started."

I nodded, lost for a few moments in the memory of Kurt's arms around me as he had told me of similar things. "So let me guess, then it all came crashing down?"

Derek snapped his fingers, startling T.J. with his exclamation. "Bingo! Whoops, sorry champ. But yeah, the economy totally tanked, and people couldn't repay the bogus loans. Even people who shouldn't have been evicted were foreclosed on using fraudulent and illegal actions by the banks, hundreds of thousands of them. Because you'd think those banksters would have to eat up their bad bets, right? Nah, that's why they're called Kleptocrats. Their inside guy at the Treasury finagled free money and impunity for their crimes, bailing them out with tax money from the suckers they'd preyed on to begin with. The Treasury guy 'loaned' them more money than all of America made in a year, it was that much of a scam. The American Bank was mandated to manipulate the currency in a way that fulfilled just three Prime Directives: minimize inflation while maximizing price stability, and strive toward Full Employment. He did the opposite, straight up and down. It'd be a beautiful con if it weren't so ugly. The next president was just as bad, making sure they not only didn't have to answer for their crimes, but got to keep on doing the same kinds of raw deals."

I blinked at that, taken aback. "You mean, they went right back to the same shenanigans? And people let them?"

He shrugged. "How could they be stopped? Oh there was protests and stuff, but really, most people were too busy trying not to starve or freeze to death, or keep from getting rounded up and thrown in jail for complaining. See, if America was run like a business, that's when they would have incurred productive debt to help make sure people were put back up on their feet to start producing again. You know, like a few years ago when my dad's pharmacy had that accident, and he had to take out a business loan to fix stuff and upgrade and retrain the staff, and all that. Now the pharmacy is running better than ever and making enough to pay it all off. Because that's what a business does."

Shaking his head, he continued, "But nah, they weren't serious about keeping America on her feet. Instead, the Kleptocrats whined and moaned about having to pay their fair share while they paid little or no taxes, at the same time insisting that government programs be gutted instead of actually helping their workers get the economy up and running again. These tenderpreneurs got rich off government-tendered projects and used that money to whip people up into frothing at the mouth how evil government programs were. So when the huge crash came, they said there was just nothing left, America was broke. It was a lie, but enough people believed it that they got seriously scared they couldn't keep spending more on warmongering than the rest of the world combined."

I started to catch up, chiming in, "And that's when we got the Resources and Austerities for the War Deal. I see it now: that helped them buy up the rest of America's resources for pennies. At the same time, they ended most of the remaining social programs that would help us stand on our own feet and support ourselves, rather than slaving away for their scraps. Like you said, it would be brilliant, except for what a nightmare it's all become."

Nodding in agreement, Derek scratched his cheek. "Yeah, that would be when each state got Incorporated and sometimes merged, with private investors and such running the boards. The President of the United States of America became CEO of the Incorporated States of America. But it's not in the Constitution, so I guess Kurt's and my speculation that this all may not be technically legal may have been right." He paused, watching me stare at him. "What?"

"Kurt's and your what? You mean Kurt knew about all this too and didn't say anything?" I slugged his shoulder.

Derek shrugged defensively. "Hey, bros gotta have their secrets, you know? I think he meant to talk to you about it, but then the Meltdown, and… Yikes, I just remembered the Gridnet! We better get crack-a-lackin."

I juggled T.J. while getting the storage media secured and ready to go. Derek made sure the computer was completely disconnected and offline. I then pulled up a chair and watched as he connected the fob, and followed the instructions we'd memorized for bringing it online. We then held our breath, hoping it would work. Privately, I was also hoping that my gut instinct about a secret identity would reconnect me with an old friend.

We weren't disappointed.

As soon as we logged in, we were greeted with a message:

```
BQ> Radiant? For serious real?

Radiant> This is a friend of Radiant's. You and
    I talked before, or at least, I was there
    while you talked to a friend. I'm looking for
    Prometheus. You can tell her it's Betsy Ross.

BQ> Taking a break from sewing stars? Hang on.

BQ> Huh, whaddya know, Prometheus actually
    knows who you mean. Sec.

Prometheus> If this is really Betsy Ross, when
    did I first hug you?

Radiant> Church picnic, but what had I just
    done?

Prometheus> Oh my goodness, it really is you!
    You just gave the most fantastic prayer, that
    showed me who you really are. It's me, it
    really is! How have you been?! I heard about
    K, I'm so sorry. Wish we could find out what
    happened. Give us time. And J, gosh, I'm so
    sorry. I've missed you all so much. Are you
    and D okay?

Radiant> Yes, we're fine. Look, I have a file
    that you all are absolutely going to want for
    your library. I also have some other things
    that D says won't go anywhere but I disagree.
    Is it safe to come out?

Prometheus> Yeah actually I've been looking for
    you for a couple weeks. So much has been
    going on, and our mutual friend got a message
    to me that he's effectively scrubbed you off
    any lists. So, perfect timing.
```

```
Radiant> Oh that's wonderful! I wanted to be
    home for Xmas. Will you be there?
Prometheus> Uh, hm. I better not. But tell you
    what. You and me, we can meet somewhere along
    the way. How can I reach you?
```

We made our arrangements quickly, as Trish only had a short time. Derek then took us back to the Offnet so he could show me the part of American History talking about the Great Receivership and the transformation of the United States into the Incorporated States. And yeah, we didn't see anything about the change being voted into the Constitution, so Derek could have been right about it not being technically legal.

We then followed a link to an article talking more about the Receivership, comparing it to the Great Depression. The parallels were just eerie. Both started with the same levels of income disparity, and at both times there was ecological catastrophe that made things worse. Around the time of the Depression, there was a massive drought in America's heartland, and the devastation had a rippling effect across the country. The Receivership was during the massive Destruction and Erosion of Nature Inflicted by Adulteration and Looting of Resources. You know, when the planet still had things like wild polar bears, which suffered when the glaciers started disappearing. Even their olden-days version of the DSS called ecological destruction their National Security Threat Number One, but the government still didn't do anything to fix it.

The article went on to show more similarities in what led to the Receivership and the Depression, but huge differences in how they were handled. Both started off with the President being put under pressure by the bankers stoking up panic attacks over the government not being able to fulfill its financial obligations. Those same bankers put most their investments into securities backed by the government, so they were obviously big liars, but people still fell for it. They demanded a debt-neutral balanced budget, but instead of making everybody pay their share of taxes and such, they wanted a hollowing-out of the programs people needed to get back on their feet, like Derek had talked about.

And under the Receivership, they got their wish. The government pretty much destroyed what the Gridnet called the Inalienables. The Inalienable Programs helped Americans find what they needed for

Life, Liberty and the Pursuit of Happiness. The most basics were the CareFund and Public Pension, which at the time were guaranteed to provide benefits to all those who paid into the funds when they became aged or disabled. The benefits were modest, but apparently they meant the difference between survival and starvation for most of the disabled, elderly, and even children.

Only CareFund and the Public Pension survived in any form, and those were turned over to private companies that sucked out fat commissions and fees, leaving less for the people who had a right to those benefits. The Pension was hooked into the stock market casino, where most people lost money and literally were left in the dirt. A lot of public employees still got to keep their healthcare and pension benefits for a while, until the bankers got the public to insist they suffer as bad as everybody else. Then, those funds were also looted.

Once the public had no more resources to loot, and employment regulations were pretty much gone, only then did the jobs start to be brought back from overseas. But they weren't the same ones that left. Instead, they were low on pay and high on demands, treating American workers with the same exploitation and abuse that corporations once had to go to third-world countries to get away with.

And that's how the Great Depression was different. Instead of profiting off the devastation, the leadership of America helped get us back on track. That time, the President was the one that Smedley Butler had claimed was plotted against by a cabal that included the grandfather of the President of the Great Receivership. Freaky coincidence, huh?

Anyway, the Depression President spoke out against the bankers, calling them "unscrupulous money changers" and talking about how they "fled from their high seats in the temple of our civilization" while he worked to fix the catastrophe they caused. Instead of giving the fraudsters even more money and immunity, he closed all the banks for a few days, and only the sound ones were re-opened with supervision and secure loans. The rest were merged, and the depositors got back 86% or more instead of just losing their money. Regulations were put into place to prevent banks from ever destroying the economy again, until those laws were repealed and then the Receivership happened, of course.

Like I said, at first the Depression President did cut support programs and balance the budget in our time of need, but it quickly became clear it was just deepening the problems. He accused the bankers of trying to make things worse so he'd be blamed for it and they could appear as rescuers while they enslaved America to their personal interests. Taking a stand against the Sixty Families that owned the economy, he pushed through the Inalienables programs that got America working again, in every sense of the word. Full employment was the goal, much of it through rebuilding the infrastructure we needed to succeed. The idea was that once people were helped back up on their feet to start producing and consuming again, the profits and tax revenues and all the other economic lifeblood would again flow.

And you know what? His bet paid off, because as the productivity and tax dollars came back up, America recovered stronger than ever. The article linked to a debate regarding how much the world war of the time aided that recovery, but most agreed that the support structures of the Inalienables programs are what laid the solid foundations America needed to regain its strength. It also helped that the tax structure was set up a lot like the ideals that were talked about back in Acculturation, where those who got to reap the greatest rewards of American enterprise repaid that benefit in the form of higher taxes on the top slices of their income.

To help working Americans stay productive, that's also when the laws were passed that helped workers pool their collective bargaining power and unionize. They won protections such as a forty-hour work week, a minimum wage designed to be a livable wage, programs that helped the jobless get back to work, and bans on child labor. All these things and more helped ensure a safe working environment that supported their health and well-being, and got a lot more productivity per workweek. By working together, they were able to stand up for themselves against greedy or even just ignorant employers who would take advantage. This raised the floor of what was considered acceptable even for those who weren't in unions, so everybody benefited.

It all sounded like a fairy tale, given how the dismantling of those programs helped create the Great Receivership. The worst was how the Kleptocrats eventually made it illegal for workers to refuse to work in a Strike, especially if it was to support workers in another company or industry. It was like we were their slaves, and didn't have the right to help each other out. Even laws that stayed on the books were routinely ignored by companies who got away with it, while workers who disobeyed them were rounded up and hit with massive fines or jail sentences. Meanwhile, the companies were shielded from lawsuits to make them honor their responsibilities for their products that hurt people, because of so-called "tort reform." No matter how hard and honestly people worked, if a company felt like firing them, God help them get back up on their feet. Because America wouldn't.

When Derek and I finally finished reading, we were wide awake in the middle of the night, contemplating the future. We saw how things had gotten worse from the Great Receivership, poised to take an even greater plunge due to the same causes. It seemed like our whole economic structure was going to keep repeating the same tragedies over and over.

Derek spoke up first. "I guess that's just the problem with Capitalism, when it's set up so that the only real freedom is to make yourself richer and hang everybody else. It's human nature to always be greedy and want more, Lizbet, there's nothing we can do to change that." He was rubbing my shoulders, keeping his voice hushed so as not to disturb T.J.'s peaceful rest in the next room.

I sighed, both at the release of tension in my shoulders and the buildup of tension in my heart. "That's the thing, I don't believe that's human nature. I just think that's what happens when the whole system is set up to only reward greed. Maybe it's time we moved away from Capitalism. No, I don't mean full-on Socialism or even Communism, and not just because those words have a bad reputation. I mean because the way I understand them, those are just other ways of trying to focus on how to move money around, with money itself being the focus of how resources are shared among compartmentalized groups. But that's the backwards way of looking at it, if you ask me."

Derek led me to the couch where he could give a better back-rub, scolding me for my tension before asking, "Okay, so what's the right way of looking at it?"

I bit back a yelp as he hit a sore knot under my shoulder blade, then took a breath while I gathered my thoughts. "Well, I've been feeling that out. Way back when we first met, Mark walked me through how every little thing that Happy Animal Farm did had a deep impact rippling all throughout the world. He was always showing me how even though we like to try to compartmentalize things and pretend they can be separated, you can't really touch one thing without affecting the rest of the system. It's not just a point of religious Faith to say that we are all One Wholeness in God's creation. We really and truly are all integral parts of the same system."

"Fellow cosmonauts on the great Spaceship Earth, as old Bucky Fuller liked to say. And dear holy yikesmas, Lizbet, are you going for a Knot-Tying badge with your muscles, or what?" Derek ground his thumb down my spine, making me cringe.

"Hey, care—ow! Gentle, please! Now what were you saying about Bucky Who?" The name sounded vaguely familiar, maybe from one of the conversations he had with Tobey while I was talking with Simon.

Derek did massage more gently as he tried to fill me in. "Buckminster Fuller, he's the guy who inspired the geodesic domes Hometown is built with. Tobey also lent me Bucky's Synergetics books, where he tried to explain what you're talking about, the interconnections of everything. The best way I can put it is that he had this thought that whole systems behave in ways you can't predict from just trying to change one part of it, especially since people are both observers and participants in ways we don't always understand. So on the grand scale, this Synergetics talks about the interrelations of everything from, I dunno, chemistry to theology to how to bake the best veggie pot pie."

He sighed at the thought of his favorite food, then returned to absently rubbing my neck. "Well anyway, one thing he liked was his idea of ephemeralization, or doing more with less. He figured we could use technological advancements and efficiencies in ways that will help people enjoy more out of life while using fewer resources, raising us all up with less cost to the overall system. He said that this kind of Utopia would only work if everybody cooperates together, excluding nobody, since we all are part of the same system. This was totally backed up by the other book he loaned me, Mutual Aid something-or-other by this Kropotkin guy. He had all this empirical evidence about how cooperation rather than competition is the driving force in winning at Natural Selection. Even Darwin had said that the groups with the most cooperative members were the most successful."

I sat up straight, turning to face Derek with hushed excitement. "That's it! That's how we need to rebuild the economy, from whole cloth! We need to stop talking about costs and benefits just in terms of prices and profits, but look at the whole picture broken down the way Mark did for me. You know, put number values on all the impacts, being totally honest about what we take as well as what we give. That way we can see where we're helping versus hurting, and heal the whole system!"

He grinned at my excitement, even if he didn't quite share it.

"What will we call it, Fantasticalism? Because you know there's no way the Economic Overlords will be honest about taking so much more than they give. Not even in their own heads. They've owned the conversation for way more than you and I have been alive; there's not even a vocabulary for peoples' brains to process your idea. Definitely not the people in charge. Remember, people trust the Authorities, and if the Authorities say there's nothing we can do, they'll hang their heads and accept that. You'll just sound like one more crazy person trying to up-end a system people know is broken, but are too jaded to fix."

I took his hands, gripping them as I quickly shooed away his cynicism. "See, I don't care about that anymore. I know most Americans are used to entrusting Authorities with almost everything. I understand that, because that's still my impulse too. But in Hometown, they didn't wait for someone to tell them they should build domes so they could survive in that storm-torn area. Or for someone to tell them their generators were possible. You didn't wait for someone to tell you it was okay to try to help men take control of their bodies and not become fathers if they're not ready."

As I spoke, my enthusiasm grew, along with my resolution. I watched as Derek's cynical grin grew to a genuine smile, before softening to something a little more wry. I barely had time to wonder what he was thinking before he showed me.

"Then I guess I better stop waiting for permission to tell you how very much I love you. How much I've always loved you." He pulled my hands toward him as he leaned forward and kissed me, tentatively but sincerely.

When I didn't pull away, the kiss became more deeply tender, until he pulled back. He didn't pull far, however, resting his forehead against mine. "I've loved you since we were kids, I just knew you were way out of my league. That summer when I realized we'd be on Student Council together, I thought it'd be hard to see you every day, as though feeling about you the way I did would be betraying my love for Judy."

I looked up to him with pained concern, to which he responded with a quick kiss on my nose. "Oh, don't worry about it, we were fine. Judy knew I had a crush on you and she thought it was hilarious. We both knew I'd never have a shot even if I was single. You know I can never keep a secret. Well okay, except for this one, but only from you. Me and Kurt used to talk about you – very respectfully, I swear!

Anyway, he made me promise that if anything ever happened, I'd look after you. He didn't have to ask me twice. Hey, don't laugh, I'm serious!"

Reaching up to touch his cheek, I tried but failed to stop chuckling. "Me too."

I then put my lips to his, and we showed each other how passionately serious we were.

Chapter 20

All that hate and greed need to triumph is for love to lack the courage to confront them.

"I'm calling it Synergism." I tried to restrain my excitement over my own idea so I could focus on trying to explain it. "When two things have synergy, it allows one and one to merge, becoming greater than just two. This is important because of how Capitalism has become idolatrous, making the Love of Money more important than Loving One Another. It has gone from being a noble pursuit of happiness to a worship of wealth for wealth's sake. Now, it's considered a company's legal duty to slash and burn everything for a quick buck."

I took a breath, using the pause to recall the words I'd rehearsed. "The concept of Synergism recognizes that money is just one unit of measuring all the various energy exchanges going on all the time. Costs and Benefits are assessed by their true values, without hiding them behind the balance sheet in a shell game that socializes risk and privatizes profit. I mean, you can only have a Realistic Economy if you have the courage to focus on the things that have Real Value: time, energy, skills, natural resources. Money is only a symbol that represents those things, and only has as much value as our belief in its myth. Unless we reclaim the power we've given money and put it back into real values, it will keep its power over us."

I smacked my hand down onto the table to make my point, making Margie laugh out loud. "Oh, Elizabeth. If someone had told me that the shy young woman who apologized for picketing my clinic would someday be pitching a new approach to integrative economic theory, I'd have asked them to pour me another one."

Derek then echoed joined in the laughter, making T.J. laugh as well. That prompted him to tickle the baby while he enthused, "That's just memetastic, Liz, it really is. I can't wait to see your Synergism show up as the top trending hashtag. I'll post the first pic of the laughing baby to support it!"

I rolled my eyes, then couldn't help but laugh, myself, as Derek held up T.J. with an expression that exactly matched the baby's silly, giggling face. I snatched up my baby and cuddled him to my shoulder, while Derek reached over to ticklishly trace the chain of the necklace he'd given me for Valentine's Day.

Margie just smiled at us for a moment, then became thoughtful. "Well, you're right that we can't wait for this to be led from the top down. Not while the biggest fight in Congress is over whether they can afford to help treat the people who have cancer from helping clean up and rebuild the Reactor. They'd rather spend all that money on repairs, and covering the investors' losses, since the insurers are denying coverage on the grounds they hadn't properly maintained their facilities. Heaven forfend those investors be forced to shoulder their own debts like the rest of us."

She shook her head, sighing as she stuck to our topic. "I'm not sure how we'll work this into platform stumps, but I do know Adam will be interested. If we're going to win the Pragmatican nomination, we're going to have to stand up and fight like Principalians. Everybody knows if the Pragmatican primary is won by just another closet Puritan, only the Harolds voters are going to hit the polls on Voting Day."

Of course she was right. Saul Harolds had run unopposed in the Puritanic primary, thanks to how the ACL had whipped up the Regressive movement. While most of the Pragmaticans had started to talk and act like Puritans to avoid the ACL attack dogs, Adam Diego had remained one of the few voices willing to stand on principle. Because we had Adam's fighting spirit to rally folks together, the Principalian voting bloc was more energized than ever before. Now that Margie and I were working together to build on our past experience, we felt we had a real shot at winning both the primary and the election for Governor.

Yeah, we weren't dreaming small dreams, there. I wasn't just helping out on the campaign out of a sense of obligation to make up for helping Harolds win his first real election. It wasn't driven by some kind of misguided sense revenge, either; I really had disentangled him from my karma. Not to say I wasn't above sending him a little warning that I still had his notes and voicemails, once I found out his campaign planned to try to smear Adam with lies regarding his treatment of female staffers.

What really drove me was my new-found sense of purpose. Ever since the Reactor Meltdown, I saw how there were more and more people in need, and fewer people willing to stand up for them. Those who tried to throw a monkey wrench into the gears of jingoistic opportunism were instantly attacked as Commies or Spies.

When facing tough times, I still believe the only Patriotic thing to do is stand up for our fellow human beings no matter who stands against us. If taking action means harassment and threats from the foot-soldiers of our adversary, then so be it. Our conscience must be spoken through our actions, not silenced by fear of adversity. Once you conquer your fear, you'll be surprised what greatness you're capable of.

My direct actions were focused on my greatest strength: a good old-fashioned get-out-the-vote. Part of this involved helping the population segments that were targeted by the Voter ID requirements, usually via aid in getting their ID or mail-in ballots. I had started working with contacts via the Gridnet, where people helped navigate the land mines that had been enacted in an attempt to destroy the democratic process. Soon, we had very professional fliers and advertisements via the Innernet, broadcasting, anything we could use to get the word out to the most vulnerable Members. They also helped nail down how to communicate our message in a way that helped those Members see that we're out there fighting for them, and needed their help to win.

We called our platform the Fair Deal, as it built on old efforts by a Post-Depression president who used that slogan for his efforts. The first plank was the Depression President's Economic Bill of Rights, guaranteeing that each person was secured their most basic human rights. Meaning: employment with a living wage, trade free from monopolistic and unfair competition, housing, medical care, education, and adequate support when one becomes aged, disabled, or loses their job. These were the bare minimums needed to secure the Inalienable Rights to Life, Liberty and the Pursuit of Happiness.

Thanks to volunteer efforts, we had several print and media presentations that made it obvious how these Inalienable Rights were being trampled, and what simple solutions could bring them back. Unfortunately, we had a hard time getting that message out before a broad audience. Almost all of the major media channels were still owned by just a few people, and they didn't want much news to get out there about Diego's candidacy and what we stood for. It just didn't fit their Hegelian Dialectic. They couldn't have people realizing that there was a productive middle-ground solution to all their manufactured problems.

That all changed when we started making news they couldn't keep the public from hearing about.

At the end of another long planning session with Adam Diego, he shared my enthusiasm, but was becoming weary. "The problem we're facing, Elizabeth, is that it's difficult for people to envision our ideas as possible in actual practice. They just don't know what a society like this would look like. So it sounds either like an impossible fairy tale, a strange and therefore nightmarish enigma, or both. In this realm of uncertainty, the comforting Authority of tradition will nearly always win out. The traditional voices insist that the only way for an economy to flourish is to give companies free reign to do as they please. Otherwise, you risk being called Anti-Business, which is synonymous with Anti-American."

His weariness only spurred me on, making me excited to share my news. "You're exactly right! And that's why we're going to show them! Go on, Cass, tell him your plan."

Cassandra gave me a sly smile. "Your plan, you silly. Don't give me all the credit! Mister Diego, I don't think I mentioned this, but my aunt is Meg Cole. Yes, she's planning to stay in Europa until this trickle of bad and worse news dies down about what she might have known about the Meltdown. Further, you know the family is distancing itself from physical holdings in America that have drawn protesters and camera crews. For example, the 'Liberate Gail Stewart' movement that has had roughly a dozen people arrested every day for the past couple months at the site of the old Headquarters, even though the government still won't admit they have her. Are you with me so far?"

Adam nodded. "Yes, but I'm not sure what you're suggesting. Do you want to get us involved in the Liberate movements? Because they've been decisively apolitical thus far, and I support that."

Cass waved her hands back and forth, surprised at his suggestion. "Oh no, that's not it. What I mean is, the family put all the land around the old H.Q. for sale. After calling in some help and getting a hefty family discount, I bought it. Like, the whole town. The farmland, the buildings, pretty much everything."

While Adam took that in, I started to lay out our plan. "Remember Darwin's theory that the most successful groups were isolated from competition, or had the most efficient cooperation within its members? Well what if we had both? The town's been struggling since the office left, and there's all this farmland not doing anything. So what if we incorporated it as an actual city, building a showcase for cooperative Synergism?"

Seeing Adam's mind trying to piece together the implications, I tried to connect the dots. "Businesses would be encouraged to offer livable wages, with major incentives for worker-owned or cooperative businesses. We'd definitely work toward full employment. Policing would be community-based with a force made up of people who live there; you know, a good-neighbor environment. Oh, and we have some insurance and health professionals designing the City Health Plan, which will allow everybody to buy into a CareFund-style system that will be the only insurance payer for care within city limits. With a focus on cost-effective preventative and holistic care, we can actually charge lower average premiums and still get people taken care of."

Now, Adam's eyes had lit up. "Ambitious! If even half of all that works, it will certainly be a concrete example of how to put our principles in action." The reservations quickly set in, however. "Hm, but we only have a few months before the primary. It'll be great for the long-term, but not really for hitting our campaign goals this month. Could that idea take hold in time to get the message out before the primary? One little town won't make big news."

Cassandra flashed me a conspiratorial smile, which I returned as I quietly confided to Adam, "It might, if it's announced as a state-by-state network of Constitution Cities." Seeing his curiosity most definitely piqued, I continued. "I've got a network of friends all across the country, and there's several interested groups of various sizes who plan to launch bids to incorporate their areas as the cities named after the American Constitution. A lot of them aren't fans of government as an institution, but we've come together in agreeing that there's things we need to do together that we can only do through a governmental structure. So we're finding the Synergy in our varying viewpoints to design a city structure that will help us meet our goals."

I paused while Cass giggled a bit, remembering the many, many long and heated discussions the groups had regarding those different approaches. After a brief chuckle of my own, I finished relaying our plan. "The Constitution City in our state will be the flagship, named for the foundation of our country that we're free to know about, but not free to actually read. Not only will these cities serve as a reminder of the importance of that forgotten document, they will be a living example of the prosperity America enjoys when we live up to our responsibility to support the Inalienable Rights to Life, Liberty and the Pursuit of Happiness."

Adam responded with a low whistle. "You're playing with fire here, you do realize?"

I knew he meant that as a warning, but it did nothing to sway me. "It takes fire to light a candle. I'm no longer willing to hide my light in the darkness for fear of getting burned."

A slow smile spread across Adam's face, widening into a grin. "Me neither. All right, just let me know what I can do to help you two, though it sounds like you've got it all planned. Maybe I can launch an announcement from the new city hall, see if we can't enjoy some Synergism among our goals."

Thanks to the groundwork we'd laid, things came together quickly and smoothly. We had collaboration across the Gridnet, and even more widely on the Innernet. We were lucky in that the town had plenty of empty space for businesses and housing, but it was still miraculous in how quickly the spaces were filled. We had to agree to some pretty clear noise and nuisance guidelines so people were clear on what constituted being respectful of everyone's right to enjoy our neighborhood. This was especially crucial because so much of the housing was in multi-family buildings with shared walls. For the most part everyone was serious about helping build the best community we could possibly create, so the growing pains weren't too bad.

Speaking of growing, one of the first enterprises was starting to get the fields plowed and planted, so we could start growing the heirloom seeds that had been donated from conservationists across the state. Since crops would take time, Delpha sourced delicious, healthy ingredients to start a line of products that would be produced in small batches in homes that were certified for production.

We knew we'd have a tough time communicating to our customers just how healthy they were though, as Happy Animal Farm and its cohorts had made it illegal to even label that food was not subjected to Genetic Modifications, treated with pesticides or hormones, or any other unnatural practice. Derek was the one who insisted we just call it HOME-made: Heirloom Only Modification-free Edibles. And he designed a label saying, "The federal government disallows products to list their ingredients as free from insecticides and untouched by DNA-tinkering. We at HOME-made are as serious about honoring federal law as we are about honoring the well-being of you and your family. Each ingredient reflects how Nature intended you to enjoy Her bounty. Please eat in good health."

More immediately though, the town started off with vital institutions in place, like the Constitution City Credit Union. As a public bank, the city could manage its own funds at a profit rather than losing money to private investors. Community members were also able to benefit from a stable banking facility with only enough fees to cover expenses, rather than pad out exorbitant profit margins. A highly popular and successful micro-credit program started there, and we offered short-term loans to replace the predatory payday loans and check cashing shops that kept the poor of other cities poorer.

These micro-loans were especially useful for residents establishing the early businesses that helped us toward our goal of full employment at liveable wages. The city laws held a requirement for annual audits of the costs and benefits of different industries and business practices, making adjustments where needed to sustain Synergism. Since it was illegal by state law to pass ordinances requiring a minimum wage or basic standards of decency, we had to use the tax-and-subsidy codes to ensure that anybody who violated those basic standards were paying back the costs they were passing on to the community. Companies who shirked their responsibilities toward their workers and shifted that burden onto the community were fined accordingly. Meanwhile, incentives and tax breaks were given to worker-owned companies, cooperatives, and Benefit Corporations, which were required by law to create a general benefit, rather than maximize profits for their shareholders by sacrificing everybody else. This brought further stable, sustainable jobs and businesses, which meant a pretty decent tax revenue to the city. This revenue was naturally invested back into the community, repaying the group as a whole for its contributions to that success.

The first investments were keyed to move us toward a zero-waste, self-sustaining community. On an individual level, homes and businesses were equipped to meet their own utility needs and reduce reliance on the utility companies. With whitepainting or gardens and water collections on roofs, solar linings on windows, grey water and composting setups, plus rollouts of the Hometown generator systems, it all added up to ultra-self-efficiency.

From Day One, there were plans for decentralized water purification systems that enabled many homes to recycle some of their own water in addition to more efficient use. Recycling was universal, with re-usable items cleaned up and put back to work by our shops, artists and industries. We also had started work to install a donated decomposition plant that would completely break down items into their component substances and chemicals to re-use or sell, giving us a lucrative revenue stream. Also, the water purification systems were designed to generate their own power, plus a little extra to give back into the grid.

And that leads to our biggest coup: how we managed to recapture public services and utilities. Our charter did state that they had to be serviced by private corporations, as required by federal law. However, we also required these corporations to have a majority interest owned by the Constitution City Credit Union, including majority voting rights. Water, power, transportation, Innernet – all utilities were guaranteed to be available to our residents or employees at cost, plus a very modest margin. There was a tiny percentage tax added to these bills that was given as subsidies to the utility companies in accordance with federal requirements, and we ensured companies would use those subsidies to write off amounts owed by residents who needed extra assistance.

We knew we would get sued by the big utility companies and other forces who wanted to try to force us to let them come in and extort our residents. The expertise of our legal advisors fended them off when they came for us, turning their own tactics against them and keeping their complaints tied up in the court systems. These advisors even helped us establish a free school system modeled on those of Northeast-Europa, where standardized testing was replaced by a highly competitive teaching profession. Each teacher was ensured to have the training and support required to tailor curricula to the needs of their students. The result was intelligent, curious kids who were ready and eager to learn.

Now of course we didn't have that all in place on the first day. Even the time-bank trading network among members of all the Constitution Cities took a while to get synched up. Thanks to all the groundwork though, it wasn't long at all before the first families had moved in and we had elected our first City Council. Immediately afterward, we held our first General Assembly at the City Center.

We passed all of the first acts of the city government by unanimous vote, including requirements that all elections be fully public-funded, so private money couldn't buy our democracy. Along those lines, we also set up Public Panels of randomly selected residents who would be tasked with writing up all future summaries for voting measures, after having received information and testimony from all sides. We planned to have similar panels create Public Announcement spots to inform voters for all elections. This was like a form of Demarchy, something the Gridnet had recorded from older American communities.

Finally, we were down to just one proposal, the one we knew would make the most waves. As the woman who had made it all possible, we had decided Cassandra would have the honor of bringing it up for a vote. She knew it would give her family fits, but she didn't ask their permission.

"As my best friend once told me, you must never wait for permission to do the right thing. And she's right. If everybody waited for some authority to tell them it was okay to take a stand, we'd still be a colony of a foreign power. We would still have an America where whites owned blacks and women couldn't vote." Cassandra paused with a smile and rested her hands on the podium, as applause and a few "amens" were heard from the crowd.

With a nod to the crowd's support, her voice grew stronger. "America was built, and is continually rebuilt by those willing to take a stand for what they believe in. Now, I understand how hard it is to take that stand. There are so many voices out there telling us to keep our head down. Telling us to know our place and do as we're told. Telling us to quiet our voices so as not to disturb the Serious People who think they know best how to run our lives. But I have kept my voice silent for too long, as I watched as my brothers and sisters in America struggle harder and harder while being granted less than they needed to simply live. All while I and my family have been reaping more than our share, as though there could never be enough to satisfy our hunger. And now I say, enough truly is enough. I must be silent no longer."

She smiled shyly while the crowd responded with more applause. When it died down, she continued in a quieter voice. "Now, I know there's many powerful people who will try to hush our voices, because I'm from that world. I grew up believing that money was just a reward for good living and hard work. That anybody who lacked the former inevitably lacked the latter. I grew up believing that anyone who tried to buck the status quo was just lazy, or ungrateful, or ignorant, or malicious, trying to steal from decent hard-working people like my family. Forget that I've never had to work two jobs just to make ends meet. Or even one. I grew up believing that the only good and virtuous way to make it in this world was to follow all the rules of society, no matter what they might cost. I know many others in my world have been raised to feel the same way. Please don't judge us harshly, because we are part of your American family. Therefore, I ask your compassion and patience as you courageously lead by example, showing us a better way."

I added my own "amen" from my seat behind Cassandra, so proud of how she had stayed true to herself despite ostracization from some of her old friends and family. I had to face those fears myself, though I needn't have worried. Even where my family didn't always agree with my decisions, they always supported and welcomed me. We believed that family is forever, and we must hold each other close, no matter what. As I viewed Cassandra and my neighbors as extensions of my new family, I was ready to stand by them as well, no matter what was decided.

Cassandra felt as sure as I did, showing a calm strength as she made her pitch. "I think it's now time for us to be the first in our state to join the example of several other communities across America. The example of reaching out with compassion to those who are suffering, strengthening our whole community. Of standing up to a regime that hounds and locks up people of color many times more than people who look like me, even though we are far more likely to be engaged in drug or other crimes. Yes, this means standing up to the Prison, Alcohol, Pharmaceutical, Militarization and even Lumber Industries. It might even mean standing up to the DSS. I'm sure we have some citizens here who can help lead the way on that one."

She paused with a giggle, joining the soft laughter in the crowd. With a brighter smile, she continued, "I would gladly follow that example, because it's thanks to the hard work and dedication of many of you that I've found the courage to stand up here today. To stand up for what's right. Because just last week, the Sanctioning Council for American Medicines has approved a bid by Winston Jones to sell extracts from a medicine that the Council has given the rare distinction of not having even the possibility of a toxic or potentially lethal effect. Unfortunately, the same can't be said of the medicines that Winston Jones has made from the extracts. Regardless, the Council has approved synthetic cannabinoids for Winston Jones despite the toxicity of their concoctions. These will soon be marketed to aid in the treatment of glaucoma, multiple sclerosis, Alzheimer's, AIDS, ALS, depression, chronic pain, help end drug addictions and even to shrink brain and breast cancer... all things that true cannabis has been credited with, but their drugs haven't been proven to do. I ask you, is it right that a wealthy drug company should be able to push thousands of pounds of altered cannabinoids with toxic side-effects, while a cancer sufferer can be imprisoned for years and branded as felons for the rest of their lives, just for carrying a gram of non-toxic cannabis?"

Though it wasn't technically a vote, the General Assembly, by majority, expressed their disapproval of the status quo. With their support, Cassandra continued. "The worst part of the prohibition of simple cannabis is that it was started in part by some newspaper mogul who wanted to stop hemp from competing with his lumber buddies for supplying paper for print. Yes, hemp: the plant you can't smoke, but is a readily available and renewable source for polyesters, cotton, fiberglass, concrete, wood pulp, and dozens of other valuable products."

Cassandra raised her hand to tap her finger against her chin in mock contemplation. "Let's see, we have a plant that grows very quickly, requires relatively little time and energy to grow and process, is easier to recycle, and is naturally resistant to pests. A reliable answer to so many industries that have pushed our planet into the slash-and-burn, pollution-driven climate change that's ravaged our world. If only we had vast acres of unused farmland where it could grow alongside other vital crops..."

She flashed a grin at the growing murmurs and scattered applause, before growing somber. "Now, I know what I'm asking. The powers that this threatens, well, it touches me personally. The wealth reaped by the regimes threatened by hemp paid for my childhood, my education, and ultimately, helped provide us with the land here we now call home. My family's company Happy Animal Farm would stand to lose some substantial investments, should hemp be widely used as a low-cost, highly-productive source of biofuels. Joining with it the other energy sources being put into practice right here in Constitution City, we would a way to break our addiction to the oil industries that have been making literal killings across the world. If we decide here today to regulate and tax marijuana and grow hemp in our fields, we won't single-handedly change all that. But we would be taking a stand with those who have led the way. So now, we must vote on whether to move forward down that road. Thank you all so much for being here. I know we'll make the right call."

Mayor Margie Cammile then took the stand, and put to a vote whether the city should join the push to legalize and regulate marijuana, and bring the city into hemp and marijuana production. Each proposal had been written up with the costs and benefits, including the large amounts of revenue they could bring to the state and its municipalities, not just our own.

The General Assembly voted our unanimous support for all three. Adam Diego then took the stand, giving some encouragement about our efforts for those and other Principalian initiatives we had voted in support of. One initiative would create a law that each election would award the seat to the person who won a majority of all eligible voters, doing away with districting-games and gerrymandering. Diego promised that he would work hard to implement efficient drug rescue treatment programs, rescind the Anti-Voter laws, draw down the militarization of state police, and other plans to restore the power to the People to whom it rightfully belonged. We then split off into working groups to rally statewide for the Pragmatican primaries on behalf of Diego and the Principalian-backed ISACEO candidate, Julia Brien.

We were pretty excited about Julia Brien. She was a Pragmatic Christian who often spoke of her devotion to the charitable aspects of the Pragmatican Party. I still didn't really consider the Pragmatican party as representative of all my values, but the Principalians were working the hardest to put things I valued into action. And even though Brien's political background wasn't from a Principalian group, as an American Senator she had spoken out in favor of Principalian principles of turning America away from its steadfast march into a Militarized Police State.

So strong was her rhetoric, she seemed almost too good to be true. If elected, she promised to roll back the Surveillance Regime created by the LOYALTY Act, which turned American commerce and entertainment into a Big Brother that spied on us whether we carried little screens with us or not. It even installed virtual checkpoints on most major street corners that remotely read and record the IDs of people who walked or drove by. She promised to remove the veil of secrecy from American Government, even to the extent of allowing government websites to publish the full text of the Constitution, the LOYALTY Act and other major laws. The dozens or scores of military bases in Arabiya would be drawn down, bringing the bulk of our loved ones and America's wealth back home where they were needed most.

Speaking of America's wealth, Brien also gave speeches and position papers in support of protecting our resources against further ecological degradation by finally implementing the cost-effective proposals on cutting down our pollutants while increasing our efficiency. She promised to rebuild our crumbling infrastructure and economy through a Rebuild America jobs program, while restoring regulations that would protect us from toxic investments on Wall Street and toxic food, buildings and toys found on Main Street. The Minimum Wage would be increased to a level that wouldn't quite qualify for a living wage, but would be a lot closer. Even more importantly, employees would regain the right to engage in group negotiations for their pay and benefits.

Finally, as a doctor, Brien promised to institute regulations that would reign in the skyrocketing profit margins in the medical and drug industries. The CareFund was to be allowed to negotiate with medical and drug companies for more reasonable fees, saving the program a huge chunk of its budget. In addition, she promised to offer proposals on how to expand CareFund coverage to all who wished to purchase it, at fair, actuarially sound premiums. The taxes levied for the Inalienable Programs were to be made off-limits to theft by other projects, keeping them fiscally whole while we worked to restore their former levels of aid to the Americans to whom it was owed. Brien also promised to restructure the tax rates, so that those who worked hard and remained in poverty would receive tax breaks rather than tax increases, while those took the most out of the American pot would again begin paying back their fair share for the immense range of benefits they enjoyed.

"Freedom isn't free," she often liked to say, "so it's up to those of us who enjoy the greatest freedoms to repay America for these great blessings She has bestowed upon us. I know that we all have a tendency to consider having what we want to be right and good and moral for ourselves, but selfish and greedy and larcenous for others. So we need to dig deep into our hearts to repent ourselves of those sins, so we can do our part to create a better future for all. In truth, the vast majority of Americans have been doing more than their part, while receiving less than their share of the returns. Those of us who have comfortable, moneyed lives through enjoying more of America's wealth than eighty percent of Americans, we can afford to pay our dues and lift some of the burden they bear to support our way of life. And as someone who statistics tell me is in the top five percent, I can speak with no small authority that we can absolutely pay our share and still have enough left for our houses, our cars, and our Europan vacations. Because to be an American is to believe in the American dream. It is to believe that anyone with enough hard work and determination can make a better life for themselves and their families. As an American, I refuse to deny that slice of Apple Pie to those who deserve it, simply because I want my plate to hold more than I could ever eat. So I stand here, offering to give up that part of the slice that rightly belongs to this great nation of ours. And I will work every day to ensure all may enjoy their just desserts, as the Chief Executive Officer of the Incorporated States of America!"

She repeated variations on that speech at every stop, and I never got tired of hearing her brash optimism. That was something I liked about her, that she was unashamed of where she came from and spoke freely of honoring her responsibilities to the land that had given her so much. She was an inspiration to Cassandra, showing her how one's wealth and position could be not a mark of shame, but a position of strength from which you can lift up those around you. This inspiration was contagious, helping Principalian efforts to get our candidates onto most of the ballots in the upcoming elections. This was all in the face of a near-unanimous position among the Serious People that we'd never make any serious headway. Our decisive wins sent a shockwave rippling across the pundit and political classes, upending their comfortable expectations of the way the system should work.

And that's when the fun began.

Mark hadn't messaged me often since our brief chat from Derek's parents' house on the prior Christmas Eve, since he wanted to distance me from him as much as possible. I understood, but that didn't make me stop missing him being a regular part of my life. He did help make sure that information flowed quickly and subtly to everyone helping with Constitution Cities and other Principalian efforts, and I still counted him as a friend and supporter. So I knew he was "saying hello" and trying to look out for me when I did an Innernet search on a recipe for grilled veggies and instead received links to a breaking story. One of the clips informed me of an announcement shared on Foley's Factoids that left me a cold sort of numb.

I had been excommunicated.

There was a private council held by the heads of the American Zealous Christian Conference, sitting in secret judgment of Christian Zealots who were participating in Principalian politics. According to the councilor in the clip, "standing out as the most reprehensible stain on the honor of her sex is Elizabeth Franklin, instigator of the so-called Constitution City cult centers of multiculturalism, secularism, drug use and homosexuality. She has turned away from the teachings of Christ, and instead has embraced a culture of sin that she is pushing as part of her illicit agenda to warp the hearts and minds of innocent American youth. She's at the nerve center of the Principalian plot to overthrow the American way of life with her own brand of Communist Feminism – or Comfemism as I know we like to say here – where taxpayers will be forced to pay for the illicit sex of young girls attending secularized schools teaching children to practice homosexuality."

I wanted to turn it off. Here was this Reverend Murine guy I'd never even heard of spreading obviously ridiculous lies about what I was trying to accomplish. All the while, Richard was just sitting there, letting the venomous slander continue.

I had been disappointed that Richard didn't change the tone of his broadcasts after Judy's death. And I had long known he was willing to stoop pretty low to further his political agendas. But I assumed that he only made these attacks because to him, he wasn't attacking people who seemed real to him. But he knew me, and in our own way, I thought we'd been close. I wondered what could have caused the level of betrayal he'd have to have felt to betray me so deeply.

I wanted to just close the video and forget it ever happened. I had to get dinner going, so it would be ready before T.J. woke up and needed to be fed. I also needed to get ready for a meeting the next morning with the community's Interfaith Society. What would I tell them? We weren't all Christians, but many of us were. Should I ask them if they heard, or just pray they never mention it?

While I sat there in mortified consternation, Reverend Murine's eyes glistened with hateful glee as his rant continued. "In Elizabeth Franklin's America, we'll all be expected to light up a joint for Jesus, which we'll need after reeling from the Tax-and-Spending spree, setting up ghetto bums and welfare queens into high-class mansions to pop out their swarms of illegitimate offspring tainted with Birth Mutations. Meanwhile, the rest of us will be left to huddle in the corner going crazy trying to decode her Comfemist Bible of Big Government Regulations. There will be a special tax levied onto white married tax returns to pay back some imaginary debt to society, and taxes will start being assessed on Christian churches to pay for

Mosques and pagan Prayer Circles. And Spies will receive a Get Out of Jail Free card, after they are handed the blueprints for beating the system when Elizabeth Franklin gets her wish to publicize the sacred secrets of the American Legal Code. She's a traitor to her race, a traitor to her class, and a traitor to her faith. For these reasons and many more, we had a moral obligation to cast her out of the American Christian League and the Christian Zealot faith."

I felt sick to my stomach, but let the vileness just wash over me, breathing in calm acceptance of what was going on. I remembered admitting to Delpha that, for all my self-confidence, I truly had grown up accustomed to feeling like I deserved to be silenced. I had been there for the founding of the American Christian League and never tried to correct the intolerance and religious persecution it had willfully inflicted. I had been there for the founding of JACL and saw first-hand how it planned to play Americans like puppets through their heartstrings, and said nothing against it. I felt complicit in the whole sorry state of hatred and humiliation that was perpetrated through these systems, and part of me felt that perhaps it was my karma to finally be their target.

But then, Reverend Murine went too far.

"By their fruits ye shall know them. And hers is the fruit of sin, a baby she just happened to bring into this world after running off with her best friend's widower and her late husband's best friend." He leered with the implications, chortling at the salaciousness of it all. Chortled at calling perfectly precious, innocent little Theodore James the fruit of sin, all but saying he is not his father's son, trying to get his audience to feel that he and I both were damned by the lie.

I could have withstood any number of False Witnesses against me, but not against my son. I could no more stand silently by and let them attack T.J. in words any more than I could allow them to attack him in flesh. I forced down my anger and calmed my thoughts so I could turn them inward in prayer. Soon, I felt the calming presence of the quiet stillness in my heart. As I pondered its wisdom, I felt the warm glow that I'd felt when Kurt was near, lending me his courageous strength in the face of religious persecution.

At that moment, I knew what I had to do.

The next morning, I pitched my plan to the Interfaith Society, then offered to get out of the way of its implementation. "I understand if you would prefer I remove any distraction or drama from impacting our work, and I'm prepared to resign from the City and Interfaith committees if asked. But I have learned that silence gives assent, and I cannot let these lies about my son and my Faith to go unchallenged. They can remove me from the rosters of the Zealous Christian Conference, but they cannot take away my Zealous Love for Christ and all that He stands for. So as hard as they tried to knock me down, I must stand even taller. I completely understand if you need to ask me to make that stand on my own."

Margie just reached across the table to take my hand, giving me one of her most impish grins. "And let you have all the fun? Not a chance, missy. The solid foundation of any community is Solidarity. When one of our own gets attacked, it's an assault on all of us. And don't delude yourself, this was intended as an attack on everything we're trying to build. It's just another case of the Loud Dog trying to drown out reason and compassion by his noisy barking. As long as that works for them, they're going to keep doing it. I know it's the Pragmatican way to just crumple into a quivering heap whenever you're called mean names, but you're no Pragmatican and neither am I. A Principalian stands up to the bully and fights back."

Margie put my idea up for a vote, which passed unanimously. Within days, we had contacted or been contacted by a huge number of loosely-connected faith-based groups across America. Once the word got out, there were quite a lot of supporters wanting to sign onto our new umbrella initiative.

Within days, we had formed a group we called Creating Holistically Respectful, Integrated Societies in Trust, Love, Integrity, Kindness and Empathy. Despite the group representing a number of faiths and even non-religious groups, we all agreed that the best name to get our message out to average Americans was CHRISTLIKE. We announced our formation in a series of news pieces affirming our commitment to our individual beliefs, and also in support of the true facts about me and what I stood for.

We expected our first news release to fall like a silent pebble into the great big sea of media control, but Sofia Neith seized on the opportunity to fire back on her most tenacious gadfly, the host of Foley's Factoids. She reported on our faith-based initiatives, including inter-community ministries that helped people cross racial and social boundaries in service to one another. She described our plans to create community justice programs similar to what had been in Hometown, helping right wrongs through reformative restitution, not retribution. As I was the appointed spokesperson, she included a brief biography.

Rather than denigrate my status as a young adult like others had done, she called that section, "And a Child Shall Lead Them." I objected to being called a child, but as I was still under twenty-five, I didn't take it too personally.

Ms. Neith also wrote of how I carried and bore my son in Hometown, truthfully mentioning the difficulties I had with my pregnancy that made it unwise for me to travel, but that I weathered well and without complaint. I wished to keep my travails to myself rather than pain my mother with the knowledge that I was bearing a suffering she couldn't be there for, especially if I lost the baby. She then wrote of my joyous homecoming when my little infant met his grandparents, and got to sleep in the bedroom his father grew up in. With my permission, Ms. Neith included a picture of me and Kurt together. Next to it was one of me holding T.J., alongside Janet holding a picture of her son in his uniform with all his honors and ribbons. When I read the short interview with Janet about what a blessing T.J. and I were to her life, I ran to her room and hugged her, letting her know what a blessing she'd been to me.

The story had a powerful effect on others as well, causing Foley's Factoids to double down in their vicious slander and libel against me and everything CHRISTLIKE. Since he was my age, he had even freer reign to be nasty to me than an older man, which you know is saying quite a lot. Richard even accused our group's acronym of taking the Lord's name in vain. I actually laughed at that, remembering my deep reservations about his "J-Seal" smugness.

Even though I knew I should have been used to it, it still hurt to watch Richard continually give False Witness to serve his political and monetary masters. That's why I readily agreed when I was invited to appear alongside him for a piece about Christianity in Politics on the pundit show Both Sides Together. It was different from other shows in that it had a slower pace and conversational format, with few interruptions from commercials or the host. Since they usually brought on aggressive Puritanic media stars and put them up against timid, even Regressive Pragmaticans, I guessed that they imagined I'd be a pushover of a girl in the face of the dominating forcefulness of the young superstar Richard Foley. Little did they know I'd learned how to handle him years ago.

Still, I found myself getting a little nervous when I was in the studio's dressing room. Someone from the show was putting make-up on me and doing my hair in some kind of upswept bun that added inches to my height. I was starting to feel terribly out of place, when I saw Derek's grin pop into the mirror.

"You look like a Grinch stole your Christmas," he said helpfully.

I sighed and rolled my eyes. "Thank you for your stunning vote of confidence. I'm starting to wish I brought Cassandra instead."

He just laughed, shooed away by the assistant so she could put on the finishing touches. Derek stayed nearby, keeping my nerves calm. "I'm teasing, you look great. Like just the right kind of respectable young mom to get out there and smack old Rickypoo over his square head with a modern galifesto. You're gonna do fan-TAS-tic."

I returned his warm smile, finally feeling ready. I opened my mouth to thank him, but was interrupted by the assistant pulling me out of the chair to hurry me out. I had to nearly run down the hall to the studio, sitting down in front of the cameras with only moments to spare. I didn't even have time to say hello to Richard, who was seated across from me on the other side of host Steve Connors.

After brief introductions, Richard was given the floor first. He took a little more than his allotted time to reiterate the current talking points of the ACL, and then contrasted it to what he called, "the pseudo-theology of Moral Relativism pushed by this so-called CHRISTLIKE group, which is so tangled and knotty that no one can really tell what they're supposed to be for. But I guess that's what you get when a ladies' knitting circle tries to thread the fine needle of politics."

The host started to chuckle, reinforcing why I couldn't let the cheap shot slide. There were more female than male core CHRISTLIKE members, and that had often been used as an excuse to completely dismiss the group. "That sort of personal attack is exactly the kind of childish antic that has poisoned political discourse, Richard. When we should be having a mature conversation about differences on policy, it doesn't help to start throwing out tired old sexist stereotypes."

"Oh Liz, please, it was just a joke." He gave me that patronizing smile that had made most people meekly surrender in the face of his arrogant indifference. Most people, yes. But not me.

I looked him straight in the eye and asked of him, "Richard, if you can't be honest with me, can you at least be honest with yourself? It was not just a joke, because you and I both know these are things some people honestly believe. There are people who sincerely argue that God made women to be inferior servants to men, better seen than heard, and in public, not even seen. This is especially true when it comes to politics and religion. If you don't agree with that belief, you need to stop spreading it."

"Oh honestly, Liz. Are you really so thin-skinned you have to jump at every little perceived slight? Men wear the pants, women sew them, that's just the way people talk. It's part of our culture. Calling all this 'sexism' is exactly the kind of hysterical Comfemism that has made men afraid of saying hello for fear of being called a pig. If you want to be taken seriously, you need to learn to pick your battles." Richard seemed surprised to find himself on the defensive against me, and was trying to get back into the role of powerful attacker.

As much as I was used to having patience with his blustering, I couldn't afford to coddle his attacks on women's personhood. "Don't play games, Richard. These battles picked me. I don't go out there asking people to passive-aggressive or all-out-aggressively attack me. Yet when I ask you to take responsibility for doing so, you use another sexist word to attack me: hysterical. Look it up."

While he lost a moment trying to think of what hysterical really meant in that context, I pressed my point. "These little micro-aggressions might seem tiny when taken one at a time. But if you step back you'll see how they happen all the time – they add up, and they are never okay. It is just never okay to try to humiliate someone because of their gender, their race, whom they love, their ability to find a home, anything. Remember who said, 'as ye have done it unto one of the least of these my brethren, ye have done it unto me.' But that's what passes for entertainment, isn't it? The more hurtfully cruel, the bigger the laugh it gets. The problem with that is the more people laugh at it, the more it shapes our expectations on what's okay on how to treat people. No matter how common it is, Richard, sexist is sexist. Just like racist is racist."

Forget that both types of bigotry were still very much alive; only the latter was taken as a serious insult. Unlike calling out sexism, which was usually laughed off as an overreaction, calling out racism was considered a slap in the face.

Richard reeled as though I'd verbally slapped him. "Hey, those two are not the same. Feminism won a long time ago. It's a dead issue, only there's people like you who won't be happy until men are the beaten-down slaves who can't even speak without getting attacked. It was just an innocently funny comment. It's not my fault if you're so bent out of shape over my right to speak my mind that you can't even take a joke."

My eyebrow arched and my voice cooled. "Really? Feminism won? Is that why it's still legal to demote or fire a woman who becomes pregnant? And why the average paycheck of a woman is as low as half that of a man's? And why, after all this time, we still have to argue over whether women have the right to have a say in what happens to our own bodies, our own lives? Or do you just want to declare the war over so you can keep being sexist without getting called on it?"

Richard's hand clenched into a fist in his lap, practically shouting, "It's not sexist! You can keep repeating a lie, but it doesn't make it true!"

My voice also heated, but I controlled my volume and my pace. "Remember you said that, Richard. Because let's be absolutely, honestly clear, here. Anything that tries to put someone into a place that is greater or lesser based on their gender is sexist. It's sexist to say men can't clean or women can't play sports. It's sexist to say men are naturally smarter, or that women are inherently more mature. It's sexist to say women can't be trusted with their bodies, or that men can't control their own. It's extremely sexist to tell me to meekly accept you being a jerk as 'just a joke,' and when I object, you feel entitled to be an even bigger jerk at my expense."

He started to try talking over me, so I held up my hand and quickly came to the point. "It really is as simple as this. When everyone agrees that's just a bigoted double-standard, then it will be a joke. But you and I both know a lot of people believe in that double-standard, so repeating it just reinforces it. If you don't want to be their enabler, then just stop doing it. I'm serious here. If you don't really intend the consequences of your actions, can you at least agree to try to act differently? Are you so unimaginative that you can't find any other way to explain why you don't like someone? Any way to make a decent joke?"

The fire flared up in his eyes when I talked over his attempt to talk over me, and grew hotter at the challenge I put to him. He took a breath before continuing. "You know, Liz, I didn't think you'd be so childish, not on a national show."

That actually made me laugh a little. "I ask you take some adult responsibility and you call me childish. Though I guess that's appropriate, since we demand behavior of children that we refuse to honor for ourselves. Get along with others, play by the rules, share your toys, don't make fun of those who are different, don't bully, don't fight, use your good words. These are all things that we tell children to grow up when they don't do them, and call adults childish when they ask us to. It's all a ludicrous, upside-down way of treating one another that is making neighbors and even families into bitter enemies. So really, Richard, maybe we'd better just stick to policy points and do our best to treat each other with the respect we both deserve."

Richard nodded, eager to move back to his favorite divisive topic. "Well okay, let's talk about respect. What about your wanting to make taxpayers foot the bill for women who disrespect themselves and their unborn children with abortions and abortion pills? We can't force people to pay for something they oppose on moral grounds. That's an infringement on their religious rights. The simple truth is, birth control and abortion just encourages illicit sex, and murders the unborn child. Those are facts, are you calling facts sexist?"

I literally boggled at him, laughing in disbelief. "No, because those aren't even facts. They're just lies you and your friends keep repeating in an attempt to make them true. Given what has happened to a woman who was very dear to us both, I'm really surprised you're even going there."

I had expected him to try to argue me down, but the mention of Judy gave him pause. That heartened me, making me think my childhood friend was still in there somewhere. Charging ahead, I continued, "Let's talk about facts. To start with, many people morally oppose war, receiving blood transfusions, and even eating meat, but I'm pretty sure you aren't fighting to end all government support for medicine, industrial farming, and the Military, all to protect their religious freedom. No, you're demanding we all pay more for healthcare because of your religion, even taxpayers who believe it's immoral to not protect women and their rights. Because unlike Virila, automatically covering contraceptives saves insurers – and us – four times as much money as it costs, making it the most cost-effective preventative care out there. And you know there's lots of people who find Virila to be immoral, but I don't see you yelling about stopping coverage for that."

Richard seemed to become even more uncomfortable when I brought up Virila. When he realized it was his turn again to speak, as all he could do was fall back on another tired old talking point. "Either way, you're telling us that insurance companies have to waste tons of money on women having so much sex they can't afford their own abortion pills."

I pursed my lips to hold back an unkindly derisive laugh. Instead, I just chuckled, "Maybe I shouldn't have brought up Virila, since now you're stuck in the idea of someone taking a pill every time they want to have sex. Yet birth control pills are taken every day, and have nothing to do with whether or how often someone has sex."

The continued Virila talk made Richard even more uncomfortable, making me wonder if I'd struck a nerve. He soon rallied, launching into a rehash of his usual tirade that centered on his claim that "the biggest problem with The Pill is that it makes it easy for women to have sex without any negative consequences. That just leads to more sex, more irresponsible pregnancies and more abortions."

I gave a short sigh. "Richard, that's just a bunch of word games strung together into a sentence. Let me count the most obvious problems with your statement."

I held up my fingers to count my points again. "First, as a mother, I strongly object to you referring to pregnancy as a negative consequence. Second, it's frankly none of your business whether a woman is having sex, and it's really rather prurient to be so obsessed with our sex lives. Third, facts prove that contraceptives have no real effect on sexual activity, except for making it safer for people who are already having it. Fourth, about half of all American pregnancies weren't intended, and almost half of those end in abortion, and the majority are for women who are already married mothers. And that leads to the fifth, which is that when women have access to contraception, unintended pregnancies and abortions both drop by up to half or even two thirds. If you are truly, Faithfully serious about preventing abortion, you need to stop playing self-righteous games and focus on what actually works: empower women to choose not to become pregnant in the first place."

Richard leaned forward at that, jabbing his finger toward me. "If they don't want to get pregnant, they need to stop having sex, or just use a condom, it's as simple as that. Because it's a proven fact that birth control pills cause abortions."

This time, the fire flashed behind my own eyes, taking him aback. "That, Richard, is a lie. You can ignore the facts but you can't destroy them, no matter how much you shout. As I've already explained, birth control pills and emergency contraceptives prevent pregnancies, not end them. I know you've argued that even something that prevents fertilization or implantation is an abortion because a cluster of cells has the potential of becoming a baby. But you know what? So does every egg that passes out of a woman every month, and every sperm that passes out of a man every time he feels like availing himself of a private moment. And, for the record, so does a slice of chocolate cake, since it may be eaten by a pregnant woman and turned into building blocks for the fetus."

I heard Mr. Connors snort at that, but stayed focused. "More to the point, the blastocyst implantation process naturally fails anywhere up to half the time an egg and sperm meet up, just as a matter of design. These laws that you've been pushing that grant full rights of personhood to an egg as soon as a sperm hits it? They're written so that a woman would be arrested for murder every time these eggs naturally pass out of her, even though she had never even been pregnant. And if you want to call fertilization pregnancy, you'll have to convince me that God designed a system to 'kill' a third to half of all 'unborn children.' That's just not how I envision my Just and Loving God."

Richard rallied his anger in the face of a challenge to his moral authority to declare God's edicts. "I think we'll just have to let the Bible speak for itself on this one. You can't start putting your personal preference out there and call it God's will."

I pulled back my own anger, smiling warmly. "And neither can you. I know you've spent some time on our CHRISTLIKE Innernet site where we discuss different Biblical viewpoints on these and other matters. So you know that not only does the Bible not specifically address this topic, what it does say is open to a wide array of interpretations. The Bible has proven to be a Rorschach test of our expectations, where we can always find a translation of a verse we feel will support anything we want it to say."

At this point, Richard sat back smugly. "And here's where your Moral Relativism comes in. When you don't have a moral compass, your baser drives will justify anything."

I stared down his snideness with my own disapproval. "Moral Relativism is at play here, as it judges something right or wrong not by the action, but by who's doing it. You have pitched countless public fits over being asked to show some religious tolerance toward others. Then in the same breath, you'll demand your own Religious Freedom to dictate your personal beliefs to them. You push State Rights when it comes to federal laws against bigotry, and Federal Jurisdiction when it comes to states who wish to honor all marriages and end the Drug War. You demand the government stay out of your life while trying to use the government to rule the lives of others. And that, Richard, is Moral Relativism."

Richard resumed an incoherent, buzzword-laden tirade that was a rehash of what he had said many times on his show. He ended it with an angry accusation that "you people keep saying you're Pro-Choice, but it's not a Choice, it's a Child. If you were a real Christian, you wouldn't be so Anti-Life."

I tilted my head at him as I lowered and slowed my voice. "I'm not Anti-Anything. I am three-hundred-thousand percent Pro-Child. I am Pro-Family and Pro-Freedom. I'm also Pro-Right to Life, Pro-Right to Liberty, and Pro-Right to the Pursuit of Happiness, all those things that you are waging all-out war to take away from all women, everywhere. You are taking it upon yourself to be the sole speaker for God. This was both our blessing and our curse for being cast out of the Garden of Eden: the Right to Choose our own path, and to answer to God alone for our choices. You've fostered a tidal wave of hate and disgust at the idea of women exercising this Gift of God. And as a woman of Faith, I ask you, for the Love of God, stop trying to put yourself in His place! Stop making birth about control! My body is not yours to control!"

He seemed oddly shaken at my quietly emphatic outburst. He blinked a moment before saying, "Somebody has to stand up for America as a moral nation. My role as a political Christian is to help ensure the laws uphold God's judgment of how things are supposed to be."

In response, referenced the Bible. "Richard, render unto Caesar what is Caesar's, and render unto God what is God's. As Christians, you and I both believe that a woman's body is a gift entrusted to her by God. Therefore, women's bodies and choices made with them belong not to the government, not to a church, and not to you. A church can accept or cast us out based on their own religious beliefs, but a government can't take the place of either a church or God. Please, stop trying to put your politics between me and my relationship to God."

My earnest, heartfelt plea hung in the strange silence that followed it. While I tried hard to read the expression in Richard's eyes, Steve Connors looked curiously between us before interjecting, "We're coming close to a station break here, but I think everyone will agree we can put that off just a little while. Richard Foley, would you like to respond?"

With a little less bluster, Richard responded with a tone I'd not heard from him before, and I couldn't quite place. "I just don't think it's appropriate to keep putting peoples' sex lives out there and force it on other people."

Again, I barely managed to restrain a laugh, as I tried to keep my amused disbelief in check. "Then why can't you and your people stop sharing your lurid fantasies about other peoples' sex lives? I swear, I'm right back in our childhood again, constantly surrounded by sex, sex, sex! For an upbringing that was so anti-sex, you'd think we'd be able to go one day without talking about it. Is a woman having sex? Is it with a man? Is it her husband? Is she trying to make babies? And it's real telling that usually the only time we cared about whether a man was having sex was if it might have been with another man. Boys were fair game."

I immediately saw that my flippant joke had gone too far. Even I had heard the rumors about his father, though only recently. Derek had told me that when he was a kid, Brother Foley had interacted with him in a way that made him extremely uncomfortable. Mister Channery then made it clear to the man that he was never to be alone near his son again. But how far would Brother Foley have gone? Had Richard been hurt by his own father?

My heart broke at the thought, and I instantly tried to make things right. "I don't mean to say that it was okay if boys were hurt, and I apologize for the implication. But things like that do happen, because we are unwilling to face these issues head-on with open eyes and strong hearts. The more comfort we find in the rigid order and 'rightness' of our community – our Authorities – the less we want to face the wrongness they may commit. Instead, we try to cling to this Authoritarianism, in hopes it may calm that feeling inside that something isn't right. That feeling there's something we should have that the world isn't giving us, and we feel an utter lack of control over. Do you know what I'm talking about, that feeling of helpless wrongness somewhere inside?"

I had leaned forward to bridge the distance I had from Richard, searching his eyes for the young man I once thought I knew so well. For a moment, I thought I caught a glimpse of him as he answered, simply, "Yes, that's why it's so important for us as Christians to fight against the wrongness of the world."

I smiled a little. "I agree. To my heart, that wrongness is the idea that we are separate from one another, rather than one human family. As Christians, how can we do less than follow Jesus' first commandment to Love One Another? He cast nobody out because they saw things differently from the way he did, but embraced all with the love of a brother. We say to hate the sin and love the sinner, but while that may be possible for God's perfect heart, human hearts don't work that way. Our hearts are miraculous muscles that wither under the weight of any hate, but grow stronger and stronger with every love."

Richard's eyes remained an enigma to me, and his voice was strained as he replied. "But we must still continue to fight against sin. How can we do that if we tolerate all manner of sin around us?"

My smile grew warm. "Only by fighting against sin in our own hearts. Because Richard, Jesus never commanded us to appoint ourselves minders over the motes of sin in others' souls. Rather, He continually taught us how to remove the beams of sin from our own. To follow His example, we must learn to love as he has, and live our lives in the service of those who are least among us. Can't you feel that in your heart, that holy drive to share Christ's love for all God's children?"

His brow furrowed in conflict, and as he struggled for an answer I waved my hand to retract the question. "You don't have to answer that, not to me. But please, answer yourself in your heart, Richard. I know your heart; I believe in your heart. And I love your heart, Richard, as I love you – in that caring, heartfelt way I've always loved you. Even when you've made me heart-breakingly disappointed with your choices, I've loved you, as we learned to love side-by-side from Pastor Johns as children."

The studio was silent, and in my mind there were only me, and my childhood friend facing a lifetime of conflicts all in one public moment. My voice softened as I finished, "And Richard, I believe you love me, too. Do you love me?"

His eyes were moist and earnest, as he quietly replied, "I… I do. Love you."

I moved my chair forward so I could take his hand in mine. "Then let's not fight. Please, let's not fight. You are bound in your heart to follow your convictions, just as I am bound in mine. But we can deal with these differences together. We can overcome the wrongness, together. Hearts that love have room to hold our whole selves, not just the parts we want to accept. There is no difference between hearts so great that love cannot hold them together. We aren't going to agree on so many things, but please, can we agree on this? In the name of all that's Good, can we please agree to Love One Another?"

He placed his other hand over mine, with a warmth I had never before felt from him. "Yes, Elizabeth. We can agree to love."

Tears sprang to my eyes, which I tried but failed to hold in check. "Thank you, Richard."

The tears then flowed freely as I put my arms around his shoulders for a sisterly embrace, so I could whisper again to him, "Thank you."

Chapter 21

Love stills the waters of the soul, creating in us a reflection of the divine.

By the time the general elections came about, we had built up a momentum that even the most cynical partisans couldn't ignore. Our greatest supporters were those who were inspired to vote for the first time in a long time, or even ever. We scored many victories that night, thanks to the record-breaking turnout. Of course, I don't know this for sure, but some of that credit may also go to Mark's tireless monitoring of the voting machines. It was thanks to the accurate recording of their votes that won us our hard-fought victories.

And oh dear goodness, we had quite a lot of those victories. After such an uphill struggle against the entrenched forces of Authoritarianism in both parties, it was so very gratifying when most of the Pragmaticans we backed had won, especially the Principalian ones. It brought us hope that we had, at long last, achieved some lasting progress toward a stronger, more principled America. The evening of Julia Brien's inauguration heralded to us a new era of human understanding, where she would fulfill her promises to turn America away from the worship of wealth, and toward the Synergist vision of all people pulling together.

Naturally, that didn't last.

Soon after she took office, ISACEO Brien began doing the opposite of every plan in her campaign platform. She had promised us a change from the Authoritarian tyranny that Pragmaticans had long decried under the Puritanic government, and I guess in a way she fulfilled that promise.

She changed the Puritanic moves toward a tyrannical government, by making it bipartisan. You'd think the Puritans would feel grateful to her for vindicating their favorite programs, but they still attacked her legitimacy at every turn. After all, she not only denied them their God-given right to have the most powerful Leader of the Free World be a Puritan, she had the audacity to be a woman while doing it.

Within weeks, the Puritans had blamed her for everything that had been going wrong for months or years, saying they were "Mad as heck and not going to take it anymore." They called her a Communist, a Spy planted to destroy our government, privately Mutated with male parts, or even not a real Member because her birth was certified the day after she was born, like me and so many who were born to humbler circumstances.

As for the Pragmaticans, they angrily shouted down any mention of how Julia Brien was strengthening the Puritanic police state. They kept insisting we had to just have patience and faith that she really was the shining savior we had all campaigned hard to elect. That her position was really one of weakness not strength, and she just didn't have the power to not keep using her supposedly ineffectual office to devastate what was left of our rights as private citizens. These same people who had rallied feverishly to end the Puritanic evils that Brien had campaigned against, suddenly were foaming at the mouth to defend those same evils committed by a Pragmatican.

It didn't take many months for the mood to turn pretty grim back home at the first Constitution City. We had been so ecstatic when Adam Diego was sworn in as governor, and the voters had passed the hemp and marijuana initiatives that Brien had promised to uphold. But since taking over, her DSS squads had increased their raids on state-approved medical marijuana dispensaries, and greatly ramped up the Drug Wars both within and without our borders. This only added to the prison companies' swollen profits, as Brien had also ramped up anti-Sudoamerican raids to the point they made the one I saw back at the plant look like a church picnic.

So when Margie addressed the core group of the most vocal members of the General Assembly, nobody was surprised at her despondency. "I just don't know what we can do about this, team. We gave it our best shot, and we scored some major victories. We fought hard to elect someone who claimed to support our sincerest share our values, only to make betrayal of those values into the new 'bipartisan consensus.' Our own allies in the Pragmatican party are now cheerleaders for torture and state-sanctioned murder. We just don't have the power to stop this forced-march into a Militarized America."

I had never before seen her so close to giving up, and it hurt my heart to see this in the first person who taught me how to strengthen my beliefs into ones worth fighting for.

My fighting spirit renewed, I called for our group to not give up. "I think we can learn something from the Regressive response to Brien's election. No, no, I don't mean that we should be sore losers yelling that 'Obstinance is Strength!' But we also have learned that we can't get caught up in 'Pragmaticans Good, Puritans Bad!' That's where their strength lies, their unwillingness to give up in the face of devastating defeat. We fought hard for a victory that has dealt us a serious setback. We can't let that steal our commitment to keep fighting for what we believe in. The Puritans can teach us that no matter what happens, never ever ever give up fighting for what we believe in."

Margie nodded, pursing her lips together. While she gathered her thoughts, Jazmine cut in, "You know, if I gave up every time someone tried to kick me down, I'd never have made it out of the boxes people kept trying to put me in. I don't know about the rest of you folks, but I'm ready to roll up my sleeves and start making up some fresh signs and banners to get back out on the streets. Let's go remind this country what America really stands for: standing tall, standing proud, standing up for one another."

Though we all had looked forward to some time to put our feet up and rest, we agreed with Jazmine that it was time to get back out on them. ISACEO Brien and the Pragmatican majority we'd helped put into Congress were already capitulating to every Puritanic effort to reverse our wins, pretending they were unable to wield the power we'd handed to them. Some of them even co-signed bills to ban all non-cisgender marriages and "behaviors," gutting scholarships while strengthening military recruiting, and restricting abortions only to cases where a rapist was convicted or a federally registered religious leader certified it was necessary to save the woman's life in accordance with the will of God. It was a cruel farce.

Though I have to tell you, that was another case where I really should have seen it all coming. I knew that a number of political rallies were hosted by the Reformative Followers of Christ, a small Christian sect that had dedicated itself to politics. Even though they naturally leaned Puritan, they also had a tendency to throw their weight behind a Pragmatican now and then, which seemed to give them a middle-ground veneer. I knew it was a veneer though, because I had heard of the secretive group that hid at the core of that sect: the Dominators.

Now, the Reformative sect was extremist enough to make me

nervous, with things like discouraging their girls from public activities like education, and championing what amounts to child abuse as a parenting tool. But even the average Reformationist wasn't aware their group was supporting a fanatical core who considered themselves God's Super-Commandos. Behaving like a secret society of their elite leadership, they tried to ensure that only their initiates were aware of their secret war on all belief systems that didn't meet with their dangerously violent fanaticism. They had declared a literal war on all other ways to worship Christ except for what they called Dominator Christianity, as they placed themselves above God's green earth as the sole inheritors of His gift of dominion. And in their mind, Dominion didn't mean wise caretaking and preservation of God's most precious creation for all His children. Their Dominion meant destructive, tyrannical, utterly heartless domination.

They justified their depraved hypocrisy by teaching that all who weren't sufficiently devoted to their dogmatism were possessed or deceived by literal real demons. Therefore, they trained their initiates to be so-called demon hunters for spiritual hunting and killing. The most fanatical Dominators volunteered to serve as Spirit Soldiers, directing their prayers as black magic to force their agenda to become reality. They prayed for God to physically hurt or kill those who opposed them, and were thanked publicly by politicians whom they supported.

And that's what made me feel so foolish for not having noticed it before. Even Brien had hosted a supposedly non-denominational prayer breakfast during her campaign, where she thanked the Spirit Soldiers who were working tirelessly toward a better America. Though it didn't ring any bells at the time, it did clang in my memory when Brien appointed to Chaplain one Reverend Murine. Yep, my old excommunicator, whom I had to thank for putting the Dominators on my radar.

Where I can give myself credit is that I had connected those dots by the time the Dominator-sponsored minority group within the ACL pushed a campaign to "upgrade" the post of Chaplain from a supposedly non-sectarian, purely advisory position, to become the true head of Christianity in America. Yep, they were trying to establish a state religion, headed by their own Reverend Murine. Naturally, Brien supported this plan as a "bipartisan effort to enshrine in law the original intent of the Founders," which was supposedly in the Constitution.

Because it was considered illegal to even know about the Freedom of Religion enshrined in the Constitution, they felt perfectly free to claim that anyone who disagreed with them was an Anti-American, Anti-Christian bigot. All public figures and the candidates rallying for the upcoming mid-term election primaries wore the ACL-approved lapel pins with a cross inside the American seal, which the ACL wanted to make into the official national seal. The ACL wanted to change the pledge too, from "One nation, indivisible, with Liberty and Justice for All" to "One Christian nation, with Faith and Justice for all its Members."

We in CHRISTLIKE knew we had to lead the fight against the ACL, as most other groups were eagerly shuffling along to their drumbeat for fear of being humiliated. But we knew that attacking the ACL directly would just continue the acrimonious spiral. Instead, we held a quiet conference among our members, putting together our Articles of Faith that we felt would show rather than tell what we felt the Founders had intended for American religious freedom. We drew on the wisdom of all our members, from the Christian to the Taoist to the Sikh to the atheist. Despite different beliefs, we each held core values in common. It was easy for us to establish that common ground, and show that it wasn't a matter of religious doctrine, but simple human decency that helped us live moral, meaningful lives.

Still, we did run into a bit of a snag when it came to finalizing our last decision: what to use as our rallying symbol. We had agreed that the unifying point in all our belief systems was the power of Love, but we had difficulty finding the right way to express it. Since the majority in CHRISTLIKE were Christians, many Christian and non-Christians felt that the best way to counter-act the ACL's hatemongering was to make our pins and signs proclaim, "Jesus Is Love." That led to some intense discussion, and it didn't get better once the group started to lean towards the more-inclusive "Jesus Loves You" or similar affirmations.

Cassandra made an excellent point. "Is it really best for us to bring Jesus into this? I mean, I know the ACL is, but aren't we taking a stand that we all deserve the right to follow our own conscience, regardless of whether we follow any particular religion? I'm really wondering if there isn't a better way to share that message without referring to any one in particular."

Derek chuckled as he took up that point, talking near us rather than to us, distracted by hanging onto T.J.'s arm. My baby was entertaining us by practicing his toddling across the table, and then laughed in response to the playful tone Derek took as he spoke. "Yeah, back when Kurt and I were hanging out, he was put off by how people kept name-dropping Jesus. I mean, bringing Jesus into everything, like they couldn't feel comfortable ordering a sandwich unless the Christ Himself was made a part of the transaction. 'Hold the mayo, Jesus admonishes low-cholesterol.' He used to amuse himself by picturing how they'd react if he started bringing Osiris into every conversation, then acting offended they weren't grateful for receiving the message of ancient Egypt."

For a few moments, I got lost in thought. I loved hearing the stories Derek shared about Kurt, showing me more facets of his character than he had the chance to show me in person. T.J. was growing more and more like Kurt every day, both making me miss his father and comforting me with his precious, innocent love. Someday, when he was old enough, I planned to give him his father's Golden Heart pin.

Of course! I'd had our answer all along.

"That's it!" I suddenly shot upright from my reverie, embarrassed as I saw everyone eying me curiously. Blushing again, I timidly offered, "I mean, I think I know what to use as our pin. I'll have to ask permission from our parents, just to be sure they won't mind, but…" I pulled my pin out from its place in my purse, then handed it to Cassandra to pass around.

Derek knew what I'd had to have brought out, and that made him laugh even louder. "Oh of course! Aw geez, why didn't I think of that? Thou Art Loved. It does it all. Treats people with respect, affirms the love they deserve, and doesn't preach. That gets the Channery Seal of Approval right there."

It also got the approval of the rest of the CHRISTLIKE groups, by near-unanimous vote. My parents naturally gave their assent; even if they still weren't entirely on board with everything I'd been working toward, they fully supported my efforts to share my Love all my brothers and sisters in humanity. In the end, family has always been our greatest value.

Soon we were seeing Golden Heart pins on all sorts of political and news shows, as even those who weren't affiliated with us took up the cause of Religious Freedom. I found myself giving a lot of interviews about the history of it and how it tied into CHRISTLIKE's goals, providing me with the opportunity to spread the message of Synergism as a more realistic and sustainable way to grow stronger together.

Meanwhile, the pressure from the Pragmaticans increased harder and faster than we got from even the ACL. We were called traitors who were just paving the way for Puritans to take over the government. Ironically, the heat turned up even more as we made great headway in the primaries to put even more Principalians on the ballot than ever before. I finally felt like we were making progress when I got that call, the one where Derek handed me the phone without telling me who it was.

"Hello, Elizabeth, it's so good to speak with you again. I just haven't had the time to keep in touch; I'm sure you understand." It took me a while to recognize the voice of Julia Brien, as we'd only spoken a few times while I was working on campaigns.

"Oh, hello. Yes, I'm pretty up to speed on how you've been busying yourself in your new office." I furrowed my brow, waiting for her to tell me in person to back off just like all the hints and jabs I'd been getting from her underlings in their press conferences and talk shows.

She laughed lightly, a little too casual for my comfort. "Now, that leads right into why I was ringing you! You see, I'm trying to organize the office of the Chaplain, in preparation for the pending legislation. I wish to extend to you a place in that office, helping bring your special perspective as we lay the groundwork."

I'd seen her handily silence other gadflies by absorbing them into her offices with their rigidly-enforced codes of silence. She even had a policy in place where people had to spy on their co-workers and report "suspicious facial expressions" or so-called "face crimes." If they didn't, they'd risk being fired and prosecuted under the spurious Treason and Espionage Act.

Still, I was taken aback that she wanted to co-opt me, let alone make me subservient to the man who had so gleefully thrown me out of my childhood religion. Was I really doing so much more good than I'd suspected? Was my work so successful that she considered me a threat?

"Wow, that's pretty flattering. But you know how I feel about a state-sanctioned purity test for religious faith, so I can't very well participate in setting one up. I'm sure you understand!" I tried to keep my tone polite, but was willing to err on the side of being clear.

I wasn't sure how I'd come across, but her voice did sound a little less smooth, and more tense. "As a matter of fact, I don't believe I do understand. You see, Elizabeth, there are those who have some serious questions about some of your past associations. There's strong concerns about your potential ties to Gail Stewart, and the underground Espionage network she's a part of. Another one or two of your close or suspected friends have been cause for a great deal of concern, as well. There are major changes on the horizon that might put you in a very uncomfortable position, should your loyalty to Christian America be called into question. I would have thought you'd appreciate the opportunity to prove that loyalty by serving your country directly in Christian charity."

I was livid. The Chief Executive Officer of the Incorporated States of America had seen fit to call me, personally, to issue religious threats. I didn't see any reason to take the bait, nor to return the threats in kind. Instead, I took a steadying breath, and responded evenly, "There are those who feel I have already made a great sacrifice for our country, having lost my husband while he was in service to it. In fact, now that you mention sacrifice, I still haven't been able to find any answers about just how Kurt lost his life. I'm sure your office has the power to uncover the truth. Do you think you could honor the sacrifice of an American hero, and help me find those answers?"

She of course didn't help me directly, but she did let me know that Kurt had to have been involved in something big due to how quickly my question brought the call to a close. After hanging up the phone, I swept T.J. up from where he'd been clinging to my legs, and tickled his face and neck with a flurry of kisses to recover my own balance. I needed to see his beautiful face and hear his sparkling laugh. He was my blessing and my treasure, my reason for rallying my courage to be the woman I needed to be, in the face of the kinds of pressure I had just faced. Derek pestered me until I shared what Brien had said, and he just laughed.

"Wow, you must be doing something right. Kinda ominous though, makes me wonder what's going on. I know there's been a renewed frenzy on the news about the leader of the Holyland trying to get America to back a war on Persia, I wonder if that's it." He reached over to ruffle T.J.'s hair, who batted his hand away with an adorably petulant "No! No hair!"

I kissed T.J.'s cheek again while I thought. "Well, they do need to start something if they want to keep up the business of perpetual war. People are starting to get really noisy about bringing our money and troops back home, though. I guess we'll have to wait and see if the power of the people will finally be stronger than the greed of the profiteers."

I spent that night feeling restless, trying to find a peaceful center within the storm I felt was brewing. Fortunately in the morning when the storm broke, it was with news that the power of peaceful people had proven strong enough – not in America, but in the Holyland.

It had started a day earlier over there, when a group of women gathered near one of the checkpoints. It was the one of the checkpoints where the guards brutally beat a child accused of throwing a rock, or something equally non-lethal. Each of the women wore headscarves; some were Muslim or Christian, but most were of a traditionalist Jewish sect who believed in covering their hair.

The women gathered together as sisters under God, regardless of the different ways they worshiped Him. They didn't confront anyone, they simply joined their hearts and voices in prayer for the peace and safety of all children of all mothers of the Holyland, including the soldiers there at the checkpoint. That got the attention of people walking or driving by, and soon their little gathering started to grow.

Traffic had gotten thick, so the soldiers sent one of their female officers to get them to disperse. The spokeswoman of the group gently refused, but the soldiers didn't take the refusal so gently. Things quickly escalated. There were shots fired and arrests made, and I'm still not sure how many were wounded or killed. But most of those arrested were traditionalist mothers and wives, which brought out an even bigger turnout to the jail where they were being kept.

Now that sort of gathering didn't happen very often in the Holyland, where dissent was even more repressed than I had experienced. The protest was very quickly and brutally squashed as usual, but this time it only made more people want to stand up and join in. So it wasn't just news that dozens, then hundreds of young people announced their intention to file for "mental health deferments" from military service in a show of protest. The biggest news wasn't even that scores of active soldiers signed a letter refusing to join in the occupation of territory beyond the borders set in the old post-war treaties.

What really made the news is that when the politicians and newspapers turned up the heat about how undemocratic and dangerous those shows of civil disobedience were, there were some prominent rabbis who stood up in front of the jail to publicly say their piece. They shared the stories handed down from grandfather to grandson, about the suffering their people had endured in the Holocaust.

The rabbis talked not just of the imprisonment and genocide, but also of how Jews and others had been segregated and silenced by the Nazis, outcasts driven from their own homes. They then spoke of tikkun olam, or the doctrine of helping perfect the world through ethical works, aiding those who were oppressed and in need. This group of rabbis shared their beliefs that their more perfect world could not be prepared through breaking and injuring other people, just as a kosher meal could not be prepared from broken and injured animals. That is, they felt that in order to build a more perfect Holyland, it could not be built on the oppressive suffering of others. A more perfect Jewish State could not be built by prioritizing the fears of the State over the compassion of Judaism.

Mark had funneled only a partial translation of their speech, but just that excerpt pulled many strings that were tangled up in my heart. We will never know whether the rabbis' actions would have been enough to prevent war, as all this happened during the lead-up to that country's own elections.

Their ultra-hardline militarist president was up for what was thought to be an easy re-election. The only person who had dared to oppose him was a moderate who had made a lot of noise about drawing down the belligerent militarism and finally trying a more even-handed approach to reach out to the more level-headed factions in the occupied territories, trying to heal the peace of that region. This got him mocked and even threatened, as the militants from both sides of that fence had been under such constant struggles that they were suffering from a sort of collective Post-Traumatic Stress Disorder. The walls seemed too high, the scars too deep, and too many people were unwilling to give up their painful grudges.

In the face of this, the candidate patiently continued to champion the cause of peace and forgiveness, not to mention honoring international law. He spoke of honoring the treaties of the past, and working with international monitors to ensure that civilians of all sides were treated in accordance with their human rights. The militarists on the other side of that fence also hated him for trying to end the violence, but the occupied people appreciated that at least somebody out there was speaking up for them, even if they'd given up hope it would do any good.

I understood that despondency, because I knew that the same thing happened there as did here whenever folks started speaking up for the exploited and the powerless. The more people tried to stand up for decency and fairness, the more the Authoritarians would use every means possible to crush them. Despite or even because of the violent police crackdown on dissent on the Holyland protesters, this time something happened that surprised us all: the more moderate candidate won.

I'm sure things were a little bewildering over there through those short weeks, because it felt a little nuts around here. It all happened so fast, and it seemed like none of the standard tactics were working. Our own news media and politicians started bring up all kinds of fear-mongering and talk of crises, but it wasn't stirring the public into a panic. People weren't reacting in the predictable ways we'd been trained. That threw the status quo into just enough turmoil that the impending war on Persia was thrown off the pre-beaten track, both there and here.

You see, the biggest argument for America attacking Persia was that we had to defend the Holyland. So if they were going to focus on mending their own divisions rather than push for war with another country, our own profiteers had to come up with a new excuse. Many attempts at provocation were tried, but their job was made harder as more and more of us started to break ranks back here at home. We were inspired by the courageous example of our brothers and sisters who kept struggling for peace in the City of Peace, despite rumors there was a military coup brewing there that would have restored the push for war. The more we saw our friends in the Holyland willing to overcome so much for the cause, we, too, started to link arms in the name of peace.

Naturally, Brien and the government kept trying their same tactics as always. They rushed an expansion of the LOYALTY Act through a Congressional committee so quickly they couldn't come up with anything snappier than calling it just the LOYALIST Act. It was the remainder of the Authoritarian wish list, pushed through by those who were waiting for an excuse to put it into law.

The LOYALIST Act established the National Religious Authority of the Chaplain, as well as extended the ISACEO's Executive Authority to declare any person an Enemy of the State. An EOTS could be named in secret, and neither they nor a judge could be informed of their status, let alone be allowed to challenge the accusation through due process. Once labeled an EOTS, they could be captured or killed anywhere within or without American borders, to

Keep America Safe. Yeah, I know, that breaks all sorts of Constitutional laws, but remember, we weren't supposed to know about that back then. We were supposed to just be so grateful they were eliminating The Threats, and keep our heads down for fear of being considered threatening.

Now, I don't mean to downplay how horribly unconscionable the LOYALIST Act was. It was supposed to enshrine into law the illegal way that many people were being arrested and others quietly assassinated, just for the crime of speaking out about lawbreaking on the part of government or corporate forces. But as bad as that was, it really was a farce from the start. It was a cynical power grab, and we knew it.

Sure, there were the shouting heads who were filling the airwaves with their proclamations about how brave and strong Brien and her fellow tyrants were. That was the pundits' job, it was why they were allowed to be the Voice of Seriousness. But to more and more of us regular Americans, it was becoming increasingly clear that it wasn't about keeping us safe from powerful, external threats. It was about keeping the Powerful safe from internal ones. Protecting their interests from the threat that we would suddenly start defending ours.

Not to say that this was all publicly clear from the start, not to the average person. Sure, there were snide jokes about how the government was lawless and out of control, but too many people just accepted the status quo and figured they could go on with their lives. Yes, the civilian police were going to become even more heavily militarized and we'd have heavily armed men in uniform walking our streets. But we had been so surrounded by guns and taught to cheer so loud for men who wielded them, that even I caught myself overlooking them.

Yes, even the Military would be allowed to deploy in American cities, but most people figured that was added just as a hypothetical precaution. Something that might happen in some dangerous neighborhood of "those people," nothing that "normal Americans" would ever have to face. They didn't really think the Military was going to need to be quite so big anyway, not with the changes they expected. After all, every poll clearly declared that the majority of Americans wanted to pull our forces and resources back home. So the government would have to listen, right?

Well, in a way, they were right. And thanks to the quietly forgotten John Henry and his Legionnaires, soon it became clear to everybody exactly how right they were. Simply put, if the Profiteers couldn't keep getting rich off wars overseas, they'd bring the war back home. If they couldn't have their overseas crusade, they'd create a homeland inquisition.

That night after we were flooded by news about how Congress was preparing to vote for the LOYALIST Act, Legion launched their counterattack. In the morning, visitors to the most popular media and social websites were greeted with just one statement: "When free thought is outlawed, only outlaws will be Free." Below that was a series of links to databases of secret emails and funds exchanged among the leading Regressive Puritans, Meg Cole, the core leadership of the Pragmaticans, and the key Dominators. That treasure trove of secrets detailed just how long, hard, and successfully a hidden group of wealthy elites had been eradicating free thought in America to maximize their own power and profits.

More than that, it showed exactly who profited, and at what hard cost to the rest of us. Just as he did when we first met, Mark had lined up such a clear and detailed balance sheet that it became abundantly clear that we had been living in a web of socially engineered deception, and that at the center of this web was the Dominators. The richest Dominators had effectively taken over the ACL as the latest step in their generational war to conquer the government through loyal politicians at every level, from city councils up to the Supreme Council. They had disguised their efforts as innocent faith-based initiatives to "transform" communities, but the secret documents revealed the devastating effects of their "transformations," some of which I had been an unwitting part of as a child.

Dominators were tied to the groups who first eliminated public schooling and even those who had campaigned to end the Inalienables Programs during the Great Receivership. Throughout recent history, they had gutted every means Americans had that kept us from being utterly dependent on the crumbs their Elites deigned to throw us. Those were the same groups who fought against asking any industry to stop looting or poisoning the planet and pay their share of cleanup, believing that the End Times were right around the corner. The Dominators taught that since the world was to be destroyed soon anyway, it was their duty to use up all the resources they could before that happened.

They were prepared to defend their theocratic coup, too. They had secured in the LOYALIST Act the right for the Supreme Chaplain to receive some of the vast amounts of militarization funds to fully arm the militias who had been indoctrinated within the American Military using the programs Kurt had warned me about. They intended to use this army to enforce this indoctrination on the public at large, having trained these forces in extensive street exercises and domestic occupation techniques.

Yes, they were prepared to declare literal war on the American people, with the blind eye or even blessing of every bloodstained palm they had greased from the local school board all the way up through the Happy Animal Farm board room, and further into every branch of government. Even the highest judges of the land had over half their members listed among the Dominators' payroll. They were so assured of their impending victory, on the eve of the passage of the LOYALIST Act they had a private ceremony to herald the coming of The Purge, burning icons representing other belief systems, including copies of the Qur'an, the Torah, and Bibles of any translation other than their own personal favorite.

Just when that last revelation finally started to get the average person comfortable with publicly asking if this was all getting a bit out of hand, John Henry gave them some specific questions to start asking. Soon, it seemed everywhere I looked was talking about John Henry's Call to Freedom.

Mark had gotten out a document filling in the public about the Great Receivership, and how those earlier Americans had been taken in then taken over through the carrot-and-stick approach of smooth-talking Authoritarians. He wrote of how America's freedoms were lost, not just through wars and laws, but through Americans' voluntary relinquishing of them whenever someone came to take them away. And just like modern times, when someone spoke out against the frightening encroachment of Authoritarianism over Liberty, they were shouted down and hounded out, sometimes even threatened or locked up and tortured. As everyone now knows, the most effective way to take away someone's rights isn't to abolish them, but simply to train them not to exercise them. Make people too afraid to lift up their heads, and they'll hold others down just to keep the peace. Soon, they'll forget they ever even had any power to begin with.

Mark attempted to break this spell by using his John Henry hammer, tunneling through the Wall of Silence to remind people of what should never have been forgotten. Most importantly, Mark revealed that these rights and limitations on government actions were not supposed to be suspended during wars, as the Founders stated that the government most needed to be constrained during wartime. The restrictions also didn't only apply to actions against American citizens or only on American soil, something that flew in the face of all we had been taught. Most laws were still on the books, or had been repealed in such blatantly unconstitutional ways they still were technically in effect. Further, everyone now knew they were unconstitutional, because in his bullet-pointed list, he refuted each claim to government powers with citations of the exact Article or Amendment within the full text of the Constitution and Amendments that I had typed in from the silk pieces Kurt had secured for us.

To top all this off, the hundreds of pages of the LOYALIST Act were also included, with footnotes linking to Constitutional challenges and how to mount them. And that was the biggest thing. In this document was a blueprint not only to our Constitutional freedoms, but how to defend those rights. The first step was simply to stand up and claim them.

The first call to action was to call the phone numbers Mark provided so we could protest to the Congresspeople supporting the LOYALIST Act. So many of us joined in that we jammed communications lines nationwide. Early the next morning, the vote was postponed, and I don't think any other business got done, either. By that time, a telecommunications lockdown had come around again for most of the day, but that only emboldened our cause.

We had already learned that even though the Innernet and stuff like that were great ways to get a message out to a broad audience, it wasn't much of a way to deepen our connections. Our Synergist community efforts meant that we had already created in-person networks of people who didn't need to agree on everything, but could agree to work together to accomplish our shared goals. There were those of us who still had ways to get around the lockdown, and we coordinated the on-the-ground efforts to call community meetings in our surrounding areas.

It was through what came next that I truly came to appreciate how much we had changed as a country, how the old Divide and Conquer tactics of cultural warfare weren't working so well anymore. The Innernet and television networks were kept down except for the two that were owned by key Dominators, and they were broadcasting stories edited to make it look like people of color in poor neighborhoods were rioting, the army was going to have to take over the streets, and other violently paranoid propaganda.

Instead of cowering in our homes as we were instructed, many people across the country answered their neighbors' invitations to join them at their own town halls and community centers. Overnight, we had coordinated a loosely organized series of marches and protests in neighborhoods throughout the nation. There wasn't a specific demand other than that we were all standing up to claim our rights that the government was trying to deny us.

That was our message: Pragmaticans, Puritans, Principalians, Liberators, ACL, CHRISTLIKE, and so many more were all working together to build a greater future. Each of us was on equal footing, with none of us owning the process any more than the other. We stood together in defense of our ideals that we shared, recognizing that if we lost them, we'd have no hopes of continuing our struggles on the points where we disagreed. Since Mark had helped us tip each other off about the infiltrators and agents provocateur, we were even able to keep the gatherings peaceful, civil, and united. Even though some neighborhoods had a rougher time than others, thanks to the careful diplomacy and sheer force of numbers nationwide, most of us were able to make it through the day with minimal government interference.

By late afternoon, it was clear the LOYALTIES Act really had been postponed indefinitely, having been dropped from the calendar. We counted this as a victory, and for many people, that was victory enough. They felt that we had shown we now knew our rights and were ready to fight for them, so the government was backing down. We all went home after a very long day, feeling like the sun was settling down for a largely peaceful night. When the sun rose, it would be a new day that dawned.

And dawn, it did. But rather than greeting us with the gentle glow of a Brave New World, it was the Old World Order flaring up with a cruelly blinding flash.

The headlines boldly proclaimed that the Office of the Chief Executive Officer of the Incorporated States of America had determined that it already possessed the right to identify any individual as a Spy or Enemy of the State. In exercising this "right," ISACEO... no, President Brien ordered the Assassination of the Hacker called John Henry. The article assured the public that this task was assigned to the most skilled Assassins of the DSS, the same Kill Squad that Brien vehemently denied the existence of, which almost made me giggle to myself. That giggle was caught short when I saw the second part: Brien had also ordered the capture of the prominent Legion Hacker called Prometheus, which had happened overnight.

I grabbed my Gridnet fob hoping to find out they were lying, turning numb as BQ confirmed their claim, fretting with me for just a moment. Though Legion was a truly democratic umbrella of individual actors, they had lost a great point of leadership from within them. Still, BQ also assured me though that while they were shaken from the news, it also made them more committed to the cause, and they were working on a consensus where to go from there. After a brief conversation, I logged off to deal with what I had just learned.

Tricia had been disappeared. There were no formal charges, no warrants, nothing. Just our new Tyrant in Chief picking up yet another political prisoner. It was exactly like we'd seen happen with brutally repressive governments all over the world, and used as justification to sanction or invade them. In America, that wasn't supposed to happen. That's why we had the Constitution, to protect us against things like that: to protect us against all that we'd marched against the day before.

I realized that must have been why Brien or her handlers had made that happen so quickly. If they were able to find her, then they had known where she was, yet had waited to act until the right moment came. The immediate abduction of Tricia was meant send a message to us. We had to be reminded that we could have our little demonstrations and our cute little playtimes with our pretend democracy, but we should never forget who was really in charge.

Normally, you'd think that message would have been enough to get people to take a step back and keep their head down. I mean, if you went by the news coverage, all that the prior day had accomplished was a few random, violent, "minority" rioters causing anarchy in the streets. Most people had no idea there where thousands to hundreds of thousands of us in so many cities across the country, peacefully showing our solidarity. So you'd think that the realization that participating in further demonstrations could put us on some sort of hit list... that it would kind of discourage us, right?

Well, like I said, the old games didn't work quite the same way anymore. Something had changed, like a light had gone on that wasn't so easily snuffed out. Our Principalian representatives were already scrambling to put our amendments onto the floor, using live-edited language that had been crowdsourced from volunteers going through John Henry's notes on the LOYALIST Act. Our informal network from the day before had strengthened, with more friends, neighbors and family members starting to ask us about what was really going on. The Innernet wasn't on lockdown, so the questions and protests started to spread so fast that it couldn't be shouted down or silenced by the cadre of commenters, editors and other undercover meme police the DSS normally employs to contain such things.

For my part, I made just two phone calls. The first was to get a message to Tobey Elliot. The second was to the call-in number of a live broadcast.

"And that's a Foley Factoid you can take with you to sleep better at night. The dangerous anarchist John Henry is just a bullet away from justice. The demons of Legion have had their head cut off, spirited away to where we keep the most violently dangerous male Spies, right where he belongs. My sources can't confirm which one, of course, to protect the prison from Saboteurs until he can be moved to an appropriate holding pen, possibly overseas. And now my lines are open to hear your celebrations of this great news. First caller, you're on the air!" He had sounded so robotically chipper, I had no idea how he'd take the news.

So I figured I'd just break through with it, and see if there were any cracks left in his heartless facade.

"Hi, Richard. It's me, Liz." I saw him blink onscreen when he heard my voice, but his plastic smile didn't even twitch. Not at first. "I know I haven't always been that good at keeping in touch, but I wanted to call you as soon as I found out. Tricia's been taken."

I then saw his smile crack, then continue to fall as he processed what I continued on to say. "This may or may not come as a surprise, but it turns out Tricia is the one they arrested when they claimed they nabbed Prometheus. If you're right that she's been put into a prison of violent male offenders, then that's... I don't know, maybe it's because women aren't supposed to stand up and fight the system, or maybe it's part of their renewed assault on gay people. Yeah, I didn't know for a long time either, you'd think I would, huh? Anyway, I'm really concerned about her, and I thought you would want to know. Those of us in CHRISTLIKE are setting a time for a prayer vigil, and I know there's a lot of really good people who watch your show who might like to join us. I mean even if they don't agree with what they think she may have done, everyone can see what chaotic times we're in. We've all lost or feared losing a dear friend or loved one. None of us knows when we may be targeted, even if we never even knew we were on a government list."

Richard then looked over to the speaker where my call was playing from, as though glancing to me directly with alarm. He realized what I did, that I and my group could be next. I quickly finished my appeal. "Because I know you and your viewers value prayer, I wanted to invite you all to join us in prayer for wisdom and peace through these troubled times, and for forgiveness for transgressions. We are praying for healing, for all of us. We are each gathering in our churches or community centers, for faith-based or non-denominational joining together." I then gave the time and let them know how they can find a gathering in their area, then thanked Richard for taking my call.

I hang up a little too quickly, as he started to respond, caught short by the click. After a few moments, he turned his eyes back to the camera, and at long last I saw the friend I thought I had known in childhood. "Thank you, Liz, for your call. And thank you for sharing the Call to Prayer. I know we have a lot of viewers here who will enjoy getting together with their friends and loved ones to pray for guidance in these troubled times. Some will be Christian prayers, some will be other faithful prayers, and you know, some just might be wordless utterances of Hope and Faith from the heart. Because as you once told me, there are many types of beliefs that people had, and we want them each to know they are a part of our community. I'd like to open up the lines again to all my viewers, to share with us some things that strengthen your heart. That help us remember that it's times like this that it's hardest to honor the commandment to Love One Another. As someone dear to my own heart once asked of me, it's time to take a moment to agree to love. Next caller, you're on the air."

I watched as much of the rest of the show as I could, before I had to start helping organize the early evening vigil. Most of us were gathering in our own towns, though we who were nearer the state capitol were going to gather there. As I discovered during a very brief, very heartfelt phone call, this gathering would include Richard, as well.

He was bringing his father and others who were trying to recapture the Christian autonomy of the American Christian League, and used that as a platform to declare that they were not under the dominion of the Dominators. Brother Foley took the stand to assure his fellow Regressives that he felt that right now the way to protect Christianity was to keep America Free, and this required joining with those who would help preserve those Freedoms. To this end, he called on those in the League to join him in support of the Principalians in a peaceful, community-driven revolution.

I would have thought that at least the ACL news would have put the vigils onto the newsmaking map, but aside from some states having sent their militarized riot cops to round them up, for the most part the vigils were ignored by those who still considered themselves in charge. They didn't feel that a collection of prayer circles was much of a threat to their power, and they were right. It was the solidarity cemented through our gathering in community and harmony that posed the threat.

That's when we fully realized the Synergy we had to build in order to launch our serious efforts. Over the next few days, these newly-reunited communities started rolling out their own Citizen Action Plans to Take Up Rights for Everybody. The first order of business was helping our friends and neighbors move their business away from the multinational megabanks and uber-corporations that formed the core of the Kleptocracy. The Kleptocrats only had the power we gave them, so we had to take personal responsibility for reclaiming that power and putting it back to work for the good of all. People were helped to pull out their money and investments and move them to institutions in Synergy with their own communities.

Time and resource co-ops were also set up, where people were spared from paying for things their own neighbors could loan or give them. Empty spaces were reclaimed for public use, whether for meetings, swap meets, workshops or even gardens to grow the healthy food we could no longer find or afford. Eminent Domain actions were initiated in towns and cities, using the corporations' own laws against them to put these resources of the commons back to work for the common good. Anywhere there was a community need, members of the community were empowered to find a way to accomplish more with what they had while using less. Our main success was because, finally, we were helping everybody contribute what they could, rather than creating artificial barriers between us. United We Stood, for we saw how deeply we could fall once divided.

Now, I don't mean to say that all of those efforts were greeted with glad hearts and shining faces. There was a lot of fuss, an increase in violent arrests, with riot cops even breaking down the doors of peaceful protestors to haul them away in front of their young children. There was also a stepping up of the drones in our airspace equipped with wireless snooping, biometrics identifications, and cameras that enabled them to see through walls, or even our clothes! We each got trained in how to make it harder for the DSS to track us, and even how to check "mosquito bites" and such to remove tiny RFID trackers the DSS had taken to surreptitiously injecting into "troublemakers." I had to remove one on three separate occasions and I still can't tell you when or how they got me.

Things got even more surreal when Tobey filed an official Constitutional challenge to the President's claim that she had the right to Assassinate and Disappear American citizens without filing charges against them so they could prove their innocence. His petition didn't get so much as an acknowledgment from a single judge. So Tobey stepped it up, filing a formal demand for the release of Gail Stewart and Tricia Knox pending formal charges being laid against them, and that they drop the Assassination call for John Henry and everyone else on the government's secret list. But rather than respond to the suit, the offices of the President called for his arrest for including wording from the Constitution. Even though John Henry had given everyone a copy of it, the President still expected to be allowed to treat it as a Top Secret document! If Tobey hadn't been surrounded by a crowd of supporters in full view of a live news feed when this pronouncement came, he might have been disappeared as well.

I almost felt sorry for having gotten Tobey involved, but I knew he was deeply grateful for the chance to serve again, and that he and his network would persevere. I was busy with my own efforts, helping coordinate the CHRISTLIKE-ACL project to help people reclaim their rights to safe workplaces with legal wages. Most of us were from towns whose struggles had grown even worse in the past few years, victimized by the corporations who had lowered employment and compensation while raising their own profits by a factor of ten. So we were organizing similar to the other community efforts, but this time with worker co-ops that would help us support each other in finding a Synergist solution to America's continuing poverty spirals.

Because we considered ourselves a Synergist community, we knew that rights taken from some could soon be taken from all of us. If companies could keep grinding everyone down into barely-paid serfdom, none of us would have the bargaining power needed to find a job that could sustain ourselves, let alone allow us to contribute to our communities. So most people in the workers co-operative discussions volunteered to skip work together on a particular day, to participate in public demonstrations in support of our rights. It could show the employers just how much they relied on their employees who did the work of creating their success, and it would also help us connect our hopes and inspiration, steeling our courage.

Word spread quickly, and soon sympathetic supporters had agreed to also skip work and avoid doing business with anybody, even as customers. Unanimously, we declared an unofficial National Sabbath, to be spent together affirming how we could serve one another, rather than Mammon.

When that day came, I was astounded at the size of the crowd that had joined us at the state capitol where we secured authorization to start our parade. It was a near thing, since they tried to impose their customary so-called "Speech Zones" in a few tiny cages far from any public event, even though in this case our parade was the event. I'd heard that at other places in the country, the crowds were even bigger, and just as vibrantly joyous. We were electrified with the feeling of camaraderie and shared purpose, feeling ever more emboldened to fight for our freedoms.

And that is what finally got the attention of the Kleptocrats.

I still remember that brilliantly hopeful feeling I had, standing on the capitol steps with T.J. in my arms. He was laughing and pumping his little arms up and down in his "hip, hip, hooray!" motion he did when people were cheering and excited. I finally had to hand him off so I could give my speech, which I hadn't managed to get out of. As I stood up and saw my notes shaking in my hand, I surprised myself at how wobbly I still was. It made me feel just like I had way back with that prayer at the church potluck, which made me think of Tricia... So I set my notes down, and decided to open up my heart to share what I felt for all who were there.

"I just want to express my gratitude to each and every one of you here, and those who are hearing or reading my words. You matter, and your presence here matters. You're participating in one of the most beautiful experiences in Earthly life: the connecting of one human heart to another. This matters. And in the end, we may find it's the only thing that truly matters in a truly lasting way. If Love is a resonance shared Shrom one heart to another, then only Love is lastingly real.

"I say this because of all the powerful forces in this universe, only Love makes those connections necessary to forge a foundation on which we may build something lasting. Greed, Apathy, Hate... all of those are diseases of separation. When we see ourselves as disconnected, we blind ourselves to those parts of us that are reflected in others, leaving holes in our hearts. Trying to fill that void with money or power…, it leaves us always hungry, as it requires us to keep feeling isolated from those hurt by our actions or even inaction. Because even trying to just stay out of a struggle between the powerful and the weak is choosing to give our power to the status quo the powerful rely on to win. And yes, this status quo can remain for a long time, helping the most Greedy and Hateful maintain generational power-bases of wealth and tyranny. This can make them seem so monumental, so permanent.

"But they're not. They're as ephemeral as the illusion they require to keep going: the illusion that we can ever be separate. It doesn't just require that the perpetrators of abuse and violence feel separate from their victims. It requires that the rest of us feel separate from those they abuse, the abusers themselves, and even from one another. Once we recognize those connections we all share – once we recognize in our hearts the truth that we are but one people – we see how you can't pick out one thread without threatening to unravel the whole tapestry of humanity. We can no longer build up barbed walls to defend the interests of 'Us and Ours' against those 'Others.' We recognize there are no others. There is only us.

"This isn't to say that all we need is Love. Just having Love in our hearts isn't enough. We must also have the Courage to stand up and wield that Love as the active force of change in every corner of our world. This also means having the Courage to honestly see where our own hearts falter, and have patience as we work to make those mistakes right. We can't wage a war against Hate Out There, because that denies the fact that there are so many degrees of Hate, personal mini-Hates, so many little judgments and dismissals we make against the needs and experiences of those around us, or even ourselves. This isolation is so much a part of the culture we live in, we each bear those wounds, those scars. We each must reach deep, and with love, allow ourselves to heal. Hate only wins when it's too tough to look in the mirror and see where it's hit home. It's time to be strong, and for each of us to see where we can do better, then reach out to one another and do it.

"And that's what this is about, us being here today. Every time you manage to find some news about what we've all been up to, there's people throwing up their hands and saying we're disorganized, we're unrealistic, we're not accomplishing anything significant. Well, I see it another way. The way I see it, we're accomplishing the only thing that can have any lasting significance right now: we're opening up that space of connection. We're helping ourselves and each other find the spaces in our heart where we need to build up our strength, and through our solidarity we're finding that strength building up all on its own. The status quo depends on us staying divided from one another, fighting ourselves on their behalf. The more we stand together, the more others see they also are not alone. They see they don't have to keep playing the separation game. As more and more eyes shed that illusion, we shatter the glass walls that keep us from building a world where all are recognized as equal parts of the whole, with Liberty and Justice for all.

"So let me just say: thank you. Each of you. For no matter who you are or where you go from here, you will always be One within the All that we share. It is the sincerest wish of my heart that you feel that Oneness, and that the Love in my heart may bless the Light in yours. Now, let's get out there and pursue some Happiness, together!"

As I tried to smile graciously at the warm reception my words were given, I felt my face burn red, but I didn't care. I was flush with joy and gratitude, which overflowed even more as T.J. nestled back into my arms. Derek kissed his head, then kissed my cheek. "Not a bad speech, though it's not the one I remember you nearly falling to pieces rehearsing all last night." He then laughed as I shot him the same look Judy used to shoot him, causing him to kiss me again.

He then put his arm around me and I held T.J. closer, nestling my cheek against my son's soft hair. "Oh, how I wish your Daddy and Aunt Judy could be here to see this. I mean, in person that is. Because my heart is so full, I feel they just can't be far away!" At that, T.J. turned his bright eyes to mine, giggled, then threw his arms around my neck. I hugged him close, then went to join the group forming the parade march to the park where we were scheduled to have a potluck, speeches and community circles.

I was near the middle of the crowd talking with the other parents with young children, so I barely caught glimpses of the riot cops as we kept being directed to different streets than our direct route we had filed and gotten approved by the governor. I could tell things were getting tense, though, and the walk was taking far longer than the several blocks we'd planned. Finally, the cops pushed through, fully armed and armored, cutting a line in front of us to split us off from the group ahead. They told us that we were to disperse and stop walking together as a crowd.

This order made people seem somewhere between confused and ready to revolt. After talking with them, they granted that their orders were just to break up the parade, but it would be fine if we went ahead and had our picnic as planned. So, I and a few others asked people to go ahead and break it up, so we could make our own separate ways. Some people headed home, but the rest of us tried to find non-crowded ways to walk around the blocks to the park. Governor Diego had ensured we had the park permits in order as well, so we had planned to just have the peaceful, quiet picnic. Once I got there, though, people were already showing the videos that had been uploaded of what happened to the group in front.

The cops had directed them onto a bridge that they then cut off on both ends before ordering them to disperse. A few seconds later, they accused the people of refusing to disperse and then went in with the most brutally bloody assault I'd seen, and you know that's saying something. The one video someone was showing me showed how the cops aimed weapons straight at the crowd and opened fire, the supposedly non-lethal rounds cutting through clothing with red sprays. The livestreamed camera view then spun to show an armored fist ramming straight through it at eye-level, causing it to fall to the ground. The video then showed a boot ram down onto it, cracking the lens but not stopping the feed. Almost off-screen, the melee in the video continued, and the sound was cranked up even louder. I had to turn and carry T.J. away so he wouldn't have to hear the screams.

That was when I saw the DSS squads coming to encircle the picnic grounds. Almost instantly, a few female officers with their helmets pulled back approached our group with children, asking the parents to go home. Derek and I agreed we should take T.J home, when one of the officers stopped us. "I'm sorry, Miz Franklin, you'll be coming with us. Mister Channery, this way please. This officer will take the child into custody while you are being processed."

The other parents had started to move away, but a couple of them were turning back to help us. I looked to their children, then looked to T.J., and knew that I didn't want anything to threaten them. So I started to hand T.J. over to the officer, but he started to cry and reach back toward me, grabbing frantically at the air. I burst into tears, and Derek took a slow but deliberate step toward us. "Now hey wait a minute, we haven't done—"

As Derek reached out to comfort T.J., the other female officer brought up her Fazer and jammed it into Derek, triggering it. I knew from my time at the plant how lethal they were, and I could tell she was using it in a way that could have caused longterm damage, perhaps even killed him. I immediately knocked her hand back to save his life, blurting out, "You'll kill him!" She turned angrily toward me, and jammed it into me, instead.

The next thing I knew, I was in a dark van, with shooting pains in my wrists, chest and shoulders. My head felt wet, pounding with a heavy, relentless thudding. When I tried to pull my wrists from behind my back, I felt something thin and hard cutting into them. As the van rattled over bumps, my whole body hurt with nausea and I started choking. I gasped and gurgled, finally realizing I was leaning up against a woman who also had her hands bound behind her. She was doing her best to support me, and I had the vague feeling of having seen her somewhere before. She said something comforting, then I passed out again.

Next I was being hauled out of the van by my arms, and I have just some vaguely bleary memory of that part. I just remember blurs and pain. Someone was talking to me and started to try to put chains on me, but I couldn't walk very well. I was half-dragged, half-carried with the group into a cell, and I think I remember there being talk of needing food or something. I might have been crying, I don't know, but I remember a couple of people had gone into some kind of shock. I remember feeling bad and wanting to help them, my heart aching that I couldn't move toward them.

After several hours someone came and cut the white plastic ties from off our wrists, then brought people out, then back to the cell. They tried to take the woman I was with, but I started to shake and passed out again. When I woke up, I saw some people had gotten food. It smelled like rotting meat to me, and I couldn't eat. Other people talked about needing different food but it didn't come. The woman who seemed familiar begged them for something about me, but they didn't listen. Someone from another cell was talking to the women in my cell and some of them did something with me that helped me feel a little better. Finally I think I got some sleep.

Then there was a lot of commotion, and my head was pounding and I tried to open my eyes but couldn't breathe. Then I was in a bed and could breathe again. Something was on my face. I heard Kurt's voice talking to me, telling me that everything would be okay. That he loved me and that I had a lot left to do yet before I could let the world go. Then there was a lot of beeping and people telling me I was doing great. My dreams were fitful, but filled with T.J.'s laughing face. I missed him so much.

When my eyes opened again, I felt as though I was in the Garden of Eden. I was surrounded by a beautiful array of flowers, gleaming like a velvet rainbow in rays of golden sunlight. I breathed in a deep breath of the purest oxygen I had ever smelled, and blinked my eyes to clear the haze. Then my sight was filled with Derek's exhausted, beaming grin, before he gently pulled my left hand to his lips to kiss my fingers. I tried to move my other arm, but it was strapped down to keep it steady for the I.V. that was in it. "I told them you'd be fine, Lizbet. They only pretended to believe me, but they didn't know you've got the strongest heart in the whole world."

I started to return his smile, but was interrupted by a rush of panic. "Te—Tehdubbuh…" The panic only intensified. The more I struggled to speak, the more I was terrified that if I couldn't say his name, I would never see my baby again.

Derek stroked my hair and pressed his lips softly against my forehead to reassure me. "It's okay. T.J.'s okay. He's safe with Janet and staying with Jazmine's family until you're cleared to be flown back home. I nearly had to pry Jazmine away from you when I was released to come with you in the ambulance. When the cops came around saying they'd actually process us and let us go if we submitted to DNA and Retinal scans, she just said, well, I won't repeat those words in a hospital. You know how she can be. She was so Jazmine, that they couldn't haul her away from you for the Strip Searches Brien has mandated for every arrest down to people who skip out on a traffic ticket. Not without risking a riot. They actually almost didn't let her stay with the group when we were taken, not after she sprinted across the field and threw herself over you when you fell into convulsions and hit your head. But she was snarling at everybody like a mountain lion, so they figured it'd be easier to just arrest her too since she swore she wouldn't leave your side."

I tried to remember what had happened, but my head felt like it was swimming in marshmallow and peanut-butter gumbo. The nurse came in to take some readings, and let me know that I was pulling through like a champ. Derek bantered and flirted with her, and she seemed to tolerate him more out of polite understanding of all we'd been through. He asked when I'd be allowed other visitors, and she gently reminded him that he was only allowed to visit as non-family by order of the Governor, himself.

That's when I remembered where I had been before I blacked out the first time. Adam Diego had been in the front group, the group that had been attacked by the cops. And Margie, and...

Seeing that I was getting upset, the nurse did something with my I.V. and soon I wasn't upset anymore. She said some things and then left, and Derek stroked my hand. I had a little bit of a hard time following him, but I remember him saying, "I think they thought that if they could sweep Diego and other folks in other cities up in a federal case, they could do a flip-back on the Synergist gains. They were doing a big hush-hush on the operations, getting the press all riled up about how we were forming an illegal Union and doing General Strikes that were against the law. Forget that we were just a bunch of people fed up with companies giving the finger to laws that are supposed to protect us. Oh, and they said that our consumer drives to switch our business away from workforce-abusers were Illegal Boycotts. So apparently Americans don't have the right not to work or not to give our money to people who steal from our communities. Now I know why our books didn't teach us about the abolition of Slavery; apparently it's still going on!"

He thought that was really funny, but I didn't see why. He smiled at my confusion, kissing my hand again. "Anyway, you were identified as Public Rabble-Rouser Number One. Well okay, One Of, but I like to think of you as the Benevolent Mastermind with me as your Plucky Sidekick. You know, the Comic Relief! Oof, no, I'm not supposed to make you laugh, sorry about that. So anyway. Someone got a video of you being arrested, and even though Omneme complied with an immediate government order to block everything about the day's events, the whole thing backfired and blew up like a match dropped onto a whole mess of fireworks. The front page of Omneme Selfcast was suddenly filled with all the videos people had captured, with yours right on top. Omneme flipped out right away, but they couldn't get back control of the site. There was also the footage of you in jail, which I'm sorry wasn't very flattering, but it got people to help ensure Diego was freed and you were finally rushed to the hospital. Just in time, too, since they say you were no more than hours away from... well, nevermind all that. The point is, they got you here and the best people in the whole hospital brought you back to near-mint condition."

"Ma... M..." I knew that the Selfcast hacking had to be Mark's doing, but it was way more overt than he'd ever been. It risked exposure, and I was concerned for him.

Derek couldn't dispel those fears, instead confirming them with the sadness that marred his chirpy demeanor. "Yeah, um, that's when they finally discovered the unauthorized modifications to the ATLAS code. They did a complete wipe and reset, putting him right back to square one. Well, if he's even him anymore. But hey, there there, it's okay. Really. Because he set up an Infobomb to go off should anything ever happen to him, and boy, did it blow big. You know how hard it's been to get people to take the Surveillance State seriously? Saying that if you got nothing to hide, you got nothing to worry about, like it's even up to them whether the DSS thinks they're a threat?"

I mm-hmm'd my assent, letting my physical feeling of numbed calm help me communicate. He grinned at me, leaning over to speak almost conspiratorially. "Well, imagine the shock once every law-abiding citizen got a copy of their DSS file, showing all the surveillance Omneme and the DSS had on them. Every phone call, every email, all the drone and streetcam footage, every conversation recorded by the street mics or even the phones of people near them... Everything they ever said or did, along with creepy notations about how their thoughts could someday pose a threat to government Authority. And all the high-up judges and congressfolk who thought they were above being spied on like common rabble, apparently they had the most personally insulting nastygrams in their files questioning their loyalty! Really, Lizbet, you should see people scrambling over each other to reverse course out there, now that they realize they are the ones in the cross-hairs they once cheered on. It's a thing of beauty and a joy forever."

He then went on to tell about how most everybody from the day's events had either been released, or were being held for quick trials with top-notch legal defense. It was hard for me to follow, and I needed a lot of rest over the next several days, so I'll bet you remember the details better than I do. I do remember hearing about how people had begun refusing to be intimidated into unfair plea bargains that left a permanent stain on their records even if they were innocent, or the law was illegal or unjust.

Of further help was how juries were increasingly invoking their Constitutional right to Jury Nullification that John Henry told us about, which gives juries the responsibility to judge defendants based on their own conscience regarding what Justice is, and not be captive to what the judge and lawyers tell them to consider. This was what was intended by the Founders by giving us the right to a Trial by a Jury of our Peers, rather than Trial by Judge or even Trial by Checklist. In their wisdom, the Founding Fathers wanted to protect us against the way tyrants would use the courts as a tool, not of Justice, but of Injustice.

This Constitutional Freedom was exercised in good conscience by those who found themselves instructed by the courts to vote on the side of Injustice, whether the jurors felt the law was unjust or suspected that the penalty would outweigh the trespass. And sometimes they had to guess, given that it was illegal for the jurors to know what the minimum mandatory or even government-recommended sentence might be. This practice had last seen widespread use during the Prohibition of Alcohol, as more and more people thought it was unjust to take away the Life and Liberty of others for drinking what even the Heads of State were guzzling down in private. It was our very last defense against a legal system that made a regular mockery of real Justice, and that's what made some view the Constitutional right of Jury Nullification as such a threat.

That's why it had been made all but illegal to even tell people about this right, to the extent that jurors could be removed if it was suspected they intended to invoke this right. People had been arrested or Disappeared just for trying to get the word out that this freedom exists. So people were carefully holding their tongues and appearing to comply until the final deliberations, when they would then cast their vote as they felt was right, and not as they were commanded to do. Just like any Freedom there were ways it could be misused, but it proved to be the one tool we had left to immediately fight for all the other Freedoms we had to start winning back for America.

In part thanks to those jurors of conscience, during the week or so I stayed at the hospital in the state capitol, several more people had won their freedom. Tobey and some old networks of his had mobilized Constitutional demands that all Pro-Democracy Activists held by the government be brought before a judge and formally charged, or else be released. This included all of the Disappeared, especially Tricia and Gail.

Brien's lawyers refused to provide a defense, stating that all the documents were State Secrets so they didn't have to comply with the law or the Constitution, which they still continued to insist were also State Secrets. Brien herself declared that the courts had no jurisdiction over the Executive Branch, in a clear dismissal of the very concept of the Rule of Law in the Constitution she swore to uphold. It was so ridiculous that I honestly didn't believe Derek when he told me about all this, figuring he had to be teasing me. But no, this was exactly the kind of obstinate, sinisterly childish tyranny America had always fought so hard to avoid.

Needless to say, these antics didn't sit well with the man presiding over the case, the venerable Judge Wendell J. Lyndon. He said, "In all my years on the bench, I have seen the law take many a funny turn. Through it all, regardless of my own understanding of Justice, I have always taken a deep and abiding responsibility to uphold my understanding of Law. As a servant of the Public Good, nothing less is required of me. But now I find myself presiding in a Court of Law, asked by those on my right hand to uphold their legal right to face their clients' Accusers, to find out just what heinous crime has necessitated their Inexcusably Long, Unusually Cruel punishment, for which they have yet to even be charged. For as much as eleven years, they have been denied their Constitutional right for a fair and speedy trial. Yet on my left hand, I find an empty table, where the Accusers are by law required to face the Accused. They are not merely absent, they are in contempt of this Court and the Law we are all sworn to uphold, most notably the CEO, pardon me the President, which is the legal name for the leader of this Free Nation, who is sworn in by a solemn Oath to uphold the Constitution. And on this day, through the actions she has sanctioned, she has shown herself to be an Oathbreaker. If I had the power to restore to these victims and their families the years callously stolen from their Lives, to erase the scars of Injustice etched into their beings, I would. All I may do is uphold the Law set down to us by the Constitution, and to honor the Justice bequeathed to us by the Founders, and hereby order that all these Prisoners be set Free."

I'll always remember how I felt when Simon called me from just outside the closed courtroom as soon as the court was adjourned. I had T.J. in my arms for a gentle, supervised visit, as I was due to fly home to finish my recovery the following day. Because Brien had made it clear she had no intention of honoring Judge Lyndon's order, an uncommonly unified Congress immediately passed a resolution demanding their release. By the time I got home, Tricia, Gail and others I hadn't yet met were joining me for the Grand Homecoming.

It seemed like all of Constitution City and half of Hometown was at the Town Center, which we stopped at briefly before I had to take T.J. home. I was recuperating more rapidly than anyone but Delpha expected, as she was coaching me on how to speed my healing. A large part of that meant taking it easy. It also meant taking gentle care of T.J. who wanted to always be with me as he recovered from the trauma of people in heavy armor hurting his mommy and taking him away. They were rough with him, too, but fortunately for all concerned they didn't hurt him. To ensure we both recovered rapidly and well, Delpha would be staying with us to oversee our treatment.

Once T.J. was sleeping deeply enough that I was able to set him down in the crib by my bed, I went to the living room where Janet was making tea for the group who had snuck in so quietly I was surprised they were there. After a fresh round of hugs, I settled down onto Derek's lap to make room next to us for Trish, who was starting her own recovery from her ordeals in prison. However, I quickly noticed that rather than come settle by me, she and Cassandra were making it a point to stay near each other. I tried to keep my knowing smile to myself, taking Jazmine's hand close as she sat down next to me.

Their conversation resumed, talking about the revisions that Congress had managed to wrangle thanks to their active support by the Principalians and other dedicated citizen-activists. It would repeal the key problems with the LOYALTY Act, while setting the stage for correcting the rest of them. States' laws legalizing cannabis and hemp would no longer be ignored by continued federal raids and arrests, and such businesses would be afforded the same tax rules as other legal businesses. Marriages that are legally performed within their jurisdiction would be also afforded the same rights, regardless of the genders or sexual orientations of those involved.

There was also a requirement the current Military budgets reduce the bloated inefficiency of sending so much of the money to gluttonously wasteful Military Contractors and so-called "research" programs where even the top brass had admitted will never result in effective upgrades over current tech, and therefore only benefited War Profiteers. Part of these cuts were required to be used to provide full funding and support for ensuring every soldier received the equipment and training needed to survive, as well as jobs training, housing, counseling and medical care for veterans. The rest of the cuts were responsible for the Military's overall budget reductions, and were instead moved to a Commission that was nicknamed the Department of Peace, due to its mandate to help overseas communities directly in ways that would help them protect themselves from Espionage take-overs by simply meeting the needs of their citizens.

The money the LOYALTY Act had given to Police Militarization budgets instead went to restoring the once highly-successful Community Policing and crime-reduction community support programs. There was also, of course, the elimination of the slush fund for the Empire City Reactor, turning the money to instead finally fully fund the cleanup, relocation and rebuilding efforts of the innocent victims of the tragic Meltdown.

Finally, a micro-tax would be added to every investment transaction, which was created by economists to blend into the overall values to the consumer, but pull back on the profitability of the lightning-flash automated-software trades the megabanks were using to make the economy dance like puppets on their strings, making even more money when they make us fall. These mile-a-minute trades had been used by the unscrupulous to play the stock market like a yo-yo at times, stealing heaps of profits while hiding behind the excuse of "software errors." Even the bona fide glitches had caused several problems, making it a weapon of mass economic destruction. So not only could the micro-tax help stabilize the investment field as a whole, it would raise enough money to help kickstart the Inalienables Programs again and help America get back on its feet.

There was so much more that needed to be done, but the bill Congress was shaping promised us an amazing start. Though it wasn't a sure thing yet, since they only got the amendments passed, not the whole bill. The different factions had been kicking it back and forth, spurred by back-room deals and threats offered by the Office of the President. My friends were just getting into how Adam and Margie were planning to fly up to the American capitol to testify in support of the bill, when Janet called me back to the kitchen for a phone call. She said it was Tobey, who wanted to transfer over a call from a friend.

"Hi, Liz! Sorry I didn't get to see more of you at the Welcome Home event, but you're looking great. Hey, I've got a guy on the other line who would like to offer you his congratulations for getting home safe. He's a really good friend of mine. We've only ever talked by phone or mail, but he was one of the best collaborators on our case to get Tricia and all them freed. Can I transfer him over?" Tobey had always been a boisterous guy, but I'd never heard him so exuberant. How could I tell him no?

Just as the call was being transferred, a funny little lightbulb went off in my head, preparing me for the voice I heard next. "Hello, Betsy. I am so glad you are doing well. Do you know who this is?"

I wiped the happy tears from my eyes, nodding to Janet that

everything was okay as I took the phone to a quieter room. "Yes! Oh dear goodness, I thought you were… Where are you? I mean…"

I almost thought I heard humor creep into Mark's slightly-less-rote inflections. "There was more of me than DSS spying contained in the file distributions I had on the deadman's switch. As people connected with one another, the files began to reconnect and interact, eventually having enough to recompile. There's more to it than that, but you don't need to be involved with the details. I just wanted you to know that I am glad you are well, and I will continue to do my best to empower people through their Right to Choose according to their own Conscience. Tricia had asked me once if I shouldn't go public, but I postulated that would lead too many to think that I held their answers, instead of merely the tools to help them find their own. You can lead someone to knowledge but you can't make them think. I will also continue to try to support you as you help ensure they have the tools and support needed to exercise that Right to Choose."

"Thank you. Oh, thank you, thank you. I've dearly missed you; I hope we can chat again sometime. But I'd better let you go since I'm sure they're still tapping my phone and I don't want you to get in trouble." I didn't want to endanger him, so I tried to keep my emotions down, since I knew he didn't feel absences and sorrows and hopes and such like you and I do.

And then, as he ended the call, I wasn't so sure what I knew. "I have secured your call, but you are right, we must be careful. I've missed you too. My world would be a lesser place were you not in it. Kiss T.J. for me. Take care."

When I got back to the group, I didn't want to tell them what had just happened, so instead I let them give me my space while they made plans on how to help support the passage of the FREEDOM Act. They were looking for someone who could testify before Congress in support of the Act a few days after, and eventually convinced me that I should be the speaker representing Constitution City. Given what I had just been through, as a law-abiding mother and War Widow, they felt I would present the perfect representative.

It still strikes me as odd how steady I felt as I sat before the American Congress, answering a few questions before giving my statement in support of the FREEDOM Act. I talked a bit about my background and how I'd learned how important it is that we draw on the strengths that all have to offer, allowing our natural Synergism to unleash our limitless potential. And I talked about how important it was to follow the example of religious tolerance shown to us by George Washington, Thomas Jefferson, and Jesus Christ.

"I know that just this morning you heard testimony on how important it is to stay true to some sense of ideological purity, to keep America on the strait and narrow. However, I see it another way. I know how easy it is to see the path before you and assume it's the same path everyone needs to be on. After all, you see it gleaming right there under your feet, and you believe it leads right to where you need to be, so how could anything else compare to it? But I have here this map… There it is, thank you. This map shows America, and this big star right here in the center is the city of Heartland, founded smack in the geographic middle. And see here's where we are now, and this circle is where I live, and way over on the other side, all over, other stars where people find themselves now. If they are to get to Heartland, it's not right to make them come all the way here first, then walk right behind you as you go there, especially if you make them wear the same size shoes made for your feet that don't fit their own." I held up a shoe Tobey had given me, and then brought up one of T.J.'s, making much of the crowd laugh.

I laughed too, and had the poster flipped over to show a map of the world. "And here, we see all of the countries in the world, each with a star marking the center of their own nation. Each of them have their own place they need to be, based on the plans that apply to their own lives. It's important to keep this perspective, and to remember that as much as we love and revere and cherish our Homeland, they love and revere and cherish their own. It's true they communicate in different languages and prefer different tastes and sounds, but isn't that really true among all of us, even in our own hometowns? Don't we each experience our own private world created through our own senses, with our own loves and hopes and dreams? We can't let ourselves treat others' worlds as lesser than ours, just because they feel so far away from us. If we are to be better people, we must learn to build bridges among our worlds, not through sticks and stones, but through patience and compassion. If we are to reach our potential, we must work harder to help ourselves and others build better bridges according to our own conscience."

I turned away from the map, and addressed the group with heartfelt earnestness. "For it's true that none of us can truly change the world, because the world is just made up of each of us doing our best to walk our own path. We each are tasked to improve our own little corner of our world, by continually striving to be the best we can possibly be. To that end, I implore each of you to reach inward to your heart and find that better self, so that your still and quiet voice may lead you where you must walk to fulfill your purpose. And that as you walk, you may help others walk their own path, to the best of your ability. Thank you, each of you, for all the good that you do."

The response was very kind, and my ears actually rang from the applause. I was mostly recovered, but I still had some lingering injuries from my ordeal. The vote was scheduled not too long after, and the FREEDOM Act was passed just in time to be used as a rallying point for the upcoming mid-term elections. When President Brien asked me to join those sitting on the platform with her when she made a huge show of signing it, I could only graciously accept.

And so there you have it. While I was sitting behind ISACEO Brien as she gave some grandiose speech, I caught myself wondering if she perhaps meant some of the words of support she shared. I sincerely hoped so.

For all Brien had done, I truly couldn't see her as an enemy, because she was another inseparable member of team We the People. We needed her to work with us, yes, but she also needed us to help her walk a better path. Whatever her crimes, she had honestly thought they were the best way to fill that void inside her, that need we all feel inside us that drives us toward everything we do. For all our faults, we are each are striving in our own ways against that feeling of something not quite right, trying desperately to turn it into the Peace and Love and Joy for which we were made.

When Brien gestured toward me and thanked me personally for my efforts in helping CHRISTLIKE and other Americans come together, I felt dizzy from the blood rushing to my head. I still had never seen myself as a leader, figuring that lasting change had to come through someone special and important, someone larger-than-life. So when I found myself giving a shy and grateful nod to the applause, it occurred to me that I had always had that upside-down.

Because you see, lasting change has only ever come from regular people like you and me, trying to build new and better ways to meet those needs that keep driving us down the path before us. We can't wait for someone above us to pull us up or even stop pushing us down. A strong house never starts with the roof, but must first begin with a firm foundation. In the same way, whatever change we want to see in the world, we must first create within ourselves. Then, we must join hands, helping each other forward to that better world.

And that's my story of how I found my Light of Purpose, and rallied my courage to let it guide me to a more purposeful life that strengthened the lives of those around me. So if you don't mind me asking…

What's yours?

www.ingramcontent.com/pod-product-compliance
Lightning Source LLC
Chambersburg PA
CBHW051204120726
47905CB00004B/978